Sweet Salt Air
&
Blueprints

Also by Barbara Delinsky

Before and Again
Love Songs
Warm Hearts
Escape
Not My Daughter
While My Sister Sleeps
The Secret Between Us
Family Tree
Flirting with Pete
The Woman Next Door
The Vineyard
Lake News
Coast Road
Three Wishes

Sweet Salt Air & Blueprints

barbara delinsky

St. Martin's Griffin New York

These are works of fiction. All of the characters, organizations, and events portrayed in these novels are either products of the author's imagination or are used fictitiously.

www.stmartins.com

Blueprints designed by Anna Gorovoy

The Library of Congress Cataloging-in-Publication Data is available upon request.

ISBN 978-1-250-26067-3 (trade paperback)

First Edition: June 2019

10 9 8 7 6 5 4 3 2 1

Sweet Salt Air

For Eve, a garden filled with magical flowers,
herbs, and a fawn

Prologue

Charlotte Evans was used to feeling grungy. As a freelancer, she traveled on a shoestring, getting stories other writers did not, precisely because she wasn't fussy about how she lived. In the last twelve months, she had survived dust while writing about elephant keepers in Kenya, ice while writing about the spirit bear of British Columbia, and flies while writing about a family of nomads in India.

She could certainly survive a *mizzling*, as the Irish called it, though the heavy mist seeped through everything—jeans, boots, even the thick fisherman's sweater she wore. The sweater was on loan from the woman under whose roof she was sleeping on this least populated of the three Aran Islands, and though Charlotte did have a fireplace in her bedroom, hot water was in short supply in the small stone cottage. She could have used a steamy shower, a thorough washing of her clothes, and a solid day of sun.

Her assignment was to write about the youngest generation of Inishmaan knitters, women who were adapting traditional patterns in breathtaking ways, and as with the pattern on her own sweater, she could now describe moss stitch, panel repeats, right and left twists, and cable designs. It was time to leave. She had to go home to put the story together and get it to *Vogue Knitting,* before heading to the Australian outback to do a piece on aborigine jewelry-making for *National Geographic,* a coup that one. Still, she stayed here.

Part of what kept her was the woman who owned the house, as warm and motherly as any she had ever met; part was the craft that permeated the place. No knitter herself, she could watch these women for hours. They were at peace with themselves and their world, enviable for Charlotte, who had no roots at all. So close to her age that they might have been schoolmates, they were trying to teach her to knit. She told herself this was cause enough to stay.

Bottom line, though, it was the island that kept her here. She had loved islands from the time she spent her first summer on one. She was eight at the time. Thirty-four now, she still felt the island aura—an isolation that made worries seem distant, a separation from the real world that lent itself to dreams.

Her eyes went to the horizon, or where the horizon would have been if the mist weren't so dense. *Thick o' fog* they called it in that other place, and it lent a sheen to her skin and a bulk to her hair here as it did there. She pulled those dark curls back now, fingers lost in the damp mass, and turned just enough on the scruffy cliff to face a few latitudinal degrees south.

There, on the far side of the Atlantic, would be Maine, but despite the shared ocean, her island and this one were worlds apart. Where Inishmaan was gray and brown, its fragile man-made soil supporting only the hardiest of low-growing plants, the fertile Quinnipeague invited tall pines in droves, not to mention vegetables, flowers, and improbable, irrepressible herbs. Lifting her head, eyes closed now, she breathed in the damp Irish air and the bit of wood smoke that drifted on the cold ocean wind. Quinnipeague smelled of wood smoke, too, since early mornings there could be chilly, even in summer. But the wood smoke would clear by noon, giving way to the smell of lavender, balsam, and grass. If the winds were from the west, there would be fry smells from the Chowder House; if from the south, the earthiness of the clam flats; if from the northeast, the purity of sweet salt air.

Oh yes, across the Atlantic would be Maine, she mused, as she opened her eyes and tried to penetrate that great distance through the fog, and this being April, she would think of it regardless of where she was. That was ingrained. Spring was when she started to plan her Quinnipeague summer.

Or used to. But no more. She had burned that bridge ten years ago with one stupid act. She couldn't go back, though she wished it sometimes. She missed the spirit of summer on Quinnipeague, so much more intense for being apart from the rest of the world. She missed Quinnie lobster rolls, which tasted better than lobster rolls anywhere else. Mostly, she missed Nicole, who had been as close as a sister to her once. She had never found another like her, though Lord knew she had searched.

Perhaps that was what staying on Inishmaan was about. The women here could be friends. They understood independence and self-sufficiency. Charlotte had felt such instant rapport with several that she sensed they would keep in touch.

Would? Maybe.

More likely not, the realist in Charlotte admitted. For all the writing she did for a living, she was a lousy correspondent. Within a day or two, she would leave Inishmaan behind and return to Brooklyn, and from there? In addition to Australia, she had go-aheads to do stories in Tuscany and Bordeaux, the appeal of the latter being the lure of Paris before and after. She had friends there—a writer, a ceramist, and a would-be fashion designer whose clothes were too bizarre for mass appeal but whose personal warmth was winning.

Would it be the same as Quinnipeague time? No.

But this was the life she had made.

Nicole Carlysle lived in blissful ignorance of the past. She had enough to handle in the present, though no one knew it, and that was the problem. No one knew. No one *could* know, which meant no outlet, no emotional support, no badly needed advice. Julian was adamant about silence, and, because she loved him, she gave in. *She* was his lifeline, he said, and what woman didn't want to hear that? But the strain was awful. She would have gone out of her mind if it hadn't been for the blog. Whether she was writing to tell her followers about a local cheesemaker, a new farm-to-table restaurant, or what to do with an exotic heirloom fruit that was organically produced and newly marketed, she spent hours each day scouring Philadelphia and the outlying towns for material. As spring took hold, the local offerings were growing.

On a different mission now, though, she sat in front of an iMac in Julian's study. There was no view of the Schuylkill from this room, as there was from most of their eighteenth-floor condo. There were no windows here at all, simply walls of mahogany shelves that held medical books Julian had either inherited from his father or collected before publications had gone digital. Nicole owned shelves here, too, though fewer in number. Hers were filled with the novels she couldn't part with, and books about entertaining that were both resource and inspiration.

Organized as she was, the papers to the left of the computer—jottings, printouts of fan comments, and endorsement requests from vendors—were neatly arranged. Her camera sat behind them, hooked to a USB port, and, in a ceramic bowl on the computer's right, lay the newly photographed subject of her upcoming blog: a head of purple cauliflower, still cupped by the veined green leaves within which it had grown. A leather sofa, with a matching side chair and ottoman, filled the room with the smell of lemon oil and age.

But that smell wasn't foremost in her mind as she read what she had already typed. "I go to farmers' markets all the time. Field-to-table is so my thing. But none of the herbs at any of them comes close to island herbs. Those herbs *make* Quinnie food—well, those herbs and freshness. Quinnipeague was growing organic and cooking local before farm-to-table was a movement, but, still, we think of the herbs first. I can't write about island cooking without talking about them, but I can't not talk about the people, either. That's where you come in, Charlotte. You've eaten Dorey Jewett's lobster stew and Mary Landry's clam fritters, and you always loved the fruit compote that Bonnie Stroud brought to the Fourth of July dinner each year. These people are all still around. Each has a story. I want to include some in the book, but I'm better at writing about food than people. You write about people. And you're so good at it, Charlotte. I google you all the time. Your name shows up in the best of the *best* travel magazines."

She paused, thinking about those pieces as she studied the mirror of her own eyes in the gloss of the screen. Just then, they were sea-green with worry, wondering what the chances were that her friend would accept. Charlotte was big-time professional, certainly used to having her own byline. She would have to split the billing here, and Nicole's advance wasn't all that much. If the book sold well, there would be more, but for now all she could offer was a small stipend, plus room and board in one of the nicest homes on the island—plus reading and talking and hanging out, all that they used to do before life got in the way.

She typed in the thoughts, rewording once, then again. Finally, tired of parsing, she added a blunt, "I need you, Charlotte. A Quinnie cookbook won't be the same without your input. I know you're busy, but my deadline is the fifteenth of August, so it's not the entire summer, and you'll get stories of your own out of this. It'll be worth your while. I promise."

Her eyes rose above the computer screen to find Julian in the open doorway, and she felt a visceral flicker of warmth. It was like that whenever he caught her unaware—had been since the first time she'd laid eyes on him in a Starbucks in Baltimore twelve years before. Back then, as a new environmental studies graduate of Middlebury, she was getting her feet wet writing publicity pieces for a state agriculture organization. Hoping to work during her afternoon break, she had set down her grande-caramel-frappuccino-with-whip on a table without noticing much of her surroundings, until she opened her laptop and became aware of an identical one, identically opened and angled on the table beside hers. Having made the same observation seconds before, Julian had an amused smile waiting.

He was a surgeon, in town from Philadelphia for a seminar at Johns Hopkins, and he had a quiet strength. That strength had been sorely tested in the last four years and yet, seeing him in the doorway of the study, she still felt the pull. He wasn't a tall man, but his bearing had always been regal. It was no less so now, though regular workouts helped with that. His hair had grayed in the last year or two, but even after a full day at the hospital, he was a good-looking forty-six. Tired, always tired now. But good-looking.

Wearing a smile, he approached. "Doing a write-up of last night?" he asked. They had eaten at a new restaurant with friends, a working night out for Nicole, who had insisted that everyone order different dishes and evaluate each while she took notes.

By the time she shook her head no, he was facing her with a hip on the desk by the keyboard. "The cookbook, then," he said as his smile grew, knowing. "You always get that look when you think of Quinnipeague."

"Peaceful?" she acknowledged. "It's April. Two more months, and we're there. You're still coming with me, aren't you?"

"I told you I would."

"Willingly? It's an escape, Jules," she urged, momentarily serious. "It may be only for a week, but we need this." She recaptured lighter thoughts. "Remember the first time you ever came? Tell the truth. You were dreading it."

His brown eyes laughed warmly. "What wasn't to dread? A godforsaken island in the middle of the Atlantic—"

"It's only eleven miles out."

"Same difference. If it didn't have a hospital, it wasn't on my radar screen."

"You thought there'd be dirt roads and nothing to do."

He gave a wry chuckle. Between lobstering, clamming, and sailing, then movie nights at the church and mornings at the café, not to mention dinners at home, in town, or at the homes of friends, Nicole had kept him busy.

"You loved it," she dared.

"I did," he admitted. "It was perfect. A world away." His eyes saddened. "And yes, baby, we need this." Taking her face in his hands, he kissed her, but there was sadness in that, too. Hoping to banish it for a few more seconds—especially in the wake of the *baby* that always turned her on—she was reaching up when he took her hands, pressed them to his lips, then smoothly slid behind her. With his arms braced on either side, cheek to her hair, he read the words on the screen. "Ahh," he said with a sigh. "Charlotte."

"Yes. I really want her on board."

He angled away only enough to meet her eyes. "You don't need her, Nicki. You can do the cookbook yourself."

"I know that," she said as she had more than once. "But she's an accomplished writer, and she has a history on Quinnipeague, too. Add her people pieces to my food ones, and the book's that much better."

"She hasn't stepped foot on the island in ten years," he said in the measured way that spoke of knowledge. Oh, he was knowledgeable—a pioneer in his field, always savvy on a personal vein.

But Nicole wasn't deterred. "How better to lure her back? Besides, if you're gone after a week, and Mom won't be there, I want Charlotte."

He was quiet. Nicole heard the argument even before he said, "She hasn't been the best friend. She called your dad her surrogate father, but she didn't even make it to the funeral."

"She was in Nepal. She couldn't possibly get back in time. She did call. She was as upset as we were."

"Has she called again since?" he asked, though they both knew the answer to that.

"We e-mail."

"Often? No. And you're the one who initiates it. Her replies are short."

"She's busy."

He touched her cheek. "You haven't seen each other in ten years. You have different lives now. If you want to lure her back to recapture what you once had, you may be in for a fall."

"I miss her." When his expression grew guarded, she insisted, "No, it is not about that. I promised you. I will not tell her." She grew pleading. "But it's like all the stars are aligned, Jules. There's the cookbook, and your being in North Carolina for the month, and Mom not wanting to go to Quinnipeague and needing someone to pack up the place—like I want to do it? That'll be bad enough, but being *alone* there while you're away? This is the last summer I'll ever have at the house, and Charlotte is part of what that place means to me."

He was quiet. "You don't even know where she is."

"No one does. She's always on the go. That's why I e-mail. She'll get it wherever. And yes, she always answers." He was right about the brevity of her replies, though. Charlotte never shared much of her life now. And yet, from the first mention of this project, Nicole had pictured her taking part in it. Oh yes, Charlotte knew Quinnipeague. But she also knew Nicole, and Nicole needed to see her. She and Julian were going through a rough patch, tender moments like this one—once commonplace—now further between. A month at Duke training incoming doctors in the technique for which he was known would be a much-needed distraction for him. And for her? Charlotte could distract her. The memories were good; she and Nicole had always been in sync. If there was any fun to be had this summer, Charlotte was her one great hope.

Julian tucked a long strand of hair behind her ear. His expression was aching—and Nicole might have reached for him again if he hadn't cupped her head. "I just don't want you hurt," he said and kissed her forehead. Then he held her back. "Do you think she'll accept?"

Nicole smiled, confident in this at least. "Absolutely. I don't care how much time has passed. She loves Quinnipeague. The temptation will be too great to resist."

Chapter One

Quinnipeague lay eleven miles from the mainland. With a year-round population of nearly three hundred, it was serviced by a daily mail boat that carried groceries and a handful of passengers, but no cars. Since Charlotte had one of those for the first time in her life, she proudly booked the ferry, boarding in Rockland on a Tuesday, which was one of only three days each week when its captain cruised past Vinalhaven to islands like Quinnipeague. Nicole had offered airfare to speed up the trip, but Charlotte flew everywhere else in life. This summer was to be different.

The car was an old Jeep Wrangler, bought from a friend of a friend for a fraction of its original cost. Giddy with excitement, she stashed the soft top in back, and, as the warm June air flowed freely through windows and roof, drove up from New York herself. She welcomed the time it would take. After a frantic two months of work to free herself up, she wanted to slow down, decompress, and maybe, just maybe figure out why she had agreed to a last summer on Quinnipeague. She had sworn she wouldn't return, had sworn off painful memories.

But there were good memories as well, all of which had flooded back as she read Nicole's e-mail in Ireland that day. She replied instantly, promising to phone as soon as she returned to New York. And she had. Literally. Right there in baggage claim while waiting for her duffel to come through.

Of course, she would come, she had told Nicole, only afterward doing the reasoning. For starters, there was Bob. She hadn't gone to his funeral because she hadn't had the courage to face even a dead Bob after letting him down—letting them *all* down—so badly. So she owed Nicole for the funeral, and owed her for the betrayal.

But obligation wasn't the only reason she had accepted the invitation. Relief was another; Nicole herself had suggested the collaboration. And nostalgia; Charlotte missed those carefree summers. And loneliness; she spent her life with people, but none were family as Nicole had once been.

And then there was the book. She had never worked on a book, had never actually collaborated on anything, though it sounded like a piece of cake, having someone else run the show. When she thought about the people she would interview, Cecily Cole came to mind first. Talk about compelling characters. Cecily *was* island cooking in many regards, since her herbs were what made the food special. She had to be the centerpiece of the book. Talking with her would be fun.

Charlotte could use a little fun, a little rest, a little make-believe—and Quinnipeague was the place for that. Even now, as the ferry passed in and out of fog, reality came and went. *You can't go home again,* Thomas Wolfe had written, and she prayed he was wrong. She expected some awkwardness; ten years and very different lives later, she and Nicole couldn't just pick up where they'd left off. Moreover, if Nicole knew of her betrayal, all bets were off.

But if Nicole knew, she wouldn't have asked Charlotte to come. Nicole Carlysle didn't have a devious bone in her body.

Leaning out from the side railing, she caught a breath. There it *was*—

But no, just an ocean mirage quickly swallowed by the fog.

After moving past empty benches, she held tightly to the front rail.

Anticipation had built since leaving New York, accelerating in leaps after New Haven, then Boston. By the time she passed Portland, impatience had her regretting the decision to drive, but that changed once she left the highway at Brunswick and started up the coast. Bath, Wiscasset, Damariscotta—she loved the names as much as the occasional view of boats, seaside homes, roadside stands. FULL BELLY CLAMS one sign read, but she resisted. Clams served on Quinnipeague were dug from the flats hours before cooking, and the batter, which was exquisitely light, held bits of parsley and thyme. Other fried clams couldn't compare.

The ferry rose on a swell, but plowed steadily on. Though the air was cool and the wind sharpened by bits of spray, she couldn't get herself to go inside. She had put on a sweater over her jeans when the ferry left Rockland, and while she had also tied back her hair, loose tendrils blew free. They whipped behind her now as she kept her eyes on the sea. Some called North Atlantic waters cold and forbidding, but she had seen others. Turquoise, emerald, teal—none moved her as gray-blue did. Seventeen summers here had made it a visceral thing.

Her camera. She needed to capture this.

But no. She didn't want anything coming between her eyes and that first sighting.

Having relived it dozens of times in the preceding weeks, she thought she was prepared, but the thrill when the island finally emerged from the mist was something else. One by one, as the fog thinned, the features she remembered sharpened: jagged outcroppings of rock, a corona of trees, the Chowder House perched on granite and flanked by twin roads that swung wide for a gentle descent from town to pier, like symmetrical stairways in an elegant home.

That said, there was nothing elegant about Quinnipeague, with its rutted paths and weathered docks. But Quinnipeague wasn't meant to be elegant. It was meant to be authentic. Shutters were practical things to be closed in the fiercest of winds, and, when open, hung crooked more often than not. Wood was gray, clusters of buoys tacked to the side of the fishing shed were bright despite their chipping paint, and the gulls that swooped in to perch on tall pilings always left their chalky mark.

Sailboats grew distinct from power ones as the ferry neared. There were fewer lobster boats than Charlotte remembered, fewer lobstermen she had read, though those who remained would be out pulling traps this Tuesday, hence moorings with only dinghies attached.

Her pulse sped when she saw a figure running down the pier, and in that instant, the bad of the past blew right back out to sea. She waved frantically. *"Nicki! I'm here—here, Nicki!"*

Like there were other people on the ferry. Like Nicole could possibly miss her. Like Nicole could even *hear* her over the thrum of the boat and the slap of waves on pilings. But Charlotte couldn't help herself. She was a child again, having traveled alone from Virginia with her heart in her mouth and here, finally, so relieved to have reached the right place. She was a teenager, a seasoned flier now from Texas, electrified by the sight of her best friend. She was a college student who had taken the bus up from New Haven to summer with a family that wanted to hear about her courses, her friends, her dreams.

For all the places she'd been in the ten years since that wedding summer, no one had ever been waiting for her.

In that moment, seeing Nicole bubbling with excitement on the pier, her own relief was so great that she forgave her the timidity, the docility, the sheer agreeableness that had made her such easy prey for betrayal—traits Charlotte had seized on over the years to forgive her own behavior.

But this was a new day. The hovering fog couldn't dull the reds and blues of the boats. Nor could the smell of seaweed overpower that of the Chowder House grill. Bobbing on her toes, she clutched her hands at her mouth to contain herself, while with agonizing precision and a grinding of gears, the ferry slowed and began to turn. She moved along the side to keep the pier front and center in her sight.

Beautiful Nicole. That hadn't changed. Always petite, she looked positively willowy standing there on the pier. Always stylish, she was even more so now in her skinny jeans and leather jacket. The wind whipped her scarf, which likely cost more than Charlotte's entire summer wardrobe—the latter being vintage L. L. Bean, emphasis on *vintage,* having traveled with Charlotte for years. Style had never been in her lexicon. The closest she came to it now were her flats, bought three years before at an open-air market in Paris.

Chug by chug, the ferry backed its snub stern to the end of the dock. The instant the captain released the chains and lowered the ramp, Charlotte was off and running. Throwing her arms around Nicole, she cried, "You are the best sight ever! You look amazing!"

"And *you,*" Nicole cried back, clinging tightly. Her body shook. She was crying.

Charlotte might have cried, too, her throat was that tight. Ten years and such different lives, yet Nicole was as excited as she was. Grasping at everything that had been so right about their summers together, she just held on, swaying for another few seconds until Nicole laughed through her tears and drew back. Running her fingers under her eyes, she explored Charlotte's face. "You have not changed a bit," she declared in the voice Charlotte remembered—high, not quite childlike but close. "And I still love your hair."

"It's the same old mess, but I love yours. You *cut* it."

"Just last month, finally. I mean, I may still sound like I did when I was ten, but I wanted to *look* like an adult at least." Blond and straight, her hair had always fallen to midback. Cut now in a wedge, it was shaped neatly around her face in a way that gave focus to the green of her eyes, which were luminous with lingering tears and suddenly anxious. "Was the trip okay?"

"It was fine—"

"But it was long, and you're not used to driving—"

"Which was why I wanted to do it, and it was good, it really was—and for the record, Nicki, you always looked gorgeous, but this cut is very, very cool." By comparison, Charlotte might have felt unsophisticated, if she hadn't known that women paid big bucks for hair like hers, and as for her voice, which was neither high nor distinct, it got her where she needed to be.

Nicole was eyeing her shoes. "*Love* those. Paris?"

Charlotte grinned. "Absolutely."

"And your sweater? Not Paris, but fabulous. So *authentic*." Her voice grew urgent. "Where did you get it? I need one."

"Sorry, sweetie. It's a hand-me-down from a woman in Ireland."

"*So* perfect for this place. It's been a dismal, cloudy June. I should have warned you, but I was afraid you wouldn't come."

"I've survived dismal and cloudy before." She glanced up the hill. "The island looks just the same." Past the Chowder House were the general store left and the post office right, both buildings long and low so as not to tempt the wind. "Like nothing's changed."

"Little has. But we do have Wi-Fi at the house. Got it set up last week."

"For just us two?" she asked to be sure. Nicole had initially told her that Julian would be up with her the week before, but was planning to leave before Charlotte arrived. If he had decided to stay on, it would change the tenor of her visit, putting the fragility of her relationship with Nicole front and center.

But Nicole was all cool confidence. "Hey. We deserve it. Besides, if I don't keep blogging, people will lose interest and wander away, and then there won't be as many to hear me when I start pitching our book—which I feel a hundred percent better doing now that you've agreed to help. Thank you, Charlotte," she said earnestly. "I know you have more important things to do."

Charlotte might have insisted that this was as important a project as she'd done in a while, if a gruff call hadn't cut off the thought.

"Hellooo." The ferry captain shot a thumb at her Jeep. "Gonna get it off?"

"Oh." She laughed. "Sorry." Releasing Nicole, she ran back onto the ferry and slid behind the wheel. By the time she revved the engine, Nicole was in the passenger's seat, sliding a hand over the timeworn dashboard. "I am paying you for this."

Charlotte shot her a startled look and inched forward. "For this car? You are not."

"You wouldn't have bought it if it weren't for my book, and you won't take money for that."

"Because it's *your* book. I'm just along for the ride." She laughed at her own words. "Can you believe, this is the first car I've ever owned?" She eased it onto the dock. "Is it real or what?"

"*Totally* real," Nicole said, though momentarily wary. "Safe on the highway?"

"It got me here." Charlotte waved at the captain. "Thank you!" Still crawling along, she drove carefully off the pier. When she was on firm ground, she stopped, angled sideways in the seat, and addressed the first of the ghosts. "I'm sorry about your dad, Nicki. I wanted to be there. I just couldn't."

Seeming suddenly older, Nicole smiled sadly. "You were probably better off. There were people all over the place. I didn't have time to think."

"A heart attack?"

"Massive."

"No history of heart problems?"

"None."

"That's scary. How's Angie?" Nicole's mother. Charlotte had phoned her, too, and though Angie had said all the right words—*Yes, a tragedy, he loved you, too, you're a darling to call*—she had sounded distracted.

"Bad," Nicole confirmed. "They were so in love. And he loved Quinnipeague. His parents bought the house when he was little. He actually proposed to Mom here. They always said that if I'd been a boy, they'd have named me Quinn. She can't bear to come now. That's why she's selling. She can't even come to pack up. This place was so him."

"Woo-hoo," came a holler that instantly lifted the mood. "Look who's here!" A stocky woman, whose apron covered a T-shirt and shorts, was trotting down the stairs from the lower deck of the Chowder House. Dorey Jewett had taken over from her father midway through Charlotte's summers here and had brought the place up to par with the best of city restaurants. She had the gleaming skin of one who worked over steam, but the creases by her eyes, as much from smiling as from squinting over the harbor, suggested she was nearing sixty. "Missy here said you were coming, but just look at you. All grown up."

A lifelong Mainer, she talked the part. Loving that, Charlotte laughed. "I was twenty-four when I was here last, no child then."

"But *look* at you. That's some sweater!" The sheer ebullience of the woman made Charlotte laugh again. "And Missy? Well, I've seen her these last years, but I tell you, the two a' you put the rest of us to shame." Her brows went up. "You hungry? Chowder's hot."

Chowdah, Charlotte thought happily. It was late afternoon, and she was starved. But Nicole loved to cook, and Nicole was calling the shots.

Leaning across the stick shift, Nicole told Dorey, "To go, please, with corn bread and fiddleheads."

"You'll be taking the last a' those," Dorey confided. "I had a vendor try to convince me to shrink-wrap and freeze, but they're never the same. I only have 'em now because they're from up north"—*nauth*—"and the growing season was late this year. They'd have been gone a week ago, if business hadn't been slow, but the price a' gas is so high, and no one's out day-cruisin' anyways when the wind's so mean. Think you can tough out the chill?" she asked, seeming impervious to it herself with her bare arms and legs.

But Charlotte was still focused on hunger. "Maybe a couple of clams, too?"

"You got 'em. Drive up top. I'll bring 'em out."

Chapter Two

THE ISLAND WAS LONG AND narrow, undulating on the surface of the ocean like a kind and gentle cobra. Its broad head, which faced the mainland, was raised to support the center of town. Once a fishing village, its narrow streets remained home to a handful of lobstermen and clammers, though most of the property was now owned by the locals that serviced newer residents. The latter, whose homes descended along the neck, included artists, businessmen, and computer programmers, all drawn to the island for its peace.

Beyond the neck was the body of Quinnipeague, accessed by a single sinuous road that slithered past mud flats, sheltered beaches, and rock ledges. The dirt drives leading to summer homes were marked by mailboxes that, come July, would be nearly hidden by wild roses and geraniums.

Nicole's house was second to last, a full seven miles from the pier and two shy of the tip of the tail. Though less ostentatious than some of the newer homes that had been built since Charlotte had visited last, it was a grand white house, two stories high with a widow's walk, black shutters, wide porches, and arms skimming the ground on either side.

Those arms held guest rooms that had, on occasions like Nicole's wedding, slept twenty.

The main house was for family. Bedrooms here were on the second floor to optimize their view, while the first floor, originally broken by doorways and walls, had been reconfigured into two large rooms, one for eating, one for living. Both opened to a wide patio that led to the sea.

Whereas life in the kitchen revolved around a trestle table of pickled oak, the Great Room was furnished to take advantage of the fireplace, which was floor-to-ceiling native stone. This was where Charlotte and Nicole now ate, sitting side by side on the floor at a huge square coffee table. Nicole had insisted on setting beautiful places, arranging their food just so, and photographing it before they started, but the camera was set aside now and the napkins unfolded.

Those napkins picked up the colors of the sofas, throw pillows, and rugs—all vibrant blues and greens that were lush against the fog outside. The logs on the grate had caught; while the heat slowly built, the chowder picked up the slack. Nicole's jacket was gone, the scarf loosely looped on her silk shirt. Likewise, Charlotte had tossed her sweater aside.

Conversation was sparse, since Charlotte could do little but moan in delight at the food. At one point, after swallowing the juiciest clam belly she'd ever had, she laughed. "How can anything taste this good?"

Having dispensed with a spoon, her elegant friend was drinking the last of her chowder straight from the bowl. She finished, put it down, and wiped her mouth. "Dorey says the key to chowder is letting the ingredients cure in the pot for a day before dishing it up, which is counterintuitive since fried clams are best right after they're dug. Personally, I think it's the chives in the chowder." Pensive, she studied her empty bowl. "Or the bacon. Or the parsley." Her eyes rose. "Maybe it's just the butter. Since Dorey's chowder is Maine style, more milk than cream, the butter shines."

Charlotte took a simpler approach. "Maybe it's just that we haven't had Dorey's chowder in so long," she said, but Nicole gave a quick headshake.

"I had it two nights ago. I have it all summer long, and it's as good in August as it is in June."

"Then you still come for the whole summer?" Charlotte asked in surprise. She had always gotten an e-mail or two from Quinnipeague—quick little holiday greetings or thinking-of-you notes—but had assumed Nicole's visits shortened after the wedding. Julian certainly couldn't be gone from the hospital for three months.

"I actually do. I started coming up with the kids"—there were two from his first marriage—"because what else were preteens going to do in Philly, and this place was perfect for them. That kind of set the pattern. When they got older and had jobs at home, I kept coming. Julian comes weekends or sometimes for a week. Same with Kaylin and John. Mom and Dad like the company." She flinched. "Liked." Looking around, she said sadly, "It'll be hard not having this."

Charlotte squeezed her arm. The house was only one part, she knew. The rest was Bob. Every available space held photos taken here and so many included him, pictured at various stages of his life. It was more a celebration than a shrine, though she knew Nicole was mourning still.

They were silent for a bit, eating more slowly now. Having finished the chowder and clams, Charlotte ate the last of her fiddleheads. There had been summers when she had come too late to catch these before they leafed out into ferns, but once tasted, they were never forgotten.

Wiping her fingers on a moss-green napkin, she cradled her wineglass and rested against the skirt of the sofa. "I feel your dad here. He was a wonderful man. I'm not sure I'd have gone to college without his pushing it. I don't think I'd have had a career. I didn't have a clue what 'work ethic' meant." Bob Lilly was a lawyer, and though he had been adamant about spending summers on Quinnipeague, he was up at dawn every morning to study the packets delivered by the mail boat the previous day. In the last of Charlotte's years here, there were a fax machine, a computer, and e-mail—and always the phone. Bob insisted on satisfying his clients before he ever went out for a sail. Charlotte remembered times when they had waited for him to finish. In each instance, when he finally joined them, he shared the bare bones of the case so that they understood the urgency. "He set an example for me that I didn't see anywhere else."

Nicole was suddenly on her knees, reaching across the table to straighten the thick candle that stood in an even thicker glass pillar. When she was done, she settled back on the rug. "Your parents died too young."

Charlotte had freed up her hair when they came inside; now she gathered the mass in a single hand and pulled it away, needing clarity against the clutter of her parents' memory. Their lives had been an ongoing orgy of self-absorption and excess. She was a freshman at Yale when they died in a fiery car crash that they might have survived, had one or the other been less stoned.

She took a sip of wine, briefly reflecting on what might have been if they had lived longer. The reflection held little optimism. And she was a realist. "They were never role models, Nicki. I try to romanticize them sometimes—y'know, their being gone and all—but I keep coming back to the mess of their lives. They were married three times, including twice to each other, and in between there were affairs and divorces and bankruptcies. They could act a part, like that of respectable renters of the house beside yours in Baltimore, but it was superficial. I was thinking about this while I was driving up today. When my parents met yours, they had just been kicked out of their apartment in Virginia, which, of course, the rental agent didn't know because back then, there was no quick way to do background checks, and she had a high-end house that needed a short-term renter, and—voilà—in walked my folks. Your parents saw through them, but they kept up the charade. Why did they do that?"

"You."

"I'm serious."

"So am I. They loved our being together. They loved that you looked up to them. They saw your potential. Besides, your parents did great barbecue. I remember those ribs."

"Likely lifted from the gourmet section of the supermarket," Charlotte muttered. She was uncomfortable with praise. It put a spotlight on the guilt she was trying so hard to suppress.

"You're too harsh."

Releasing her hair, she let go of the turmoil of her parents' lives. "I guess. And even if they did steal the ribs, I met you in the deal, so it wasn't a horrible thing." She and Nicole had hit it off from the start, becoming inseparable during the year they were neighbors. After Charlotte moved away, there were overnights, though always at Nicole's house, and, of course, there were summers on Quinnipeague. "My parents would have been at a loss to find something for me to do. Your parents were a windfall when it came to that."

"But it worked both ways. My parents got me a sister at a time when my mom was still having miscarriages. I think your being here helped her accept that I would survive without a sibling. Besides, they trusted you more than they trusted some of the island girls." Eyes wide, she clamped her mouth shut against a smile that escaped anyway. "Remember Crystal? And *Brandy*?"

Charlotte laughed. "Bizarre Brandy. To this day, I've never seen so many piercings. What's she up to now?"

"She's a hairdresser on the mainland. Crystal's still here. She married Aaron Deegan, who lobsters with his dad. They have five kids."

"Five? Whoa. And Beth Malcolm? She was smart. I was always afraid you two would be friends, so you wouldn't need me here."

"Are you kidding? I was too shy to do much with her. I didn't mix with locals until you showed up. You were bolder than I was. You got me out. My parents loved that."

"Beth was a reader, too," Charlotte recalled, then thought. "What are you reading right now?"

"*Salt*. It's about—"

"Maine!" she broke in, delighted. "So am I! It was on sale at JFK when I flew in from Australia, and when I saw the island on the cover, how could I not buy it?"

"It's not our island—"

"No, but you can feel it, smell it, almost taste it. Are you loving it?"

Nicole grinned. "Loving it. Loving the setting, the characters, the magic."

Charlotte dittoed each point, which on one hand wasn't surprising. She and Nicole had always liked the same books. They used to spend hours on the beach, passing them back and forth while the surf pounded the shore.

On the other hand, ten years had passed. While Charlotte was building houses in post-earthquake San Salvador or post-tornado La Plata, Nicole had been decorating a plush Philadelphia home. While Charlotte was in remote towns writing about doctors, farmers, and artists, Nicole had been in Center City blogging about food. Granted, *Salt* was on every bestseller list. But that they would both be reading it right now was evidence of ways in which they were still the same.

"At first I thought the author was a woman," Nicole offered. "Chris Mauldin—it could go either way. There's no photo, and the bio is vague."

Charlotte had wondered it, too. The sex was powerful but exquisitely tender. She didn't know guys who made love that way—which was probably part of the wide appeal of the book. Chris Mauldin was serving up dream stuff to an audience that craved it. At least, Charlotte did. She wasn't sure about Nicole and certainly couldn't ask. "Well, if he was trying to hide being male, he's given up. I googled the name, and a 'he' came right up. Does anyone know his real identity?"

"Not on the forums. I swear that's part of the phenomenon. Think about it. He's self-published—"

"Only in e," Charlotte cautioned, sucking cornbread crumbs from her finger. "My hardcover copy has a big-time logo."

"Right, but *Salt* was an e-bestseller for weeks and weeks before he sold the print rights. Can you imagine his marketing genius? He knows how to work the Web and does it in total anonymity from wherever."

"Anonymity is part of what makes the success of the book such a phenomenon. It's the big tease. Here's this mystery guy serving up our dream, and we don't know who he is, where he lives, or what he looks like."

"Like it matters who he is?" Nicole asked. "He had me hooked on page one. I mean, what a great first line. *Every man wants love, if he can get past the fear of exposure.* We like him because he's honest. At least, I do." Scrambling up, she added a log to the fire. "I like him because he's willing to put himself out there and be vulnerable and maybe end up being hurt. Let me tell you, though, *I* would never hurt this man. I'd buy anything he writes—and I say that though I'm only halfway through *Salt*."

Charlotte wasn't even that far. "Is he working on a second book?"

"I hope so, but he's being vague about that, too. One thing's for sure. He's blown away the competition. I'd love to do that with a book." She jumped up. "Stay. I'm getting dessert." She was off.

"Where am I supposed to *put* dessert?" Charlotte called after her. Nicole hadn't finished the fiddleheads or clams, but she was up and down, wearing off what little she'd eaten.

"You'll find room," came the voice from the kitchen, along with the open-and-shut of the refrigerator door. "I cannot have a guest here for take-in without adding something of myself to the meal." She returned with snifters of small, wild strawberries. "These are the first of the season. I picked them this morning."

"On the roadside?" Charlotte asked, tickled by a dozen memories. Nicole had always known how to spot the best patches, like her eyes could see the tiny red glow beneath the leaves from fifty feet away. She had been known to yell *Stop the car!* at odd times to fill either a bag or her hands.

"No. One of the families on the neck has wide open meadows loaded with fruit. They started a little pick-your-own business, with strawberries now and blueberries soon. They cultivate wildness, and they don't use herbicides. I go there as often as I can."

"These are *so* small," Charlotte marveled, though she knew they'd be packed with flavor. "It takes forever to pick a pint."

"It's about the process," Nicole said with a smile, seeming to relax just thinking about it.

So did Charlotte. And yes, she could find room. Slipping a berry into her mouth, she savored it, before returning to the interrupted discussion. "Maybe you will."

"Will what?"

"Blow away the competition. I read your blog, Nicki. You get hundreds of comments on every post—and on Facebook, how many friends?"

"Seventy thousand." This, said with quiet pride as she scooped up their chowder bowls and headed off again. "Cappuccino?"

"No, thanks. You are amazing, Nicki."

"The machine does it, not me."

"I meant your blog." She had taken a more traditional route herself, studying journalism at Yale, followed by a postgrad year at Columbia. It was all very safe—precisely why, needing to break the mold, she had signed on as a Web correspondent in Afghanistan, where danger was a constant. The deal was for six months. Back in the States, she poured herself into hands-on charity work while the nightmares receded. Writing was her therapy. Between pieces she did in Appalachia—or in communities struggling to rebuild after a hurricane or fire—and those from Afghanistan, she caught the eye of magazine editors, who signed on for the pieces she pitched.

It was a career trajectory that had been taken by scads of journalists before her. But Nicole—quiet, introverted Nicole—was breaking new ground. "How'd you do it? How'd you get so big?" she called.

There was silence from the kitchen, then a dry, "God works in wondrous ways."

"I want to know how it *happened,*" Charlotte insisted. "Nicole, are you going to come in here and sit?"

She reappeared with a small ceramic creamer from which she topped the fruit in each snifter with something that looked far thicker than cream. "Sabayon, made with Dad's favorite Riesling," her high voice announced. "I forgot how much wine he'd stored here."

"Oh, yumm." Forget the strawberries; Charlotte tasted the sauce. "*Yummm.*" Of course, a mouthful of fruit *with* sauce would be even better.

She was about to dig in, when Nicole said a sharp, "Wait!" Up again, she grabbed her camera, arranged the snifters just so, and took several shots, before setting aside the camera. They were on the sofa now, the fire crackling around another new log. She didn't eat, simply sipped her cappuccino with her eyes on the hearth.

Charlotte sensed a melancholy. "Thinking of Bob?" Eating sauce made with his favorite wine would do it.

"And Jules." Nicole was suddenly teary. "He gave me the cappuccino machine a couple of summers ago. We have one just like it at home. He used to make cappuccino every morning and bring it to me in bed." Darting Charlotte an awkward glance, she added a quick, "He's too busy now."

Charlotte felt a twinge of envy. It wasn't about Julian. It was about loving and being loved in return. "You miss him."

"Yes." She gathered herself. "Hence my blog."

"Go on," Charlotte urged gently.

Sitting straighter, Nicole wet her lips. "Well, you know I like to cook. And entertain."

"Martha Stewart Living." It had always been around the house. Even now, there had to be a dozen issues stacked on the coffee table. Granted, a second stack held copies of *New England Home, Summer Cottage,* and *Cooking Light,* but the *Living* pile was higher.

"My bible," Nicole admitted. "It still inspires me, but since I never have exactly the same ingredients she does for, say, a roast duck or bouillabaisse—or the same materials for a centerpiece—mine come out a little different. So Julian and I were having people for dinner a lot—doctors, hospital administrators, friends who'd bring friends—and afterward they'd ask for recipes, or menu suggestions, or how to arrange wildflowers in a vase, or where to buy grass-fed beef. After a while, I thought it'd be cool to have a place to post the information so that everyone could read it. Suddenly people I didn't know were e-mailing. They were picking up on organic and local and homegrown."

"It's a hot topic."

"I wasn't thinking about that when I started to blog, but by the time the site was built, most of my posts had to do with eating organic, buying organic, supporting local farms and markets, and identifying restaurants that did the same, because that's what people were asking about. I began tagging along with Julian when he traveled for work, so it wasn't just Philadelphia, but Seattle, Denver, and Chicago. And it was Quinnipeague. People here didn't give it a name, but they were living farm-to-table before farm-to-table was a movement. They didn't call their produce organic, but they let you know that they didn't use artificial pesticides and fertilizers, and you knew the result—all delicious and safe. Organic was ingrained in me. Majoring in environmental studies at Middlebury was a logical next step, but I swear I didn't put two and two together until I started blogging about Quinnipeague. It's amazing, Charlotte. Those blogs get the most responses. People love reading about local farms and hand-made goods and free-range chickens, and it's all about farm-to-table."

"Hence Nickitotable.com." Charlotte was still amazed. "How many people read you now? Say, a single post."

"Over time, maybe thirty thousand."

"And Twitter?"

"The same number."

Charlotte sat back. "That's *amazing,* Nicki. All from nothing in how long?"

"Six years. Mostly the last four." Pushing up, she was off for the kitchen again. "I have cookies."

"I'm *stuffed,*" Charlotte cried, but the words of protest were barely out when Nicole returned with a dish of chocolate almond cookies.

"From the café." Settling back into the sofa, she retrieved her cappuccino.

Charlotte took a cookie, but didn't eat. "Did your dad know about the book?"

"He knew I was talking with a publisher. He'd have loved this." She frowned at her cup and said quietly, "I think about your parents, who weren't there for you. Then I think about Dad and me. To be so close to a parent—I was very lucky."

"You still are. You have Julian and his kids. You have Angie. They keep you anchored. I envy you that."

"You do not," Nicole scoffed with a small smile. "You love freedom. You love *adventure.* I'm the one who needs support." She stood, pausing as she reached for the fruit. "You've had enough, right?"

"For now." But before she could tell Nicole to sit and relax, Nicole was collecting utensils and plates. "Did you finish the Australia story?"

"I did." Gathering up wineglasses and napkins, Charlotte followed her into the kitchen. "Seriously. You have an incredible life. Freedom has its downside. There are times when I'd give anything for a real home. You—you have stability. I can't believe you and Julian have anniversary number ten coming up. Will you do something big to celebrate?"

"Maybe. What did you do about France?"

"Postponed. I'll go in the fall. But you need to do something for your tenth."

"We were in Paris two years ago," Nicole said as she loaded the dishwasher. "Julian delivered a paper there."

Julian Carlysle was cutting edge when it came to prenatal cardiac surgery. A brilliant surgeon, he had been a rising star at the time of his marriage to Nicole. Charlotte assumed Paris wasn't his only big-time venue. "How often do you two travel?"

"Every few months." Her green eyes lit. "Want to take a walk?"

"Where?"

"Wherever you want."

Having been in the car all day and just overeaten, Charlotte liked the idea. "The beach," was all she had to say.

Bundling up, they slipped out the sliders, crossed the stone patio, and went down two wide granite steps. Typical of the North Atlantic, the shore was rocky. The beach grass that sprouted between boulders was its only softening touch. Even the sand at the water's edge was hard packed and strewn with stones. But the ruggedness didn't detract from its lure. Here was nature in its raw beauty. The tide had ebbed, leaving behind swaths of seaweed. Drawn by its fishy smell, gulls squealed as they dove to peck marine life from the tangle.

Since it was still light, they walked toward the tail of the island. Sand and surf were rougher at this end, but invigorating. The breeze was steady, blowing hair, scarf, and grass. When Nicole looped an arm through Charlotte's, they walked as they had when they were kids—and for a time Charlotte was one again, on her own personal escape.

Then they passed the spot where she had been with Julian, and the escape turned dark. She had never retained the details of that hour. There had been too much wine, too much exhaustion, too much fog that night. There had also been subconscious baggage, at least on her part, though she didn't admit that for weeks. At the time, all she saw was a gigantic mistake. Julian had sworn her to silence the next morning, and she had readily agreed.

His life hadn't changed. He married Nicole a month later and had gone on with his career. For all she knew, he had convinced himself that nothing had ever happened.

She had tried to do it, too. There had been no love involved, no forethought. It was a gross error, a lapse in character, and while she might blame her parents for the example they set, she had no one to blame but herself. Julian had started it, but she had gone along.

Feeling ten years' worth of guilt now, she freed her arm under the pretense of scrambling over a cluster of rocks. When she returned to Nicole, she walked sideways. "So, how is the good doctor?"

"Fine," Nicole chirped. "Really busy."

"Still working long hours?"

"Uh-huh."

"Does that bother you?"

"He loves his work. What about you, Charlotte? Who do you date?"

"No one special. But you didn't answer my question. Do his hours bother you?"

"How can they?" Nicole returned. "He's in the prime of his career. He lectures, he sits on panels, and he's even on TV now, which is a total no-brainer since he's handsome and articulate. They call him when they're reporting on anything related to fetal surgery. He's their expert." Her fingers quoted the word.

"So he's in demand," Charlotte said and couldn't resist adding, "I'm glad. I was worried he'd have hung around here longer if I hadn't been coming." As tests went, it was subtle. His absence might be entirely innocent; any man would be wary of spending time alone with two women writing a cookbook. If Nicole knew about the sex, she hadn't let on in any of their earlier discussions.

Indeed, she seemed appalled now. "Oh no. He would have loved to see you, but he wants to be at Duke a week before the new doctors arrive, and he has to settle everything in Philly before he leaves."

"I'm amazed he can leave his own work for a whole month."

She waved a hand. "It's for teaching, which is honestly and truly, I mean, *really* his strength. Hold on." Having apparently felt a vibration, she dug the phone from her pocket, saw the screen, and picked up the call with a grin. "Hey. She did, got here just fine. What?" She covered her free ear. "I'm sorry, the ocean is pretty loud. Oh, wow, that's great. Beijing? You *should*. Uh, honey, we're just walking the beach. Can I call when we get back?" She listened for a minute, bowing her head at the end. "Oh," she murmured, walking faster, and said something Charlotte thought was *shit*, though Nicole didn't usually use that word. "Okay. I'll call. Love you."

Ending the call, she stuffed the phone back in her pocket, and, head still down, strode on.

Charlotte's legs were longer, but she had to hurry to catch up. "Everything okay?"

Nicole raised her head, eyes blank for a beat before refocusing. "He was invited to China. May have a conflict. It'll be okay." She didn't sound sure, but before Charlotte could ask, she glanced at the sky. "It's getting dark."

"Rain clouds?"

"Or dusk." She brightened. "Remember when we used to walk out here with the sun going down?"

"I do." Charlotte smiled. "We were taking a chance, going a little farther, a little farther, closer and closer to Cole land." She squinted, trying to penetrate the fog and spot the marker. "Cecily Cole is at the top of my list. I can't wait to talk with her."

Cecily's herbs grew in the garden of her home at Quinnipeague's outer tip, but to call her an herbalist was to understate her place in island lore. Her herbs were pure in flavor and powerful in use—and she knew how to use them, both gastronomically and medicinally. She had a way of appearing with remedies when they were needed most; this was the light side of Cecily Cole. But there was a dark side, or so island men claimed. They swore that when they suffered heartburn, it was one of Cecily's herbs punishing them for an alleged offense to their wives. A diminutive woman with silver hair that protected her back like a gossamer shawl, Cecily was alternately loved and feared.

"Oh Lord." Nicole was gaping at her. "You don't know. Cecily died five years ago."

Charlotte stopped walking. "Died? But she's key to cooking here. How can we do this book without her?"

"Her herbs are still around. Didn't the chowder and clams taste as good as ever?"

"Yes, but you can't talk about island food without talking about Cecily."

"We can still talk about her. We just can't talk *with* her. Not that we ever really could."

Charlotte remained stunned. As legendary as Cecily was, she had always been something of a mystery. She had come to the island at the age of twenty—or eighteen or twenty-two, depending on which version of the story you heard—after a disastrous love affair with an influential mainlander. Likewise depending on the storyteller, she had either chosen to leave the continental U.S. or been driven away, though it was generally agreed that she bought her house with a payoff from the affair. She had brought her plants with her, along with the seeds of legend, and lived quietly at her end of the island. Her interactions with islanders were limited to trips to the store for supplies and, increasingly, gifting herbs to those in need. Habitually distrustful, she did not welcome guests to her home. Rumor had it that she would put a curse on anyone who trespassed on her land.

But that was rumor, and in the interest of the cookbook, Charlotte had the perfect excuse to approach.

"I think we should go back," Nicole said.

Charlotte had done stories on some highly intimidating characters, not the least being a Native American on Martha's Vineyard, who claimed to be the descendent of Wampanoag medicine men and had a trail of miraculous doings to prove it.

Cecily Cole? She might have been an epic challenge, with the potential for information just as great.

But it was what it was. "She's dead," Charlotte said. "She can't do anything. I think we should go see if those herbs still grow."

"I wouldn't do that," Nicole warned. "Her son lives there now."

"I thought he was in jail."

"Not anymore. Come on. I'll race you back." She turned, facing home.

"Did he dig up the herbs, or are they still there?"

"I don't know."

"Someone must."

"Well, I'm not asking," Nicole said. "The last thing I need right now is more bad vibes."

Charlotte studied her face. The sky was indeed darkening, taking detail with it, but she could see tension. It seemed out of place on such an innocent face.

Likewise, the awkwardness with which Nicole waved a hand. "You know what I mean—Dad dropping dead, our selling the house."

"He would have loved your doing this book."

"I could have used his encouragement."

Charlotte slipped an arm around her waist. "You have me. I'll be right here until the book is done."

Nicole smiled. There may have been tears in her eyes, though it could have been the reflection of the ocean in the dim light. "I love you, y'know."

Charlotte hugged her. A moment later, exhilarated to be the object of something so rich, she dared Nicole with a look. They set off down the beach at a fast jog, trading the lead as they dodged obstacles in the sand. By the time they reached the house, they were out of breath and laughing.

Their movement on the beach steps set off floodlights from the patio all the way around to the kitchen door. Nicole stopped, sniffed. "Strange," she said and began walking toward the side garden, where a profusion of reds and pinks blurred at the edge of the beam. "I was out here this morning. The lavender was nowhere near being in bloom. It's been way too cold. But how could I not have smelled this?"

Charlotte hadn't smelled it earlier, either, but she couldn't miss it now. This lavender was in full bloom, its tall spikes clustered with purple flowers that looked too soft for the wind but apparently weren't, since they held their form well.

"My mind must have been somewhere else," Nicole said. "But this is *perfect*." Moments later, she had clippers and began handing sprigs to Charlotte, who was absorbing their smell to the point of stupor. Finally, Nicole stood, closed her eyes, and inhaled. "Ahhhh. Amazing." She took half of what Charlotte held and sang softly, "Those are for your pillowcase, these are for mine."

"Don't we have to dry them first?"

"And dilute the smell? Lavender has calming properties. I'll take it full strength, thanks."

Charlotte didn't need calming—or rather, didn't want it. She wanted to bask in the glow of hope. She was being given a second chance to prove she could be a loyal friend, which was more than she might have asked after living ten years and a huge secret apart. She had expected awkwardness, wariness, reticence—*something*. But her arrival on Quinnipeague had been as smooth as the ocean was not.

Besides, after leaving New York at dawn and driving for hours, she was exhausted. If the lavender sprigs did anything beyond making her smile, she had no idea. Minutes after her head hit the pillow, she had fallen into a sleep so deep that she heard nothing of the conversation coming from Nicole's room down the hall.

Chapter Three

NICOLE WAS A BUNDLE OF nerves. She had wanted to call Julian back sooner—hell, had wanted to talk with him there on the beach, but it was impossible with Charlotte along. And even when they were back at the house, what could she do? Sneak off to the bathroom to talk with him about life-and-death issues, then return to Charlotte like nothing was wrong?

"Hey," she said the instant he picked up, "I'm sorry. I thought she'd never go to bed. Tell me again what happened."

"My left leg went numb," he said quietly. "I was just getting up to leave at the end of a team meeting."

At the hospital, in clear view of doctors and nurses who knew him. *Nightmare.*

"I sat down again and picked up my cell, like I had a call, while everyone else left. The numbness let up after a few minutes, but my leg's never done that before."

"Maybe it just fell asleep," Nicole said hopefully. "That happens to me all the time, and if it went away—"

"It was numb, Nicki. Not asleep. Not trembling. Plain-out numb. That means this medication is not working."

"Maybe it just needs more time," she tried.

"It's been three months. It either works or it doesn't."

"Maybe the numbness is a side effect of the drug itself. You often have those."

"Numbness isn't a side effect. It's a symptom."

"But it'll pass." She had to believe that. He saw the best doctor, took the best drugs.

"New symptoms are not a good sign."

"Did you call Peter?" Peter Keppler was a neurologist. His office was in New York, where they could visit him without Julian's world knowing.

"He says it could be a fluke, but, cripes, this is getting scary."

Julian had multiple sclerosis. The MS diagnosis had come four years earlier, and though he felt near-constant fatigue, his symptoms, mostly blurred vision and tremors, remained intermittent and mild. Still, the diagnosis was devastating for a surgeon who was not only entering the prime of his career, but in a specialty where the tiniest wrong move of the scalpel could damage a fetus.

So, with the ink still wet on his diagnosis, he had stepped back from the work that he loved. When he scrubbed up now, it was to teach other surgeons the technique for which he was known. No one questioned this; it was a natural progression in a brilliant career. Nicole knew that, but it was little solace when she saw how much Julian missed not doing the work himself. Saving the lives of unborn children was heady stuff.

But there was no choice here. If he had continued to operate knowing he was impaired, he would have risked not only patients, but reputation and self-respect.

The key was controlling the disease, to which end he had tried every gold-standard treatment, but nothing had slowed the frequency of his symptoms. Adding to Nicole's own misery was his insistence on secrecy. Since no one at the hospital knew, she wasn't allowed to tell her friends, her personal physician, even her mother.

"Peter is the best, Jules," she said now. "There's always something else to try."

But he was discouraged. She could hear it in his murmur. "We're running out of options," he said, and he would know. An academic at heart, he had read every theory, every study, every paper there was to read on MS.

Nicole had married a positive guy. She didn't know what to do with this one. "I'm flying home tomorrow," she decided.

"No. You need to be there."

"I need to be with you."

"I need to be alone." He had said that before, and no matter how he tried to soften it, it hurt. "I love you, baby, but sometimes I'm so concerned about you that I can't think about what *I* need to do. Right now, I need you there doing your book." There was a meaningful pause. "You haven't told her, have you?"

"You made me promise not to," Nicole charged, releasing her frustration in this peripheral way. "Do you know how hard that is? I mean, talk about awkward. There were a dozen times when it would have been totally appropriate to share it—like when I realized I hadn't told her Cecily Cole was dead, which has major impact on this cookbook, but I must have been so preoccupied each time she and I talked that I hadn't said it. I mean, who's she going to tell, Jules? She doesn't know anyone you know. She can be trusted with a secret. Same with the kids." His son was eighteen, his daughter twenty-one. "It's been four years, and we see them a lot. Don't you think they'll be hurt when they finally find out?"

"So I should tell them now and have them terrified that I'm going to die—or worrying that *they'll* get it someday? There's no test to tell them that. What can they do?"

"Support you. Support *me*."

He didn't answer, simply said a despondent, "Well, I just wanted you to know about the leg."

"I want to *help,* Julian. What can I do?"

"There isn't much."

"You're my rock," she warned, only half kidding. His solidity was one of the first things she had loved about him. He knew what he wanted and made it happen.

"Rocks don't have tremors. They don't go numb in front of a roomful of colleagues."

"Being a rock is a state of mind. You're usually upbeat."

"So maybe I'm human," he snapped, but eased in the next breath. "Oh baby, I don't want to argue. I hate it when I get like this. It's just that I don't understand my body. I don't know why I react negatively to the best of the meds. Shortness of breath, high blood pressure, stiffness—so we change meds, or I take another pill, cut out salt, stretch more, add yoga. I can't operate. Barring a miracle cure, I won't ever operate again. So what's left? My self-image. I want to be *seen* as healthy, at least. But the longer this goes on, the greater my chances of being publicly exposed, and once that happens . . . *pffffhhh*."

"You'll always be able to teach," Nicole said, though her eyes had filled with tears. "You can do research and write papers. Your mind is brilliant. That won't go away."

She must have said something right, because he seemed to regroup. "I know," he said. "I just feel weary sometimes." He took a breath. "Not the kind of future you expected, huh?"

No. It wasn't. She tried not to go there, but it was hard not to—hard not to google MS and read about its progression; hard not to think about Julian being there in not-such-a-long time. MS didn't kill. It disabled. Sometimes badly. And as his wife, she was totally helpless.

"Let me come home," she begged again. "You're all alone with this. At least I *know*."

"I don't want pity."

"I have *never* pitied you," she shot back. "That's such an unfair thing to say. But I could cook, do errands, pay bills—"

"Paying bills is *my* job. My income may be down, but I'm still the earner here. Don't rush me into a wheelchair, Nicole. I'm not debilitated yet."

"I didn't say—"

"You focus on your business, I'll focus on mine."

"That's not how a marriage is supposed to work."

He was silent for a time, then sighed. "Oh God. I didn't ask for this. I'm just trying to deal."

"So am I. I love you."

"Love can't cure tremors. Let me concentrate on what will, okay? Talk later. Bye."

"Later" was twenty minutes. Nicole had spent the time sitting on the bed, alternately rocking forward and back, side to side, trying to soothe the shakes inside and to think of something to do. When her cell rang, she jumped.

"I'm sorry," he said quietly. "I shouldn't take it out on you."

Her eyes filled again. "I'm just trying to help."

"I know. But this is the hardest thing I've ever faced. I grew up wanting to be a surgeon. I never wanted to be anything else." They had talked about this before. Each time he started, she let him vent. "My father is still operating, and he's sixty-eight. I know, I know. He's in orthopedics. It's not fetal. But it still requires a steady hand. Me, I was supposed to have another twenty years. I was supposed to discover newer forms of in-utero intervention. This was just supposed to be the start." He was silent. Then, "You there?"

"Yes."

"You're very quiet."

Nicole might have said that he had already made his mark with a breakthrough technique, which was more than most surgeons ever did—and as for his father, *he* would know that getting MS was not Julian's fault, but Julian refused to tell him, too, so he was without that support as well.

Right now, he was feeling self-pity. He had a right, she supposed.

"Nicole?"

"I don't know what you want me to say."

He sighed. "I guess there isn't much you can."

Lately, that was the state of their marriage, which was nearly as upsetting to Nicole as MS.

"My patients could teach me about dealing with illness," he murmured. "The frustration, the fear. I never knew. It's humbling."

Nicole knew about frustration and fear. For four years, her mantra had been *It's okay, something will work, there are new treatments all the time.* But it was starting to sound empty. She knew what the future could hold, and it wasn't the illness that terrified her most. She could deal with the illness. She just wasn't sure Julian could.

"Beijing will be great," she tried by way of encouragement. The invitation to speak there was a coup.

He was suddenly hesitant. "Should I be that far away if something goes wrong?"

Timidity was new. Not a good sign. "You're speaking at a hospital. Peter can get the name of an MS person there."

Julian was quiet. Then, "So, was it great seeing Charlotte?"

Nicole doubted his heart was in the question, but she welcomed the diversion. "It was. She's just the same. We still get along really well. We're both even reading the same book."

"Did you cook dinner for her?"

"I was going to, then Dorey met us at the ferry and started talking about chowder, and we couldn't resist. We brought it home and ate in front of the fire. Did you eat out?"

"No. I picked up chicken at Whole Foods. Is the weather still cool?"

"For sure. There?"

"Warm and humid."

"I wish you'd come up," Nicole said. In the old days, he would have eaten at restaurants with colleagues when she was gone, missing her enough to not want to eat home alone. Now he was hiding—not that she dared say that.

"I have to get ready for North Carolina."

"You could do that on Quinnipeague, then fly straight to North Carolina from here. Charlotte would love to see you."

"Nah. There's too much to wrap up here. Let me see if this numbness recurs."

"Will you let me know?"

"You won't be calling to check?"

She sensed he was teasing her, but she saw nothing funny in the question. "If I call, you'll jump on me for it, so I don't *dare,* but that doesn't mean I won't be thinking about you all the time."

"I thought the point of having Charlotte there was to think about something else."

"It is. But you're my husband, and everything in me is saying I should be in Philadelphia and *not* Quinnipeague, only you won't allow it, so will you do this for me, at least?"

"What if Charlotte's right there?"

"I'll say I can't talk."

He waited a beat. Finally, "Okay, baby. I'll call."

Nicole hung up the phone and cried. She did this a lot when Julian wasn't around, just lots of quiet, helpless, frightened tears. They always slowed in time, as they did now. She blew her nose and wiped her eyes. Then she spotted the lavender on the pillow. Lifting the sprigs, she held them to her nose. She breathed in once, then again.

Two sniffs wouldn't do it, of course, and the more she consciously tried to relax, the more she worried. Coming off the bed, she put on a robe and fluffy slippers, then, opening the door with care so that its creak wouldn't wake Charlotte, she crept down the stairs. In the kitchen, she made passionflower tea, turning the jar of loose leaves in her hand while a teaspoon's worth steeped in her mug. The tea was local, made from an herb that rarely grew in New England but did on Quinnipeague. A natural sedative, passionflower was another of Cecily Cole's gems.

The tea was still steeping when she decided she was hungry. On impulse, she took a jar of strawberry jam from the cupboard. It, too, was local, put up the fall before by one of the island women. Unscrewing the lid, she pried a layer of wax from the top and, taking a spoon, sampled it straight from the jar. She closed her eyes, isolating the sense of taste for the greatest enjoyment. Strawberries . . . and vanilla? Eyes popping open, she peered into the glass until she spotted the bean among the berries. A single bean. No surprise there. Vanilla beans came from a variety of orchid that had no business growing on Quinnipeague, but did. Not only was the flower a more vivid yellow than elsewhere, but the bean was potent.

After scooping out a glob of jam and adding crackers, she set the plate on the large oak table, but she didn't immediately sit. Distracted, she ran a hand over the pickled wood. She loved this table. If she and Julian had a bigger place, and she could take one piece of furniture, it would be this. Happy memories filled the chairs here, crowded in with hopes for three babies, maybe even four. As a lonely only, she had always wanted a big family, and Julian had been on board with that. But Nicole was only twenty-four when they married, and Kaylin and John, who lived with them part-time, were preteens. There was plenty to do before her own babies came, and when they finally started trying, instead of a pregnancy came Julian's diagnosis.

Her father was aching for grandkids. In his last years especially, he used to ask. *So, toots, any good news coming? Your mother and I would love to babysit.*

Bob hadn't known about Julian, either.

Her throat tightened. Determined not to cry again, she sank into the chair, opened her laptop, and logged on to Nickitotable.com. Blogging was her escape. It had struck her more than once that if Julian had not been diagnosed, she wouldn't have this site, this following, this book contract—and she would have been perfectly happy. Now, it was a godsend. What else would she do when she woke up in the middle of the night and couldn't sleep? Talking about what she did know was ten times better than imagining what she didn't, and she did know restaurants and farmers' markets, flower arrangements and menu planning. These were safe things. They were *happy* things.

Today, there were questions to answer from readers as well as ones from a woman named Sparrow, who had created her blogsite and now handled requests for everything from reviewing a new farm collaborative to submitting guest blogs. So sweet little Nicole, who had never aspired to work, had a staff. And businesses actually paid her to post ads. Initially, they'd been local to Philly, but increasingly they had a national reach. She was actually bringing in enough to net a profit. It wasn't as much as a book would bring in, but it made the blog self-sustaining, like the agro-elements she promoted.

Tonight, the readers' questions were easy—what different salad to serve with lasagna, how to store limes, suggestions for an anniversary party placecard. She suggested, in order, a beet salad, the refrigerator, and a Hershey's kiss with names on strips sticking out of the top. Yes, she wrote to Sparrow, she did want to advertise beef online but said a "no thanks" to the company selling frozen hors d'oeuvres. She knew the brand and didn't care for it. Money was money, but she did have standards.

Paying bills is my job, Julian had said. *My income may be down, but I'm still the earner here.* And if that changed? She shuddered to think. But it was one of the reasons she was doing this book. She wanted to be able to help.

Thinking of it made her hands tremble even without MS, and the irony of that?

Pulling up a blank screen, she began to type quickly, though it was a minute before her fingers stopped hitting wrong keys and found their way. "Charlotte arrived today, but we didn't even mention the cookbook. There's plenty of time for that. For now, it's about us. I've told you about Charlotte—Charlotte Evans?" She added a link to Charlotte's most recent piece. "She's the one who's collaborating with me on the cookbook. We've known each other since we were eight, which makes it so special to be working together. She's one of those friends you don't see for a long time and then pick up where you left off. Our lives are radically different—I'm married, she's not; I'm a homebody, she's always gone—but once she got here, we didn't stop talking.

We're even reading the same book—*Salt*. Have any of you guys read it yet?"

She described Charlotte's arrival and talked a little about Dorey, because the beauty of these summer blogs was to seed interest in the book. She had written about Quinnipeague many times in the past, though more out of love than ambition . . . not that ambition hurt now. "We brought dinner home from the pier, but I couldn't just plop it down on the coffee table by the fire. You know my mantra. It's all about the presentation, which is pretty easy if you keep the right materials on hand. Up here we do, because my mother loves pretty things, which is probably where I came by the trait. I used woven place mats that were a heathery blue. The dishes were a deeper blue. So were the napkins—and not paper ones, either. I like cloth. Linen, actually. I know you all hate to iron, but if you buy a whole bunch, and basket the dirty ones until you have enough to wash together, then hauling out the ironing board isn't so bad."

She reread the words, paused, dropped her hands to her lap. Julian loved cloth napkins. He loved lit candles and fresh flowers. His first wife had been a corporate type who was out several nights a week and, even when not, had no desire to cook. The second time around, he had wanted a homemaker. Old-fashioned? Maybe. But Nicole loved homemaking. She loved playing backup to her husband. This was what her mother had done. It was all Nicole had ever seen, all she'd ever wanted.

The words on the screen blurred. Her mind jumped ahead to a future in which Julian would be unable to work, unable to travel, unhappy.

She blinked, took an unsteady breath, dragged her thoughts back to Charlotte, dinner, and presentation.

"What else?" she typed. "We have low stacks of books on the table, along with a grouping of hurricane lamps and votives. I didn't light them. It would have been overkill, with the fire going and the sun still up. But they were pretty just sitting there unlit. Take a look." Leaving the table, she retrieved her camera, connected it to the laptop, and inserted the pictures she'd taken of the table with its books, candles, and place settings. Refusing to be distracted again, she hurried on. "People usually pair white wine with seafood, but this being summer and our meal being mostly shellfish, the rules are loose. I found a fabulous Pinot Noir in the cellar."

She chatted about that for a bit, before posting several more pictures, these of food and wine, and she shared her recipe for sabayon sauce, right down to the Riesling. Then, pulling up a shot of Charlotte, she cropped to the head and sat back. Long, thick, wavy brown curls, a mouth that was too serious but had always been that way—Charlotte looked good. She did look older. But *good* older. Her skin wasn't heavily moisturized or made up. She had never been one for that, had never been able to afford it, and though Nicole guessed she could now, she apparently chose not to. And maybe she was right. She didn't seem to need it.

Nicole did. Lately, her eyes looked tired and her hair dull. There were times, worrying about Julian, when she felt ancient. So she went a shade lighter, bought new makeup, had a facial or a manicure—anything to give her a lift.

Charlotte was lucky. She didn't care if her nose burned in the sun or if the wind chapped her lips. And because she didn't care, neither ever happened. Nicole envied her the indifference, though it was easy to be indifferent when you had so little to lose. Nicole had a lot to lose—home, husband, lifestyle. Charlotte had never had any of that.

So is it harder to dream about what you don't have, than to live in fear of losing what you do?

She didn't know the answer. But she heard self-pity. And she had thought *Julian* had that?

Remorseful, she refocused on her screen. No, Charlotte didn't have a husband or kids. She didn't have time for them, what with chasing stories all over the world. By comparison, Quinnipeague was tame. Nicole was lucky she had agreed to come. She wanted to make it a nice time in spite of MS.

Which raised the issue of breakfast. French toast? Frittata?

Definitely frittata.

Leaving the table again, she transferred a small packet from freezer to fridge. It was salmon, home-smoked on the island and more delicious than any she had ever found elsewhere. Smoked salmon wasn't Cecily Cole's doing, but the dried basil and thyme she took from the herb rack were. Taking a vacuum-sealed package of sun-dried tomatoes from the cupboard, she set it on the counter beside the herbs. Frittata, hot biscuits, and fruit salad. With mimosas. And coffee. That sounded right. Eaten out on the deck maybe?

No, not on the deck, unless the prevailing winds turned suddenly warm.

They would eat here in the kitchen, with whatever flowers the morning produced. Surely more lavender. A woman could never have enough lavender—or daylilies or astilbe, neither of which should bloom this early, but both of which had looked further along than the lavender, yesterday morning, so you never knew.

Returning to the computer, she finished her blog post. Finally, entering "It's all about the setting" as the title, she signed it, dated it, and published it. She surfed for a while after that, checking her usual farm food Web sites for news, but there was little since she'd checked the day before. So, taking her copy of *Salt* from the counter, she settled in the Great Room with her tea and, in the wee hours, began to read.

Chapter Four

Charlotte awoke to the sound of the surf, the smell of sweet biscuits, and a sense of peace. Some of that peace was from the lavender in her pillowcase, its scent a halo around her still, but she was convinced that what she felt went beyond that. Just as her coming here as a child had been crucial, so was this.

Redemption was part of it now. She could help make this cookbook special.

But there was more. This summer would be a turning point in her life. How else to explain the sense of rightness she felt?

True, it could be wishful thinking. She had felt rightness that February in Rio, when she was sent to do a piece on samba and ended up teaching girls in the slums how to write—and again that summer in Sweden with a guy she thought might be the one. Both trips had been great, but she had returned home alone, exactly the same.

Still, she knew that at this moment in time, she was supposed to be here.

Slipping from bed, she crossed to the window. The view from her room was of the rougher northeast stretch of beach that they had walked last night. As the morning fog shifted, the breakwater came and went. Likewise a fishing boat farther out. At least she thought it was a fishing boat, though it wasn't visible long enough to let her know for sure. Staring harder, she caught a glimpse of sails. No fishing boat then. In the next instant, though, the sails, too, were gone.

A ghost ship. That was an exciting thought. She could weave up a whole slew of imaginative stories around a ghost ship. Pressing her palm to the cool windowpane, she smiled. She was good at dreaming up stories, used to do it all the time. Imagination had been her escape when she was a child.

Here, reality was the escape. Choosing hot biscuits over a ghost ship, she layered a sweatshirt over her T-shirt and sleep shorts, pulled on a pair of wool socks, and followed the smell.

An hour later, she was stuffed. Frittata, hot biscuits, sliced kiwi and grapes, two mimosas, and endless coffee—Nicole kept plying her with more, refusing to let her move from her seat to either serve food or clean up. She was feeling pampered, but then, she always did when she came here. Nicole was mothering her the same way Angie used to. Back and forth between stove, sink, fridge, and coffeemaker—she didn't stop moving.

Nor did she stop talking. She mentioned the blog she'd just posted and the preliminary book cover her editor had sent, but these were only en route to discussing Charlotte's own work. She seemed to have read it all—humbling for Charlotte, who had spent the same years in ignorance of Nicole's life and wanted to hear about that, but Nicole wouldn't allow it.

Finally, when she was about to make one more trip to the sink, Charlotte caught her hand. "You're making me dizzy, Nicki. *Sit.*"

Nicole was quickly apologetic. "I'm sorry. I love doing this."

"The dishes can wait. I want to talk."

"We are talking."

"Not about what I want." She softened the words by jiggling her friend's hand. "I want to know about your life."

Nicole looked cornered. "My life? My life is great."

"So's mine. End of discussion." She stared in challenge.

Nicole stared back, then laughed. "You haven't changed. Same blunt Charlotte." When Charlotte continued to stare, she finally settled back into her chair. "What do you want to know?"

"Start with Kaylin and John," Charlotte said. "Are you guys close?"

Nicole's smile held affection. "Very. Julian and I share custody with Monica . . . well, shared, past tense, because they're both over eighteen now. Come fall, Kaylin will be a senior at Penn and John a sophomore at Haverford, but right up through high school, they were at our house all the time."

"House or condo?"

"Condo," she acknowledged. "We kept thinking we'd buy a house, but Kaylin loved playing Eloise in a high-rise, and Johnny loved running up and down the halls—and it was only ten minutes from Monica, who did have a house with a yard, and like I said, there were summers up here. Mom and Dad loved it. And the kids adored them. They've taken Dad's death hard."

Charlotte believed it. Bob was one of the warmest people on earth. Right from the start, he had considered Julian's children his grandchildren. But those two were supposed to have been a prelude to more. There had been lots of talk about that during the wedding summer.

So—yes, *same blunt Charlotte*—she asked, "Why haven't you had more kids?"

"Because we already had two to raise."

"You always talked about having your own."

"There's no rush. I know"—a dismissive wave—"I'm thirty-four, but that doesn't make any difference. All that talk about the biological clock? Sometimes I think it's a crock of you-know-what. Women today are having kids in their forties. *Lots* of women are. I know three doing it right now."

Her response was a bit too emphatic for Charlotte. "Is there a problem?"

"Like fertility? No. We'll have kids. We're just taking our time."

"If Kaylin and John are both in college, and Julian is forty-six, what are you waiting for?"

"Charlotte. You're as bad as my mother!"

But Charlotte wasn't being put off. She needed to know that Nicole's marriage was okay. "He didn't change his mind about having more, did he?"

"Oh no," Nicole insisted. "He wants them as much as I do." She glanced at the window and brightened. "Sun's breaking through. Let's take coffee out to the patio." Before Charlotte could respond, she was heading for the mudroom. She returned carrying two parkas, and though her step remained light, her eyes had misted. "Mom's and Dad's. I was thinking I'd give them to the church. They'll know who can use them. You take Mom's." It was red. She held it out.

"I'm taller than you. Give me Bob's—"

But Nicole's arm was firmly around the larger blue one. "I need his," she said in a single fast breath.

Charlotte took the red one. Helping with the coffee, she carried mugs while Nicole grabbed biscotti. Minutes later, they were outside. The patio was a patchwork of granite slabs that had been quarried in Maine and set in an arcing pattern to mirror the shore. Two heavy wood chairs stood to the right of the beach steps, facing the sea. Closer to the house and more protected were the table on which they had so often eaten back then—glass on top, iron below—newly cleaned and surrounded by chairs.

Off to the side were a trio of lounges. They pulled two of these closer to the house, under a pergola whose vines would be overrun with peachy roses within the month.

Cupping her coffee for its warmth, Charlotte tucked her legs under her jacket and angled toward Nicole. "Are you happy?"

Nicole's eyes were bright over her mug. "Happy?"

"With Julian. With your marriage."

"Of course."

"Is he good to you?"

"He's an angel. Why do you ask?"

Charlotte wanted to believe that Julian loved her, that there was no pattern of infidelity, and that nothing about that one awful night lingered. "Just curious. You always had energy, but it feels nervous now."

"I've told you—lots on my mind . . . Dad, the house, the book."

"As long as it's not Julian. I want to know you're happy."

Nicole jumped up and, all but lost in Bob's parka, crossed the patio. "I *would* be happy if the gardener had done his job, but look at the mess here." She knelt at the creeping cypress that bordered the stone and began plucking brown tips from the lowest fronds. "They think we won't see these, but it isn't only about looks, it's about the health of the plant. If you want new growth, the old stuff has to go."

"Is George Mayes still doing your work?" Charlotte recalled him being a character, as likely to show up tipsy as not, but intent either way on talking the plants and shrubs through the toughest of times.

"George tries," Nicole said as she searched for anything dead she might have missed, "but he's in his eighties, so his son Liam does most of the work." Stuffing what she'd pruned in her pocket, she returned to the lounge. "Liam isn't as good, but they need the money, and it's not like there are dozens of landscapers on Quinnipeague to choose from, and then there's Rose." Wife of George, mother of Liam, Cheryl, and Kate, with however many grands, even great-grands by now. "Her slaw is still the best." She looked quickly around. "Where's my coffee?" Spotting it near the cypress, she scrambled up again. When she returned, she said, "I'm not sure if it's the celery seed or the dressing, but Rose is definitely on our list. Mayes Slaw is the perfect side."

Charlotte burrowed deeper into her parka. The memory brought a smile. "The best. And she made it for the whole town. I always imagined she had the grandkids lined up in a row, slicing cabbage at the counter like Santa's little elves."

Nicole laughed. It was a welcome sound. "Granddaughters. The boys'd be doing the physical stuff. They're a traditional family. Not all on Quinnipeague are. Wait'll you meet some of the new ones. We've gotten more diverse." Up again, she curved back toward the garden on the side of the house.

"What are you *doing*?" Charlotte called, perplexed by her constant up and down.

"Checking the flowers," Nicole called back. "Mom'll want to know if the sweet William is in bloom. That's the pink one. The lisianthus is ready to pop. It'll be a deeper purple than the lavender. Wait'll I tell her about *that*." She returned to the lounge. "By the way, I think it's mustard seed in that slaw."

"Is that an herb?"

"Mustard seed? No, it's a spice."

"What's the difference?"

"An herb comes from the leaves of a plant, a spice from the seeds," Nicole explained. "Some plants produce both, like cilantro and coriander. Salt is a mineral. We call it a spice, but it isn't."

"What's pepper?"

"A spice. A peppercorn is the seed from a pepper plant."

"Did Cecily Cole cultivate mustard plants?"

"Sure did."

Charlotte grinned. "Q.E.D."

Nicole laughed again. "That proves nothing. We don't know for sure what herbs Rose uses in her slaw."

"We'll ask. What we really need to do," Charlotte decided, "is to explore Cecily's gardens—you know, take pictures and all. She's the matriarch of island cooking."

"Tell that to her son."

"I will."

"He has a gun. He shoots gulls for sport."

Charlotte winced. "What does he have against gulls?"

"I don't know, but I'm not looking to find out. Cecily's plants are all over the island. We can get what we need from everyone else."

"But her garden is the source," Charlotte argued, as Nicole got up again. "Where are you going now?"

"I'm cold," came her little-girl voice. "I want to get dressed."

"Just grab a blanket from inside. It's gorgeous out here." She breathed in. "This air is amazing. Sweet."

"Charlotte, it's salt air, and there's no sun." She shot a hateful look at the clouds. "I honestly thought it was coming out, or I wouldn't have suggested this. Sun is cheerful. That's what I want. Actually," she called over her shoulder as she headed toward the house, "I think we should drive into town. It'd be good to let everyone know we're here."

Nicole had trouble sitting still. Charlotte couldn't shake the feeling that she was running from something and that the something was *her.* There were times when Nicole wouldn't look her in the eye, which meant maybe she did know about Julian and her, and was trying to move on.

Chastened, Charlotte got dressed. She offered to drive, but Nicole insisted on taking the old SUV that her parents kept at the house, giving her good reason for sadness. "Dad never worried about my driving here," she reminisced. "There's only one road, so you can't get lost, and you can't speed because it's bumpy."

"Do they ever repave?" Charlotte asked, jouncing now that she didn't have a steering wheel to hold.

"Not often. It's not a Quinnie priority. We're the spoiled ones. I was thinking I'd give this car to Eleanor Bailey, kind of as a thank-you. She was always bringing over crab cakes—remember those little minis? She knew Dad loved them."

"I loved them, too. That's another recipe we'll need."

Nicole was silent, staring out the windshield with both hands on the wheel, which would have been fine if her knuckles hadn't been white.

Charlotte touched her arm. "You okay?"

She nodded, cleared her throat, brought herself back. "Just thinking of Dad."

"As long as there's nothing else."

Nicole shot her a glance. "What else would there be?"

"Me," Charlotte dared say. "Are you sure you want me here to do this?"

Nicole looked stricken. "You don't want to be here. You have something better—"

"Better than *this*?" Charlotte cut in. "*Nothing* is better than this. Helping you with a book? I'm *honored*."

"Then don't say anything else," Nicole said gently. "We have the ingredients for an amazing team." More fiercely, she added, "And, please, don't even *think* of leaving." She drove on.

Paying penance. That was Charlotte's first thought in response. Her second was more poignant. "Maybe I bring back too many memories."

"Like, they won't come anyway? At least with you here, I have a shoulder to cry on."

"Promise you will?"

"Yes, but I'm fine. Really, I am."

And she was at first. They stopped at the post office, ostensibly to let the postmaster know that Charlotte might be getting mail, but since he did lobster bakes like no one else on Quinnipeague, and since he was a major conduit of island news, greeting him was good politics.

Then came the island library, which was connected to the hardware store, which the librarian owned with his wife, who made a great clam macaroni and cheese, hence a dual purpose there as well.

Neither visit was brief. Charlotte had forgotten how different island time was from time in the rest of the world. People weren't satisfied with a quick, "Hey, nice to see y'again." No matter what chore they were doing, they stopped to feed the wood stove and then stood there for the warmth, and you couldn't just walk away with them clearly in a gathering mood. They wanted to talk about Bob, of course, and Nicole graciously accepted their condolences. Since they had seen her over the years, though, it was Charlotte who was the novelty. They asked where she lived now, how long she had lived there, whether she had a husband or kids. When Nicole told them about her writing, they wanted to know how she came to doing it, whether flying bothered her, what Paris or Belize or Bali was like.

At times, it was a grilling. Take the hair salon. They stopped there because the owner was known for the quiches she brought to town breakfasts. When they arrived, the woman was in a cloud of scented styling mist as she finished with one client and started on another, and the questions came fast and furious. All three wanted to know *everything.*

Charlotte was beginning to weary of it, when they turned to Nicole. "And you, you're too thin. We'll fatten you up this summer. I didn't get to see your husband last week. Still curing the ills of the world, is he?"

"He is," Nicole said, slipping her elbow through Charlotte's and adding a singsongy, "We're off. We'll be back another time. Bye-bye." They were barely out the door when her elbow tightened and she muttered, *"Still curing the ills of the world?* Is that supposed to be funny? It's disrespectful, is what it is. Why can't people keep their mouths shut, if they can't say something nice?"

Charlotte was startled. "She thought it was." When Nicole didn't respond, she tried to smooth things over. "But hey, I'm glad we left. I'm usually the one asking the questions. It's hard being on the other end. I need a snack. Does the Café still have scones?"

Nicole was a minute settling. Then, she said, "Sure does."

"Are you game?"

"Sure am."

The Quinnie Café was as charming as Charlotte remembered. Relics of whaling days hung on dark-paneled walls, though the main attraction was the windows that looked out to the sea. Weather permitting, they would be open under awnings. This morning, though, it was all about the woodstove, whose dry scent flowed over armchairs, five round tables with chairs of a sturdy birch, and a counter with stools.

The tables looked new, as did the pendant lights that hung over each, but the biggest change since Charlotte had been here last was a profusion of outlets. Just then, two tables held people at laptops, newer Quinnies whom Nicole introduced as an op-ed writer for the *Times* and a computer programmer.

Since the Café was at the far end of the island store, hidden behind shelves of dog-eared magazines, jigsaw puzzles, and toys, those having coffee might not have been seen by those shopping for food if Bev Simone, who ran the store, hadn't spread the word, which she did—but only after following them in and updating Charlotte on ten years' worth of births, deaths, and marriages. "But Nicole and Julian, their wedding was the best," she concluded. "We still talk about it." She squeezed Nicole's shoulder. "Your daddy, God rest his soul, knew how to throw a bash. And such a handsome couple, you and the doctor. When'll he be back?"

"I'm not sure," Nicole said without blinking. "His schedule's tight. He's hoping maybe August."

"Hoping isn't good enough," Bev scolded.

Nicole's smile didn't budge. "It's the best he can do."

"He is one busy guy," Charlotte told Bev, who seemed mollified by that and, hearing a distant jangle, returned to the store. But she wasn't done. Since she viewed Nicole and Charlotte as celebrities—*writing a book, on us!*—she sent in one islander after the other to say hello.

So there were lots of questions in the Café, too, again aimed mostly at Charlotte, whom they hadn't seen in so long. Seeming happy to be left out, Nicole busied herself going back and forth in turn for scones, cappuccino, spoons for the cappuccino, knives to spread jam on the scones, and napkins.

Then came Beth Malcolm, the one who had worried Charlotte so many years before. She taught at the island school, which had just finished for the year, hence her being at the Café midday, midweek, and what she carried as she joined them was *Salt*.

"I must be the last person on Quinnipeague to read this," she remarked when Nicole and Charlotte exchanged a glance. "Have you read it?"

"Reading, present tense," Charlotte said.

"And you like it?"

"We do."

"Isn't it amazing?" she asked, then, seeming startled, abruptly turned to Nicole. "I saw Julian on TV. It was *so* awesome. I didn't recognize him at first. He was wearing a suit and looking so serious, but *good* serious, like you just knew he knew what he was talking about, and then there he was wearing shorts and a shirt here last week. The electrician—you know, the one who just did the wiring at your place—his wife had a baby in April and for a while before that they thought there was a problem with his heart, so everyone was talking about Julian and the miracles he does with preemies."

"Fetuses."

"We love it when he's here. When's he coming back?"

Nicole rolled her eyes toward Charlotte in a way that might have passed for indulgent if Charlotte hadn't known her so well. Here, it was pleading.

"Everyone's asking that," Charlotte told Beth, "and he's hoping for later in the summer, but he's swamped with work—"

"And besides," Nicole added in a high voice, "if he came back, he'd be on vacation. He wouldn't want people staring at him. He'd want privacy."

"Which," Charlotte quickly put in, because that high voice held an edge, "is the island specialty. How many kids are in the island school now?"

Distracted, Beth talked about that, then about her own two kids and her husband, whom she had met in college and brought back. He was a sculptor, creating masterpieces out of metal and struggling to be recognized, though after confessing the last, Beth said a contrite, "I promised him a sticky bun. Gotta go. Hey, we have a book group. You guys want to come?"

"Are you discussing *Salt*?" Charlotte asked with interest.

"Oh no, we all read that out of curiosity. But we're doing *Caleb's Crossing*. It's also about an island."

Charlotte had read it. "Maybe we will," she said and waved as Beth left. She would have asked if Nicole had read that one, too, if Nicole hadn't been looking in alarm at her scone. "What?"

"Currants," Nicole cried. "In these scones. *Not* grown here."

Charlotte was unsettled by what almost sounded like panic. Currants were no cause for that. Besides, the Nicole she had known was easy-going. Either she had changed, or something else was up, and it wasn't Bob. If she were thinking of Bob, she would be sad, not panicked.

They finished eating with little talk. Bev sent in another shopper, but the woman was innocuous and brief. As soon as she was gone, they slipped out themselves.

That was when they bumped into the publisher of the island weekly. He lit up when he saw them, though he quickly focused on Nicole. "I heard your good news. A book, huh?"

"Cookbook," Nicole corrected with a plastic smile. *Cornered* was the word that came to Charlotte's mind. She had thought it once yesterday, too.

"Good for you," the man said, "though I'm not surprised. Y'always had that little something special, right down to bringing that husband of yours to Quinnipeague. Say, I'd love to have a sit-down with the two of you to talk about your book—cookbook—and about his work. When's he comin' next? I'd do a story for the paper. This is front-page stuff. And hey, I'm sorry about Bob. He'll be missed."

Nicole nodded. She neither blinked nor stopped smiling.

The newspaperman barreled on. "He would have loved my doing a profile of the doctor and you—y'know, photo spread and all. Think Julian would agree to do it? Ahh, well of course he would. The paper's just for us Quinnies, and he loves it here." He reached for the door. "The wife needs elbows. She promised me lobster mac 'n' cheese, and I don't turn *that* down. If you want the best island recipes, you'll need that one. I'll tell her. She'll be excited about being in a book. So will you let me know when the doctor makes his plans? I'll come out to the house. That's worth profiling all on its own, but now we have you two stars in it. Book, TV—you're the power couple. Po-wer coup-le," he repeated, marking each syllable with a fist, before proceeding into the store.

Charlotte was thinking that it was true, when Nicole turned owl eyes on her. "I *remember* her lobster mac," she brayed, "and if she wants her dish in my book, she'll have to add something to it to make it different from every other mac 'n' cheese recipe out there today!" Charlotte drew her away from the store, but Nicole ranted on. "Power couple? *Power* couple? He doesn't know what he's *talking* about." She sounded frantic. "There are a gazillion cookbooks out there, I'm one of millions writing more, and Julian spends more time teaching than doing. *Power couple*? That is such a crock of *shit*."

Language, tone, look—all were so unexpected that Charlotte couldn't let it pass. Before she could ask, though, Nicole broke free and stormed off, away from the SUV and down the street.

"Where are you going?" Charlotte called.

Nicole stopped and looked around. Turning right, she headed for a cluster of rocks overlooking the pier. In summer, the rocks would hold visitors eating lunch, but on as cool a day as this, they were deserted. The only thing Charlotte could imagine was that she planned to jump.

She ran, catching Nicole's arm just shy of the rocks. "What is *wrong*?" she cried, frantic now herself.

Nicole's eyes were large, her face nearly as pale as her hair. "Nothing! Everything's fine!"

Charlotte shook her. "What *is* it, Nicki?"

Nicole put both hands to her head and pressed, her eyes suddenly confused.

"Please tell me," Charlotte begged gently.

"I can't." A whisper, pleading. "I can't."

"I'm here to help. I want to. It can't be that bad."

Nicole exploded. "MS *not that bad?*"

Charlotte gasped. "You?"

"Julian!"

The words echoed. Nicole looked around, thinking that someone else had said them, because if she was the one, it would be a betrayal of the worst kind.

But the only person in sight was Charlotte, who couldn't have known about this, and wouldn't have yelled it at her anyway, and Charlotte's face was blank.

Nicole felt a great sinking inside.

"He has what?" Charlotte whispered, cupping her shoulders.

She couldn't say it again. Julian hadn't wanted her to tell anyone, least of all Charlotte. Hadn't he specifically asked that last night? Now she'd gone and done it. She hadn't planned to, but that didn't matter.

He would be hurt, disappointed, *angry*. Their relationship had been rocky lately. This wouldn't help.

Thinking that she simply wouldn't tell him, which meant another secret to keep, she felt a great wave of despair and, sinking to her knees, burst into tears.

Chapter Five

Charlotte was stunned. Of all the possibilities to explain what was going on, she hadn't imagined illness. The Julian she remembered was too active, too fit. He was too dedicated, too *famous*—which, of course, was an absurd thing to say. Famous people got sick all the time. Famous people *died* all the time.

Not that Julian would die. MS was doable. Charlotte knew this for fact. But it was chronic, and chronic illness changed lives.

Kneeling, she wrapped her arms around Nicole, but her friend didn't allow it for long. Pulling back, she said in a voice that was broken but urgent, her eyes a haunted green, "You can't tell anyone, Charlotte. Promise you won't?"

"I won't."

"Not a single person. If Julian finds out I told you, he'll divorce me."

"He will not. He loves you."

She pulled a tissue from her pocket. "I used to be so sure of that, but he's changed." She pressed the tissue to her nose. "He used to be open. He used to be easy-going and confident, and he's still that way with everyone but me. With me, all the worry comes out. I'm the only one who knows—other than you now."

Charlotte didn't understand. "You can't be the only one. His dad's a doctor." She remembered meeting the senior Dr. Carlysle at the wedding. While not as academic as Julian, he had been impressive in a quiet way.

"Not his dad, not his mom," Nicole said. "No one but his doctors, and they aren't even in Philadelphia—and I totally understand that his future depends on people *not* knowing, but do you know how hard this is for me?"

Charlotte struggled to imagine. She was self-sufficient, but Nicole? Nicole was more dependent, more *social*. To be under a gag order with friends? "How long have you known?"

She brushed the tears from her eyes. "Four years."

"*Years?* Omigod. Through everything with Bob? Angie must be devastated."

"Charlotte. *Listen* to me. Mom doesn't *know*."

"But she's your mother."

Nicole stared at her.

"He wouldn't let you tell your own mother?" Charlotte asked in dismay, then held up a hand. "I'm sorry. I shouldn't criticize him. I haven't walked in his shoes." She tried to take it in. "I thought . . . I thought maybe you guys were estranged, like he had an affair or something."

"Julian? Not Julian. He's totally loyal, but me? I didn't make it a *day* without blabbering."

"You shouldn't have waited even that long," Charlotte scolded. "You should have told me the second I got here." She was puzzled. "Four years, and no one could *see*?"

"That's the thing. You don't see fatigue, which is what he feels most of the time, and the other symptoms come and go. No one looking at him sees a problem." Her voice went higher. "But MS is progressive. He isn't responding to medication, so we know where he's headed. And sometimes I think I'm being totally selfish because his symptoms are still mild—but think of what he does. He's a surgeon who works on the smallest creatures, and if his hands start to shake at the wrong time, it's a disaster. He isn't operating now, he just teaches, and he's dying inside, and no one knows that or knows why. It's like he's leading two lives—one in public, where everything is normal, and one in hiding, where he's worried and angry." She stopped, eyes welling again. "I shouldn't have told you, but you and I always talked about everything, and now, here we are, with everyone asking when he'll be back." She caught a breath. "He made me promise not to tell you. Is this disloyalty, or is it not?"

There it was again, that word. Charlotte might have said a thing or two about Julian and disloyalty, if that hadn't been the last thing Nicole needed to hear, and she wanted to help, *needed* to help. So she gentled. "Not disloyalty, Nicki. Survival. You're human. You have feelings and needs. You're a saint for having kept this to yourself for so long." Tugging her down so that they were sitting with their backs to a boulder, she said, "Tell me everything."

Once started, Nicole couldn't stop. The cork had popped, and four years of agony poured out. In the telling, she relived it: being in their condo when Julian had first told her the results of his tests, being with him in New York when his doctor laid out a course of treatment and again, repeatedly, when one regimen was abandoned and another begun, living on the roller coaster of hope and disappointment, hope and discouragement—and through it all, long night after long night at her computer, reading way too much about MS.

Boats creaked at their moorings far below as the surf washed the pier, the fishing shed, the shore. Though the stone protected them from the brunt of the wind, the salt air still circled, mixing with wood smoke from every building in sight. It was soothing. More soothing, though, was the unburdening. Julian would be furious. But she *was* human. She had acceded to his needs for so long, but this was *her* need.

Charlotte didn't have answers. She just listened. She didn't call

Nicole spoiled and self-centered when she cried that it was unfair, that Julian had such a promising future and *why did this happen to us.* Nor did she sugarcoat things, like Nicole's mother would have done. Her questions were brief and to the point. And afterward? Charlotte drove back to the house—just took over, and that felt wonderful, too—while Nicole summed it up. "It's a juggling act. We need to find a treatment that slows the progression of the disease, but doesn't throw him into cardiac arrest in the process."

"Has that happened?"

"Not yet, but only because they watch him closely. With one drug, he had to sit there for six hours after the first dose, and then his heart slowed so much that they refused to give him a second dose. That's been the story. Some of the most promising treatments cause such a bad reaction in him that he has to stop. That cuts the options way down. If nothing works—*ever*—the whole thing is . . . omigod, so awful. When I think of where we could be in a few years, I go into an all-out panic, which would be so bad for Julian that I try not to think, but I can't escape it, y'know? He comes home, and he's down. He's thinking it's only a matter of time before the wrong thing happens at the wrong time. I mean, he's already removed himself from the OR, but no one's figured out why so he's still in demand. And there's *another* thing," she hurried on. "He likes being on TV or onstage doing symposiums in front of thousands of doctors. He likes being invited to London and Paris and Beijing. I mean, who wouldn't? It's totally flattering. But once they learn he's sick, they'll assume he's lost his edge and won't call."

"How bad are the flare-ups?"

"Not awful. They only last a day or two, so he cancels things in Philly, and we take the train to see his doctor in New York."

"Corticosteroids?" Charlotte asked.

Nicole was startled. "How did you know that?"

"I did a piece once on a small clinic in the English countryside—"

"I read it. It was about cancer."

"I know, but for a little while afterward, I dated one of the doctors there. His specialty up to then had been MS. It was a bad relationship, but I learned a lot. Corticosteroids are used to treat flare-ups."

"They help," Nicole confirmed, "but you can't take them forever. Julian has to find something that prevents flare-ups in the first place. The thing with MS is that what helps one person won't always help another. We hear success stories about a new medication, then either he has a bad reaction to it or it does nothing for his symptoms."

They were back at the house, on the patio again, sharing a single lounge like they did when they were eight, now sipping hot tea under a finally warming sun, when Charlotte asked, "What about yoga?"

Nicole studied her, relieved—*so* relieved—to be able to finally share all this and with someone in the know. "Your doctor must've really talked."

"Mostly about himself," Charlotte replied, only barely amused. "At least the MS part was interesting. He mentioned yoga as an alternative treatment."

"Not alternative for us. Complementary, like *with* meds, not without. Julian isn't taking chances. Same with diet. There are so few studies to prove that things like macrobiotics will help, so he's just careful about what he eats. He always has been. And he exercises. He runs, he works out." She understood Charlotte's surprised look. "Sure, he falls. He blames his sneakers or the treadmill or the *curb*. It terrifies me." She felt terror even in the telling, though it wasn't as jagged as usual. Isolation magnified things, but Charlotte knew now. She understood. "He goes for a run, and I wait for the police to show up at the door to tell me he fell and was hit by a car."

"You can't do that to yourself."

"How not to? I know that it's selfish of me, when we're so much better off than most—"

"Hold it, Nicki. Don't say that again." Charlotte turned to fully face her. "Pain is pain. You have a right to feel it. You didn't ask for this."

"But I'm not handling it well. I don't know what to *do*. Tell me, Charlotte. I want to help him, but I don't know how. He says I hover, but I hover because I want to help. Then I say the wrong things . . . *do* the wrong things. I really am a very small person."

Charlotte looked genuinely astonished. "Are you kidding? Another person would be paralyzed, but not you. Look what you've done in the last four years—helping Angie, mothering Kaylin and John, blogging well enough to win a book contract. Give yourself credit, Nicole."

But she had trouble doing that. She tried to hold it together when she was with Julian, but when she was not, she worried about everything. "The blog takes my mind off MS. Maybe he's right about my needing to get away. And he's been pushing for this book. He is totally supportive." She was intense now. "I need it to be a success, Charlotte. Oh, not for my name—I don't want recognition—but if the book sells, there could be others." She framed hopeful headlines in the air. " 'Nickitotable does Quinnipeague.' 'Nickitotable does Chicago or San Francisco, or New Orleans.' It's about . . ." Not fame. Not even distraction. "Security." The word popped out. Now she considered it. "I'm spoiled. I took it for granted that Julian would always have a job."

"He will."

"But he won't earn what he used to," she said, hearing the words aloud and feeling their impact. "I can't talk about this with him. He goes nuts when I try. But if nothing works and he gets really bad . . . I need a source of income, Charlotte. I mean, I know this is just a cookbook, and cookbooks don't sell a gazillion copies, but I need it to sell well." She felt a qualm. "Am I setting myself up for failure?"

Charlotte smiled. "What did your dad always say?"

"Aim high, hit high," Nicole reeled off. "But look what happened to Julian."

"Right. He aimed for a great practice and got it. He aimed for a close family and got it. I'd say he did pretty well."

"Okay. He got his dreams," Nicole conceded. "But what about *mine*? I had dreams, too."

She saw the exact moment when Charlotte got it—a certain tick in otherwise steady brown eyes. "That's why you haven't had a baby?" She seemed stricken. "He can't have sex?"

A week before, Nicole would have minded the bluntness, but not now. With everything out in the open, she was feeling so relieved that Charlotte could have said *anything* and she wouldn't have minded.

"Oh, he can. It's not that. The crazy thing is, we deliberately put off having kids. Kaylin and John needed attention, and I could give it, and they gave me back so much. Now, Julian's the problem. He's afraid he won't be able to pay for clothes and education—he's afraid he won't be able to physically *hold* a child—and I keep telling him it's okay, that we'll find a way to make it work, that people with MS have kids all the time, but he doesn't want to hear it."

"Is MS hereditary?" Charlotte asked.

"They don't know for sure. I mean, there's *so much* they don't know—like why women get it more than men . . . like whether there's a relation between MS and mono . . . like why there's more MS in the northern U.S. than down south. Julian's had every test in the book, and they have no idea why he got this. He won't tell his friends or his parents. And he won't tell Kaylin and John. He says there's nothing they can do. Maybe he's right." She was thinking about that, trying to move on, but something still rankled. "The power couple? Not quite. We may look happy and successful and powerful to the world, but inside we're not. Julian is sick, and I am a fraud."

"You are not a fraud."

"Writing a cookbook to fill a hole in my life? Pu-leeze."

"That's how half the world works, Nicole. You've always been passionate about organics, and the farm-to-table movement is right up your alley. What you're doing is called sublimating, and it can produce *the* best things."

Nicole let the words float around her, wanting so badly to believe. This was why she had brought Charlotte here. Feeling a swell of gratitude, she studied her friend as, cupping her tea, Charlotte studied the sea. She was somber, brooding even, and Nicole didn't question it, after everything she'd dumped on her. It was a lot to take in.

For her part, though, Nicole felt lighter than she had in months.

Impulsively, she gave Charlotte a hug. "I'm lucky to have you. Your coming here has saved my life."

"That's melodramatic."

"I'm serious. I'm glad I told you. I feel *so* much better. It's like . . . it's like the sea shadow moved," she said and felt her father's presence. "Dad talked about that, too. Remember? Directly under clouds, the black patches on the water where it's dark and freezing cold? Well, I just moved. I can still see the shadow, but it's warmer and brighter where I am now. Thank you, Charlotte. You're the best."

Chapter Six

YOU'RE THE BEST, NICOLE HAD said. But Charlotte didn't think so. While she had been traveling around the world, picking and choosing assignments in a carefree, self-indulgent spree, her friend was at home going through hell. And if she'd known it, would she have hung around? Hanging around would have meant seeing Julian, and she wasn't sure he would have wanted that any more than she did.

Now that Nicole had confided in her, though, she shared the burden. Needing to know everything about MS—part refresher, part update—she spent the afternoon on the patio with her laptop. There was no fog now, and the only clouds were fluffy ones. The sun warmed her arms and legs, allowing her to unbundle, but the warmth didn't spread far inside. The advances in the five years since she'd broken up with Graham, her British doctor, were marked by new drugs, new theories, new trials. For every blog post touting a miraculous recovery, though, there was one claiming a hoax, and side effects were a recurrent issue.

Then came stem cell transplants, which had been niggling in the back of her mind. Graham had mentioned them as an MS treatment with future promise, and from what she read now, they were coming into their own. The process involved taking adult stem cells from bone marrow, tissue, or organs, and infusing them into the body to replace diseased cells with healthy ones. In the case of MS, a malfunction in the immune system caused damage to nerve coverings, disrupting the sending of electrical signals through the brain and spinal cord. This disruption was what caused MS symptoms. The aim of a transplant was to give the body fresh, new, healthy cells that could generate healthy nerve coverings.

Current thinking leaned toward autologous transplant, which entailed using a patient's own cells in the hope of minimizing the risk of rejection. Beyond that, embryonic stem cells held hope, though these cells carried a slew of political issues. Not so umbilical-cord stem cells, though from what she read, use of these remained experimental.

The whole thing was chilling. It took everything she had to hide her worry at dinner. But Nicole, in cookbook mode now, had recreated individual seafood potpies from a Chowder House recipe. She set places at the trestle table—bright orange place mats on the pickled oak, napkins in shell rings, and an aged Vouvray in unetched goblets—and again she insisted on photographing the whole thing before allowing Charlotte to eat.

"What do you think?" she finally asked after a period of pensive chewing. The absorbed look on her face said she was breaking down elements of texture and taste, pitting one ingredient against another, weighing their proportions against the whole.

This was the Nicole that Charlotte knew—the detail person, who remembered every subplot of every book she had read and could cite a reason why it worked for the whole. Charlotte, who usually moved on without looking back, had alternately loved and hated her for that.

It wasn't love or hate now, but admiration. Nicole wasn't moving on. She was simply pushing one thing aside to focus on another.

Inspired, Charlotte focused hard on the merits of the dish. "I like the lobster. And the crab. And I *love* the mussels. The shrimp feels . . ."

"Overdone," Nicole prompted.

"But this was frozen, right?" She certainly didn't want to imply that the shrimp had been miscooked, didn't want to even *hint* at criticism when Nicole was in escapist mode. *MS*? *Mind-boggling.*

Nicole chewed another mouthful. "Yes, frozen. Shrimping around here runs from December to April. They actually ended the season early this year because the catch was so big." She singled out another tiny shrimp and chewed. "Definitely tough. And there's already a crunch from the fennel, so I don't need anything this firm. Maybe I should use cod instead of shrimp?"

"That would work," Charlotte said thoughtfully. "But I do like this salad with it. And the bread."

The plan was to include menu suggestions with each recipe—what side would go with an entrée, what entrée would go with a side, what starter or sweet would complement each choice. Nickitotable.com was known for this. It was also known for presentation, which was why Nicole went to such pains to artfully lay out and photograph each meal. Of course, she didn't consider either a pain. She loved doing it.

Trying to follow her lead, Charlotte sat back now to look at the whole—a ramekin with a half-eaten pastry disc resting on what remained of a cream sauce chunky with seafood. Islanders didn't dilute their seafood dishes with dozens of sides, hence the simplicity of salad and bread. But there was an element of Cecily Cole in the cream sauce. "The parsley adds just enough green."

"And the ramekins add a chestnut brown," Nicole mused. "I got them at the island store a few years ago, and they weren't expensive. By the way, I'm making a resource list to put at the end of the book. Not everyone has access to our ingredients, and it's not like we can get fresh ones to them, but the island store ships ramekins, and since they're locally made—"

"By Oliver Weeks?" Charlotte cut in with an enthused grin. "Still? What a character. Big interview, there."

"The book has to focus on cooks."

"He makes implements for cooks."

"I don't know if my editor will go for Oliver Weeks."

"Then I'll interview him for me," Charlotte vowed. "I can sell a profile of him in a snap. Still here? Wow. Still single?"

"He's dating Alicia Dean."

Charlotte was appalled. "Alicia Dean? Bo-ring."

"You're only saying that because you thought Oliver was hot."

"He *was* hot." Growing cautious, she asked, "What's he like now?"

"Wrinkled."

"Really? He's not terribly old."

"Same age as Julian. Mid-forties."

Ten-plus years older than they were, which was one of the reasons Charlotte had never actively flirted with Oliver. Not that she'd flirted with Julian. Not that she'd ever thought Julian was hot. Not that she cared if Julian was wrinkled or gray now—other than as a bellwether of his health. To this day, she couldn't give what had happened between them any explanation remotely related to physical attraction. Loneliness? Perhaps. She had just broken up with yet another guy she thought might be the one, so she could add heartbreak to the list of excuses. Add wine and exhaustion, and the outcome was doomed.

"Alicia spent a couple of years on the mainland," Nicole said, "so there's a little more life to her now. She does PR for the Chamber of Commerce."

"The Chamber of Commerce," Charlotte droned. "Now there's an exciting organization, particularly since Quinnies hate tourists."

Nicole looked to be fighting a smile. "Day-trippers are okay. Dorey loves them." She pointed at the potpie. "She'll give me other Chowder House recipes, but I think this one's worth including. Potpie is an island staple."

And potpies on Quinnipeague weren't only for fish, Charlotte knew. She remembered ones that contained chicken, pork, and beef, though the latter was usually ground. "Shepherd's pie," she breathed in sudden euphoria. "Topped with mashed potato laced with horseradish descended from a plant in Cecily Cole's garden. Think her son still grows it?"

Nicole held up both hands and, in a very high voice, said, "Don't go there, Charlotte. You *know* the trouble I already have in my life."

"MS isn't trouble. It's worry."

But those hands covered her ears now. "I don't want to hear. We have to talk about the book." She left the table to grab a folder from the counter and, as she returned, pulled out two sheets of paper. Pushing the first to Charlotte, she said, "These are chapter headings, beginning with BRUNCH and ending with SWEETS. My editor thought there should be chapters for STARTERS and SALADS. I did add STARTERS, since they can be a whole meal if the portions are large, but salads are part of the menu plans, so they'll show up in different chapters. Besides, ten chapters feels right. See? I've already included POTPIE."

Charlotte also saw CHOWDER, FISH, FOWL, and FILETS, plus SIDES AND SNACKS. What she saw as she read, though, was Nicole in the kitchen, living and breathing food for the blog and the book. Charlotte wasn't much of a cook, but when she was home, she ate. When she was bored or tense, she ate. And there was Nicole—at home, certainly bored at times, definitely tense—wallowing in food but thin as ever. Nervous energy had to be nearly as good as gastric bypass.

"People of interest," Nicole said, putting the second sheet on top. "My editor doesn't know Quinnipeague, so I made this list myself. All of them are major players here."

Charlotte looked over the names, suddenly struck by how irrelevant these people were—how irrelevant the whole *project* was—compared to issues like illness and infidelity. And friendship. Friendship was definitely on the line here.

Misreading her expression, Nicole spoke in a rush. "You don't have to do these exact ones if you don't want. I just kind of went through the chapter headings and listed some of the people I'd want to ask for recipes, and then picked people from that list whom I thought were interesting, but if they don't interest you, they won't interest my readers, so that's a good litmus test. I mean, these are just suggestions."

"It's your book," Charlotte said, feeling like the *worst* kind of friend.

"But you're the writer."

"It's *your book,*" she repeated, testier now. If Nicole had been more demanding of Julian, he would never have followed Charlotte to the beach. End of story. "You're the one who knows your audience, and you're the one who signed a contract. I don't know what your publisher wants. And I haven't been here in ten years, so I'm not the one to make executive decisions. Tell me who to interview, and I'll do the interview."

Nicole had recoiled.

Only then realizing how sharp her tone had been—and how old and one-sided her anger—she was immediately contrite. "I'm sorry. I'm probably tired."

"It's everything I told you this morning," Nicole wailed.

"No. It's cumulative. The last few months . . ." She let it go at the suggestion. *Of course* it was what Nicole had told her that morning. "But I really do want you to direct me in this, Nicki. You know what you're doing."

Nicole didn't look entirely convinced, but at least she didn't argue the point. Rather, as they finished eating, she went through her list, gaining confidence as she explained why she had chosen each islander on it.

Charlotte managed to express enthusiasm, though she had no idea how Nicole could so completely immerse herself in this. But then, Julian's MS wasn't news to her. She was used to smiling when things were dark. Charlotte had always thought of herself as the tougher of them. Not so just then.

They finished dinner and cleaned up, and still Charlotte was thinking about MS. She felt she had a lot of knowledge now with nowhere to go. What she wanted was to hear more about the different treatments Julian had tried. Four years wasn't a long enough time to run out of options. Some of the blog postings she read were from patients who had gone from one protocol to another over the course of twenty years.

But Nicole didn't raise the subject; she simply lit the fire as dusk fell, grabbed *Salt,* and curled up on the sofa. Since she was further ahead than Charlotte, she refused to discuss the book lest she spoil it, and the more Charlotte asked, the firmer Nicole's headshake.

Charlotte picked up her own copy, but not even *Salt* could keep her mind from going places she didn't want to be. For every three pages read, she had to reread two. Setting the book aside, she went to her room and returned with her knitting—though why she had brought it along, she didn't know. The women on Inishmaan had started her on what they claimed was the easiest of their sweaters, and she'd actually finished the back since then. Was it easy? No. Thinking that a smaller piece might be more manageable, she had started a sleeve. Did she know what she was doing? No. She studied the pattern, knit half a row, unknit the stitches, and tried again.

Eventually, she gave up and, sitting on the floor by the bookshelf, looked through picture albums. At one point, she got up to show Nicole a shot of the two of them, gawky and mismatched at thirteen, but Nicole held up a hand and shook her head *no* without taking her eyes from the page she was on.

Putting the album away, Charlotte returned to the sofa. *Salt* was the story of a fisherman, his dog, and a woman who had burst onto the scene unexpectedly, but with whom he was falling in love. Each of the characters had a vulnerability that tugged at her heart. But even love seemed irrelevant to her right now. So she concentrated on the writing style, which was clean and succinct but musical, ebbing and flowing as the ocean would do.

Thinking of the ocean made her crave air. Saving her place with the cover flap, she put the book aside and stood. "I need to move. Want to go for a walk?"

There were tears in Nicole's eyes when she looked up. "I can't leave now. I'm at a really good place." She swallowed. "And I want to call Julian. You go. I'll leave the door open."

Layering up with her humiliatingly perfect fisherman's sweater and a scarf, Charlotte went out the kitchen door. But she didn't head for the beach. She didn't want to pass the painful stretch that would make her think of Julian. She didn't want to think *at all.*

So she made for the road, where she would be able to walk faster, and headed west, toward town. A minute later, she made a U-turn. Town was safe, and safe was okay. If she wanted distraction, though, risk was better.

She walked at a clip back, past the Lilly mailbox and on, speeding up once her muscles warmed. Nervous energy? Oh yeah. She needed to get it all out—needed to *exhaust* herself if she hoped to sleep that night. And the fact of "that night" being only the second of her time here?

Leave, a tiny part of her begged. Julian sick, Nicole needy, Charlotte feeling responsibility—this was the kind of tension from which she had always run. She could easily claim a problem that demanded she return to New York or, better yet, to the site of one of her stories. She could be on the first ferry out, whenever that was.

But she kept walking. She couldn't leave. Totally aside from the fact that Nicole was counting on her, it was a matter of self-respect. And besides, she'd been looking forward to this last summer on Quinnipeague. She did love this place.

Not much to see now, though, she thought with a shiver as she gathered the mess of her hair and tucked it under her scarf. Darkness was dense this far from town. There were no cars here, no streetlights, no welcoming homes, and whatever glow had been cast from Nicole's house was gone. Trees rose on either side, sharing the narrow land flanking the road with strips of field, and beyond was the rocky shore, lost now in the murk.

But there was hope. As she walked, she saw proof of a moon behind clouds, etching their edges in silver and spraying more to the side. Those silver beams would hit the ocean in pale swaths, though she could only imagine it from here. But she did hear the surf rolling in, breaking on the rocks, rushing out.

When the pavement at the sides of the road grew cracked, she moved to the center. This end had always been neglected, a reminder that Cecily didn't invite islanders for tea. The fact that no repair work at all had been done said the son was the same.

Turn back, a tiny part of her begged. Nicole was right; they could get plenty on Cecily without coming here. But to see the gardens again, this time with purpose? How to resist?

She passed a string of birches with a ghostly sheen to their bark, but between the sound of the breeze in their leaves and, always, the surf, she was soothed. The gulls were down for the night, hence no screeching there, and if there were sounds of boats rocking at moorings, the harbor was too far away to hear.

There was only the rhythmic slap of her sneakers on the cracked asphalt—and then another tapping. Not a woodpecker, given the hour. Likely a night creature searching for food, more frightened of her than she was of it. There were deer on Quinnipeague. And raccoons. And woodchucks, possums, and moles.

The tapping came in bursts of three and four, with pauses between. At one point she stopped, thinking it might be a crick in her sneakers. When it quickly came again, though, she walked on. The closer she got to the Cole house, the louder it was.

The creaking of bones? Skeletons dancing? That was what island kids said, and back then, she and Nicole believed it, but that didn't keep them away. Bob and Angie had forbidden their coming here, so it was definitely something to do. Granted, Charlotte was the instigator, but Nicole wouldn't be left behind.

Feeling chilled now, she pulled the cuffs of her sweater over her hands as the Cole curve approached. That curve was a marker of sorts, as good as a gate. Once past it, you saw the house, and once you saw the house, you feared Cecily. As special as her herbs were and as healing as her brews, she could be punitive. Or so said the lore.

But what was lore, other than imaginative efforts to entertain? Cecily was dead, and Charlotte was curious. A look wouldn't hurt.

Slowing only a tad, she rounded the curve. The thud of her heart felt good. She was alive; she was having an adventure; she was breaking a rule, irreverent person that she was. The salt air held a tang here, though whether from the nearby pines or adrenaline, she didn't know.

Then, like a vision, Cecily's house rose up at the distant end of the drive. It was the same two-story frame it had always been, square and plain, with a cupola on top that housed bats, or so the kids used to say. But there were no bats in sight now, no ghostly sounds, nothing even remotely scary. A floodlight was trained on the upper windows, spraying unflattering light on an aging diva. And the sound she heard? A hammer wielded by a man on a ladder. He was repairing a shutter, which would have been a totally normal activity had it not been for the hour.

Wondering at that, she started down the long drive. The walking was easier here, the dirt more forgiving than broken pavement. An invitation after all? She fancied it was. The house looked sad. It needed a visitor, or so she reasoned as the trees gave way to gardens left and right where Cecily had grown her herbs. In the darkness, Charlotte couldn't see what grew here now, whether the low plants were herbs or flowers or weeds. She could smell something, though the blend was so complex that her untrained nose couldn't parse it. Unruly curls blew against her cheek; wanting a clear view, she held them back.

Cecily's garden. There was power here. She could feel it. But a man on a ladder in the nighttime? That was risky.

Her sneakers made little sound on the dirt as she timed her pace to the pound of the hammer. When he paused to fiddle with what looked to be a hinge, she heard a rustle in the garden beside her, clearly foraging creatures alerted by her movement.

Alerted in turn by that rustle, the man stopped pounding and looked back. He must have had night eyes; there was no light where she was. Without moving a muscle, though, he watched her approach.

Leo Cole. She was close enough to see that, astute enough to remember dark eyes, prominent cheekbones, and a square jaw. She remembered long straggly hair, though a watch cap hid whatever was there now. He wore a T-shirt and paint-spattered jeans. Tall and gangly then? Tall and solid now.

But thin-mouthed in disdain. Then and now.

"You're trespassin'," he said in a voice that was low and rough, its hint of Maine too small to soften it.

"What are you doing?" she asked, refusing to cower. She had met far more intimidating people in far less hospitable spots.

His eyes made a slow slide from her to the window and back. "What does it look like?"

"Repairing your house in the dark." She tucked her cuffed hands under her arms. "Is that so you won't see the broken windowpane over there, or do you just like being reckless?"

He stared at her for another minute. Then, holstering the hammer in his jeans, he climbed down the ladder, lifted a shutter, and, somewhat awkwardly, given its bulk, climbed back up. The shutter was wide, clearly functional rather than decorative. Though he carried it one-handed, he stopped twice on the way up to shift his grip. At the top, he braced it against the ladder's shelf while he adjusted his hands, then lined up hinges and pins.

He had one hinge attached but was having trouble with the second. She knew what this was about. She had worked with storm shutters. They were tricky to do alone.

Resting the shutter on the shelf again, he pulled the hammer from his waistband and adjusted the hinge with a few well-aimed blows. Then he tried the shutter again.

Watching him struggle, Charlotte remembered more about Leo Cole from her early days here. Not too bright, they said. Troubled. Stubborn. She had never known him personally; she was only there summers, and he ran with a different crowd. Actually, she corrected silently, he didn't run with a crowd. A lone wolf, he did damage all on his own, and it was serious stuff. The stories included stealing cars, forging checks, and deflowering sweet young things.

Her last summers on Quinnipeague, he was in state prison, serving time for selling pot. Rumor had it that Cecily was the one who grew it. The islanders always denied that, of course. They didn't want the feds threatening their cures.

Leo had been nabbed for selling it on the mainland. Did he still grow it? She couldn't smell it now, and she did know that smell.

Having returned the shutter to the shelf, he was readjusting the hinge.

"Want some help?" she called up. Wasn't this was about risk?

He snorted.

"Four hands, and you'd have that right up," she advised.

"Two hands'll do."

Charlotte looked past him toward the cupola. She didn't see any bats yet, didn't feel any ghosts. If Cecily's spirit was floating around, it hadn't cast a spell to keep Charlotte here. She remained because she was stubborn herself.

He was staring at her.

"I've done this before," she said.

"Uh-huh."

"I have. I've built houses."

"That so." He didn't believe her.

"Half a dozen in El Salvador after the big quake there, and at least as many when tornados hit in Maryland. I know how storm shutters work."

He continued to stare.

"All you need," she said, freeing a hand to hold back the hair that blew loose again, "is someone to steady it while you fit the pins in the hinges."

"Really. I didn't know that."

"Okay. So you did. But you could've had that hung and been down five minutes ago. Aren't you cold?" She was appreciating every thick inch of her sweater, while his arms were ropy and bare.

"I'm a man."

She waited for more. When nothing came, she said, "What does that have to do with anything?"

"Men run hot."

"Really." Refusing to be baited, she returned her hand to her armpit, shifted to a more comfortable stance, and smiled. "Great. I'll watch while you get that shutter hung. Maybe I can learn how you do it alone."

Apparently realizing he'd been one-upped, he grunted. "Fine. Since you know it all, here's your chance." He backed down, put the shutter on the ground against his leg, and gestured her toward the ladder.

"I'm not lugging that thing up," she warned.

"No, but if you climb the fuckin' ladder, I can hold the shutter while you to do the fitting. Assuming you can see. Your hair's a mess."

"Thanks," she said brightly and gripped the rail. Two ladders would have been better. She wasn't sure she liked the idea of climbing this one with him at her butt. She would be at his mercy. But she did have a point to prove.

So she began to climb, looking back every few rungs to see where he was. When she reached the top, she felt his shoulder against the back of her thighs. If she hadn't known better, she would have thought he was making sure she didn't fall.

But she did know better. Leo Cole had no use for women. If he was standing that close, he was toying with her.

She didn't like being toyed with—and, yes, her hair was in her eyes, but she wouldn't give him the satisfaction of pushing it back. Fortunately, she knew enough about hanging shutters to do it, hair and all. While he bore the weight of the wood, she easily lined up both pairs of hinges and pins, and that quickly it was done.

Nearly as quickly, he backed down the ladder. By the time she reached the ground, he was stowing the hammer in a toolbox. The instant she was off the last rung, he reached for the ladder.

"You're welcome," Charlotte said.

He shot her a scornful glance.

"I'm Charlotte Evans."

"I know." He looked up to reel in the top half of the ladder, which clicked and clanged as it doubled on itself. "You're doing a cookbook, and you want my mother's stuff. Forget it."

He didn't look like Cecily, she decided. He was too tall, too dark. According to what islanders said, Cecily's hair had been pure silver from the first day she set foot on Quinnipeague. Charlotte recalled it being long and flowing, the woman herself petite, almost spritelike. "I'm sorry about her death."

"Her gardens aren't public."

"How'd she die?"

When the ladder was fully compressed, he secured the extension and carried the whole thing around the corner. The clink faded into the rolling surf, or into a garage or a shed, though she didn't hear a door. He was empty-handed when he returned, walking past her to collect an assortment of tools from the ground near where the ladder had been.

Charlotte was thinking he had tuned her out, when he knelt by the toolbox not far from her feet and said, "She got sick."

Cecily. "With what?" When he didn't answer, Charlotte said, "She was a healer. Getting sick shouldn't have been a problem."

Angling away, he dug into a pocket.

"Did she die at home? Is she buried here?"

After dumping a handful of nails in the toolbox, he stood again, went to the pole that held the floodlight, and turned it off.

The darkness was a shock. But the moon was out now. As her eyes adjusted, she could see the gardens. Oh yes, something grew there, and it wasn't last year's crop. This was new growth, full-bodied and fresh. Several of the taller plants had even been staked.

With a rustle, a small, fat creature appeared from a row on the left, crossed the dirt drive, and waddled off down a row on the right. Charlotte might have asked about it if she hadn't suddenly spotted a deer. It was watching them from the edge of the trees, its pelt a tawny glow in the moonlight.

She took a breath. "How beautiful."

"You should see her fawn."

"Where?"

He hitched his chin toward the staked plants. "She leaves it while she goes looking for food."

"Why go anywhere, when she has a feast right here?"

"Oh, she won't eat any of this. She knows it's mine."

Charlotte looked at him, but if there was humor in his eyes, the night hid it. "Seriously?"

He didn't smile. "You need to leave. I have work to do."

"I'll say," she dared. "Your window's cracked, your drainpipes sag, and the shingles on your roof are lifting. Storm shutters are all well and good, but they won't keep rain from coming in the roof."

He straightened an arm, pointing back toward the road.

"But this was just getting fun," she protested.

He stared.

"Tell you what," she tried. *Aim high, hit high.* "Just say I can come back one day to see the gardens. One day. That's it. Then I'll disappear, and you'll never hear from me again."

"Sneakin' pictures with your iPhone, so the world knows what's here? No way." He hitched his chin toward the road. "You're gratin' on my nerves. Bear doesn't like that."

"Bear?"

"My dog."

"If you had a dog," she countered, "it'd have gone after the deer and her fawn and whatever that little fat thing was."

He snapped his fingers. From behind a bush by the house, a creature emerged that was large, black, and hulking. It plodded forward on huge paws, stopping several yards from Charlotte, and stared at her with what she could only call feral eyes.

She wasn't afraid of dogs. But she didn't like them. And this one? Not friendly. "O-kay," she said lightly and backed away. "I was just being neighborly."

The dog continued to stare. Its ears were alert, its jowls wet enough to reflect a sliver of moon.

After retreating a few more steps, making her intent clear as she put just that little distance between herself and Bear, she faced forward, chin up, and strode down the drive. She listened closely for the thud of paws or the jingle of a collar, but if the dog followed, it was silent.

She didn't look back until she was on the safe side of the Cole curve, and then it was only for a quick glance over her shoulder. She wasn't surprised to see the road deserted. Leo Cole didn't want her around, but she hadn't sensed untamed anger. Nor, in spite of the dog, had she sensed danger. Leo just wanted to be left alone.

She could do that. She had no interest in the man.

But those gardens . . . those gardens held her thoughts as she walked along the road. The promise of them was a drug, and she didn't mean dope. That smell she couldn't parse? It was fertility, healing, and hope all at once. She had to get back there, and not with an iPhone. She wanted to use her Nikon, ideally up close with a wide-angle lens, but with a zoom from afar and on the sly if need be. She could make those gardens come alive in print. She could capture that scent. Nicole's readers would love it.

So would Nicole. It was the least Charlotte could do.

Chapter Seven

Charlotte didn't tell Nicole that she'd been to the Cole place, simply because other things took precedence—namely, the arrival of summer. She knew it the instant she got out of bed Thursday, could see it in how the beach grass stood tall and hear it in the languid cry of the gulls. When she opened the window, she felt a special Quinnie warmth. This wasn't the sticky heat of the city, but rather a gentling of air that was balmy and sweet. It was also very possibly fleeting, she feared, having spent enough summers here to know how quickly the cold could return. Seizing the moment was key.

To that end, once they finished breakfast on the patio and felt the true warmth of that sun, she suggested the beach. Nicole looked at her, looked at the ocean, grinned conspiratorially, and rose.

An hour later, with no mention whatsoever of the cookbook, they were in the Wrangler, driving in the direction of town only enough to pass the clam flats and reach Okers Beach. Two other cars were already parked on the sandy berm by the path; had it been the weekend, there would have been more. Houses like Nicole's had their own beaches, but most were on the north side. Okers, being on the south and tucked into a Quinnie curve, offered calmer surf and softer sand. It also offered drive-bys from the Chowder House with sandwiches, chips, and drinks, though when Charlotte and Nicole arrived, lunch was still a ways off.

Dropping their bags, they set up low beach chairs, put on sunscreen, and reached for their copies of *Salt*.

"You'll finish today," Charlotte said, eyeing the small wad of pages Nicole had left.

Nicole grimaced. "I know. I'm trying to read slowly. I do not want this to end."

Charlotte, who was barely halfway through, wasn't rushing to finish either, and not for lack of interest. If she was bored, she wouldn't finish; she liked books to sweep her up, and if one didn't, it was gone. *Salt* offered contentment in a slow savoring, luxury in knowing there was more to read. "What is it about this book?" she asked. "It's not like the plot is unique. Man and dog are alone. A perfect woman comes for the summer. They try to make a go of it."

"You make it sound trite."

"But the way he writes, it isn't. That's my point. What is going on here that has us holding our breath?"

Nicole spread a hand on the page before her. "We love the hero. He's vulnerable. He really needs her. I mean, he's capable of living alone. He's done it for years. But his life is empty." She paused before adding a quiet, "We die for this. Every woman wants to be needed."

Even with the surf diluting it, Charlotte heard sadness. "Julian needs you."

"Does he? I mean, if he doesn't want me with him now, what does that say?"

"It says he doesn't know how to handle this any more than you do. It says he doesn't know what he's supposed to be doing."

Nicole stroked the book. "That's what we love about *Salt*. This guy knows what he wants. He's out on his lobster boat all day long, but he knows he wants to come home to this woman." Her voice melted. "She's his dream come true. Is that the sweetest?"

"They won't end up together," Charlotte warned.

"How do you know that?" Dismay, then accusation, "Charlotte Evans, you rat, you read the ending!"

"I didn't," Charlotte protested, laughing.

"You always used to, and it's just as bad now as it was then, because I *do* want them to be together." She swatted at Charlotte's arm. "You are a spoiler!"

Still laughing, Charlotte fended off another swat. "I have not read the ending. I swear. It's just that I understand this woman. She lives in Dallas. She's used to glitz and restaurants and shopping. How can she trade that for life on a small island?"

"Easy, if she loves him enough."

"You are such a romantic."

"And you aren't?"

"Of course I am," Charlotte conceded. "I love this book, too." She had a hopeful thought. "Tell me there's a twist coming that'll allow her to stay."

"I'm not telling," Nicole said and, lowering her sunglasses, began to read.

Thursday was the kind of day Charlotte had dreamed of when she agreed to come to Quinnipeague. They read, they walked the beach, they swam as much as the cold ocean water allowed. By the time the Chowder House van arrived, there were others on the beach. Nicole knew most as summer people, and while there were warm hellos, they kept to themselves.

Summer people were that way. Most were escaping busy lives and welcomed the hush. Locals were the ones who talked.

Today, there was just the smell of sunscreen and surf, hours without awareness of time, and when the sun was at its highest and warmest, crab cakes on buns, topped with Dorey's special tartar sauce. "Did you know," Nicole remarked, blotting her mouth with a napkin, "that the French were the ones who first popularized tartar sauce, which was named after the Tatars from Russia and the Ukraine, and that those early versions contained white wine vinegar and capers?"

Charlotte peeled back her bun. "I don't see capers."

"No. Dorey uses sweet pickle, parsley, and chive."

The Cecily Cole effect, Charlotte thought, but didn't say it aloud. Rather, they went back to eating, back to a serenity stroked by the tempo of the surf and undisturbed by talk of either the cookbook or Julian. The only tears were Nicole's when she finished reading *Salt*. And they were voluminous, punctuated by multiple *omigods* and a hand pressed to her chest to steady her heart.

Still she refused to tell Charlotte how the story ended. Rather, after a dinner that night of pecan-crusted cod—a test, since it was one of the Chowder House's signature dishes, and Nicole wanted to be sure the recipe was right—she let Charlotte clean the kitchen while she dove into a new book. Charlotte, who liked to linger with characters when she was done with a book, was dismayed that Nicole could so quickly put all that emotion aside, but she claimed she needed to immerse herself in another to compensate for the loss. It was escapism at its finest—denial of *Salt,* denial of MS. True to her word, she was quickly absorbed.

So Charlotte went for a walk. There was no heading toward town this time. Right off, she went in the other direction. The night was mild and her step steady. She rationalized, telling herself that she'd been a slug all day—sitting, reading, *eating*—which was true. But she was also curious about what was happening at the house.

She walked in moonlight this time, enjoying the mild air, the sweet smells of nascent blooms. One day of warmth, and the shrubs lining the road added the scent of roses to that of sea salt all the way to the Cole curve, where the tang of pine sap took its place.

She slowed at the curve. She didn't hear anything tonight. And sure enough, when she went on, all was dark. She walked until she came abreast of the gardens, which, too, were more strongly scented than before. There were flowers here, not just herbs. She would stake her novice nose on it.

Stopping, she sat down right there in the middle of the drive. Far beyond trees, rocks, and the house, the surf rolled in, but its sound was muted enough by those objects not to hide that of small creatures on the move. A chipmunk darted across the drive, its tiny tail straight up. A frog jumped, croaked, jumped again, and disappeared into the plants with only the occasional diminishing croak.

Focusing on the woods, she let her eyes adjust to the shadows, separating one tree from the next and—ahhhh, there was the doe. Standing straight and still, it might have passed for a tree had Charlotte not known to look. It was watching her. She held her breath, wondering if it would accept her benignity—wondering, actually, if it would proceed to eat Leo Cole's goods now that he wasn't around to see. It didn't. In time, it simply turned and, without a sound, stepped gracefully into the pines.

Charlotte was thinking that she really wanted to look for the fawn, only that would likely bring the doe back, and this wasn't her land to disturb—when a dog barked. The sound was muffled; Bear was in the house. Anxious to get out and chase whoever trespassed?

Sitting in the dirt without moving, she waited for the front door to open. Alternately, her gaze skipped to the side of the house from which she half expected a hulking brute of a black dog to burst. What would she do if it did?

Run. Fast.

But there was no sign of Bear, either in that minute or the next twenty, which was how long she sat filling her lungs with Cole air. Its intricate blend of flowers and herbs, warm now and intense, was hypnotic. She half expected that her legs would refuse to move if she decided to leave.

But they didn't balk when she stood. They were rested and filled with energy—actually took her back to Nicole's house at a speed she would have marveled at had she been watching the time. Her mind, though, was filled with less honorable thoughts. She was wondering whether, if she returned another night, she might walk through that garden. She was wondering if the light of the moon would allow her to take pictures of the herbs there. She was *wondering* whether, if she was undetected then, too, she might *borrow* a few.

* * *

She might have shared the plan if Nicole had been in the kitchen when she returned, but she was asleep, and by the time Charlotte went downstairs Friday morning, the urgency had passed.

Nicole was late joining her. Carrying her laptop, she had apparently been working into the wee hours, not sleeping at all. After reading a tip in one of her favorite farm reports, she had researched and blogged about a new artichoke cultivar with a heart was so tender it could be eaten without being cooked. It was the kind of cutting-edge news she liked passing on to her readers, and having done that at length, she said, she had earned the right to play.

So they spent another warm day at the beach. There were more bodies on towels today; weekenders had arrived, delivered early by the ferry with a guttural noise that could be heard from the pier, and the beach was the go-to spot. Though there was no boisterousness, there were iPod docks and earbuds aplenty. There was also lots of talk, with Nicole in its midst. Many of those newly arrived were people she had known for years but hadn't seen since fall.

Watching her, Charlotte thought she looked better. She was in her element with people, and though there were questions about Bob and Julian, she handled them well. She even accepted a dinner invitation from friends of her parents, who had half a dozen others coming as well.

"They want you, too," Nicole informed her when she returned to their towels and stretched out again, but Charlotte shook her head no.

"Why not?"

"I'm not a dinner party kind of person."

"Are you kidding? You'd be the most interesting one in the room!"

"I hate small talk."

"You can do it."

"Oh, I can. I just don't want to."

Nicole must have sensed she was serious, because she said, "Then we'll go another time. You're my guest. I can't leave you home alone."

"Of course you can," Charlotte scolded. "You love the McKenzies. And besides, this breaks the ice for you. It's better to see some people now, than everyone all at once Sunday morning at brunch." Bailey's Brunch was an annual event, ostensibly to celebrate the summer solstice, though truly to welcome back seasonal Quinnies. Held at the church, it would be the first townwide gathering of the summer, and therefore an important one for Charlotte and Nicole to attend. "Besides, these are your people, not mine." She paused and said on a lighter note, "See the heads on the bluff?"

Nicole glanced up at the rocks that anchored the far end of the beach. The heads were attached to bodies of local teenage boys, for whom hours on that bluff each summer weekend was a rite of passage. "They're still at it."

"Obviously a different crew."

"For sure, but they do love taking it in. Warm bodies."

"Warm *female* bodies."

"And you in a one-piece suit. What happened to the bikinis you loved?"

"The French Riviera," Charlotte remarked, and at Nicole's curious frown, said, "Bikinis all over the place, looking great on some bodies and horrid on others, and the occasional one-piece suit looking so much better."

"But you have the body for a bikini."

Charlotte couldn't comment further. "Not like yours. You look amazing, Nicki. You absolutely have to go to the McKenzies' tonight. Trust me. You'll light up the party."

Nicole leaned close to be heard over the sounds of laughter and waves. Her eyes were a crystal-clear green. "Do you know how *glad* I am that you're here? Come? Please?"

But Charlotte shook her head and smiled. "After a day here with all these people? I'm socialized out. You go. I'll sleep."

* * *

She didn't sleep, of course. She planned to, but wasn't tired, and what she wanted, really, was to photograph herbs. Shouldering the Nikon, she walked down the road, familiar enough now with the terrain to move to the center even before the pavement worsened. She listened for hammering or barking but heard only the reverberating surf, and when she rounded the curve, there was nothing but moonlight on a dark house.

Flash would be a problem. Not only would it skew the true color of the plants, but a sudden glint, no matter now brief, might alert Leo Cole. So, no flash, just moonlight, which gave a silver glow to the plants and was actually charming. She had a steady hand. She also had enough experience taking pictures in the wild to know how to brace her body for greater stability.

By the time she thought this through, though, the smells had sunk in and were distilling her plans. Oddly mindless, she went to the same spot on the drive and sat down. *Take pictures,* ordered the tiny voice in her head. But she wasn't in the mood. *Borrow,* said the voice. But she didn't want to do that, either.

She felt lethargic.

No. Not lethargic.

Relaxed. Content. *Seduced.*

Legs folded, hands limp on her thighs, she dropped her head back, closed her eyes, and slowly inhaled. Basil? Mint? Cilantro? There were threads of each—but also of others far beyond her ability to name. And fertile earth. And sweet salt air. The moment was rich.

Then came breathing. She righted her head and opened her eyes. The road to the house was empty, but when she looked left down an aisle of staked plants, she saw the dog.

It came toward her on paws so large that she vetoed the idea of running. She wouldn't get far, and the damage of lunging jaws could be worse. So she held her breath while it approached and sniffed her face, her neck, her camera. Its nose was wet. She wanted to recoil, but didn't dare move.

"Caught," came a low voice from behind her. And still she didn't take her eyes off Bear.

"Call off your dog," she said through lips that barely moved.

"He doesn't like trespassers, either."

"I'm just sitting."

"On my land."

"Call off your dog and I'll leave."

He snapped his fingers—once, softly—and the dog lumbered past. Only then, with care, did Charlotte turn. Leo Cole was barefoot, bareheaded, bare armed and legged. Shorts and a tank, that was it. His face was shadowed, accentuating its hard lines, while the dog at his thigh watched her with distrust.

"Fancy camera," he said in that flat voice of his.

"It's part of my arm."

"Which you stand to lose if you lift it."

"No lifting. It's too dark. Call off the dog."

"If it's too dark, why'd you bring it?"

"There were flowers back on the road that were pretty in the moonlight."

"And I'm a leprechaun."

She might have snickered. He was way too tall and deep-voiced to be any kind of magical creature, and with a menacing dog, foaming at the mouth beside him? Well, maybe not foaming. But scary enough. Trying to stay calm, she took a slow breath.

"Were you meditating?" he asked.

"No." With movements measured enough not to alarm the dog, she rose. "I was . . . being. There's something about this air. It's like a drug."

"You with the FDA?"

"No. With the cookbook lady."

That was nearly as bad, to judge from the tightness of his mouth. "Yeah. Looking for pictures. And recipes. You won't get either, y'know."

"Why not?"

"Because I'll put out word that I don't want you to."

"Why will islanders listen to you?"

"Because I grow the herbs."

"I thought people here grew their own."

"I control the parent plants, and the parent plants control theirs."

Charlotte failed to make the connection. "Like, your plants decide whether their plants grow? That's imaginative."

He shrugged, clearly not caring what she thought.

"What's it to you anyway, our cookbook?" she asked.

"Publicity stinks." He moved aside in silent command, and made the smallest *scoot* with his thumb in case she missed the message.

She might have asked more—about Cecily, about the herbs, about what he did out here on the far tip of the island besides repairing his house in the dark—if it hadn't been for the dog, and while, looking down on it now, she didn't see any more viciousness there than last time, she wasn't taking chances. Leo didn't want her around. And Leo controlled the dog.

That said, she wasn't exactly sure how to get past them. Between him, the dog, and one narrow drive, there wasn't a whole lot of room. If she went to the left, she would be close to the dog. If she went to the right, she would be close to Leo.

She was trying to decide which was safer when, sounding vaguely amused, he asked, "Are you afraid of Bear?"

"I was bitten by a dog once." She saw no point in denial. As far as she was concerned, caution was a good thing when you didn't know the beast. "That one was supposed to be friendly. Yours looks anything but."

He touched the dog's head with the tips of his fingers, apparently another signal, because, seeming suddenly bored, the dog looked away.

Charlotte didn't trust that it wouldn't look back and lunge. Opting for the right side, she walked slowly past Leo and continued on down the drive.

* * *

"You what?" Nicole asked in disbelief. They were in the kitchen, topping off breakfast with seconds of coffee. Nicole had just given a blow-by-blow of dinner at the McKenzies'—good company, a pork tenderloin, from a local pig farm, that had been laced with rosemary and grilled and was surprisingly good, though pork wasn't her favorite meat, and a stunning centerpiece of wildflowers floating in a hollow gourd about which she had just blogged—and she wanted to know what Charlotte had done.

"I was at the Cole place."

"What do you mean, *at* the Cole place? Like walking around? Ringing the *bell*?"

"I don't think there's a bell," Charlotte said. She had her knees up, bare feet on the edge of her seat, hands cupping her mug. "The house is old and run-down. Leo was fixing a shutter. I gave him a hand."

"You what?"

"Helped him out."

"Leo *saw* you? Charlotte, you are not supposed to go there. If there's one thing Quinnies say, it's that. Leo is dangerous."

Charlotte remembered being up on that ladder Wednesday night. He might have easily tossed her off or touched her inappropriately, but he hadn't done either. He had steadied her until the job was done, then backed off. Granted, he was more annoyed last night, but hindsight cast a softer view on that as well. "I don't think he is. I've been there three times—"

"Three? *When?*"

Charlotte felt marginally guilty. "The last three nights. It's really no big thing, Nicki. That's just the direction I walk. The distance from here to there is just right."

"He's the island bad boy."

"Not a boy anymore."

"Which makes it worse. Three nights, and you didn't tell me? What else haven't you told me?"

Charlotte felt a stab of serious guilt. What to say to that? "He has a dog."

"He has a dog," Nicole repeated with a considering nod. "You hate dogs."

"Only because that Dalmatian bit me, but my father kicked it first, so it thought it was being attacked and went after the weakest thing in sight, that is, me. I've met some nice dogs."

"If this was Leo Cole's, it was not."

"You don't know that," Charlotte warned. "When it came at me, I felt threatened. But it didn't attack." She paused. "Have you ever seen Leo up close?"

"No. The day I got here, he was storming through the center of town. He was way down the street, but if looks could kill, I'd be dead."

Charlotte hadn't felt anything murderous. "He didn't seem so bad to me."

"What did he look like?"

She retrieved the image, considering it now as she hadn't before. "A man."

"Obviously."

"Fit."

"Muscular?"

"No. Just . . . fit. *Clean,*" she added, though she wasn't sure why the word popped up—maybe because he had been anything but clean in the old days, so she had expected the opposite? His hands had been smudged while he worked on his roof. But she wouldn't have called him dirty.

"You must've seen more than I did," Nicole remarked. "Of course, you did. You were up close. Remember that long hair?"

"It's short now," Charlotte said. "Brown. Maybe with flecks of gray, though that could have been the moon. How old is he?"

"Four or five years older than us."

"So, late thirties. That fits."

"What was he wearing? When I saw him last week, he was dressed in black."

"The same last night, I think, though it might have been navy. He was wearing shorts."

"Oh boy," Nicole drawled. "Falling off his butt, I bet."

"Actually, no. They were nylon—long, like basketball shorts—and they hung at the right place."

"His waist."

"His hips." The shorts had been drapey in a modest way. "Slim hips. Ropy arms. What does he do, Nicki? I mean, he needs food, and for that, he needs money. I can't imagine Cecily left him much, so how does he get it?"

"He was a handyman for a while," Nicole said. "We never used him. He smelled."

Charlotte laughed. "Who said that?"

"Everyone."

"Well, he doesn't now. At least, I didn't smell anything."

"Not even the dog?"

"No. It didn't smell. It was short-haired."

"A pit bull."

"Uh-uh. Too big. He calls it Bear."

"That figures. He could be trouble, Charlotte," she advised. "He could charge you with trespassing. He could go to court to prevent us from mentioning Cecily in the book. He could sue my publisher for a cut in the profits."

"He won't do that."

"And if you really piss him off," Nicole went on, "he could get—I don't know—some kind of *injunction* to prevent us from printing any recipe that uses her herbs, which means the book is dead. Promise me you'll stay away from him, Charlotte."

"But there's a whole other side to this," Charlotte reasoned, thinking of the camera she hadn't yet mentioned. "What if I can get into his gardens?"

Nicole reached across the table and grabbed her hand. "There's nothing in those gardens that we can't get anywhere else."

"Yes, there is. There's—" *A photo op,* she might have said, but Nicole cut in.

"Herbs? There are herbs all over the island. We don't need any from Leo Cole. Promise you'll stay away?"

"There are roots."

"What—like parsnip, turnip, beet?"

"No," Charlotte said but stopped. The business about Leo's plants being parents that controlled their offspring was ridiculous—but she wouldn't put it past Nicole to buy it. At the very least, it would make her nervous. Besides, Charlotte wasn't sure if that was what she meant by roots. She wasn't sure what she meant. The word just popped out. Like clean.

"Promise, Charlotte?" Nicole begged. "Please? For me?"

Charlotte had nodded. It wasn't exactly a swear-on-the-Bible promise, which she would have had trouble making. But she couldn't go to the Cole place today, anyway. Weekends on Quinnipeague offered choices. Many involved food, others sport, yard sales, or entertainment. This weekend being the kickoff of the summer season—and Nicole being committed, for the sake of the cookbook, to being seen by as many Quinnies as possible—their day was filled.

They started at a library book sale, to which they brought bags of books culled from the shelves around the house. It was the first of the cleaning-out Nicole would have to do, but between the two of them, they worked with such speed and left so quickly, that the emotional impact was minimal.

From there, they hit a cookout on the pier—actually, a cookout on Susan Murray's forty-foot party boat. Susan was the CEO of a software company in Portland, which meant that, while she wasn't a full-time resident of Quinnipeague, she lived close enough to visit year-round. A born manager, she loved to party, but there wasn't an ounce of pretension about her. Her boat was an old pontoon, and the menu—Susan's standard—was hamburgers, hot dogs, and chips, with mounds of s'mores cookies. The cookies were a must for the book, as was Susan.

After lunch came softball on the school field. The school itself was small, limited to pre-K through five, with higher grades shuttled to the mainland, but the field was the largest open spread on the island. Two games were played simultaneously, with Nicole in one and Charlotte in the other, and there were cold drinks afterward.

Returning home sweaty, they went for a swim at the house and sat on the patio wrapped in towels until the shadows deepened, at which point they returned to town, grabbed salads at The Island Grill with six seasonals who happened to show up at the same time as they for dinner, followed by movie night at the church. This week's showing was *Titanic,* which everyone in the place had already seen, but the island ambience—the smell of hot popcorn bagged by the minister and his wife as quickly as their little machine could produce it, the whirr of fans in the cathedral ceiling, and the creak of old wooden chairs—added a special flavor.

The church was the go-to spot for every large island gathering. Saturday night was the movie, Sunday morning a service, and then, in a transformation that never failed to amaze Charlotte with its speed, came Bailey's Brunch.

The place was packed with islanders ranging from a ninety-year-old to a newborn, from weekend regulars to summer people to one-time guests. Charlotte and Nicole divided up here, too, working the crowd as much for the sake of the book as for fun. Charlotte had always been drawn to the less conventional of island residents, and though few of them were foodies and, hence subjects for the book, she remembered many and enjoyed catching up.

And, of course, there was food, which was set out on long tables where an hour before parishioners had filled rows of chairs. The presentation was nothing to write home about, with paper goods and plastic utensils in piles. And still, in all her travels Charlotte had never seen as appealing a spread. There were quiches of every variety, French toast casseroles, fish hash, and a curried fish that she adored, plus tuna mousse, salmon cakes, and crab fritters. There were chowders—no island event went without. There were cruelly delicious sticky buns, cranberry scones, and tuna muffins. There was the fruit compote that she loved, and chewy chocolate candies, each with an almond inside, individually wrapped and filling a bowl. She knew that the makings for those, not to mention the coffee beans behind the rich coffee in her cup, were from another part of the world. Nearly everything else, though, was locally caught or grown.

Charlotte mingled, catching up with people she hadn't seen in ten years. She booked interviews, often now alongside Nicole, who sampled every dish in an evaluative way, ever-so-subtly shaking her head or nodding to indicate which they wanted and which they did not.

They stayed even after the crowd thinned, enjoying themselves, which was a good thing. The enjoyment ended abruptly when Nicole's phone rang on the way home. It was Julian, apparently having been trying her for several hours, though Nicole couldn't have heard her phone over the voices at the church.

He was having trouble breathing. It was one of the more rare side effects of the drug he was on, and usually passed quickly. This time it hadn't. His doctor wanted to see him Monday morning. So rather than flying south, he was taking the train to New York. He suggested Nicole meet him there.

Charlotte drove her to the pier, where a boat was waiting to take her to Rockland. From there, she would taxi to Portland, then fly to New York. Though Nicole didn't tell her much beyond the basics, Charlotte felt the weight of worry. "You'll call me with updates?" she asked when she pulled Nicole's bag from the Jeep.

"It'll be hard. You're not supposed to know."

"But I do, so I'll be thinking of you the whole time. Text me. Or go down the hall and call."

"I'll try," Nicole said and gave her a hug.

* * *

Back at the house, Charlotte wandered. She tried not to let her imagination do the same, but it was hard not to think of what-ifs. *Salt* helped; the hero was rebuilding a boat, the process of which Charlotte found intriguing. But reading meant focusing in on words, and she was too antsy to do that for long.

So she knit for a while. It turned out that those incredibly good chocolate almond candies had been made by a newcomer to Quinnipeague who owned a yarn store in town. Charlotte planned to visit. That meant making progress on her sleeve, so that she didn't *totally* embarrass herself. Having finished the ribbed cuff, though, she was following the Aran pattern chart when she made a mistake. She ripped two painstaking rows, knit them again, and discovered she had dropped a stitch, which was now lost three rows back.

Frustrated, she set the knitting aside and went outside. She walked the beach. She swept the patio. Opening her laptop, she checked her friends' Facebook pages and looked at Twitter for the first time in days.

Dusk kept her waiting. But the minute it arrived, she was off.

Chapter Eight

LEO COLE WAS DOING SOMETHING different. The sound Charlotte heard as she approached was a sporadic clattering, like he was hurling something against metal. She couldn't tell what it was until she rounded the Cole curve and saw the floodlit slope of his roof. Two ladders stood there; near the top, a board stretched between them. Boots on the board, Leo was prying up shingles, tossing one after another into the Dumpster below.

She looked for the dog, didn't see it, and walked slowly forward. When she was close enough, she linked her hands behind her and watched for a while. Oh yeah, she had told him that his shingles were lifting. Watching him, though, she guessed he had known it. The way he went at the task spoke of experience. His movements were methodical and sure. From time to time, he grunted with the effort of removing a stubborn piece, but for the most part, he seemed untaxed.

In time, he stopped, pushed a forearm up his brow, hitched the claw tool to the next shingle in line, and reached for a bottle of water. That was when he spotted Charlotte, though if she hadn't been looking closely, she wouldn't have known. He didn't jump, didn't even fully turn, simply looked sideways as he drank. When he was done, he wiped his mouth with the back of his hand.

"Why am I not surprised," he muttered just loud enough for her to hear, then reached for the claw and continued his work.

She heard derision. But anger? Not really. "You knew about the roof problem."

"Yup. I ordered shingles a month ago."

"Why do you do this at night?"

He was silent. Then, "Why do you want to know?"

"Human interest." She shrugged. "Boredom."

He pried up several more shingles and tossed them back before saying, "Sun's down. Wind's down."

"When do you sleep?"

Another shingle fell. "When I'm tired."

"Studies show that the less sleep you get, the greater your chance of stroke."

"Studies get it backward," he countered. "Insomnia is caused by stress, which causes high blood pressure, which causes stroke. I'm not stressed."

She might have argued for the sake of argument, if he hadn't made total sense. So maybe he worked all night and slept all day. "You don't have a nine-to-five job?"

He worked on, finally said, "Nope."

"How do you pay for the shingles?"

He glanced down, sounding annoyed. "What's it to you?"

"Nothing. I'm just curious." Looking around, she spotted the toolbox. "If you have another roof ripper, I could help."

He snorted. "Dressed like that?"

"I'm not dressed any different from you." A tank top and shorts. His tank was chopped unevenly at the waist, the shorts as dark and drapey as always.

"You don't have boots."

No, but her sneakers were designed for traction. She turned one to show him the sole. When he simply went at another shingle, she said, "Seriously. I can help."

"You've done this, too?"

"I have."

He worked on for a bit. Then, "Nah. Only one claw." Moving to the right to reach a new spot, he said, "Want to make yourself useful, pick up the shingles that missed the Dumpster."

With the floodlight aimed at the roof, the ground was dark. Only when her eyes adjusted did she see what he meant.

But she didn't move. Climbing a ladder was one thing; groveling around on the ground with her arms and legs exposed was another. "Where's the dog?" she asked.

"In the bushes."

"Will he attack?"

"Not if you pick up the shingles and leave."

Trusting that he could control his dog, she collected an armful of shingles and dropped them in the Dumpster. After a second, then a third, she was done. Brushing off her hands, she called up, "What else can I do?"

"Get away from the Dumpster. Stay there, and you're gonna be hit."

"You wouldn't aim at me."

He barked out what might have been a laugh. "If my aim was perfect, you wouldn't'a had anything to pick up just now."

He had a point. Moving away from the Dumpster, she folded her arms on her chest and watched him work. He must have been trying harder, because every shingle went into the Dumpster, so there was nothing to do. After a bit, she sat.

"You said you'd leave," he charged.

"You said that. Not me." Her curiosity was far from satisfied, and the dog hadn't appeared. "What's it like being in jail?"

He shot her a look. But he didn't call the dog. "That's a dumb question. It *sucks*." He pried up several more shingles, tossed them down with greater force. One hit the ground, but he didn't seem to notice. "How'd you know I was in jail?"

"People talked about it back then," she said, standing, waiting. As soon as he tossed down the next shingle, she darted in for the one on the ground and tipped it into the Dumpster.

"You were here before?"

"Well, now you've hurt my feelings. I spent seventeen summers here. So I didn't make any impression?"

He stretched to reach higher shingles. "I don't remember much."

"High on Cecily's cures?"

Bracing the claw against the roof, he scowled down at her. "One of the reasons I work at night is because it's quiet. If you're gonna stay here, you have to shut up."

At least he wasn't harping on her leaving. This was progress. "I can shut up."

"Do it. Please." He moved farther right to work on a final swath of shingles. "And you're wrong. I wasn't high all the time. I was angry."

"Seriously," Charlotte mused. That scowl was what she remembered, but she didn't hear anger. "What did Cecily die of?"

He worked for a bit. She guessed he was ignoring her, but she had interviewed reluctant subjects before. She was about to lob up an easier question, when he said, "Pneumonia."

Pneumonia. That surprised Charlotte. Cecily would have known how to treat pneumonia. "I was thinking it had to be cancer."

"It was. She went to the hospital for that. While she was there, she got pneumonia."

Charlotte had heard similar stories, but it suddenly made Leo more human. "That's bad. I'm sorry."

"Not as sorry as I am," he said, grimacing against a stubborn shingle. "I was the one who dragged her to the hospital."

Since Quinnipeague had no hospital, that would have been on the mainland, and what Charlotte heard went beyond regret to guilt. Gently, she asked, "Is that why you hang around here, to keep up her house and garden?"

"Among other reasons."

"Like what?"

He looked down, annoyed again. "Don't you need to be somewhere?"

"Actually, no," though, sitting still, she was feeling a chill, so she unwound the sweatshirt from her waist. "Nicole's in New York. It's just me at the house." She looped the sweatshirt around her shoulders.

"Should you be telling me this?" he asked.

"Why not?"

"I'm dangerous."

"So they say," she remarked, because she was still alive now after, what, four visits?

"You know different?"

She smiled. "I know karate."

The movement of his cheek might have been a smile or a wince, though it was lost when he hung his head. After a minute, he straightened and took another drink of water. Then he climbed down the ladder.

Not trusting him, Charlotte stood. "Another few minutes, and you'll be done," she said, studying the small strip of remaining shingles. "What's next?"

He stood an arm's length away, seeming taller than he had the night before, when she'd passed him on the drive. "If you've done a roof, you know," he warned. The slightest pat of his thigh caused a rustle in the bushes.

Tar paper was next. But the dog was at his side now, so she put a smile on her face, turned, and sauntered off.

Karate might protect her from the man, but the dog? She didn't know which was more dangerous—or whether either was, certainly a thought there.

One thing was for sure, though. Both paled next to MS, which was what rose up in her mind the nearer she came to the house.

* * *

Nicole knew the drill. After landing at LaGuardia, she took a cab to the small hotel where they always stayed. It was an easy walk from the hospital, but this night even that seemed too far. Shortness of breath? A tight chest? Both were documented side effects of the meds Julian was on, but they were also classic symptoms of a heart attack. She suspected Peter Keppler had suggested he go straight to the ER in Philadelphia, but that he had refused.

Much as she told herself that, being a doctor, Julian would know the difference, she was terrified about what she would find.

Having already checked in, he had texted her the room number, so she pulled her roller bag straight to the elevator. Eight anxious floors up, she went down the hall and knocked softly. Praying he was still alive, she listened for sound. But he wasn't a heavy man, and, as it happened, he was barefoot. The relief she felt when the latch clicked and the door opened was intense.

He looked pale, but not blue. Though clearly tired, he stood straight.

Slipping into the room, she closed the door and wrapped her arms around his neck, relieved to be able to drink in everything that was Julian and strong. When he hugged her back, she imagined there was an element of clinging in it. He did need her. That was gratifying.

Finally drawing back, she studied his face. "How is it?"

"Better."

"But still there. Which one—tightness or short breath?"

"Both, but better. What did you tell Charlotte?" he asked, and she wanted to yell that Charlotte wasn't what mattered, *he* was.

But Julian, being Julian, was neurotic about secrecy, and if he was worried about Charlotte, she could help him with this at least. "I told her one of your colleagues died and I wanted to be with you at the funeral. I've gotten good at lying." Wasn't she doing it right then? Oh yes, she was good. If he had suspected she wasn't telling the truth, he would have pushed it.

But he simply asked, "Flight okay?"

"I guess. I wasn't really focused on it. I kept thinking I'd walk in here and—"

"Don't say it, baby."

"I know I know I know," she whispered, as much in contrition as anything else. "Were you sleeping?" Though he was still dressed, his hair was disheveled and his eyes heavy.

He shook his head, made the face that said he had been doing nothing worthwhile, which meant he was likely sprawled on the bed, staring at the ceiling, worrying about the same things she was and then some.

"Thanks for coming," he said.

And suddenly, out of the blue, she was livid. Growing up, the only child of adoring parents, she had been indulged on every level. She hadn't had to filter her thoughts back then, and though life experiences had taught her something of self-control, when she was upset—really upset—she still lost it.

That happened now. After a long day of travel, hours of worry, and months of strain, *thanks for coming* hit her wrong. "Where else would I *be*?" she cried. "You're my husband. I should have been in Philly with you. You take care of me, Julian. Would it be so awful if I took care of you once in a while?"

"There's nothing to do," he said, pulling away.

"There *is*," she said, telling herself that this wasn't the time, what with that lingering tightness in his chest, only this *was* the time. "You've cut yourself off from everyone who means something to you."

"Not true. I talked with my parents yesterday. I talk with friends all the time."

"But not about the truth, so it's all a show. And this, now? I'm your cover, Jules. We both know that if we're in the hospital tomorrow and you see a colleague, the idea is that I'm the patient—and that's fine, if it makes you feel better. But it doesn't make me feel better, because I'm your wife, and you're shutting me out, too. Is that all I am, your cover?"

He stared at her. *Ease up, you're making things worse, don't nag, don't hover.* She heard it all.

Turning away, he began unbuttoning his shirt. After that came his pants and his socks. It used to be that his boxers would follow, and that when he turned back to her, his need would be clear. MS affected the sexual response of some patients, but not Julian. He remained perfectly capable—*amazingly* capable. But it had been weeks since he had allowed himself to feel the need.

Granted, they couldn't make love with his chest tight, regardless of how he tried to minimize the problem.

Still, watching him undress, she couldn't help but remember the days when sex was a constant, when all he had to do was to call her *baby*—such a macho word for an academic guy—and the attraction flamed.

She felt the longing.

Leaving the boxers on tonight, though, he slipped into bed, snapped off the light on his side, and closed his eyes.

Peter Keppler was thorough. Nicole had always liked that about him. It meant hours of waiting for tests, but by the end of the day, he had enough data to make an informed decision. They were in his hospital office, which was little more than a glorified examining room, but Nicole wasn't complaining. Julian looked better, she thought. He always did when they were with Peter, like he could finally, fully let someone else take charge. And he had slept well, moving so that their bodies touched. She wasn't sure it was conscious, but she had cherished it nonetheless.

They were in separate chairs now, Nicole trying to be calm, while Peter reviewed the day's tests. The good news, he reported, was that Julian's heart would be fine, the bad was that the daily charts he kept at home in Philly confirmed that there was no improvement in the symptoms.

"We'll change the cocktail," Peter decided. "It's a small tweaking, but I don't like these side effects."

"Forget the side effects," Julian said in his informed way. "I'm worried about the efficacy of these drugs. After three months, there should have been improvement. These meds are the newest and best. If they're not working, I'm in trouble."

The neurologist made a sound that was halfway between a grunt and a laugh. "Doctors are the worst patients. They're always one step ahead."

"You bet," Julian said. "My hands are shaking as often as ever. And numbness? Sitting in a chair when it hits is bad enough, but what happens if I'm walking down the hall with colleagues?"

Peter studied him. "I wish I could operate and correct the problem with a scalpel like you do, but MS isn't that way. You're stable. One new symptom isn't much in the overall scheme."

Nicole agreed. Three months wasn't very long. The research she had done suggested that it often took far longer on a medication for the disease to get the message.

But Julian wasn't on that page. "One new symptom is one too many," he said. "I'm getting worse. This is my life, and it's heading in the wrong direction."

"You have MS," Peter reminded him. "For all we know, your symptoms would be worse without the treatments you've had." *Precisely,* Nicole thought, as the doctor went on. "I've worked with some patients for ten years before finding a path to remission. You and I, we've only been at it for four."

"The wrong direction," Julian repeated ominously.

Charlotte spent the morning sorting through a ragtag collection of cups in leftover colors and designs, mismatched plates, napkins, picnic tablecloths, and plastic cutlery. Nicole had waved a dismissive hand at the pantry in which these were kept; she far preferred the real stuff to paper and plastic, and had suggested a wholesale cleaning. Charlotte figured she could help with this, at least.

After filling two large bags, she drove them to the church. Though she kept her phone in her pocket, Nicole didn't call.

Having stowed her camera in the backseat, she continued on to the farm where Anna McDowell Cabot raised the chickens that produced eggs for so many island specialties. Anna was a rotund woman who waddled and clucked like her hens, but her clucking was informative.

A lifelong Quinnie, she knew as much about the island as anyone. She talked for hours about the ways in which the island had changed, and, with Charlotte's frequent rechanneling, how those changes had affected the food.

Having been the beneficiary of herbal remedies for acid reflux, she considered Cecily Cole a saint. But when Charlotte mentioned Leo, she grew cautious. "He's very private."

"A bad boy."

"Bad?" With a soft clucking, she considered. "Not so much bad, as misunderstood."

"By whom?"

"Everyone for a while. He was an unhappy child. Now, he just keeps to himself."

"What does he do for a living?"

"Oh"—a specious sigh—"a little of this, little of that," which told her nothing.

"He still grows Cecily's herbs," she tried.

"Leo does not." A wise smile here. "Those herbs grow themselves."

"Does he sell them?"

"I never heard that."

"Does he give them to people who need them, like Cecily used to do?"

"I guess."

"Does he trade them for food?"

Anna frowned. "Why the questions?"

Charlotte wasn't about to suggest there were personal reasons, when there was reason enough on a professional vein. "Cecily's been dead five years, but her herbs are going strong. We're assembling a cookbook. How can I not ask about the herbs?"

"You know what they say about curiosity and the cat," the hen-keeper clucked.

Charlotte certainly did. Curiosity killed it. Bob Lilly used to warn her about that, though he loved her questions and never once refused an answer. There was, of course, a rejoinder to the adage—*and satisfac-*

tion brought it back—but Charlotte let it go. Having taken pictures as they talked and walked, she was more than satisfied with the interview. While others on the list could talk about specifics, Anna provided an overview that would be crucial for the book.

Charlotte left the Cabot farm feeling a new enthusiasm. Wanting to share it with Nicole, she sent a quick text. When she didn't hear back, she grew uneasy and tried calling, but Nicole didn't pick up.

It wasn't until late afternoon, when they returned to their hotel to pack, that Nicole was able to call Charlotte. Texting wouldn't do it. She needed to hear a comforting voice. Julian was taking a shower—wanting to wash the patient from his body, he said. She stood in the farthest corner of the bedroom, hunched over the phone with her eyes on the bathroom door.

"It's me," she said in a low rush. "I can't talk long. If the shower goes off, I'm done. We're heading to LaGuardia for a flight to Chicago."

"Chicago?" Charlotte asked in alarm. "What happened to Raleigh-Durham?"

Thinking how glad she was to be able to share her frustration, Nicole murmured, "Postponed for a couple of days, and I'm not happy about Chicago, either. I mean, things were fine today. It wasn't a heart attack, just a problem with the meds. His doctor wants to alter the dosage and give it more time, but my husband is impatient. We're going to Chicago for a consult."

"Aren't there other specialists in New York?"

"Yes, but Julian knows who's doing what where, and this one's into different therapies."

"What kind of different therapies?" Charlotte asked with what sounded like rising alarm—but even that was calming for Nicole, who welcomed validation of her own worry.

"This particular doctor is into stem cell transplants." The words shimmied around in her belly. She pressed a steadying hand there. "Julian is willing to try something unproven, if there's a chance it'll work. This scares me to death, Charlotte, but he's getting desperate." The shower went off. Straightening, she spoke casually. "So Anna was good?"

"Desperate to do something radical?" came the voice at the other end, but before she could answer, Julian opened the bathroom door. Toweling off, he came into the bedroom, eyes questioning.

"Just letting Charlotte know I won't be back tonight," she explained.

Charlotte exhaled audibly. "Okay. Well, you got my text. Anna's a great resource."

"Did she give you her recipe for layered eggs?" Nicole asked lightly. "By the way, I don't know why she calls it layered eggs, since it's really about ham, zucchini, and mushroom, but she uses incredible herbs. Did she list those for you?"

"She did."

"Good. I'll do a test batch once I'm back." She relished the thought, and it had nothing to do with food. Immersing herself in even this tiny bit of work was a respite. "Did you and Melissa Parker agree on a time to talk?" she asked. Melissa provided baked goods for the Chowder House, the Island Grill, and the Quinnie Café. Not only was she a must profile, but Nicole had given Charlotte a dream list of Melissa's recipes for inclusion as well.

"Tomorrow," Charlotte said. "So you're flying out tonight?"

"We are." She reverted to alibi. "It's been tough on the family. I'll do some cooking and bring over a few meals."

"How long will you stay in Chicago?"

Now that he was off the offending drug and he knew he would live, Julian wouldn't stay more than a day. He wanted to get to Duke before anyone suspected something amiss. Besides, the consultation was strictly informational. He had even offered to go alone, but in that case, Nicole knew she would get an abridgement of the discussion and would forever worry about what she had missed.

She had a stake in this; she wanted to hear exactly what was said. "I'll fly up Wednesday," she told Charlotte. "Can you make it without me until then?"

Chapter Nine

Charlotte held the phone to her belly for a long time after the call ended. Nicole wasn't the only one who was scared. When it came to experimental treatments for MS, stem cell transplants held great promise. But there were stem cells—and then there were *umbilical cord* stem cells. Umbilical cord cells came from the blood that remained in a baby's umbilical cord after it was cut, blood that was drained and whisked to a blood bank where it was frozen and stored for future need. The ethical issues surrounding embryonic stem cells didn't apply here. This was blood. There was no egg, no fertilization. A baby couldn't grow from it. But increasingly, in research labs and hospitals worldwide, stem cells taken from umbilical cord blood were being found to have properties for healing and regrowth in humans with different diseases.

Such were the facts. Nicole surely knew them.

But Charlotte knew something Nicole did not. She knew something *Julian* did not. If she had to tell what she knew, the damage might be catastrophic.

Dreading that, she sat on the beach for a while. The ocean air was warm, blowing her hair, skimming her skin. She watched a gull swoop into the shallows for a catch, then a pair of sandpipers flipping stones in search of crabs. The sea was eternal, she told herself. Life went on. Traumas came and went.

It was small solace.

Needing a dose of comfort, she drove to the Chowder House for a lobster roll and fries, drove home again, and returned to the beach, where she proceeded to devour every last crumb in the bag.

Did she feel better? No. If anything, she felt worse now, like a terrible *fat* friend.

She needed to walk, and not to Leo's. She needed to *really* walk. Heading for town, she moved as quickly as her stomach allowed, going faster as the lobster and fries settled, finally turning and running home. She wasn't a runner. She had always wanted to be, but her knees disagreed. No doubt, they would be screaming by morning.

The Jacuzzi in Angie and Bob's bedroom would help. Nicole would have insisted, as would Angie, which was why she couldn't do it. She was a traitor of the worst kind—betraying Nicole, betraying Angie and Bob, even betraying Julian.

She was a bad person. If Leo Cole was, too, they deserved each other, or so her thinking went as she scrunched her mutinous hair into a wad and set off for the island's tail. She was so absorbed in her own guilt that she didn't hear anything—not the roll of the surf, the hoot of an owl, or the slap of her own feet—until she reached the Cole curve and the sound of hammering registered.

He would be applying tar paper to the roof he had exposed the night before. She knew that even before she saw him at it. Moving steadily along makeshift scaffolding, he unrolled the paper left to right, and hammered nails at regular intervals to secure it.

She watched for a while unobserved. For a bad guy, he had nice legs. He also had a tight butt, though his shorts were loose enough so that the shape came and went.

"Can you hammer?" he finally called down.

Not unobserved at all. "Can I hammer," she murmured in wry affirmation.

He gestured toward the second ladder. When she reached the top, he picked up a new roll of tar paper, anchored it, handed her a hammer and a tin of nails, and let her at it.

Tar paper came in different weights. This one was of the heavier variety, which made sense given the climate. Until she had unrolled and secured a healthy swatch, it was awkward, but she refused to complain.

"Utility knife?" she asked when she reached the edge of the roof.

He walked it to her. Warm from his tool belt, it did the trick. She went back in the other direction, cutting again when she reached the paper he had laid. He touched her arm once to move her aside so that he could better work the edges together, but she was soon on her own again. When they finished one row, they climbed higher and started the next, then the next. In time, they reached the cupola, which was harder, closer. Their arms touched more than once, legs touched more than once, none of it unpleasant.

The air was still. He was right about the wind being down at night. Or maybe it was just this particular night, capping another long summer day. Even with her hair off her neck, it was heavy and hot. Not that she was alone. The floodlight picked up streaks of sweat on Leo's face and neck. He paused often to swipe at it with his arm.

"That's it," he finally said, taking a long look at what they'd done before collecting his things and backing down the ladder. As soon as Charlotte was on the ground, he lowered the ladders and carried them away. He returned with two bottled waters, handed her one, and drank the contents of the other in an unbroken series of gulps.

Charlotte was feeling better, like she had accomplished something, had earned her keep in an odd regard. She looked up at the roof. Still lit by the flood, it was dark and even. "That's good-quality tar paper," she said.

"What's the point of making the effort, if you don't do it right?"

She smiled. "I just read that in a book. The guy is building a boat and wants to use the best materials, which are taking forever to arrive, but he's adamant about waiting."

Leo was staring at her.

Puzzled, she stared back. "What?"

"You read that crap?"

"What crap?"

"*Salt.*"

She was amused. "What do you know about *Salt*?"

"It's all people are talking about."

"You read?"

He frowned. "Sometimes."

"But not *Salt*. Because it's crap. For the record," Charlotte remarked, feeling proprietary of the book, "I don't think it's crap. I think it's well written and tells a great story."

Leo stared for another minute, then said, "So does *Moby-Dick*. Lots of copies of that in the prison library."

"So they let you read there. That's not so bad."

He turned up his lip. "I also learned how to pick locks and hot-wire cars."

"I'll watch my Jeep. They used to say you stole money from the church box."

"They never caught me at it," he countered, not quite answering the question.

She shot a puzzled look at the house. "So how do you pay for repairs?"

"Embezzlement."

Charlotte didn't believe it for a minute. "Did you ever force a girl to have sex?"

"I never had to. They were willing."

"Did you ever make one pregnant?"

"I'm not that dumb," he muttered and, seeming to have had enough talk, walked back to the house to turn off the floodlight. Then, in long strides, he headed off through the herbs. As he walked, he pulled his shirt over his head.

"Where are you going?" she shouted as the moon glanced off his bare back.

"Swimming. Go home." He turned into the night woods and dissolved.

Charlotte wasn't about to go home. She wanted to see where Leo swam. If her calculations were correct, that path would lead to a stretch where the shoreline was rocky and forbidding. She and Nicole had never walked that far down the beach. Like broken pavement on the road, the message was KEEP OUT.

Now, though, she could approach it from a different direction. If Leo had cut through the woods, so could she.

She was about to do that when a rustling came from the bushes by the house. As the dog emerged, she held her breath. A black hulk in the moonlight, it looked first at her, then in the direction Leo had gone. She had no idea what its thought process was; she only knew that, after what seemed an inordinately long time, it set off after Leo. It walked slowly, plodding toward the woods. The word *gingerly* came to Charlotte's mind. As she watched, she didn't think the dog looked dangerous. She thought it looked old.

It hadn't gone after the doe or its fawn. It hadn't lunged at her. She had never seen it do anything but lumber along. Old. She couldn't rule it out.

Not that she was taking any chances. She waited until it was gone, then silently followed. Something sweet hovered in the garden, but her focus was beyond. There was definitely a path. Forest brush snapped under her sneakers, but the surf grew progressively louder. Then it appeared, reflecting the moon like a light at the end of the tunnel. Large boulders, small rocks, and flat little stones flanked a patch of wet sand. Had the tide been in, that sand wouldn't have been visible at all. Even now it was hard-packed. Leo's clothes were there, alongside his boots, kicked off and askew.

Hidden just inside the path, Charlotte searched the water. Moonlight bounced off the waves, which rolled gently in, but it was a minute before she was able to separate out a pair of arms. Pale white in the moonglow, they stroked steadily away from shore. A risky thing to do? She would think so. But he had to know what he was doing—had probably done this hundreds of other nights. He swam easily, rising and falling with the waves, seeming as comfortable in the water as he was on his roof.

Mesmerized by the rhythm of those arms, the turn of his head when he breathed, an occasional kick that broke the surface behind him, she barely breathed herself until something wet touched her leg. Startled, she whirled around. It was the dog, looking up at her with baleful eyes.

"It's okay," she whispered shakily. "It's okay. Good Bear. No harm."

Baleful? Or simply sad? In the rays of the moon that wove through the trees, she saw furrows on its brow, and patches of brown near its eyes and snout.

Heart pounding, she extended a hand. The dog sniffed it for a minute. It didn't growl, didn't bare its teeth or back away—it actually seemed to want something more. She put her fingertips to its head, much as Leo had done that first night. Its fur was short and coarse on the flat stretch between its ears, but those ears looked silky. Curious, she touched them.

The dog sat.

Charlotte's heart continued to pound, though no longer from fear. Now it was the pull of the moon, and before that the smell of temptation in the garden. She was hot. "I'm going for a swim," she whispered to the dog. "Okay?"

When Bear didn't move, Charlotte looked at the sea again. Leo's arms were distant, but they had reversed direction. He was heading in. If she planned to join him, it had to be now.

"Stay," she urged softly, and with only the quickest glance back to make sure the dog didn't follow, she hurried to the beach. The moon was bright, turning the ocean into a play of contrast, midnight and silver, dark and light, good and bad. This was her life. She had no business being here. She was playing with fire.

But that didn't stop her from stripping down to her underwear and running into the surf. The water was cold, taking her breath for an instant, but she didn't turn back. When she was thigh-high in it, she dove over an incoming swell and submerged in its wake. Surfacing a body length beyond, she gasped at the cold. Then, pausing only to locate Leo, she started to swim. Her body rose with each swell, working harder on the climb, but the effort warmed her. She stroked steadily until one ill-timed breath met the rolling surf. Just shy of swallowing a mouthful, she spit it out and, straightening, looked for Leo. She didn't have to look far. He had stopped swimming and was watching her. Dark head, dark eyes, wet face white, he was as much a contrast as the rest of the world.

Treading water, she remembered the warnings about Leo Cole. Just then, though, none seemed to matter. If Leo had done bad things, so had she. And danger? She had once dived off a cliff in Acapulco. It hadn't been pretty, and she wasn't about to repeat it, but she had survived and remembered the rush. Being in these waters with Leo couldn't be worse.

The surf brought him closer. She couldn't tell whether he helped it with his hands, since they were submerged, as were hers. Her hair had come loose and trailed behind her. Only her head and shoulders broke the surface as she kicked to keep herself afloat.

He stopped an arm's length away, staring at her with shadowed eyes. After a minute, he blew out a short breath. From the exertion of swimming? Not likely. It might have been a question: *What did I expect?* Or a warning: *You're pushing me.* Mostly, it felt like a bald statement: *We're in trouble.*

But wasn't that what she wanted? If there was a price to pay for this, what was one more price? And it wasn't just her. *We,* his expression said. This wasn't a one-way thing.

His leg tangled with hers. At the same time, he tethered her by the hair and brought her to his mouth. The loss of breath then was for real.

Part moon, part ocean, his kiss was like nothing she'd ever experienced. It was commanding, but not hurtful—thorough in the way she needed. By the time it was done, her arms were around his neck, her legs around his waist. The cold water should have depressed his need, but did not. The next wave brought a taunting undulation.

Breathing hard, he propelled them toward shore. They were barely in the shallows, their legs still washed by the surf, when he set her on the sand and levered up only enough to tug at her panties. She helped, but one leg was all they managed. Holding that leg, he looked at her, giving her one last chance. *Are you in or out?*

"In," she whispered, and he was. Head back, eyes closed, he held himself there for what seemed an eternity, before looking at her again. He seemed surprised. So was she. She hadn't been conscious of wanting him, hadn't drooled over his body while they worked or dreamt about it afterward. The way he fit into her now, though, satisfied something deep inside.

Wanting another kiss, she brought his face down, and the hunger was fierce on both sides. In time, she needed air, gasping at the power of what she felt. His thrusts went beyond the rhythm of the surf, creating sensations so strong that she cried out.

He went still. "Hurt?"

She laughed into a moan, moved her head no against the sand, and, crossing her ankles, pulled him deeper. It went on and on and on, both the lovemaking and the spasms at the end. Her body or his? She was too into it to know or care.

When he finally slipped to the side, she lay back, breathless and limp. Eyes closed, she refused to see anything around her. He stayed close, his abdomen to her hip and one leg over hers. She didn't fall asleep, though the sense of release was so great that she might have. She simply lay there for however long, totally drained.

Then she felt something. It was his hand, moving over her belly in a slow, tentative way that had nothing to do with sex—and in a flash, reality returned. Sitting up fast, she turned away and hugged her knees. When she looked back, he was on an elbow, frowning.

"You have a baby," he said.

She swallowed, shook her head no.

"Those are stretch marks," he stated.

She had always been careful to hide them. One-piece bathing suits were good for that. Same with silk camis. But she had never been so taken with sex as she'd been with Leo, and it was night. The dark should have kept her secrets.

Not that she had thought any of this out ahead of time. She had come to Leo's to be punished. But sex? *Punished?* He hadn't been a brute of a lover at all. Powerful, yes. But far from cruel, and that was as upsetting as the other. Sex with Leo had been . . . amazing. It wasn't supposed to be like that.

Frightened, she looked around for her clothes and quickly pulled them on. Leo was sitting up now, watching her, but he didn't speak, and as soon as she pushed her wet feet into her sneakers, she made for the path. She didn't pass the dog, barely heard the crunch of the forest floor or felt the sand matting her wet hair. When she came out into the garden, she hurried through the rows, down the drive, and onto the road. She didn't look back, *couldn't* look back. And when she reached Nicole's house, she closed the door and sank to the ground.

She had run to Leo's to escape a mess. Now she had created another.

There was only one thing to do. After showering away all signs of the night, she wrapped herself in a fleece blanket on the sofa downstairs and, picking up *Salt,* escaped into a world where love beat the odds.

At least, she thought it did. An hour later, though, she was worried. The lovers were perfect for each other, but they were rooted in such different worlds that only a sea change in one would keep them together. She didn't see it happening. The author had painted both in fine detail; she knew them well. They had overcome silence and secrets, and had changed in the deepest possible ways—but their differences remained huge. They simply couldn't change more and stay in character.

Unable to bear the suspense, she flipped through to the last pages, the ones Nicole had sobbed about. Minutes later, she slammed the book shut, buried it under a pillow in the corner of the sofa, and, heartsick, went to bed.

Chapter Ten

TUESDAY'S MEETING IN CHICAGO WAS tough from the start. Whereas Peter Keppler had an easy way about him, Mark Hammon was an academic. A slender, bespectacled man who wasn't prone to small talk, he studied Julian's file at length, turning from one page to the next, frowning, going back, removing his glasses to rub the bridge of his nose, glancing at Julian, replacing the glasses, returning to the file. When he finally spoke, he expressed serious reservations about Julian being a candidate for a stem cell transplant.

What little relief Nicole felt was offset by Julian's frustration. His face was tight with it.

"You're thinking that I've only been at this for four years," he argued, "but my reading says that stem cell treatment is the most promising when it's done in the early stage of a disease. I'm the perfect candidate."

Hammon didn't look convinced, though he considered it a while before saying, "You tend to have serious side effects. There are less risky things to try first."

"What we've tried hasn't worked." When Hammon named two

drugs that Julian hadn't tried, he only waved a dismissive hand. "The side effects of either one can be worse than the disease, and the promise of payoff isn't as good as with stem cells."

"Given your physiology and your history of reaction, an autologous transplant would be better."

"Using my own cells? With another patient, I might agree. But I've been on so many drugs that I doubt my own cells would be any good, and testing for that would only waste time. Time is the issue, Mark. If there's any chance of salvaging my career, I need to act now. I want to take a step that holds real promise. I know the risks."

Frowning, Hammon pushed at his glasses. "You know them? I've seen them. In some cases after we introduce cells, we can't control their growth, so tumors result. In other cases, the drugs we use to depress the immune system and avoid the rejection of transplanted cells turn out to be toxic. One of my early patients died from the chemo itself."

"What if we found a good match with donor cells?"

"Even then." But he stared at the file. "No mention here of tissue matches with family members."

Julian was silent.

"Parents? Children?" He asked, including Nicole in the discussion.

"They haven't been tested," she said, darting a nervous look at Julian, whose eyes warned her against saying more.

Hammon tipped his head; testing relatives would be a logical first step.

"What about umbilical cord stem cells?" Julian asked. "My kids were born before freezing cord blood was an option, but even if they were tested now, umbilical cord cells are the ones that hold the most hope. They don't require an exact match, and they carry regulatory T cells that can repair the damage and possibly even reverse the disease. That's from your own research."

"True. But using cord blood cells is even more experimental. In your case, there's still an excessive risk of rejection. Infusing those cells into your body could be lethal."

"I could go to Mexico," Julian dared.

Hammon didn't blink. "You're too smart for that."

"For *sure,*" Nicole told Julian, horrified by the thought. Desperate for an alternative, she turned to the doctor. "What if Julian tried another standard therapy and it didn't work? If the disease begins to progress beyond what it is, would you consider donor stem cells?" She didn't want anything experimental, period, but if Julian was determined, later was better than now.

"I might, but the risk would remain." He was looking at Julian. "Stroke, pervasive infection, paralysis—any one of those could leave you worse off than you are. Your mind is good. You have years of productivity ahead, whether you're in the OR or not. Besides, I'm not the only one doing research. This is an emerging field. In six months or a year, we'll know more."

"He's right, Jules," Nicole begged. "Six months won't hurt."

Julian turned on her. "Six months could be *forever* for me. What part of this picture don't you see?" Dismissing her with a look, he faced Hammon again, but Nicole heard little of what they said. Nor did she speak. She had been silenced as surely as if she'd been slapped.

They were there for another thirty minutes. She managed to shake the doctor's hand when they left, but her stomach was in knots. Fear? Worry? There was also anger. She told herself that she had no right to feel it, that Julian was just trying to survive and she had only upset him more, but the arguments were empty. There was a whole other side to this that *he* didn't see. She couldn't seem to put that fact aside.

He took her elbow as they entered and left the elevator, and, as soon as they reached the street, drew her out of the stream of pedestrian traffic to the privacy of a granite wall. "What was *that* about?" he asked in a voice that was uncharacteristically emotional. "Was it necessary to embarrass me in front of a colleague?"

She might have pointed out that he had embarrassed her right back, if she hadn't been reeling from it still. "All I did was to say that the doctor had a point."

"You sided with him. That's not what I needed in there."

"You'd go to Mexico and have a procedure done in a no-name clinic? Jules, this isn't only about *you*."

He might as well not have heard. "Hell, Nicole, don't you *get* it? Experimental treatments are done at the insistence of the patient, and they can't express doubts the way you did. I've been there, baby. I know how it works. A doctor believes in his technique, but until he's done it a certain number of times, he can't know for sure if it'll work and, if so, on which patients. The first patients are always the ones who demand the procedure and are willing to take the risks. You sided with him. That was counterproductive."

"I'm frightened," she tried, wanting to diffuse the situation, much as she had wanted to do in the doctor's office, but it didn't work now, either.

"*You're* frightened?" Julian countered. "What about me? This is not a walk in the park. I know the risks, but the alternative is worse. You aren't the one who stands to lose everything!"

Turning abruptly, he set off at a rapid pace toward the hotel. She had to trot every few steps to keep up, but he was so lost in his snit that he neither noticed the occasional waver in his gait nor seemed to know she was there.

She was acutely aware of both, and while the first tugged at her heart, the second stoked her anger. His health wasn't the only thing at risk. It looked like their marriage was going right down the tubes. *And it wasn't her fault*. She was trying to understand what he felt, was trying to ease things for him. But she could do no right. He needed someone to blame, and she was it—like *she* had given him MS.

He wanted it to go away. Damn it, so did she. But it wasn't going to happen, and the longer he denied that, the more miserable he would be. Life didn't always go as planned. There were graceful ways of dealing with bad things that happened. What he was doing was only making it worse.

Back at the hotel, they packed and checked out, then took a cab to the airport. They didn't speak, other than to direct the cabbie to their individual airlines, Julian for a flight to Philadelphia, Nicole to Portland. She didn't offer to go home with him, and not simply for fear of rejection. Just then, she needed Charlotte more than Julian, therapy more than another fight.

Her drop-off came first. When the cab stopped at the curb, Julian reached for her hand and gave it a squeeze. She tried to smile, but couldn't. Oh yes, she feared for her marriage. But anger percolated, and, being a new emotion for her, she had little control. Scowling, she climbed out, took her bag from the cabbie, and set it on the curb. Then she ducked back in.

"For the record," she told Julian in a shaky voice, "you are dead wrong. I love you. You are my husband, my *life.* If I lose you, I *do* lose everything." Not trusting that she wouldn't burst into tears, she slammed the door, grabbed the handle of her bag, and wheeled away.

Charlotte felt every inch of her body that day, but she refused to think about Leo. It was easier with each passing hour and no call from Nicole. That gave her plenty to worry about. She had always been in charge of her life—as a child because her parents were emotionally absent, as an eighteen-year-old heading to college on full scholarship, as a pregnant twenty-four-year-old with a secret no one else in the whole world knew.

Now her future seemed to weigh on forces she couldn't control.

So she took refuge in ones she could. She spent hours that morning on Anna McDowell Cabot's interview, adding to what she had written the night before. After driving out to the farm to ask several follow-up questions—and still no word from Nicole—she met with Melissa Parker. Whereas Anna was in her seventies and had lived in Quinnipeague all her life, Melissa had married into it at thirty. Now forty, she was a pastry chef here. Since she had studied in New York prior to meeting her husband, she and Charlotte had an instant rapport. She worked out of her home, which boasted a spanking-new industrial kitchen. This was where they met.

Though Quinnies under thirty would make a beeline for Melissa's marble macadamia brownies, her specialty was an herbed brioche, a warm batch of which were on the counter when Charlotte arrived. Naturally, she didn't refuse a taste, but she didn't stop there. When Melissa raved about island sage, Charlotte sampled a sage croissant, then a roll laced with rosemary and basil, then a scone rich with thyme. Melissa felt that her skill had evolved since coming here, that Cecily's herbs had enhanced her baking in ways she couldn't begin to explain.

"Did you ever meet her?" Charlotte asked, wondering if she'd get a different perspective from someone who wasn't native to Quinnipeague.

"Several times. She was sweet. Reserved."

"Reserved, as in secretive?"

Melissa considered that. "More like private. I don't think she had any friends in the conventional sense. I couldn't grow her herbs. I tried, but they didn't take. It's too shady here. My soil doesn't drain well."

"You must have done something to upset Cecily," Charlotte said only half in jest. "Or Leo." She couldn't resist. "Do you know him?"

"No. He's happy staying out there at the house."

"That has to be isolating. He must come into town sometimes." Those roofing materials hadn't just risen from the sea.

"I'm sure he buys food at the store."

"Doesn't he have any friends?"

Melissa shrugged.

"Or *travel*?"

"Travel." She sputtered a wry laugh. "He doesn't even go to the mainland."

Charlotte was startled. *"Ever?"* she asked, wondering what kind of man could bear the solitude. Even year-rounders, who did mix with other islanders, made regular trips to the mainland. "Does he work for people around here?"

"He used to. I guess he still does. He's good with his hands."

Charlotte wasn't going *near* that one. "What does he do with Cecily's herbs?" she asked, because his garden was a treasure trove, and he didn't strike her as one to cook, himself.

"That's an interesting question," Melissa said, seemingly puzzled. "I don't really know. Maybe he sells them, but he isn't my source. I buy mine from Shari Bowen, whose soil does drain well and who needs the money. I think that's what Cecily planned."

Sensing that she couldn't push more on Leo without arousing suspicion, Charlotte simply nodded at the last. When it came to Cecily and the mystical, Melissa was preaching to the choir.

Her phone remained silent. As she left Melissa's, she checked it, saw four bars, shook it, waited and watched. Nothing.

Frustrated, she returned to the Wrangler. She was passing through town en route to the neck road, when she spotted a deep purple awning hanging off the porch of a small frame house. SKANE'S SKEINS, read orange script on the awning.

Thinking that a piece of chocolate almond candy would lift her spirits, Charlotte pulled in behind several other cars. The shop was the living room of the house, refitted with floor-to-ceiling bins that contained more yarn than she would have thought a lone island would warrant. That said, the yarn was nearly as yummy as Charlotte knew the candy to be.

Discipling herself on the latter, she browsed while other customers were helped, then introduced herself to the owner. A pear-shaped woman with bright red cheeks and hair, Isabel Skane had a pleasantly calm voice. Calm actually described the shop. Rainbow colors, softness, texture, low spa music—it was soothing. Charlotte browsed through the yarn, browsed through notebooks of patterns, put her favorites on a Wish List, and said she'd be back. Then, after helping herself to one candy from a bowl by the register, she popped it in her mouth, took a second to go, and returned to the Wrangler.

She was back at the house, typing up a rough outline of the material, when Nicole finally called.

Her voice was small. *"Omigod."*

Charlotte's pulse began to race. "What happened?"

"Oh, Charlotte." Defeat.

Charlotte was thinking that Julian had a heart attack after all, that he was hospitalized, in intensive care—when she heard background announcements, the likes of which she knew all too well. "Are you at the airport?"

"Yes." Nicole said in the same small voice. "He's at his gate, I'm at mine. Is that poetic?" she wailed softly. "What a nightmare."

"Tell me."

"Tomorrow. I don't have the strength right now." Coming from a woman who usually ran on at the mouth, the confession spoke volumes. "Would you believe, the flight's way late. There's bad weather just east of here, so nothing's landing." The PA system came on. She went quiet, then said a weary, "Finally. My plane's in range. But here's the problem, Charlotte. I won't get to Portland until ten, which means that I won't get to Rockland until midnight, so there's no way I can get to the island until morning."

"Where can you stay in Rockland?"

"There are some nice inns. I'll stay in one."

"Are you sure?"

"I don't have much choice, y'know?"

Charlotte would have gone to get her if she'd had a way of doing it, but boats that shuttled Quinnies to the mainland always did so in daylight. The occasional sunset cruise went out, but by the time darkness fell, every slip in the harbor was full.

She wanted details on that meeting with the doctor. Waiting was an agony, but it sounded like what Nicole had been through was worse. What to do to make things better?

Had she been a baker, she would have whipped up a batch of those marble macadamia brownies, and had them waiting. Since she didn't bake—and since marble macadamia brownies would be nothing new to foodie Nicole—she wrote up Melissa's interview and, after polishing Anna's, printed both out. Nicole would be pleased.

Placing the pages on the kitchen table beside a vase, which she would fill with fresh flowers the next morning, she took a breath, put her hands on her hips, and looked outside. Denial worked as long as you had something else to do, but she had just run out. It wasn't dark yet, but she couldn't wait a minute longer. She had to talk with Leo.

Chapter Eleven

FEELING AS MUCH URGENCY AS trepidation, she set off. The breeze crossing the road was stronger than it had been the past few nights, rustling the leaves in the trees, cooling her arms and legs. Uneasy, she glanced at the sky. Clouds were gathering in the west, likely from the storm system that had delayed Nicole's flight. The humidity was already up, and along with it, the volume of her hair. And then there was the thick sea smell.

Rethinking the walking plan, she returned to the house, changed into jeans, and took the Jeep. Minutes later, she parked just beyond the Cole curve.

If he worked on the roof tonight, he would be putting down plywood. But it wasn't night yet. And with a storm coming on? She wasn't sure he would work at all.

Rounding the curve, she saw the house in daylight. The shutter Leo had hung was straight, but others were not, and while the tar-papered roof was an unbroken expanse, the clapboard body needed a coat of paint. The poor thing was threadbare.

The foliage around it was another matter. Even in the overcast, she saw myriad shades of green, one more vibrant than the next.

When Charlotte had asked Leo where Cecily was buried, he hadn't answered. Now she half suspected that the ashes were sprinkled over these grounds, a fertilizer in perpetuity to chalk up to the Cecily mystique.

As Charlotte started down the drive, she studied the front windows for signs of life. Where she thought she remembered curtains from Cecily's time, now there were blinds, and though they were slatted open, she couldn't see much. She did smell the gardens, though, and stopped when a certain sweetness hit her. It whisked her back to the night before, when she had cut through on her way to the beach. Following her nose down that row now, she stopped at the end near the woods, where the shrubbery was nearly as tall as she was. No herbs here—these were small white flowers in bloom, their petals star-shaped, smooth to the touch and strong of scent. When she brought her fingers to her nose and inhaled, her insides quickened.

Frightened, she wiped her hands on her jeans. She didn't know what Cecily's message was, but it made her feel less in control. She had come here with a purpose, and it wasn't sex.

Backing away from the flowers, she continued down the drive. As she approached the house, the bushes moved, and Bear came out. A long-ingrained fear whispered, but it died down when he shuffled to her side, head up, eyes beseechful. He was a sweet old thing, nothing to fear.

The man was something else. She had no idea what to expect.

The house had no porch, just three steps and a landing. A tarnished knocker waited. Needing time to gather herself, perhaps to take courage from the scent of herbs, rising now over that of the small white flowers, she settled on the second step with her feet on the ground. Bear came and sat close beside her. Elbows on her knees, she touched the coarse hair between his ears and traced the furrows on his brow. He closed his eyes, seeming enraptured.

That ended abruptly when a whistle came from the back of the house. Ears perked, eyes worried, the dog looked toward the sound, then at Charlotte again.

"He's with me!" she called to Leo. She didn't look around until bootsteps approached, and even then she hesitated. Stretch marks were only part of it. There was also the sex.

But both were fact. She couldn't change them. Stoical, she raised her eyes.

For an alleged thug, he was clean-cut. Short hair helped. Likewise the shadow of a beard where scruff had been. And attractive? The same prominent cheekbones and firm jaw that had screamed *attitude* when he was younger were now just plain male. Same with his very adult body, which explained the physical side of what happened last night. The other side was what made her nervous.

He seemed unsure, though his face didn't betray much. It was all in his eyes. Seeing them for the first time in daylight, she realized they weren't black, but a very dark blue—and wary as they went from her to the dog.

"Figured it out, huh?" he said.

Charlotte stroked Bear's head. "How old is he?"

"I don't know. I got him from a shelter when I first got out of jail. The vet there guessed three."

That would have been ten years ago, making Bear thirteen. "What's the life span of a dog like this?"

"Nine to twelve. He's part Rottweiler, part mutt. Mutts live longer. I'm counting on that." He stood six feet away, staring at her with barely a blink. "So you know my secret. What's yours?"

It was all she could do not to look away, but she owed him this. Quietly, she said, "I did have a baby. I mean, I gave birth to it. But I gave it up."

"Why?"

"I wasn't married. The father was." Hearing it aloud, she felt rotten to the core—in recklessness and depravation, very much her parents' daughter, which she had never, ever wanted to be. That was one of several things that had haunted her these ten years.

"Why were you with a married guy?"

"He wasn't married at the time. He was engaged." She swallowed. "To my best friend."

She waited for judgment, but Leo remained expressionless. "Did you love him?"

"Lord, no. That's what was so *stupid*. It was once, and it was totally meaningless. We'd had too much to drink."

His eyes held hers. "We weren't drinking last night."

"Yeah, well"—she did look away then—"that's the other part of this that scares me."

"You were scared because I saw stretch marks?"

Something struck her then. "How did you know what they were?" she asked. He was so sure about it. Yet he didn't socialize. He wasn't married, wasn't a father. At least, he didn't have a wife or kids on Quinnipeague. Maybe elsewhere?

"I used to spend weekends on the bluff." Overlooking Okers Beach. "With binoculars."

With binoculars. "*That's* bad," Charlotte said. "They're still at it, y'know. We saw them last weekend. And yeah, some of the women weren't bothered that their stretch marks showed."

"But you were," he said, dragging her back to the subject at hand. She supposed it was good, if difficult on her end.

"I don't let them show," she admitted. "I don't tell people about this."

"You told me."

"I kind of had to, after what happened."

"It was just sex."

That hit her the wrong way. "It was *honest*. If you didn't see that, then I wasted my time worrying about it all night. Sex is sex, but that was something else. Don't ask me what, because I've been trying to figure it out, but that's the only word that comes up right now. Honest."

His expression did change then, mirroring her anger. His voice was low and hard. "Okay. Let's talk honest. Why are you here?"

His tone took her aback. "Today? Now?"

"No. Every night since last Wednesday."

"I didn't come Saturday," she said meekly.

"Why come at all?" he shot back. "Here you are, just perfect for me, knowing how to put on a roof, like you were recruited to seduce me. Is it the cookbook? The herbs?"

She sat straighter. "*Seduce* you. I didn't *plan* what happened. Did you *not* get the bottom line of what I said before? The last summer I was here I made a major mistake. Why would I want to make another?" She realized she'd said more than she should have, but the words were out. Honest? Oh yeah. She stared at him for another minute, then stood, bowed her head, pressed her brow. "This is not working. It's getting dark. I should go."

"Don't," he said quickly, with what she actually thought sounded like vulnerability. When she dared a look, his expression was guarded. "I just needed to know."

"Whether I'm using you?" she asked. "If that was true, would I be as obsessed as I am about what we did?" She reconsidered. "Maybe 'obsessed' is too strong. Troubled, is more like it. I don't do this, Leo. I don't travel around the world having affairs, and if you're worried you might have made me pregnant, don't. I protect myself. I've seen the downside of carelessness."

His voice was lower than ever. "A baby isn't a downside."

To her horror, her eyes filled with tears, but she couldn't stop either the tears or the words. "It is if you grow it for nine months and feel it move inside you, then watch it being born and hold it in your arms and love it even when it's covered with blood, and just when you're thinking you can't give it up, a nurse takes it away and you know you'll never see it ever again—" She stopped short. Folding her arms over her middle, she forced herself to calm.

He didn't speak for the longest time. "Sit," he finally said, adding a low, "Please."

She sat mainly because her legs wouldn't carry her far. They were limp, like they'd been pulled tight, stretched, and suddenly released.

Her whole body felt that way, no doubt from the run she'd taken earlier, though the emotional element now didn't help. She didn't usually talk about the baby—didn't *ever* talk about the baby. Truth be told, she didn't think about it much. The girl was with good parents. She was benefitting from the kind of life Charlotte couldn't begin to give her. All things considered, Charlotte had made the right decision.

Leo sat at the other end of the step, leaving a body's width between them. Bent forward, he had his elbows on his knees. His hands were linked, his eyes on the drive. "That was an eloquent argument."

Charlotte watched Bear. The dog was oddly soothing. "I didn't intend eloquence. Usually I have to work at it."

"You mean, your writing. I googled you. You've been doing this a while. Did you always want to be a writer?"

She was about to answer the question when she paused. "You googled me?" She eyed him askance. "You're connected out here?"

"Aren't you?"

"Yeah, but I don't live the life of a hermit in a house at the far end of the road."

"I'm not . . . entirely a hermit." He seemed uncomfortable. "I surf. I know what's going on." He sat back, elbows on the upper step, not quite nonchalant but as close as she'd seen him to it. "The pieces you write—how long do you edit?"

"Until it's right."

"How do you know when it is?"

"I just do. I guess that's part of the skill. I'm not the best writer in the world, but I'm a picky reader. When I reread a piece and feel like my subject has come alive, I'm done."

He considered that. Then his brow furrowed like Bear's. "Do you ever spend a long time on a piece and end up throwing it out?"

"Yes."

"Because an editor says it's bad?"

"Because I do."

"What if an editor asks you to do something you think is wrong?"

"Wrong?"

"Something that would compromise you as a writer. Has that ever happened?"

Charlotte didn't have to think long. "You mean, like the time an editor asked me to fabricate a piece?"

"Did you do it?"

She met his eyes over her shoulder. "No. She won't ever hire me again, but that's okay. There are other publications."

When he looked off down the drive again, she studied his profile. Though dusk softened its lines, they were surprisingly intelligent for a guy who wasn't supposed to be bright. And for a guy whose social skills should be primitive? Okay. So he surfed the Web. That certainly wouldn't make him a master of small talk. She had been with countless sophisticated people who couldn't think to ask her anything more than how many pieces she wrote in a year.

Leo Cole was a surprise. She had known that last night on the beach, when he had been worried he was hurting her. She had no idea who he was.

Seeming to gather himself, he looked at her. "What now?"

"What what?"

"Want to go back to the beach and screw?" There was a lift at the corner of his mouth that might have suggested a smile. Humor, too?

"No," she said, though not sternly.

"Why not?"

"First, because I don't like that word. Second, because both of us need to know I'm not easy. And third, because it's going to rain."

"No, it isn't. Not 'til morning."

"How do you know?"

"I have a weather station inside that gives me an hour-by-hour. It's never wrong."

She had expected something organic, like his knowing when a storm approached from the angle of the herbs. "A weather station. And a computer. To look at your house, you'd think there's nothing inside that didn't come from the last century. Tell me you have a sixty-two-inch flat screen."

He shook his head no, then glanced up at the roof. "It's getting dark. Want to help nail plywood to that tar paper?"

Charlotte wasn't about to refuse. Leo asking for her help was a first. Was he sly? Oh yeah. Four-by-eight sheets of plywood were nearly as bulky as the storm shutter had been. It was a perfect task for two.

Raising two ladders, they clamped on scaffolding and carried up the first of the sheets. Once it was there, he positioned it, then she held it straight while he secured it with a *pop-pop-pop* of the nail gun. Between them, they had a second and third sheet up in no time. She would have liked to use the gun, would have liked to feel a little power. But there was only one gun, and he didn't offer to share. She allowed him the machismo by way of thanks for making what might have been a nightmare of a discussion less painful.

They didn't talk. Charlotte was fine with that. Her day had been filled with internal chatter, and though the issues hadn't gone away, working with Leo was a respite.

They were nearly at the top of the roof when her phone vibrated. It was Nicole, texting to say that she'd landed in Portland. When Charlotte finished reading, she found Leo studying her.

"Who?" he asked.

"Nicole." She returned the phone to her pocket.

"Still in New York?"

"On her way here." She looked up to find his eyes on her mouth. He returned to work in the next breath, but her mind wandered. Even aside from recognizing stretch marks, he was a talented lover. She wondered where he normally satisfied himself.

"Do you have a girlfriend?" she asked.

"No." *Pow pow pow.* "Do you have a boyfriend?"

"No."

"Why not?"

"I travel too much."

"Where's home?" he asked.

"I have an apartment in New York."

"Was Nicole staying there?"

"No. She was with her husband. My place is in Brooklyn, and it's barely big enough for one. They can afford a hotel suite in Manhattan." For what it was worth, she reflected. Money certainly didn't buy happiness. She could still hear the misery in Nicole's voice.

They put up another two sheets before Charlotte had a thought. The hero of *Salt* cruised through the night sea to pick up his friend. Leo wasn't exactly a hero, but he did live on an island. He was physically adept, a heroic swimmer, and if he was macho enough to wield a nail gun with command, he had to know something about a cockpit.

"Can you drive a boat?"

He snorted.

Taking that for a yes, she said, "I need your help, Leo. She'll have to stay over in Rockland if we don't get her."

He seemed amused. "We?"

"I can't go alone. And you owe me."

"For what?"

"Helping with your roof. Do you have a boat—or one you can use? Oh." She remembered. "You don't go to the mainland."

"Who said that?" he asked, seeming offended.

Charlotte wasn't about to bring the Cole curse down on Melissa. "It doesn't matter."

"It sure as hell does." Letting the nail gun hang, he looked at her. It was only eye to eye—no mouth this time—but she felt it. Those dark blue eyes had depth, and what she saw there was pride. "I know how to get to the mainland. If I don't go, it isn't because I can't, but because I won't. I can get you there."

She wanted to believe. Getting Nicole back tonight would be the answer to a prayer. "How?"

"Magic carpet," he said with a quirk at the corner of his mouth. Then, "When'll she get to Rockland?"

"Midnight."

"What time's it now?" The only thing on his wrist was a spattering of hair where a watch might have been.

"Ten fifteen," she read from her own.

"Help me finish, then get your car and pick me up at the curve."

Having issued the order, he put nail gun to plywood, and the popping resumed.

Charlotte assumed he had his own car and wondered what kind, how old, and whether he was embarrassed to use it. Not that it mattered. She didn't have to go home for the Jeep. It was waiting on the road just beyond the curve.

Excited to be able to do this for Nicole, she texted that news, then helped Leo finish.

Once the ladders were stowed, Leo went around back with neither explanation nor invitation and came back shortly, wearing his watch cap and jeans. The jeans were old and fit him well. She spotted a bulge in the back pocket, likely a wallet, though she didn't see keys. As soon as he slid into the Jeep, he moved the seat back to make room for his legs.

Cool air whipped her hair as she drove. She might have worried about rain if she hadn't trusted Leo in some odd way. He knew the weather here as well as anyone, and he did have Cecily on his side.

That said, his arms were bare. *Men run hot,* he had said; still, she wondered if he would be cold once they hit the water. She was none too warm on land. As soon as she parked at the pier, she grabbed her fisherman's sweater from the backseat and pulled it on.

The harbor was deserted. Other than those few people cleaning up at the eateries, Quinnipeague was asleep.

"I'll meet you on the dock," Leo said and loped to the back of the Chowder House. With the slap of a screen door, he went inside, returning moments later with a takeout bag and a set of keys. "Dinner," he explained and, without commenting on the keys, led her to a slip on a side arm off the dock.

Charlotte had no idea whose boat they took, but it was relatively new and decidedly sturdy. With a minimum of effort, he untied the lines, backed out of the slip, and guided them away from the pier before gunning the motor and shooting them into the moonless ocean night. With the fading of Quinnipeague, she did feel a qualm. The boat's headlight bounced off the occasional patch of fog, but otherwise it sank like dead weight in the waves.

Standing beside him, she struggled to see a horizon. "How do you know where to *go*?" she finally called over the wind, clutching a handbar on the dash as the boat surged ahead.

"Done it before," he called back. "Nervous?"

"Yeah, I am. I can't see a thing."

He pressed a button, and the GPS came on. "We're here." He pointed. "Your friend is there."

Charlotte studied the screen. If it was accurate, they were headed right.

"Where's the bag?" he asked.

She pulled it from under the seat and opened it. Even diluted by the wind, the smell that rose from inside was unmistakable. "Little bits?" she asked in excitement. Little bits were one of Dorey Jewett's gems: small, sweet lobster knuckles that were sautéed in butter. There were no herbs involved, just enough of a Ritz-cracker coating to absorb the butter for ease of eating.

"Want some?"

Charlotte was sorely tempted. "Oh no. I had dinner."

"There's enough for two," he said and, taking a handful from the bag, popped one after the other in his mouth. He didn't exactly roll his eyes in ecstasy, but he looked content.

She watched, salivated, finally sighed and reached into the bag. He was right; there was plenty for two. Wondering if this was Leo's idea of a dinner date, she savored every bite. When they were gone, she crinkled up the bag, stowed it in a side pocket where it wouldn't blow away, and returned to Leo's side.

They didn't talk then. It seemed a wasted effort, what with the roar of the motor and the crash of the boat as it flew through the waves, but there was something exhilarating about standing beside Leo Cole with her hair flying back from her face. One thing was clear. He was as comfortable at the helm as he was on the roof of his house. He didn't seem bothered by the bite of the wind. Nor was he bothered by the darkness, either truly knowing his way or simply putting his faith in the screen on the dash.

In a surprisingly short time, the lights of Rockland appeared. Deftly, Leo slowed, turned, and let the waves carry the boat the last few feet to the dock where Nicole stood, a lone, frail figure with her luggage beside her and the woes of the world on her huddled shoulders.

Scrambling out, Charlotte wrapped her arms around her, and Nicole started to cry. She didn't speak, just sobbed softly for what seemed the longest time. Finally, she drew back, wiped her cheeks with the backs of her hands and looked around for her roller bag.

"He put it on the boat," Charlotte said gently, at which point Nicole looked closely at who the "he" was.

Her wet eyes widened. "Leo Cole?" she mouthed to Charlotte, and, with a look of alarm, whispered, "You *promised*."

But Charlotte was guiding her to the boat. "We'll talk about it tomorrow. Right now, you need to be home."

Chapter Twelve

Charlotte spent most of the night in the Great Room, anxiously imagining every possible scenario, and distractions didn't work. She wanted to read but couldn't focus, wanted to write but couldn't create. Finally, picking up her knitting, she got the sleeve of her sweater back on track, only to realize three inches later that the cables weren't right. She studied the pattern, studied the cables, studied the pattern again—and pushed the whole thing aside in disgust.

Through it all, she was listening for Nicole, but the only sound she heard came at dawn in the form of wind-driven rain. It slapped the patio stones, bowed the beach grass, and whipped up the waves. It would be a good morning to talk, she thought, but when Nicole finally came downstairs, talk seemed the last thing she wanted. Her face was pale, her hair flat, and she reached for the coffee like she couldn't think beyond that.

"Did you sleep?" Charlotte asked once they both held steaming mugs.

Nicole was uncharacteristically quiet. "Barely."

"Can I get you something to eat?"

Smiling sadly, she shook her head and sipped her coffee.

Rain gusted against the windows, its earthy smell mixing with that of the dark brew in what would have been a soothing blend if Charlotte hadn't been so keyed up. "Was it really bad?"

A nod, another sip.

"How?" Charlotte asked.

Eyes on the mug, Nicole lifted it again. When she put it down this time, she sank deeper into the chair and finally looked up. "What's with Leo Cole?"

Charlotte would rather talk about Julian's condition, but Nicole clearly needed a warm-up. "I've been helping him, so he helped me. I have no idea whose boat it was, but he knew how to drive it."

"It was Hayden Perry's," Nicole said. "He and Dad used to talk boats all the time. I wonder if Hayden knew he took it."

"He must have. Leo got the keys from Dorey, who wouldn't give them to just anyone. Besides, twenty-two miles full-throttle in a boat like that, and the fuel gauge will be way down. He'd have to notice."

Nicole looked to be considering that. Frowning, she pulled Charlotte's interviews close, thumbed the first few pages, but didn't read. Her eyes rose. "Does this mean you owe Leo something?"

"No. It's the other way around. He owed me for helping with his roof."

"Will he give you access to Cecily's gardens?"

"I'm working on that," Charlotte promised. It was a major goal of hers. "The idea is to befriend him. I'm not sure he has many friends." Then again, she wouldn't have guessed that a prominent islander would loan his expensive boat to Leo Cole. "It's weird," she mused aloud. "There are times when I feel like the thug act is a show. He can be as well-spoken as you and me."

Nicole sighed. "Well-spoken didn't get me far yesterday." Her eyes filled with tears. "I think my marriage is in trouble. And I'm not the only one who thinks it. Kaylin called last night right after I landed in Portland. She had just talked with Julian, and she knows something's wrong. She said he sounded removed. That was the word she used—

removed. She asked me if he made a mistake in the OR and was being sued, or if the hospital was being sold and his department was going somewhere else. When I said no to those, she asked if we were getting divorced." Her expression turned stricken. "She actually asked that."

"She was just tossing out wild fears, Nicki. That doesn't mean she believes any of them."

"Why wouldn't she? The reality is that he divorced her mother, so he could divorce me. It's easier to do if you've done it once."

"You're nothing like Monica. You fill a gaping hole in Julian's life. He *loves* you."

"After what happened yesterday, I'm not so sure," Nicole said. The fact of her voice being so quiet—so *dull*—said something. "It's like he's pushing me away, too."

"Maybe he's trying to protect himself."

"From *me*?"

"Maybe he's building a wall, in case you leave him."

"Why would I leave him?"

"Because you're young and healthy, and you want a child."

Nicole sat up straight. "That is so wrong, Charlotte. I wouldn't leave him. I'd have gone to North Carolina with him in a heartbeat. I'd have done the book another time, and if my publisher bailed out, I'd have found another. He knows this. I told him more than once."

But Charlotte was into the psychology of Julian's situation. "Monica abandoned him. She chose her business over him. Maybe he fears that because he's sick, you'll choose a younger guy over him. Maybe"—she was thinking—"he's afraid your book will be such a success that you won't need him at all."

"I would *never* dump him for a career," Nicole argued, "and I would *especially* never dump him because he's sick. That's not how marriage works—at least, it isn't in my life—and if you think it does work that way, well, maybe that's why you aren't married yourself!" Silence hit. Seconds later came remorse. "I'm sorry, Charlotte." She grabbed her friend's hand and held it tightly. "I shouldn't have said that. It was mean."

Charlotte understood that she was upset. She was actually grateful to see spunk and fire, rather than pure sadness. And Nicole raised an interesting point. Quietly, she said, "I'm not married because I can't find the perfect guy."

"No guy's perfect."

"No, but if you don't think it at least at the start, you're sunk. Forget my parents' experience. Half the people I meet are divorced."

"And that terrifies you?"

"What terrifies me," Charlotte said in a measured way, speaking from the heart as she couldn't with anyone else, "is falling hard, getting hurt, and having to put my life back together again." The truth was, she had lousy taste in men, dating ones who turned out to be either chronic playboys, profoundly needy, or married. Maybe she went for the bad ones to keep from falling hard in the first place.

She had thought about this. She had analyzed it in depth. When you live alone, travel alone, exist solely on the outskirts of other people's lives, you do have time to wonder why what you want most in life is out of reach. You also have time to tell yourself that you don't want it at all, though whether you can ever be completely convinced is something else.

She sighed. "Not your worry, Nicki. Besides, I'm in agony waiting here. Tell me," she begged. "What happened yesterday?"

The diversion had helped. After taking another drink of coffee, Nicole sank back in her chair. "He agreed to try a different medication."

Charlotte breathed a sigh of relief. "Ahhh. That's good, isn't it?"

"I don't know." She was studying her coffee. "There's a new one that's supposed to work on the immune system to keep it from eroding the myelin that covers the nerves, because when the myelin erodes, the nerves don't communicate with the brain, which is what MS is all about." The words were rote; clearly, she had read the same description of MS hundreds of times since Julian's diagnosis.

Charlotte already knew what the disease was, though she let Nicole take her time.

"This new treatment means injections every day," she finished, raising her eyes. "No problem there. Julian's a doctor."

"What's the drawback?"

"Liver damage. He'll need constant monitoring. But he's willing to risk it. He's convinced he's just sitting around watching himself fail." She pushed an arm high on her forehead, baring resignation. "He's always been on the cutting edge of medicine, so he takes risk for granted. And he's made up his mind. He wants to try a stem cell transplant. He's only taking this other drug to show the doctor it won't work. I would put money on the fact that this minute, as we sit here talking, he's calling around to find a doctor who wants a guinea pig. He doesn't seem to care that the risk of rejection is worse for him, and he still refuses to tell his parents or his kids, any of whom might be a donor."

"He's talking about adult stem cells, then?"

"Actually not," Nicole breathed defeatedly. "He wants to use umbilical cord cells."

Charlotte was horrified. *"Now?"*

"He's tired of going from one drug to the next. He feels like he's wasting time. Bottom line? He wants it all: stop the symptoms and reverse the disease. UCB cells may do both."

"They don't know that for sure."

"Tell me about it," Nicole breathed. "When I talk about the risk, he says it's *his* life—only, it isn't just him." Ardent, she sat forward. "It's my life, too, but I don't think he gets that. He refuses to anticipate what the worst would mean to me. I might lose him. A transplant like this could leave him a vegetable."

Charlotte let a beat pass before saying a soft, "Or cured." She had a vested interest in what happened, and would much rather Julian not want to use UCB cells, but she had read enough about them to know the promise. She couldn't lie to Nicole about this.

"Yes," Nicole admitted, deflating again.

"How impatient is he?"

"Very. He'll look around until he finds someone who's willing to do it."

Charlotte felt a sinking inside. If Julian went ahead, she had a moral obligation to tell him about the baby. A better match could save his life. But then Nicole would know the truth.

Charlotte could make Julian promise not to tell. He could simply say that the doctor had found a good match in a cord blood bank. But that would be lying, nearly as wrong as what they'd done in the first place. "Have you talked with him today?"

"No. We texted. *You okay?* I wrote. *Fine,* he wrote back. That's it. *Fine.* He's removing himself from me, too. Like, who's left?"

Not me, Charlotte thought. She didn't want any part of Julian Carlysle, other than to save him for her best friend, who wouldn't be her best friend then, but was still for now. Desperate to preserve that, she reached for Nicole's cold hand. "Okay. Here's a plan. Text him often, but be brief, just a line or two to let him know you love him. Don't *let* him remove himself. Keep at him with lots of little thinking-of-you notes."

"And if he doesn't answer?" Nicole asked in a woeful voice.

Charlotte remembered that voice. It was a throwback to her childhood Nicole, who shied from the limelight and was socially unsure. That Nicole was long gone, replaced by the one her parents had trained to be confident and adept. Everything she had accomplished in the last four years, all under an ominous cloud, was proof of that.

She had a right to occasionally regress. But the answer was obvious. Charlotte didn't even have to say it, simply pointed at Nicole's laptop, the stove, and her own printouts.

Nicole craved sweets. Her list included peach pie, rhubarb pie, and pumpkin pie, all of which would be on hand the following week for the Fourth of July cookout on the bluff, so she knew Quinnie cooks would have their recipe cards nearby. In addition to pies, she wanted recipes for blueberry cobbler, apple crisp, molasses Indian pudding, Isobel Skane's chocolate almond candy, and, of course, Melissa Parker's marble macadamia brownies.

Since the book was her baby and she was the cook, gathering and testing recipes was her job. Some would have to be resized, but she had experience with this. Others wouldn't need testing at all, assuming she trusted the donor and had personally sampled the result. She needed signed releases for each recipe, which meant return visits once she either cooked or read through each for discrepancies, so she had double reason for starting today.

Immersing herself, she spent the morning in town. Oh yes, islanders talked, though mercifully now about themselves and their recipes, rather than about her—and she loved what they said. Realizing that she could add sidebars with tips from those not being profiled, she took careful notes, and though she returned to the house at midday with fewer cards than she'd hoped, one of them came with a quart of fresh blueberries, from which, following the donor's recipe, she made a bubbling cobbler.

Topped with yogurt, that was lunch.

She spent the afternoon typing up notes, answering readers' questions, and blogging about a new online source for organic cinnamon and nutmeg, either of which she could have used for testing the island recipe for Indian Pudding that afternoon. Both spices were produced from a tropical evergreen that, Cecily's miracles notwithstanding, did not grow on Quinnipeague, but since Indian pudding was a prized dessert here, Nicole refused to leave it out. Typically, Quinnie Indian Pudding called for cider molasses made from island apples. The recipe she had been given listed bottled molasses, which she supposed made sense, given its wider availability, though the taste wasn't quite the same. She made a mental note to ask Bev Simone about her supply of the real stuff.

Meanwhile, Charlotte interviewed Susan Murray, who was on Quinnipeague through the Fourth and was a good example of a part-timer drawn here for food and fun. She was flattered to hand over her recipe for s'mores cookies, which Nicole baked, and which they sampled along with the Indian Pudding that night.

* * *

Waking up Thursday morning to another dreary day and the sense of being physically stuffed, they focused on FISH. While Charlotte interviewed the postmaster about the origin, techniques, and ingredients for his best-in-Maine lobster bakes, Nicole set off to gather recipes for glazed salmon, baked pesto haddock, and cod crusted with marjoram, a minted savory unique to Quinnipeague, and sage.

She baked the crusted cod for dinner using fresh herbs from the island store and cod filleted that morning at the pier. Other than adjusting the amount of savory to compensate for a lack of mintiness off-island, Nicole thought the recipe was perfect and blogged as much before going to bed.

She also told Julian that. Since arriving in North Carolina, he had begun calling her each night before he went to bed, which she took to mean that her short texts were working, and though he sounded tired, they talked about work, not MS. He was pleased with what he was accomplishing. So was she. The month apart would be productive at least.

Work was a distraction for Charlotte as well. Even when Friday morning brought sun, she wasn't tempted to play. Totally aside from Leo, or from Julian and Nicole and umbilical cord stem cells, the amount of work to be done was daunting. The more she and Nicole talked, the larger the project loomed, and collecting raw material was only the start. Every profile had to be written, edited, and polished, with accompanying photos cropped and enhanced. Nicole would be the menu-planner, as Charlotte knew nothing about that, but since she was the professional writer, she would tie everything together. It was a lot to do in a brief period of time that might be made all the more brief if Nicole had to leave on a moment's notice to be with Julian again.

Today being the start of a long weekend, they addressed BRUNCH. Holiday weekenders would start arriving by noon, but islanders generally rose with the sun, which made seven in the morning doable. At least, that was the plan the evening before, altered when Nicole slept late after working long into the night.

Still, they were on their way to town by eight. While Nicole drove off in search of recipes for fish hash, clam fritters, and salmon quiche, Charlotte settled in at the Chowder House with Dorey Jewett, who, well beyond the assortment of chowders she always brought to Bailey's Brunch, would be as important a figure in the book as any.

They sat in the kitchen, though Dorey did little actual sitting. Looking her chef-self in T-shirt, shorts, and apron, if she wasn't dicing veggies, she was clarifying butter or supervising a young boy who was shucking clams dug from the flats hours before. Even this early, the kitchen smelled of chowder bubbling in huge steel pots.

Much as Anna Cabot had done for the island in general, Dorey gave a history of restaurants on Quinnipeague, from the first fish stand at the pier, to a primitive burger hut on the bluff, to a short-lived diner on Main Street, to the current Grill and Café. Naturally, she spoke at greatest length about the evolution of the Chowder House, whose success she credited to her father, though the man had been dead for nearly twenty years. Everyone knew Dorey was the one who had brought the place into the twenty-first century, but her family loyalty was endearing. It was particularly evident when Charlotte asked about Cecily's role in her cooking.

Pausing with her chop knife midair, Dorey was suddenly puffed up. "Jewetts have been cooking here since before Cecily was born. We did fine with our own herbs, thank you." The knife came down with a *thwunk.*

Charlotte modified the question. "Then, island cooking in general. You can't deny that her herbs play a role."

"No, I can't deny it," Dorey conceded, though the speed with which she proceeded to chop onions spoke of annoyance. "Some of your so-called cooks aren't what I'd call cooks. Their heirloom recipes would be downright awful if it weren't for those herbs."

"You do use Cecily's herbs, though?"

"Hey, I'm not stupid. If you need fresh basil or thyme on this island, there's only one source, and I'm not talking about her garden. I have Cole herbs in my own greenhouse. You won't find better anywhere else. I wasn't saying you could." She scraped the onions into a bowl with the broad of her knife, then ran a wide forearm across her watering eyes. "I'm just saying the Jewett recipes are more than herbs."

Charlotte was thinking that competitiveness was a side of Dorey she hadn't seen, when she saw another. Out of the blue, the woman asked, "What's Leo Cole to you?"

"Excuse me?"

"You were with him Tuesday night on Hayden Perry's boat."

Charlotte should have known Dorey would keep tabs on the harbor even at night. But there was a perfectly good explanation for what Dorey had seen. "I asked him to take me to Rockland. Nicole is my friend. We were picking her up."

Dorey studied her. Her tone softened, though her eyes remained serious. "Leo hasn't had it easy in life. Cecily wasn't the best mother. He's finally at a good place. I'm worried you'll mess it up."

Charlotte laughed. "Me?"

"He was different coming in here that night. He likes you."

"I like him, too."

"Why?"

Charlotte opened her mouth, then closed it and considered what she understood about her feelings. Finally, puzzled, she said, "I have no idea."

"You need to," Dorey warned. "He isn't one to play with."

"Because he's dangerous? That's what everyone says, but I don't feel it in him. Who *is* he?"

"What do you mean?"

"Is he a handyman? A carpenter? A *gardener*?"

"You don't know?"

"No. We don't talk much about personal things. It's the silence that kind of works—for both of us, I guess."

With a sigh, Dorey lightened up. "Well, I wouldn't know about silence. My life is filled with noise. If I didn't like it, I'd be doin' somethin' else besides running this zoo." She reached for another onion. "Gotta get back to work. Any more questions?"

"Actually, yes. Was there ever a father in the picture?"

"I meant, questions about the restaurant. Anything about Leo, you have to ask Leo. I know you've been asking other people, but I'll tell you one thing, Missy," she added, prodding the air with the tip of her knife. "For whatever else he is, Leo's a born and bred Quinnie, and we protect our own."

Hands up, Charlotte backed off. "Got it."

"That's good. No one here wants him hurt."

Charlotte did get it. She was summer; Leo was forever. He could be the worst of the worst, but Quinnipeague was his home. Islanders related to that. Black sheep or not, they would side with him.

Thinking how nice that was, she emerged from the Chowder House into the sun. It was ten thirty. Pickups filled the spaces outside the Café, suggesting that locals were taking advantage of the last hours of quiet before weekenders began to arrive. She looked through the lineup, but didn't see Nicole's SUV. Wondering if it was parked elsewhere, she looked down the street, then up. That was when she saw Leo. He was leaning against a dark blue pickup, parked nose-in at the head of a narrow driveway beside the library.

Her pulse skipped. With his hands in the pockets of his jeans and his booted feet crossed, he looked for all the world like he was just passing the time—except for his dark eyes, always his dark eyes. There was nothing nonchalant about those, and they were focused on her.

She started toward him, walking casually to avoid attention, though there was no one about. He had parked in a discreet spot. Their relationship—whatever it was—was secret.

She smiled, said a soft, "Hey," when she was close. He didn't answer, simply drew her in against the truck, and, with his hands flat on the window by her head, caught her mouth with his. It was the first time since Monday night, but as quickly as that she was back on the beach, naked in the moonlight, and turned on as that lean mouth moved hungrily over hers. Her arms were around his neck before it was done, holding on lest she fall, though his body would have prevented that. It held her against the truck, shielding her from the world. She was breathless when, after a final long kiss, he raised his head.

His eyes were wide and midnight blue. She couldn't look away. "What was that for?" she whispered.

"Wanted to see if I was imagining," he said in a low, rutted voice.

Imagining the fire. He didn't have to finish for her to know. Nor did she have to ask if the fire was real. She could hear it in the roughness of his breathing, could feel it in the lower body that wasn't lifting from hers so fast.

Those midnight blues roamed her face. "You haven't been out to the house."

"I've been with Nicole. She needs me around."

"For her cookbook?"

"There's also personal stuff. Plus, it's been rainy. You couldn't lay shingles in the rain, and now you have to wait at least a day for the plywood to dry."

"So you're not coming over tonight?"

"That depends on Nicole. If she's having dinner with other friends, I can get out."

"I'm Plan B."

"You're Plan Z, if you ask Nicole. She's afraid you'll sabotage her project."

He didn't respond to that. "What'd you tell her about us?"

"That I didn't know what in the hell it was, which I don't. Do you?"

"No. All I know is I want more."

So did Charlotte. Taking his face in her hands, she initiated the kiss this time. He let her lead it for a breath before taking over, and she didn't protest. Something happened to her when she was with him, like *this* was where she was supposed to be. When he raised his head this time, she should have been aching for more. But she felt peaceful, like she was home. With a contented sigh, she closed her eyes and rested her forehead on his chin.

"What was that for?" he asked in hoarse echo of her earlier words, but it was a minute before she was willing to draw back.

Then, with an inhalation to steady herself, she said, "Just wanted to make sure."

His eyes were inscrutable. Finally, he asked, "What's your cell number?"

She gave it to him and, sliding out from under him, backed away with a glance at the truck. "Is that yours?"

He nodded.

"Nice." It was dusty, but late model, which raised more questions, but she was tiring of them. So he had a source of income. What did it matter? If the island was in his corner, it couldn't be *too* disreputable.

Smiling, she faced forward and started walking. Her smile faltered, though, when she saw Nicole at the Chowder House. Apparently having come from the opposite end of the street, she had pulled up to the front door, set her blinkers, and looked to have been ready to go inside if she hadn't seen Charlotte. Having stopped beside the hood, she was staring at the dark blue pickup.

Frowning, she waited only until Charlotte was close. "Were you kissing him?"

Charlotte shrugged. "I guess so."

"Kissing him," Nicole repeated, like she wasn't sure she understood. When Charlotte nodded, she asked, "Is something going on? Like, more than helping with his roof?"

Good question. She remembered Leo saying, *Here you are, just perfect for me.* And Dorey saying, *He was different coming in here that night, he likes you.* Charlotte might have blamed making love on the beach to the moment, but there was the kiss just now. It had taken her out of herself.

Her escape. Not a mess of the summer as she had first feared. Her own personal escape from stem cell anxiety and deadlines.

Not that she could tell Nicole that. Needing a minute, she opened the door and climbed into the passenger's seat. Nicole stared, before rounding the car and sliding in, but she didn't let it go. As soon as she switched from reverse to drive, she asked, "Is there?"

"Yes."

"What?"

"There's a physical attraction."

"Is it real? Or for the sake of the cookbook?"

"It's real," Charlotte said. "For what it's worth, he hasn't mentioned the book. I think he's okay with it."

"Because he likes you?"

"Maybe. Or because he's knows I won't steal Cecily's herbs. I still want to take pictures. Those gardens are something." She was thinking of the white flowers with the incredibly arousing smell. She wondered what they were.

"Have you slept with him?"

Admitting it made her feel cheap. So she said, "No." It wasn't exactly a lie. There had been no sleeping that night.

"Do you think you will?"

"Why does it matter?"

"Because I worry about you. He's an ex-con."

"Oh, so was my dad," Charlotte tossed out in a second's exasperation.

"He was not."

"He was. He was convicted of domestic abuse and spent ten days in jail."

"Domestic abuse?"

"Of wife number two, who, not being a lush, didn't have alcohol to keep her from talking back. He didn't like back talk."

Nicole seemed horrified. "You never told me this."

"I'm not proud of it."

"Did he ever hit you?"

"He threatened to."

"Did he hit your mother?"

"No. She knew enough to steer clear when he was in a snit."

"I had no idea," Nicole said meekly and was quiet as they passed the road to Okers Beach. They were passing the clam flats when she returned to the other. "Still, ten days is different from four years."

Charlotte didn't want to discuss this. "Maybe Dad had a better lawyer than Leo. My point, Nicki, is that there are lots of reasons why people get sent away. We shouldn't pass judgment on Leo until we know what his are."

Nicole shot her a look. "You want to find out."

"Yeah, I do. He's interesting. So many things about him don't fit. I want to know who the real Leo is."

"And then what?"

Charlotte took a biding breath. "Then I get gorgeous pictures of his gardens for your book, after which I go back to New York, and then Paris, and then wherever work takes me. That's the lesson of *Salt,* is it not?"

Nicole's eyes lit. "You finished it?"

"I didn't. I got to the point of caring so much and feeling like things would end up wrong, so I read ahead."

"Charlotte!"

"I couldn't help it," Charlotte declared, unrepentant. "I refuse to finish. This is my protest."

"But you just said you'd do the same thing!"

"Right. That's reality. But fiction is fiction. Chris Mauldin took my heart and twisted it. That's pure manipulation."

"It's pure brilliance, if you ask me," Nicole mused and pulled up at the house.

Charlotte didn't argue. Not only didn't she want to further the discussion of *Salt,* which might lead back to her relationship with Leo, but now that they were home, she had other things to do. Having loved her interviews with Anna and Melissa, Nicole wanted her write-up of Dorey ASAP, so that she could impress her editor with their progress.

At the same time, Nicole began reading through the newest recipes in her pile and found a problem.

Chapter Thirteen

CHARLOTTE WAS AT THE KITCHEN table when she heard a soft, "Strange." She stopped typing and looked up.

Nicole stood at the counter, frowning as she thumbed back and forth through a handful of recipe cards. "No thyme in Rebecca's fish hash? There's always thyme. It's one of the reasons I like her hash. And salmon quiche without parsley? Without *dill*? Marie's quiche has both. Goat cheese would be bland without dill, and even aside from taste, parsley adds color." Studying another card, she seemed baffled. "Mint extract in peppermint blondies? *Extract*? There's nothing organic in that. What happened to fresh mint?" She turned anxious eyes on Charlotte. "Quinnipeague is known for its herbs. They're supposed to be a major part of the cookbook. Remove them, and you lose what's so unique here. These cards have to be wrong."

Feeling a chill, Charlotte left the table. "All of them?" There were several dozen in the pile.

"Not all. Some are good. But these others? And *these*?" She singled out several lower cards that were marked with Post-its. "I got these earlier in the week. It's the same thing, either use of a commercial product or a clear-out omission. Two or three could be innocent mistakes. But eight? Nine? What is going on?"

Charlotte took the cards and glanced through. Original recipe cards would be dog-eared and stained; these were clean. "They're fresh copies. It could still be innocent."

But Nicole was shaking her head. "I know these people. They're not careless. This was deliberate."

"Sabotaging their own recipes?"

"Protecting them. Someone told them not to give away island secrets." Her implication was clear, her green eyes direct.

"You think it was Leo," Charlotte said.

"Who else could it be?"

"Dorey. Or Anna or Melissa." She had asked each about Leo. "They protect him."

"From what?" Nicole asked, clearly skeptical.

Charlotte searched for an answer, but her mind was stirring an uncomfortable brew. She had a personal stake in this. How to be objective?

"Aren't they protective of me, too?" Nicole asked, hurt now. "I've summered here all my life. They love my family—you heard how they gushed last week. Besides, these people aren't timid. If they didn't want me doing the cookbook, they'd have said so." Her eyes darkened. "It has to be Leo scaring them off. He didn't want us doing this in the first place. Ask him to stop, Charlotte, please? There are times when I feel like I'm hanging on by a thread. The last thing I need is a complication, when we finally have momentum going."

They did have that, in spite of the ongoing heartache of Julian. Nicole missed him—no doubting it—and he shared that, to judge from his frequent texts. *Tired, but okay,* he would say in response to her query. Or, *Just finished a great session with a bunch of top-notch MDs.* Or, *Taped a clip for the local news. Link to follow.* Charlotte assumed that their phone calls were more personal, since Nicole's anger had faded.

Not so the fear, which shadowed her eyes at odd moments. But she didn't talk about this as much now, either. *Tiresome* was the word she used when Charlotte asked. And true to that, she was upbeat and smiling when they were in town. Working on the cookbook gave her focus. She was right; the last thing they needed was a glitch.

Charlotte saw an easy fix. "Can you correct the herbs yourself?"

"If I alter the recipes, they won't sign a release. Please, Charlotte, ask him to stop?"

"I don't think it was Leo," she said, though she was unsettled. Hadn't Leo threatened to prevent their getting recipes? *I'll put out the word that I don't want you to,* he had said.

But that was before they were . . . whatever they were. Now it seemed impossible that he would do this. He had been too caring on the beach Monday night, too understanding on his front porch the next night. And his kiss this morning? Too honest.

"Then how do you explain this?" Nicole cried, holding up the cards. "I didn't sense guilt when I was collecting these. If leaving things out was deliberate, they were clearly comfortable with it. Did they not think I'd *notice*?" She grew beseechful. "Call Leo?"

"I don't have his number."

"Someone must. Maybe Dorey."

"Uh-huh, like she'd give it to me? She made it clear that I shouldn't mess with Leo Cole."

"She was right," Nicole said, deflating, "and *she* didn't see the two of you this morning. Are you going to his house this weekend?"

"I don't know."

"You don't have to babysit me, y'know."

"It isn't babysitting. I *choose* to be with you." That said, Charlotte's thoughts jumped ahead. If she wanted to get to know Leo, they needed more time together than an hour here and there. But she didn't want Nicole to be alone. "Has Julian committed to the Fourth?"

Quietly, Nicole said, "He can't come. He feels that since the doctors he's working with won't be leaving town, he shouldn't, either, and besides that, it's too far to travel. I think he means for him. And he's right.

Raleigh-Durham to Quinnipeague is a haul." She regarded the recipe cards with renewed desperation. "What're we going to do about these?"

The answer, of course, was to go door-to-door getting corrections, but that meant putting people on the spot when nothing about the underlying problem had changed. If island women were being pressured, the pressure would remain until its source was found.

Leo was the logical first stop. Charlotte could have walked to his house Friday night, but something held her back. It might have been the fish hash that Nicole made with fresh halibut, the rest of Rebecca Wilde's ingredients, and what she intuitively knew to be the right amount of thyme. They didn't eat until late, and after finishing off a white Burgundy from Bob's stash, they were too sluggish to do more than watch a restored version of *Gone With the Wind*.

Then again, it might have been fear keeping her from Leo's that night. If he had carried through on his threats, they had no future.

Or, it might have been simple procrastination. Better she learn that tomorrow than tonight.

Saturday dawned foggy. Nicole played in the kitchen most of the morning, testing first a French toast casserole, then Anna Cabot's famed layered eggs. Mercifully, these recipes were correct. They were actually perfect, she declared in an ebullient text to Julian following a tasting session with Charlotte.

No answer on the other? he wrote back.

Not yet. Maybe later. Charlotte has assured her Leo would be in touch, and Nicole figured that collecting more recipes would be ridiculous until he was stopped.

On one level, she was stymied.

On another, she was freed. When the fog burned off, she took that as an invitation to sit on the back patio and read.

* * *

Midway through the afternoon, Leo texted Charlotte. *I'm doing shingles tonight. Want to help?*

Since it was a clear, warm night, Charlotte walked. A navy dusk was just settling in when she rounded the Cole curve and saw him setting up the ladders. He wore his usual black, but his tool belt was still on the ground. Bundles of shingles were stacked on a pallet nearby.

Halfway down the drive, she stopped to wait. She smelled herbs, plus those white flowers, which were near the woods on her left. Refusing to be charmed by any of it, she thought of the recipe cards and stayed where she was.

Leo finished with the ladders and was about to open the first bundle when he saw her. He waited. When she didn't move, he gestured her forward. When she didn't come, he set down the box cutter and started toward her.

"Something wrong?" he asked as he neared.

She nodded. "We started collecting recipes cards. The herbs were misrepresented on a bunch of them."

"Misrepresented?"

"Given as dried, rather than fresh. Or left out completely. Like people were afraid to mention them. Like someone told them not to."

He seemed amused. "That so?"

"Was it you?"

His amusement faded. "No."

"You threatened."

"Yeah, and Bear was dangerous."

All talk, then? She wanted to believe it. "Well, it wasn't Cecily."

He snorted. "You sure about that?"

"Come on, Leo. Dead people don't go talking around town."

"Not in the traditional way."

"Which means?"

"The legend lives on."

Charlotte was intrigued. "Which *means*?"

"People believed things about Cecily. Most were wrong, but tell that to the faithful. If they think she can reach out from the grave, they might try to avoid upsetting her."

"By passing on recipes that used her herbs? Why would that upset her?"

He shrugged. "Go ask. She wasn't always the nicest person."

"Most Quinnies worship her."

"They weren't her son," he said with a head-on stare of those midnight eyes.

Charlotte caught her breath. "What did she do?"

He stared at her for another minute before looking away. "Not my place to criticize. I wasn't easy to raise."

"What did she do?" Charlotte repeated, but this time to his back. He was wandering off into the herbs. Halfway down the row, he bent to snap sprigs of tiny red buds from a broad-leafed plant. Stuffing them in his pocket, he reached for more. "What's that?" she asked, coming abreast of him.

"Sorrel." He shot her a quick look. "You know sorrel?"

"No."

"Most people don't. It isn't glam'rous," he said, sounding more Maine, "but it has a really nice lem'ny taste. The leaves cook up into a cream soup. Sorrel's also good for poachin' fish."

"What do you do with those buds?" Charlotte asked as he stuffed several more in his pocket.

"Throw 'em out. Sorrel grows easy, as long as you keep it trimmed. It's the young leaves that have the best taste. Buds like these"—he picked off another—"retard the new growth." He straightened, eyes resigned, enunciation less Maine and more Leo. "I know all this because I worked these gardens for her. It wasn't by choice. If I didn't do it, I didn't get fed."

Wondering why that sounded ominous, Charlotte was tentative. "That's a good work ethic."

"For a kid who's four? Five? Six? She home-schooled me to keep me around. I used to sneak off—jump on the back of a pickup headin' in town—and when I got there, I'd steal a little of this, little of that. Town was a whole new world. Candy? Potato chips? Comic books? They'd catch me and bring me back home, and she'd make me sleep outside with the plants. Great in summer, not in winter."

Charlotte tried to imagine it. "She imprisoned you here?"

"Not entirely. I used to stow away on fishing boats that left the harbor at dawn. She must've thought the male company would help because she didn't raise a stink. When I got a little older, she sent me around the island on my bike delivering her packets. They did help people. Gotta give her that."

"But you're describing child abuse. Didn't anyone know it?"

"How would they? They didn't come out here, and she wasn't telling. Me, neither. She was my mother."

He wandered to the end of the row, absently touching the white flowers as he passed. Following him, Charlotte asked, "How'd you finally end up going to the island school?" He didn't answer. She guessed there had been outside force. "Weren't they afraid of crossing her?"

"Islanders were. Not authorities on the mainland."

"Child welfare?"

He hesitated, then said, "Close enough. She did love me. She was afraid of losing me." Chewing on a corner of his mouth, he stood with his hands at his back, fingertips tucked in the waist of his shorts, and his eyes on the woods. With the sun gone and the moon not yet up, the trees blurred into a moss-green mass, making it a good place to get lost.

Not that Leo was lost. Entirely focused, he took several steps into the murk and scooped the fallen end of a branch from the forest floor. Studying it, he turned it slowly and with purpose, before tossing it gently toward the garden.

"What's that for?" Charlotte asked.

"Whittling. Pine's soft, but the knots can be tough." Retrieving the branch, he showed her. "There aren't many knots here. This one's good."

"What do you whittle?"

"Nothing much. I'm bad at it. It's about the process."

Like her knitting, but the thought was a distraction. "Go on," she urged gently. "About growing up. I want to hear." He looked at her then. Even with a minimum of light, she saw vulnerability—or felt it. "Friends tell friends things like this," she coaxed.

"Is that what we are?" he asked, sounding discouraged.

"Yes."

"Then that's a first for me. I don't have friends. I never learned how."

She had trouble believing that. He was a nice enough guy.

He must have seen her doubt, because his hand tightened on the branch. "I was ten when I started school in town. I'd never been with other kids. I didn't know how in the hell to act. Obviously, I did it wrong. Cecily saw that as a validation of what she'd been saying—that the plants were the only friends I needed, and that if you loved them, they'd love you and would thrive. They did. They still do. But they shouldn't." He glanced over the rows. "The climate here is all wrong for most of these plants. So maybe she was right. About the love part, at least." Hunkering down, he dropped the branch and brushed a hand over the grass. "How can something that grows in the shade be this green?"

It did look green, Charlotte realized. Even at night. But something else struck her. It had to do with the way he'd touched those white flowers and, now, brushed the grass. "You love the plants."

He shifted to sit. "I do. I like taking care of them." His knees were bent, boots planted in that surprising green grass.

"For her?"

"For me. I tried to kill them once," he confessed, sounding more guilty than proud. "It was right after she died. I was angry she'd croaked in that hospital, like she'd done it to show me how bad my judgment was, so I came back here and hacked all this down. It was fall. Most of it was gone for the season anyway, but I dug everything up, roots and all. Next spring, it all came back. Bigger, stronger."

"Did her ashes do that?" Charlotte asked.

He recoiled, staring up at her in distaste. "Hell no. I didn't cremate her. She's buried in town behind the church. I figured folks'd visit her there." His mouth quirked. "Part of the legend, y'know? She helped those people. Me, I was just the drug runner."

"A bad lesson."

"Hey, she gave it away for free. I was the one who sold it. She didn't know I was doing it 'til I got caught."

"Didn't she see her marijuana disappearing?" Charlotte asked, frowning back at the garden. "I don't smell it, by the way."

His expression turned wry. "It's the only thing that didn't grow back. Mother didn't want me tempted."

"So, you do believe that the dead reach out?"

"No. Hell, I don't know. But there's something poetic about the pot just dying off."

"Would you have been tempted?"

"Nope. Not to use, not to sell."

Charlotte wasn't surprised. Nothing about him spoke of either. All she could think about in the silence that followed, though, was the way Cecily had used him. *Wasn't the best mother,* Dorey had said. Charlotte hadn't followed then, but did now. Her own parents had never been that bad, their major crime being neglect. But she felt a new affinity for Leo. To have to struggle against a parent at home and then face the rest of the world . . . she didn't imagine it had been any easier for him than it had been for her.

Lowering herself so that she sat cross-legged between his boots, she leaned on her thighs. "Do you have a father?"

He snickered. "Cecily was good but not that good. Immaculate conception was beyond her."

"Do you know who he is?"

"Oh yeah."

"Do you see him much?"

"No. He doesn't come here, and I don't go there."

"Where's there?"

"Rockland."

The mainland, and so close. "But you two talk."

"Not if I can help it. He didn't treat my mother well. Just left her alone to raise me herself. I'm guessing she was bi-polar. The swings were dramatic. So it was hard. Money. Me. That."

Hard on Leo, Charlotte heard, though he tried to frame it otherwise. Needing to comfort—to let him know that he wasn't alone just then—she wrapped a hand around his calf. "You're good to take her side," she said, but he was staring at her hand.

"Is that pity?"

"No."

"What then?"

"Just me wanting to touch you."

"If it's pity, take it back."

She left her hand where it was—actually moved it in lightly. There was no padding here, just warm skin covered by a spatter of dark hair.

Slowly he calmed. "About what you said before. I have my own side. I just try to see hers is all. She helped a lot of people. That was her calling."

"So you keep up her house and her herbs."

"What else do I have?"

It was a throwaway line, but Charlotte took it to heart. He might have filled in a few blanks about the boy, but there were still major holes in the story of the man. He was an ex-con; that was fact. But other things didn't fit—like his talking as if he had an advanced degree in psychology. Giving his leg a squeeze, she said, "You tell me. What do you have?"

His eyes swept the night land. "This. My home."

"Did you never want to go elsewhere?"

"I've been elsewhere. It was worse."

"Where?"

Eyes glazing, he was suddenly years away and angry. "When I got out of jail, they set me up doing construction on the mainland. My boss was a woman who didn't like that I wouldn't fuck her. When she accused me of selling drugs on the site, they locked me back up faster'n you could say *frame-up*."

Charlotte gasped. "Did you?"

"Sell? Hell no. The prosecutor figured that out. That's when I came back here." He calmed. "I lived in an old shack down by the pier and did odd jobs. When Cecily got sick and wouldn't get help, I called the prison doctor. He'd been a kind of mentor, bringing me books and stuff. He said if I took her to the mainland, he'd meet us at the hospital. He never showed."

"Betrayal," Charlotte whispered.

"You could say."

She sensed he had other words for it, any of which he would articulate if she pushed him. He was intelligent and intuitive—unexpectedly so, she thought not for the first time.

But the silence was comfortable.

Finally, he came forward, took her hand, and linked their fingers. "Anyway, it wasn't me warning people against helping you out. I don't like the idea of your cookbook, but I wouldn't ruin it for you."

She could see it in his eyes, which in that moment were unguarded and direct. "Do you know who would?"

"No."

"Then how do we fight it?"

"We?"

She had meant Nicole and her. But he had a point. "Would you spread the word that Cecily's okay with the cookbook?"

"I'm not sure it'd help. I don't connect with her, Charlotte. I don't even go to the cemetery. Islanders know that. Cecily and me, it's definitely a love-hate thing."

"There," Charlotte said and, sitting straight, took back her hand. "That's what I don't understand. How do you know to call it a love-hate thing?"

He frowned. "Because it is."

"But how do you know that term? Have you been in therapy?"

"No."

"Which is weird. You describe a childhood that should have left you scarred, but you seem totally balanced to me. You live alone out here, but you don't sound like a hermit. You don't even speak Maine much. You do sometimes, but then it's like you forget to do it. Words, intonation, rhythm—you don't sound like a high school dropout. You say you have no friends, but you talk like you've been talking with friends all your life. Your dialogue is just right."

"I read," he said quietly.

"We all do—"

"I read," he repeated, eyes unblinking.

"I thought that started in prison."

He seemed to relax at that, giving her a curious smile. "Why?"

"Because I heard you were lousy in school."

"To put it nicely, but that had nothing to do with brains. I didn't like discipline. And I didn't like their books."

She considered that. It fit into the picture that was starting to emerge. "So you were reading back then?"

"Gotta thank Cecily for that. Next to plants, she loved reading most. I fought her—didn't like her books much, either. She called them her magic carpet, only her carpet didn't take *me* away. My own didn't take off until I was five and stole that first comic book. From there, I got into paperback books. Then I hit the big-time."

"Big-time?"

"The library. I used to love stealing from there. They knew I was doing it. Looked the other way, maybe out of compassion, maybe fear."

"But you returned the books when you were done."

"I did not. What fun would that be?"

"Leo."

"I'm not saying I'd steal now. But those books were my lifeline. I'd be up all hours reading. I never needed much sleep."

Hence, his doing the roof at night. The question of what he did during the day remained. But she didn't want to ask just then and risk the good feeling between them. "What do you read?"

"Whatever. Reading's always been my out."

She studied his face. It was shadowed, but jaw and cheekbone were strong, and there was a depth to his eyes that the night couldn't hide. Or maybe it was that she knew it was there. Or that she was touched by his words. Or that her hand still shaped his skin. Or that his letting her into a place few had gone made him all the more attractive to her. Or, simply, that her heart was squeezed.

Whatever, coming up on her knees, she took his face in her hands and gave him a long, slow, nibbling kiss. Sweet scents hovered, adding to a sense of rightness.

When she finally allowed an inch between their mouths, he whispered a hoarse, "What was that for?"

"Because I like you," she whispered back, hard-pressed for a better answer, though it seemed to do the trick.

Pulling her so that she straddled his lap, he returned the kiss with growing hunger. She was starting to feel it in her belly, when he took off her T-shirt and unhooked her bra. The bra had been on the whole time at the beach, but his mouth on her breasts was not something she would have wanted to miss this time. She held his head, fingers in his hair. Needing more, she cried out.

As he had done at the beach, he paused at the sound. "Too much?"

"Not enough," she moaned.

He helped with her shorts, but she pushed his aside only enough so that she could take him in. They both went still then, forehead to forehead, taking deep, quivering breaths as they savored the possession, and when that wasn't enough, he rolled her beneath him and thrust.

He took her away—just took her out of herself to a place she could only go with him—but, when it was done, there was nothing scary about the return. He felt solid. Rooted. *Real.*

They sat for the longest time, his back against a tree with his arm around her and her cheek to his chest. That chest was finely textured, leanly muscled, and smelled of Leo. Feeling a sense of peace, she could have stayed there forever.

But Leo wanted to work on the roof. "Long's you're here," he reasoned a short time later as they climbed the ladders. The idea was to work sections from left to right, bottom to top, each section overlapping the next. "Two hammers or one?" he asked.

"One," she said. "I'll hold, you hammer." She had done it this way before and thought it the fastest and most efficient. After Leo positioned each shingle, she held it while he nailed. As he pounded in the last nail, she brought a new shingle up for positioning. Once they got into the rhythm, they moved right along. They stood close, arms or legs brushing at times. It wasn't sexual, but pleasant.

"Definitely anticlimactic," Charlotte remarked at one point, to which Leo chuckled. She had never heard him do that before, and eyed him in surprise. He seemed surprised, himself, to which she said, "It's a good sound."

"Y'think?"

A warmth spread inside. "I do." She might have kissed him again if they hadn't been standing on scaffolding clamped to the roof. And then came a *whoosh* in the garden. Looking back, she caught her breath. "The fawn." A sliver of blurred spots reflecting the moon, it darted here, darted there. "What's it doing?"

"Chasing a chipmunk. Or a mouse."

"I thought it was supposed to be sleeping."

"Did you always sleep when your parents put you to bed?"

Knowingly, she smiled at the fawn, then, feeling Leo's leg behind her, smiled curiously at him. "You think I'll fall?"

"Better safe than sorry."

Bob Lilly used to say that. Same with the hero of *Salt*. "I'm really fine," she assured him, but did brace herself with a hand when, at a renewed rustling in the garden, she turned quickly. The fawn was jumping and pouncing through the lowest of the herbs.

She watched in enjoyment for a minute, then had a thought. "Where's Bear?"

"In the shrubs. It's past his bedtime."

"Is he okay?"

"Oh yeah. Just old."

"Do you worry about him?"

"All the time. He's my best friend in the world."

Best *animal* friend, Charlotte might have corrected if she had wanted to get into that discussion, but she didn't. Each time she looked at Leo—each time their eyes met—she felt that spreading warmth. It might be pure chemistry. But she had known chemistry before, and it wasn't like this.

Their system worked. With Leo adept at repositioning ladders and planks, they lost no time moving from section to section. Still, it was close to midnight when they finished. Charlotte was yawning as he walked her down the drive, though she wasn't so tired as to be numb. The herbs were sleeping, but not those white flowers. They were night creatures like Leo, stronger than ever in the dark. Their pull kept her awareness of him high.

"Are you sure I can't drive you?" he asked when they reached the Cole curve.

"I'm sure." She needed to keep these parts of her life separate. He was here, Nicole was there—fantasy here, reality there.

Say good night, she thought. *Kiss his cheek. Give him a hug.* But the scent of those flowers was in her head, pushing for more. So she did nothing, simply stood in silence, watching him watch her.

"This is starting to make me nervous," he said quietly. "You're leaving at the end of the summer, right?"

"That's a ways off."

"But you are leaving."

She tried to keep it light. "Mid-August is the plan."

"So we should keep this low-key."

She laughed. "Like that would work? Like we should just tell our bodies there's nothing to feel?"

He studied the road underfoot, then raised questioning eyes. Even in the dark, their message was clear. What he was asking, she knew, was whether there was a chance she would stay.

But she had a life. She had friends in far places. She had assignments lined up. "I can't," she whispered, though the words tugged at her insides.

He took a breath and nodded. "Okay. Just so I know."

That, she thought, was reality. But these night hours, the moon, the fawn, that incredible smell—this was fantasy, wasn't it? Or not? Shouldn't he argue, fight, plead?

Annoyed that he was so accepting and apparently didn't feel the same tug she did, she glared back down the drive at the only thing that might have been its source. "What *is* that smell?"

"Me?"

"No, those white flowers. Back there in the garden."

His voice held a reluctant smile. "Jasmine."

"Jasmine."

"It's an aphrodisiac."

An aphrodisiac. She hung her head, then righted it and sighed. "Silly me. I should've guessed."

Chapter Fourteen

Nicole lay in bed Saturday night listening for Charlotte to return. Ten o'clock came and went, then eleven, and she grew uneasy. She wanted to know what Leo had to say about the recipes. More, though, she was starting to wonder what was really going on between Charlotte and Leo. If it would further hurt the cookbook, she didn't want it. She had a deadline to meet.

Somewhere around midnight, she fell asleep. When she awoke, it was two. Checking the hall, she saw that the front light was off and Charlotte's bedroom door closed. At least she was home; Nicole had half feared she would spend the night at Leo's. That kiss had been a wake-up call. Charlotte at thirty-four might be very different from Charlotte at twenty-four. For all Nicole knew, this Charlotte had lovers wherever she went.

Having married young, Nicole had never experimented much. Other friends had, and she didn't judge them for it. Nor was she judging Charlotte. She just wanted her here at a time when no one else was.

Feeling alone and lonely as she lay in a bed built for two, she decided to call Julian when morning came. He had sounded more tired than usual tonight. She was worried something else was going on.

As it happened, she didn't call Sunday, though she thought of it a hundred times. He had told her his plans, which started with rounds at the hospital and would be followed by brunch with the team he was training, then an afternoon with his laptop in a quiet alcove of the university library, drafting lectures for his fall series in California. He would be busy. She didn't want to disturb him.

But she couldn't not wonder how he felt. So she texted the question at seven, to which he texted back, *Starting rounds in five minutes,* which told her nothing. She wanted to know if the new drug was helping, whether he was feeling side effects, whether he was actively pursuing the stem cell route. She wanted to know how his hotel accommodations were and whether the laundry service was decent. Mostly, she wanted to know if he missed her, but was afraid to ask that, too.

After a subdued call from him Sunday night, her imagination was going wild. She shot off a handful of Monday morning texts, but his answers were unsatisfying enough to force her hand. Choosing her time with care, she waited until late morning, when he would be in his office-on-loan and hopefully alone before heading to lunch.

"Hey," she said lightly and, pulse racing, held her breath.

"Hey, baby. How are you?"

At the upbeat sound of his voice—that oh-so-intimate *baby*—she dared breathe again. "I'm good," she replied in relief. "You sound better."

"I slept well. Everything okay there?"

"It is. The weather's gorgeous." It was small talk. But after last night's worry and now his sounding like the old Julian, she could happily pretend there was no angst in their lives and enjoy what was right about them as a couple. "The stone on the patio is like a heater once it absorbs the sun. And the ocean is starting to warm up. I wish you'd come," she added, not nagging, but excited.

Good-spiritedly, Julian said, "I wish I could." Then, "Did you get the recipes fixed?"

"We did," she said, allowing for the evasion. She liked that he was concerned about her work. "We spent the morning in town. Leo wouldn't commit to calling around, but the people we talked with agreed to make changes. I'm guessing he told one person, who then spread the word."

"Did they say why they changed their ingredients?"

"They said they thought we'd want recipes that people anywhere in the country could follow, but it was kind of a canned line, you know? Like it was either the one he fed them or one they agreed on among themselves."

"It doesn't matter, as long as it's fixed."

"Assuming Leo lets it go at that. Charlotte still claims he had nothing to do with it, but she's biased. I don't trust him. If their relationship ends, he could attack out of sheer spite."

"Nicki. You're more positive than that."

She sighed. "I know. You're right. I just get frightened sometimes."

"Did you decide what to do with your father's clothes?"

It was another evasion, this one picking up on something she had said last week. She liked that he had remembered. "Well, I did, but Mom has other ideas. She called last night after you and I talked. She had a long list of questions, some of which I could answer and some I could not. It's be so much easier if she was here."

"It's an emotional thing for her."

"It is for me, too, but it has to be done, and she has opinions on all of it. You know what'll happen, Jules. She'll refuse to come here and will—quote, unquote—leave the decisions to me, then she won't like the ones I make. Dad's clothes are a good example. I thought I'd take them to the consignment shop in Rockland—and it's not about the money, which I was planning to donate to the animal shelter there, because it's a cause

Dad loved. When I mentioned this last night, Mom first said she didn't want me *touching* his clothes yet. In the next breath, she said the minister would know what to do with them. But honestly, I can't see someone here on Quinnipeague walking around in Dad's clothes. Whoever it is would look ridiculous—like an imposter. Books or furniture or pots and pans are one thing. But something as intimate as clothes?"

"Isn't it really about what your mother wants?" Julian asked gently enough.

"I suppose."

"It'll sort itself out, Nicki. So, with the recipes good, you're feeling better about the cookbook?"

"I am. Charlotte's profiles are great. Want me to e-mail you a few?"

"Sure," he said, but he was only indulging her. He had never been overly interested in Charlotte's contribution, preferring to think of the cookbook as Nicole's alone, and she did love him for that.

"Anything new?" she asked gently.

"I talked with Grendjin about the Beijing trip," Julian offered. Antoine Grendjin was president of the hospital. He and Julian used to play golf together, though they hadn't done it since Julian had developed chronic tennis elbow, or so he had told Antoine. It was a good enough excuse—tennis elbow being more of a problem for golfers than golfer's elbow, and an injury that fit in well with Julian shifting to a teaching role in the OR. "He's fine with my being gone the week."

"Did you sign the contract?" Nicole asked. The speech was for the following February; typically, there would be paperwork sent straight to him in Durham now.

"Not yet. I have it here."

She felt a glimmer of unease. "But you haven't signed it, because you're not sure how you'll be in February? Are you feeling any better now?"

"I haven't signed the contract because I haven't gotten to it," he replied sharply and, seeming to hear his edge, asked more quietly, "How about you? Now that there's progress, when do you think the cookbook will be done?"

"They want it by mid-August. I'll need all that time. Even after we have the recipes and Charlotte is done with her profiles, I'll have to pull the whole thing together—you know, write the foreword and the afterword, make menu plans, edit it so that my voice in the book is consistent with my blogging one. I still get the heebie-jeebies about it sometimes. Me, write a *book*? Charlotte was always the confident one. She's such a professional."

"So are you."

"Not in the same way. She knows what it's like to work under a deadline. She knows what it's like to see something of hers in print."

"So do you. Your blog is in print. I'd warrant a guess that your following is much larger than hers."

"Well, anyway, she keeps me in line. But we're not working over the Fourth," she ventured. "Everyone'll be here, Jules—all the people you like. You'd be able to sleep and swim and take a quick break from Duke. Are you sure you won't come? I miss you." She was careful to keep her voice light, not wheedling. She wasn't a nag, just a wife loving her husband.

"Maybe in another weekend or two."

"But this is a long one with the Fourth on a Thursday," she coaxed. "You could—"

"Not now. Gotta run, baby. Enjoy that sun."

He was gone before she could point out that he hadn't said how he was feeling.

But he had sounded good. And she hadn't wanted to rock the boat. With the connection cut now, though, she could only worry about what wasn't said.

She worried in silence—not venting more to Charlotte, simply so that she didn't have to hear it all again herself. There was nothing fun about trying new medicines and waiting for improvement, watching for side effects, praying that a tingling foot was an aberration and not a symptom. Charlotte found it upsetting; Nicole could see that. So she was protecting Charlotte by not going on and on—but she was also protecting herself. She couldn't be entirely sure of this Charlotte, who had done her own thing for ten years and now had something or other going with Leo Cole. There were parts of Charlotte that she didn't understand. But she needed her. She couldn't risk driving her away.

Besides, she had been silent for four years through no choice of her own. Being silent now because she did choose to be was okay. It was a comfort knowing that she could talk if she wanted to, and she no longer felt guilty doing it. This wasn't a betrayal of Julian. At a time when Julian was doing what he needed to do to survive, so was she.

So she kept up a bright front. They spent Monday afternoon throwing mugs on Oliver Weeks's pottery wheel, Tuesday morning focused on CHOWDER, and Tuesday afternoon at the beach. Nicole thought it was a good blend of work and play, though under it all the worry was there. Evening calls were increasingly brief, and Julian only texted in reply to notes she sent. Granted, she kept asking how he was feeling, which possibly irritated him, but she couldn't help herself.

You won't tell me how you are, so I imagine the worst, she finally wrote, to which he replied, *Status quo,* which did little to ease her mind.

Charlotte sensed it. "You're not sitting still," she said at breakfast Wednesday morning. "Last time you were like this, you exploded by ten. Tell me what's wrong."

The invitation was all it took for Nicole to let loose about the worry, the frustration, the anger. If she repeated herself at times, she didn't care. Charlotte hadn't seen Leo since Saturday, so Nicole felt like she had her back. "I have this sense of impending doom," she concluded.

"That's melodramatic."

"I'm serious. Impending doom."

"More now than before?"

Nicole considered that. "No. But doom can only be impending for so long. At some point, it has to hit, right?"

"No," Charlotte said. "Multiple sclerosis is a chronic disease. It can go on for years with little change."

Julian wouldn't put up with that, she knew, but she didn't want to repeat it. Better to try to believe what Charlotte said. "You're right. Definitely right."

"You're working yourself up for nothing."

"I am. You're right. And I shouldn't criticize Julian. He's doing the best he can." She took a deep breath. "That's better. Thank you."

"Want to go to Rockland?"

"Today?" she asked, liking the thought. "To play?"

"Absolutely. I didn't bring enough clothes. Besides, tomorrow's the holiday, so there'll be extra ferries shuttling guests in today. We've done a lot on the book. We deserve a day off."

They took the early boat to Rockland and spent the day shopping, viewing the Wyeth collection, even catching an afternoon movie at the Strand before heading back to the dock. In a different place, Nicole had an easier time focusing, though she regularly glanced at her phone. By the time they returned to Quinnipeague, every bit of her worry was back.

Charlotte was on edge simply because Nicole was. She didn't believe in the business of impending doom, but Nicole was so serious about it that she wondered if there were things she didn't know. There had been moments in Rockland when she was the same old chatty Nicole, other times when she was silent. Charlotte couldn't force her to talk. All she could do was to stay close.

That said, her mind did wander occasionally when she saw a man who was of the right age and build to be Leo's father. She didn't mention it to Nicole. Leo remained a sore spot with her.

* * *

It was late afternoon when they got back. They were dropping their things in the kitchen when Nicole's phone rang. Her heart was thudding even before she saw Julian's name. He didn't usually call this early. "Hey, Jules," she said in breathless surprise, praying that he had either changed his mind and was coming after all, or simply missed her enough to want to hear her voice. When he didn't speak, she asked a frightened, "Everything okay?"

His voice was quiet. "No. It's out."

She gasped. "What do you mean, out?"

"I was at a grant meeting with half a dozen surgeons when my right hand started to shake. I tried to put it in my lap, but it was pretty obvious."

"Maybe they didn't see."

"They were staring at it, Nicole. Surgeons don't like hand tremors."

"But these doctors don't know you. Maybe they think that's just how you are." The argument was absurd, of course. Shaking was shaking. "At least it wasn't in front of your team in Philly."

"Dan Ewing was there," Julian said quietly. "He flew down last night and was at the meeting. He stayed behind when the others left and asked point-blank. When I didn't immediately answer, he said he knew something was wrong—that he'd known it for a while—but didn't know what it was. So I told him. I didn't have a choice, Nicki. Giving evasive answers is one thing, lying outright is another."

"I understand," she tried, "but Dan's a friend. He'll respect your need for privacy. He won't go blabbing all over the hospital."

"Not all over the hospital, but he has an obligation to make sure certain people know. He's head of the department. That puts him in a precarious position vis-à-vis responsibility and liability."

"But you haven't operated in four years."

"It's about transparency. He said I needed to tell Antoine. I just called him."

Nicole gasped again. "Omigod. What did he say?"

"He went through the mumbo-jumbo about legalities and ethics, only it isn't mumbo-jumbo. It's what any hospital would do."

"He can't ask you to leave."

"He can, but he didn't. He was sympathetic."

"Like, upset?"

"Stunned. He asked all the right questions. But friendship only goes so far. As president of the hospital, he has to put certain wheels in motion."

"What wheels?"

"Whatever's needed to protect the hospital. I won't have to leave. I just have to pull back from everything related to treating patients. There's paperwork involved. I have to notify my insurers. I have to document the history of my illness, so that if there's a patient problem from two or three years ago, I can show that I'd already stopped holding the scalpel."

"It's all there in the records, isn't it?"

"Yes, but it'll take some digging to put it together. I took every precaution, Nicole. I was careful even before the diagnosis, because I wasn't sure of my hands." His voice shook. "The point is, it's over. I need to talk with the department head here. I can assure him that I haven't gone near patients, but he'll have lawyers at his back, too. He may or may not want me to stay." He exhaled. "Oh God. The consequences keep mounting. They may not want me here. I won't be asked to talk at conferences. Same with being on TV. My career is done."

"No, Julian," she argued, though her eyes had filled with tears, "it isn't done. It's just shifting."

"Same difference."

"But how are you feeling? You won't tell me that."

"Because you don't want to know."

"I do," she insisted.

"Okay, then. I'm feeling like this drug is having no effect at all. There's no improvement. It's just getting worse. The tremor today lasted for a good long time. The hand was shaking in my lap." Nicole swallowed, about to speak when he added, "If this drug was going to help, it should have done so by now. I've read the literature, baby. The old 'give it time' routine won't cut it, so save your breath. Once the holiday's done, I'm calling Hammon."

Remembering his remark about Mexico, she felt a tiny spark of hope. "You haven't gone looking elsewhere, then?"

He was silent, then very quiet. "No. I said I would. But I've had to think about it. This isn't an easy choice for me, Nicole. You think it is, but I do know the risks."

"I know."

"You don't. You don't know what I'm feeling inside."

"You won't tell me!"

"No man likes to tell his wife that he's scared."

Nicole's heart broke for him. "You have a right to be scared. I'm scared, too! It's nothing to be ashamed of."

"It is if it paralyzes you. I don't want to be paralyzed. I'd rather be a guinea pig."

Her stomach was churning. "Julian—"

"Don't worry. It won't happen tomorrow. He'll want to try an autologous transplant first."

Using his own cells was less risky, but her stomach continued to churn. "What would that entail?"

"Maybe nothing. If my blood counts are too low, it's a no-go."

"Then what?"

"We use donor stem cells."

And if he resorted to donor cells, she knew exactly which ones he'd go for. "You want to try umbilical cord cells, but that's *so* experimental," she cried.

"I have nothing to lose."

"You *do,*" she argued, frantic. "You react badly to these things. Okay, so this drug isn't showing improvement yet, but if you've been tolerating it well—"

"I haven't. I'm jaundiced. Even Dan saw that. Jaundice means liver problems, which is what the blood work is starting to show. It'll only get worse if I stay on this drug."

She hadn't known about the blood work. He had kept that from her, knowing she would panic. Struggling for control, she tried to think. "What does Keppler say?"

"I haven't told him yet. This is beyond him now, Nicki. Mark will search cord blood banks to find as close a match as he can."

"There has to be another drug—"

"I've tried the best."

"Then something off-label."

He made a frustrated sound. "This isn't nicotine addiction. I've made up my mind, Nicole. I want treatment with umbilical cord stem cells."

"You could die."

"I could live. Either way, I'll have done something for medical research. Look at it from my point of view. I can't treat my own patients anymore. This is one way I can still give."

My point of view. My patients. I, I, I. "What about me?" she shot back. "What about our marriage?"

"Our marriage means the world to me, baby, but look at me. I can't be the kind of husband I want to be," he said with such defeat that her anger dissolved.

"I'm flying down," she said. "If I can't get a flight tonight—"

"Don't," he ordered, then entreated, "Please. I need to talk with Kaylin and John. And I need to call my parents. Explaining it is going to be hard for me. I need to be alone with it for a bit."

Nicole would have argued, if she hadn't been so devastated. She was losing him, and there didn't seem to be anything she could do to stop it.

Chapter Fifteen

Charlotte had been rooted to the spot, barely breathing lest she miss a word. If it was wrong of her to be listening in on a discussion between husband and wife, her personal stake justified it. Besides, Nicole hadn't turned away, though she wondered if Nicole even knew she was there. Her eyes were glazed, her hand trembling as she very quietly lowered the phone.

Charlotte waited. When she couldn't stand it any longer, she whispered, "What?"

Nicole looked up. Her face was ashen, her eyes the palest ghost of green. She moistened her lips, then swallowed.

Rounding the table, Charlotte reached for her cold hand. "What happened?" She had been able to piece together parts of it, but not all.

Nicole's eyes welled. "It's over."

"What is?"

"Everything."

Horrified, Charlotte said, "He wants to *kill* himself?"

"Not directly. But that's what it amounts to." Tears trickled down her cheeks. "He's just giving up."

"Because someone found out."

Nicole nodded. She seemed numb, which was nearly as frightening to Charlotte as anything else. Pulling her friend down into a chair, Charlotte took the one beside it and, holding both of Nicole's hands tightly, said, "Talk to me, Nicki. Tell me what he said."

Nicole let out a long, tremulous sob and, in a broken burst, told her what had happened. By the end, Charlotte was holding her, trying to comfort her as she had done that first morning in town, though this time without success. Nicole was shaking all over when the story was done, eyes bleak, cheeks streaked with tears.

"I can't help him," she whispered, looking helpless and confused. "He won't let me in. Is that fair, Charlotte? Shouldn't this be a decision we make together?"

"It should be," Charlotte said, though her mind was rushing in a frightened direction. If Julian was determined to use umbilical cord stem cells, she had a decision of her own to make.

"He's become totally selfish and self-absorbed," Nicole cried. "I don't know this man."

"You love him."

"Not *this* man." Her eyes held shock at the words, then instant grief. "You're right. I love him. I'd do anything to help him. But I'm out of the picture."

"You're not—"

"He doesn't want to hear what I have to say. There's nothing I can do."

"Maybe there is," Charlotte begged, desperate to give her hope. "Maybe he's right about trying something totally different."

"He'll die!"

"He doesn't have to."

"Like you can prevent it."

"Not me, but maybe—" She stopped. She wasn't ready for this, knew that it would cause damage and that once out, it couldn't be taken back. She didn't know if it was the right thing to do at all. But remembering the sense of purpose she had felt in returning to Quinnipeague, she had to believe it was tied to this.

"Maybe what?" Nicole cried, then begged, "Tell me, Charlotte. Anything."

In mere seconds, with Nicole looking at her like she was the only one who could possibly help, Charlotte wavered a dozen times, weighing the knowledge that Nicole would be hurt against the possibility that Julian might be saved. In the end, it was a moral issue. Hurt could be handled; death could not.

"Umbilical cord cells," she said with barely a breath.

"No no! That's what I *don't* want! I don't care how close the match is, Julian's body will reject it. It's rejected everything else. If I'd had a baby, we'd have frozen the cord blood and had a better chance with that, but I don't *have* a baby."

"I do," Charlotte mouthed, afraid to say the words aloud.

Nicole's eyes widened. "What?"

"I had a baby," Charlotte said softly. "I gave her up for adoption, but there's cord blood. I own it until she turns eighteen."

Nicole let out a frustrated breath. "That won't help. You can't just take any cord blood and think it'll work, not with Julian's body."

Charlotte stared at her, frozen in a last minute of indecision. There was still time to take it back, just say that she'd gotten pregnant after she left here.

But she couldn't say that. It would have been an outright lie—and through all of this, ten summers before and now, she had never lied outright to Nicole. Sweet, innocent, generous, and kind Nicole. Impending doom? Absolutely. It was ready to hit. But as painful as the truth was, life was life and still the most precious thing in the world.

So she didn't take anything back, simply stared at Nicole until she figured it out.

It took a minute, not because the idea didn't come, but because it was so off-the-charts impossible that Nicole couldn't believe it. But

Charlotte had to know she was thinking it and didn't correct her. Not impossible, then. But wrong, so wrong that she had trouble taking it in. *"Julian's* baby?"

Charlotte's nod was so small that Nicole might have missed it if she hadn't been watching closely.

Sitting straight, she put a hand on her chest. "You had Julian's baby? You and Julian . . . together?"

"Just once. Before you were married."

In a sickening instant, Nicole saw a tangle of arms and legs, the lock of undulating bodies. With the scrape of chair legs on the tile floor, she rose and stepped back. "You and *Julian*?"

"It was an accident. We were drunk."

Nicole wanted to misunderstand, but the guilt on Charlotte's face wouldn't let her. She backed up farther, needing to distance herself from the words, but they didn't fade. Barely able to breathe, she continued to stare at Charlotte, seeing something totally different from what should have been there, someone she didn't know at all. And Julian? Her *husband*?

For a minute, she felt faint enough to pass out. All it took to recover was Charlotte coming toward her and she shot out a hand, *stop*.

"Don't *touch* me," she whispered and fled into the Great Room, which was as far as her legs would take her. Sinking against the edge of the sofa, she tried to take in what Charlotte had said, but her thoughts were fragmented, torn by questions that had nowhere to go but out.

Jumping up, she ran back to the kitchen. Charlotte hadn't moved.

"When did this happen?" she asked. She needed to know. Didn't know why. Just needed to know.

Charlotte looked terrified. "A month before the wedding. It was like a circus here. We were painting guest rooms, moving furniture, trying to decide where the tent would go."

It was a blur to Nicole. "What night?"

"Saturday, I guess, because he left the next day. You have no idea how sorry—"

"What time?"

Charlotte flinched. "I don't know. We were all exhausted. Julian had been making margaritas."

"Where was *I*?"

"You were with us for a while." She swallowed. "Then you went to bed. We could feel the margaritas, so we switched to wine. We were drunk, Nicki. It didn't mean anything."

And that was supposed to make it *all right*? Nicole stared at her in disbelief. Unable to even *begin* to respond, she walked out. Seconds later, though, she was back. There were more questions. Asking them seemed her only link to sanity. "When did you know you were pregnant?"

"Not until after I left here."

"And you're sure it was Julian's?"

"I hadn't been with anyone else in ten months."

"Ten months," Nicole echoed. "Exactly ten months." Were there that many men? "You keep count?"

Charlotte held her gaze. "Not the way you mean. I agonized afterward. Getting drunk isn't my style. I wanted to know why I did it that night. So I dug back. I remember feeling lonely. There was so much happiness here, but I remember feeling alone."

"We included you in *everything*."

"Yes, you did, but you were planning a wedding. I had been planning one the year before—not planning, just dreaming. I'd done a piece in Sweden and met a guy and thought that was it."

Nicole was skeptical. It sounded like just another excuse. "You never mentioned it."

"It ended badly. I couldn't talk about it. I didn't want to *think* about it. But after a few drinks, I must have been. I must have been wondering if I was right to break up with him and if there was something wrong with me that I couldn't find love and if I'd ever have *my* day walking down the aisle."

"So you screwed my husband instead."

"No, I got *drunk* instead. I'm guessing that I was desperate to feel wanted. It could as easily have been the gardener as Julian."

"Blind sex? *Indiscriminate* sex? You were my *maid of honor,* Charlotte. How could you be that after what you'd done?"

"How could I *tell* you?" Charlotte cried.

"How could you *not*? You were pregnant by my husband."

"Your fiancé, and I didn't know I was pregnant until after the wedding."

Unable to look at her a second longer, Nicole started out, but she hadn't even made it past the door when another, horrible thought made her pivot. "Did *he* know you were pregnant?"

"No. I haven't talked with him since I left here ten years ago."

"You didn't think he had a right to know you were *carrying his child?*"

"By the time I found out, you were married. I couldn't do that to you."

"You did it!" The words *carrying his child* were bleeping front and center. She started to cry, but stopped herself and screamed, "How *could* you, Charlotte? You knew I wanted a baby."

"I didn't plan it," Charlotte cried. "I didn't plan that night, didn't plan a *baby.* It was the most difficult thing I've ever lived through."

As was this for Nicole. Anger was the only thing keeping her erect. "Am I supposed to feel sorry for you?" she asked, tasting bitterness and hating that, too. But how not to resent Charlotte for having the baby she should have had? More quietly, unable to shake the image, she asked, "What was it?"

"Oh, Nicki, don't—"

"Don't ask? Don't *wonder*? If not now, when?" A detached part of her said she had to know these things, that as long as she kept asking questions, the awful, *awful* whole of it wouldn't hit. "What was it?" she repeated.

"A girl."

"Where is she now?"

"Washington."

"D.C.?"

"State. It was a private adoption. The parents were at the hospital for the birth."

"And you didn't think Julian should have been there?"

"He was married to you. It would have killed you."

"Didn't you think he should have had a say about what happened to his child?"

Charlotte's mouth tightened. "No. I didn't. We avoided each other that last month, then he was married to you, and I was gone. He never asked if there was a chance I'd get pregnant. Neither one of us wanted to remember that night." Her voice softened, pleading. "I agonized, Nicole. I was pregnant. I was terrified. I thought of every possibility. I knew you'd be the best mother in the world, but how could you raise a child conceived this way? And if I told Julian, he'd either have to keep it from you or risk ruining his marriage. Adoption seemed like the only choice."

"Did you hold her?" Nicole asked quietly. How many times had she imagined holding her own child immediately after its birth?

"This won't—"

"Did you?"

"For a minute."

"Did you name her?"

"No."

"Are you in touch with her now?"

"No."

"But you kept the umbilical cord cells." Charlotte nodded. "Why?"

"In case I had other children who might need them. Or me."

"What about Julian's other children?" Nicole added, thinking of children she might have had herself, children who would have been half siblings with this one. The question hung in the air without answer. "Did your friends know?"

"What friends? I was doing community outreach in Appalachia when I found out. I didn't know anyone there."

"They must have seen that you were pregnant."

"By that time, I was gone. I got my first writing assignment. It was for a story in Oregon. I spent most of the pregnancy there."

She looked ashamed, but that didn't help Nicole. Somewhere in the back of her mind was Julian . . . guilty Julian . . . *cheating* Julian.

But Charlotte was here, and Nicole wanted to hit back. "It makes sense in a sick way. Your parents were always fooling around. You said you hated that."

"I did."

"But then you did the same." The numbness was starting to wear off. Trembling inside, she wrapped her arms around her middle. "Do you have any idea how I feel? Did you think about that at all?

Charlotte nodded. "It's haunted me for ten years."

Resentment flared. "I loved you like a sister."

"And I you," Charlotte said, forearms on the table now, earnest and intense. "What I did was wrong, Nicole. I never wanted you to know. Then I got here and you told me about Julian, and I've been praying ever since that it wouldn't come to this. But if he needs those stem cells, how could I not speak up?"

"You could have told *him,*" Nicole fired back. "Why me first?"

"Because you're the one I care about."

"By wrecking my marriage?"

"That's the last thing I want. I went away after the wedding and I stayed away. I tried to remove myself from your life. But you invited me back, and I've missed you. Everything seemed so right when we talked that I hoped the past was done and we could regain what we had. I did something awful, Nicole. If these cells give you hope, I'll have been able to give something back for all I've taken away."

"Really," Nicole said in a swirl of fury, because fury was the most obvious thing to feel. There was also disbelief and disappointment. There was emptiness. She had always thought she and Julian were the couple. Now to learn that it was *Charlotte* and Julian? She had no idea where that left her.

Charlotte didn't speak.

Nicole's fury did. "You had my husband's baby."

Still nothing.

"I can never forgive you for that."

"I understand," Charlotte said, turning beseechful, "but listen to me. This isn't *about* the baby. It's about stem cells. I have them. They could be the answer."

"Answer to *what*?" Nicole shouted, letting anger give her strength. "Saving my husband's life? Right now, I couldn't care less. He betrayed me as much as you did."

"Neither of us knew what we were doing."

Nicole didn't buy that. She could understand a lapse of morals in Charlotte, in whom they were poorly rooted to begin with. But Julian? Her *husband*? Even with his being married before—even with his dating other women between—she had assumed faithfulness, and if not on the eve of their wedding, when?

Charlotte drew her arms from the table and, in a faint voice, said, "Do you want me to leave?"

"Yes," Nicole said, then, "No." She thought about the cookbook, which was why Charlotte was here. On one hand, the cookbook seemed irrelevant right now. Food . . . place settings . . . tens of thousands of followers? Her whole *career* seemed irrelevant.

On the other hand, it was all she had. And Charlotte had committed to help. And kicking her out would only let her off the hook.

What to do? Nicole's thoughts were muddled by thick globs of emotion. Dismayed, she simply said, "I can't look at you," and, turning on a heel, ran through the Great Room and up the front stairs.

Charlotte waited for her to return. There was no sound from above—no crying, no yelling at Julian, not even the slam of a door. *I can't look at you*. Charlotte deserved that. She deserved worse. Still, it hurt.

Needing the comfort of the ocean, she went out the kitchen door. In the distance, the boom of fireworks at the pier marked the start of festivities for the Fourth, but festive was the last thing Charlotte felt. Crossing the patio, she settled on the beach steps and hunched over her knees. The tide was out, leaving a deep stretch of seaweed-blotched sand. Beyond it, the surf frothed in, broke, rolled out, echoing down the Quinnipeague coast. She tried to see the poetry in it; life ebbed and flowed. Bob Lilly had talked about that when she first came here, an eight-year-old child, troubled by what was happening at home. His voice, his words, and the echo of the poetry had given her strength during the loneliest times in her life.

None of it helped now. She had betrayed Bob, too. Wondering if Nicole was right—if she was as defective as her parents had been—she felt worse than ever. She rocked lightly. She put her head to her knees, listening, waiting, but though the ocean thundered rhythmically, it didn't soothe.

In time, she raised her head. Midnight had come and gone, but she doubted Nicole was asleep. She couldn't go to her. But she could wait in the Great Room, all night if need be, glad to be a whipping post if that would help Nicole.

She had just started back when the house lights went out. Uneasy, she made her way through the dark to the kitchen door and turned the handle, but the door didn't budge. She tried the patio sliders, then the front door, without luck.

She was wondering what to do next, when she heard footsteps inside. In a moment of fantasy, Charlotte imagined Nicole throwing open the door, saying that she understood, that people made mistakes, that those stem cells were the answer to a prayer.

The only thing reality brought, though, was the realization that the footsteps had been going *up* the stairs. Nicole had locked her out.

Chapter Sixteen

CHARLOTTE STOOD IN THE DARK, wondering what to do. She couldn't ring the bell. This wasn't a case of Nicole being distracted. She knew Charlotte was outside and didn't want her coming in.

Feeling like scum, she sat on the steps in the moonless night, arms around her knees, eyes on nothing at all. She had made a gross mistake ten years ago. It seemed she had compounded the error tonight. In weighing hurt against help, she had misjudged. Everything she had wanted *not* to happen *had*. And now the damage was done.

She thought to drive to the pier and wait there until morning to catch the ferry, but she didn't have money or even her car keys. Besides, running away wasn't the answer. She had spent her life running from one unpleasant relationship or another. But Nicole wasn't an unpleasant relationship. Charlotte loved her like a sister.

Anxious, she jumped up and started to walk. The night was cool. Still in the blouse and shorts she had worn to Rockland, she felt chilled, though she suspected part of it was grief. When easy walking didn't do it, she walked faster.

Five minutes later, though, she sat down on the side of the road. She had no business going to Leo's. She didn't deserve comfort. But she had never felt this alone. Even during the years when she hadn't seen Nicole, Charlotte had known the Lillys were there—an emotional, if fanciful touchstone. But no more. The loss was crippling.

She didn't know if Leo would understand. But she had nowhere else to go.

She walked with increasing speed, trying to escape an unspeakable sadness. Distracted, she didn't see the decaying road until her foot twisted in a rut. She caught herself and limped on, barely slowing, welcoming the pain. Shortly before the Cole curve, she started to run, pushing herself mercilessly down the dirt drive. She didn't notice the shadows of plants, the scents, the rustle of leaves. Not even the ocean registered.

Running straight to the house and up the steps, she sagged against the door. Her breath came in short gasps; her forehead, palms, and torso braced the wood. Shifting, she glanced at her watch. It was 2:10. All was silent inside.

She shouldn't have come. But she couldn't leave. She was cold and shaky, and that was totally apart from her mental state.

With only the faintest move of her hand, she knocked, then paused to listen for sounds from within. Hearing none, she repeated the knock. This time, Bear barked from the back of the house. She knocked again, still softly. The bark came closer.

When the door opened, she nearly fell forward. She caught herself just in time and looked up. Leo's hair was messed, but he didn't seem groggy. Though barefoot, he wore a T-shirt and jeans.

She must have looked like a madwoman, with her hair every which way and her face desolate, because he stared at her in stunned silence before whispering a frightened, *"Jesus,"* and pulling her inside.

As soon as the door shut, she slumped against it. In the next instant, her legs gave way and she slid down the wood to the floor. Covering her face, she burst into tears. Uncontrollable, they came in gut-wrenching sobs that went on and on. Mortified, she pressed her face to her knees and covered her head with her arms.

She felt a hand on her nape. "What *happened*?" he asked.

The connection was enough. Something inside her snapped, and the whole of it poured out. The words were broken, but, like the tears, they kept coming. She told him every last little private thing—about herself, Julian, the baby, Nicole.

He didn't say anything, just listened. When she ran out of words, he helped her up, led her through the dark house, and put her to bed.

She woke up feeling a wonderful warmth, a heartbeat under her ear, an arm around her back. Not daring to move, she opened an eye. The room was dark. It was a minute before she noticed a sliver of light where the drapes met, another before her eyes adjusted and she realized where she was. She sat up quickly, clutching the sheet to her chest, though she was fully dressed—and looked beside her. Leo half sat against the headboard with pillows at his back. His chest was bare, but he still wore his jeans. The arm that had held her lay empty on the sheet, the other was folded behind his head. His eyes, reflecting that sliver of light between the drapes, were on her.

Everything flooded back—her confrontation with Nicole, her flight here, her blubbering confession—and she was stricken. "My God," she breathed, thinking of Nicole, who was broken, then of Julian, who would damn her, then, in horror, of Leo. "I can't believe I told you all that!"

"Why not?" he asked quietly.

"It was private. I've betrayed her again."

"You think I'd tell anyone?"

"I don't know. Would you?"

He stared at her a minute longer, less relaxed now if the rigidity of his jaw was a clue. She was thinking she had offended him, when he rose from the bed and opened the drapes—and even then, she might have continued to watch him if he hadn't glanced around the room in daylight, inviting her to do the same.

The bedroom was a surprise. From the looks of the outside of the house, she would have expected something shabby, but nothing here was. The king-sized bed was sleek and black, the walls sleek and white, the carpet a nubby blend of both. French doors surrounded by windows faced the ocean, but there were also built-in dressers, paintings hung floor-to-ceiling, and Bear sprawled beneath a wall that held a huge flat-screen TV.

If this had been Cecily's bedroom, it was no more. Everything here was masculine, definitely Leo's. Everything in it was new and of fine quality, from the sheets and quilt to the carpet and art—all of which raised more questions than they answered. Confused, she looked back at him.

"We all have secrets," he said sadly and, opening a door to the outside, hitched his chin. When she joined him, he led her over a planked deck, across a well-kept beachfront, and down a long dock that extended out into the waves. At its end, sails furled, was an elegant sloop of fiberglass and teak.

A bell rang in Charlotte's head. This was the ghost ship she had seen the first morning she was here.

"Yours?" she whispered, stunned.

He nodded. Far from gloating, though, he seemed troubled. When her eyes asked why, he turned her so that she looked back at the house.

She sucked in a breath, thinking that this couldn't be the same house she had helped to reroof. That one was old, this one new. That one had peeling brown paint, this one was artfully set stone in myriad shades of sand. That one was two-storied and boxy, this one a single level with high ceilings, a handful of skylights, and an extension on the right that was nestled into the trees as sweetly as if it were part of the woods.

Oh, it was the same house. She could see the cupola up high behind the bedroom roof. But it had been totally rehabbed on this ocean side.

"When . . . ?" she asked, not sure where to begin.

"This year."

"You did it yourself?"

"I had help."

"Who?"

"Islanders."

"They *know* about this?" Being on the remote end of the island, it wasn't a part of Quinnipeague that they would normally pass.

"Some."

She hadn't been able to take her eyes from the house, but at his cryptic tone now, she did. He was chewing on the inside of his mouth, looking nervous, which, of course, made her wonder yet again where he got his money. Her first thought was grand theft, which would have been something a guy might do after he'd quit selling pot. But like the house, this guy wasn't what he seemed. Insider trading?

She finally had to ask, albeit in a confused hush. "Materials, labor—how did you pay?"

He stared at her with what actually looked like fear, and she might have questioned *that* if it hadn't slowly faded. Seeming resigned, he walked back down that long wooden dock and set off across the sand toward the room on the right. He didn't have to wave her along. Desperate for answers, she went.

As with the bedroom, the ocean-facing wall of this room was glass, reflecting the seascape so effectively that Charlotte couldn't see anything inside until he opened one of the doors, and then, her eyes were on him. He was chewing on the inside of his mouth again, clearly torn. But he did cock his head, gesturing her to pass him and go in.

Even with trees draping the skylights, there was enough sun pouring in over the ocean from the east to show endless shelves packed with a motley assortment of books. The only break in the shelves was for a machine of the copy-fax-scan variety. A large desk stood in the center of the room. Like the shelves, it looked to be cherry. It held a large computer screen that was surrounded by papers, some in neat piles, others not. This was a working desk, she realized and shot him a puzzled look.

He had his hands in his pockets. His jeans clung to lean hips, with his chest an inverted wedge above, but his shoulders seemed slumped. Clearly uneasy, he tipped his head toward one of the bookshelves.

She followed his gaze. The abundance of books was no surprise; he had already said he was a reader. As she approached the shelves, though, she was drawn to a familiar spine. She pulled it out. *Salt.* And it wasn't alone. There were three other copies—actually, *six,* if you counted three that, glancing around in bewilderment, she saw in the shadows of the copy machine. Eyes whipping back to the shelves, she spotted the title *Salt* on the spines of three others, though these were different. They were paperbacks.

But *Salt* wasn't out in paperback, at least not yet, or it would have been on sale in the airport.

Curious, she pulled out one, then another. Their covers had different designs, like someone was trying to decide which one to use.

Someone?

In the space of a stunned breath, little things came together—things Leo had said that reminded her of *Salt,* his familiarity with island life, the fact that the boat at his dock was like the one the hero built, even his disdain for the book, which might ward off suspicion.

Her gaze flew to his. *"You?"* she whispered, incredulous. *"You* wrote *Salt?"*

He didn't speak, didn't smile, didn't show a trace of emotion.

Trying to grasp it, she put a hand on the top of her head. "Self-published. Self-promoted."

"It isn't rocket science."

Disbelieving, she looked at the book again, then back. *"You* wrote this?"

A touch of color hit his cheeks. "Is that so improbable?"

"Yes! To hear Quinnies tell it, you're just a troublemaker who shoots gulls." Her own suspicion dawned. "None of it's true, is it. They were protecting you." That brought another thought. "They all know?"

"Mostly. The guy driving the mail boat sees me getting books and bags of forwarded mail. He's a gossip."

"Why 'forwarded' mail?"

"I have a P.O. box in Portland."

"So no one can track you here."

"I don't want publicity."

"Like the kind our cookbook could bring?"

He sputtered wryly. "Looks like I've ceded *that* fight."

Charlotte felt a dull pain. "Maybe me, too. Nicole won't want me touching it now." But she couldn't think about that, with the reality of Leo Cole sinking in. Feeling Bear's warmth by her leg, she touched his head for balance. "You wrote the hottest book of the year, and the world hasn't a clue. This is mind-boggling."

He said nothing. Clearly, he didn't think it was so mind-boggling. Clearly, he was feeling vaguely threatened that she knew his secret. "Does your publisher know your real name?"

He shook his head. "Everything goes through a lawyer in Boston."

"Even phone calls?"

"Those, too."

She scrunched up her face. "You don't want even a *little* of the glory?"

"No."

Well, he certainly knew what he wanted on that score at least. Fanning the three paperbacks, she held them out. "Which did you choose?"

"I haven't yet. The hardcover's doing well enough so that this won't come out for a while. Which do you like?"

Charlotte didn't have to study them. "The blue one," she said. It was a stylized ocean scene with a boat, though whether at sunrise or sunset, she didn't know, which added to the poignancy of it. She fitted the books back on the shelf and, puzzled, returned to Leo. "How did you learn how to do this?"

"I didn't design the cover. My publisher did."

"No, I mean, writing a book. I agonize over a piece that's twelve pages. *Salt* is four-hundred and eighty-three."

His mouth slanted, though not exactly in a smile. "You remember that."

"Oh, I do," Charlotte replied, clear-minded on this. "I was loving the reading so much that when I started to worry where it was headed, I skipped to the end. I hated that ending. I haven't finished the book."

"Are you angry?"

"Absolutely. You tugged at my heartstrings, then tore them all out and threw them away. I like my fiction happy. Real life is bad enough." Again, she thought of Nicole. Pushing the thought away again, she approached the desk. Some of the notes there were handwritten, others typed. One of the neater piles held what looked to be letters. "From fans?" she asked.

He nodded.

She was in awe. In the next instant, though, her eyes flew to the screen. "A sequel?" she asked excitedly, desperate for a happy ending.

"No. *Salt*'s done."

"Then this is a whole new one?" She looked at the header. *Next Book,* it said.

He pushed his hands deeper into his pockets. "It's not going very well."

"Why not?"

He shrugged. "*Salt* wrote itself. This one's a struggle. Maybe it's the interruptions, you know, doing stuff on the Web to promote *Salt*. It's time-consuming."

"But you don't need much sleep," she remembered him saying.

"The issue isn't sleep. It's fear."

"Fear?"

"That a second one will bomb."

"What does your publisher say?" She pointed her chin, about *Next Book*.

"Nothing. I haven't sold it to them yet."

"Can I read it?" Omigod. *That* would thaw Nicole.

"No."

"Why not?"

"Because it isn't worth shit. I'm thinking *Salt* should be the first and last."

"But you have a special talent."

"Lots of people do. They just don't know what to do with it. I figured out that part." But he was reaching inward, troubled again. "It isn't just fear. It's the next part."

"What part?"

"Success. Fans, bloggers, the media—they all want a piece of you, and the more successful you get, the more demanding they are. I won't leave the island to do what writers usually do."

Knowing him even in a small way, Charlotte could understand that. He liked his privacy.

Actually, she liked his privacy, too, though that thought took her by surprise. She was trying to understand it, when he said, "What're you thinking?"

Perplexed, she was trying to decide. Touching Bear again, she said, "You wrote *Salt*. I'm not sure I like that."

"Why not?"

"I don't know." She was unsettled, but couldn't put her finger on it.

"It should make you like me more. It means I'm loaded."

She grunted at the absurdity of that. "Money means diddly to me. Actually, knowing you're loaded scares me to death."

"Because you're jealous."

"Of what?"

"My success."

"No *way*. I can't compare my job to yours. Every assignment is different. I get to go different places and talk with different people. I don't want to write a book." Thinking of the cookbook, she added, "At least, not a novel."

"So what scares you?"

She tried to think it through. What she liked about Leo was that he was self-contained, that his ties to the island were exclusive. Her future was strewn all over the world, but he wasn't going anywhere. He was rooted here. She found comfort in roots. When she was with him on his private little tail of Quinnipeague, she felt safe.

How to reconcile that with the concept of international bestsellerdom? And how to reconcile any of it with the future? She had no idea.

So she simply said, "I liked your life when it was simpler. The real world is complicated. Yours is basic and down to earth. At least, I thought it was." Needing a break from the hot seat, she asked, "Why are you telling me all this now?"

He didn't blink. "I know about you and Julian. You were worried I'd tell. Now you have something on me. That's insurance, isn't it?"

Insurance. Charlotte wasn't quite sure there was such a thing. Life did what it wanted whether you had insurance or not. Take the situation with Nicole. Julian could have had any number of other diseases, and this wouldn't have happened. That he should have MS, that no treatment was working, that his body had a rejection problem—Charlotte wouldn't have dreamed it in a million years.

And yet, it was all she thought about as she walked back to Nicole's. Leo had offered to drive her, but there was too much going on in her head. She needed exercise. She needed fresh air. She needed a buffer between his life and hers.

It didn't completely work. She got caught up remembering what he had said when she asked if she could tell Nicole about *Salt*.

He had shrugged his consent. "You have something on her. She won't tell."

"Is that what it's all about," Charlotte asked sadly. "Having something on someone?"

"It isn't the way I want life to be. But life never is."

She wondered if he was preparing himself for her leaving, which made her wonder exactly what their relationship was. She didn't know—didn't even know what she wanted it to be.

Inevitably, though, as she neared the house, Nicole replaced Leo. There were immediate issues here, starting with getting inside. For all she knew, the doors would still be locked and Nicole would refuse to answer the bell. For all she knew, her luggage would be on the front steps.

But oh yes, she did have a bit of insurance against that. She couldn't dream that Nicole was angry enough to turn her back on those stem cells.

There was no luggage on the front steps, and the door was unlocked. Cautious, Charlotte let herself in. She smelled coffee and was desperate for a cup, but didn't feel she had a right to help herself. For all she knew, Nicole had left the door open only so that she could get her things. Her welcome here remained in serious doubt.

Nicole was in the Great Room. She didn't rise or even turn, though she must have heard the door. Only the top of her head, blond hair uncombed, showed above the sofa cushions. She sat facing the sliders, which were open to salt air and a frothing surf.

Charlotte went only far enough to enter Nicole's periphery, and the sight tugged at her heart. She was a knot on the sofa—legs tucked under her, elbows at her sides, profile tense.

"I'm sorry," Charlotte said with her heart in her mouth. "If I could erase that night, I would. It meant nothing."

"I wish it had," Nicole murmured. "At least then someone would have gotten something out of it."

But someone yet might, Charlotte thought. "The stem cells are yours. Say the word, and I'll have them sent."

Nicole didn't acknowledge the offer. She lifted her mug, sipped her coffee, tucked the mug back in her lap. Finally, sounding curious but detached, she asked, "Why did you agree to work on the cookbook? Did you *want* me to find out about this?"

"God, no. I only agreed, because I figured you wouldn't. Ten years had passed. I was dying to see you. Maybe I felt that helping with it would go a little way toward compensating for what I did."

"Nothing can do that."

"Maybe not. Tell me what you want me to do. I'll leave, if you want."

Nicole turned her head only enough to suggest she was looking at Charlotte, without actually doing it. "And let you off the hook? No. I have to think of myself right now. The cookbook is my future. You agreed to help. You owe me."

"I do," Charlotte said, knowing it would be easier for her to leave, but feeling that for once she just couldn't run. "I'll help any way you want." She paused. When Nicole simply took another sip of coffee, she asked softly, "Did you tell Julian?"

"No."

That puzzled her. The stem cells alone would have been reason for her to call, and as for the affair? The old Nicole had been so angry last night that she would have yelled at him for an hour.

But the Nicole on the sofa seemed different. This Nicole was subdued. She was more controlled. In a cool voice, she said, "I told my mother. Not about you, just about Julian's MS. So that's one good thing. She's coming up."

Charlotte loved Angie and wanted her there for Nicole's sake. Facing her now? That would be hard.

Nicole did turn then, finally emotional. "You bet, it'll be awkward for you. But I don't really care. You should feel guilty every time you look at her. I hope you suffer."

It wasn't the suffering that bothered Charlotte, as much as the hatred. Nicole wasn't a hater. Knowing that she had caused this was as bad as everything else.

"But you'll have to look at me, too," Charlotte said deferentially enough. "Are you sure you want that?"

Nicole's nod was slow and long. "I want my cookbook done. Besides, if you think you can run off with those stem cells, think again. Julian will go after you." She paused, bewildered. "Did you always want him?"

"I *never* wanted him."

"Was it jealousy—you had no one and didn't want me to, so you did what you could to spoil my marriage?"

"If I'd wanted that," Charlotte argued, "I'd have told you about this long ago. I know you're trying to figure out why it happened, Nicole, but I've already told you all I can. I was lonely, so I drank too much. Julian wasn't any more aware of me than I was of him."

Nicole's eyes were cold. "But he wasn't calling my name when he made love to you."

"We weren't making love. There were no words at all. It was an animal act."

Nicole stared at the ocean again. Then, recomposed, she said, "You were at Leo's, weren't you?"

"I didn't know where else to go. For what it's worth," she added, because she couldn't let the inference go unchallenged, "there were no animal acts there. I was distraught, and he is a friend."

"Did you tell him?"

Charlotte wanted to lie. But that would only add to her guilt. "Yes." When Nicole shot her an alarmed look, she said, "He won't tell."

"How can you know that?"

"Because he told me something personal that he doesn't want getting out. If he talks about you, I tell the world."

"Like the world would care about Leo Cole?" Nicole asked in disdain.

Charlotte would have leapt on that disdain if the situation had been different. But leaping anywhere wasn't wise, when she was already on thin ice. She waited until Nicole sank deeper into the sofa before saying, "It would."

"Honestly. The *world*?"

"He wrote *Salt*."

Nicole snorted. "And I'm Lady Gaga."

"I saw his office. I saw the books there—including paperback copies that won't come out for a while. I was just as skeptical as you, Nicole. But think about it," she said, unable to keep the excitement from her voice. "He's the perfect one to write about island life."

"And about caring for women?"

"The bad things we heard were rumors. He isn't that way."

"So he says. But men lie." Another cutting look. "We both know that."

Here, too, Charlotte couldn't let the inference go. "Did Julian ever lie to you?" she asked, mildly annoyed. She was starting to hear self-pity, which never sat well with her. "Did you ever ask him if he'd slept with me? Did you ever ask if he even *liked* me?"

"Yes. When you two first met. You were my best friend. I was desperate that he like you." She seemed to know that Charlotte had made a point, though, because she hit back. "He didn't want you involved in the cookbook. He didn't want you here with me this summer. I don't think he ever really liked you at all."

"That's what I'm *saying,*" Charlotte insisted, turning the argument around. "What happened between us was impersonal. It was once, and it was mindless."

"That doesn't mean it was right."

And what could Charlotte say, other than to return to the purpose of the firestorm? "You need to tell Julian about the stem cells."

"I don't need to do anything."

"Okay. You're right. But you said he might die. Using those cells would lower the risk."

"If they're a match."

"The match will be at least half, since he's the parent."

"Are we sure he is?"

Charlotte was suddenly weary. "Oh, for goodness' sake. If you doubt it, do a DNA test. Honestly, Nicole, would I lie about something like this, knowing it could be disproved"—she snapped her fingers—"like that? The bank I used did a DNA test before it froze the cord blood. Compare those results to Julian's DNA, and you'll have your proof."

Nicole was silent. Though her coffee had to be cold, she sipped it anyway. She was going through the motions, Charlotte realized, holding it together as she wouldn't have thought her friend could do. Not that she'd thought Nicole could build a hugely successful blog, either. But this was different. This was emotional. Maybe those four years of secrecy had given her a hidden strength.

Charlotte waited, allowing her time to ask more. Into the silence, she finally said, "So what do we do now?"

Nicole looked at her. "Now?"

"You don't really want to play Scrabble with me. So where do we go from here? I'd be glad to take a room in town if that'll make you more comfortable. Tell me what you want me to do."

Nicole was quiet for another minute. Then, "Stay here. The house is big enough for two of us. Today's the Fourth. Do what you want during the day, but we should go to the barbecue together tonight."

"Together?" Charlotte asked in surprise.

Nicole was impassive. "I don't want it any more than you do, but we have to pretend nothing's wrong. I don't want anyone doubting that this cookbook will come to be. We have to look like a team."

"Can you do that?"

"Easily. I'm good at putting on a show. I've been doing it for four years."

Since Julian had been diagnosed. "Nicole, about the stem cells—"

"Do you ever think about her?" Nicole cut in, albeit with a chink in her indifference. "Do you wonder what she's like?"

The child. "I try not to."

"You're her mother."

"Only biologically."

"But you have to wonder."

"I gave up that right when I signed the agreement."

"What if Julian wants to know about her?"

Charlotte should have seen where this was headed. Of course, Nicole would be worried about that. Suddenly, Charlotte was, too. "I hope not."

"Why?"

"She has a life."

"What if *she* wants it?"

"She's only nine. She's too young now. Besides, would he really want it? He didn't want you getting pregnant because he was afraid he wouldn't be able to do the things a father does."

"This is different. The child is born. Is his name on the birth certificate?"

"No. I told them I didn't know who the father was."

"Did you keep anything of hers—a hat or blanket?"

Charlotte shook her head. "Only the stem cells. You have to tell Julian about them, Nicole. That's the whole point of this hell."

But Nicole had risen. "I need to shower. I feel dirty. Try to interview Rose Mayes. Her cole slaw can fit in a couple of different places. Get the recipe while you're there. And check out the ingredients. Let's see what your precious Leo Cole does this time."

"Leo didn't—"

"Meet me here at six. We'll get to the barbecue when it's in full swing."

Chapter Seventeen

Charlotte drove to the Mayes house, but there were so many children and grandchildren underfoot that Rose, who was a strikingly energetic seventy-five and totally apologetic, couldn't talk. She was, however, in the process of making her slaw, so Charlotte was able to copy the recipe while it lay on the kitchen table. She watched closely as Rose mixed the dressing—all the while wondering whether she was one of those who might have feared Cecily enough to be secretive. If so, someone had assured her that sharing was fine, because she specifically said that the mustard seed she used was a descendent of Cecily's plants, and the rest of her ingredients were organic and fresh.

Wanting to validate Leo, Charlotte returned to the house, only to find it empty. Nicole's laptop was gone as well, likely taken to a place where she could work without seeing Charlotte. And though Charlotte felt the sting of that, a small part of her was relieved. They would go together to the barbecue. That would be bad enough.

Making herself a ham sandwich, she unearthed her copy of *Salt* from under the sofa cushion and took it out to deck. This time around, reading the book was a different experience. For one thing, since she knew the ending, the worry was gone. For another, knowing the author, she read it thinking about the prose, the vocabulary, and the plot in terms of Leo's life. Several times, she stopped to reconcile a remark or event with what she knew of him. More often than not, though, it raised more questions.

Even forewarned, she cried at the end. The characters were so well drawn that she felt what they felt, and their parting hurt. No doubt, given the turn her own life had taken in the last twenty-four hours, she was hypersensitive. But *Salt* had become personal.

She cried herself to sleep right there on the lounge chair, awoke late in the afternoon to find that the wind was blowing in, that she had no Leo to warm her, and that either the glass slider had blown shut—an unlikely prospect—or Nicole had returned. Fearing she was locked out again, she quickly tried the door, but it opened easily.

Nicole had her laptop open on the kitchen table. Charlotte might have asked how she was, if she hadn't been typing steadily, clearly ignoring her. Nor did she want to talk during the drive to town. When Charlotte complimented her on her blouse, which was red and sleeveless with touches of lace, she simply nodded. Same when Charlotte asked if she'd written another blog.

The silence was so uncharacteristic—so telling and sad—that Charlotte might have cried again. And once they parked and walked together to join the crowds on the field beside the church, Nicole spotted friends and, with a superficial smile for Charlotte, smoothly moved off.

Wisely, Charlotte had her camera. On the chance that Nicole would want to include pictures of island events in the book, she photographed everything in sight. Huge grills lined the sides of the field, serving up hot dogs, hamburgers, and grilled chicken. Long tables, covered with the requisite red-and-white oilskins, held platters of buns, baskets of chips, and condiments of every kind. More interesting, Charlotte thought, was the lineup of sides for which recipes would be printed. There were pasta salads and vegetable salads. Mayes slaw was only one of several slaws. And there were bean casseroles, with meat and without.

Charlotte photographed them all. She photographed groups sitting on quilts that were strewn across the field, and others getting refills of soda and beer. She photographed squealing children playing tag.

In time, the light got too low for pictures. She was debating getting something to eat herself, looking back over the crowd to see which group she might join, when she spotted Leo. Wearing a muted plaid shirt and jeans, he sat alone on a split-rail fence at the far end of the field. Overhanging trees might have hidden him in the lengthening shadows if he hadn't already been in the back of her mind. His feet were on the bottom rail, his legs splayed, elbows on knees.

Taking her first deep breath since leaving his house that morning, she decided that he hadn't eaten, either. Loading a plate with enough goodies for two, she crossed the field. After setting the plate on the flat of a post, she went between his legs and looped her arms over his shoulders.

His smile was small, but so sweet that it took her breath. He kissed her softly. When he drew back, she mirrored the smile. "You came," she said.

"I don't usually."

She had figured that. Even here, he was solitary. "Why now?"

"I wanted to see you."

A warmth spread inside, clogging her throat so that she couldn't reply.

His smile faded. "How'd it go?"

Her confrontation with Nicole. For those few seconds, she'd actually forgotten. Finding her voice now, she said, "It went."

"Uncomfortable?"

"Very."

"If she doesn't want you under her roof, you can stay with me."

Charlotte might have loved that, but she had vowed not to run away. "Her mother is coming. I want to be there to help."

"Is her mother trouble?"

"Could be. She doesn't know about Julian and me, but she will. There's no way Nicole will be able to hold it in." Retrieving the plate, she settled beside him on the fence and shot him a wry look. "Keep that invitation open, though. I may need it."

He took the hamburger she offered. After several big bites, he asked, "Have you thought about the other?"

"What other?" Charlotte asked back.

He was self-conscious. "My writing the book."

She chewed and swallowed, then said, "I finished it this afternoon. It's brilliant."

"Not the book. Have you thought about me as the writer."

"I'm trying not to."

"Because it's too complicated?"

She nodded. "I need simplicity right now. And friendship."

And sex, his dark eyes said. *A given,* hers replied. She could feel it even then, as they sat thigh to thigh on the fence. His hair looked like it had been combed before the wind had fingered through, and the lines of his nose, cheeks, and jaw were marked. He wasn't attractive in the classical sense, though something about him screamed *man*. At least, it did to her.

He glanced at the crowds on the field as he finished off his burger. "People are looking, y'know."

"I'm surprised they aren't mobbing you."

"They know I'd leave if they did." He took a handful of chips. "Being with me could ruin your reputation."

She laughed. "Sorry, but my reputation is long gone."

They didn't talk again until every chip, every bean, every bit of salad on the plate was devoured. He handed her his beer to wash it down, then said, "She's headin' our way."

Charlotte choked on a gulp and wiped her mouth with the back of her hand. "Nicole?" she whispered. He nodded. "Does she look angry?" When he shook his head, she looked around.

To the unknowing eye, Nicole looked on top of the world. Her blond hair swung comfortably at her jaw, the red blouse was chic, her white slacks snug. Even in the hovering dusk, she glowed. No one but Charlotte would see the faint smudges under her eyes as anything other than the style. Nor would anyone but Charlotte see past the stunning green of those eyes to their bite.

They were on Leo. "Charlotte tells me you're Chris Mauldin," she said civilly enough.

Leo gave a faint shrug.

"*Salt,* huh?" she went on. "Where'd you get the name?"

"Sea salt. Sailor. Tears." Nothing was new here. He had given similar answers in numerous online forums.

"No," Nicole said. "Where'd you get the name Chris Mauldin?"

"The phone book."

"You said it was real in one of the posts."

"It is. Just not mine."

"Was it the Quinnipeague phone book?"

She would check it out, Charlotte knew.

But Leo muddied the waters of that plan. "The library has phone books from all over Maine. It was a random choice. I don't remember what town."

Nicole gave the kind of soft *hmph* that could have shown either admiration or frustration, if her follow-up hadn't been telling. "I hear it's being made into a movie."

Charlotte hadn't heard that.

Nor, apparently, had Leo. "Not that I know of," he said.

"It should be," she stated. "I mean, how can you resist a love story like that? Arizona and Maine—they come from such different places."

"Actually," Leo corrected politely, "she's from Texas."

Charlotte knew that Nicole knew exactly where the heroine was from. She was testing Leo, and none too subtly.

"And her mother?" she asked, pushing further. "That's a tough one. There's no way she could disregard the feelings of *that* woman."

"Nicole," Charlotte chided softly.

Leo was more blunt. "You and I both know her mother was dead." His voice held an edge. "You don't have to believe me. I'm fine with that."

"You have to admit, it's a pretty preposterous story."

"So's yours," he said.

Here was the unpolished Leo, Charlotte realized, charging when charged, and it didn't bother her. She rather liked that he said what he felt, and that she could choke on her beer and not be ridiculed.

But Nicole was startled and that quickly brought her back to being the woman whose life had suffered a series of shocks. "I couldn't dream mine up."

"Nor me mine." When she had no comeback, he said, "Let's call it a draw."

She didn't answer. Seeming wounded, she turned to Charlotte. "Can he drop you home? The Matthews invited me over for coffee after the fireworks."

"I can do that," Leo said before Charlotte could ask.

"Great," Nicole said to no one in particular and, turning, walked away.

Charlotte slid off the fence and ran after her. "Are you okay?" she asked, catching her arm.

Nicole stopped and stared at her. "He's despicable. My story preposterous? Like I could have made it up? Like I was responsible for *any* of it?"

"You attacked him. He lashed back. His skin isn't very hard."

"And that's the kind of guy you like?" Pulling her arm free, she set off again.

Charlotte watched her for a minute, hurting for her but unable to help. She could help Leo, though. Returning, she settled in between his knees. "I'm sorry," she said softly.

"Don't be. It could have been worse."

"She's feeling humiliated."

"Because her husband was with you before they were married?"

"Because she didn't know, and because now *you* know."

"Did I mention it?" he asked with a last bit of defensiveness.

She slid her arms around his waist. "No. She just feels exposed."

He snorted. "I know *that* feeling."

Charlotte studied his face. The light had faded enough to make its lines more stark, reminding her of those first nights at his house. Recalling how little she had known of him then, she realized how much there still was to learn.

"Who was she?" she asked gently. When Leo seemed reluctant to answer, she said, "*Salt* had to be partly autobiographical."

His eyes fell to the place where their bodies met, middle to middle, though there was nothing sexual in it.

"Was she from Texas?" Charlotte asked to get him started.

"Arizona," he said. "Ironic?" That was how Nicole had tried to trip him up. "She was here for the summer."

"A regular?"

His head moved no. "She came with her family. First and last time."

"When was this?" Charlotte asked, and, moments later, felt his surrender.

He met her eyes. "I was back here two years. I was living in town, doing construction or renovation or handiwork—whatever. Her father was a real estate developer. He was successful—y'know, headed an empire. He bought the house that April and wanted to do it over. I was doing a lot of the work."

In *Salt,* the father was an investment banker and his daughter a partner in the firm, but the house in that version needed work, too.

"We met. We clicked. We had an affair."

"What was she like?"

"Physically? Like Nicole. Fragile-looking. She was sweet. She wasn't the kind of person you'd picture in finance. She wasn't tough." He paused. "Her daddy was tough enough for two."

"What about her mom? She wasn't dead, was she?" He would have changed that kind of detail.

"She might as well have been. She was a ditz. That's probably the only way she could avoid her husband's iron hand—y'know, zone out. She didn't know what to do with herself up here other than sit in the sun and burn to a crisp. Two brothers came and went, but when push came to shove, it was just the dad and his little girl."

"How old was she?"

"Twenty-seven."

"She wasn't a little girl."

Leo seemed puzzled. "Her father accepted that on some level. He didn't freak out when she met me at night. He didn't even freak out when she told him she loved me. Marrying me, having my kids, that was different."

"Did she say she would?"

"To me? Many times. She hated her life. She hated the pressure and the expectations. She hated the fact that her father favored her over her brothers. She said she could set up a little office in town and still work for the firm. She thought it'd be easier if she wasn't under his thumb. I was her escape."

"So she said?"

"Oh, she meant it." His eyes held hers. "But Quinnipeague isn't the real world. Leave here, and the best of intentions fall apart." Slipping a hand under her hair, he cupped her nape. He might as well have flashed his message in neon lights.

"I can't promise you anything," she whispered.

"I know." Lowering his head, he opened his mouth and, done with talk, kissed her until her knees were weak. "Can I drive you home?" he asked in a voice whose huskiness went further.

Fireworks lit the rearview mirror, but Nicole's house was dark when they reached it. Charlotte felt only a brief hesitation. Nicole wouldn't be back for a while, and she wanted Leo too much to wait. So she led him up the stairs, closed the door to her room, and quickly undressed.

He watched, not so much waiting as entranced, though there was nothing seductive in what she did. When she was naked, she helped him undress, leaning in to kiss his neck, his chest, his belly as each was bared, and when they joined, they held still for the longest, most trying moment, before breaking into a movement that could only be called fierce. They made love against the door, the floor, the bed, none of it gentle, but this was about truth. It was about needing to be together and needing release. It was as raw as anything Charlotte had ever felt, and it was real.

Afterward, mindful of Nicole's imminent return, they lay together for only a few minutes before silently dressing and, hand in hand, walking down the stairs and out to Leo's truck. He was behind the wheel, Charlotte standing on the running board, kissing him again, when he made a noise against her mouth. She drew back.

"I almost forgot," he said and lifted her to the ground. Climbing down, he went back to the bed of the truck and pulled out a trio of pots, each containing tall, staked stems. Above fernlike leaves on each were clusters of white flowers. "For Nicole's garden," he said.

Catching a sweet scent—not arousing like jasmine, quite the opposite—Charlotte leaned in. "Mmmm. What is this?"

"Valerian," he said. "The root was used during World War I to treat shock. You know, PTSD. You don't need to touch the roots with these plants. The smell usually does it. I meant it as a peace offering to Nicole, but from the looks of her, it'll have to be pretty potent to work. I'm not sure even my mother has that much power," he remarked only half joking, then added, "Plant these in the sun, but don't worry after that. Cecily will take care of them. She likes you."

Charlotte might have asked how he knew that, but he was off, carrying the pots around the side of the house, setting them carefully at the edge of the garden before straightening and dusting off his hands.

She followed him back to the truck, kissed him lightly before he climbed inside, then watched his taillights until a cluster of trees blocked their view, and even then she didn't move. *I can't promise you anything,* she had said, but feeling a new ache as she watched him leave, she wished it wasn't so.

Chapter Eighteen

By the time Nicole pulled into the driveway, she was exhausted. Putting on a show was hard work when she was being pulled every which way at once. She missed Julian, but dreaded seeing him. She missed Charlotte, but didn't want to talk. She wanted to tell all to her mother, but didn't want to tell the half.

She had never thought of herself as a prideful person, but she was too proud to tell her mother that her marriage was failing. She had never thought of herself as unreasonable, but she couldn't listen to Charlotte's apologies. And Julian? She didn't know where to begin. She had never thought of herself as cynical, but wondered why he had married her; had never thought of herself as mistrustful, but wondered if he had a woman at work; had never thought of herself as *spiteful,* but couldn't tell him about the cells. She was furious at him, but thought about him all the time. He had called while she was at the Matthews', which excused her distant tone, but she didn't offer to call him back.

Letting herself in the front door, she went through to the kitchen. Charlotte's purse was on the kitchen counter, meaning that she was back but apparently asleep. Nicole would have given anything to sleep.

Her eyes were heavy and her thoughts spent, but her body was keyed up. Caffeine with dessert? Not a good idea.

Blog, she told herself. But she wasn't in the mood. Check for messages from Sparrow, she suggested. But it could wait. Shop online for organic tea, she proposed, but why do that when she already had the best in the cupboard?

After steeping a mug of Cecily's passionflower tea, she carried it through the Great Room door and, pulling out one of the patio chairs, sat in the dark at the table outside. The ocean soughed gently over midnight sand. She took one deep breath to calm herself, then another, and, puzzled, turned toward the garden. Something smelled good, but it wasn't lavender. Rising, she followed her nose to the three pots that hadn't been there earlier. She touched the green fronds and, bending to the white clusters on top, inhaled.

She wasn't sure what they were, but she was pretty sure where they'd come from, and while a part of her wanted to hurl them into the sea, her better instinct held back. Sitting down on the garden path, white pants and all, she inhaled, exhaled, inhaled, exhaled. In time, she felt calmer—possibly from the simple act of breathing deeply, more likely from the plants. She couldn't be prideful when it came to these. They were definitely medicinal. They were also pretty. And she was tired of being angry.

Reasoning that since she had already benefitted from the tea, she wouldn't be damned for accepting a second Cole gift, she looked at them and breathed of them until she was calm enough for bed.

Friday had the dubious distinction of starting a weekend that had effectively begun two days before—meaning that the ferry schedule was off, which Nicole didn't discover until she reached the pier and waited twenty minutes for a boat that didn't come.

"Not due 'til eleven," advised the harbormaster, Roy Pepin, as he sauntered toward the dock from the Chowder House kitchen with a take-out mug in one bony hand and a half-eaten cruller in the other. "Ten minutes mow-a. G'won up and see Dorey."

Nicole smiled, nodded, and was grateful when Roy went on his way. Since there wasn't much for a harbormaster to do in a harbor as small as this, he tended to talk even more than other Quinnies. Holidays always brought him out, and if he was rarely seen on the pier itself, it was because he was chatting it up at one slip or another.

But Nicole wasn't in the mood to socialize with Dorey, either. She was trying to gear up for her mother's arrival, feeling the old pull and push, wondering how much to say when. Before leaving the house, after filling a ceramic ewer with fresh-cut peonies from the garden, she had snipped off a few valerian sprigs. Yes, valerian, Charlotte had said. Taking them from her pocket now, she held them to her nose. That they remained fragrant was a tribute to Cecily. That the scent alone, rather than tea brewed from the roots, brought relief, was also a tribute to Cecily. Nicole refused to credit Leo with this, much less Charlotte—though that anger was less raw this morning. The hurt remained, along with a certain disgust. But breakfast hadn't been as awkward today. Granted, Nicole had finished her own before Charlotte came down, so it wasn't a question of having to cook for or eat with her.

Nicole no longer felt she owed Charlotte for coming to Quinnipeague. A few profiles for the cookbook were a drop in the bucket, given what Charlotte owed her. Nicole feel guilty? No more! Still, she was able to ask about the flowers in what she thought was a reasonable tone, and, when Charlotte said they were from Leo, she actually told her to thank him.

She also didn't ask the impossible—which, in hindsight, was what she had done, expecting Charlotte to approach Rose Mayes on the holiday. She did suggest talking with the minister and his wife, who, being parentless and childless, had no weekend guests and would be eager to talk. Given the number of island events held at the church, they were major players in Quinnipeague's social scene—not to mention the mean banana-raspberry smoothie the wife kept in reserve as an alternative to popcorn on movie nights.

The wind blew her hair about, and still Nicole held those petals to her nose. When the ferry finally appeared on the horizon, she felt a yearning. She needed her mother here—needed to talk about MS and babies and the future, all of which Julian had forbidden her to discuss. And yes, she needed to talk about Charlotte and Julian. Angie was the mother, and, right now, Nicole the child.

But it wasn't Angie who stepped off the ferry when it turned and backed up to the pier. It was her stepdaughter, Kaylin. Long dark hair caught up in a ponytail that had lost stray wisps to the wind, she wore jeans, layered tops, and tall UGGs. A large duffel hung from one shoulder, a backpack from the other.

Confused, Nicole ran to her and gave her a hug, but in the next instant she was searching the boat. Other weekenders had debarked. There was no one left.

"Mom was supposed to be here," she said worriedly, knowing that Kaylin, who had spent so many summers with Angie, loved her, too.

"She's coming Sunday," the girl said.

"No. She said tomorrow, which is today."

"She was planning to," Kaylin explained, words coming in her typical rush, "but when she saw me at the dock in Rockland, she said you and I needed time alone."

Nicole didn't understand. Angie was the one she needed. "So where is *she* supposed to go?"

"She's driving up the coast."

"Alone?"

"She was grateful to see me. She said she needed more time to gather the courage to come. There's no cause for worry, Nicki—"

But Nicole was already on the phone and, moments later, heard the same thing from Angie. The call was brief. Angie sounded fine.

Nicole was disappointed but relieved—though she couldn't dwell on either, because Kaylin said in a frightened rush, "Dad told me he has MS, Nicki. I. Am. Staggered. I mean, thank God I wasn't at work when he called, because I was a total mess. I don't know anyone with MS but I've heard plenty, and now my own father has it. I can't believe it, I just can't *believe* it."

Nicole took her backpack. "How was he when he called?"

"Tired. I mean, like, I've seen his hand shake, but I thought it was too much caffeine. And his balance is sometimes off. I've seen him kick at the carpet like it's the carpet's fault, which I always thought was just how he was getting older. But he sounded really, really down. He's been sick for four years, and I didn't know? What was he *thinking*?"

"He was trying to protect you."

"Like I'm ten or something?" Kaylin asked, sounding indignant. She had her father's dark looks and regal carriage, but her mother's attitude. "I'm twenty-one. I'll be graduating from college next year."

Attitude had served Monica well, propelling her up the corporate ladder, but Kaylin wasn't quite there yet. "Speaking of which, why aren't you in New York?" Nicole asked. "You said summer interns don't get time off." The girl had landed a plum spot at a major television network, hence no time planned on Quinnipeague.

"I left after Dad called. And I'm not going back. You're right. We don't get time off. It's sweltering in the city, and they have us running all over the place for stupid little things like mauve-and-white polka-dot place mats for this set or a red linen scarf for that personality—which is what my supervisor calls his anchors, though the only personality those people have is on air. They treat us like furniture."

That fast, Nicole was on overload. She had spent the night preparing to be a daughter and wasn't up for being a mother. Struggling with the transition, she heard her father's voice, and, in the void, repeated his words. "It's called paying your dues."

"Dad said that, but I've been there a month, Nicki. That's long enough to know what I don't want. Besides, his being sick puts it all in a new light."

"He'll be okay," Nicole said.

"Not to hear him tell," Kaylin remarked and, during the drive back to the house, gave a rapid-fire blow-by-blow of the discussion. "He says he's taking part in a trial," she ended. "He says it's his best hope, but it's dangerous."

"He told you the risks?"

"He had to. I made him." Kaylin could be dogged when she wanted something, very Monica at times. More than once over the years, Nicole had been a buffer between father and daughter.

But she felt little sympathy for Julian now. He had made his own bed, which was another of Bob's pithy points.

Suddenly Kaylin was more frightened than confrontational. "Maybe he was exaggerating the danger. Do you think he was?"

"He was probably talking worst-case scenario."

"I told him I'd be a donor, but he says umbilical cord cells offer more hope. Is it true?"

In lieu of taking a stand, Nicole shared what she knew. Without quite dissing stem cell treatments, she tried to put the emphasis on more conventional ones. Kaylin, bless her, kept coming back to the other.

When they reached the house, Nicole made fresh lemonade and led the girl to the garden. "Talk with me here," she said. "I want to plant these flowers." She needed a little soothing herself, but if the valerian helped Kaylin at the same time, so much the better.

Besides, garden work was therapeutic. Having no garden back home, Nicole only did it here, and then only when George Mayes wasn't around to put in his tipsy two bits. In passing, she pulled spent blooms from her mother's red snapdragons and drying leaves from the purple lisianthus, but her goal was those white valerian plants. They were doing just fine in their pots, but Nicole knew they would do better in the ground and, though she doubted the soil was right, Charlotte had insisted that Cecily's spirit would make them grow.

Okay. So maybe Cecily was trying to butter her up into thinking more highly of Leo and Charlotte. But Nicole could play the game, too. She could pretend she felt better about them as a couple. She was good at hiding things. And she did like these plants.

"Here or there?" she asked Kaylin, indicating the site options.

Never without an opinion, Kaylin pointed. "There. Dad shouldn't be alone, y'know."

"He isn't alone," Nicole said as she took a gardening fork to the soil to loosen it up. "He's in Durham surrounded by doctors."

"That's his job, and it isn't the same. Shouldn't you be with him?"

Nicole kept working. "It's been four years, Kay. He and I know what to expect." She looked up. "Did he call your brother?"

"Johnny?" She make a sputtering sound. "He's no help. He's been working on my mom's cousin's farm, which is two hours from Des Moines, and they were in the middle of some soybean emergency."

Nicole twisted the fork in the soil. "How did he take it?"

"Oh, he's Mister Cool. He says Dad's a doctor and knows what he's doing, and I always thought so, too, only he was wrong for not telling us. I mean, like, we have a personal stake here, too, don't we?"

Nicole pointed at the trowel and, when Kaylin passed it to her, lengthened the hole to allow for three sets of roots. "They don't know that it's hereditary."

"They don't know that it isn't," the girl argued. "Okay, so if MS has to do with the autoimmune system, maybe that's the hereditary part, which means that I may have the same disorder but it'll develop into some whole *other* disease."

She sounded frightened again, clearly needed a mother's reassurance. But Nicole wasn't her mother, damn it, and right now, she was emotionally handicapped. Julian really needed to be here answering her questions. Hell, Julian really needed to be here answering *Nicole's.*

But he wasn't. And Kaylin was.

Grasping at straws, she eyed the valerian. Handing the girl a bag of fertilizer, she nudged her nearer the blooms. "Mix a little into the soil while I get water."

"Will I?" Kaylin called as Nicole put a watering can under the nearby spigot.

"I don't know," she said when she returned. "None of us knows when it comes to health. Look at my dad. He dropped dead out of the blue."

"That's my *point,*" Kaylin said with feeling. "I could kill myself working as hard as Dad always did, then get sick, and, zappo, it's gone."

"Excuse me," Nicole said, darting her intermittent glances as she poured water into the hole, "your father isn't done working by a long shot, and even if he were, he's already contributed more to his field than many doctors do in a lifetime." Nicole might fault Julian's judgment on personal matters, but she couldn't fault his work. "He's made breakthroughs that totally justify the effort it took to get there. Even if he doesn't discover another single thing, he'll always have that."

"Well, he was lucky. He didn't get sick until he was forty-two, but most people get MS in their twenties or thirties, and I'm twenty-two, which puts me right in the line of fire. If I have limited time—"

"You don't have limited time!" Nicole cried, unable to bear that thought. Taking one of the pots, she held the flowers to her nose and breathed deeply.

"But if I do," Kaylin said in a more measured way, "shouldn't I be doing something I like? I won't ever be a news anchor or host a talk show, and I know more about set design than my bosses do, because I've taken courses that they haven't. This internship sucks."

After another inhalation, Nicole gently pulled the plant from its pot, positioned the roots in the hole, and scooped dirt around them. When the stalks stood on their own, she reached for a second pot. "There must be something you can get out of it."

"Oh, yeah. A line on my CV and maybe a reference, but if it leads to another job like this, what's the point? I'm not having fun."

Nicole thrust the pot at her to hold and reached for the third. "There's more to life than having fun."

"But look at you. You're here having fun, while he's back there alone."

Having *fun*? Nicole might have laughed at the irony of that if she hadn't known the laugh would speak of hysteria, which would open up a can of worms she couldn't possibly, *possibly* discuss with Kaylin.

So she simply emptied the second pot, secured the roots in the ground, and sat back on her heels. Only then, when she was feeling a little calmer, did she answer the criticism. "I offered to be there, Kaylin. He thought it would be better if he made those phone calls himself."

"I don't mean right now. I mean all summer. You knew he was sick. How could you come to Quinnipeague?"

The question was so like one Charlotte had asked, that it seemed only right for Charlotte herself to return from town just then. When Nicole looked up, Kaylin swiveled. "Omigod," the girl cried. "Charlotte?"

They had spent only that wedding summer together—Kaylin and John here for the first time, getting to know the island, Angie and Bob, and even Nicole—but ten weeks of living in the same house with a person involved more shared time than could be forgotten.

Charlotte smiled. Rather than launch into social niceties, though, she was typically blunt. "Your dad had a full schedule in Durham and wanted Nicki here. It wasn't her choice." She glanced at Nicole. "Sorry. I overheard. Do you guys want to be alone?"

"No," Nicole said. Charlotte, Cecily's valerian—she would take whatever help she could get.

Kaylin picked up where she'd left off, challenging Charlotte now. "He may say that, but I don't believe him."

"He wanted Nicole to work on her book."

"He was totally lonely. Why else would he have suddenly decided to tell John and me?"

Nicole broke in, puzzled. "Didn't he tell you why?"

"Tell me what?"

She wasn't protecting Julian in this when there was a perfectly good explanation. Taking the last of the three pots from Kaylin, she said, "He was outed down there, and word spreads. He wanted to tell you himself before you heard it from someone else." That someone else would have been Monica, who had been married to Julian long enough to know his colleagues in Philadelphia, any one of whom might be learning momentarily that Julian had MS.

"And anyway," Charlotte said, playing bad cop to Nicole's good, "if you're so worried about his being alone, why aren't *you* down there?"

"I offered, but he said no. So I'm doing the next best thing, coming here to get Nicole to go."

Setting down the pot, Nicole caught the girl's hand. "He doesn't want that."

Kaylin's face crumbled. "You guys *are* breaking up?"

She gave the hand a little shake. "*No.* I talk with your father all the time."

"Did you agree with him not telling Johnny and me until now?"

As angry as Nicole was at Julian, she didn't want to bad-mouth him to his daughter. But if she was dealing with character issues in him, this related to one in her.

Releasing Kaylin's hand, she removed the last plant from its pot and said a quiet, "No."

Charlotte was less restrained. "Different people handle problems different ways. Nicki wanted to be in Durham; he wanted her here. She wanted you to know way back; your dad didn't."

"But he's right about the internship," Nicole put in, because he had shared Kaylin's earlier complaints. "He told you to stick with it, didn't he?"

Kaylin nodded and, finally calmer, said, "He said I was being impulsive, but he doesn't understand what I'm feeling. I tried to tell him, but he didn't get it. Bob would have understood."

"Excuse me?" Nicole burst out. "Mr. Law and Order? He was a pushover with you and Johnny, because you never tested him on big things, but this is a biggie, which is what he'd tell you if he was here. He believed that if you made a commitment, you had to stand by it."

"It's called paying your dues," Charlotte added.

Smiling, Nicole fitted the plant in the hole. "I already used that one on her."

"It bears repeating," Charlotte stated, focused on Kaylin. "I worked for no-name publications, writing pieces *no one* read, before I finally sold to a magazine big enough so that the byline got me better assignments. All that early time, I kept remembering what Bob said."

Kaylin knew how successful Charlotte was. Nicole had told her back in the spring, had even looked over Kaylin's shoulder while the girl read several of Charlotte's articles. Nicole might criticize Charlotte, like Julian, on moral grounds now, but that didn't take away from the quality of her work.

Kaylin was properly subdued.

"So you'll go back?" Nicole ventured, tamping soil around the plant.

"I can't," the girl said meekly.

"Why not?"

"I called my boss this morning." When Nicole eyed her in alarm, she hurriedly said, "There was only a month left anyway. They let you go after the first week in August so you have time before school."

She had quit. Stunned, Nicole sat back on her heels. "What did your father say?"

"He doesn't know."

"So you just did it. Can you call your boss back?"

Kaylin looked sheepish. "It wasn't a good ending. I told him there was a family emergency. He actually asked me what. I couldn't tell him about Dad, and I think I stammered a little and then finally said it wasn't really his business—and he and I hadn't been on good terms anyway, so the discussion went downhill." Her voice went now.

It was done then, Nicole realized in dismay as she pounded the last of the loose soil with her palms. She wondered if Kaylin had picked her timing, thinking that Nicole would be more understanding than either of her parents. As flattering as it was, it put her in the position of having to call one of the others.

But no. Kaylin was of age. The decision had been hers.

"You can't stay here," she warned, gathering up the garden tools. Kaylin couldn't ever know about Charlotte and Julian.

"Why not?"

There were plenty of innocent reasons. "We're getting ready to put the place on the market, which means weeding out and cleaning up. Besides, the summer's just starting. You can't do nothing for the next six weeks," she said as Julian would have, though she did agree with him on this. Having Kaylin hanging around, watching, listening, already worried that her father was heading toward his second divorce—it would be beyond dismal for Nicole.

"I could hostess at the Island Grill like I used to," Kaylin offered.

Nicole stood. "The season's underway. They've already hired their staff."

"I could help with your book."

"I have Charlotte for that." She grabbed the watering can with her free hand.

"I could help pack up the house," the girl tried, adding a timid, "or babysit Angie."

"Angie won't stay long," Nicole said, though it suddenly occurred to her that she had no idea how long her mother would stay. It suddenly occurred to her that she might have *two* more houseguests for however long, watching her every move through what had to be the darkest period of her life.

For the first time since Kaylin stepped off the ferry, she felt a moment of panic.

"I can work with Kaylin," Charlotte offered quietly, beside her now. "We'll make it a journalism internship. There are personal stories here that have nothing to do with the cookbook—like Oliver Weeks and Isabel Skane. Kaylin can hang around with them on my behalf. She can even do online research for my fall assignments."

Nicole was uneasy, but she was in a bind. As wounded as she was herself, she did love Kaylin. None of this was her fault. She had deserved better from Julian, too.

Besides, much as she didn't want it to be so, Charlotte's plan made sense.

Nicole was no pushover. But as soon as it was decided that Kaylin would stay, she knew she had to call Julian. Sure, Kaylin could do it. But Nicole owed him a call, and here was something relatively neutral to discuss.

Not wanting to be overheard, she took her phone to the beach and, facing the house to make sure no one came, punched in his cell number. With each digit, she grew more tense, but that was a good thing. Anger kept her spine straight, her hand steady, and her resolve intact.

He picked up after a single ring. "Hey. I was starting to worry. You okay?"

She had been abrupt the evening before and hadn't called him back. Hearing his voice now, it all rushed back. She wanted to tell him what a bastard he was, wanted to scream and carry on about betrayal—and maybe she would have done that once. But the ocean was at her back, grounding her to a world she had been safe in long before Julian had entered it, and as for the anger, rather than pushing her into hysteria, it gave her control.

She refused to apologize for not calling sooner. Nor could she get herself to ask how he was. "Kaylin's here," was all she said.

He was silent for a beat, then resigned. "I figured she'd try that. She wants to quit the internship. She wasn't happy with me when I said she couldn't."

"She's twenty-one."

"And thinks she knows everything. I assume you told her she had to go back."

"Actually, she's staying here."

"For the rest of the summer? Who made that decision?" he asked, marginally indignant, the father whose child hadn't behaved.

Nicole refused to cower. *She* wasn't his child. "Kaylin did. She's twenty-one." It bore repeating. "She called her boss and quit before she ever got here. Charlotte offered her an internship. She'll help with interviews."

"There?"

"Yes." With Charlotte. If that made him nervous, so be it.

He was silent again. Then, "Are you all right? You don't sound like you."

No more childish voice? Funny, how disillusionment made you

grow up fast. In many ways, his betrayal was worse than MS. At least, MS hadn't been his fault.

"I'm fine," she said, and the steadiness anger gave her was only the half. The other had to do with stem cells. She knew something that Julian did not. That was empowering.

"Are you sure?"

"Absolutely."

"Does this have to do with Charlotte?" he asked in a way that might have been casual if she hadn't known what she did.

She couldn't resist. "What could Charlotte have to do with anything?"

Problems with the book, he might have said. Or getting under each other's skin at the house. He might have even come clean. But he let it pass and simply said, "Nothing. You just sound strange. I worry."

Of course, he did. And she said nothing to ease his mind. He didn't need to know it all now—and if there was some reason he did, he certainly wasn't telling her. Was she being spiteful? Yes. Did she hate herself for it? Yes. Could she reverse it? No. After feeling powerless for so long, she needed to cling to this just a bit.

Besides, if he was worried about her for once, maybe that was good. For four years, he had been totally self-absorbed. Four, she caught herself? Try *ten*. He hadn't thought about her—hadn't considered how small she might feel learning he'd had sex with her best friend on the eve of their wedding. Small. Yes. That was it. Small. Insignificant. Worthless.

But she wasn't. If her parents' faith had meant anything, she was substantial and significant and worthy of being respected and loved. *He* was the small one here—at least, when it came to marriage. He had accused Monica of leaving him out of her life. Wasn't he doing the same to Nicole, and if so, was he the problem? Had he never considered that?

If not, it was time he did.

Actually, it was long *past* time he did.

That thought strengthened her, but her resolve lasted only through the call. The instant it was done, everything rushed back like the incoming tide, dumping at her feet the debris of ill health, a rotting marriage, and a muddy future. When the waters receded again, she was left with the realization that Julian might be the biggest asshole in the world, but he was still her husband, and that though she might hold a winning card in those stem cells, that didn't make up for the loss of love. Love was all she had ever wanted.

Turning toward the sea, she burst into tears.

By the time Nicole was composed enough to head for the house, Charlotte was approaching. They met at the patio's edge. Done being the perfect hostess who had to greet everyone with a smile and kind word, Nicole pulled her sweater tight and waited.

"Kaylin saw you crying," Charlotte said quietly. With her hands deep in the pockets of her jeans and her hair pulled starkly back, she looked subdued. "She's convinced you're lying about you and Julian."

Nicole glanced at the house. Kaylin stood at the glass sliders. "She thinks we're separating? Maybe we are."

"You confronted him then?"

"About you two? No. If my marriage falls apart, it won't be because of that. It'll be because my husband is an uptight jerk who refuses to include his wife in his life."

"He's sick, Nicki. You said it way back—he isn't himself."

Nicole remembered those words. They had totally new meaning now. "Maybe not completely," she said, "but I'm suddenly wondering about all the things I didn't see. I wasn't looking for anything wrong. He dictated and I obeyed. I was too soft."

"But we all *love* you for that."

Nicole wanted to say that it hadn't gotten her far and to ask whether Charlotte thought she should obey now or hold her ground, to rush to Durham or stay here, to give on the issue of stem cells or object. She wanted to pour out her fears, confiding in Charlotte as she'd always done, and not only during summers. During those growing-up years, they talked on the phone during winters, too. Charlotte had known about her first bra, her first kiss, her first serious crush. She had helped Nicole write her college essays and had been the first person Nicole called when she got into Middlebury. During their sophomore year, they had driven hours, meeting halfway between schools to sing their hearts out at a Shania Twain concert.

Nicole wanted the closeness back. She wanted Charlotte's help with Julian. Charlotte was smart. She would know what to do.

But she was still the enemy. Nicole wanted to forgive her, but couldn't.

Feeling a pervasive sadness, she said, "I never could understand why we grew apart. I told myself you were giving me space, like you knew you couldn't be part of my marriage and were stepping back. When it got worse, I blamed it on your work. Then on our having such different lifestyles. But all along it was the other, wasn't it?"

Charlotte's eyes were dull. *Yes.*

That quickly, Nicole was stung all over again. "You were my BFF."

"I *am.*"

"A BFF is supposed to be loyal. She's supposed to be honest and considerate and generous. She's supposed to sacrifice something she wants if she knows that getting it will hurt the other."

"I did all those things," Charlotte claimed helplessly.

"You did *not.*"

"Once. I screwed up *once*—and I was so drunk I didn't know I was doing it. Haven't you ever made a mistake?"

Oh yes, Nicole thought. She had trusted blindly. But no more. "Don't tell Julian about the stem cells, Charlotte. He doesn't need to know yet."

"But shouldn't he at least know they're an option?"

"He needs to consider other options first."

"You said he was going straight to stem cells."

"He will if I tell him what you have. Don't you see? Even with cells from his own child, he could die."

"Do you care?"

"Yes!" Nicole exclaimed, then quieted. "I shouldn't. But I do."

They stood for a moment, facing each other in silence while the ocean pounded and the gulls screeched. Finally, Charlotte said, "Are you afraid he'll want to know the child?"

Nicole considered the question. She wanted to deny it, but her anger wasn't that strong. "Maybe."

"The adoption papers forbid our contacting her."

"You. But not him."

"Both of us. The parents know how to reach me, but they've never tried."

"Why did they let you keep the stem cells?"

"She can use them if she needs them. That was part of the agreement."

"But why did you want them? Was it to keep some little last thing of hers?"

Charlotte looked vulnerable now. "I thought that if I had other children—"

Nicole cut her off, feeling a trace of impatience. "Yes, you said that, but wasn't there even a little bit of wanting something of hers?"

There was silence, then a reluctant, "Maybe subconsciously. But they're yours, Nicki. I'm serious about that. I can't think of a better use."

Nicole had wanted the admission. She wanted Charlotte to know she did understand the emotions involved. Now, though, she turned away. "I don't want them."

"He might. Please tell him."

"I can't."

"No one would have to know," Charlotte argued, her voice low and quickly taken by the wind. "You could just say he used donor cells. No one but the three of us would know their source."

Nicole knew it wasn't that simple. Kaylin was here, still watching from the sliders. And Angie was coming. And then there were Johnny, Julian's parents, and Monica, plus dozens of friends and colleagues, all of whom would ask questions if a stem cell transplant went bad.

But she couldn't think that far. One step at a time was all she could manage. "I'd better go talk with Kaylin." She set off, then stopped and, wary, turned back to Charlotte. "What about Leo? Will your working with Kaylin interfere with that?"

"No. He has his own work."

Nicole still wasn't sure what Charlotte saw in Leo Cole. She found him abrasive. But she hadn't been able to trip him up. "He really did write *Salt*?"

"Yes."

"Has he sold the rights to a second book?" Charlotte shook her head. "Why not?"

"He's keeping his options open."

"About writing the next one, or about who to sell it to?"

"Both."

"So if the world already knows Chris Mauldin is male, why's he's hiding out on Quinnipeague?"

"This is his home."

"But he never leaves. Is he agoraphobic?"

"No. He just prefers life here."

"Is he not interested in broadening his horizons? In growing as a writer?"

"He's not interested in what it would cost him. He figures he can grow just doing more of what he's done."

Nicole thought it a waste. Not in her wildest dreams did she have publishers fighting each other for the rights to her second book. Leo Cole was either very brilliant or very stupid—though she couldn't say that to Charlotte, who was clearly biased. So she settled for, "Well, anyway, thanks for giving Kaylin a job."

"Don't thank me," Charlotte insisted. "*Use* me. Please?"

Nicole knew Charlotte was feeling guilty—but so was she. Yes, she should tell Julian about the stem cells, but she wasn't ready, just wasn't ready. So she converted guilt into productivity. On a wave of antisentimentality, she attacked her bedroom closet, bagging up clothes she hadn't worn in years. That took her into Saturday, when, with Kaylin's help, she opened the Great Room cabinets and boxed up childhood games, jigsaw puzzles, old cassettes and CDs. After dinner at the Chowder House with her stepdaughter—Charlotte had gone down the road in the opposite direction, the details of which Nicole didn't want to know—she blogged about lobster rolls, adding a photo from her stock source, and when the posting was done, she spent several hours reading farm journals.

The thought did cross her mind that with Kaylin here, Charlotte could leave when the interviews were done. Kaylin could help organize the book, and if not Kaylin, her own editors. Wasn't that what editors were for?

She was getting ahead of herself with this, but it was nice to have a choice.

Feeling marginally in control, she slept soundly and awoke Sunday morning on the same positive note. She lost a little of it during the drive to the pier as she faced the thought of her mother again and wondered just what to say. But it wasn't until the ferry ramp lowered and her mother came down that her confidence imploded.

Driving up the coast these last few days, Angie hadn't been alone.

Chapter Nineteen

NICOLE KNEW THE MAN. TALL and robust, Tom Herschel had been one of Bob's law partners and was an old family friend, a widower who had lost his wife to breast cancer three years before—all of which, *including* two nights in motels along the coast, might have been totally innocent, if it hadn't been for the look on Angie's face. Her eyes were larger than normal, and it wasn't from makeup, though Angie was an expert at that. She was also an expert dresser, and though she weighed five pounds more this summer than last, she was still stunning in her sweater and slacks. What Nicole saw most, though, in these first instants, was nervousness.

Perhaps she was uneasy coming here for the first time without Bob? Or she was anxious about Nicole's mental state?

"You remember Tom," Angie said after they'd hugged—and it was such a ridiculous comment, what with Tom having been at the house all the time during the dark days after Bob's sudden death, that Nicole just *knew.*

How to behave? Speechless, she kept her right arm around her mother and extended her left for a genial clasp of Tom's hand, but she faced Angie again in the next breath.

"Up the coast?" she managed to say.

Angie's smile was stilted. "We went to Bar Harbor. Acadia is a fabulous place to hike."

Nicole had never known her mother to be a hiker but couldn't say that with Tom right there at her elbow. Rather, an inbred politeness kicked in, and she nodded and smiled, at which point Angie drew her into a motherly hug and deftly changed the subject. "I've been worried about you since I learned about Julian. I talked with him again this morning. He's worried about you, too." Holding Nicole back, she scowled. "For what it's worth, I'm furious at him for making you keep this all to yourself. There was no *reason* why you couldn't tell me. You poor thing."

Not wanting to dwell on what "poor thing" could mean, Nicole reached for her mother's bag before Tom could and led them to the car. Once the engine turned over, though, Angie picked up where she'd left off. "He sounded okay. But, of course, I couldn't see him. This has to have been such a strain on you. He was right to want you here, though this has to be bittersweet for you, too. Well, maybe it's different for me. My memories go so far back. Even standing on that ferry and watching Rockland recede, how many times your father and I did that." She sucked in a breath. "Has the island given you any kind of a break?"

Nicole checked the rearview mirror, then turned left and started down the neck road. She didn't have time to answer before Angie said, "Of course, you have the cookbook to do. That must be a diversion. How's it coming? Have islanders been cooperative? I don't suppose they wouldn't be, but asking for something as intimate as a personal recipe has to be challenging. Recipes *are* intimate, don't you think? Many of them have been in families for generations. I was telling Tom about the project, and he raised the issue of getting signed releases for everyone whose recipes you print. Have you thought about that?"

"My publisher did. They gave me a form."

"Oh, good. Do you think that's okay," she called to Tom, who was in the backseat, "or should we have someone in the firm check it out?"

"I'm sure it's fine," he reassured her, much as he had done dozens of times during the funeral planning—and suddenly Nicole had a thought that would have made her apoplectic, if she hadn't already been numb. Angie and Tom, even before Bob died? She couldn't bear to *think* it!

But here was her mother, giving a running commentary on whose drive they passed and how *were* the Warrens or the McKenzies or the Matthews? Yes, she jabbered. Normally Nicole would have given her competition, but since she wasn't saying much now, Angie had the airwaves all to herself. Still, she sounded . . . what? Apprehensive? Uncomfortable? *Guilty?*

By the time they were home, Nicole's head was throbbing. While she filled a glass with water and downed two Tylenol tabs, her mother opened the refrigerator and, after studying its contents, extracted boxes of blueberries, raspberries, and strawberries. Setting a colander in the sink, she put the berries under the spray.

She paused only to ask, "You haven't washed these, have you?"

"No. Uh, Mom . . ." What to say? "I was going to grill steaks for dinner, but I don't have enough for five."

"No problem. I thought we'd go to the Grill."

Nicole swallowed. "Okay. And, uh, how do you want to handle bedrooms? The master is the only one free—"

Hands stilling, Angie gasped. "Oh no, I couldn't sleep there. The memories would keep me up all night! When your father and I walked out of that bedroom last September, we had no idea he would never be back." She resumed washing the fruit.

"So you came here with *Tom*?" Nicole asked, because berries were nothing next to the memory of her father, which felt like it was being shoved into a dark, dusty corner.

Angie shushed her and glanced at the door. "Don't rush to judgment, honey. Tom didn't have to come. But he knew I'd have trouble here."

"Well, you can't both sleep in my room," Nicole said, bewildered.

"Why would either of us want to, when there are six other perfectly good rooms in the wings?"

In two bedrooms or one? That was what haunted Nicole. But it wasn't until after lunch, when they had exhausted the issues of Julian's diagnosis, treatment history, and current symptoms, that she was alone again with Angie and able to ask. Charlotte had offered to show Tom around the island, and had drafted Kaylin to narrate the tour.

They were on the patio, Angie rearranging the furniture there as though nothing was wrong, while, in Nicole's world, nothing was right. With growing astonishment, she watched her mother bend to check under the table for traces of where the legs had stood on the stone the summer before. Straightening, she moved one chair after another aside, all the while ignoring Nicole, who simmered.

"What is going *on,* Mom?" she finally cried. "Are you *with* Tom?"

Having pulled out all six chairs, Angie was struggling to move the table. "Take that end, like a good girl, would you?"

Nicole helped her inch the table to the very spot where it had likely been last year, then dropped her hands and asked, "Are you?"

Angie began returning chairs. "Would that be so awful?"

"Yes! Dad hasn't been dead seven months!"

"It's been seven months and three weeks."

"You said you loved him."

Angie stared at her. "I did love him. With all my heart and soul."

"Did you always have a thing for Tom?"

"Nicole," she warned. "That is very wrong. I've always loved Tom as a friend. So did your father. What you're suggesting is an insult to all of us."

Nicole knew her mother enough to recognize honest outrage, but she was only marginally appeased. She couldn't get her head around the idea of Angie dating. "He wasn't around the last few times we visited. All this time, I've pictured you alone."

"I've been telling you about dinners with friends."

"I assumed you were talking about couples, like the Farringtons or the Spragues." But that raised another awful thought. "Does the firm know about this? Dad's friends?"

"They don't think twice about Tom's support. In some regards, they're happy to have me off their hands, and they trust Tom." She grew crestfallen. "I knew you'd be upset."

"How could I not be?" Nicole cried.

"Tom is a *friend,* honey. When someone dies, everyone gathers around for the first week, then little by little they wander off. Tom didn't."

"But he's nothing like Dad." Bob was affable, outgoing, a rainmaker. Tom was none of those things.

"That's the point. I'm not looking for someone to replace your father."

Nicole barely heard. "I thought you loved him."

Angie's voice shot up. "I *did. Listen* to me, Nicole. This has nothing to *do* with Dad. Dad is *dead.*" There were tears in her eyes. She held the chair so tightly that her knuckles were white. "Maybe I shouldn't have brought Tom. But I wanted to be here with you and didn't think I'd be able to handle it all on my own. Look at this table. I remember when your father and I bought it. And that planter . . . and those mushroom lights. Back home, I took care of these kinds of things while your father worked, but up here, we did everything together. This house may not much resemble the one your grandparents built, but I look at this one and see that one. It's where your father and I were married."

Nicole tried to understand, but she kept picturing Bob looking down from heaven at the sight of his best friend in this house with his wife. Wasn't it a betrayal, not totally unlike Julian and Charlotte?

She must have looked like she would cry, because Angie had a quick arm around her. "I'm sorry, sweetheart. I didn't think you'd take it this badly."

Nicole couldn't speak.

"So much happening in your life," Angie cooed, squeezing her sweetly. "I can understand why you're numb."

Nicole had a hysterical thought. *Numb? After four years? No way. It's seeing my mother with another man after seven months!*

There was more to it, of course. She had taken a breath—tempted, oh so tempted by that loving arm to let loose about Charlotte and Julian, trust and betrayal, and how little Angie knew of it all, when she spotted movement in the Great Room. The island tour was apparently done.

Angie gave her a last squeeze before letting go. "There's a fellow at our church whose wife has had MS for thirty years. You'd never know she was suffering from anything worse than aging. Julian will be fine, honey. I know he will."

"How can you be sure?" Nicole asked, knowing that no two cases of MS were alike, but willing to grasp anything that would make her feel better.

"Because God wouldn't take your father and your husband in the same breath."

"Mom—"

"Remember what Dad used to say when things didn't go the way we wanted? What doesn't kill us makes us stronger."

Nicole was stunned. Mention of death did not make her feel better.

Angie must have taken her inability to speak for thoughtfulness, because, after pressing a cheek to hers, she went inside.

Nicole watched in despair. There was no PDA, but Angie was smiling for Tom. Or maybe the smile was for Charlotte or Kaylin. She didn't know what to think.

Retreating into numbness, she wandered up the path and into the garden to sit with the plants. The valerian was thriving. Same with the lavender. She didn't know which would help her more and didn't care, as long as one of them worked.

Charlotte joined her a short time later. "I'm sorry. I tried to draw it out, but there just isn't much to see." She settled down on the path, not quite invading Nicole's space in the garden, but not going away, either.

And Nicole didn't want her to. There was something to be said for not feeling entirely alone. "Are you scandalized?" she asked Charlotte with a sideways glance.

"About Tom? Surprised when I first saw him."

"Do you think she's wrong?"

"I'm not one to judge," Charlotte had the good grace to say.

"But what do you think?"

Another person would have given Nicole the answer she wanted, but Charlotte would be truthful. This was why Nicole had asked.

Her dark hair was a wild riot caught in a hair tie, but her brown eyes were more restrained. "I think they're both alone," she finally said. "They're not breaking any rules."

"What about Dad's memory?"

"That'll always be here."

"But buried under a mountain of new ones?"

Charlotte smiled sadly. "There would be new ones anyway. Angie is young—"

"Sixty-two."

"That's young," Charlotte remarked. "Women in Appalachia—or Ethiopia or Zimbabwe? Sixty-two is old in those places, but not here. Not the way Angie has lived. She's still full of life. She'll never forget Bob—never in a million years—but you can't expect her to close up like a clam and wait to die. You wouldn't want that for her."

Nicole supposed not. "But so *soon*?"

"He's helped her through a hard time. He seems like a nice enough guy."

"He's bland."

"Anyone would be bland next to Bob."

True, Nicole thought. Still, having Angie show up with another man was not what she needed just then. "She should have warned me. All these months, and she said nothing. Did she have to hide it?"

"Did you ask?" Charlotte argued gently. "She was protecting you, Nicki. Think about it. Would this have been easier two or three months ago?"

No, Nicole admitted and watched a bee hovering over the sweet William, which were in full bloom and lovely, their frilled edges framing petals layered with deep shades of pink. The buzzing was loud enough to survive the rumble of the nearby surf. She listened, breathing in wisps of the spicy clove scent of valerian, a soother in the salty sea air.

One thing about Charlotte; she knew when not to talk. She waited a full five minutes, until Nicole was feeling calmer, before quietly asking, "Did you tell her?"

About the affair, the child. "No."

"Will you?"

Nicole had come close. But something had stopped her, and it wasn't only the return of the others.

"If I'm going to talk about stem cells, I have to," she said, though Charlotte had already made the opposite point. No one had to know the identity of the donor. Anonymity was expected with donor banks. Julian would have to know, of course, but he wouldn't want the source of the cells advertised. Nor would Nicole. What had happened was humiliating enough without.

But she had no intention of sharing those thoughts with Charlotte, who deserved to worry a little.

Chapter Twenty

Charlotte was apprehensive entering the kitchen Monday morning, wondering whether Nicole would have spilled all to Angie overnight and, if so, what manner of condemnation would greet her. But Angie smiled brightly at her from the counter, where she was slicing kiwi, and someone must have already driven into town, because not only was Tom reading the *Wall Street Journal* in print, but Nicole was slicing bagels, fresh from a Quinnie Café bag.

Kaylin was a no-show; she wouldn't be up until ten. Charlotte might have stayed in bed late, too, if she hadn't been edgy thinking of Nicole and Angie alone. If it was going to happen, it would happen, but she wanted to be able to defend herself when it did.

That said, there was safety in numbers. Nicole wouldn't spill the beans in front of Tom, and since Tom sat there through breakfast, seconds of coffee on the patio, and cleanup back in the kitchen, Nicole and Angie weren't alone. By the time Angie took Tom back into town to browse in the shops, Kaylin was awake, so Charlotte was safe for another little while.

Under the guise of scouting out potential interviews, she left the two on the patio in the sun and went to visit Isabel Skane. There were others in the shop, two browsing the floor-to-ceiling bins of yarn, three at the table knitting. Charlotte had brought her sweater, which elicited more *ooohs* and *ahhhs* than it deserved given the number of mistakes, and Isabel quickly saw the problem with the cables.

"Once you slip stitches to the holder for a cable, whether you place the holder in back or in front determines the look of the finished cable. See these early ones?" Isabel spread out the lower sleeve. "You've consistently given the cable a left twist here, meaning the holder was in front, but you lost track of that as you moved up the arm."

Charlotte didn't like the implication. "So I need to tear all of this out?"

"Not if you think the Native American way," Isabel offered gently. "They deliberately knit a mistake into each piece to let the recipient know it was hand-knit with love."

"Well, that would work," Charlotte remarked, "except for two things. A, I'm the recipient and, B, there was nothing deliberate about these mistakes."

Soft laughter, a grin, and a knowing nod came from the three at the table.

"Want me to rip?" Isabel whispered. She was definitely a perfectionist, though that had never been in doubt in Charlotte's mind, given the samples on display in the shop. Each was flawless. Charlotte wasn't sure she would ever reach that stage.

"You're doing a great job," Isabel encouraged her, taking the sleeve. "This pattern would challenge even me."

Charlotte doubted that, but the remark opened the door for her to dig deeper into Isabel's knitting background and, unaware of her own professional purpose, the two shoppers joined in. Day-trippers, they were avid yarnies, asking questions Charlotte wouldn't have known to ask but the answers to which were fascinating.

Isabel paused from ripping only to ring up their sales. By the time she had the sleeve back to the first wrong cable, Charlotte was on her third chocolate almond candy and feeling no pain.

The pain returned, of course. Driving back past the beaches and flats, she could think of nothing but that Nicole had either told Angie or *hadn't* told Julian. Either way, there would be increased tension in the house.

But lunch was underway with no added tension, just hearty turkey sandwiches on thick slices of Melissa Parker's anadama bread. And so went the day. Nicole read through recipes with Angie for a while, then they all went to the beach. Charlotte stayed behind to edit photos, and when they returned she held her breath, searching faces to see if anything had changed.

Something actually had. Nicole confided to her in a private moment that Angie was urging her to fly to Durham despite what Julian wanted, because, after all, a wife should be with her husband, and what did Charlotte think about that?

Charlotte thought it was a good idea. She hoped—but didn't say—that if Nicole were there, she might be more apt to tell Julian what she knew about the affair, the baby, the stem cells. Charlotte was starting to think of telling him herself, and not only for his sake. Nicole was suffering holding it in.

But Nicole was adamant about picking the time. And since Charlotte didn't want to betray her again, she waited.

By the time the patio grill had cooled and the dishes were done, Charlotte needed to get out. Staying nearby to help Nicole was all well and good, but the tension was getting to her. When Trivial Pursuit, which was best played with exuberance, was retrieved from the giveaway box, she pleaded a need to see the ocean and excused herself from the room.

Can I come over? she typed into her phone as she climbed the stairs for a sweater.

Since when do you have to ask? Leo texted back, then, seconds later, *Want to go sailing?*

Now?

Why not?

Don't sailors return to shore at night?

Not me. I know these waters. Do you trust me?

Charlotte thought about racing with him from Quinnipeague to Rockland for Nicole, pouring her heart out to him in a flood of tears, and believing all the unbelievable things he said. Did she trust him? She figured she did.

Be there in five, she typed and, pocketing the phone, went for her keys.

For the first time, she drove right past the Cole curve and down the dirt drive between all those well-tended rows of flowers and herbs. Leo was a dark shadow on the front steps. Dropping his knife and wood as she approached, he rose and gestured her to the side of the house. Once she had parked beside his truck, he opened the door, helped her out, then pressed her against the car for a slow, tongue-dance of a kiss. She was beginning to think he had changed his mind about sailing, when he took her hand, led her out back, and picked up a duffel.

"Jackets and a blanket," he explained. "In case you're cold."

She wouldn't be for a while after that kiss, and, anyway, she had her fisherman's sweater along. But his consideration was endearing, as was his care when he lifted Bear onto the boat after the dog followed them down the dock.

In no time, he had stowed the bag, pulled in bumpers that hung between the boat and the dock, and released the lines. When he turned a key, navigating lights came on. With the press of a button came a healthy thrum.

"Motor?" she asked, surprised, since there was a good wind.

"Just 'til we clear the rocks," he said as they moved away from the dock. "They come on with no warning."

One did just then, seeming barely a foot from Charlotte's side, though she wouldn't have seen it if Leo hadn't pointed. A chiseled mound of wet granite, it rose only enough to break the waves. But he steered comfortably around it and between several others before he finally cut the engine and hoisted the sails. There were two, one fore and one aft; both winched up in no time.

Though the air was mild, the wind held steady as they tacked away from Quinnipeague. When they were far enough out so that the crash of the waves against the shore was barely a beat, he steered into the wind until the sails flapped, then lowered them and secured the lines. Pulling a thermos of cocoa from the duffel, he produced mugs and filled each.

"Warm enough?" he asked, settling beside her on the padded bench.

"With Bear on my feet, cocoa in my hands, and a hot guy beside me?" She gave a satisfied sigh, then, looking up at the star-filled sky, said, "Tell me what I see."

He began to point. "Saturn's too low this late, but there's Jupiter. See it? And way over there's the horse, Pegasus." His finger shifted, drawing. "Big Dipper. Little Dipper."

Charlotte had to focus hard to see each. Then she saw something else. "A shooting star." She squeezed her eyes shut.

When she opened them, Leo was watching her. "Wha'dya wish for?"

"I'm not telling. That'll jinx it."

"Tell me."

But she wouldn't. Instead, she nestled closer—which, if he had known her a little better, would have told him what her wish was—and said, "It's nice being out here, just floating." She listened. There was the lap of the water against the hull, the soft clink of the rigging as the boat swayed, Bear's low snoring, and Leo's steady heart. "It's quiet."

"Are things loud at the house?"

"Tense. Nicki still won't tell Julian about the stem cells."

"Can you?"

"I'm trying to respect her wishes. But she can't hold out forever. Those cells are a valuable tool."

"She's using them as one."

Charlotte was about to say that she wasn't using them at all—when she realized what he meant. "A tool against Julian."

"Punishment for the affair."

She tipped her head back on his shoulder so that she could see his eyes. "How did you know that?"

He shrugged. "Just a guess."

"It's the kind of thing the hero of *Salt* knew. Natural intuition. Have you worked more on *Next Book*?"

"Some. I got distracted by hate mail."

"What kind of hate mail?"

"One guy says I stole his story and wants a cut of my royalties or he's taking me to court. Another says my research sucked, because if anyone built a boat the way I described, it'd sink."

"People like finding fault. It's the culture."

"You don't get hate mail."

"Only because I'm small-time. Ninety-nine point nine percent of your mail must be positive."

"It's the point one percent that haunts me. Like the lady who says I'm irresponsible not addressing birth control with so much sex going on." He stopped talking, watching her intently.

"I told you."

"Tell me again."

"I'm not an impressionable young girl." Pregnancy was not a worry. She made sure of that.

"Once burned?"

"You could say. For the record, there haven't been many men."

"I wasn't asking that."

"But I want you to know. I'm particular about who I'm with."

The night sky was bright, accentuating his eyes. "If you wanted to have my baby, I wouldn't walk away."

Charlotte's heart stopped for a split second before resuming its beat. The remark might have been innocent but for the intensity in those eyes.

"Be careful what you say," she warned softly.

"I'm serious," he said. "But you won't stay here, will you." It wasn't a question.

"Would you come with me to Paris in September?" she asked. It wasn't a question, either, though, so she simply slipped back into fantasy by nestling closer.

They drained the thermos and drifted for a time until Leo raised the sails again and returned to the dock. "Come in for a few," he whispered when they reached the beach.

And how could she not? She wasn't able to put into words what she felt for Leo Cole, but making love came in a close second.

Chapter Twenty-one

ANGIE STAYED THROUGH THE WEEK. Nicole certainly couldn't ask her to leave, since it was her house, but increasingly they were at odds—and not about the small things they bickered about when Nicole was growing up, like music, makeup, and clothes. Their disagreements now had to do with the role of a wife, and it was two-sided. Nicole felt Angie was disloyal; Angie felt Nicole was negligent. Bob had always been the great diffuser, which gave Nicole double reason to miss him now. Add to that her turmoil about all the things her mother still didn't know—things about which Nicole was so torn—and she was touchy whenever her mother appeared.

On Tuesday, when Angie again raised the issue of her joining Julian in Durham, Nicole snapped, "He can come here, too, y'know," which led to a remark about *Tom being there,* which led to another argument about that.

On Wednesday, when Angie asked how Julian was feeling, Nicole said, "I haven't talked with him today," and when she asked why not, Nicole said, "Mother, it's barely eight. He needs sleep. I am not waking him up." When Angie argued that Julian was *always* up early, Nicole said, "Well, he isn't now," and left the room in a huff.

On Thursday, Angie waited awhile longer to launch in, but that only made the words more pointed when they came. "Do you *ever* call Julian?" she asked, and when Nicole said that they talked *every night,* Angie said she seemed angry and that if the anger was toward Julian, it was disappointing. "He didn't ask to be sick, Nicole, and if your anger isn't at him, it's at me. Where did this selfishness come from?"

Stung, Nicole held up her hands in surrender and turned away.

"She's worried about you," Charlotte tried to reason later, but when Charlotte, too, asked how Julian was feeling, Nicole was more defensive than ever.

"I could call him ten times a day, and there wouldn't be anything new. He's tired. He's *always* tired. End of conversation."

And then there was Kaylin, who announced she was returning to New York.

Nicole was bewildered. "But you have no job."

"I can get a job waitressing."

"What about working with Charlotte?"

"She doesn't need me, Nicki. I mean, like, it was sweet of her to offer, but she always does her own stuff herself, and you guys are totally on top of the cookbook." Her ponytail swished as she turned away, then quickly back. "And don't ask what Dad will say, because waitressing is a totally responsible job. And besides, Mom says it's okay."

Feeling shut out and separate, Nicole didn't share the text she received from Julian a short time later. He was returning to Philly. Having had done most of what he wanted to do in Durham, he was tired.

He was tired. He was always tired.

But something felt different this time. *Tired how?* she texted back.

Just tired.

Is it the drugs?

I think I just want to be home.

End of conversation.

Nicole worried.

She worried that his MS was getting worse.

She worried that everyone knowing about it now had demoralized him.

She worried that there *was* another woman in Philly, and that he missed her.

And yet, she couldn't get herself to call him. *It'll upset him,* she rationalized. *It'll make him angry. It'll cause a greater rift.* She knew she should offer to meet him at home, but there was no way she could see him and not confront him about Charlotte, and she just wasn't ready for that.

Burying herself in work, she spent the afternoon reviewing her to-do list for the book and seeing far more there than on the all-done list. Actually, she realized in a frightened moment, there was precious *little* on the all-done list. Yes, they had addressed BRUNCH, CHOWDER, FISH, and SWEETS, but not all of the recipes had come in—and those were only four of ten chapters. They hadn't even started the other six, and her deadline was barely a month off.

"Can we do all this?" she asked, offering the lists when Charlotte found her on the patio in a particularly discouraged moment.

Charlotte studied them briefly and looked up. "Absolutely."

But Nicole's stomach was churning, as it used to when she was eight or nine or ten, facing something new and different. She hadn't felt panic like this in a while.

Charlotte must have known that. Taking her friend's arms, she looked her in the eye and said a quiet, "It's been a rough week for you with everyone here. I love your mom, but she brought new issues with her, and she raises all your old insecurities. For what it's worth, I'm disappointed in Kaylin, too, but you can't control her. They're leaving Saturday. Once things settle, we'll work through these lists. I've had deadlines before, and I promise you, this one's doable."

Doable. Doable. Doable. Nicole chanted the words, and it helped.

What helped most, though, was Nickitotable.com. This was her escape. Community farms, pure food, spreading the locavore word—this was her mission. Whether describing the fresh-from-the-sea haddock they grilled for dinner and served with corn salsa, pushing handwoven place mats that Bev carried at the island store, or promoting the return of roadside food stands, she was in a world she could manage. She took to using her laptop in a far corner of the patio, where she immersed herself and, with the sea providing white noise, refused to look up.

Charlotte had taken to using her laptop at Leo's, though she wasn't as productive as she might have been on the patio with Nicole. After moving his computer over to make room on the desk for hers, he produced a second chair, which was totally sweet. But seated so close, she was distracted—first, by the glasses that he put on when he was at his computer for a stretch and which startled her each time he put them on; then by his surprisingly speedy forefinger pecking; then by the way he would sit back after a sentence or two, mouth the words, come forward and type more, lost in the world he created for however brief a time.

And brief it was. Though he never discussed specifics, and continued to refuse to let her read what he had written, he always grew frustrated. Inevitably, Charlotte would hear him swear, tap the keyboard to bring up new screens, and settle in to do marketing. This he shared with her—posting responses to Facebook fans, responding to questions posted on his Web site, tracking down blogsite reviews of *Salt* to thank a reviewer, or weighing in elsewhere on a discussion of his characters or plot. When she asked why he made the effort, he said he did it for *Salt,* and when she asked why it mattered, given the book's jaw-dropping success, he said it was a fair substitute for the touring his publisher would rather he do.

At one point toward the end of the week, he set down a thick folder. She hesitated before opening it. "More hate mail?" she asked warily.

He shook his head and hitched his chin at the folder, urging her on.

She opened it to find letter after letter from publishing houses and production companies, all addressed to his post office box in Portland. In some instances, there were multiple letters from the same source, sent when he hadn't responded to a first or second one. With each, the money increased. The amounts were staggering.

"This is every writer's dream," Charlotte breathed in awe.

He looked terrified. "Y'think?"

"I do." She singled out a glitzy header. "This one's for a feature film. So's this," she said, pushing at another. "And these?" She fanned out several more. "These are the best publishing houses in New York." She looked at him. "Have you called any of them back?"

"No. That's my lawyer's job. But he knows I'm not ready to sign another contract, not with my current publisher or any other. I like being in the driver's seat and working at my own speed. I don't want to have to finish the next book if I don't want to. And if they get fed up and lose interest, I can do another e-book myself."

"What about a movie? You can't do that yourself."

"Do I need a movie?"

"No." Neatening the letters, she closed the folder.

"You think I'm crazy," he said. With his hair slanting in short, dark spikes, his jaw hard and his lips thin, he looked tough, but the toughness didn't reach his eyes. Those eyes always betrayed his vulnerability, which was what Charlotte saw now. But there was more. She sensed he wasn't only thinking of his future as a writer. He was thinking of his future with her.

"You're not crazy," she said, addressing the first, easier to do than addressing the second. "Anyone who offers this kind of money isn't going to let you stay anonymous. If you were to take any of these, your life would change."

He seemed to relax a little.

"And I know what you mean about being in the driver's seat," she reasoned. "That's how my work is, and I love it. I couldn't have come here this summer without that freedom. I just wish . . . just wish . . ."

"What?"

She wished he would give a little, wished he would agree to go to Paris with her or at least visit her in New York. As for the rest, she didn't care about it any more than he did. Sure, the money was good, but if it wasn't what he wanted, it wasn't worth a dime. She loved him the way he was—honest and pure, naïve in his way, certainly vulnerable, all of which might be lost if the world found out who he was, and then where would her haven be?

Leaving the desk, she wrapped her arms around his waist and put her head on his chest. "This is nice," was all she said, and he seemed content to leave it at that.

Driving home a short time later, she thought of just how nice it was. She liked working with Leo. Distractions and all, she had done some good work. Whether it was the man, his beautiful office, or poor old Bear—who had taken to finding her leg wherever it was and sleeping against it—she was inspired.

Nicole knew it, too, because the interviews Charlotte gave her were top-notch. They captured the spirit of the island in ways Nicole couldn't have done herself, which—totally aside from Charlotte being her sole cheerleader—justified Nicole having insisted she stay. The rawness of her anger had passed, leaving a nagging hurt, but even that paled in the face of Angie's needling.

She did her best to regroup after each argument, determined to be more mature and restrained. But with Angie's departure near, and few mentions made about how sad the house was without Bob, how strong his presence remained, or what to do with his clothes, Nicole was growing suspicious.

Saturday morning, when they were in the kitchen alone and Angie remarked that being here wasn't so bad, that they should put a hold on packing, that maybe selling the house was a rash idea, Nicole lost it.

"Rash?" she cried. "Mom, you've been talking about selling since Dad died. You haven't had a single doubt, not once. The only thing that's changed here is Tom."

Angie drew back. "Was he unpleasant to be around? Did he get in your way? I know you avoided the west wing, but if you'd gone there even once, you'd have seen that Tom and I did not share a room—and if we had, would that be so bad? Would it be so bad if I kept the house and spent time here with someone other than your father? Bob loved having people come."

"Tom is not people," Nicole argued.

"Right you are. Tom is special. He's the one person your father would have trusted with me. Tom knows me. He respects what I had with Bob and lets me talk about him. He would never ask me to give up those memories, any more than I'd ask him to give up his memories of Susan, rest her soul. But this week has been really good. So no, I'm not selling."

Nicole swallowed hard. If this was Angie's call, it was done. "It's your house. You can do what you want." But there was another side. "I don't have to be here."

That caught Angie, who looked suddenly stricken. "You wouldn't want your children to experience Quinnipeague?"

"I don't *have* any children!" Nicole shouted, wondering how her own mother could be so insensitive.

"But you will."

"*When?* My husband is sick. He might die."

Angie straightened. "So you'll sit around and wait for that?"

"Mother!"

"I'm serious. Are you counting on his death?"

Nicole took a short breath. "Please don't say that word."

"So what's planned for the fall?" Angie asked with a calm that took nothing from her momentum. "Julian says he has a week of work in California and then something in China in the spring. Are you going, too? There's great sightseeing in China. Or are you afraid to make plans?" Her face was suddenly harder, the lines over her lip more pronounced. "Life doesn't follow our orders, Nicole. Things haven't worked out the way you want, but you have to accept them—"

"I can't."

"Accept and move on," Angie finished.

"Is that what you're doing, just giving up on everything you had that was good?"

Charlotte appeared at the door and stopped. At the sight of her, Nicole took a deep breath, held up her hands, and started to back off.

But Angie cried, "Oh, no no no, don't run away. We need to discuss this right now. You are stuck in the past, Nicole. Your father is dead. Nothing can bring him back."

"I refuse to forget him."

"Then remember this," Angie said in a rising voice. "He wasn't perfect. He never made the bed or did the laundry, not even when I was sick. We would eat in five-star restaurants, with him using their fine linen napkin to blow his nose, though I can't tell you how many times I asked him not to." Her voice kept rising. "He never wanted to hear complaints about my day, because my problems were petty compared to the ones he saw. He could be judgmental, and he was impatient. It was fine for *us* to wait for him, but he didn't like waiting for us. And he *died* on me, Nicole," she charged as her voice hit a high note. "He left me alone just as we were reaching what should have been the easy years of our lives. There are times when I'm *furious* at him for that." Winded, she sagged. "Does that mean I didn't love him? No. I loved him faults and all."

Nicole wasn't so angry that she didn't hear what Angie was saying.

She just wasn't sure where it was headed. "What does this have to do with me?"

"Do you love Julian?"

"Of course I love Julian."

"Then make it work." The words hung in the air along with all that Nicole hadn't said about the state of her marriage. Nicole was trying to decide whether to deny problems or admit to them, when Angie said, "And while we're talking about your father, here's one more thing. I lived through dozens of court trials with him, and the one thing he always said was that you had to look at the hand you're dealt and be creative. That's how he won cases. Look at the hand you're dealt, Nicole, and be creative. Make your own reality!"

Nicole couldn't be creative with so much else going on in her mind. One step at a time. That was all she could handle, which was why she did laundry, made lunch, made marginal peace with Kaylin as the girl packed, and, at the appointed time Saturday afternoon, drove the trio to the ferry. She was pleasant enough saying good-bye to Tom, and felt true emotion saying good-bye to Kaylin.

How to deal with her mother? She had wanted to tell Angie about Julian's illness for so long, yet now that she had, she was as bottled up as before.

Seeming to sense it, Angie let the others board first, then took Nicole's hands. Her voice was gentle, her neatly made-up eyes sad. "I can't know everything that's going on with you," she said. "I shouldn't. You're a grown woman. But you always used to be tolerant. I don't see that now. Honey, life isn't black or white. There isn't only one picture that's perfect. It's about piecing together shades of gray to make something quite stunning. And the picture shifts. That's another Dad-ism. Remember his sea shadows? Each time the shadow moves, there's a new image. Only sometimes those clouds are stuck up there, so we're the ones who have to move to see it."

* * *

At some point during the night, Nicole moved. Come dawn, she saw a different picture. Angie was right; she was a grown woman. She would never act on the say-so of her mother, though the phrase that stuck in her mind came from her. *Make your own reality.*

And with that came the conviction that she had to go home.

Charlotte drove her to the ferry. "Are you sure I can't come?" she asked as she lifted the Rollaboard from the back.

That scenario was actually one of many Nicole had considered during the night. But what had happened before her marriage was something that she and her husband had to work out. Same with their future. "I need to do this myself."

"If you want me to talk with him, I'll be here."

"What I really want," Nicole said, "is for you to keep at the book. I'm freaking out about that. The timing of all this couldn't be worse. I've done the menu planning, and if I'm not back right away, you have my notes on the rest." She had added more during breakfast. "Will you keep things going?"

"Absolutely," Charlotte said, looking her most earnest. "I'll do anything, Nicki. Name it, and it's yours. I'll even blog for you."

Feeling sad, Nicole smiled. "And take away the one thing I do well?" She gave Charlotte a spontaneous hug, only afterward realizing that she probably shouldn't have. But it was done, certainly the tolerant thing to do. Her mother would have been pleased. Forgiveness? She wasn't quite there yet. She had to hear Julian's side of the story. For now, though, that hug had filled a void.

"Don't underestimate yourself!" Charlotte called when Nicole was at the top of the platform. Moments later, with the rumble of its engine, the ferry cast off, and she was on her way.

Chapter Twenty-two

HAVING MADE THE DECISION TO return to Philadelphia, Nicole was impatient. Unable to find a taxi in Rockland, though, she had to wait for the shuttle bus, then wait again at the Portland Jetport for her flight. She didn't land in Philly until early evening, but even in all that time, she didn't change her mind. The only qualm she had as her cab neared the condo was whether Julian would be alone. She hadn't called to say she was coming. There was nothing she wanted to say on the phone.

She felt a headache coming on, but willed it away and produced a smile for the doorman, who took her bag from the trunk and wheeled it inside.

"Good to see you, Mrs. Carlysle. Would you like help taking this up?"

"No, thanks, John," she said, reaching for the handle as she entered the elevator. "It's light enough." The only things she had brought were ones she didn't have doubles of, like makeup and a favorite outfit or two, though generally she wore different clothes here. She didn't know how long she'd be staying. That depended on what she found.

John pressed the button for the eighteenth floor and, seeming unaware of Julian's illness, gave her his usual smile as the door closed. By the time it reopened, she had her keys in her hand.

Quietly, she let herself into their place. Julian's wallet and keys were on the nearby credenza, but there were no signs that anyone was with him—no handbag, no shoes or discarded clothing. Part of the reason she had come without warning was to check, and though she hated herself for the suspicion, it was one of the things they had to deal with.

He wasn't in the living room. Nor was there sound from elsewhere—no television, no music, no shuffle of feet in the kitchen. Guessing that he was working, she set her shoulder bag on the carpet by the suitcase and went down the hall, but the study was empty.

When she turned from there, though, she saw him. He stood at the bedroom door, wearing khakis and loafers, but that was where normalcy ended. His shirt was unbuttoned, his hair messy and his skin sallow. Most uncharacteristic, though, was the fear in his eyes.

Because he wasn't alone in the bedroom?

No. She knew in the instant that he was *profoundly* alone, his eyes tearing up now—her husband, whom she loved with the kind of irrationality that kept love alive even when anger should kill it.

"I'm sorry," she whispered, that quickly becoming the deferential Nicole who had been told not to come. "I can't leave you alone. I have to be here."

She approached, but he was reaching for her even before she arrived, pulling her close and holding her to him with a strength she wouldn't have imagined he had from the looks of the rest of him.

"You came," he murmured, his voice shaky in her hair. "I wasn't sure you would."

"You didn't ask me to come," she said in surprise, pulling back. The fear remained in his eyes.

"You sounded so distant. I thought you wanted out."

"I thought you did."

"I'm not good at talking about some things," he said, but before she could tell him that had to change, he ducked his head and caught her lips in a kiss that, yes, held fear and relief, but also the warmth of the good times. When it was done, he held her close for a while, right there in the doorway, and she didn't complain. When he kissed her again and she felt his arousal for the first time in months, her own excitement grew.

Nothing mattered then—not Charlotte, not the stem cells, not even a tremor in the hand that searched and uncovered. She gave him what he wanted, but the hunger was mutual—and if there was a subconscious anger in her greed, it became desire. She was forward in ways she had never been, reacquainting herself with his skin and his scent, taking the lead when his arms tired, refusing to let him rest until they were both sated.

Mine. The word echoed in her mind when finally she lay against him on the bed, listening as his heartbeat grew steady, as her own did the same. Tired or not, he kept an arm around her, holding her close, and when he dozed off, she followed.

She woke up to see city lights glowing under a purpling sky. Pushing up in alarm, she found him awake, head on the pillow, eyes watching her. "How long did we sleep?"

"A couple of hours," he said, then quietly added, "This is the best I've felt in days."

"Really?"

"Really."

She took a deep breath, let it out, and, when he gave a tug, returned to his side. No way was she raising the issue of Charlotte and spoiling the moment. Yes, she wanted what she'd had in the past. She wanted nothing more than to turn back the clock to the days before Julian got sick. And yes, she knew she couldn't. But if, for whatever reason, this intimacy had survived, she needed it.

Apparently, so did he, because he didn't speak, simply continued to hold her, letting her go only to get food, which she did in the form of grilled cheese and arugula sandwiches, but once those were gone, he wanted her with him again.

She was tired enough, relieved enough to sleep in his arms through the night. When morning came, though, she couldn't put it off. They were lying together in bed, his fingers moving lightly on her shoulder.

She spoke against his chest. "Tell me what happened with Charlotte."

His fingers stilled. When she didn't try to modify the question and let him off the hook, he let out a defeated breath. "I was afraid it was that. There had to be a reason you were different."

"I want to hear your side," she said, sitting up now, with the sheet under her arms and determination in her eyes. In fact, she didn't want to hear *anything*. But knowing Charlotte's side, she had to know his.

He began with the obvious—exhaustion from juggling work and wedding plans, too much to drink, little remembered the next day except that what had happened was wrong. But he had looked deeper, too. "At some level," he confessed awkwardly, "I was worried about getting married again. It was easy to blame Monica for what happened the first time, but a marriage takes two. You were younger and more vulnerable. I felt a greater responsibility for you." His voice fell. "I wasn't sure I was up to the task. But there we were with the wedding coming closer and closer, and the arrangements growing more and more elaborate. I panicked and drank too much. I was trying to forget the fear."

"Were you hoping to call off the wedding by having sex with someone else?" Nicole asked. It was a logical follow-up to what he was saying. She had to ask or would forever wonder.

"Lord no," he said with force and, reaching for her hand, hung on. "It was an insane thing—an *animal* thing that had nothing to do with what I wanted."

"Was the wedding too over-the-top?" she asked, still trying to understand.

"No. No, baby. The wedding was perfect. The problem was me. I got overwhelmed and did something I have regretted ever since. I am so, so sorry." He had always been modest. But humble? Ashamed? Never before. "It's the worst thing I've ever done. I told myself that I hadn't betrayed a vow, since we hadn't exchanged them yet. But that was a technical distinction. The whole thing was wrong." His eyes skittered off, only to return seconds later. "I was hoping it would go away. I thought it had."

It might have had it not been for the baby, she knew, but she wasn't mentioning that yet.

He had pushed himself up against the pillows, though there was nothing relaxed about the pose. "When did you learn—" He stopped himself. "Ahh. Right before the Fourth. That's when you pulled back."

She didn't apologize, didn't say anything at all. In the morning light, his jaundice was unsettling, but she wasn't ready to deal with that. He still had more explaining to do, and though he was visibly uncomfortable with it, she held her ground.

He sighed and looked away. "I barely knew her. I had only met her that summer, and I was only on Quinnipeague weekends. It wasn't something I planned." He looked back at Nicole, more troubled than ever. "Did she?"

"No." Nicole believed that. "She regrets it, too."

"Why did she tell you?"

Because she had to, Nicole might have said. *Because I was falling apart thinking that you were desperate enough to sacrifice your life for the sake of experimental medicine, and she wanted to give me hope.*

Still she held back. The argument now wasn't about stem cells. It was about her marriage.

So she simply said, "She probably thought I already knew."

"Did you ask her to leave?"

"No. I need her help with the cookbook."

"How can you stand looking at her?"

"How can I stand looking at you?" Nicole replied. "I'm trying to understand, Julian. I tell myself it was a long time ago, but I'm suddenly seeing things differently."

"Like what?"

"The late nights you work. Business trips."

He gave a spasmodic shake of his head. "Never."

"Not even while I'm on the island for weeks at a time?"

"Never," he repeated.

She started to rock, couldn't help herself. "But it happened with Charlotte. My best friend." Her breath shook, with deep, dark fears breaking through. "I know women whose husbands cheat. I never saw myself as one of them. But I am. It happened."

He came forward fast. "Not an affair, not willful—"

"Was it *me*?" she had to ask. "Was I not strong enough or smart enough or independent enough?"

He cupped her face with tremorous hands. "It wasn't you. You're all I wanted. It was me, feeling inadequate and being stupid enough to try to drown my own insecurities in drink."

"You? Inadequate?"

"You put me on a pedestal, Nicki. But I'd already fucked up one marriage when I met you. Have I fucked up a second?"

"I don't know," she said. The MS issue had to be discussed. But they weren't done with the other. "I hear the excuses you both give, and she's doing everything she can to help, but I still feel betrayed and angry."

"I'm sorry," he said, but mention of anger had stirred it up in her again, so she reached for a robe and went into the kitchen.

Minutes later, knife in hand, she had emptied the refrigerator of apples, pears, kiwi, and pineapple, and was chopping them to bits. After scooping the tiny cubes into a bowl, she added lime juice and sweetener and put the bowl in the fridge. Ten minutes later, she had turned frozen baguettes into cinnamon French toast enough for two, added a mound of fruit salsa to each plate, and put them on the breakfast bar—not because Julian deserved it, but for the sheer therapy of it.

Wearing a sweatshirt and jeans, he watched from the door. His hands were tucked under his arms, his feet were bare. "Feel better?" he asked when she was done.

Had he been smug, she might have lashed out. She still felt threads of anger. But the only thing in his tone was a knowledge borne of familiarity, a reminder that they had been married for ten years and that she wasn't ready to end it.

Yes, she felt better. Not great. But better. Nodding, she pocketed her hands, and met his gaze.

"So help me God, Nicole, there have been no other women. What happened that night was sobering."

"You were with women before me—"

"But never while I was married to Monica," he broke in, "and never while I was married to you. For what it's worth, I haven't had any contact with Charlotte since the wedding."

Nicole knew that. The whole issue of the baby made it so, because there was no way in hell Julian could have known about that and not let it slip now.

Coffee. She wanted coffee. Turning away, she was in the process of making it when he came from behind, wrapped his arms around her middle, and buried his face in her hair.

His voice was muffled. "I don't want to lose you, Nicole. You are the best thing in my life."

The words haunted her. She finished setting up the coffee, then turned. "Would you have said that even if I didn't know about you and Charlotte?"

"Yes. I would have told you last night if we'd stayed awake."

"Why did it have to take my going silent for you to realize it? Because I'm normally so sweet and trusting? Because I was an airhead ten years ago and too naïve to make you worry about it before now?"

"No," he insisted, framing her face with his hands, but he was frowning again. "And you aren't an airhead. You're an amazingly smart woman who never gave herself credit for that. You never demanded much. I took you for granted. And now with MS? You were the only one I could take my anger out on."

"Is the anger gone?"

"No. But I have to make a decision, and I can't do it alone."

"Other people know now," she argued. "You could talk with them."

"They're not you. I need you on my side. I've been miserable these last ten days."

She wanted to believe, wanted to think that the tears in his eyes last night had been sheer relief that she was here. It was an encouraging thought.

Gesturing for him to sit, she poured two juices and was in the process of carrying over their coffees when he took a mouthful of salsa and set down his fork. The tremor in his hand had been pronounced.

"No better?" she asked softly, taking the stool beside his.

He shook his head.

"How did your parents take it?"

"Stoically." He cradled his coffee with both hands. "Dad was quiet. My mother refuses to consider the ramifications for my career." He hesitated. "They haven't called you?"

She shook her head. She had never been close to Julian's parents, had always guessed that they viewed her as the second wife, maybe the trophy one. Maybe it was her childlike voice, or the fact that she hadn't given them a grandchild. She bought them Christmas gifts, sent birthday cards, and pulled out all stops when they visited Philadelphia, though that wasn't often. And she had her own parents, little more than an hour away.

"It's okay," she said to Julian now. "They're dealing, just like you. Has word spread at the hospital?"

"Some. I didn't get in until midday Friday. A few friends came by then. It's awkward until they realize I'm still me and"—he tapped his head—"all here. Dan was great in Durham. And Antoine wants to play golf. He says it would be good for me, though I think it's guilt on his part. But I have to hand it to him. He isn't running away." He stopped short.

"Others have?" Nicole asked.

Julian held up a hand and left the room, walking with the slightly uneven gait that he usually tried to hide. He returned a minute later, wearing wool socks.

"Who ran away?" she asked.

"The support staff. Hey, I was only in for half a day, and the whole idea is still strange to them. They don't know what to say. You'd think they would, given what they do for a living. But this isn't a patient. It's me."

"How's the limp?"

"You saw. It comes and goes. There's some relief not having to worry that someone will see." He rose again and, heading for the living room this time, fiddled with the thermostat.

When he returned, Nicole touched his hand. It was cold.

"I get chills," he admitted quietly and busied himself with the French toast.

Chills were a side effect of the meds he was on. Between that, the yellow tinge to his skin, and the pronounced tremor in his hand, it was obvious they weren't helping.

She ate silently beside him for a short time, liking the good will between them, liking that he was eating, liking that he seemed more relaxed with her, his old self in some regards. From having sex? Maybe. Men took pride in that.

But there was an elephant in the room, looming hairy and large. Sitting back with barely half of her breakfast eaten, she said, "Have you done anything about the other?"

"Stem cells?" He eyed her French toast, and asked, "Do you want that?"

She moved her plate closer and waited until he had finished most everything there. Naturally lean, he was now leaner than ever. For missing her? Disinterest in food? Nausea, which would be another side effect of the meds?

"Stem cells?" she prompted softly, gearing up for what she feared hearing. Impending doom? It seemed so long ago that she'd used the phrase with Charlotte. She had managed to push it aside for a while, but here it was again, front and center.

Setting down his fork, he rested his bad hand in his lap, and looked at her. "No. I haven't done anything yet."

"Why not?" she asked in surprise. He had been so determined when they'd discussed it last.

He reached for his coffee, but she took the cup before it reached his mouth, and topped it off with hot, fresh brew. As before, he held it with both hands.

"Why not, Julian?"

He was studying her strangely. "This is not a discussion you want to have."

"I know that. But I don't want to be ignored anymore."

"I never ignored you." He considered, modified. "I just turned away when you said things I didn't like."

"If you want me involved in your life, you have to let me in."

"I want you involved in my life," he said. "That's one of the reasons I haven't moved forward on this. I knew you were against it."

Wow. "Does that matter?"

His eyes were intense. "Yes. It matters a lot."

"Because you want me to support what you do?"

"No, because I want your opinion. You have common sense. I depend on it."

"You do? But you're the doctor. You know more."

"Maybe about medicine. Not about life."

Nicole didn't know what to think. Julian depending on her was a heady thought.

As she watched him, he grew self-conscious. "I also have questions. It isn't an easy decision." He looked out the window, then back. "Can we go for a walk or something?"

"Don't you have to get to the hospital?"

"Why?"

Here was bitterness. She was waiting to see if it would become anger and snowball into an accusation against her, when he let it go.

"I have a two o'clock meeting," he conceded, slipping into the old Julian, professional and composed. "It's a first pregnancy. There are early signs of left ventricular hypoplasia in the fetus and, understandably, the mom is off the wall. I can't do the surgery myself, but since it's my technique, I may be able to reassure her. My name is still worth something." He rose. "Out?"

* * *

They walked leisurely. Though the heat and humidity were high, the familiarity of the city was reassuring at a time when their lives were in flux. Julian held her hand and, later, looped her elbow through his. He seemed to want the connection. Hungry for it herself, Nicole refused to think beyond the moment.

Eventually reaching the park at Rittenhouse Square, they found an empty bench by the fountain, where the movement of water could soothe. Pedestrian traffic was light, but the normalcy of other people was calming as well. Julian stretched out his legs, ankles crossed, and though his arms were folded, their elbows remained linked.

When he asked about Kaylin, Nicole described her visit in a level-headed way. She even remained composed when he asked about Angie. From the perspective of Philadelphia and Julian, the issue of Tom just didn't seem as important, though Julian asked all the right questions regarding loyalty to Bob. Same with not selling the house. Nicole was still trying to process the meaning of that.

The questions ended. Tearing her eyes from the fountain, she found him studying her. She smiled, puzzled.

"Your voice is different," he remarked. "The way you speak. It's more blunt."

"Like Charlotte?" she asked, feeling a fondness she wouldn't have thought herself capable of not so long ago. Either old habits died hard, or new ones were, yes, more forgiving.

Whatever, he gave a short shrug with his brows. "I couldn't say. I barely knew her."

Accepting that at least, Nicole explained, "She's had to deal with a lot in her life, so she doesn't waste words. When she speaks, you listen. People tune me out sometimes. I feel like I need to fill the silence, whether I have something to say or not. It's the insecure me."

"It's the sociable you, and I like your voice," he said gently. "It's unique."

"Childlike?"

"Sweet."

She sighed. "Then along came reality." She waited. He looked torn, but they had to discuss the next medical step. Sitting in the midmorning quiet of a public garden was as good a place as any. "Your turn," she cued.

Releasing her arm, he leaned forward, put his elbows on his knees, and knotted his hands. He was slow to speak, seeming to struggle, unsure where to start. Finally, with the quickest glance back at her, he said, "I've been reading MS blogs."

That surprised her. He had always resisted. "You said they didn't relate to you."

"They don't in the sense of work. It's what I do for a living that makes this so bad for me. But that doesn't mean others don't have problems. And some of them don't have access to the kinds of doctors we do."

She might have said he was right, that it was about time he moved past self-pity and looked outside himself. But that would have been filling the silence again, and she was through doing that. Julian needed to talk. She waited for him to go on.

Finally, frowning at the ground, he said, "I feel like I'm on a precipice. I know that sounds melodramatic, but I've never been in a situation like this. My patients have. They put the lives of their babies in my hands all the time, or they used to. I was the one in control. But I'm not now. I can't control the doctor, can't control the process, can't control the results. I read those blogs and tell myself that if I return to a more conventional treatment plan, I could go on for a long time with maybe minimal decline. Then I think of the things that I love that I wouldn't be able to do." His frown deepened, dark brows more pronounced in profile. "I ask my patients to take risks. Can I not do it myself?" He considered that, hands clenched tighter. "So I'm here on the edge, knowing that if I decide to jump, I could either fly or fall." When he looked at her, he was fighting tears. "I don't know what in the hell to do."

Heartbroken, she came forward so that they were arm to arm, thigh to thigh, and leaned into him for several minutes. Then, feeling trepidation, she turned her head on his shoulder. "You still want that cure."

His eyes were frightened when they met hers, his voice low. "Yes."

His fear somehow modulated her own. "Umbilical cord stem cells," she breathed, just to be sure.

He nodded. "If I'm going for it, I'd rather go for it all."

"In spite of the risks?" she asked, and held her breath.

He hesitated, then said softly, "I want a cure. I tell myself that it doesn't matter as long as I'm alive. Only it does. I want it for me, but I also want it for you, for *us,* so that I can be the kind of husband you deserve. And I want it for others who are facing what we are." Voice still low, he said, "Here's another way I'm different from those bloggers. I've seen the success that can come when you take a chance on a new technique. I know how breakthroughs happen. It has to start with someone being willing to try."

"It could go bad," she whispered, feeling like she was on a precipice herself. He wanted her support. She could be the one pushing him over the edge.

"I know. That scares the shit out of me. But these meds aren't working. I don't need blood work to tell me what's happening. If I'm not off them soon, my liver is gone." His breathing was unsteady. "I want to try, Nicole."

And there it was, a choice as simple as loving him and wanting him happy. This was the hand they'd been dealt. The cards said that if he ever had a shot at winning, he needed this.

His eyes mirrored that need. She was lost in them for a final, pleading moment, before ceding the fight. "Then you should."

He gave a little jerk, clearly surprised. "You didn't think so before."

"I didn't understand how torn you were. I wasn't sure you'd thought it through."

"Oh, I have. I've thought it through six ways from Sunday. I could die. I could live and be cured and still not be allowed in the operating room. I could live but be severely debilitated just because of the treatment. I could live and be a vegetable. I know the risks."

The final, pleading moment was hers now. Once the words were said, they couldn't be taken back. But he wanted this. She could only imagine how much.

Taking a last breath, she swallowed, then said softly, "There's something that could lessen them." She loved him and, fly or fall, she owed him this. "Charlotte had a baby."

His expression was blank. *Which has to do with what?* it said. After a minute of utter silence, though, the blankness dissolved.

"She had *my* baby?" he whispered in horror. Sitting up straight, he exhaled in a sharp gust. "*My* child?"

"It isn't yours or hers now." Briefly, she explained.

His expression went from shock to confusion. "She said nothing."

"What could she say? Think about it. What were her choices?"

He sank back against the bench. To his credit, he remained stunned. "And you're sure it's mine?"

"She says she wasn't with anyone else. If she had been—if there was the slightest chance the baby wasn't yours—she wouldn't have confessed to having the cells."

"Cells from a child guarantee at least a partial match." But he was still struggling with the other. "She carried my child for nine months without a word? Who helped her?"

"No one. She was alone."

He considered that in silence.

"Would you have fought her?" Nicole finally asked, because that did impact her. Oh, abortion wasn't an option. None of them would have wanted that. But had Julian taken the baby, Nicole's life would have radically changed, and not only in the sense of having a baby to raise. Surrogate motherhood was one thing, but a baby conceived in a moment's betrayal? Charlotte would have forever been part of their marriage. The marriage might not have survived.

He was a while thinking about that, before finally shaking his head.

"Do you want to know about the baby?" she asked cautiously.

He thought again, then shook his head once more. "I can't. Not now. Tell me about the cells."

"They're frozen. Charlotte owns them until the child is eighteen."

He considered that, then let out another breath. "I'm not sure if this makes my decision easier or harder."

"Why harder?" she asked.

"It's suddenly real." Un-Julian-like, he pushed a hand through his hair, then clung to the back of his neck. "If there's a match, I'd have an edge. That may be too good to pass up. But it could still backfire." His eyes shot to hers. "I could still die."

"Not a good word, Jules," she warned quietly. "Do you trust Hammon?"

"Yes."

She took his hand—so cold again—and held it to the pulse at her throat. "Like your patients trust you?" When he nodded, she said, "Then if anyone can minimize the risk, it's him."

They were quiet returning to the house. Julian didn't rush to pick up the phone, but sat in the living room, brooding. Nicole guessed that a small part of him was still trying to process the fact of that night ten years ago having produced a child. More, though, to judge from the indecision on his face, he was revisiting those six ways from Sunday with this new information.

When she came to sit on the arm of his chair, he slipped his own arm around her waist. When she brought him lunch, he ate everything she served. And when he went off to his two o'clock meeting, she gave him a hug and let him go. She didn't ask what he was thinking, and though she was dying to know, she wouldn't hover. They were in this together. She believed that now in ways she hadn't before. She knew her husband. He was a self-contained man. He would speak when he had something to say.

When he returned from the hospital, he did. While there, he had called New York. Peter Keppler agreed with him about the liver problem and, understanding the next step, returned him to a more conventional drug. Julian also called Mark Hammon, who apparently began the conversation holding to the idea of an autologous transplant, until he electronically accessed the latest blood work.

"My counts are too low," Julian told Nicole now. "We won't be able to get a good collection of cells from me, so it'll have to be donor cells. If Charlotte is telling the truth, those UCB cells would be a gift. Mark is excited. That's the first time I've heard it from him. But he's cautious. He wants me to think through everything again. He also wants me to recuperate." Cautious himself now, he said, "I want to go to Quinnipeague, Nicki. It's the best place to rest. And Charlotte's there. She and I have to talk."

Nicole's first high little voice cried *no no no.* She had just found her husband again and couldn't bear to risk losing him to a woman with whom he'd had an affair, or whatever you wanted to call it. Seeing them separately was one thing, but together—and on *Quinnipeague*? *Her* island? Her *haven*—which wasn't the haven it used to be, thanks to these very same two people?

When the deeper, grown-up voice emerged, though, it said that, of course, Julian had to talk with Charlotte. Nicole had opened the door to that herself by telling him about the cord blood. He and Charlotte had a connection that wasn't ending anytime soon.

She wasn't sure which frightened her more—his having a stem cell transplant or his seeing Charlotte. But both were part of the new reality. If Angie was right, Nicole had to accept it and move on.

That said, moving on involved Charlotte in more ways than one. That cord blood could either save or kill. Having encouraged Julian to use it, Nicole felt the weight of responsibility. She wanted to share it with the woman who had made it possible.

Chapter Twenty-three

CHARLOTTE FELT THE WEIGHT. IT had been on her shoulders for more than a month, heavier after she told Nicole about the baby and even heavier now. Hour after hour with no word? She was dying to know what was going on but was reluctant to inject herself into what had to be a difficult time between Nicole and Julian.

When finally, *finally* on Wednesday morning Nicole texted, she was relieved only until she read the note. Sitting at Leo's desk, she reread it in dismay, then held the phone away and cried, "I've been waiting to hear for two days, and this is the best she can do? *Returning tomorrow, can u pick up at pier?*"

"Text her back," Leo suggested and, of course, it was the sensible thing to do, only Charlotte hadn't been good at being sensible since Nicole had left. Too much was at stake—Julian's health and Nicole's marriage, not to mention the future of her friendship with Nicole.

Now she texted, *What happened?*

I'll tell you tomorrow, Nicole replied, to which Charlotte made an exasperated sound.

Leo was reading over her shoulder. "Write her back."

Does he know? Charlotte texted.

Yes.

And . . . ?

Tomorrow. Can't talk now.

Tossing the phone across the desk, Charlotte turned on Leo again. "Here is a woman who can find a dozen different ways of saying the same thing in one conversation, and she refuses to talk now? Does she not know that I've been waiting?"

"Waiting *anxiously,*" Leo remarked, dropping into his chair and tipping back.

Supersensitive, she studied him. "Are you mocking me?"

"No no. But your mind hasn't been here." He glanced at her laptop. "Get any good work done today? Yesterday?"

"You know I didn't," she remarked, "but look who's talking. You say it's because *Next Book* sucks, but you won't let me read it, so I can't even give you encouragement. I want encouragement, Leo." If they had any future as a couple, he had to learn. "That's what I need right now."

Lowering his brows, he considered, then said, "I think you've done all the right things."

She sighed.

"What?" he asked defensively.

"Tell me that Julian and Nicole will be okay."

"You want me to lie? I don't know what's going to happen." His brows went even lower. "And anyway, why does it matter so much? You hadn't seen her in ten years. You drifted apart."

"Which was totally my fault," Charlotte stated, "and which I seriously regret and had hoped to move past by coming here this summer. Nicole's the only friend I have who knew me when we were kids. There's something to be said for that."

Leo righted his chair. "I wouldn't know," he said quietly, his dark eyes penetrating. "But you weren't close to your parents, either."

Livid, she said, "Excuse me, is the pot calling the kettle black? My parents are as dead as your mom, but your dad is not. What does he do, by the way? When Nicki and I were in Rockland, I kept thinking I'd see someone who looked like you."

"Not likely. He'd have been the one strutting around in khakis with a bill cap, dark glasses, a patch on his arm, and a gun at his hip."

"He's a *cop*?"

"Chief of."

"Seriously?" But he wouldn't kid about something like that. His father, the chief of police? Whoa. "When was the last time you talked with him?" Leo was silent. "Don't you think you should? Don't you think he should know what you're doing with your life? He isn't a nobody, Leo. Don't you think he would be *proud*?"

He stared at her. "No. He would not be proud."

"Why not?"

"Because he said I'd never make anything of my life if I stayed here, so he'd have to eat crow, and that's not his favorite meal."

Leo rarely spoke of his father. The fact that she rarely spoke of her parents was a thread they had shared. But his father was alive, and clearly a sore point. Speaking of him now brought the vulnerability to his stare that got to her every time. Parts of his past were as dark as his eyes.

Remorseful, she reached for his hand. "I'm sorry. I didn't mean to push."

"You did," he said flatly. "It's been in the back of your mind."

"Maybe, but it isn't my business."

He didn't answer, simply continued to stare at her in a way that said it was her business, because whatever they had was growing deeper by the day, so they had to know each other better if they had a prayer in hell of understanding why he wouldn't leave Quinnipeague and she couldn't stay.

So much unspoken. Charlotte knew it, too. A cop? Amazing. "What do you hate most about him?"

He finally blinked, took a breath, lowered his eyes to their linked hands, seeming to take comfort in them. "That he never came here.

Like it wasn't worth his time." He studied their fingers, woven so well it was hard to tell whose was whose.

"He must have been here when you were conceived."

"It happened there."

"How do you know?"

He met her gaze. "When I realized I didn't just sprout like her plants, I asked Cecily."

"At which point, she explained the facts of life?"

"Oh no. I got those from other kids. Took a lot of crap for not knowing. Not that they knew much. They knew nothing about the beauty." Lifting their hands, he separated out fingers enough to kiss hers.

And again, her heart clenched. He could do this as no other man ever had—could turn distance into something utterly sweet. Or maybe it was his way of expressing love, because she sensed that he felt that, too.

"I'm sorry," she said again. "I can be a bitch."

"Not all the time." He smiled his tough-guy, poignant smile.

She lingered on it a minute before sliding a discouraged glance at the phone. "I tell myself that I'm just the messenger. They tell me they want the cells, I make a call, that's it. Only it isn't. Each step of the way, I care what happens." She thought about the moment. "And then there's the cookbook. I expected Nicole to be gone a week. You're right. I haven't written much."

"But you knitted." The yarn bag lay on the floor. Having gotten the knack of the cables, she was nearly done with the second sleeve. "Who's it for?"

She sighed. "Me. I guess. At least, the process is. I feel better when I knit. Like you do when you whittle." Totally the process for him. Though he never seemed to finish anything, he wasn't bad at it. She could always tell what he was trying to make.

His expression turned wry. "My alternative isn't wandering around aimlessly."

"Do I do that?"

"Sometimes." He gave her hand a little shake. "Why don't you call her? Be honest. Tell her the wait's killing you."

She considered doing that. "But if Julian is there, she wouldn't be able to talk and, besides, my impatience is petty compared to what she's living through."

Leo tipped back again, though nowhere near as nonchalantly this time. He looked like he wanted to help but didn't know how. "You're a good friend," he finally said, which did help, as did a reprise of that poignant smile, not to mention the rest of him. His hair was tousled, his eyes intimate and direct. He wore his black gym shorts and a tank top that showed a little chest hair and a lot of shoulder. He was barefooted, which seemed to be his preference, though she was barefooted now herself. The day was warm. The French doors were open; the ocean rolled in on the shore less than fifty feet away, directing the sweetest of salt scents their way.

Taken as always by both it and him, she wheeled her chair around so that she faced him, slipped her hands up his thighs, and sighed.

"What?" he asked in amusement—because he could read her thoughts, which were lewd. What with the splayed way he sat, the shadow on his jaw and the engaged look in his eyes, he was good enough to eat.

But she had already done that earlier.

Sex with Leo continued to amaze. And the amazement wasn't hers alone. A lot of what they did was new to him, too. They were well suited to each other in this regard.

But sex couldn't sustain a relationship. And it didn't work long distance. Having been on Quinnipeague for four weeks, she had another four to go. Then Paris. Which she loved. Then Tuscany. Which she loved.

She sighed again. "Can we do something?"

He smirked. "That?"

"No. Like sail."

He thought for a minute. "How about Jet Ski?"

She eyed him askance. "I do not see a Jet Ski at your dock."

Hauling her up by the armpits, he kissed her firmly on the mouth and said, "Being a best-selling novelist has its advantages. People are eager to please. I know one we can borrow. Interested?"

In a distraction? "You bet."

Zooming around the island on a Jet Ski was a fine distraction.

Same with having dinner at the Chowder House, which meant confirming what most Quinnies already knew about their being involved. Even Dorey Jewett's arched brow, less warning than intrigued, gave Charlotte a warm feeling.

And making love on the sand that night? Lying naked under the stars afterward? Washing the salt off in his Jacuzzi, then making love all over again in his bed?

Distractions all, but finite. Wednesday came soon enough, and Charlotte woke up worried. That was when Leo led her through the garden and into the forest. He spent a few minutes searching before Bear sniffed it out, at which point Leo knelt and pulled back a mass of fern fronds to reveal low clusters of what appeared to be red four-leaf clovers. They looked oddly mystical.

"What *are* they?" she asked, squatting beside him.

"I don't know. But they make wishes come true."

"Seriously?"

"That's what Cecily said. She hid them around the forest."

More than happy to set reality aside a bit longer, Charlotte was charmed. "Make wishes come true, huh?"

"That's what she said."

"Like regular green four-leaf clovers?"

He shrugged.

"Then you don't know for sure?"

"If they work? Cecily claimed they did. She only gave them to very special, very loyal friends, and they don't talk." Picking one, he held the bud by its tiny stem. "Close your eyes and make a wish."

Charlotte closed her eyes and wished for Leo. Then she looked at the bed of petals. Regular four-leaf clovers were one in ten thousand, but when it came to red, there had to be hundreds in the clump. "Can I make more than one wish?"

Tucking the first clover into her tank top, under the lace of her bra, right by her heart, he picked another. "Close your eyes."

She closed her eyes and wished for a cure for MS. "One more?" This time, she wished for Nicole and Julian to live happily every after.

She now had three petals tucked in her bra, but when she went to remove them, Leo covered her hand.

"They have to stay with you for three days."

"On me?"

"Or in a pocket."

"What happens after three days?"

"They dry up and die. By that time the wish is either rooted or not."

Charlotte eyed him skeptically. "Are you kidding me?"

"Would I risk Cecily's wrath by lying?" he asked, fully serious.

No. She guessed he wouldn't. Still, red clover that made wishes come true? "Could I take a little clump and plant it in Nicole's garden?"

Leo looked like he was about to refuse. Then he paused, frowned. "I guess you could. The valerian is still alive." He held up a hand, *stay,* and loped off for a trowel and pail.

Charlotte planted the clover with care, encircling the small patch with wire mesh so that one of the Mayes men didn't mistake the clover for weeds and pull it out. She tamped the soil a final time, watered it, then went inside to clean up. Taking the petals from her bra, she showered, dressed in a clean tank and shorts, and slipped them into her pocket. They were wilting, much as ordinary clover would do. She wasn't sure they were magic at all, but could she risk it and throw them away?

* * *

The ferry was due at two and, sure enough, several minutes before that it appeared on the horizon, etching a *V* of foam in the waves. Reaching the pier, it turned and slowly backed in.

Of the half dozen passengers waiting at the top of the ramp, Nicole was the most stunning. She wore white capris, a turquoise silk blouse from her Philly stash, and a multicolored scarf, just taken from her hair, which, with just a touch of the wind, looked as chic as ever. Eyes on Charlotte, she waited until four others debarked before starting down.

That was when Charlotte saw Julian. Startled, she caught her breath.

But of course he would come. He would want to talk with her, which she didn't particularly want, which was likely why she had blotted out the possibility and why Nicole hadn't mentioned it. Not that Nicole had mentioned much.

Ten years, four of them ill, had aged him. He still stood straight, and was trim and well dressed. But leaving the ramp, he walked with a deliberateness that wasn't quite natural, and he looked exhausted. That didn't keep him from staring at her with a handful of questions and a glint of accusation.

The accusation hit her the wrong way. This was the first time she'd seen him since learning she was pregnant—and he was accusing *her* of something? What about *him*? While he had been enjoying newly married bliss, she had been dealing with loneliness, fear, and pain. *Why hadn't he worn a condom?* A responsible man would have done that, drunk or not—or so she had reasoned quite unreasonably when life had seemed dark.

Once the baby was gone, she had put the anger behind her and moved on. Now it roared back.

What to do? She touched a cheek to Nicole's in token greeting. But Julian? What could she bear? A nod? A handshake?

Following his lead, she did nothing. Ignoring him as best she could, she took Nicole's bag and carried it to the car.

* * *

Her anger eased during the drive to the house, but not without great effort and ongoing internal monologue. *It's over, Charlotte. Let it go. You were the one who chose to freeze cord blood. Focus on that.*

Julian rode shotgun for the sake of legroom, but Nicole proceeded to fill what would have otherwise been an uncomfortable silence by leaning up between the seats to talk to him about seasonal changes. Charlotte might have asked her to put on her seat belt, if she hadn't been so grateful to have a head between Julian's and hers. Each time she felt his stare, she wanted to shout, *Yes, I had your baby and gave her away, but you were married and I was alone.* Each time, she returned to her mantra. *It's over, Charlotte. Let it go.*

Anger and guilt mixed in waves, building on an awkwardness that neither the ocean air that blew through the open windows nor the bursts of coral and red flowers that lined the route could touch. As soon as they had settled in at the house, with Julian on the patio and Nicole searching the fridge for dinner-makings, Charlotte approached her.

"Would you rather I not be here? I could stay at Leo's. That way you'd have the house to yourselves."

"What would you rather?" came a distracted reply.

"I asked first."

Nicole rifled through the vegetable bin, then the freezer. "He needs red meat," she murmured, straightening with one hand on the refrigerator door and another pushing up the back of her hair. "I want fresh everything. I'll go back to town."

"I'll go," Charlotte offered, perhaps a bit too readily, but if she couldn't get answers, she needed an out.

Letting the fridge close on its own, Nicole went through the kitchen door to the garden. Following her for a shopping list, Charlotte found her bent over the valerian.

"These are doing well," she said, putting her nose to the petals and inhaling. Still doubled over, she peered up at Charlotte. Her distraction was totally gone. "What did it feel like seeing him? Be honest with me. I need to know."

Oh, she did. It struck Charlotte this was why Nicole hadn't given her fair warning that Julian was coming. She also suspected that he hadn't known she would be at the pier. Nicole had wanted candid reactions.

Like Charlotte could hide hers? "It did not feel good," she stated.

Nicole studied her with sharp green eyes. "Worse than during the wedding?"

"Way worse. I mean, hell, he was looking at me like I was an ogre, but it wasn't like I did this on my own. He was careless—"

"I thought he was drunk."

"Drunk *is* careless," Charlotte cried, not caring if Julian heard. "He's a fine one to be accusing me of *anything*. I was the one who took the hit for that night—and since it nearly killed our friendship, you did, too. *He* got off scot-free. I didn't have to mention those stem cells, Nicole. If he wants to use them, he should be damn grateful I did."

Nicole was taken aback. "I hadn't realized you were angry."

"Yeah, well, seeing him brought it all back. So there's your answer." Taking the lavender for herself, she leaned in, closed her eyes, inhaled, calmed. When she straightened, she felt better, not that she regretted the outburst. Catharsis had value on many levels. "Besides," she went on, in answer to Nicole's question, "during the wedding, we could ignore the whole thing. Now we can't." *It's over, Charlotte. Let it go.* "Does he want the cord blood or not?"

With a last inhalation, Nicole stood. "Yes. He wants it. We're here because he needs to rest first. He fights the fatigue, but it's constant, and you saw how jaundiced he is. The neurologist put him back on safer drugs. He needs to stabilize and regain strength before the other."

The other. Charlotte tried to interpret her tone, but this Nicole wasn't as transparent as the old one. So she asked, "Are you still against it?"

"Terrified," Nicole cried. "I mean, have the two of us signed his death warrant?" Seeming desperate for comfort, she eyed the flowers. "But how can I tell him no, when it means the world to him?" Her gaze wandered, stumbling into the fenced-in patch. "What is that?"

"Red clover," Charlotte said, explaining the how and why of it as she approached. Picking a single leaf, she offered it to Nicole. "Make a wish."

"You believe in this kind of thing?"

"Don't you?" Charlotte asked in surprise, because where gullible went, Nicole usually led the pack. "This is a Cecily thing."

Nicole let out a breath. "I've grown up. I don't believe like I used to." But she was eying the clover with something that looked suspiciously like longing. Finally, grabbing the tiny leaf, she said, "Screw that. I am in dire need of a wish," and closed her eyes tightly. When she opened them, she seemed calmer.

Taking advantage of that, Charlotte repeated her original question. "Should I stay with Leo while Julian is here?"

"Were you with him while I was gone?"

"Back and forth."

"What do you see in him?"

"There are times when I haven't a clue. He has serious baggage."

"But you're spending nights with him."

"I *love* him."

Nicole's green eyes widened. "Seriously?"

Startled by her own admission, Charlotte considered the words. Thinking them was one thing, saying them aloud another. Forcing herself to breathe, she said, "I guess so."

"But you're leaving in four weeks."

"I know."

"And he won't leave."

"No."

Shifting to the adjacent topic, Nicole asked, "How's work going?"

"It's going."

"What's left?"

Charlotte reeled off the list. She tried to make light of its length, but with most entrées and their related interviews still not done, not to mention intros, connectors, and closings, there was lots to do.

Nicole let out a frightened breath.

"We can do it," Charlotte assured her.

"But I may have to leave again," she warned. "If the doctor wants Julian in Chicago, I can't let him go alone. Should I ask for an extension of my deadline?"

"No." An extension wouldn't help Charlotte. She had to be on a plane in four weeks. "I'll make it happen if I have to pull all-nighters the whole last week," she promised. This wasn't only about work ethic. It was about atonement and redemption.

That said, three was a crowd. Tension between Julian and her could make for uncomfortable days. "I'm happy to work at Leo's."

"No," Nicole said, suddenly decisive. "Work here. Julian needs to talk with you, anyway. You're one of the reasons he came."

Julian didn't seek her out until the next morning. Charlotte had already been into town for an interview and was at the patio table, typing it up on her laptop, when he emerged from the house. Wearing surprisingly stylish cargo shorts and a wool crewneck sweater—Nicole's doing, she bet—he looked marginally rested.

Deliberately, she finished typing her thought. Then she sat back in the chair and waited. He owed her something after all she'd done for him.

"I'm sorry," he said wisely, conscious at some level of her anger. Nicole's doing, too?

"Do not judge me," she warned softly. "My sympathy for you only goes so far."

He glanced at the nearest lounge. "Do you mind if I sit?"

She moved her head. *Whatever.*

He stretched out, crossed his ankles, and pushed his hands into his pockets.

And since he had opened the dialogue, Charlotte was only too happy to take part. "The last thing you should be is angry at me," she said. "I did what I had to do. I wanted Nicole to be happy."

He sat, seeming deep in thought. As she watched him, she wondered for the gazillionth time how she could have ever been in his arms. She felt no physical draw at all.

Finally, he said, "I had no idea." About the child.

"That was the point. I never wanted this to spoil your marriage."

He made a sardonic sound. "Funny how health issues can trump most else."

He didn't have to elaborate. Annoyed as she was—unsympathetic as she wanted to be—Charlotte hadn't missed the tremor in his hand when he ate or the way he favored his right leg and too casually touched the backs of chairs to steady himself when he walked past.

"Did she look like one of us?" he asked quietly.

Feeling a twist of the old pain, Charlotte was somber. "I don't know. She was covered with gunk. And I was crying, so everything was blurred. They took her away right after that."

"Did you ever regret it?"

"Of *course* I regretted it. She was my child, my baby. But keeping her would have been wrong. I thought it then, and I think it now." She was clutching the wrought-iron arms of the chair. With a conscious effort, she relaxed her grip. "It's done, Julian. You can hate me forever, but she has a happy life."

He still seemed troubled. "Did you ever think about looking for her?"

"I'm not allowed to do that. Nor are you." She glanced up at the pergola with its lavish canopy of small, peach-colored roses, but their fragrance failed to take her to a happier place.

"Even just going to her school and watching her on the playground without her knowing?"

She struggled to stay composed. "What I'm *saying*, Julian, is that letting them take her from my arms was the hardest thing I've ever done, but she isn't mine anymore. Do I wonder sometimes? I wouldn't be human if I didn't. But to spy on her, then walk away a second time?" She gave a slow headshake.

"What if she comes looking for you someday?"

"Please. I can't go there. This isn't about the baby. It's about the cord blood."

"That's fine for you to say," he argued with an anger of his own. "You've had ten years to come to terms with it. I haven't."

He stared at her. She stared back.

"Does she know about the stem cells?" he finally asked.

"I doubt it."

"If she needed them and her parents came to you, what would you do?"

"If I had them, I'd give them. If they've already been used, I can't."

"Is she well?"

"I do not know. There is no contact at all. Nothing."

Seeming to finally get the point, he stared at the ocean again, before meeting her gaze. "How do you retrieve the cord blood?"

This was better. This she could handle.

Then again, perhaps what she felt was relief. Venting her anger at Julian gave a kind of closure to that night on the beach. What came next was part of moving on.

"I call. The bank will overnight whatever you need. They froze separate one-milliliter samples for the sake of matching. They also did DNA testing when the cord blood first came in."

"Is that standard?"

"I don't know about other banks, but it is for this one. They use the results for identification purposes as much as anything, kind of like a serial number. So if you doubt she's your child—"

He waved off the possibility.

Grateful for that at least, Charlotte mellowed. "You should know, Julian, that I hadn't planned on telling Nicole any of this."

He swallowed. "It worked out. We're stronger, she and I."

"I'm glad. She's my best friend. I would do most anything for her sake."

He took a deep breath and raised his eyes to hers. "Then it's time. I want the cord blood. Will you make the call?"

Chapter Twenty-four

Singling out the small rectangular tag from others on her key ring, Charlotte called the number there and gave the necessary information. After a follow-up fax to confirm her identity, the cord blood was on its way to Chicago.

And what was there to say then?

Julian had already been in touch with the doctor, but called back now with shipment details.

Nicole sat beside him on the patio, looking like her heart was in her mouth as the arrangements were defined. She left him only for the minute it took to go to the garden, pick another clover, and return.

And Charlotte? With her part done, she headed for the beach and walked until she found a sheltered rock. Nestling in, she hugged her knees and stared out. Under a steady wind, the ocean was a mass of whitecaps that hit the shore in a reverberating rush, all wet and mired with spume. But she didn't feel the wildness inside. She wasn't upset. Nor was she gratified, though. And she certainly wasn't smug. Sitting alone with granite at her back, cold sand under her butt, and the wind whipping her hair over her face, then away, over and back, hiding then exposing, she wasn't sure what she felt at all.

"You okay?" Nicole asked, seeming surprisingly strong against the elements in her jeans, sweater, and thick-wrapped scarf.

Charlotte felt a prick of annoyance. She had left the patio to give Nicole and Julian private time. But this was hers. "Everything good back there?" she asked in what was, in essence, a polite dismissal—as in, *unless you need me, please leave.*

"I guess. Once Hammon gets the cells, he'll start work in the lab."

With a brief nod, Charlotte returned to the sea, but the hint must have been too subtle, because rather than leaving, Nicole began to talk.

"Once the cells are thawed, Hammon has to select out the regulatory T cells. They're the ones that hold the secret to a cure, and you only find them in umbilical cord blood. Know why? A baby may not be compatible with its mother—like, different blood type or whatever. Regulatory T cells make it possible for the baby to thrive in the womb regardless of that. This is the same reason you don't need a perfect match when you do a transplant using regulatory T cells. They're like magic bullets. We're just beginning to understand the kinds of illnesses they may help."

Holding her hair back on the side farthest from Nicole, Charlotte glanced up as a seagull flew past, but it was another subtle gesture missed.

"He cultures the T cells and expands them," Nicole went on. "I mean, the numbers are ridiculous. He may get a few million from the original sample and then expand them in nineteen days to, like, a thousand *times* that, so he'll have enough for an adult transplant. This guy is good, Charlotte. This is all research for him, so he'll keep track of every little detail. He's going away in September, so he wants to do the transplant by the middle of August to make sure he's around for two or three weeks afterward to be sure Julian's okay."

She was trying to sound confident, like this was all just another medical procedure, and she wanted reassurance. But Charlotte wasn't in the mood to coddle her. Pushing up from the rock, she said, "I think I need to walk," and set off.

"Want company?" Nicole called, sounding frightened.

But Charlotte tuned that out. "No." She didn't understand what she was feeling, she only knew she didn't want Nicole around.

Walking toward the tail of the island, she crossed patches of sand, skirting boulders and low rocks. She stopped when she reached the spot where she had been with Julian. There was no pain from that memory now. Nicole knew what had happened and was benefitting from it.

But Charlotte felt pain from something. Trying to figure it out, she stood for a time, oblivious to the punishing wind, before continuing on.

As she neared Cole land, the route roughened. Boulders were larger at spots, spilling at length into the sea. She debated swimming around them. Hell, she was wading in and out of the shallows already, and with the gush of the incoming surf, her sneakers and lower jeans were wet. If the rest of her got wet, too? She would dry.

That said, she wasn't suicidal. The water was wild, the depth of the rocks unknown, and undertow a possibility. So she turned inland, climbing up over granite, plodding through heath and thick grass, then scrambling back down when sand reappeared. Two, three, four times she did this, the last being the hardest. Here was the forested patch bordering the spot where she first swam with Leo. The boulders were more jagged here, the woods dense. She stumbled over roots and tangled underbrush, and scrabbled on all fours over the trickiest rocks before reaching sea level again.

The beach where they had made love was a puddle. Splashing through, she continued on over a floor of stones, over a last granite patch, through the overhang of trees and around the curve to the tip of the island and Leo's house.

The office door was open. He would be working.

But she didn't go in. This wasn't about him. It was about feelings that disturbed her but that she couldn't name, and about needing to be at the most soothing spot on Quinnipeague.

So she walked all the way to the end of the dock and sat cross-legged with her elbows on her knees. The ocean was as wild as before, but the last outcropping of rocks over which she had climbed was a natural breakwater, calming the surf at the dock. In keeping, his boat rocked gently against its lines.

No, this wasn't about Leo. But she didn't feel the full effect of the soothing until his footsteps vibrated on the dock.

Bare feet was all she saw. He scratched the top of her head, then leaned over her. "You okay?" he asked just as Nicole had, but with an entirely different effect. Lowering her face to her knees, she began to cry.

"Hey," he whispered, lowering to his haunches. His hand slipped to her nape, stroking gently, but he let her cry.

In time, she took a ragged breath and, wiping her face, raised her head. "Oh God," she whispered, embarrassed. "Where did that come from?"

He didn't answer, simply sank down, folded his legs, and faced her.

"He wants the stem cells, so I made the call," she said, looking anywhere but at him. "I should feel pleased that I was able to help. Or relieved that it's done." Her eyes filled again, her voice high and broken. "So why do I feel so . . . nothing?"

"Empty."

She pushed her fingers against her eyes. "Yes."

"They were yours all this time, Charlotte. Now they're gone."

"But it was just blood, frozen away in some anonymous repository."

"It was a link."

"I gave her up. I've been just fine without her."

"It was a link," he repeated quietly.

Chin in her hands, fingers spread over her face, she admitted a soft, "Yes." And now the link was gone. "But that isn't why I kept them—" She caught herself. "Or maybe it was and I didn't know it? Why else would I be upset now?"

Unfolding his legs, he turned her and pulled her close. With her back to his front, he cinched her in with his arms, but the quiet of that only lasted until she looped her fingers around his wrists.

"Jeez," he breathed in horror, "what in the hell happened to your hands!"

She straightened them, only then seeing the scrapes. Some were a superficial white, some more pink, others outright crusted with blood. "I had to hike to get here. It was either that or swim."

"You couldn't *drive*?"

"And spoil my dramatic departure from the house?" she asked, self-mocking. "Absolutely not."

"Let's get those cleaned," he said, but when he started to stand, she clamped her arms on his to prevent it.

"Let's sit here. Just a couple more minutes, okay?"

After a healthy disinfecting with sage soap and a cup of passionflower tea sipped for calm, Leo dropped her back at the house. Nicole was at the kitchen table with her laptop, eyes on the door in anticipation when she came through, but she didn't speak, for which Charlotte was grateful. The cells were gone. Nothing Nicole said could bring them back.

Determined to move on, Charlotte asked, "Are you blogging?"

"Just finished. There was an interesting piece in today's *Wall Street Journal* comparing farm-raised and wild salmon. Readers always wonder. So I talked a little about PCBs. I mean, we don't know exactly how harmful they are, but they're definitely there in farm-raised fish. Right now, I'm writing the introduction to the chapter on FISH."

Charlotte heard nervousness in the chatter. But if the talk was of fish, she could bear it.

"No PCBs here, it's pure sea-to-table," Nicole went on, "but I want to change the name to SEAFOOD. A lot of people think of FISH as white fish or fish with a soft skin as opposed to SHELLFISH, like lobster and scallops. But I don't want two separate chapters. SEAFOOD covers it all, don't you think?"

"Yes."

She frowned, thoughtful. "That's actually a good idea for a blog—fish versus shellfish, what each includes and why. Cookbooks sometimes confuse the two, but they really are different."

She babbled on, definitely nervous energy, Charlotte realized. She would be second-guessing the stem cell route, wondering if these weeks would be the best she'd ever have with Julian again and whether he would be functional after this treatment was done.

Had Charlotte been the frenzied type, she might have babbled, too, though not about fear for Julian's health, and not about losing the cells. She understood herself more now, and while she hadn't expected to feel buyer's remorse, it was what it was. Leo had said it; those cells were a link. Gone now, she had to let go.

Her own nervous energy was quieter, and it had less to do with UCB cells than with time. She was leaving in four weeks. The comfort Leo had given her just now was sweet, so sweet, and perfect for her. She would never find it in another man. She had been around long enough to know that. But it was the same old same old. He wouldn't leave and she couldn't stay. What to do?

"Hel-lo?" Nicole called softly.

Charlotte blinked. "Sorry. What did you say?"

"I said we need to brainstorm. I am freaking out about what we have left to do in a very short period of time, and the only way I can see us getting through is to make lists and assign dates and put everything on a schedule. They want a completed draft by August fifteenth, but I don't even think I'll be here then. Can we redo the schedule to speed things up?"

We just spent two hours with a calendar, Charlotte e-mailed Leo later that afternoon, while she was organizing the interviews on her laptop. *Made an accelerated outline for the rest of the cookbook. She printed out four copies of the schedule—one for each of us to keep in clear sight, one for the note board in the kitchen, one for her purse. Nicole likes organization.*

Too much? he wrote back.

Maybe, but who am I to judge? I slipped through Yale on the seat of my pants, while she graduated magna from Middlebury, so clearly this works for her.

I didn't graduate from college. I didn't even go.

And look at you now, Charlotte replied, knowing he was testing her to see if she cared. *You're more successful than any of us.*

That was beginner's luck. I'm writing squat today.

Because you were busy playing shrink. Thank you, Leo. You helped.

Anytime, Charlotte. Another session tonight?

Charlotte wanted to be good. That meant trying her best to be attentive to Nicole, perhaps out of guilt for still feeling annoyed, more likely because the cookbook was her project, too.

That said, the time issue loomed. *Be there at nine,* she e-mailed.

Late dinner?

I'd like that.

Leo knew how to cook. His offerings were simple, like the strip steak he grilled that night, but he had a wicked way with herbs. Not that she was surprised, given his background. Still, the sight of his lean, long fingers expertly wielding a chopping knife in his new, relatively sleek, definitely state-of-the-art kitchen was such a contrast from dirt-crusted ones wielding a hammer, callused ones hauling up sails, and literary ones typing a book, that she found herself watching him in awe. Barefoot, he wore jeans and an open-neck shirt. When she found herself imagining how well he would fit into her Brooklyn neighborhood, she determinedly dragged herself back to the reality of the moment—which was tarragon butter, freshly drawn and dribbled over the steak, served with a salad that contained chives, basil, and a slew of other herbs she couldn't name.

"You know parsley," he said and pointed in turn at dill, marjoram, and arugula.

"Arugula? Huh. With these others, it looks like an herb."

"It is an herb."

"I thought it was a lettuce?"

Midnight-blue eyes were indulgent as he shook his head.

"Do you grow it in your garden?"

Amused, he nodded.

She took another taste of the salad. The dressing was a simple blend of olive oil and lemon juice that she had watched him squeeze. He had added fresh-ground pepper, but no salt. The salad didn't miss it. "Can I have this recipe for our book?"

He shook his head no.

"Even if I keep it anonymous?"

Another headshake. "You'll get other recipes like it. Herbs are a Quinnie thing."

You were right about that, too, Charlotte texted from town the next morning. *I just interviewed Carrie Samuels, and she gave me three different herb salad recipes.*

Three? he typed back.

Parsley, mixed herbs, and fennel.

Fennel. Good one. Why were you interviewing Carrie?

Age. And family. She's younger than me but with six siblings and four times that in aunts, uncles, and cousins, she has very deep roots. I envy that.

You envy roots?

Yeah. I don't have any.

Roots can be shackles.

Her thumbs hovered. Shackles were a negative, right? Was he complaining? If he wanted to cut roots and wander afield, she could help.

But he typed before she could reply, *I have plenty to share. Want some?*

She sighed. *You're the root guy, I'm the wanderlust girl. Is there a way to graft the two?* She sent the question, then, fearing a discussion that texting couldn't handle or, worse, an argument, quickly typed, *What's with fennel? Carrie gave me a quart of fennel soup for Julian. She says it's medicinal.*

It is, he replied, *but not for MS. Ask about her mother's pregnancies.*

Carrie's mother's pregnancies. That had not come up during the interview, but she figured if he had mentioned it, it was something to add. Climbing from the Wrangler, she ran back to the small cottage where Carrie lived with her husband and three kids, knocked on the door, and smiled apologetically. "One last question?"

Back in the Jeep a short time later, she typed, *Constant morning sickness, for which only fennel helped, and with seven babies in twelve years, she lived and breathed the stuff. Carrie wanted to know how I knew to ask, and while I was trying to think up an answer, she said she knew it was you. Is there something I don't know, Leo Cole?*

I used to deliver fennel to her mom. Carrie followed me around.

Puppy love?

(Snort.)

Well, Charlotte wrote, *I didn't confirm or deny that you were my source, so your virtue is safe.*

Thank you, Charlotte.

Thank you for the tip, Leo.

That afternoon Charlotte was pro-active. *I'm off to interview Mary Ellen Holloway,* she e-mailed before closing her laptop. *Anything special I should ask?*

The zucchini lady? I thought you were doing salads today.

Nicole says we have too much to do to limit ourselves.

What about the schedule?

She revised it again. So while she does a blanket sweep for recipes, I'm interviewing whoever commits to a time. She set up matching files on our computers for sorting. Zucchini is both a side and a snack. I've never had zucchini chips like Quinnie ones. (Sigh.) Why aren't you working????

Because I'm e-mailing you.

That won't pay the bills.

Neither will Next Book. *I told you. It sucks.*

When can I read it?

When it starts getting better. (Sigh.) Ask Mary Ellen about blossoms.

Blossoms?

Zucchini blossoms. She fries them.

OMG, Charlotte texted when, after two hours with Mary Ellen, she returned to the Wrangler. *ZBs are AMAZING. She just fried up a batch. Why didn't I know about them?*

Because she doesn't make them for island events. Didn't Nicole know?

She must not have, since she didn't have them on our list. Mary Ellen sent me home with what we didn't eat just now, plus zucchini bread for Julian. She knew all about him, BTW.

Quinnies talk. Are you coming over tonight?

Nicole wants to work. But I told her I'd be gone for the night tomorrow. Are you free?

They spent Saturday night grilling fat hot dogs on sticks over a fire on the beach, and, undressing only enough, made love on the sand in the embers' warmth. Taking refuge in his bed from the cool of the night, she fell asleep in his arms while he read Grisham's latest. His body heat held her close until the arrival of Sunday's sun, and when she awoke to his hands on her body, she was ready again.

"How do you do that?" she breathed after an orgasm that was stronger, deeper, more mind-blowing than any other.

His heart was thudding under her cheek. "Do what?" he asked hoarsely.

"Make me feel so much."

He didn't answer at first, simply stretched a hair-spattered leg between hers. Gradually, his pulse steadied. "Do I?"

She tipped her head back. Her fingers had left his damp hair a mess of dark spikes. The lines of his face were softer, but the midnight blue of his eyes was dark, and not with passion, she realized. She saw worry.

"What?" she asked softly. She wanted him to say it—say that he loved her and that she should stay. They weren't texting. They were together and naked. They could discuss this now.

But he simply drew her closer, kissed the top of her head, and held her until it was time to bring her breakfast in bed.

Charlotte spent Monday with Eleanor Bailey, owner of a must-have recipe for mini crab cakes as well as the biggest Quinnie heart. If there had been a formal hospitality committee on Quinnipeague, Eleanor would have chaired it. Since this was the crux of Charlotte's profile, they drove the island roads together, stopping to visit shut-ins, deliver groceries to others unable to get to the store, even prepare lunch for the four young children of a woman whose preemie baby was taking huge chunks of her time.

Eleanor was storing the leftovers from lunch in the fridge, when Charlotte's phone pinged.

S'up? he wrote.

I'm at the Blodgetts' with Eleanor. Too noisy to think. I'll get back to you. An hour later, she typed, *What a zoo.*

Lotsa little creatures?

Oh, yeah. S'up with you?

Down. Weekend sales. Just got word.

Why? When he named a new release, she wrote, *Ahh. That author's a biggie. Give him a week or two, and Salt'll be up again. Are you writing?*

No. Counting my direct deposits. Is it OK to text that? Which is safer—e-mail or text?

Text. It's through phone lines and doesn't go anywhere but your phone. E-mail sits on a server.

Why don't we talk on the phone?

Because Eleanor is two feet away.

I hope you're not driving and texting.

She's driving.

She's hell on wheels.

Now you tell me.

Can you come over later?

We're testing recipes.

Later later, then.

Absolutely.

Ten tonight? I'll be waiting between thyme and turmeric.

Turmeric. Sounds phallic.

TURMERIC, not tumescent. You have a dirty mind.

Takes one to know one. I've never seen turmeric.

It's related to ginger. The rhizome treats arthritis.

Rhizome?

Root.

That won't help me find you, she typed. "Work," she told Eleanor. "I'll be done in a sec." *Describe the above-ground part.*

It's phallic.

She snickered. *Ha ha.*

I'm serious.

So it'll look like you?

Am I phallic?

Part of you is.

Is this sexting?

No. We're not sending pics.

Want to?

Funny boy.

Is that a no?

Absolutely. You may be Mr. Anonymous, but I am not. She sent the note with a touch of resentment but quickly sent another. *Back at Eleanor's. Gotta finish up here. See you at ten.*

Nicole and Julian were upstairs when Charlotte left the house that night. She hadn't said she was going out. She didn't owe this to Nicole, especially after the ton of work she'd done for her that day, and when she crept back in early Tuesday, the kitchen was empty.

Feeling guilty for negative thoughts, she put on a pot of coffee. It had just finished brewing when Nicole appeared in her fluffy robe and slippers. Her face was bare and pale, her eyes tired. She reached for a mug. "You went out last night."

"Uh-huh."

"I heard the door."

She seemed about to say something more, but simply closed her mouth and reached for the cream—which was wise, in Charlotte's humble opinion. She had no intention of discussing Leo. She didn't want to be explaining herself, much less invite criticism.

But Nicole's worry lay elsewhere. Holding back a swath of blond hair, she said, "I know you're pissed at me, Charlotte, and I'm not sure why, but here's the thing. I jump every time the phone rings, because, if it's Hammon, we may have to leave. He needs time to culture the cells, but if he wants to run tests on Julian before the nineteen days are up, and if I'm in Chicago and not here, the cookbook is in trouble. The cookbook may be totally silly compared to MS, but it's like"—her green eyes went foggy as she tried to explain—"it's like something of *me* is in it, and I need that to make it through all this." Scowling, she pulled a handful of red petals from her pocket. Some were faded, others more fresh. "Do these actually *work*?" she asked in despair.

"Do we know that they don't?" Charlotte countered, closing Nicole's fist with the clover inside. "We're making good headway on the cookbook—"

"But mostly on collecting raw material. There's still so much left to write." She scooped her hair back again, baring frantic eyes. "Five chapters are done now, but another five are not, and that's not including the long, detailed, *witty* foreword and afterword that my editor wants."

"Write them now," Charlotte suggested calmly.

"I am so not in the mood for witty."

"You'll add wit later."

"What if I can't?" Her eyes foreshadowed the horror of paralysis, coma, death.

"Nicki. You have to think positive. Give me the chapter intros you've already finished," she suggested, coming up with Plan B there and then. "If you have to leave, I'll use those as a model and write the rest myself."

Nicole studied her, then sighed. "What a mess. I should never have signed that contract. I knew Julian was sick."

"Which is why you signed it, and it's good," Charlotte argued, taking her arms. "Don't do this to yourself. You made a commitment. It's done."

"But you're with Leo all the time."

Silence.

Astonished, Charlotte dropped her arms. "Much of the time I'm with Leo, I'm writing for you, and the rest, you're with Julian. Why do I need to hang around here? You have the cells. I paid my dues. Don't bring Leo into it."

"But I'm losing you *anyway*."

The silence this time was sadder. Charlotte felt it and let out a tiny breath. "No, Nicki. You're not. I'm just having a hard time accepting that the stem cells are gone, but I'm telling *me* the same thing I'm telling you. It's over and done. Get. A. Grip."

"This is a nightmare."

"Given everything, that is probably an understatement," Charlotte acknowledged, folding her future with Leo into the mix, "but we'll get through. Trust me on this. I've done it before."

When Wednesday dawned cloudy and cool, they headed for the island store, where the potbelly stove filled the sitting corner with the scent of glowing pine logs and warmth. Though they knew that this was the place to see and be seen, their real target was Bev Simone, who, as owner of the store and the Café, was second only to the postmaster in the daily number of Quinnies she met. Indeed, through the hours Nicole and Charlotte were there, Bev rarely sat, but talked about the evolution of the store while standing at the ready, elbows on the back of a fat armchair. When the door jangled, she was off, but she always returned with something that helped—either a recipe card, a release form, or a foil-covered package for Julian.

Quinnies were curious, but tactful. They could easily pass an hour chatting up the weather, the radish harvest, or a bad stretch of planks on the pier, but to make small talk with Nicole at this time would have been considered gauche. Likewise making a big deal about bringing a plate of brownies, a bowl of fresh-picked strawberries, or a pan of lasagna. As for their curiosity, Bev was able to satisfy that with the bits of information Nicole purposely gave.

Did you ask Bev about her arthritis? Leo e-mailed midday, to which Charlotte replied, *I didn't have to ask. She knows I'm with you and mentioned it right off. Devil's Claw. She says it's indigenous to South Africa, but, if so, how did Cecily grow it?*

Under lights inside. When I tore the greenhouse down, I stuck the roots in the ground and it keeps coming up. It's ugly as hell, but it just won't die. ARE you with me?

She wasn't thrown by the change of subject, since it was never far from her mind. *I am if you'll come to Paris.*

I don't speak French.

I do.

I don't own a suitcase.

I do.

I don't have a passport.

Apply now, and you'll have one in time.

He didn't respond to that, and Charlotte didn't see him that evening. She and Nicole worked late, and by the time they were done, she was too tired to do more than fall into bed. She woke up Thursday morning thinking about him and wanting to tell him as much. But he had to write back first. It was his turn.

* * *

You're very quiet, he finally texted after Charlotte had suffered through a long morning.

Waiting for word on your passport, she wrote. She had been able to distract herself with work, but seeing his text brought a rush of emotion. She was feeling relieved, impatient, and needy, all of it unsettling.

Why Paris?

Because it's where I'm going after here.

Why do I need to see Paris?

You don't. Her need to type kept her from throwing her hands up in frustration. *It could be Tuscany. Or Montreal, or Boston, or Brooklyn. The point is that it isn't Quinnipeague.* If he didn't see that, then she had overrated his brain.

What's wrong with Quinnipeague?

NOTHING! I just can't live here full time. Some of the time, yes. But if you can't spend some of your life elsewhere, we have no future.

There was a brief pause then. She wondered if she had gone too far. It wasn't an ultimatum, exactly.

Yes, it was.

Why are you raising this now?

Because it's been weighing on me. I love you.

The instant she clicked SEND, she would have pulled it back. Texting wasn't the right place to say this. But it was done. Too late. Gone.

Chapter Twenty-five

Charlotte had typed the words in exasperation, and no, texting wasn't the right place for a first declaration, but wasn't she stating the obvious? The man had written *Salt.* He was sensitive and insightful. He had to have felt what was going on here.

But the flow of notes abruptly stopped, leaving her suspended, wondering if she had misjudged him, fallen for an irreparably damaged soul or, worse, an empty shell. At the very least, it looked like she had scared him off.

But she refused to take back the words. *Aim high, hit high,* Bob Lilly had always said, and, emotionally speaking, Charlotte was finally doing it. She had never fallen in love—as in, aching at the sight of someone, wanting to live with him and have kids with him and to grow old with him, and being willing to modify her life to make it happen. But she felt all that now, and it *couldn't* be all one-sided. The recluse, who had once accused her of trespassing and told her to leave, had opened up. Totally aside from physical attraction, he seemed drawn to her thoughts, willing to listen, wanting to share with her what he did for fun. He had taken her into his own private space—had *let* her fall in love. He wouldn't have done that if he hadn't felt even just a teeny little bit of the same, yet with each minute that crept by, she grew more distressed.

After a full hour of silence he wrote, *I've heard that before,* at which point she gave up all pretense of working, went outside, and phoned.

He had barely picked up when she said, "I know you've heard it before, but she was not honest. I am trying to be, and it isn't only for your sake. It's for mine, too. I stand to be hurt really, really badly if this falls apart, because I feel things for you that I've never felt before. I don't want to be hurt, Leo. I can't afford to lose everything again."

"And you think I can?" he argued flatly. "This isn't easy for me, either."

"Why not?" *Say it,* she thought and held her breath. *Say it.*

But he was quiet. Finally, "Can I come over?"

Releasing a breath, she lowered her head. "No. Not now. I need to work and you need to think."

How's it going? he texted later that afternoon.

It's going, she wrote back.

Can I see you tonight?

No. I need to think, too.

She knitted for much of the night—knitted frenetically—first propped up in bed, then curled in a chair, later standing by the floor lamp when she got up for a drink of water and couldn't quite get herself to return to bed. Her fingers weren't kind to the sweater; working on the front now, she made constant mistakes. Leo was a thread worked right into the popcorns, cables, and twists, but no matter how long or hard she pondered their relationship, no new insight popped up. She loved him. How many ways could you parse that? It wasn't rocket science.

By Friday morning, she was in a snit. It must have been written all over her face when, after a whopping two hours of sleep at dawn, she awoke to the smell of coffee.

Julian was reading the paper, while Nicole made bacon and many more pancakes than the two of them would eat. "Blueberry," she told Charlotte, gesturing toward the pile. "Help yourself." Then, "You don't look great."

Charlotte poured coffee into the largest mug she could find. "I didn't sleep well."

"Did you go out?"

"No."

"Problems with Leo?"

The woman didn't have a mega-following for nothing, Charlotte thought dryly, wondering at what sounded like satisfaction in her voice. But of course, Nicole would like the relationship to implode. She had been against it from the start.

Not wanting to discuss it now, Charlotte asked, "What's on for today?"—which was a ridiculous diversion, what with printed schedules everywhere. But if Leo was off-limits, what else did she have?

Work would save her. It always had. After all, what was wanderlust if not having nowhere better to stay?

Hey, he texted at ten.

That was it. *Hey.*

At eleven, he wrote, *Are you there?*

Yes.

Ignoring me?

Trying to. I have work to do.

I'm wounded.

He had been kidding. She was not. *That makes two of us.*

Can I take you to lunch?

In town? She couldn't bear it. Or at his house? With dreams scattered everywhere and Bear—she hated dogs but loved Bear—plopped against her leg? Worse.

I have to work, Leo. Really.

You're pushing me away.

Yes, so I can work. Please respect that for a change.

For a change?

Sighing, she typed, *Delete that. It begs a whole other discussion. I'm working now. Please.*

She put the phone in her pocket, determined to ignore it, reasoning that the beauty of being uncommitted was that you didn't owe anyone anything. The downside, of course, was that you felt unloved, which was why she kept checking for notes from Leo. By the time he finally texted, her hackles were back up.

Do I have a prayer in hell of dinner? he wrote.

She might have considered it if he had texted sooner, but while he'd been taking his own sweet time, she had made other plans. *I can't. We're going to the Warrens.*

So after. I'll pick you up at their house.

But Nicole had wanted her for the evening, and Charlotte had every intention of drinking enough wine to put her to sleep as soon as she got home, thereby keeping her from agonizing over why Leo couldn't commit. *Tonight isn't good, Leo. Sorry.*

She dressed up, which by Quinnipeague standards, meant a blouse and skirt. That the skirt was short and paired with high wedged sandals made her feel like she might have been able to pick up a guy if there had been anyone there of interest. There wasn't. Moreover, the wine plan didn't work, largely because Julian's presence reminded her that bad things could happen when too much wine was consumed. So she simply smiled a lot, nodded a lot, and spoke when addressed, but her heart wasn't in any of it. Slumped in the backseat on the way home, she felt empty, which annoyed her, which was why, when they approached the house and she saw a dark blue pickup parked on the edge of the road just past the driveway, she rediscovered her spine. The instant the SUV parked, she was out and, ignoring the echo of slamming doors behind her, strode toward the house. She wasn't halfway there when a hand closed on her arm.

"We need to talk," he said.

She stared at his hand. "Not tonight."

"Don't shut me out."

Her eyes met his, but the night was dark, making them as opaque as his jaw was tight, all in a shadowed face. "Should we discuss who's shutting who out?"

"We can discuss whatever you want."

Charlotte felt she'd been doing that internally for the better part of the day, and hadn't she told him tonight wasn't good? "I'm tired."

But his hand was insistent, its grip just shy of hurtful as he drew her toward the truck.

"Hey," Nicole shouted. "You can't just drag her off. What part of *no* don't you get? She doesn't want to go."

He stopped and murmured, "Tell her to mind her own business."

"She loves me," Charlotte said.

His hand fell, his mouth went flat. "Fine. She's your future? Fine. She's all you need? Fine." He took a step back.

Charlotte's heart was curling up on itself, aching with want and need. "She's not my future, and she's not what I need, but she's my friend and she loves me, so she cares."

"I care."

"Is that the best you can do?" she shot back.

"No."

She glared at him, thinking that one word didn't do it—*two* words didn't do it—that she *knew* there was more inside him, and that she couldn't turn away from him yet.

Glancing at Nicole, she held up a hand, said a terse, "I'm good," and stalked off across the grass, across the road to the truck, around the truck to the far side, where she stopped, leaned against the door, and angrily folded her arms.

Leo was there in a heartbeat. Pinning her to the metal with his hips, he pried her arms free, anchored them over her head with one hand, and held her face with the other. His mouth tore at hers, lips angry, tongue insistent in ways it had never been before. In those seconds, he was the dangerous recluse who threatened trespassers and shot gulls for sport.

But she wanted the man she knew. So she returned his aggression with aggression, asking for more, tearing her arms free so that she could search with her hands. She was clutching his hair when his mouth found her neck, and when his hands found her breasts, she slipped hers in the back of his jeans to pull him closer. Mouth to mouth, he gave her breath, and when he began rocking hard against her, she forced her hands between them to touch him there.

"Jeeeez," he groaned and, covering her hand, held it still. Struggling for control, he leaned into her, pressing his mouth to the top of her head.

Charlotte gasped for breath, but with each breath came more of Leo. He always smelled clean, though not in the herbal way she had once imagined. He might bathe her with peppermint and sage, but he was Irish Spring all the way. Now, between that and man and arousal, she was desperate with need.

"Do it," she gritted between her teeth, pulling at his snap.

He swore when her hand closed around him.

"Here?"

"They're inside. *Do* it," she ordered, aching for him. If this was the only way they could communicate, she would take it for the sake of sheer affirmation.

Frenzied, he pushed her already-hiked skirt to her waist, tugged her panties until they tore and, lifting her legs, slammed inside.

She cried out at the sudden fullness, then again when her back lashed the truck, but if he had tried to slow down, she would have screamed. He was rough, but she wanted rough. In this, too, she gave as good as she got, kissing him, clutching his shirt, riding him fiercely until a guttural sound came from his throat, at which point she broke apart herself.

After a climactic eternity, he sagged against her, holding her up when her body went limp. And he stayed in her for a while, panting with decreasing force, before slowly withdrawing. Even then, he held her close.

The truck, the muted crash of a distant surf, their state of undress, her anger—item by item, her awareness returned. With it came the idea that he had just punished her for the hurt he had suffered years before, but if that hurt was exorcised now, she couldn't object. They needed to move on.

She let her legs slide down his until they took her weight, pressed her face to his chest, and listened to his heart. It calmed, but only to a point.

"I can't say the words you want," he finally murmured.

She didn't move. "Because you don't feel it?"

"Because I can't say the words. I don't know where to go with this."

"What do you *feel*?"

"I feel . . . like I'm doing what I swore I would never do. I told myself I would never commit that way again."

Though it wasn't quite the declaration she wanted, it was something.

"Things change."

"Do they? Look at me. I am what I am." He pushed a hand through his short, dark hair not so much in frustration as bewilderment. "I didn't expect any of this—the book, you. I'm clueless here, Charlotte. Don't know what in the hell to do about any of it."

Hearing the echo of Angie's thought, Charlotte said, "Life is like a game of cards. It deals you different hands at different times. You don't have that old hand anymore, Leo. Look at what you have now."

"I'm looking at her," he whispered. And she was lost in the midnight blue complexity of a deep, darling man.

Framing his face with her hands, she kissed him until that lean mouth softened. She didn't say anything else. He was uncomfortable with words, and she couldn't bear to spoil the moment. Back at his house, though, when she bundled up in one of his sweatshirts and they went out to the dock, she thought about the few weeks she had left.

Words weren't necessary; she could show him how she felt. She would get under his skin so that by the time she left, he would feel the loss. And yes, he'd been there before, the difference being that she was willing to meet him halfway.

It was his choice.

Nicole had remained in the dark at the front window long after the truck pulled away. Lost in thought, she gave a start when Julian slipped his arms around her waist. She leaned into him, appreciating that he'd sought her out.

Quinnipeague had been good to him. After nine days here, he was rested and stronger. He had even put on a few of the pounds he had lost while on that last dismal drug. His symptoms remained, neither better nor worse. Even now she felt a tremor in his hand, but steadied it with her own. He wasn't debilitated by a long shot. And yes, she was committed to the stem cell transplant. Hadn't she been the one to suggest it? Still, a tiny part of her wished that they were taking it more slowly, adapting to his illness, waiting before taking this next iffy step.

His thoughts were elsewhere as he rested his chin on her head. "Why does he make you so angry?"

Leo. She sighed. "Because he's all wrong for Charlotte."

"How do you know?"

"Because he's nothing like you."

"Nicki," he said with a curious laugh, "why should he be like me? Charlotte's nothing like you. You're sweet and giving. She's independent and edgy."

"Do you ever wish I was more of those things?" Nicole asked, because always, *always,* in the back of her mind, there would be an image of them together—always, *always,* in the back of her mind, there would be the worry that she was somehow lacking as a woman.

"No, I do not. I love you for who you are," he said, giving her the reassurance she feared she would need again and again.

Closing her eyes, she turned her face to his neck. These nine days had been good for them as a couple, too. They had talked, made love, slept close. Fear of the future was never far, though she knew that the stronger he was, the better he would withstand the transplant. Still, she wondered if he was living on borrowed time. She guessed he was wondering it, too. He was softer, gentler, mellower.

And forgiving. When she said that one aloud, he asked, "Where does forgiveness come in?"

"Charlotte's baby."

"It was my baby, too," he said, mellow indeed. "I can accept that she's gone, but having a shot at these stem cells is something. Charlotte didn't have to come forward with them. She didn't have to come here at all this summer."

"You didn't want her to."

"No," he said with a modicum of shame for his evasiveness then. "But it worked out. And now she deserves happiness, don't you think?"

Nicole truly wanted that for her, but something about Leo rubbed her the wrong way. "Can she get it with him?"

"I don't know. But neither do you. Only Charlotte can answer that."

She angled her head to try to see his face in the dark. "She says she loves him. After five weeks? That's all it's been, Jules. Five weeks. Did you see how rough he was tonight?"

"He wasn't all that rough. And she handled him."

"But what is he? Okay, so he lucked out with *Salt,* but can he repeat that? People may buy his next book, but if it isn't as good, they won't buy him again. And how can it be as good? The guy is *Quinnipeague,* Jules. I mean, I love it here, but living nowhere else—oh, he was in prison for a while, sorry, I forgot about that. Like he'd get material for a follow-up to *Salt* there? I mean, really. *Salt* was a place just like this. He can't repeat it. My dad would call him a flash in the pan."

"Wrong," Julian said quietly. "Your dad would have been intrigued. He'd have invited the guy over for dinner to talk about how he made his book such a success."

Nicole was appalled. "You want me to invite Leo to *dinner*? Omigod, Julian. That would be like giving Charlotte a green light to do whatever she's doing with him."

He sighed. "Baby, you are not her mother."

"But I love her, and she is being totally stupid. He's taking what he can get while he can get it."

"You may be wrong," Julian said more firmly, at which point Nicole grew defensive. She was going along with what he wanted when it came to treatment, even though it wasn't what she wanted. And still he found fault.

"Wrong, like I hover? Like I smother you?"

He pressed her lips closed. "I was taking my frustration out on you when I said those things. But you're doing the same thing now. You're worried about the cookbook and angry at your mother, and we're both on edge waiting for Hammon. But none of this is Leo's fault. You're making him the receptacle of every other bad thing. That's not fair, Nicki. It's not right."

Nicole wasn't sure if she agreed, but she didn't want to argue more with Julian. Things had been too good between them for that, and if time was short, she couldn't waste it. So she turned in his arms and kissed him. "I love you," she whispered against his lips.

She felt his smirk. "Is that meant to shut me up?"

"Yes," she mused, then reflected. "It's like right now, at this moment in time, I'm arguing with Charlotte about Leo, Leo about Charlotte, Mom about Dad and Tom and the house—or I would be, if I was talking to Mom—even Kaylin, who is doing absolutely nothing but playing in Manhattan until school starts again, and when I ask her about it, she starts in on MS, and I can't go there with her right now. I don't want to argue with you."

He didn't pursue it, simply guided her up to bed, though when he teetered on the stairs, she was the one to steady him.

She hadn't shut him up, she knew. If she were to resume the argument the next morning, he would pick up his side of it again. And maybe he was right. Maybe she was demonizing Leo for no reason. Only it did feel like a reason. And she was worried about Charlotte.

Whatever, she'd be damned before she would encourage Leo Cole.

Charlotte didn't have to encourage him. In lieu of not saying The Words, he was attentive and gentle all on his own. Whether it was prepping her for interviews while driving her into town, making the effort to talk with other Quinnies at the end-of-July potluck dinner Sunday, or making sweet love to her in the shower, the bath, the bed, or the boat—he was an interesting companion, a devoted helpmate, an exquisite lover. And the irony of that? Despite her determination to sink her teeth deeper into *him,* she was the one falling harder herself.

Nicole was the thorn. She clearly hated Leo and kept her distance the few times their paths crossed. Charlotte told herself she didn't care. But she did. She wanted Nicole's blessing. Wasn't Nicole one step removed from Angie and Bob? Wasn't she as good as a sister in Charlotte's lonely-only family of one? She was going out on a limb with Leo and wanted someone to say she was doing the right thing.

Knowing Nicole wouldn't say it, though, she didn't ask. When they were together, she focused on work, but the silence regarding Leo would have been comical if it hadn't been so sad. After all, Charlotte was with him whenever she wasn't either with Nicole or working on her behalf. She was with him most evenings and some overnights. She was brushing her hair more, using mascara more, buying a sweater, scarf, or necklace at the island store—all because she cared more about how she looked. Nicole had to notice, but she said nothing.

"She's preoccupied," Charlotte told Leo when he came to pick her up for dinner Wednesday night and Nicole turned away. "She's worried about what's coming for Julian. She isn't herself."

"Hey," he said, opening the door for her to climb into the truck, "if you're afraid my feelings are hurt, don't be. I'm fine."

If he was fine, she decided, she was done making excuses. "Well, I'm not. This hurts me. What is her problem with you?"

"Maybe her problem's still with you."

She waited until he rounded the truck and slid in behind the wheel before saying in an indignant tone, "*Why?* I could have blamed *her* for what happened with Julian. I mean, why wasn't she with us on the beach that night? Was she afraid of getting sand in her pretty little open-toed shoes?"

"She's angry about that night, about the baby she wanted but you had, about the fact that you've come through with stem cells that could save his life." He cupped her face, fingers skimming her ears. "Don't agonize over this, Charlotte. She's afraid. She can't take it out on Julian so she's taking it out on you."

"On you," Charlotte insisted. He was right about everything else.

"Okay, on me, but I have a hard skin." He started the truck. "I'm hungry."

The Island Grill was packed. As luck had it, a window table opened minutes after they arrived, adding an ocean backdrop to blue linen, a vase of balsam, and the scent of sizzling steak. Having had steak the day before, Leo ordered swordfish, Charlotte ordered scallops, and they shared—and during the time they ate, no less than three people approached to quietly ask if Julian had gotten his call. All three were longtime family friends, which explained why Nicole kept them in the loop.

None of the three were year-round Quinnies, and still *they* weren't bothered by Leo, Charlotte observed. He was well dressed, well groomed, and ten times better looking than any other man in the place, which made her wonder if Nicole was plain old envious. There was nothing rakish about Julian. Distinguished, yes. But not exciting.

Leo was exciting. At least, Charlotte thought so, but then, she knew how he could be in private. Here at The Grill he was comfortably reserved. Though he was polite when people approached, he didn't seem to care if they did. He didn't look around for familiar faces, didn't need to see people he knew. He didn't order the most expensive wine on the list, though he could easily afford it. And while he looked the part of someone comfortably disposed, no outsider would have taken him for a number-one *New York Times* bestselling author, which served him well this night.

Their strawberry-rhubarb crostini was brought to them with two spoons by no less than the owner of the restaurant. Michaela Bray never failed to startle Charlotte. While the food here was unfailingly straightforward, the fifty-something woman had pink streaks in her short, silver hair, exquisitely made-up blue eyes, and a tattoo that crept up the side of her neck. She had only last week returned to Quinnipeague after tending to a sick mother in Sacramento, so Charlotte hadn't interviewed her yet. They had set a time; she assumed Michaela was delivering their dessert herself to confirm it.

But she pulled up a chair, leaned in close, and murmured, "Don't both of you look at the same time, but there's a woman in a red blouse at the back corner table. She's media."

Charlotte looked only at Leo, who barely glanced around. Though he showed no outward change, she felt a new tension in the leg that touched hers.

"Why's she here?" he asked, eyes on Michaela.

"Her parents are renting for a couple of weeks."

"So she's not working," Charlotte said, wanting to define the threat.

"Not officially," Michaela warned, "but she let everyone know she just finished a piece on Clooney for *People.* When you get ones like that who are full of themselves, you know that if they get whiff of a scoop, vacation or not they'll grab the nearest camera. No Quinnie will let on who you are," she told Leo, "and you're not loud, so she won't hear it by accident." She stood, leaning back in for a last, "Just wanted you to know," before straightening again and saying to Charlotte in a fuller voice, "Friday at ten?"

Charlotte nodded. "I'll be here."

The crostini was the restaurant's signature dessert, but neither of them could appreciate it fully—Leo, because he was working too hard to be nonchalant, and Charlotte, because she was wondering how to help him.

When they were back in the truck, she asked, "Does that happen much—you know, outsiders?"

He backed out of the space, shrugged, and, shifting gear, set off for home.

"Would it be so awful if the outside world knew?" she asked.

"I don't know." He drove down the neck before leveling off and asking, "Do you?"

"No."

They continued on past the clam flats. "But if I go public, and readers come here in droves, I'm not the only one who suffers. Tourism is great, but not when it decimates the feel of the place. That's why Quinnies keep my secret. They're scared, too."

Charlotte had a thought. "So you're deliberately letting it die?" When he shot her a quick look but said nothing, she added, "Not really wanting *Next Book* to happen?" Still he was quiet. "What about the offers you've had? You got a privacy clause once. You could do it again."

"Don't put money on that," he warned. "My lawyer says they're hounding him. He says they want the publicity of a public appearance when the paperback comes out."

"If they want a second book enough, they'll agree to whatever you want, and if they don't, another publisher will."

"Like I have a second book to sell?" he murmured. "I do want it to happen, Charlotte. I'm just not inspired."

"What inspired you with *Salt*? That book was so rich. All from Our Lady of Phoenix?"

The epithet made him snicker. "No."

"Then what?"

"My dreams." He kept his eyes on the road.

"You didn't have it with her?" she asked in surprise.

"I thought I did. Looking back now—" He shook his head no. "It was all a dream. With her, with *Salt*. I wouldn't have chosen that ending, but the rest of it was what I'd always wanted to happen."

The fact that he didn't look at her, that he seemed self-conscious, touched her deeply. She thought of the opening line of *Salt*: *Every man wants love, if he can get past the fear of exposure.* Here was exposure. *Salt* might be fiction, but the man behind it was sensitive and complex. And then there was that *looking back now.* If he was saying that Charlotte was the one who had shown him what true love really was, this was huge.

He parked behind the house and helped her out of the truck, but then, seeming lost in thought, wandered off. She followed him into the garden, where the scent of lavender rose above the rest.

Sitting beside him on the dirt, she tucked his hand in the crook of her arm. "You don't have to hide, Leo. You have so much to be proud of."

"One thing."

"More than one. You have depth."

He studied their fingers, rubbing a long thumb against hers. "I've let you in more than anyone else."

"More than her?" Charlotte asked, needing confirmation of that at least.

"Our Lady of Phoenix?" A wry smile in the dark. "No comparison. I was young. If I'd been a little smarter, I'd have known she wouldn't stay. The signs were there. She didn't like Quinnies. She hated Bear. She was allergic to fish." He smiled sadly. "I never talked to her like this."

"The conversations in *Salt* were imagined."

"They were what I wanted a relationship to be."

We have it, Charlotte thought, but she knew that he knew.

"I've gotten better, haven't I?" he asked.

"From the uniword guy on the roof?"

His smile was as beautiful a thing in the dark as the crescent moon. "Uniword?"

"Grumpy. *Guarded*. But yeah, you're better." She paused, thinking back to those first days, and swept her chin toward the herbs. "So when are you going to let me photograph all this?"

"How about tomorrow?"

She gasped. She had been fully expecting a refusal. "Seriously?"

"The herbs need to be thinned. I'll have to get supplies at the hardware store so I can pot and deliver."

"Deliver?"

"To Quinnies who'll grow them. Now's the time to divide the plants."

"You'll let me use pictures in the cookbook?" She had to be sure she understood.

He nodded.

"For Nicole?"

"For you. Come at dawn. The light's best then."

Charlotte was dying to tell Nicole. Forget bragging rights, though she certainly could claim those. This would make Nicole feel better about the cookbook. More important, it would make her feel better about Leo.

Nicole was in fact waiting for her at the kitchen table, her fingers opening and closing around a handful of tiny red leaves. When she spoke, though, her voice was low and filled with fear.

Mark Hammon had called earlier that evening and wanted Julian in Chicago the next day.

In the frenzy of packing, last-minute instructions, and getting Nicole and Julian to the pier, Charlotte pushed everything else aside. Pictures of herbs were petty. This was life and death.

To Nicole's credit, where Julian was oddly scattered, she held it together. Only after the mail boat sputtered to the dock and he boarded, did Charlotte pull her into a tight hug.

"You are incredible," she said quietly. When Nicole's resistance gave way to trembling, she said, "You're strong. He'll do fine; you'll get him through." Holding her back, she gave her a stare. "Do not argue with me about this. You are *so* doing the right thing. I will always love you for that."

Nicole's eyes were awash with uncertainty. She was the one to do the pulling this time, clinging to Charlotte until the mail boat beeped. "You're the best," she finally whispered and, drawing back, took a breath. Putting on a confident face, she turned and climbed aboard to join Julian.

Chapter Twenty-six

As she watched the boat disappear that Thursday morning, Charlotte wondered what condition Julian would be in when she saw him again. Given the experimental nature of UCB treatment, he could end up anywhere between cure and death. Add to that the testing, waiting, and worrying that she knew would come in Chicago, and she figured her own days would crawl.

That didn't happen. Leo had put off thinning the herbs for a day, knowing she wouldn't have had the heart to leave the house that morning, so she began at the top of her to-do list, interviewing a few last Quinnies, collecting late recipes, cross-checking for releases and going after ones that hadn't yet come in. She still had most of her profiles to write, but she knew she could do that under pressure at the end.

More important first, since Nicole was stressed about it, was reading the rest. Not that it took much effort. Nicole was a good writer. Her style was warm and personal, much as in her blog, and it set a perfect tone for the book. Charlotte found herself smiling as she read, hearing Nicole's voice with its enthusiasm and pop, all the more remarkable considering the darkness in her life during the writing. She caught a few typos and removed the occasional "like" or "I mean" that interfered with the flow, though she was careful not to change the flavor.

After e-mailing those files to Chicago, she pored over the notes Nicole had left and, emulating her style, which actually turned out to be a hoot, wrote the last few chapter intros from scratch.

And then, yes, came the photos. Leo had been absolutely right about the time. The light of dawn gave a magical glow to the garden. But then, midmorning light was flattering to the taller plants, while noon light more evenly lit the leafier ones. All told, she took hundreds of pictures, both of the garden and of Leo working there. None of the latter would appear in the book; he had made that clear at the start.

"Trust me," she said at the time. "These are for me." And they were. After transferring Leo shots to a separate SD card, she spent hours editing the rest.

Once she had sent Nicole enough material to keep her spirits high, she turned to her own work and the southwest of France. She hadn't thought about the assignment in weeks, but it was suddenly rushing at her. After two nights in Paris, she would be taking the high-speed train to Bordeaux to profile the owners of a small winery. Her editor called to confirm travel arrangements and to share thoughts on the piece, after which Charlotte spent hours at her computer getting background information. She e-mailed a heads-up to her *amie Parisienne,* Michelle, with whom she would be staying at the start and the end of the trip, and since she was heading to Tuscany after that, she touched base with the editor who was paying her for that piece.

All told, she would be gone for three weeks. For the first time in her life, the thought of being so far for so long was unsettling, and she had Leo to blame. More than once as she studied him, with his dark head bowed to computer or phone, his lean legs splayed, his clever hands holding or poised, she heard the clock ticking so loudly that she considered rescheduling her flights and staying on Quinnipeague until after Labor Day.

But that would only defer the inevitable. Her work was part of who she was.

That said, with Nicole gone, she made no pretense of sleeping alone. She stopped at the big white house each day, the caretaker of this, too, and though Leo often went with her, he wasn't comfortable there. His own home was truly his castle; it was where he felt safe. And he had plenty to do. If he wasn't studying e-book sales analytics, relaying lawyer-to-publisher new thoughts on the paperback release, or surfing the Web for marketing ops, he was removing summer storm debris from his roof or cleaning the boat. He seemed to have temporarily given up on *Next Book,* though she guessed it was in his mind as he walked around in the night, dressed in those long gym shorts or nothing at all. He got regular deliveries of other authors' books and read while she slept, leaving whatever novel, memoir, or biography it was open and facedown on the bed. Always, he had breakfast ready when she woke.

Three weeks without Leo, three weeks back in the life she had known before him, three weeks with no guarantee he would want her when she returned—the fear never quite left her. And she *knew* he was feeling it, too. She could see it in his occasional lost look, and that, too, needled its way to her heart.

And then there was Bear, in some regards the more vocal of the two, who growled his way into a blissful purr when she rubbed the lean leg that he favored or stroked the silky spot on his brow. She had no idea how she could have ever thought him vicious. He was a softie, but an old one. She did worry about him—and about Leo come the day Bear died—and about herself if she learned of it after the fact.

Yes, Bear was definitely a player in her desire to stay, but so was the island. Quinnipeague in August was a lush green place where inchworms dangled from trees whose leaves were so full that the eaten parts were barely missed. Mornings meant *thick o' fog* that caught on rooftops and dripped, blurring weathered gray shingles while barely muting the deep pink of *rosa rugosa* or the hydrangea's blue. Wood smoke filled the air on rainy days, pine sap on sunny ones, and wafting through it all was the briny smell of the sea.

At Leo's, still and always, the smell of herbs rose above. She would miss this, too.

No. Time didn't crawl. It was slipping away with alarming speed.

Slipping away. Nicole had thought the same words often of late. Memories of her father, communication with her mother, interest in food and clothes and even the cookbook—she was losing a grip on the familiar.

Part of it was leaving Quinnipeague with its link to her past.

Part of it was the silence on her mother's end.

Part of it was spending hour upon hour at the hospital, where individuality gave way to utilitarian scrubs and sterile gowns.

Mostly, though, it was Julian, whose preoccupation had grown deeper since they landed in Chicago. Time and again, she found him staring blindly at the carpet, the window, or whatever TV was in view. When he opened his iPad, he was more apt to zone out on the home page than read any of the journals he had loaded there. He responded when she spoke, looking at her then, even smiling, but he didn't initiate conversation on his own.

They offered Nicole a counselor. *Often harder on the family than the patient,* they said. But Nicole doubted that. Julian was suffering emotionally. She didn't need a counselor to tell her he was terrified, but when she reminded him that he didn't have to go ahead with this, he insisted he did. In her darkest private moments, she wondered if his slipping away from her was a prelude to what might be.

Friday morning, members of Hammon's team did scans of Julian's brain and spinal cord. Both tests were brief and noninvasive. The spinal tap that afternoon was more involved. He tolerated it well right up to the recovery, which required that he remain lying down for ninety minutes in the care of a nurse who was constantly asking—hovering, *nagging*—if he felt a headache or tingling or numbness. *I'm a doctor,* he finally snapped. *I know what to look for, thank you.* Nicole might have reminded him that the woman was only doing her job, that he demanded the same attentiveness from his own team, and that doctor-patients could be pains in the butt, if indulging him hadn't been more important. Mercifully, there were no headaches, and the only tingling or numbness he felt were the same-old-same-old from his illness.

Saturday, after a morning of blood work, he began to drag—literally, his left foot worse than ever, though whether from MS or simply the enervating effect of giving so many vials of blood, Nicole didn't know. But she couldn't complain. Clearly, Mark wasn't leaving anything to chance. He wanted to be sure that every one of Julian's vital organs was functioning well before attempting something as risky as this transplant would be.

While the tests were being done, Nicole either sat in a nearby waiting room or stood alone in a corridor just beyond the room where Julian lay. And this waiting wasn't so bad. Though she knew that each test inched the process forward, she was in a personal holding pattern, wherein Julian was alive as long as the testing went on. Moreover, the fact of others tending to him gave her a break, because if Hammon was the director of the event, she was its facilitator. She had a written schedule, a watch, and a mandate to keep track of where they had to be when and get them there on time. This was no small feat with Julian spacing out.

"Are you okay?" she asked him at first, but after a few days, it was more a statement of affection than a question demanding a response. No, he was not okay. He was on a train that was picking up speed, headed to a place none of them knew. He was physically shaky and increasingly tired. He missed seeing patients, worried about his kids, and couldn't talk about any of it. She might have asked if *he* wanted to see a counselor, if she hadn't known the answer. Her Julian prided himself on being self-contained. With Hammon's team scrutinizing his every bodily function and the dignity he lost in the process, she couldn't force him on this.

* * *

Sunday was a rest day. Hammon ordered it, and Julian was tired enough not to argue, but it did mean that he had idle time in a strange hotel with little to ward off unwelcome thoughts. While on Quinnipeague, he had kept in touch with people at work, albeit with declining frequency. They knew where he was now and why, and sent notes of encouragement. But his passion in life was working with patients. Since the satisfaction of that had been taken from him, contact with colleagues was only a reminder of what he missed.

Had he been stronger, Nicole would have taken him to the Art Institute. She had never seen the Modern Wing, though she had studied much of the art housed there and might have been able to distract them both by playing the docent.

But Hammon had suggested he catch up on sleep, and he seemed exhausted.

So, leaving him with the bedroom drapes drawn, she settled in the living room of the suite to catch up on work, which was a touchy subject itself, now that he was without his. But she did have a deadline, and her work was her joy.

Focusing on immediate experience, she blogged about defying convention by having eggs, sunny-side up, with bacon and wheat toast for dinner at the hotel restaurant the night before. She talked about what made organic eggs organic, how organic bacon differed from regular bacon, and where pork could be found that was antibiotic- and hormone-free.

When Julian continued to sleep, she turned to the cookbook. Charlotte had been sending files, both edited and new, but she hadn't had the wherewithal to look at them until now. With that deadline only eleven days off, though, she read each file, made counteredits, and sent them back. *These are awesome,* she wrote in the accompanying note. Had she really not written those new chapter introductions herself? Hard to tell. *Did Michaela come through with the recipes we wanted?*

She did, Charlotte replied with barely a moment's lag. *I sent them on to New York.*

Why are you working today?

Same reason you are.

I doubt that. Unless Leo's sleeping.

She sent off the last, wondering if Charlotte would answer. Leo's name had been conspicuously absent from their notes, and it wasn't that Nicole was fishing for information. But Charlotte had been unfailingly solicitous in the last few days, texting to ask about her, Julian, the tests. A small mention of Leo seemed only right.

Not sleeping. Reading Sue Grafton, Charlotte wrote back as though discussing him was the most natural thing in the world. *He knows I want to get this done. Is Julian sleeping?*

Out cold. Two days of tests did him in. At least they're done. We get the results tomorrow. Hold your breath that Hammon doesn't see a problem that will nix the trial. Nix the trial, kill the hope, destroy stem cells that then could not be refrozen. *I lose sleep thinking about this.*

Why? Charlotte wrote back. *His liver was the only question, and those symptoms are gone. Hammon wouldn't have come this far if he didn't think Julian could go all the way. He's still culturing the cells, right?*

Right. They could be ready by Thursday. He'll have to medicate Julian first, but if that goes okay, he'll do the infusion Friday. Her stomach turned at the thought. Five days until the reckoning.

Medicate how?

He'll give him a chemo drug to suppress his immune system and lower the risk of rejection. The cells aren't a perfect match, only four out of six, which is totally consistent with his being the father, she added, lest Charlotte think anyone questioned that. *Hammon actually prefers a partial match like this. I'm not sure why. I know that if a baby inherits a genetic condition, his own cells won't help him because they would carry that condition, so maybe with Julian, it's the mismatched cells that hold the most hope. Hammon actually thinks T Reg cells may work with no matching at all, but at this stage, the FDA won't let him use a total mismatch. They want the extra precaution.*

She sent the note, thinking how much she knew about this and how little it mattered if the experiment went wrong. She had to be strong for Julian. But those dark private moments kept coming.

Her e-mail dinged again. *Is the Wi-Fi there good enough to handle a super big file?*

Absolutely, she wrote back, suddenly in desperate need of a lift. *E-mail marble macadamias, and I'll eat every one.* Warm, soft, fragrant brownies would go a long way toward covering up the smell of hospital that had taken over her life.

Of course, Charlotte couldn't e-mail brownies. Wondering what would be in a super big file that hadn't already been sent, she waited for the computer to ding again. When it did, she found a photo album waiting. She caught her breath at the title. *Cecily Cole's Garden.* Inside, one after another, were portraits of plants, some individual, some grouped into thick clusters of herbs and flowers, captioned left to right like guests at a party. Some were tall, some short, some broad of leaf, others narrow, some spiked, some feathered. They covered the spectrum of green, from olive to pea to lime. The flowers were in different states of bloom, but all looked rich, healthy, and so . . . so *Quinnipeague* that Nicole felt a wave of homesickness that brought tears to her eyes. What a comfort it was to be back there for these few virtual moments!

And oh yes. The pictures would be *amazing* in the cookbook.

Grabbing her phone, she pressed in Charlotte's number and said a breathless, "He let you do it."

"I wore him down."

"And we can use them in the book?"

"Of course. He wouldn't have let me shoot them if he wasn't okay with that."

"Do I have to pay him for the pictures?"

"Absolutely not."

"Are there any conditions?"

"Only that we not use his name. We can label them as Cecily's plants, but the implication should be that the pictures were taken all over the island. Obviously, he doesn't want readers coming to his house—not his readers or ours."

"I understand," Nicole said, willing to grant him as simple a request as that. At the start of the summer, she had feared he would sabotage the cookbook, which he could have easily done, since his herbs were at the heart of island cooking. To this day, she believed he might have been the one inhibiting those early contributors. The fact that he was helping them out now spoke either of remorse for that, his feelings for Charlotte, or generosity. If the latter, he was also forgiving. Nicole hadn't been particularly nice to him.

Admitting that to herself, she was humbled. But the sound of Charlotte's voice more than compensated. It warmed her, soothed her. She did want Charlotte to be happy. What had happened ten years ago was at this moment very far away, and totally aside from the stem cells, Charlotte had been beyond-belief-helpful this summer. These photographs would make the cookbook special.

"He's not a bad person," Charlotte said softly.

Nicole wasn't ready to fully concede that, but she offered a conciliatory, "Please thank him for me. And Charlotte?"

"Yes?"

She lowered her voice. "Pick another clover for me?"

"I do. Every day."

Nicole insisted that they have lunch in the lobby restaurant, where she had a grilled salad to Julian's short rib sliders. She took notes and snapped pictures of both, telling him that this was food for a blog, which was a good excuse for having gotten him up and out for a little while at least, but she didn't push for more. If Hammon wanted a quiet day, there was nothing more quiet than golf. Julian loved the game, and the PGA Championship was on. So they went back upstairs after lunch to watch in their suite.

Since he was with her now, she wasn't comfortable working, and since she didn't want to leave him, she couldn't shop, walk, or go to a movie. Not being a lover of golf, she sat beside him, trying to get caught up in the game, but her mind wandered.

She didn't like where it went.

Opening her iPad, she downloaded what sounded like a good book, but when she started reading, the characters didn't grab her. So she pulled a magazine from her growing collection and flipped through. Magazine articles were usually short enough to hold her attention. But she had already read the good ones.

She pulled up the pictures Charlotte had sent and showed them to Julian. Needless to say, pictures of herbs intrigued him about as much as golf intrigued her, which meant he was quickly back to watching the game.

Staying with the photographs, she found comfort in the profusion of green. That led her to think about Quinnipeague, which led her to think of the house that apparently wouldn't be sold. Her feelings about that had changed since returning to the island with Julian. In the past, her parents had always been around, but if she could have time alone there with Julian, it wouldn't be bad at all. That had been nice—or would have been, if there hadn't been a sword hanging over their heads.

The weight of that sword grew heavier as Sunday slowly ticked away.

Monday morning, with a report that the test results were good, the ticking sped up. Once Julian nodded his agreement, Hammon produced a ream of release forms.

I didn't expect that, Nicole e-mailed Charlotte a short time later. *Julian did, since his patients have to sign releases, too. He says it's as much about educating the consumer as it is about avoiding a lawsuit, but, geez, is it intimidating. You sign your life away in multiple copies. I mean, we knew about most of the potential side effects, but seeing them in print? It was bad.*

Anything would probably seem bad to you right now, Charlotte replied, making total sense as Nicole knew she would, which was one of the reasons Nicole had been quick to e-mail her. *He plans to do it Friday?*

Unless something goes wrong between now and then, but he doesn't see that happening, Nicole wrote. *I guess I'm glad, since this is what we came for. And I'm being calm. You'd be proud.*

Do you FEEL calm?

Are you kidding? I'm terrified!

Is Julian?

Nicole considered that. *Not right now. It's strange. He's been so out of it since we got the call to come here, like the reality of it hit him over the head and he was stunned. He's been in a daze. Then, as soon as he signed the papers, he woke up. Just like that, he's lucid. And eager. I thought it was just being there in the office with Hammon, but when Hammon left the room and Jules looked at me, his eyes were clear and he smiled, like he was back.*

Does he worry about the risk?

He does, but it's a measured worry. He says it's like with his own work. He's scared when he tries something new on a patient, but if he's done the testing and practiced the technique, and if he knows the risks and has plans for handling them, he's excited. That's what he says. But how crazy is it to be excited about something that could kill you?

He believes in the trial.

Oh yeah. He and Mark get what this could mean for people everywhere with MS, and it's true, only Julian isn't just "people" to me, he's my husband. The old Nicole returned. She needed reassurance. *What if it goes bad, Charlotte?*

It won't. It can't. When does he start the drug?

They just did! It's called fludarabine. The infusion takes a little while, and they'll keep him here for a couple of hours to make sure he doesn't have an allergic reaction. Me, I'm the one who reacted. I got light-headed and turned green. They told me to wait out here in the hall. I should probably go back in now.

He'll do fine, Nicki. So will you.

Keep telling me that.

I will. Xoxox

Charlotte clicked SEND and, whispering a what-a-nightmare groan, raised her hands high in the air and stretched to ease the tension from her shoulders. Suddenly Leo was behind her, leaning between her arms to read the last of the exchange on the screen. Looping her hands around his neck, she watched him read. Talk about light-headed? From this angle, she couldn't see more than a square chin and jaw and his neck, but the neck was strong. She loved that, loved how clean he smelled and how solid he felt.

When he finished reading, he held her arms and looked down. "Bet you want to be with her."

"I do. She's been hit with a lot, and she's been so strong. I know she's with Julian. But the frightened part of her is all alone."

"Why don't you go?"

"Because you won't." When his eyes grew ocean-turbulent, she said, "Would it be so bad? You could wear a ball cap and your Ray-Bans. No one would know who you are—not that anyone knows you're Chris Mauldin or even what Chris Mauldin looks like. And you'd be with me. I know my way around."

"I don't like off-island," he said in his old, flat, stubborn voice. It was an old, flat, stubborn *wall,* she decided, and, twisting, went up on her knees on the chair.

"You don't *know* off-island. You know prison. You know a construction crew headed by a bitch. You know the father who ignored you. But there's a whole other world out there, Leo, and it isn't bad. I could show you that."

His eyes were clouded. "Don't you like Quinnipeague?"

"I *love* Quinnipeague. But I also love New York and Paris. And Juneau and Rio and Oslo. I love the variety."

He thought about that, clearly troubled. "Do I bore you?"

Feeling helpless, she breathed. "*Never.* But a person can love clams cooked a dozen different ways, and still love steak." She framed his face with her hands. "Know what the best part is about going different places?"

He knew the answer. He had read enough, dreamed enough. He was certainly smart enough. But he was in the moment, a silently turbulent package of pigheaded fear. Eyes holding hers, he shook his head.

"Coming home," she chided softly. "My place in Brooklyn is tiny.

It's shabby, and it smells of whatever my downstairs neighbor is cooking, and clouds in New York aren't like clouds here. My furniture is secondhand, my refrigerator may be dead when I get back, and there are *roaches.*" Mention of those made her shudder, in response to which his mouth quirked, but she went on. "Brooklyn is nothing like Paris or Tuscany, or Ireland or Bali, but right now it's where my roots are."

He didn't blink. "Roots can be moved. Look at the herbs. We transplant them all the time."

"Right," she said with meaning and held his gaze.

Still he resisted. "I am who I am. If you loved me, you wouldn't want to change me."

Deep inside, she felt something deflate. If he didn't know she loved him after the last few days, he was thicker than that wall he had built to protect himself from the outside world. She had certainly said it enough, and not only when they had sex.

But it was test time. She let out a quick breath. "I could say the same to you."

"I never said the words," he said.

She sat back on her heels. "Right again." But he got an F. Shifting around in the chair, she rose and headed for the office door.

"Where are you going?" He sounded afraid.

"To the dock."

She barely made it halfway before he caught her arm and pulled her against him. "We don't fight. It's not who we are."

"Who *are* we?" she asked weakly.

The ocean rolled in, washing over the sand before being sucked back.

"I don't know," he finally said against her ear. "I'm trying to figure it out."

Charlotte didn't sleep well that night, but found herself obsessing over the larger picture. She felt fear for Nicole and guilt at not being there. She worried that she had inherited her parents' dysfunction in matters of the heart. And when she projected herself into the future and tried to anticipate adventure in Bordeaux, all she could think of was the weirdness she always felt the first day in a new place.

Between each thought came Leo. She imagined spending a lifetime here on Quinnipeague and realized she had a problem: She could do it in a heartbeat. While she lay here in bed, curled to his back and held there by his hands, which grasped hers in the dark, she could feel the pull of nascent roots. She had come to know the island more this summer than ever before, thanks to the cookbook, thanks to Leo, thanks even to her own maturity. She liked the people, liked the pace, liked the sweet salt air. She also liked the feel of those roots.

But there was still the rest of the world, which she loved. And the fact that she was tired of going places alone. And the realization that if downtown Quinnipeague counted for anything, she liked going places with Leo, which brought her right back to the rest of the world. She wanted to travel with Leo.

He knew how she felt, but wasn't budging. And when she was no longer here? That might get him going. He might be lovesick enough to act. Or he might just suck it up and do fine alone again, might even get another book out of it. If his writing was his catharsis. If he wanted revenge for her leaving. If he really didn't love her all that much.

The last possibility was like . . . like the pea under the mattress of the princess. And where had *that* thought come from? She had to dig back to remember. Her mother. Her mother had been into fairy tales. She would have liked Quinnipeague for that reason. With its wood smoke curling, its mystical herbs healing, and its symbiosis with the sea, it was the ultimate fairy tale.

How to fold that into real life? Lacking an answer that would work for Leo, she could do nothing but lie there and listen to the soft, steady sound of his breath.

Nicole did the same thing, though she didn't take the steadiness for granted. Hammon hadn't expected that Julian would react to the light dose of fludarabine he had prescribed, and the nurses who monitored him in the hours after the infusion had seen no cause for alarm. She was the one who had visions of sudden death, to which end she kept one body part or another—arm, leg, or hip—touching him at all times on the premise that as long as he was warm, he was fine.

She glanced at the clock: 2:27 A.M. Returning her head to the pillow, she went still and listened, but his breathing was steady.

She dozed and woke again to what sounded like wheezing, but turned out to be laughter in the hall.

She drifted off again, bolting up this time to what sounded like choking, but turned out to be the rumble of a truck on the street far below.

Charlotte's words became her mantra. *He'll do fine, Nicki. So will you.* She had Team Quinnipeague rooting from afar—lavender to calm, valerian to uplift, red four-leaf clover with the alleged ability to make wishes come true.

Nicole hadn't told Julian about those. He was a scientist. Scientists didn't do alleged.

Nicole wasn't as doctrinaire. Had she been on the island, she would still be picking that clover, still be holding it close for three days to let her wish take root. She liked knowing that Charlotte was doing it for her now that she was gone. With Friday only three days off, she needed all the help she could get.

Chapter Twenty-seven

Early Tuesday morning, Julian had a second chemo infusion, and when there was no sign of trouble this time, either, he said he was bored. He couldn't run, couldn't work. He wasn't interested in the art museum or the planetarium, and as for other options, there were limits. Hammon didn't want them going far on the chance of a delayed reaction. Nor did he want them in tight spaces where, with Julian's immune system low, he might pick up an infection.

For Nicole, finding the right distraction on a moment's notice was a challenge, which was in turn a welcome distraction. Taking to heart her mother's advice on creativity, she worked with those medical parameters and the hotel concierge, and came up with a plan.

By noon on Tuesday, in a rental car that came with a programmed GPS and box lunches, they drove to the Brookfield Zoo and, on Wednesday, the Botanical Garden. Julian's gait was more stilted both days, perhaps from the fatigue he was trying to ignore, but since they walked arm in arm, she could help. Both venues were quiet and open, with plenty to see. At night, they either watched movies in their room or slept, all of which took their minds from The Main Event, as

Nicole thought of the transplant in her sane Jekyll moments. The harried Hyde moments were when she texted Charlotte, who had a stake in this, too, and who could calm her.

Julian had no injection on Thursday. Hammon wanted to check him out a final time and review the details of the procedure with them, which precluded another day trip. So they simply walked through Navy Pier that afternoon, stopping when Julian tired but otherwise just . . . walking. They ate dinner at a restaurant that Nicole had heard about, taking care to sit at a secluded table, and watched another movie in their room, but they had more trouble this last night denying what was to come. There was a poignancy in the arm Julian kept around her. He was the one who seemed to need physical contact through a toss-and-turn night.

All too soon, it was Friday morning. As instructed, they were at the hospital by six, at which time Julian was admitted, settled in a room, and hooked up to monitors and an IV. With Hammon supervising, he took a single Tylenol by mouth and a ten-minute IV infusion of Benadryl, both prophylactic treatments of possible reaction to the T-regulatory cells. The Benadryl made him seriously drowsy, which was a good thing, Nicole decided, since she was a bundle of nerves. It was worse once the actual infusion began. She studied first Julian, then Mark, looking for a reaction from either of them to what was finally happening.

Julian was fuzzy. She saw no clues there.

But Mark? Intense. As he stood by the IV pole on the opposite side of the bed, she couldn't decide whether he was simply concentrating hard or downright frightened. He was more a thinker than a talker; she knew that. But she needed to know now if he was having second thoughts.

"Doubts?" she asked aloud.

Her voice startled him, he was that absorbed. His eyes flew to hers, but it was a minute before he raised his brows and pressed his glasses to the bridge of his nose. "I always have doubts. The process wouldn't be experimental if I didn't."

It wasn't the unequivocal thumbs-up she needed. But he had to have a feeling one way or another. "Are you worried?"

"I'm always worried." He glanced at the monitors that showed Julian's vital signs. "That's why we're watching so closely."

"I'm fine," Julian murmured sleepily.

Nicole rubbed his arm. "Mark was about to tell me that." Her eyes put the question to the doctor. She didn't care if he made it up. She needed the reassurance and wanted Julian to hear.

Hammon pushed at his glasses again and finally said, "If I didn't have faith in T-reg cells, I wouldn't be trying it. The lab tests were good. The first human trials were good."

"Those weren't with MS," she whispered.

"No," Mark confirmed. "Julian's my first."

At mention of his name, Julian opened his eyes. "How'm I doing?" he asked Mark, seeming to have drifted in and out of the conversation. Turning the arm with the blood pressure cuff, he reached for Nicole's hand.

"So far, so good," Hammon said.

With a satisfied murmur, he closed his eyes again. He looked pale but peaceful. The monitors held steady.

"Don't take my distraction for doubt," Mark said, finally opening up to Nicole. "Someone in my position is constantly reviewing a huge amount of information. The responsibility can feel overwhelming at times. Julian knows how that is. He's a risk-taker, too."

Eyes closed, Julian nodded, at which point Nicole decided that she was with two men who were either very brave or very reckless. Whatever, watching the slow drip of the cells, she was a nervous wreck. She had half a mind to ask for a little of that Benadryl herself.

They stood in silence for a time, she to Julian's right, the doctor to his left. Her eyes went from the IV, to Julian, to Mark, and back.

They reached the fifteen-minute mark; the infusion was half done.

"So, if something happens, when would it be?" she asked Mark. And it was strange. No one here was talking about the effect the cells might have on MS. At this point, it was solely about getting Julian through the treatment alive.

Mark shrugged a brow. "It could be any time—now, tonight, tomorrow. Different bodies react different ways. Some patients have no reaction at all."

But others did, Nicole knew. Stroke, heart attack, respiratory failure—these were three of the worst possibilities, but the list included dozens, running the gamut from mild to severe, all of which Julian had signed off on, as if complications were expected, as if they were perfectly acceptable. Of course, he'd had no choice. Without his signature, the procedure would have been off.

The infusion ended. Julian remained the same. Mark watched him for a while, then left to monitor vital signs from an office down the hall.

Alone, Nicole held her husband's hand. He opened his eyes from time to time, and gave her a smile, but it was small. "Feel okay?" she asked, to which he nodded each time. She poured him water and held the straw while he sipped. She poured herself a cup, but it didn't slow her own inner shakes.

After a bit, she began to feel dizzy. Not wanting to leave Julian's side, she ignored it, but it didn't ease. When the world went a milky white, she backed into a chair, hung her head to restore the flow of blood, and focused on breathing in and out, in and out. In time, she was well enough to look up again. Julian continued to sleep.

Pulling out her phone, she texted Charlotte. *He made it through the infusion. Now we wait for a reaction. Tell me we did the right thing.*

The speed of Charlotte's reply said she had been waiting for news. *We did the right thing. Julian wants this. Is he nervous?*

No. Dopey. They have him on a heavy dose of Benadryl.

When will you know if the transplant works?

Nicole took a tempering breath. She had asked the same question not only of Mark, but of various members of his team, not to mention the nursing staff, and the answer was unsatisfactory each time. *That depends on how he reacts. Seizures will mask the disease. Same with stroke.*

Why are you expecting the worst?

Because I'm terrified. So much is riding on this.

But it's done. You can't take it back. You have to look ahead. Be optimistic.

Charlotte set down the phone. She was sitting cross-legged on the single step outside Leo's office while, across the beach and in the surf to his thighs, the man himself was sanding the dock.

She had promised to help. Right now, though, she wished she were in Chicago, and it had nothing to do with messy jobs like sanding and restaining a dock. If Julian was groggy and the doctor was focused on looking for trouble, who was there for Nicole?

Catching her eye, Leo waved her over.

Raising a just-a-sec finger, she opened her contact list, selected a name, and put through the call.

Nicole felt washed out. She wasn't dizzy now, more sick to her stomach, but she hated to leave the room. Something could happen at any time. She had to be there if it did.

Julian awoke enough to ask for the TV. Encouraged, she turned on a news station, though he seemed to drift more out than in. Nurses came to check the flow of fluids from the IV, and they couldn't have been nicer. They brought him Jell-O. They brought him pudding. They even brought Nicole chowder and crackers, which she ate only because she knew she needed nourishment, though it was the worst chowder she'd ever had. Naturally, she was comparing it to chowder on Quinnipeague, where she was desperate to be.

She texted Charlotte. *Are you working?*

Yes. Just sent you SIDES and SNACKS, all done. Do NOT look at them now.

Nicole was torn, more Jekyll and Hyde stuff. While her heart was with Julian and about as distant from the cookbook as could be, Nickitotable stamping her foot, pointing at the computer, telling her to work. *Maybe tonight,* she typed. *My editor wants everything by Thursday.* She had been so caught up in the countdown to the transplant, that she had slackened off. But Thursday was less than a week away.

Your editor won't even look at it until after Labor Day, Charlotte wrote back. *Trust me. The last two weeks in August are dead in New York. Let me call her and explain. You have more than enough reason to ask for extra time.*

I hate to do that. It says something about me.

Are you kidding? Every writer is late. Deadlines are a starting date. Editors give them out in hopes of seeing something a month later.

Nicole was tempted. Six days from deadline meant six days from Charlotte's departure, after which she was truly on her own. *How close are we?*

You need to review the last of the recipes. I need to write the POTPIE intro, collect three releases, finish two profiles for SWEETS, but that's it.

Nicole tried to grasp all that Charlotte had done—and, P.S., it wasn't like nothing was going on with *her* life. There would be Leo, surely an issue for Charlotte with only six days left on Quinnipeague. And though Nicole was starting to get used to the idea of their being together, she still couldn't ask. So she simply typed, *What would I have done without you?*

You'd have gotten an extension on your deadline, and you still should. You need to read everything I've written, and you'll want to make changes. It'll be easier because the structure is there, but this is your book. Can I call your editor?

Nicole let out a shaky breath and typed, *Not yet. Let's wait another few days and see what happens.*

She sent the last, but continued to stare at the words. *See what happens.* If Julian had a stroke, it would be more than a few days before she could focus on food. Likewise, if he was paralyzed or recovering from a heart attack, and if he died?

No. Better to get the cookbook done before Charlotte left.

* * *

She spent hours that evening at her laptop in Julian's room, poring over what Charlotte had sent. Each time Julian stirred, though, she was quickly up and leaning over the bed, asking how he felt, telling him how well he was doing.

Mark, who had been in and out all day, stopped by at ten to say that he was going home for a few hours of sleep. He looked more ruffled than his usual neat self. She doubted he was often at work this late.

"Are you worried?" she whispered again, not wanting Julian to hear.

The doctor's reply was similarly low, though likely more from exhaustion than secrecy. "No cause for worry yet."

"Is this a good sign for the success of the treatment?"

He shot her a glance over his glasses. "It's too early to tell. You should probably get some sleep yourself. Can I drop you back at the hotel?"

"No. I'll stay a while longer."

"They'll call if there's a problem. You're only five minutes away."

The night nurse said the same thing a short time later and again an hour after that. By the time she said it a third time, the room lights were low and Nicole had fallen asleep curled in the chair. She jolted awake at the touch of a hand on her arm.

"He's still sleeping," the woman said, "and that's a good thing, because if he sees you here at this hour, he'll worry."

Nicole went to the bed, saw for herself how peacefully Julian was sleeping, and gave in.

The call came at five on Saturday morning. Having fallen asleep only three hours before, she was dead to the world when the ringing jarred her awake. She was a minute getting her bearings and another searching for the phone in the folds of the sheets.

"Yes?" she breathed, sitting up. She was shaking as much from being startled awake as from fear.

It was Mark, his voice tight. "His temperature spiked. I'm at the hospital now. I won't call it an emergency yet. But I told you we'd let you know if there was any change."

"Temperature spiked," Nicole echoed and swallowed, trying not to panic. "What does that mean?"

"He's having some kind of reaction. This may be the worst of it."

Or the start, she knew, pushing the sheets aside. "But you can get his temperature down, right?"

"I'm upping the acetaminophen, but I have to be careful."

He didn't have to elaborate. The fear was damage to a liver that hadn't fully recovered from the last MS drug.

They should have waited. She knew it, *knew* it. Another month, and he'd have been stronger. Another *two* months and he'd have been even stronger.

"Is he awake?" she asked, pulling a blouse from the closet.

"Yes. He says he's okay."

Of course, Mr. Cool-and-Calm would say that. Mr. Risk-taker would say this was part of the game.

Nicole was neither cool, calm, nor risk-taking. "I'm on my way," she said, and, ending the call, rushed to get dressed. Having in essence cut Mark off, she didn't know whether he would have told her to wait, that it wasn't crucial, that she should just come at eight. But it didn't matter. No *way* could she have gone back to sleep.

The sun hadn't yet risen when she was through the lobby and out the revolving door. Hopping into a cab, she hugged her bag to her chest, only marginally aware of a paler horizon between buildings to the east. In no time, she was at the hospital and taking the elevator to Julian's floor.

At first glance, there was no imminent trauma—no red lights flashing above his room, no emergency gear in sight. Mark stood just outside the door talking with two of the doctors from his team. Pushing at his glasses, he separated himself from them as she approached. She saw concern on his face, certainly fatigue, but no panic, not yet.

How is he? she mouthed. The floor was still in night mode—lights dimmer, sounds softer—but her own lack of sound wasn't so much consideration of others as pure anxiety.

"Still hot," he said quietly.

"Getting worse?"

"Up a notch."

She was still clutching her bag, needing to hold something solid with the bottom of her world shifting. "Not what we want."

"No."

And what more was there to say? Frightened, she entered the room. Julian's eyes were closed; he would still be on Benadryl, still half zonked. Flags of red touched his cheeks just above the shadow of his beard. His forehead was damp.

He opened his eyes, saw her there, and gave a vague smile. "Hey."

"Hey, yourself," she said brightly.

"What time is it?" The words were slurred.

"Early." She didn't want to alarm him with the actual time, which was five fifty. Slipping her bag to the floor, she leaned in to softly kiss his lips. They were as hot as his cheeks looked. "I couldn't sleep. How do you feel?"

"Okay."

"You look like you've just finished a run."

"Don't I wish," he murmured and held out a shaky hand for hers. He had a surgeon's long, slim fingers. She had always liked their warmth against her usually cold ones, but this intense heat was something else.

She told herself that it was the fever that was causing his hand to shake.

He closed his eyes. "This is a blip. It'll pass."

"Absolutely," she said and brought his hand to her throat. "Mark expected things like this." She glanced at the tray table with its small pitcher and half-filled plastic glass. "Is that drink still cold?" Ice had to be the way to go.

But he said, "It's fine."

And she didn't want to let go of his hand. "Are they letting you eat yet?"

"Only Jell-O."

She saw none on the tray. "Can I bring you more?"

Eyes still closed, he shook his head. If she couldn't bring him drink and she couldn't bring him food, she could at least cool his face. She ran her free hand along his jaw, up to his temple, across his brow and down. He hummed his pleasure.

She repeated the circle once, twice, three times, by which time her fingers had warmed. He was hotter than ever.

Hugging his hand to her neck, she put her elbows on the bed rail and watched him. He didn't actually sleep but seemed to hover in a twilight one step above, opening his eyes to smile at her every so often before drifting again. Nicole didn't move, not when the nurse checked him, not when Hammon checked him. She counted his breaths, reassured by their steadiness. She wasn't reassured by the color on his cheeks, though, which was flaming compared to the pallor elsewhere. When her legs tired, she pulled the chair close and, clasping his hand now between the rails, put her forehead to the cool metal and closed her eyes.

"Tired?" he mumbled.

"Mmm."

"Go for coffee."

She looked up. "For you?"

"You," he said, clearly wanting to sleep himself.

Still she stayed. She might have even dozed, vaguely knew that others came and went, but she was tired enough not to move and encouraged enough by the curl of Julian's hand around hers not to bother with anything else.

She was starting to stir, needing to stretch and use the bathroom, when Charlotte texted. *How's he doing?*

He has a fever.

As in a reaction? Call me when you can.

Rising then, she leaned over the bed. "Jules?" she whispered.

When, with visible effort, he opened his eyes, she asked, "How do you feel?"

"Okay," he mouthed and returned to wherever he'd been, but he didn't look as peaceful as he had earlier. His skin was moist, his brow furrowed; he seemed to be concentrating. Trying to control the fever through sheer force of will? She touched his cheek. He was burning up.

"I'm going for that coffee now," she said softly. "Can I bring you anything?" His headshake was small. She kissed his forehead. "Be right back," she whispered and slipped out of the room.

"I only have a sec," she said the instant Charlotte picked up. "The fever was 102 when I got here at six and it's 103.5 now. They can't control it. I want to bathe him with cool cloths, but they say no." She had just checked, frantic to do something.

"Is Hammon worried?"

"He doesn't say it in as many words, but he's not a word man to begin with, and when I talked with him a minute ago, he was down to two per response. *This isn't trending the right way,* I say. He says, *I know. Isn't there anything you can do?* I ask. *Not yet,* he says. So I'm thinking," she told Charlotte, "that a reaction means his body is aware of the treatment, but when I ask Mark if this is good or bad, he says, *We'll know soon.* Three words. Yay."

"You have a right to be upset—"

"Scared."

"Scared, but if this is the worst it gets, it isn't so bad. I'm sure Hammon's doing what he can," Charlotte reasoned and, coming from anyone else, Nicole would have shot back with a dozen arguments to the effect that Mark knew this might happen and should have had a plan, that it was a fever, for pity's sake, and if a teaching hospital couldn't deal with a fever, *it* had a serious problem, and that maybe Mark's best wasn't good enough.

But this was Charlotte, whose voice brought comfort.

"I wish you could come," she pleaded. "Any chance?"

After a pause came a soft, "I can't, Nicki."

"Because of Leo?" There. She'd had to ask.

Charlotte didn't deny it. "I only have five days left here," she said, sounding like she was agonizing. "I need this time. Besides," she hurried on, "given the circumstances, it isn't really appropriate. I still regret what happened that night. I'll always regret it."

"I don't," Nicole said, unable to hold anything against Charlotte just then. "He would have had MS with or without you. Same with this treatment. He was itching for it, and if it wasn't these cells, he'd have used donor ones. These ones feel better to me. I just want it to work, Charlotte. I keep wondering what I'll do if it ends badly. Julian has his heart set on a cure. If there's no hope, what's left?"

"If he's alive—"

"He'll be devastated. I want to criticize him for putting all his eggs in one basket, but there just isn't any other basket."

"There will be," Charlotte reasoned. "Research is ongoing. If this doesn't work, something else will. You have to keep telling yourself that."

"That's fine for me, but what do I tell Julian?"

Discouraged, she bought coffee and a muffin, and carried them back upstairs. Hammon was just leaving the room. The stark lines of his face said there was no improvement.

Setting her food on the tray table, she sat on the side of the bed where the rail was down and held Julian's hot hand in one of hers while she nibbled and sipped with the other. When she'd had enough, she pressed his fingers to her mouth, willing the scent of coffee and blueberries there. They smelled antiseptic, but his hands often did, given his work. Everything else was strange, though, from the heat of his skin to his utter stillness. She told herself that he was conserving energy, focusing on fighting rejection of strange cells in his body, but it was small solace.

His temperature continued to rise. It had hit 104 by noon and 104.5 by three.

"How high can it *go*?" she asked in a panic.

"Higher," the nurse said calmly, clearly used to fevers.

They gave him more acetaminophen. Hammon came and went, came and went, assuring her that Julian was strong enough to fight this, but she could see that he was concerned.

"Is there nothing more you can do?" she begged. "Nothing else to lower the fever?"

"Not yet," he replied but seemed disinclined to say more.

What are you waiting for? she thought frantically when he left her alone again with Julian, who continued to float, tethered to the bed by a tangle of sensors and wires and the hum of the mother machines.

Then she knew what they were waiting for—or, at least, what they feared. The humming went on, but there was something else. At first, she thought Julian was snoring and gently shook his arm. When he opened his eyes, though, she could hear each breath he took.

"Call Hammon," he managed.

Racing to the hall, she was looking around in bewilderment when a nurse, having seen the problem from her station, rushed past. Minutes later, Hammon and his team came at a clip from the computer room behind the desk.

Nicole followed them in, but stayed clear of the bedside while they listened and examined and discussed what to do. In addition to the wheezing, Julian's blood pressure had dropped, both of which raised mention of anaphylactic shock. From time to time, she heard Julian speak in a low, whistly voice, and even in spite of the sound, he was forceful. He clearly had an opinion. Nicole guessed what it was.

Separating himself from the others, Hammon joined her. "We could use steroids. They'd control the reaction. But they might kill the T-regulatory cells."

"Julian wants to wait."

"Yes. He knows the risk."

Of killing the cure. But the risk went beyond that, and in a moment of panic she could only see the other. "At what point do you opt to save his life?" she asked in a high voice.

"When we feel it's in danger. Let's see how long this lasts."

She held her tongue. Raw with emotion in a world of science, she was out of her depth.

Hammon returned to Julian's side. Feeling weak, she backed up to the wall by the door and listened as they went back and forth, weighing pros against cons with none of the emphasis she would apply. After a time, she didn't hear the words, only the awful sound of Julian's laboring breath.

It went on and on and on. She must have begun to look sick, because a nurse gently took her arm and guided her out to the hall for air. No, she didn't want water. No, she didn't want tea. She stood there feeling frightened and alone, arms wrapped around her middle in an attempt to self-soothe. And when the nurse asked if there was anyone she could call to be with her through the evening, she gave a jerky shake of her head.

Oh yes, she had friends. And family. And a following that clung to her every word.

But the friends were back in Philadelphia, thinking that Julian was on vacation in Maine. They didn't have a clue about this.

Same with Kaylin and John, both of whom should be there if their father was failing. They knew he was in Chicago consulting on a new treatment, but he had refused to tell them the rest.

And the following? They knew Nickitotable, not Nicki Carlysle.

Had her father been alive, she would have called him. He would have boosted her spirits.

Or . . . or maybe not. She didn't want to hear *Aim high, hit high* right now, and as for *What doesn't kill us, blah blah blah,* that was *so* not what she needed. She had adored Bob, but he was optimism to the point of denial. It struck her now that if he had been more proactive about his family history of heart problems, he might still be alive.

Realism was her mom's domain. Just then, she wanted Angie. They had parted badly, with ill will and ugly words. But she wanted Angie. She looked down the hall toward the elevator, willing her to emerge, aching for it.

And then suddenly there she was, a blurred image through Nicole's tears, surely a mirage. But the closer she got, the more real she was.

They hadn't talked in the four weeks since Angie had left Quinnipeague, but four weeks couldn't negate thirty-four years.

"Mom," Nicole breathed. Just Mom, and the estrangement was done.

Angie's face held only concern. When her arms opened, Nicole went there and began to weep, and those arms tightened around her, which was what she needed most. She had been strong for Julian, supporting his decision, steadying his limbs, filling in the blanks when they had time on their hands. And she had vented to Charlotte. But it wasn't the same.

Angie was her mother. Mothers were for those times when only a total meltdown would do. And tears were only the first part. After that came talk. As they sat side by side in the family lounge, Nicole poured out every bit of her fear—the rising fever, the falling blood pressure, the wheezing that could escalate to anaphylactic shock, the ominous hand tremor, the steroid dilemma.

Angie was sympathetic and concerned—but yes, realistic. She didn't pretend to have answers, simply listened and asked questions. Her presence alone was calming. It was also well-timed. Nicole was about to take her to Julian's room when Mark appeared in the lounge. "We're transferring him to the ICU," he said quietly.

She was on her feet in a flash. "He's worse?"

"No, but we can watch him more closely there."

"He's still refusing steroids, isn't he?" Julian wasn't flashy in manner or dress, but when it came to medicine, he was definitely out there. Granted, he was careful. He studied every angle. But once committed, he didn't turn back.

"He's still hoping to preserve the T-regs."

"Do you agree with him?"

"I see his point. I also see the other side. Right now, I'm torn. That's why we want to watch him more closely. If he gets much worse, we won't have a choice."

"Should I try talking with him myself?" Nicole asked and answered, "No, no point. If he wouldn't listen to you, he won't listen to me."

Mark gave her a brief smile. "You're probably right. I admire him, though. He'd rather die trying."

Die trying, Nicole thought and turned frantic eyes to her mother.

Angie stood then and put a restraining hand on her arm. After introducing herself to the doctor, she said, "Can we do anything while you move him?"

"You can take Nicole somewhere for dinner."

Since Nicole refused to leave the hospital, they went to the cafeteria, but she couldn't think of a thing she wanted to eat. She sat at a table, fingers knotting, while Angie filled a tray, paid the cashier, and set the tray neatly before her, but all she could hear-see-feel was ICU ICU ICU.

"It sounds worse than it is," Angie offered gently as she divvied up napkins, forks, knives, and food. "It's just a precaution."

"What if he does die?" she asked as she could only with Angie.

"Don't go there, honey. He's a long way from that."

But Nicole couldn't stop. If the doctors were worried enough to want intensive care, *they* were thinking he might die. She had known this was a possibility. But a future without Julian? Unthinkable. She should've told him that back in Philadelphia, should've said it on the island and again last Friday morning at the hotel, before all of this had begun. She could've made him fight harder. She would've done it, if she hadn't been determined to be strong for him herself. And now, intensive care?

"An ICU is just another room with more machines," Angie mused, taking a forkful of chicken salad. "Dr. Hammon simply wants to get as much information as he can. He's covering his bases, and I don't say that in criticism. He doesn't strike me as the type who'll let his patient die trying unless he's pulled out every stop. He'll overrule Julian when he feels the time is right." She eyed an unappetizing piece of fish before pushing the chicken salad toward Nicole. "Please eat."

Nicole picked up a roll. Setting it down again, she eyed Angie in despair. "I'm trying to be realistic. That's what this whole summer's been about. It's what this whole *year* has been about. Talk about wake-up calls. Talk about *growing up*."

"Oh sweetheart, you've been grown up for a while. Look at the last four years. Keeping all that to yourself, accepting Julian's limitations, dealing with flare-ups? And your blog? And the *book*? You don't give yourself enough credit."

Charlotte had said the same. But Nicole couldn't take credit for anything when Julian was en route to the ICU. "How does one prepare for something like this?"

"One doesn't. It's all about how you react when it happens."

"This isn't what I wanted."

"No." Her mother smiled. "But look at it this way. If you'd died at twenty-five, you wouldn't have had to deal with it."

"What an awful thing to say!"

But Angie didn't take it back. She simply straightened the straw in her diet Coke and sipped—and of course, in the silence, Nicole realized she was right. This was what always happened. Mother-daughter disagreements were, in hindsight, basically mother stating the truth and daughter taking her own sweet time coming around. That had been the case with boys and sports. It was certainly the case with Tom.

"I was not nice to you when you were on Quinnipeague," Nicole said softly.

"No, you weren't."

"I'm sorry."

"Apology accepted."

Nicole paused. "Just like that? No discussion."

"No. Not now, at least. I understand what you're feeling, sweetheart. Trust me, I've felt a lot of it myself. I also know how frightened you are right now. You're thinking that you can't lose Julian, that your life would be totally empty without him, that there has to be something you can do; only you don't know what it is. Your mind is filled with coulda shoulda wouldas."

Nicole was amazed. Hadn't she thought those same words five minutes before? "How did you know?"

"Because I loved your father like you love Julian. He was in the ICU, too—the difference being that he was basically gone when he got there. Julian is not. You will have your life with him, sweetheart. I have to believe that. You will."

Nicole breathed more deeply. Angie couldn't know for sure that Julian would survive. Plus, there were different levels of survival, any one of which might be worse than what they'd had before now and, in so being, impact their lives forever more.

But she did trust her mother. And she did want to believe.

Reaching for Angie's hand, she linked their fingers as she used to do when she was little and whispered, "How long can you stay?"

"As long as you want, honey. I'm here for you."

Moments later, when Angie went to dump the uneaten food and buy cheese to nibble on upstairs, Nicole pulled out her phone.

Thank you, she typed very simply and pressed SEND.

Chapter Twenty-eight

Charlotte was rowing. The boat was an old wooden thing that she had spotted in Leo's shed, but since, unlike the sailboat, it was something she could drive herself, she had made him take it out. Leo, being Leo and a handyman, had sanded, painted, and sealed it before he would launch it, and then, though he let her row, he insisted on going along.

The sun hadn't set, but it was heading that way, spattering gold across the waves under a brooding sky. As mild as the waves were, the boat bobbed more than it actually moved. Pulling on the oars with her back to the bow, Charlotte was fully absorbed for the first time that day.

When her phone vibrated against her hip, though, Chicago came back in a rush. Dropping the oars in their oarlocks, she pulled it out, saw Nicole's text, and smiled in relief.

"Her mother got there," Leo guessed. Facing her in the stern with his bare feet braced wide, he was uncorking a bottle of wine and, with remarkable steadiness given the rock of the boat, half-filled two plastic cups.

An OK exec decision? she typed.

Very OK, Nicole replied.

Satisfied, Charlotte took the cup he offered. After tapping it to his—they always did this—she sipped.

"How is he?" Leo asked.

Charlotte glanced at the phone again before sliding it into her pocket. "Must be the same, if she didn't say."

"She should have called her mother herself." As sympathetic as Leo was for the situation, he hadn't warmed much to Nicole.

"Uh-huh," she said, sipping the wine. "We know all about that." He still refused to call his father.

With a you-know-what-I-mean look, he reached into a plastic baggie, pairing cheese with pear slices for her and with crackers for himself.

She took a bite, then said, "If it were me, I'd call Kaylin and John, too. They ought to be there. She needs all the support she can get." She pushed the rest of the snack in her mouth.

Leo's eyes were level. "Go to her."

She shook her head no, leveled a gaze right back at him as she swallowed. "I choose you." It was one step removed from *I love you,* which she didn't say other than in moments of passion, when she had no control over what came out. Those words were too threatening for other times. And that was fine. He knew how she felt.

The oars clinked loudly against their locks. Leaning forward, he pulled them into the boat, then reached into the baggie and doled out seconds.

"Maybe you shouldn't," he finally said. "There are too many problems."

"Tell me something new." He didn't travel. That wasn't new.

"Kids," he said.

Whoa. That *was* new. He hadn't mentioned kids before. *Salt* hadn't gone that far, and she hadn't dared ask. "You want them?"

"Yes," he said, seeming wounded that she wouldn't have known.

"That's part of the dream, but we can't have kids if you're flying all over the world."

The fact that he was thinking of these things was something. But a step forward or just an extension of the wall? "So the problem is me."

"It's *me*. I'm Quinnipeague."

"You're sophisticated, educated, and worldly on paper. You could do it in real life," she argued.

But he was stuck on the other. "And even if you went back and forth from here, we'd still be apart for weeks at a time. That's a recipe for disaster."

"Oh, come on, Leo," she said gently, "that's what we see on TV and read in books, both of which need trauma to keep the plot moving. But I know lots of couples that have families and jobs and still travel. Everyone gives a little, and it works. If you're talking babies, though, you'd *really* have to meet me halfway."

"You don't want more kids?"

"I do. *Absolutely*. But I did it alone once, and I won't do that again. And excuse me," she frowned, "where would I give *birth* to these kids? There is no hospital here." Quinnie babies were customarily born on the mainland in the kind of hospital where Cecily had died after Leo had dragged her there, for which he still felt deep regret.

He seemed confused, clearly hadn't considered that. Brows knitting, he leaned forward, then sat back again, elbows on the transom, long legs splayed outside hers. The pose was more defiant than relaxed. "What if someone finds out who I am? That'd be a problem if you were my girlfriend, wife, mother of my kids, whatever."

"Wouldn't be a problem for me. You're the only one who has a problem with success."

"Okay, then the reverse. What if I can't write another book? What if the money I've made on *Salt* is a one-time thing? What if I can't support a wife and kids?"

Charlotte stared at him. "Listen to you, Leo. You're dreaming up problems, and every one of them is small. Money is not an issue. You have enough to last a lifetime, even *before* the paperback comes out, and that's not counting what you could make if you let them turn *Salt* into a movie. You invest. I've seen you do it. You're making money on top of money."

"I worry."

"So do I, but not about that. Right now, I worry that Julian Carlysle might die. All the money in the world didn't keep him from getting MS, and it can't assure his survival now." She felt a chill just thinking about it, though perhaps that was a murky cloud crossing the path of the setting sun. They were definitely in a sea shadow. She had to move, but to where?

Nicole would have said sea shadows were for fools because, try as she might to hang in there and be positive and maybe see things differently—as in, these reactions are just part of a larger picture that includes reduction of MS symptoms—come Sunday morning, Julian was no better. As Angie had warned, there were more machines in the ICU. And the staff checked on him so often that it was like having a private nurse. But his temperature remained high, and the wheezing was exhausting him in a way that went well beyond the drowsiness of Benadryl.

Still, he refused to take steroids.

By Monday morning, when there was no improvement, she was worried enough, frustrated enough, angry enough to take a page from Charlotte's book and to make an executive decision of her own. Julian's parents, being in San Diego, were too far away to come running, but his children were not. They were adults, or close to it. They had a right to be there.

Charlotte was constantly checking her phone for word from Nicole, but other than the occasional *Still the same* or *No change*—all sent from outside the ICU, since cell phones were banned inside—there was nothing of substance until Monday afternoon.

Then, *I called Kaylin and John. They'll be here tomorrow. He's going to be mad, but tough shit. It was the right thing to do.*

Absolutely. They SHOULD be there. You did GOOD, Nicki. Any improvement yet?

No. Hammon is still agonizing over steroids. If Julian asked him to do it, he would. I'm telling you, my husband's priorities are fucked up.

The language was totally uncharacteristic of Nicole, but she was clearly at her wits' end. Not that Charlotte was about to scold, since every other thought in her mind was that *Leo's* priorities were fucked up, too, in those very same words. She knew that Leo loved her at some level. But enough to admit it? Admitting it meant you acknowledged what it meant, which meant you did have to give a little, and he wasn't ready to do that.

Time was running out. She was up late Monday night working on the cookbook and at it again at dawn on Tuesday, working straight through midafternoon, when she was finally able to call Nicole.

"How is he?" she asked first, because that remained the priority.

"The same," Nicole replied, sounding tense. "Kay and Johnny just landed. They'll be here any minute. He won't be happy. I'm gearing up for that. So tell me something good."

"I think we're done."

There was a moment's silence, then a surprised, "You and Leo?"

"The cookbook," Charlotte corrected with barely bridled excitement. In spite of everything dark going on, there was still a sense of accomplishment when she finally closed her working file, sat back, and let her hands fall from the computer. As for Leo, he was in her good graces at that moment, having been genuinely excited for her. Knowing she would call Nicole, he had gone into town to pick up groceries for a celebratory dinner.

Nicole's voice lifted. "Seriously?"

"I just e-mailed you the last of the files."

"Omigod! You. Are. Amazing!"

"Don't say that until you read what I sent. I love the profiles, but you may want to reorder which goes where, and tweak menu plans to coordinate with that, and there's still all the me-writing-as-you business."

"I'm barely halfway through. I'm so far behind!"

"But that's the second part of my news." Charlotte was nearly as pleased about this. "You have more time."

Nicole's laugh was shrill. "Not from what *I* see."

"So I called my favorite editor," Charlotte went on. "She and I get along really well, like we have lunch together just for fun, and I asked if she knew yours. Turns out that they're good friends. Do you know about the baby?"

Nicole was clearly puzzled. "Yes. It's due at the end of September."

"It came last *week*. She must have e-mailed you."

There was a pause, then a gasp. "Omigod. *That* e-mail?" She switched to speaker phone, apparently checking her inbox while she talked. "I didn't open it, because I felt so guilty not being done." She gasped a second time. "A little girl. Five pounds, one ounce. Deadline extension until the end of September, when she'll start working from home." She let out a long, soft, clearly relieved sigh. "Omigod. I don't believe it. This is the best news!"

So, just like Charlotte when she'd called, Nicole had two pieces of good news to share with Julian. She knew he would be pleased about the cookbook, but she didn't get to that until much later, because just as she turned off her phone, Kaylin and John arrived. Kaylin looked the New Yorker in skinny jeans, blousy layers, and impossibly high heels, while John, with an untucked shirt, jeans, and an impossibly pale face, just looked scared.

Nicole had called them for Julian's sake. Seeing them coming toward her, though, she felt a little of the same relief she had felt seeing Angie. This was her family. With each new arrival, she felt less alone.

Though Angie was included in the hugs, Nicole was the one to explain what was happening. She had told them on the phone about the treatment and his reaction. Now, without quite saying he might die, she detailed his symptoms. "He sounds worse than he is," she said, which wasn't necessarily the truth, but they would be frightened enough.

Leading them into Julian's unit, she directed them to the hand sanitizer, and then, leaning over the bed, gently shook his arm. He opened his eyes, but it was a minute before they focused on his children. There was an initial instinctive flare of pleasure, then understanding and a glower at Nicole.

"I didn't want them to worry," he croaked between wheezy inhalations.

"They're here to cheer you on." She stood back to give each of the kids time. Kaylin took more, though she talked so steadily about how glad she was that Nicole had called because she wanted to be there, that nothing was demanded of Julian. John was more emotional, as, ironically, was Julian.

"I'll be fine," he managed to tell his son while struggling for air and composure, but he seemed to find new strength when the kids retreated and Nicole took their place. His brown eyes, still dull with fever, were full of censure, his words sharp around the whistling of his breath. "I told you not to."

"They love you."

He rasped, "What's love." It wasn't a question, more a holier-than-thou dismissal, and that hit Nicole the wrong way.

"It's *everything*," she said, eyes wide open. "It's why I've been here with you for the last week and a half, even when I would have rather waited longer to do this, and it's why you need to *fight*."

"But not . . . the kids."

"Yes, the kids," she shot back with a fire she wouldn't have dared a day or two ago, but if not now, when? *If not now, when?* Her father had been big on sayings; this one was hers. It was what reality was about. Growing up—being strong—this was her summer. And it absolutely felt right. "They love you. They want to be part of your life. Well, illness goes with that. They aren't babies, Jules. They're young adults with lots of good sense and positive vibes, and they *love* you." With Julian staring at her, seeming stunned by her voice, listening with greater awareness than he'd shown since Friday, she felt a surge of strength. "They're here because I called them, because this is what people do when they love each other, this is what families do—and aren't you lucky to have this? Some people don't." As an inner steam built, she pressed a hand to her chest. "Omigod, I feel so blessed to have them here right now. You should, too, and if you can't see that, then you don't deserve us." Clutching his hand, she leaned in and, more determined than ever, said, "If you can't fight for yourself, fight for us. Do not throw this away, Julian Carlysle. Do not be a total . . . total . . . *prick.*"

He stared at her. His forehead was still dewy and his cheeks flushed, but something gave in his eyes, and his lips curved. "Prick?"

She hedged. It was an ugly word. "I was going to say asshole, but that's what came out."

He made a strangled sound that might have been a chuckle. "Prick, huh?"

"You can be," she said softly.

"But you love me anyway."

"I do."

Smiling, he closed his eyes. The smile lingered, but he said nothing more. He was quiet. Too quiet.

Dead.

The thought stole her breath.

Terrified, she leaned close again and gave his hand a sharp shake. "Julian."

He opened his eyes. "Just resting. Want to ease up on the hand?"

* * *

He's better! Charlotte read a short time later. *Wheezing, blood pressure, fever—everything broke. It'll be a while before he's totally out of the woods, but Hammon is beside himself. Me, I just can't believe it. More later. Going back in now.*

Tears in her eyes, throat tight, she showed the text to Leo, who hugged her until the kitchen timer drew him away. Beyond joy for Nicole, she felt extraordinary relief, as though the hell of the summer—memories of the affair, Nicole's anger, the loss of this only link to her own child—had a purpose.

The book was done, and Julian had turned a corner. It was a double-celebratory dinner.

Leo had bought lobster fresh from the sea that afternoon, and cooked it live, which she refused to do herself after hearing the scrabbling of the claws against the pot years before. He also grilled ears of sweet corn and sliced zucchini, both fresh from Quinnipeague fields, while Charlotte heated a round of Melissa Parker's buttery rosemary bread.

Silence between them had never been a problem, and it wasn't now. Charlotte couldn't help but think of Julian and smile in relief from time to time, but increasingly her thoughts were of Leo. His features were soft now, his midnight eyes warm. He tucked a strand of hair behind her ear; she wiped butter from his lip with a thumb. Again and again, they raised their wineglasses in wordless toasts, and when the wine was gone and the food eaten, they lingered over coffee, sitting on the dock with Bear. When Charlotte leaned down at one point to rest her head on the dog's neck, her eyes filled with tears. By the time she straightened, though, the tears were gone. She refused to cry on this special night.

Later yet, when the moon was up and the surf down, they walked the beach, toes gripping the sand, hands separating only to scramble over large rocks. In time they reached the spot where they had first made love seven weeks before. It might have been their destination all along, but they didn't speak of it aloud. Leaving their clothes on the beach, they swam, though once they were in over their heads, it was more treading water, with Leo keeping them afloat while Charlotte wrapped her legs around his waist and her arms around his neck, and their mouths fused.

They made love once there in the water, then again, slower and more savoring, on the beach. When it was done, they stayed until the ocean air chilled them. Then, carrying their clothes in the hands that weren't linked, they returned to the house, where they lay in bed for the longest time, bodies curled into each other as they listened to the roll of the tide, which was as rhythmic as Leo's breathing when he finally fell asleep.

Charlotte didn't sleep, simply listened to the ocean, his breathing, and that life-sustaining beat of his heart. Minutes passed, then hours. If she dozed, it wasn't for long. More important, she knew, to feel the soft brush of his chest hair against her cheek and the strength of his thigh under hers. More important to commit his scent to memory.

Shortly before dawn, leaving Leo prone on the bed with his head turned away, she quietly rose. Bear looked up from the floor, but a simple touch to that silky spot between his eyes had him sleeping again. Her duffel was on a chair; never having formally moved in, she had never fully unpacked, which made the task easier now. Adding the last of her clothes and toiletries, she carried the bag to the kitchen. Wanting to say some last thing to Leo, she took paper and pen from a drawer, but words escaped her. Finally, with a simply *XOXOX,* she left the note on the pillow, let herself out the front door, walked down the drive with her duffel and on to Nicole's.

Leo didn't follow. He didn't come or even call, but she hadn't expected either. She wasn't even sure he had been totally asleep while she was packing. They both knew this had to be done.

That said, the hole inside her gaped. She tried to fill it by doing laundry and cleaning her room, but both were quickly done. So she knit. After a summer of it, she was totally familiar with the pattern and, miraculously, made no mistakes. By early afternoon, she had cast off and was driving to Isabel Skane's for instructions on putting the pieces together. She took detailed notes, thinking it might take her a while to get it done. But the finishing turned out to be the easy part, especially since she had nothing else to do but sew on the patio, seeking comfort from the last of the pergola roses, the salty breeze and the thunder of the surf.

More than once, she wandered to the garden where lavender, valerian, and red clover thrived. She smiled, pleased that they remained alive, though they had certainly done their job. Word from Chicago was good. Julian was better, steadily recovering from the transplant. Even his MS symptoms were improved, Nicole reported, though only time would tell if that would hold. Likewise, only time would tell whether the stem cells could actually mend damage to the myelin sheath that four years of the disease had caused. But Nicole didn't care about that. She had her man back. She couldn't be happier.

In a moment's whimsy, thinking that the plants remained alive and fresh just for her, Charlotte picked a single clover, made a wish, and tucked it by her heart. She didn't know if she believed in all this. Too often in her life, she had dug deep inside and come up with the same calming that the plants had offered, and as for making wishes on red clover, was this truly why Julian was better? Medicine was medicine, science was science, physiology was physiology—and had Leo said he loved her, for all the clover she'd picked and wishes she'd made? No!

Discouraged, she returned to the sweater, working into the evening, weaving in ends and wrapping it up just before exhaustion hit. Having not slept the night before, she slept soundly—a good sign, she decided Thursday morning as she made a last check of the house, packed up the Wrangler, and set off.

As planned, she reached the pier before the ferry arrived. Taking the tissue-wrapped package from the passenger's seat, she went into the Chowder House. The scent of chowder was strong, accompanied by that of fried clams. Dorey was in the kitchen, getting ready for lunch. One look at Charlotte, though, and, wiping her hands on a cloth, she left the stove.

"You look like you lost your best friend," the woman said, uncharacteristically subdued.

"Actually, there's good news." Smiling, Charlotte told her about Julian.

"Good news but not surprising," Dorey decided. "The heart of Quinnipeague was with them." She paused. "It'll be with you, too."

Charlotte struggled not to cry. "A favor?" she managed to ask and held out the package. She didn't have to say who it was for or what to do with it. Dorey nodded and took it. Then her crinkled eyes grew pleading.

"Are you sure you can't stay?"

"Yes. I have to work."

"Will you be back?"

"I don't know." Choking up, she turned to leave. When she felt a stocky arm around her shoulders, she paused, eyes on the old wood floor.

Dorey's voice was filled with compassion. "And I was worried about him," she remarked with a *tsk*. "Take care of yourself, Missy. I'll keep the chowdah hot for you."

Chowdah. So Maine, so *Quinnie,* the word echoed in her head until the ferry horn blasted it out. Once she'd driven the Wrangler aboard and the ramp was raised, she took a seat in the stern. How not to look for him then? How not to hope he had changed his mind? How not to envision a happily-ever-after in this place that was a fantasy in so many ways?

All she saw, though, was the island growing smaller as the ferry plowed through the waves toward the mainland.

She did fine all the way to Rockland, did fine all the way to New York. She even did fine when she got to Brooklyn and found her third-floor walkup sweltering, the AC on the blink, and no air to be had outside. She called her landlord, stopped at her coolest favorite sushi place for dinner and, after, at her coolest favorite café for a tall, iced raspberry tea to go. Back in her apartment, she was fine going through her closet for clothes to take to France.

It was when she was taking Quinnie things from her duffel, reaching in a final time, that she touched something hard. Puzzled, she pulled it out. It was a piece of pine, six inches of increasing detail from tail to nose, its head a near-perfect replica of Bear whittled by the man who knew him best.

Charlotte's heart began to pound. For all the nothings Leo had started that summer, all the while claiming that he wasn't good at it and that, like her knitting, it was all about the process, this was exquisite.

Holding the tiny dog, with its small, widespread ears, its muscular flanks and lean legs, and, in her mind's eye, seeing the real thing with its master close behind, she burst into tears.

Chapter Twenty-nine

PARIS WAS AS MUCH FUN as Paris could be without a beating heart, or so Charlotte felt. In the two days she was there, she robotically followed her friends, smiling and nodding even when their French babble went over her head. She didn't tell them about Leo, didn't want to talk about him, and they were excited enough just seeing her and taking her from market to market, café to café, club to club.

Did she think about Leo? Of course, she did. She had deliberately packed different clothes from ones that would remind her of Quinnipeague, but she had tucked the little whittled Bear in their midst—couldn't leave it home alone, much less sleep without it—and she thought of Leo each time her hands warmed the wood. He had taken great pains, particularly with the detail of the head, and with pine being knotty and soft, she wondered how many times he'd had to restart with a fresh piece when one didn't work. While she slept? While she was at Nicole's or in town? Was it a 'til-September gift or a final good-bye? She just didn't know.

She also thought of him each time Nicole sent an update, which was often. Julian had been removed from intensive care on Thursday night, and when Charlotte landed in Paris early Saturday morning, a waiting e-mail said he was up and walking around. Charlotte was pleased for them both, though here, too, it was a knee-jerk response.

By the time he was discharged from the hospital, it was Monday, and she was en route to Bordeaux. Here, amid imposing châteaux and lush vineyards, she was more engaged. This was her baby; she had to be *on*. Her assignment was to profile an American family who had recently bought a small vineyard here. It was a remarkable clan—three generations' worth, including two grandparents, two sons and their wives, and seven children under the age of ten—facing a remarkable challenge. Having owned a smaller vineyard in California, they were following a dream, and though the former owners were there to guide them, it wasn't going quite the way they had planned. Between a weakened economy, a foreign infusion that was driving prices too high, and the sheer veneration of the competition, they had been forced to rethink their goals. Marketability was their new byword. Their wines had to be affordable, which meant cutting margins of profitability, which meant retooling the dream even more—all of which meant stress. And yet they were happy. During the ten days Charlotte spent in their aging château, she saw optimism at every turn.

For the first five of those days, Nicole and Julian stayed in Chicago to return to the hospital for daily checks. By the time Charlotte left Bordeaux, they were back in Philadelphia, and Charlotte was welcoming Nicole's texts as ties to her past. She knew the minute they settled back into their condo with new hope, the minute Nicole hit her favorite farmers' markets, the minute she realized—again—that nothing was as fresh as Quinnie-fresh.

Fresh described Tuscany, though in totally different ways from Bordeaux. Rather than verdant rows of manicured vines rolling up and down hillsides, in the small Italian village where she stayed, the olive groves were more drab, their trees rangy and staggered. Rather than the moist scent of Bordeaux, the smells here were drier and more piquant, often of *focacce* or fish or meat stew, all cooked with olive oil straight from the press.

The challenge here wasn't optimism, but evolution. The subjects of her story were an olive farm and the Italian family that had run it for generations, and their constant reinvention had more to do with the personal interest of the members than the economy. Money meant little to this family. To them, life was about trying different things, most notably—and the reason Charlotte was there—establishing a cooking school to showcase the glory of the olive.

She spent hours with growers, pruners, pickers, and pressers. She interviewed local chefs and sat in on a session with current students. Much like what she'd done those last days on Quinnipeague, she was in the process of choosing recipes for her piece, when Nicole and Julian returned to the island.

His tests are all good, Nicole wrote, *so Hammon says the risk of further rejection is remote. He's still weak, but it'll be a while before we know whether it's from the transplant or the disease.*

Is he discouraged?

Hard to say. I don't think he's thought about work yet. He's focused on getting out and walking. He's determined to be running in another week. That's his litmus test for recovery.

Picturing them on the road, the patio, the beach, Charlotte felt a wave of homesickness. *What's it like there?*

Gorgeous. The nights are cooler and start earlier, but the crowd's gone. I've been taking my laptop to the Café and working there. Am almost done. I mean, there are no changes—NO changes—to what you did. How do I thank you—for that work, for the stem cells?

He'd have made it through. It was meant to be.

But so much more meaningful this way.

More painful? Charlotte had to ask, because nothing could ever erase the betrayal behind those cells.

Maybe a little, Nicole typed. *But being back here, I miss you. Are you okay?*

I'm good, Charlotte replied. *Back in my old routine,* she added. Only she wasn't really. Try as she might to recapture the excitement of traveling freely without ties to home, she failed. She was with people all day long, but she was lonely. And then there was the whittled dog.

What's the word from Leo? Nicole asked.

Charlotte felt a deep, dark pang. *Zip. We aren't in touch.*

Why not?

Taking a break. That was the gentlest way to put it.

You BROKE UP?

No. Yes. Maybe. I don't know. Having typed the words on impulse, she positioned her thumb to delete. But this perfectly expressed what she felt, which was total confusion. She loved Leo but didn't know what to do with it. She had hoped he would text, or call, or get on a *friggin' jet* in a burst of courage, and surprise her with a declaration of undying love on the banks of the Seine, in a vineyard in Bordeaux, or under a Tuscan olive tree.

Such romantic notions. This wasn't who she was. It might be what she liked to read. But in real life?

Leaving the first words as is, she typed, *It's like Julian, I guess. Time will tell.*

Then you're not coming here after Italy?

To Quinnipeague? No. I take the train back to Paris Wednesday and fly to New York Friday. I'll work there for a while.

I'm sending you flowers. When do you land?

You are not sending me flowers. Flowers were unnecessary. *Thanks* were unnecessary. She would never quite feel she deserved either, where Nicole was concerned.

When do you land? Nicole repeated.

Knowing that she was determined enough to figure it out, which meant that arguing now was absurd, and that, anyway, flowers would be pretty and bright in her lonely walkup, she typed, *1:25* P.M. *Friday.*

In fact, she arrived a day early. Once in Paris, she felt a yearning for American soil, and when a can't-hurt-to-try phone call offered a flight change, she booked it. The flight was smooth and, despite headwinds, landed early. Her duffel was one of the first to emerge; she sailed through customs, and was still early enough to be in a cab en route to Brooklyn before the Friday afternoon rush. The AC worked perfectly, quickly cooling her apartment. In no time, she had unpacked, putting clean in the closet and dirty in a basket. Her laptop, camera, and a folder of pamphlets and notes went on the breakfast bar in her galley kitchen.

What to do then?

Craving to reconnect with her roots, she began calling friends, some of whom she hadn't talked with since spring. She left three messages before, desperate for a human voice, she called her friend-the-editor, took the subway into Manhattan, and met her for drinks. Whether being jostled on the subway, crowded in pedestrian traffic, or ignoring pick-up looks in the bar, she was comfortable. This was her old stomping ground, loud and busy and familiar. She was glad to be back.

Since she was on Paris time, she was asleep by eight, and the next morning she met one friend for breakfast, another for coffee. Keeping busy seemed the way to go, so when she returned to her apartment she did laundry, dusted, vacuumed. After checking for e-mail, she went down the street for lunch. The café was a favorite of hers, another familiar spot. The yarn shop, though, was new. She went in, introduced herself, and browsed, but left empty-handed when nothing there was as beautiful as what Isabel Skane sold.

Home again, she kicked off her shoes, put on shorts, and, after tacking her unruly hair into a tortoise-shell claw, opened her Bordeaux folder and shifted papers around. And shifted papers around. And did it a little more.

Lacking incentive, she looked around for something else to do, but nothing appealed. Feeling hollow, she went to the window, folded her arms over her middle, and stared out through the thin blinds at nothing at all.

It was a minute before she saw the man. Leaning against the stoop of the town house across the street, he wore a ball cap, dark glasses, jeans and sneakers. A backpack lay by his feet. He was looking up at her window, his body alert. She might have thought he was casing the joint if it hadn't been for the bunch of yellow flowers he held. From Nicole? Not quite. Something about the way he stood—the way his jeans fit his hips, not quite loose, not quite tight—the way his legs were braced like he was on a boat—was very familiar. And then there was his sweater.

Her heart nearly stopped when the last registered. She had dreamed, but hadn't dared hope. Romantic wasn't reality. And this wasn't Quinnipeague on a cool, *thick o' fog,* wood-smoke summer morning, but Brooklyn on a warm and hazy September afternoon.

In a split second, heart pounding now, she realized what it had taken for him to come here, and still she stood for disbelieving seconds after that, feet rooted to the faded carpet.

She blinked, and he remained.

Real.

Suddenly not rooted there at all, she flew from the apartment and raced down two flights in her bare feet. Flinging open the front door, she darted out, but stopped on the top step. With the glasses and cap, with the jeans, sneaks, even the flowers, he might have been any man. But no other one would be wearing an Irish knit sweater in 78-degree heat, much less a sweater with a lopsided cable on the left front and bunchy shoulders.

Holding the wrought-iron rail, she went slowly down the stairs, never once taking her eyes from him lest he disappear. She didn't stop at the bottom, but crossed the sidewalk and stepped off the curb without a glance either way.

His face was bronzed after a Quinnie summer, but his cheeks were flushed beyond that, and though she could see little of his brow beneath the big Q on the visor of his ball cap, his jaw, throat, and what little neck showed above the sweater looked damp.

"Do I know you?" she asked with her heart in her throat.

"I hope so," he replied in a low and shaky voice. "I sure as hell don't."

"Feeling strange?"

"Very."

"Because of the city?"

"Partly."

The thought crossed her mind that he had come to say good-bye, which would surely account for unease. But all this way? "Did you fly?"

"I don't fly."

"You don't leave Quinnipeague, either," she reminded him gently, inching closer as hope gained strength. "So you drove."

He shot a nervous glance down the street, where his dark blue pickup was parked. In that split second, she remembered making love against its side and felt a stab of want deep in her belly.

Inching closer still, desperate to touch but afraid to assume, she said, "You'll get a ticket parking there."

"I can pay a ticket. Will they tow?"

"Depends how long you're here." But she didn't want to go there yet. "How's Bear?"

"Nosin' around looking for you."

Her throat closed up. Bear always did that to her. But why Bear and not Leo? Perhaps because Bear's love was unconditional. And because loving a dog was allowed.

But Bear wasn't here, and Leo was—and she ached to be allowed to love him, too. Eyes filling, she pressed her lips together to stop their trembling, but it wasn't enough. On tiptoe, she snaked her arms around his neck and buried her face in his throat. He smelled of sweat and soap—and balsam and pine, lavender, valerian, sage, thyme, and mint, and fried clams and *chowdah*, and the beach, and the ocean. He smelled of Quinnipeague, because he *was* Quinnipeague.

Unable to contain the sheer fullness of it all, she began to weep—Charlotte, who never wept except with Leo. With a guttural sound, he wrapped one arm around her, anchoring her tightly to him, while the other smoothed tendrils of hair from her face before pressing the back of her head to his throat. He kissed her hair and was inching closer to her temple when she drew back.

"What *took* you so long?" she charged in a nasal voice.

He might have argued that she had been away and only now returned, and that she was the one who had left in the first place—and she would have thrown back words like cell phone, e-mail, and text.

Instead, succinct and wry, he said, "I'm a slow learner."

Just like that, her anger was gone, and her heart was melting in puddles. She could live with this kind of honesty—speaking of which, as she tried to blot her tears, she said, "I look awful."

"You look beautiful." He held her gaze.

But his eyes were only shallow shapes on the far side of dark. Needing to see the whole of them, she lifted his Ray-Bans—and then barely breathed. Here was a stunning midnight blue with not a trace of defiance or disdain, nothing of the wall, just deep, deep need and want and fear.

Then his lips moved. Had her eyes not been wet, she might have read his lips. But tears blurred the words. So she asked, "What?"

He whispered it this time.

Her heart caught. "Again," she whispered back.

"I love you," he said, not quite full voice, but intimate and exposed and so *Leo* that she had to believe.

Her tears threatened again. But his eyes remained so dark, so worried, so fearful, that she could only blink and hold her breath.

"Is it still there?" he asked in that same not-quite-full voice.

Releasing the breath, she smiled. "It doesn't go away, Leo. It's always there. That's what I've been trying to tell you. When it's real, it stays."

"This is real?"

She nodded. Her eyes fell to the bunch of flowers that still hung from his hand. And suddenly, with a clumping of little threads of thought, she frowned. "When did you get here?"

"An hour ago. I was thinking you'd come in a cab. Your flight must've been early."

"Nicole told you."

"Oh yeah," he drawled, facetious in a way Charlotte totally got. "In no uncertain terms. She hates me."

"She does not. I'm sure there's pride involved, and stubbornness. But if she called to tell you when I was landing and that you had to be here with flowers—"

"The flowers were my idea," he said and, as if in proof, a van pulled up just then with the logo of a local flower shop on the side.

Minutes later, Charlotte was holding the bushiest arrangement of wildflowers she had ever seen. It was actually pretty ugly, but of course, Nicole was making a statement about how much prettier wildflowers were in a Quinnipeague fall, and that Charlotte needed to come see for herself.

"These'll be dead in no time," she decided as her eyes moved to the yellow roses, "but not those. They need water. Want to come up?"

"Christ," he breathed, "I thought you'd never ask. It's hot as hell out here."

"That's because you're wearing a heavy old handmade sweater. Why in this heat?"

"It was the only thing holding me together."

They were barely able to put the roses in water, before the sweater came off, then shirts and pants and the rest—all this with perfect air-conditioning, but the need to be together was overwhelming. They made love a dozen ways, from floor to bed to shower and back. Charlotte had never been as insatiable, but then, she had been without Leo for a month, and she was in love.

Not that Leo flagged. He was, in a word, awesome. Actually, he was also *wordy,* telling her that he loved her over and over again. She didn't think she would ever tire of that.

As afternoon morphed into evening, though, there were practical matters to consider, like stashing the truck and buying food for dinner, but both were easily handled. The truck went behind the Jeep in the alley of a friend several streets over, and they brought in Thai, which Leo had requested, and since he'd never had it before, Charlotte ordered a selection. He liked some dishes better than others, but long before the food was gone, he was starting to drag. Having made the crossing from Quinnipeague to Rockland with the truck the afternoon before, he had left there at three this morning to allow for traffic and terror and getting lost.

So Leo, her man of the night on Quinnipeague, dragged her back to bed in Brooklyn and made sweet, sweet love to her one more time before falling asleep. Not her. She wasn't tired in the least. She was too pumped up to sleep, too enthralled by the sight of Leo in her bed to want to close her eyes at all.

Besides, moments before dropping off, he had reached into his backpack and pulled out a manuscript.

"Next Book?" Charlotte asked excitedly.

He shook his head and nudged the wad of papers into her hand. Then, lying on his side facing her, he pushed the pillow to fit his neck, and closed his eyes.

Charlotte stared at him. When it became clear that he wouldn't explain—that he was actually that quickly asleep—she turned to the cover page. *Roots and All That Other Dirty Stuff,* it read. She turned to the next page. *For Charlotte.*

Swallowing, she started to read.

It would never be published, of course, though not because it wasn't beautifully written. He was a natural; that was clear from the start. He had put several hundred pages together in three weeks, and the prose was as lyrical as in *Salt,* though Charlotte knew he couldn't have had time for much editing. Here was catharsis in its most raw form—a spilling out of thirty-eight years of brief victories overshadowed by anger, resentment, and fear.

This was Leo's own, very personal story, written perhaps for Charlotte but surely finished for himself. He had told her the basics before, but now he elaborated on the feelings he'd had for his mother and the island. He wrote of his dreams of having a father. He wrote of defiance and sadness, of confusion and floundering. He wrote of island girls and sex and his lover from Phoenix, none of which Charlotte found offensive, what with the wrongness of those relationships so clear in light of the man she knew. He wrote about seeing Charlotte in the dark of his drive that first night, of what their summer together had meant to him and how, when she left, he was paralyzed at first, then disgusted enough with himself and his fear to know what he had to do.

And what he had to do, for starters, was to see his father. It wasn't an easy visit for either of them, what with no history of communication, no guidelines for father-son relationships, no filters to soften hair-trigger emotions. Leo had been brutally honest, largely angry and accusatory, surely arrogant when he told the man about *Salt*. He hadn't planned on doing that. He knew the risk of exposure, and he didn't trust this stranger.

But *Salt* had seemed a vital connection to make. With its ties to the sea, to longing and dreams, it was a big piece of who he was.

His father was older than he remembered, newly retired from the police department, outwardly defensive at times, but listening. Would there be a détente? Leo didn't know. But hours of blunt talk—this act of tearing up negative roots and leaving the ground tilled and waiting, as Leo put it—was what he had to do before leaving the State of Maine for the first time in his life.

And he did have to leave, or, at least, had to be able to do it. Having taken Charlotte's arguments to heart, he spared himself nothing on that score. Narrow-minded, he called himself. Selfish. Cowardly. As insecure as that little boy sleeping outside with the herbs, he didn't paint himself in the best of lights, not even with the success of *Salt*. And yet he came across shining in Charlotte's eyes.

By the time she finished reading, it was three in the morning, and his words had brought her to tears a dozen times. Leo slept through it all. She didn't know how. Hadn't he wanted to see her reactions? But no, she realized. He was using sleep so that he wouldn't see, wouldn't worry or fear. Through it all, though, he kept a physical link, be it the touch of a toe, a hand, a leg.

Seeming to sense when she finished, he stretched, opened one eye, then the other as he regained awareness, and quickly grew wary. He waited for her to speak, but what could she say? He had lived through the kind of angst that, for all her own loneliness, she couldn't imagine. And his father? The man claimed Cecily had threatened mayhem if he interfered with Leo's life, and he had felt just bewitched enough by her to believe it. Cecily hadn't known that he was the one directing the lawyer who got Leo off with five years in prison rather than ten, or that he was instrumental in having charges dropped the second time around, when Leo was falsely charged.

Reaching up, he touched the tears on her face, but she didn't want that. Nor did she want sex. Sliding down, she squirreled one arm under, stretched one arm over, and held him tightly enough so he'd know she wasn't ever letting go. In time, he switched it up, holding her while she slept with her ear to his heart.

When she finally awoke, a midday sun was heating the carpet, and he announced that he wanted to go into the city. Charlotte was startled. "Manhattan?" She would have thought he'd have wanted to take it slow, fanning out from her neighborhood in baby steps. Manhattan was a shock for people from other cities, let alone those from tiny islands.

But he nodded. "Fifth Avenue." He was sure.

That said, when they left open air to go underground for the subway, he held her hand as though his life depended on it. Stop to stop, he was guarded, and when they emerged in Midtown, his eyes held a mix of terror and awe. But he was cool—oh, he was cool. Betrayed only by the bob of his Adam's apple, he studied the street signs. He had clearly done his homework; he knew how the grid worked. After several blocks, he began checking numbers. When he found the one he wanted, he opened the large door and stood aside.

Charlotte, to whom the number meant nothing, but the store name etched over the stone portal did, shot him a questioning look. He simply hitched his head, indicating that she should precede him. Once inside, he went to the nearest salesperson and, in a quiet, confident voice, asked for Victoria Harper, who, it turned out, was the assistant manager with whom he had talked earlier that week. If Charlotte hadn't already been stunned by his *savoir-faire,* she would have been moments later when the woman guided them to a display case filled with diamond rings. The elegant Ms. Harper proceeded to pull out several that, apparently, she and Leo had agreed to on the phone.

Charlotte pressed shaky fingers to her mouth, though she couldn't have talked if she'd wanted to. All she could do was to stare at the rings, then at Leo, who smiled with equal parts shyness, excitement, and pride. "What did you expect?" he asked.

Blindly, she groped for his hand, which seemed the only real thing in the place. "I, uh . . . I didn't . . . I-I hadn't planned—"

"Is that a no?"

"It's a yes yes *yes,* but . . . *Tiffany's*?" she cried and added in an astonished whisper, "It's too *much.*"

"Not for me," he said, "not if you love one of these."

She loved Leo. She didn't need a ring. But he had planned it all out, and he seemed to know exactly what he was doing. If he had learned sophistication from fictional characters, they had taught him well. As suave as he was in as fabled a store as this, his eyes were earnest. He wanted her happy.

She studied the rings. Each was stunning. Most women didn't have a choice; she could see the advantage of that. With a hand pressed to her chest, she went back and forth, but it was overwhelming.

"If you don't like these, there are others," he said, nervous now. "Or we can have one designed."

"Omigod, *no,* Leo," she said, clutching his hand to her throat. "These are *exquisite.*"

"He knew what he wanted," said Victoria with a hint of something British in her voice. "He has very good taste."

Charlotte doubted that her own taste was as good, but her eye kept returning to one of the rings. It was a pear-shaped diamond flanked by tapering baguettes. She liked the simplicity of it, liked the spark the diamond emitted.

Within minutes, it was on her finger. She could hardly breathe.

It had to be sized, but smart Leo had made that part of the deal. The chosen ring went to the in-store silversmith for an hour, during which time they walked outside and, for the first time, he took in the grandeur of Manhattan in general, and Rockefeller Center and St. Patrick's Cathedral in particular. Charlotte was the one who clung now—to his arm, his hand, his side—more amazed at the courage of her husband-to-be than anything the city had to offer.

When they returned to Tiffany's, the ring was waiting, sparklingly alive in a velvet-lined box. Charlotte inhaled a stunned gasp, again thinking it was way too expensive, way too large, way too *flawless* for someone as flawed as she. But Leo was removing it from its bed, dropping to one knee, and offering himself to her. He didn't speak. Didn't have to. She heard the words loud and clear in the sweet, shy, vulnerable look on his face.

Grinning, she held out a shaky finger. He slid the ring on, then rose and, slipping his hands into her hair, tipped her face up for the simplest, most honest kiss. Only when it was done did she hear the applause of onlookers, at which point, embarrassed in a delighted way, she tucked her face into his neck.

It couldn't have been better scripted if he had written the scene himself.

Epilogue

JUNE WOULD ALWAYS BE CHARLOTTE'S favorite month on Quinnipeague. She loved the purples and pinks of new flowers and the smell of moist earth. She loved the frothy roil of the sea as it recovered from a day of rain, and in those early mornings, before the fog lifted and sun warmed the island, there was nothing, *nothing* better than a wood fire, wool socks, and hot chocolate made from scratch.

She had the hot chocolate this morning, but with Leo back in bed, she didn't need the fire or the socks. Propped against the headboard, he was typing away, but looked over when he felt her eyes on him.

"Happy anniversary," she whispered, cradling the warm mug as she lay on her side.

He raised a brow. "Not 'til October."

"It was one year ago tonight that I first walked here and saw you on your roof."

Amused, he considered that. "Only a year?"

"Weird, isn't it."

He opened an arm for her to scoot closer. Hadn't they been this way forever? But no. They had come from totally different places, which should have made compatibility a challenge. And yet, as easy as it was for Charlotte to see his side, what gratified her most was how safe he now felt in moving toward hers.

Not that they had ever disagreed about getting married quickly and on Quinnipeague. Leo wanted a small wedding, and Charlotte would have been happy exchanging vows at the end of the dock or in the herb garden. But Quinnies were vocal about wanting to attend, and she loved this community she was marrying into. "It's a tribute to you," she told Leo when he hedged at the thought of a crowd. "They're saying that they know your childhood was hell, they're sorry they didn't do more, and they really like you. They do, Leo."

In essence, Quinnies ran the wedding, which was fine with Charlotte, who didn't know the first thing about running anything beyond a dinner for four . . . and that, with take-in. Nicole had offered to help and did take her wedding-gown shopping. But Nicole was busy shuttling between Philadelphia and New York, working with her editor to get the cookbook into production, and giving Julian emotional support at a time when his future hadn't quite taken shape.

The ceremony was held in the church. Charlotte wore a stunning white gown, which was as close as she came to traditional, what with her hair loose and curling, her fingernails painted blue, and Bear walking her down the aisle. They went slow. Bear's excuse was arthritis, hers the four-inch heels Nicole had insisted she wear, though the heels came off for the progressive celebration that followed, starting with champagne on the front steps of the church, moving on to appetizers at the Island Grill, dinner at the Chowder House, and dancing under a heated tent on Nicole's patio.

Leo's dad, though a Mainer with a long history of public service, was awkward with Quinnies. He knew many of those there, but if they didn't resent him for abandoning Cecily, they did for abandoning Leo. They were polite, but there was clearly no love lost on his behalf. Julian, who didn't know all that many Quinnies, enjoyed discussing law enforcement, so kept an eye on him.

"What're you thinking?" Leo whispered now. He had a hand on her belly, which was seriously swollen. She was seven months pregnant. Four more weeks on the island, then they would shift to New York for the duration.

"Your dad. We should take him to dinner on our way to New York."

"Why?"

Charlotte gave him a chiding pinch. "Because he's your dad. And because he's LL's grandfather." LL was little Leo, though Leo was adamant about not naming the baby after him. He wanted Ethan, after the hero of *Salt*. Charlotte loved that name, too, though she felt that, in the absence of in-utero clothing, LL was more boyish than LE.

Leo didn't reply. She knew he would come around about his father. He usually did, not that they saw the man often. He certainly wasn't an active player in their lives. Still, he and Leo did share genes. Charlotte, being Charlotte and incorrigibly curious, had found common ground with him discussing granite quarrying, which was part of the midcoast Maine history and about which it appeared he knew a great deal.

It was about roots. Charlotte was finally growing them now and was greedy. Not the least bit ashamed of that, she snuggled in.

He drew his head back to see her face. "That's a smug smile. What now?"

She shrugged, grinned, eyed his computer. "I'm thinking how far you've come."

"Literally?"

"That, too."

He was on his second book—actually, the second one after *Salt*—and just starting Chapter 16, if the screen was to be believed. He claimed Charlotte was his muse, but she knew better. Having exorcised a raft of demons, his mind had opened. He would never love traveling as much as he loved Quinnipeague, but his world had begun to grow. After New York had come a honeymoon in New Zealand, then a week in Eastern Europe, where Charlotte was on assignment, then one in Iceland. Though he would only admit it when forced, new places inspired him. Once the baby was big enough to tuck in a carrier, they would be traveling not for her work, but his.

With the help of his lawyer, Leo had hired an agent who sold the second Chris Mauldin for bigger bucks than he had ever dreamed. He had written it in four brief winter months, and, having proven to himself that he *could,* had signed another contract. The deal specified that Chris Mauldin would neither tour nor do anything else to reveal his identity, and though his publisher fought him on the issue of confidentiality, Leo wasn't budging. Moreover, he would only meet with his agent or editor in the office of his attorney. Slightly paranoid? Perhaps. But they were hungry enough for his books to agree.

With the advance he received for *Salt*'s successor, he had bought a brownstone in Brooklyn, where they spent much of their work time at catty-cornered desks. Bear was with them, sleeping through the long drive, too old to care about the change in location or even about having to wear a leash. Leo was probably more aware of the leash than Bear was. Tethered to the dog, he ventured farther afield on his own. And then there was the reality of a hospital. Having accepted that Charlotte absolutely would *not* give birth at home, he used tours and birthing classes to mitigate his unease. It helped that Nicole and Julian were doing the same in Philadelphia; Nicole was due three weeks after Charlotte.

And Julian? Eight months after the transplant, he was remarkably well. Though his symptoms had improved, the hospital wouldn't allow him to operate. He had known that would be so. Still, it was a door that had closed once and for all, and he took it hard. Then alternatives had sprung up. He was on television more than ever, as something of a poster child now for MS, a motivational speaker at events, an advocate for pushing the envelope of medical trials—all of which was great publicity for Nickitotable and her cookbook.

A vibration sounded on Charlotte's nightstand. Rolling herself over, she put the mug there in exchange for the phone.

"Just wanted to hear your voice," Nicole said. Pregnancy had left her breathless, which ratcheted up her voice to the pitch it used to be. But she didn't babble as much. She had grown up that last summer. It wasn't a bad thing.

Actually, it was a good thing for Charlotte, since they were in touch every day—often multiple times—sharing advice, complaints, fears. And since Charlotte was trying to get ahead on her own assignments, brief calls or texts worked best.

"Feeling okay?" she asked now.

"I do not like this extra weight. But there's good news," Nicole said, clearly struggling to contain her excitement. "We're into a third printing." The cookbook had come out in time for Mother's Day, with promotions planned for summer sales. Since those had yet to begin, something was working even without. "They are thrilled. And my editor says, by the way, that heartburn is not necessarily a sign that the baby will have hair, since she had heartburn the whole time and her baby turned out bald."

Charlotte laughed. "I don't have heartburn, just hiccups. What does that mean?" She felt the bed move as Leo slid down behind her.

"ADHD?" Nicole ventured.

"I seriously hope not," Charlotte said, covering Leo's hands when they covered her baby bump.

"Maybe he'll be a dancer."

"Uh-huh," Charlotte drawled. "Tap."

"Or a workout guru. Hit it big in that, and you can do really well. Mine, now mine will be an inventor, kind of like its dad."

Charlotte only heard part of the last. Leo was nibbling her ear. "Okay, Nicki, I have to run. Talk later." She hung up, pushed the phone under the pillow, and smiled at the far wall. "What are you up to?"

"Up," was all he said, though she could certainly feel that. He snaked a hand under her tee—his actually—and stroked her breast. "When's she coming?"

"Soon," Charlotte murmured, there so quickly, given his clever fingers and mobile hips.

His breath was warm against her ear, his smile audible, his up larger. "Not you. Nicole."

"Next week," she managed, breathing shallowly. Angie was already on Quinnipeague, beside herself in anticipation of *two* births as she opened the house for the season. Tom had come to help, but would be leaving before Nicole arrived. That said, Nicole was starting to come around, with Bob gone now for eighteen . . . uh, twenty . . . uh, however many months—Charlotte couldn't think straight with Leo's hand between her legs. When his leg raised hers and he entered her from behind, she gasped at the beauty of the fullness. There had always been physical chemistry between them, but add emotional chemistry to it and the pleasure exploded. This was one of the pieces that Charlotte had never had with anyone else.

Though he barely moved, the heat was searing. Ever so slowly, it built and burst, and for a time after that, all she knew was a residual panting at her ear, the rapid rise and fall of his warm, now-damp torso against her back, and fading spasms inside.

When it finally ended, she rolled herself over, cupped his chin, and met the deep blue eyes that she desperately wanted their son to have.

"I hate not looking at you," she whispered.

"I don't want anything between us."

"Not even your own child?"

"Nope, not even him," Leo said and grinned. He did that a lot now. It wasn't the mean grin of a guy with a chip on his shoulder and a fear of flying, but the smug one of a happy man.

Lost in it, she couldn't speak, but could only look at him and feel the love link they shared.

Raising a brow, he made a show of turning his ear her way. "Nothing to say?"

She smiled back, as smug and happy as he was, and simply shook her head.

Acknowledgments

Sweet Salt Air marks the start of a new phase in my career as I begin work with the talented and energetic team at St. Martin's Press. There are so many people to thank. Topping the list, though, have to be my editor, Hilary Rubin Teeman, whose in-depth notes reflect the in-depth thoughts that I need, and my publisher, Matthew Shear, who quickly asked me where I want to go and, as quickly, pointed me there. Still, yet again, I thank my agent, Amy Berkower, for her sound advice and unflagging support, both professionally and politically.

Thanks to my assistant, Lucy Davis, for one very special contact above and beyond the rest—to wit, Dr. John Wagner, whom I thank profusely for his dedication to umbilical cord stem cell research. I asked him to share his thoughts of the future with me, and he did. I dreamed that by the time this book was published, treatments such as the one described here would be the norm. They aren't yet, but we're getting there.

In that sense, I would be remiss if I didn't acknowledge the estimated 2.1 million people who, at this writing, have multiple sclerosis. You helped me understand the frustration, pain, and fear this disease brings. I wish you all the very, very best as medical breakthroughs approach.

More generally, I thank my readers for their loyalty and patience as they allow me time to write a better book.

Finally, always, I thank my family for its love. I am one very lucky soul. I wake up every morning knowing that.

Blueprints

to finn,
for sweet blueprints
and love always

prologue

The rain let up just in time. The final day of taping for the spring season of *Gut It!* was about to begin, and though the sun hadn't yet appeared, Caroline MacAfee's hopes were high. Well behind the stream of work vehicles pulling up on the road, the western sky was giving way to scattered patches of blue, as the June breeze pushed gunmetal clouds east, toward Boston and the sea.

How to describe what she felt as she stood at the head of an all-new cobblestone drive looking at the rebuilt facade of what once been a weary old Cape? There was relief that the hard work was done, and surprise—always surprise—that everything had come together so well. There was also a sense of ownership. Caroline hadn't asked to be the mouthpiece of the show, but after nearly ten years as host, it was her baby as much as anyone's.

Gut It! was a local public television production, a home renovation series headlined by women—specifically, the women of MacAfee Homes. It touted neither high drama nor celebrity antics, just real work by real people with whom an audience of real women identified. The taping was done by a single cameraman, who was male but good, and directed by an executive producer, who was female and smart. If said producer was also prickly at times, the success of the show forgave it. Over the course of twenty projects, *Gut It!* had built a cult following that Caroline believed would only grow with this one.

Glancing skyward, she rubbed her hands together and grinned at the camera. "I wore yellow today to inspire the weather gods." She hitched her head at the approaching blue. "But how perfect is this? Welcome back to Longmeadow, Massachusetts, where we're putting the finishing touches on the latest *Gut It!* redo. As you can see"—she stepped aside for a worker shouldering a large roll of sod—"things are pretty busy right now." She skipped back again, this time with an excited "Hey," for a pair of furniture movers carrying a sofa toward the house. "Great fabric," she called after them and told the camera, "Our homeowners are planning to sleep here for the first time tonight, so we're hustling today. Lots to do."

Inviting viewers along with her chin, she started to walk. Talk came easily. She hadn't expected that, when she stumbled into this role, but she and the camera had become friends. "It's been six months since we began work on the small Cape that Rob and Diana LaValle put in our care. They needed more space, but since the house was originally built by Diana's grandparents and held the emotions of four generations, a teardown was out of the question. Our challenge was to preserve the heart of the house while we doubled its size, updated its features, and made its systems state-of-the-art efficient and green. Today is the day of reckoning. Let's see how we did."

Feeling a visceral delight, she guided the camera to her daughter, who was consulting with the general contractor as they watched the last of the exterior shutters being hung. That contractor, Dean Brannick, was the only male who appeared in every episode, but he had become such a fan favorite that no one minded. As he loped off, Caroline called, "Catch you in a bit, Dean," and slipped an arm around Jamie's waist. It was the kind of spontaneous gesture she had hesitated to show at first. Turned out, viewers loved it. Second to the female angle in appeal came the mother-daughter connection.

The resemblance between them was strong—same wide mouth, fern-green eyes, and auburn hair—but their differences were nearly as marked. Caroline let her hair wave, while Jamie blew hers straight; Caroline was five-seven to Jamie's five-three; Jamie wore the sophisticated neutrals of a young architect, but master carpenter Caroline, when not behind goggles and a chop saw, was known for color. Her yellow jeans were paired today with a matching tank under a slim-fitting turquoise sweater, all in contrast to Jamie's gray slacks and jacket.

"Talk to us, Jamie," Caroline invited. "As the architect of record for this project, you've been involved since Day One." She gestured toward the house. "Whaddaya think?"

"I'm *pleased,*" Jamie replied as they walked on. "The best part of an architect's job is seeing a house go from modest to amazing, and this one did." Her pride showed; the camera hung on that. Cutaways of detail work would be inserted later, as would second or third takes, but for now it was all about feeling and flow. "The original structure had one and a half stories and a steeply pitched roof. By raising that roof, we were able to create three generous bedrooms and a loft on the second floor, with an expanded kitchen and a whole new great room underneath."

"Everything energy-efficient."

"Totally, from insulated floor joists to double-thick insulation and dual-pane windows."

"And that's just the inside." Caroline raised admiring eyes. "This exterior is something."

"I agree. The homeowners wanted to dress things up without losing the flavor of the original Cape," Jamie reminded viewers, "so we bumped out the front foyer and added fieldstone to the facade. And new gables over the second-floor windows? Wow." Her eyes touched the brackets under each gable. "Gotta love those corbels."

"Amen," smiled Caroline, who had carved them herself.

"Not *amen,*" broke in the producer with a hand on the cameraman's shoulder to signal a cut. "This isn't about religion. Jamie, sweetheart, repeat that last line."

Jamie did. This time, Caroline managed a whole other kind of smile and said, "Absolutely," before moving on to the colors Dean had picked. The man was multifaceted. In addition to ordering supplies and hiring subs, he could handle any aspect of construction, including the egos of men who did grunt work in a world of women, and homeowners who had no clue about exterior paint. Here, cedar shingles picked up a deep gray from the stonework, while the trim was a startlingly pure white.

"Crisp and fresh," Jamie breathed. "And it all blends with the architectural shingles he chose for the roof."

"What we don't see from here, of course . . ."

". . . are the triple-junction solar cell panels. They're another aspect of the energy-efficient reconstruction of this house."

"All of which we'll get to later. For now, I'm just stunned at how elegant a Cape can look."

Jamie laughed her agreement. "This house used to be old. Now it has a reinvigorated sense of tradition. Take these cobblestones. Dean found them in a mill warehouse in New Hampshire. They date back to the turn of the twentieth century." She glanced at Caroline. "Remember the detached one-car garage that was here?"

"It was an eyesore."

"And inadequate. The LaValles have four kids who'll be driving soon, hence a new three-car attached garage at the back of the house. By leveling the old one, we not only removed a visual distraction but gained valuable land abutting the kitchen." A cutaway would show the new patio, replete with trelliswork and a raised fire pit.

After a discussion of the challenges posed by the topography of the lot, Caroline drew the camera's eye back to the front porch. "The stone columns add an arts-and-crafts element, which enhances the curb appeal tenfold. And just look at the front door. It's taller and wider than it was, and the sidelights make it grand. Jamie, you always envisioned an imposing entrance—"

"Wait," the producer cut in. "Caroline, you're talking too much. Let Jamie speak."

Caroline felt an inkling of annoyance. She wasn't doing any more than she ever did, but the point was too petty to argue. Thinking that she was ready to be free of Claire Howe for a few months, she said, "Okay. That's fine." She glanced at Jamie, who nodded.

"Let's start fresh with the front porch," Claire instructed, at which point Jamie re-created her mother's narration. Since there was no formal script, the words were slightly different, and Jamie's manner of speech reflected her age. She tripped once, but started again and went smoothly on.

They were heading inside when Caroline was distracted by the women in the shrubbery beds. Stopping Jamie with a hand on her arm, she called, *"Annie."* Annie Ahl was the show's landscape designer. Wearing mud-crusted boots, gloves, and a satisfied expression, she stepped out from between a pair of newly planted junipers. The pixie cut of her pure silver hair suited her diminutive size.

Caroline was looking beyond the junipers. "Do I recognize those?"

"Good eye," Annie said in the high voice that had nearly nixed her place in the show. Like the cameraman and his feel for light, though, her instinct for design was too good to pass up. She was the senior landscape architect at MacAfee Homes, and Caroline's close friend. "We removed those azaleas last fall to protect them from the mess of construction. They wintered over in my nursery, and now here they are, back home. They actually bloomed two weeks ago. See the last of the flowers?" There would be a cutaway of those. For now, the camera stayed on the talent. "Naturally, we'll have to wait to see how they do here next spring, but I'm confident they'll make it. They're hardy."

"And they have company now." Caroline took in the new plantings.

"Uh-huh. One row—"

"Not *uh-huh,*" Claire cut in. "I've asked you not to say that, Anne."

Annie said a particularly high-pitched, "I'm sorry. It's just natural."

"I like natural, but not *uh-huh*. And watch the voice. It's too high."

Caroline had never once read a complaint about that on their Facebook page, which she personally monitored. But Claire was the boss. In a voice that wouldn't reach the woman, she told Annie both of those things. Once Annie gathered herself, they resumed.

"When I first saw this house," she said perfectly, "the shrub beds were long and narrow, which was typical of beds at the time the house was built. I wanted greater depth to complement Jamie's new designs, so we widened and reshaped them. The taller shrubs in back are Andromeda, holly, and yew. I've planted juniper in and around the azaleas, and we're just now putting in perennials."

"Good job, guys," Caroline called to the two still planting, and let Annie go.

As she and Jamie climbed the stairs to enter the house, Caroline pointed out the solid walnut front door with its raised panels and bronze hardware. In the foyer, they saw Dean coming down the hall from the kitchen. "We're just tweaking the security system," he said. "Want to see the control room?"

The cameraman signaled a break. After cold drinks all around, they picked up in the basement with the security specialist, who was giving a rundown on the advanced features of a system that went far beyond security to include remote control of heating, cooling, and irrigation. Dean took the lead; he was easy on the eye and ear, and he understood electronics. When the plumbing and heating expert joined them to explain the environmental soundness of the new systems, Caroline backed off completely.

The sky continued to brighten, offering the dispersed natural light the cameraman loved. Dodging hustling crews, Caroline talked with the stone specialist, who was polishing marble in the first-floor lav, and the tile expert, who was finishing the kitchen backsplash. These scenes, largely included for DIY addicts who wanted to watch the process, would be saved or cut after the producer and her editors had a chance to log the videotape and decide how much time to spend on what.

When taping resumed in the afternoon, Caroline was in the kitchen with the homeowners, highlighting what was old, new, and repurposed, but the excitement quickly turned to the great room, where the show's interior designer, Taylor Huff, was supervising the placement of furniture. Sectional sofas complemented cushiony chairs, whose upholstery coordinated with window valences and chair cushions in the kitchen. Then came the media specialist, who was programming the remote for a huge flat-screen TV. *Gut It!* had worked with her before; she was at the forefront of technology and reliable to a fault when it came to installation. Unfortunately, she flustered easily. Even before Claire could intervene, Caroline stopped the taping to calm the woman, then reshaped questions to help her along.

One by one, the crews finished up, and neighbors and guests began to arrive. By early evening, as the lowering sun spilled through the dining room into the foyer, production assistants were arranging nearly forty family, friends, craftsmen, and crew for the group shot that had become a *Gut It!* tradition.

Caroline was front and center. Facing the camera a final time, she said with satisfaction, "There you have it, a recap of this season's *Gut It!* We took a sixty-year-old Cape that was too small for a growing family, too dated for a modern couple, and too wasteful in an energy-conscious town, and we turned it into a larger, younger, greener home. Now, we're here with homeowners Rob and Diana, at the foot of the stunning winding staircase that they always dreamed of having. I'm Caroline MacAfee, the host of *Gut It!* Thanks so much for being with us this season. We hope you'll join us next season for a whole new project." She looked around. "Everyone set?" Facing front, she slid one arm around her daughter and the other around Diana LaValle. "O-*kay,*" she said, then, "Squish in, you guys," when the cameraman gestured as much. Seconds of compression passed. "All eyes on the camera." There was one click, then a second and third, then a communally held breath while the cameraman checked his playback. When he smiled, Caroline turned to her friends and raised a triumphant fist in the air. *"Yesss!"*

one

Jamie MacAfee would always be her parents' child. It didn't matter that she was twenty-nine and financially independent. When it came to her mother and father, she was still the little girl whose life had been shaped by their divorce and her need to please them both—which was why she was increasingly anxious as she drove across town for a quick breakfast with her dad.

The streets were early-morning quiet. School buses hadn't yet started to roll, lawn mowers remained stowed, and what other noises there might have been at seven were muted by a thick and ominous heat. June wasn't supposed to be this hot in New England. Humidity that had been oppressive the evening before remained trapped under the dense maples and oaks that lined her route, and the silk blouse she wore stuck to her skin. Her convertible top was down. Two streets into the drive, she jacked up the air and aimed the blowers at her neck, but her anxiety remained.

It ticked up a notch when she passed the corner of South Main and

Grove, where the teardown being rebuilt by her major competitor as a Dutch Colonial was starting to look a little too good.

It ticked up further when she passed an Audi A5 that looked exactly like her fiancé's but, of course, was not. Brad Greer had left her condo at six that morning after what should have been a sweet cup of coffee in bed turned into a set-to about picking a wedding date. They had been engaged for six months, and she hadn't done it yet. Her fault. Totally. Between taping *Gut It!* and working on a dozen projects in various stages of design, she hadn't had time to breathe. Brad was vulnerable when it came to love, though, and it tore at her when he got all down in the mouth, as he had earlier.

He hadn't called, hadn't texted. She would have driven to his place if there'd been time.

But there wasn't, which brought her to her father. He was the real source of her angst. He knew she had a special reason today to be with her mother, and for Jamie, there should have been no contest. Caroline wasn't just her mother; she was her best friend—and Jamie was all the family Caroline had. Roy, conversely, had moved on. Twice. Jamie hadn't cared for his second wife and wasn't sorry when the brief marriage ended, but his third and current wife, who was close to Jamie's own age, had become a friend. Moreover, Roy was absorbed enough with Jessica and their young son to leave Jamie to her own life.

Unless he needed her for something.

Which he apparently did now.

Still, she should have put him off.

But he had been dogged last night on the phone, evading every attempt she made to discuss whatever it was there and then. *This is about work,* he had finally said with unusual gravity. Work meant MacAfee Homes, where Jamie and every other local MacAfee was employed. She offered to be at the office by nine, but Roy had been adamant about seeing her before she saw her mother.

Those were his words. *Before you see your mother.*

That was what frightened her. The implication was that he wanted to talk about Caroline, but what could he say? Caroline had been a master carpenter for MacAfee Homes since before marrying Roy, and their parting hadn't slowed her rising star. Roy's father, Theodore MacAfee, who headed the business, blamed his son for the divorce far more than he did Caroline. Theo adored Caroline. Whenever Roy tried to exclude her from plum assignments, Theo overruled him. Likewise when Caroline wanted birch burl or some such exotic wood and Roy claimed she was over budget.

Then again, Jamie realized, Roy's current emergency could be as simple as his wanting her to babysit two-year-old Tad while he and Jessica vacationed in Europe, which would certainly impact Jamie's work. Being a full-time mom was hard; she had watched Jess struggle, and Jess did not have a career outside the home. But Jamie did love her father, and she was totally smitten by her half brother, which meant she could never say no.

Jamie didn't think that warranted drop-everything-and-come insistence, but he wouldn't be denied. The best she'd been able to do was get him to meet at seven, so that she could still see Caroline before work.

And there he was, crossing the lot at Fiona's as she pulled in off the street. She waved through her open top and parked. Glancing in the rearview mirror, she ran quick fingers through her hair, but all she saw, to her dismay, were the freckles on her nose. So much for her expensive new concealer. The heat apparently melted makeup just as it swallowed up breathable air.

Resigned, she groped around for her shoes in the floor well and slipped them on, then slid out of the car as deftly as her short black skirt and those high heels allowed. The skirt showed off slim hips; the heels added inches she desperately needed. Pairing them with white silk, she was dressed to impress, though not solely for her dad. This was her typical take-me-seriously look for days that were filled with meetings. Most architects doing her level of work were older than she was, and while the family business gave her a leg up, it also gave her a name to uphold.

Freckles didn't help, but there was no erasing them now. The best she could do was to put her shoulders back and set off with a pretense of confidence—only to ricochet right back when the long strap of her shoulder bag caught in the door. *That* wasn't impressive, she mused, though it was nothing she hadn't done before. As physically coordinated as she was when focused, when distracted, she was pathetic.

Freeing the bag, she strode forward.

Fiona's was an upscale diner that offered the best breakfast in town, which meant that even this early in the day, it was humming. The parking lot was comfortably full; the air held the lure of hot corn muffins, chunky hash browns, and local maple syrup.

By the time she caught up to Roy, he was talking with two of Williston's finest, on their way home after a night on patrol. They had admiring smiles for Jamie as she hurried to keep up with Roy, who was entering the diner. He immediately began working booths filled with real estate agents, lawyers, plumbers, shopkeepers, husbands and wives—all local, all friends. Williston lay twenty miles west of Boston. Home to fifteen thousand residents, it was ruled by a Board of Selectmen, but if there had been a mayor, Roy would have been it. He was always smiling, always up for a meet-and-greet, always remembering names. Theo had done this for years until age crippled his mornings, at which point Roy smoothly stepped in. As the single largest employer in town, not to mention the raison d'être for many town shops, MacAfee Homes treasured local goodwill.

Roy made it happen. That he was strikingly handsome didn't hurt. With his keen brown eyes and perpetual tan, he looked younger than fifty-two. The gray that had spattered his hair a decade before had miraculously turned sandy, and, though Jamie didn't know for fact, she would bet that his forehead was medicinally smoothed. Not that she criticized him for it. He put in the effort to stay in shape—had likely gone running at dawn that morning, even in the heat. Now, dressed in a crisp blue shirt and fine gray slacks, he had a fresh-from-the-shower sheen.

For Roy, it was all about looking young—young body, young face, young wife. The irony, of course, was that with Jamie always trying to look older than twenty-nine, they were occasionally taken for brother and sister. Roy loved that, and while Jamie was proud of her father for his efforts and, yes, for his looks, she found the brother-sister comparisons awkward.

This day, she didn't get a formal greeting from him—no hug or kiss, no *hey, honey, thanks for coming*—just a possessive arm around her shoulder, drawing her into the small talk.

But small talk wasn't her strength. She could speak at length about architectural design, energy efficiency, or repurposed barnboard, but she wasn't good at keeping track of whose mother was sick, whose son had gotten into college, or which tree service would take down the rotting pine in the center of town. Roy knew all that and more, in part because Jess picked up gossip at the local hair salon and shared it with him. Jamie would have forgotten it in two seconds flat. Not Roy. He remembered every last detail, pulling out whatever was appropriate in a way that endeared him to his audience.

Today, the talk was of the weather. *Beastly hot . . . not right . . . fierce storms coming.* Jamie smiled and nodded, but after a minute began to shift from one high heel to the other.

Her mother was waiting. Today was her birthday. And she'd had surgery on her wrist less than twenty-four hours before. Jamie had texted her earlier but wanted to *be* there.

Finally, Roy guided her to a free booth. Fiona's wasn't so much a single railroad car as a square of four cars framing an open kitchen. The decor was a virtual history of the town, Fighting Falcon–blue wall after wall of framed high school senior class photos dating back to the mid-1900s, and laminated front pages of the *Williston News,* née the *Williston Crier,* memorializing the town during major events like the fire of '56, which wiped out half the town center, the blizzard of '78, which paralyzed town life for weeks, and the '04 Red Sox capturing their first World Series title in eighty-six years, which had been out-of-the-park *awesome* for a town in which two team members had lived. More old newspaper clippings covered the tabletops and were covered in turn by a thick sheet of glass, but the clutter ended there. Benches were upholstered in a soothing gray, place mats woven to match. Cloth napkins, knotted around silverware, filled a slim tin by the wall. Jamie automatically reached for two as they slid into the booth, passing one to Roy, who placed his cell beside it.

They were barely seated when the waitress brought the mud-strong coffee he liked and a pitcher of cream. Once both mugs were filled, Roy ordered his usual three-cheese omelet, Jamie her usual egg-white frittata.

What she really wanted was a side of the thick, sizzling bacon that smelled so good, but ordering it was out of the question, (A) because it was unhealthy and (B) because Roy would have felt the need to discuss that, and the last thing she wanted was to distract him.

Cupping her mug, she leaned in, anxious to hear what was on his mind. Before she could ask, he confided in a hushed voice, "See that guy behind me at the end of the row, the one with the red hair? He's a Barth."

Not urgent news, Dad, and nothing to do with Mom. But Jamie glanced at the redhead in question. "Barths are blond," she said for lack of anything wiser.

"Not this one. He's buying the house on Appleton and plans to live in it. He just moved back from California with his wife and kids and is rejoining the business. The Barth Brothers teardown at the corner of South Main and Grove? It has location, magnitude, and visibility. They're making a statement with it. They want to make inroads here."

"Why here? Williston's our base. They have the North Shore. MetroWest is ours." MacAfee Homes had dominated the suburbs west of Boston since before she was born.

"They want the Weymouth acreage," he said, referring to the largest privately owned parcel in town.

"It's not even on the market," Jamie argued, though she knew that preemptive buys, negotiated directly with the seller, were common. "Is it?" she asked on an uneasy note.

"Not yet. But Mildred Weymouth has been dead nearly a year, and her kids can't agree on what to do with the place, much less afford the upkeep. The grounds have gone to shit, and property taxes are in default. Mildred's trustee says they have no choice but to sell." With a soft whistle and both hands on his mug, Roy sat back. "Thirty acres of prime wooded land? Pretty tempting."

Seriously, Jamie thought. Speculation had run wild since Mildred Weymouth's passing, and Jamie was deep in the mix. She envisioned a hybrid community of single-family homes and condos, all developed by MacAfee Homes. "We can outbid the Barths."

Roy checked his phone, put it down. "They'll drive up the price."

That was a problem, Jamie knew, but nothing MacAfee Homes couldn't handle. A single Barth moving to town didn't supplant the power of three generations of MacAfees who had lived here forever.

Roy proceeded to say as much in different combinations of words, and all the while, the little voice in Jamie's head was saying, *Come on, Dad. We could have discussed this at the office. Why here? Why now?*

Their breakfast arrived, but she barely looked. Teasing—not scolding, never scolding—she said, "This wasn't why you wanted to see me before I saw Mom."

Roy smacked the ketchup bottle over his omelet. "Hell, no. I only thought of it because that Barth was right there." Setting the ketchup aside, he softened. "I hear you saw Taddy the other night. Sorry I missed you. I was at the selectmen's meeting. How was he?"

Jamie gave a helpless smile. "Adorable. He calls me Mamie. I love that he's talking."

"Mostly he says *no*. Jessica's struggling with that."

"She seemed okay to me."

Roy frowned. "I'm talking tantrums. She has no idea what to do when he throws himself on the floor and kicks and screams."

"But all kids do that. Sometimes it's the only way they can express themselves. I saw one of his tantrums. It was actually pretty cute—I know, easy for me to say, since I leave when the going gets tough." But that couldn't be why her father had wanted to see her, either. "So, Dad. You got me here good and early."

"The early was your doing."

"And you know why." Caroline.

Ignoring the bait, Roy checked his phone, this time swiping once, then again. It wasn't for work, Jamie knew. He was checking Twitter and sports news. "There's a good point guard on the summer league team," he murmured, "but if the Celts don't trim their roster to get under the max . . ." With a grunt, he returned the phone to the table, then brightened. "How's Brad?"

Jamie sighed. There was nothing urgent about Brad—well, there was, but her father didn't need to know that. "Brad's awesome," she said, as was expected.

"You know that I think of him like a son."

How could she not? He said it often enough.

"He's good for you, good for the business. Someday . . ."

He didn't have to finish. Someday, Brad would head MacAfee Homes. He had come to the company straight from law school, hired as an assistant to the in-house lawyer, who had become pregnant soon after and opted to be a stay-at-home mom. Though barely thirty, Brad had taken over. That was three years ago, and he had more than proven himself since. In his quiet, competent way, he had shown an understanding of the business that went beyond law. Since Jamie had no interest in these things, once they were married, Brad would be right behind Roy in the line of succession.

Theo liked that idea.

So did Roy, who, while he certainly wasn't ceding any real power to his future son-in-law yet, had already begun to share some of the more onerous tasks that he didn't care to do himself.

Grinning in a self-satisfied way, he tapped the plate with his fork. "I have to tell you, the stars are aligned. I thought Brad was the icing on the cake, but now there's more on top of that, and it is sweet indeed." Fork in midair, he came forward, brown eyes alive. "I met with Levitt and Howe yesterday to discuss the future of *Gut It!*" Brian Levitt was the general manager of the station that hosted the show, Claire Howe the show's executive producer.

Jamie was confused. As far as she knew, the future was decided. The fall project was in its final stages of production prior to taping, and the spring project had been picked, preliminary designs drawn, permits filed.

Roy's mouth curved into a smug smile. "You're the new host."

She drew back in alarm. "Mom's the host."

"They say we need a change. Things have been the same for a while. It's time for a facelift."

Scrambling for an explanation, she said, "A facelift would mean changing the format or the graphics or maybe taking on different projects. But

I've been giving them cutting-edge designs. Don't they like them? Do they not want me to be the architect anymore?"

"They love your work, honey. They love *you.* That's the point." His fork urged her to eat her frittata.

Wishing it were bacon, she managed a small piece, but there was no comfort in it. She was thinking how much more satisfying the bacon would have been when he said, "They want you to continue doing what you're doing *and* be the show's host. It's really a no-brainer. You're beautiful and smart and talented. This would make your career, honey. You couldn't ask for better exposure."

"As an architect," Jamie said, setting her fork down with care. There was a whole other problem to changing the host. "What I do is intellectual. I'm more of a paper person than a people person."

"Who says? Not me. Not Claire. She gave you a leading role in several segments this season. Why do you think she did that?"

"Because the segments dealt with architectural design?"

"Because she was trying you out. You passed. You were great." Chiding, he added, "You told her you loved it."

Jamie might have, but specifics were a blur. "What else would I say? Claire's our EP, and she's tough. But talking about my own field is one thing. Talking about every other field in home construction is something else. And anyway, *Mom's* the host," she repeated, more loudly now, because this was the other half of the equation, and it was huge. "Our audience loves her. Ratings are good."

Roy ran a napkin over his mouth. "They could be better."

"Says *who*?" Jamie asked, frightened now, because, despite dozens of meetings with Levitt and Howe to prepare for the fall, no one had mentioned a ratings concern.

"Brian," Roy said. "He speaks for the network, and when he speaks, we listen. He got the show off the ground ten years ago, and he's been fighting for us ever since. If it weren't for him, *Gut It!* wouldn't be in half the markets it is. He's our guardian angel." His voice tightened. "He's the GM, and when the GM has his mind made up, crossing him is not wise. We need *Gut It! Gut It!* is good for MacAfee Homes."

The issue wasn't money, Jamie knew. The station funded the show through grants and syndication fees. It paid MacAfee Homes on a contract basis, and MacAfee Homes paid cast members from that sum. What remained in company coffers was less than the profit from a major construction project—less than the condo complex they had built in Foxborough last year, and certainly less than the potential for development of the Weymouth land.

No. *Gut It!* was about exposure.

"Do you understand what a marketing boon the show is for us?" Roy asked, clearly irritated that he had to explain. "Easily half the work we get is from people who either watch it or know someone who does. And then there are endorsements. Tools, 'as seen on.' Gloves, 'as seen on.' And the books documenting each season? The Barths have brochures; we have stunning coffee table books. They're a powerful marketing tool, but they're worth zip if the show is canceled."

"I know," she conceded. "We need the show. But Mom should stay on as host."

"It's done, Jamie." He lifted his phone, checked the face, put it down. "The station is not renewing her contract as host. She's out."

"Just like *that*?" Jamie asked, appalled by both suddenness and finality. She knew the station could do it. But out of the blue? With no warning? That was no way to operate. Forget that Caroline was Jamie's mother; she was a human being who had basically shaped *Gut It!* with her bare hands. "Aren't our terms with the station meant to be negotiated? Can't we call our agent?" When Roy gave her an arch look, she winced. "Our *agent* thought this was a good idea?"

"He understands how things work."

"And how is that?" she asked quietly, but Roy got the point.

Blunt now, he held her gaze. "We're targeting a younger demographic."

Jamie wanted to weep. She had known this was his bottom line—of course it was—but hearing the words was something else.

"We want to win the couple buying a first home," he went on, "or the gold-mine techno-kids, or the Gen-Xers with a growing family."

"They think Mom is too old."

"I didn't say that."

But it's what you mean, said her little voice. *It's what you always mean.* Jamie loved her father, but she had no illusions. When his marriage to Caroline floundered, Roy had blamed his infidelities on her age and appearance, claiming that she had "let herself go," that he needed a more sexy wife. His second one was ten years his junior. His third was ten years younger than that.

"This isn't me, honey," he insisted. "It's Brian and Claire."

"But you can convince them they're wrong," Jamie pleaded. Her father was a consummate salesman. He could convince anyone of anything. "Mom is a master carpenter with incredible people skills. She's authoritative. She's experienced. She's reassuring."

"She's fifty-six."

"That's not old."

"For television it is. Age makes a difference."

"She looks *fabulous.*"

"She looks fifty-six."

"And not only does she *look* great," Jamie rushed on, panicked on her mother's behalf, "but her work gets better and better. She's just hitting her stride."

Roy bounced an irritated glance at the window, then whined, "No one's asking her to retire. Brian and Claire want her to stay on the show. She just won't be its public face. TV needs young."

"Roy needs young," Jamie blurted out, because her little voice simply couldn't control the frustration, to which her father shot her a *watch it, honey* look. She might have taken it back, purely for the sake of keeping peace between them, if she hadn't had a sudden, awful thought. "Oh hell, Dad. Are you breaking this to me while someone else breaks it to Mom? Is someone at the house right now telling her—like, giving her the birthday present from hell—because today *is* her birthday, you know that?"

"Yes, I know it. And no, no one's there. I wanted to talk to you about how to break it to her."

"Well, *I* don't know," Jamie cried, feeling helpless. "How do you tell a woman she's too old for her dream job? Because that's what this is, Dad. Mom stayed with carpentry even when other opportunities opened up for women, because carpentry is what she loves. Then she got roped into hosting *Gut It!* She didn't want to do it at first, remember?" There had been an outside host the first season, but the chemistry was off, and Caroline had spontaneously filled in the gaps. "It was like she discovered strengths she didn't know she had."

"So will you."

"But Mom knows construction—I mean, *knows* it. She can as easily help frame a house as carve a crown molding. I can't be on a roof the way she is. I hate heights."

"She or Dean will narrate those parts."

"But those parts," Jamie said with air quotes, "are ninety percent of the series. Framing, plumbing, heating, wiring—you name it, she can explain the entire process in lay terms. I can't do that. And handling the cast? Calming them when they're rattled? Mom has stature. We respect her *precisely* because of how long she's been doing this." When he said nothing, she whispered, "How can you ask me to kick her out?"

"This is about the survival of the show." He returned to his breakfast.

"What about Mom?" Jamie asked softly. When he simply continued to eat, she begged, "Fix this, Dad. Make them change their minds."

Midway through a triangle of toast, he said, "Honestly, Jamie. I want this for *you*."

"I don't want it." The words simmered over a backdrop of utensils, kitchen activity, and conversation. Jamie had never actively challenged Roy before. Even when she saw his face harden—even when she recognized the look as one he usually gave Caroline—she didn't soften her words. No, no, no, she didn't want to take sides, but if ever there was cause, it was now.

Eyes drilling hers, he sat back in the booth. "That wasn't the impression you gave Claire two weeks ago when she asked how you would handle the objections of the historical society to the new project." Jamie blinked, feeling used, but he wasn't done. "Or when she asked your opinion on those reluctant neighbors, and you assured her you could bring them into the fold. You knew where this was headed."

"Someday, maybe, but not *now*."

"Yes, now. It's about leadership. Tennis, architecture—hell," he said glancing at her blouse, "the way you dress—you're a natural competitor. It's what you do."

"Not against Mom." She didn't want to fight with Roy. Did *not* want him displeased. She had never, not once, criticized him for criticizing Caroline. She had certainly never said a word about the divorce. But punishing Caroline solely because of the date on her driver's license was unfair, and using Jamie as the tool to do it only made it worse. Lifting her mug, she took refuge behind it, sipping, as she struggled.

She heard Roy's fork scrabbling into the last of his omelet. She imagined he was regrouping and steeled herself.

Finally, sounding puzzled, he asked, "Don't you want to be a star, even a little?"

"Of *course* I want to be a star," she cried. She had done it in tennis—USTA junior champ for two years, ITF second seed in Paris—and had the trophies to prove it. When it came to architecture, she had won local awards. To be recognized for her work on a larger scale would be special.

The problem was Caroline. Jamie would rather die than hurt her mother, and this would hurt.

She gave it a final shot. "And even aside from the Mom issue, I don't have *time*. The host of the show does a ton of behind-the-scenes work, but I'm already in over my head." There were currently three licensed architects in MacAfee's design department, but their head architect, Jamie's mentor, was finally retiring after threatening it for years and had bequeathed his major projects to Jamie. "We're talking ten private homes, a library, two office buildings, two banks, the *spring Gut It!* project, for goodness sake, and that's not counting anything the Weymouth property may produce—and then there's planning what *I'm* supposed to be saying on air this fall about the design plans alone."

"You always do great on tape days."

"Because Mom leads. She sets the tone and asks the questions. Mom is *perfect* for this job. I am not."

Roy drained his coffee, set down the mug, and sat back. "If it's not you, it'll be someone else. Like I said, it's a done deal."

"For *fall*? Can't they wait another season or two?"

"Ratings don't wait. Consider that redheaded Barth over there. If he ratchets up the competition, we may need all the help we can get. Do you want MacAfee Homes to fall behind?" When she didn't answer, he said, "Claire's calling Caroline later to arrange a meeting."

Jamie sat back. "Please, not today."

"It has to be soon. Brian and Claire want this sewn up so that they can start putting together promo material. You know your mother best. What approach should Claire take?"

Jamie also knew her father. When his sentences came short and as fast as they did now, he was immoveable. Oh yes, the decision had been made, and it infuriated her.

She wasn't impulsive. She was a thinker, a studier, a strategizer. But her parents were her weakness, and what he proposed was untenable.

That was why, without thinking beyond the moment, she said something she would come to regret.

two

I'll tell Mom. Claire can be abrasive, and this'll be hard enough on her without that."

Too late, Jamie saw his slow smile and realized that she had played into his hands. This was what he had wanted all along. It fit the image of a MacAfee family that was united and strong. To Roy, Caroline's age was dirty laundry that should stay in the bin, handled quietly and in private.

But two could play the game, Jamie decided in a moment's defiance. If she was the one telling Caroline, then she could do it in her own words and her own time. That gave her an element of control, which, given the anxiety she felt, helped her sit through Roy's prattle about how wonderful she was and what a great host she would make. The little voice in her head was answering each line with a sarcasm she hated, until finally the head of the local Lions Club appeared at their table. Thinking that the interruption hadn't come a moment too soon, she slid out of the booth, gestured the man into her seat, gave Roy a quick peck on the cheek, and left.

Back in her car in Fiona's lot, she was hit by the heat and a wave of second thoughts. She jacked up the AC as she turned onto the street, but those second thoughts weren't as easily fixed.

What have I done? Did I seriously agree *to host the show? How can I* ever *tell Mom?*

Brad would know how. Diplomacy was his thing. But he still hadn't texted or tried to call, and she couldn't very well call him without mentioning their own issues, which seemed small by comparison.

She left Fiona's upset. By the time she'd driven two blocks, though, she was angry. She didn't want to think that Roy had put the bug in Brian's ear, though it wouldn't have been out of character. Roy saw Caroline as his aging ex-wife. He was constantly making little digs about her hair or her face, and when Jamie told him Caroline was having surgery on her wrist, he sighed and said, "That's what happens . . ."

Like there weren't crow's-feet at the corners of *his* eyes?

Like *he* didn't wear orthotics in his running shoes to help a bum knee?

Like she hadn't caught him *napping* in the office after a late night out with Jess?

So Jamie was angry at Roy, who at the very least hadn't argued when mention was made of removing Caroline as host. And she was angry at Brian Levitt, who was behaving like a chauvinist. And she was *furious* at Claire Howe, who was a woman, for God's sake, and should understand a female audience better than Brian.

Another two blocks, though, and her heart was breaking for her mother. Caroline's self-esteem was higher than it had been at any time since the divorce. This would be a terrible blow.

How to deliver it?

One thing was for sure. Jamie wasn't breathing a word to Caroline today, not on her birthday, and likely not tomorrow, since she would be gone from dawn to dusk. And if she could convince Brian and Claire that this was a bad move, she might not have to tell Caroline at all.

She tried calling Brian, then Claire, but both calls went to voice mail. Vowing to try again later, she dashed into the bakery, then the grocery store for orders she had called in the day before. Back in her car, she sped through a world that was a myriad lush shades of green, with historic houses on every block and the scent of fresh-baked goods rising from the seat beside her. Habit had her waving at a MacAfee truck, then again when she passed a neighbor from her condo complex, and as she crossed through the little shopping area that marked the center of Williston, random townsfolk acknowledged her with a chin or a hand.

The closer she got to Caroline's, the better she felt. *Forever the child?* she wondered again. She hadn't lived at home since before college, and never at Caroline's current house, yet she was soothed simply turning onto her mother's street. It was one of the most untouched in Williston, which was why, in a preemptive strike that only a town insider could make, Caroline had snapped up the house before anyone else could make a bid. MacAfee Homes would have renovated; Barth Brothers would have torn down and rebuilt. And wouldn't that have been a crime? There was no place for new construction here, certainly not of the mega size the Barths would build on this kind of lot. A McMansion would change the entire character of a street where shade trees were old and luxuriant, lawns were thick with meandering roots, and drives were dirt or stone. The houses themselves were vibrantly painted Victorians, and while Caroline's was smaller than most, its Queen Anne style heightened its charm. Teal clapboard was below, mint shingle above, all of it framed by intricately carved trim in pale blue with navy accents. Asymmetrically designed, it had a scrolled eave, a big bay window, a handsome turret, and a modest play of steep-sloped roofs, but it was the encircling veranda that Caroline claimed had sparked love at first sight. Rounding out into an open turret at the corner to allow for a wrought-iron table and vintage chairs, it was a fresh-air parlor ringed with hanging petunias in a riot of pinks. In good weather, this was where Caroline spent her free time.

Sure enough, there she was as Jamie drove up, lounging in a wicker love seat that swung from a thick chain. Her bare feet were crossed on the front rail. A smile lit her face.

With a popping of tires on gravel, Jamie turned into the driveway.

Her convertible was red, the same color as the pickup parked at the garage, but while Caroline's truck was the epitome of practical, with tools under its bed cover, dirt on its tires, and the logo of MacAfee Homes on its dusty flanks, Jamie's car was pure indulgence.

Gathering bags from the passenger's seat, she climbed out. Those feet on the rail twitched in a little wave as she started up the walk. Her mother's toenails were orange; she had seen them the day before. Pedicures were one of Caroline's weaknesses, and bright toenails were only the start. She had been wearing jeans that were yellow, purple, or green long before they became a fad. When she coordinated those jeans with shirts that were striped or plaid, she was a standout. *Gut It!* addicts also loved the bright sweaters she wore in cool weather and the hot-red parka she wore in snow. When the executive producer once suggested that she try for sophistication with black, the Facebook uproar had been fierce. Viewers wanted boldness, and her mother gave them that. There was nothing stodgy about her. Too old? No way!

Jamie swallowed her dismay.

Caroline was pink and braless today, her soft tank and shorts a tribute to heat and a well-earned hiatus. Her hair was a messy knot of waves at her crown, her face bare of makeup and gorgeous in a totally natural way.

Less gorgeous was the thick bandage around her right hand and wrist, but the absence of last night's sling was a relief. More reassuring, though, was Caroline's face, which was back to its natural glow. Her recovery-room pallor yesterday had terrified Jamie.

Carrying the bags, she bypassed newly budding roses and climbed the front steps. "Is it better or worse now that you can feel the pain?"

"Better," Caroline said with warm fern eyes, "but anything would be. There's nothing more disconcerting than having a body part that feels like it belongs to someone else. You look beautiful."

Jamie bent to kiss her cheek. It smelled woodsy, like lily-of-the-valley body wash, which meant Caroline had managed to bathe, another good sign. "Happy Birthday," she sang and drew back. "How do you feel?"

"Lazy."

"Lazy is good on a day like this. Warm, huh?"

"I've worked in worse."

"Yeah, well, the doctor said not to do anything today," Jamie warned and looked around. The laptop was blessedly absent.

Not so Master, Caroline's cat. Shimmying its massive gray coat out from under the wicker chair beyond the swing, the Maine Coon gave Jamie's leg a rub. "Poor baby must be roasting," she murmured, before refocusing on her mother's wrist. "Does it hurt?"

"Compared to raging tendonitis? Nope."

"So yes, it hurts," she deduced, because Caroline wasn't a complainer. She saw wrist problems as an occupational hazard that couldn't be helped. No one on the set had known she was in pain, and had that pain not grown progressively worse, she would never have agreed to surgery. Officially, now that taping was done, she was just "taking a few days off."

She looked thoroughly pleased with herself, which made Jamie suspicious.

"What are you taking?"

"Tylenol."

"You look too happy for just that."

Caroline laughed. "I'm relieved. I hate surgery. So now it's behind me, and here I am in my favorite place with my favorite person." The sultry quiet of the front porch was a far cry from recent days on the set. The only sounds here were the buzz of bees in the roses, the hum of a Weedwacker several houses down, and the gentle creak of Caroline's love seat as the chain moved to and fro. She eyed Jamie's armload. "Whatcha got?"

Wedging a drained iced-tea glass between her bags, Jamie managed to open the screen door. Master scooted into the house so close to her legs that she nearly bobbled the glass. "Food!" she called back as the door slapped shut.

The air inside smelled of age in a hallowed way, and though it was marginally cooler after the night, Jamie knew that wouldn't last. Her heels ticked along the dark hardwood of the hall as she passed a whitewashed grandfather clock and an L of stairs. The walls of both stairway and hall were navy, which should have closed in an already close space. But Caroline had known that between moldings, balusters, and newel posts, the white trim would bring the navy alive.

A window at the landing three steps up was open, with Master now frozen on the sill, stalking an invisible dove that cooed in the maple's depth. The living room on her right was also navy, here over peach panels. It had originally been built in the old English style, with front and back parlors, but the walls between the two had long since come down, leaving only striking trim work to mark what had been. Caroline had accessorized the room in burgundy and placed a dining table at the far end. Large and round, it was a magnificent walnut piece—she had made it herself—and was the focal point of the room for many who entered. For Jamie, though, the pièce de résistance was the swatch of Victorian lace that hung in a frame on the wall. Taken from Caroline's mother's wedding dress, it was a Rorschach test of sorts. Jamie had grown up seeing her moods in the lace.

Rather than confirm turmoil there now, she simply checked to be sure the two ceiling fans were whirring at either end of the room and strode on.

The kitchen was a sage cubby at the back of the house. High wainscoting covered its modest wall space and was topped by a wide plate rail holding rescued antiques. Though Caroline had added a line of ceiling cabinets, the storage space was sparse.

Setting her bags on the lone counter, Jamie opened the fridge and stashed what needed chilling. The rest went on the stove simply for lack of space, not that any cooking would be done here today. The room was already warm, and the heat would only rise.

In anticipation, she turned on the ceiling fan. Then she took a small plate from a glass-front cabinet. The china was hand-painted, though sturdy enough to have survived her childhood with only a single small chip. The plate she held was blue-rimmed with an apple in the center; others beneath it in the stack had different colored rims, different fruits. And oh, the memories served up on these plates—of apple wedges sprouting in eighths from a slicer (*Let's count, baby, one, two, three*) of pound cake topped with strawberries and whipped cream, of s'mores oozing marshmallow over chocolate over graham crackers.

Tucking nostalgia back inside, Jamie took a sticky bun from one of the bakery bags, a mini scone from the other, and napkins from the drawer.

After refilling the iced-tea glass from the pitcher she had brewed the night before, she tucked a slim package with a red bow under her arm. Unsure, she set it back on the counter. Seconds later, she grabbed it again and headed back out to the porch.

She reacted more sharply this time to the slap of the screen door. "A pneumatic closer would eliminate that," she advised, placing the refilled glass on the swing's wide arm beside Caroline's phone and bandaged wrist.

"But I like the sound," Caroline said without apology. Taking the sticky bun from the dish Jamie held, she bit a pecan from the top. "The slap of a screen door adds something."

"Noise."

"Flavor. It's part of what I love about this place. MacAfee Homes builds a great house—we *renovate* a great house—but recycling and repurposing and replicating, say, period millwork can only go so far in adding character. Character has to mature. It takes years for that." The love seat shifted when she lowered her legs for Jamie to pass. "I have it here now."

Jamie sank down beside her. "Air-conditioning has nothing to do with character. That sun's heading for brutal today. You need central air."

Caroline slid an indulgent glance at the paddle fan whirring softly overhead. After taking a full bite of the bun, she offered one to Jamie.

Jamie shook her head. Having deprived herself of bacon, she had every intention of eating the scone. How else to deal with frustration? She *so* wanted to do something for her mother. Caroline just gave and gave. She was too independent to ask for much, and now, if she was going to lose something she loved, there had to be something Jamie could give in exchange.

"Okay. Forget air. What about the kitchen? We could punch out a wall and double the space."

"Why do I need more space?"

"Wouldn't you like more counters? Even a desk, think of *that*. Dedicated laptop space in your kitchen? If you don't want granite or quartz, we can use butcher block or maple or hand-painted ceramic tile, any one of which would work with this house. I'd add an eating island with barn board siding and bookshelves—"

"—for the cookbooks I don't own, because I rarely cook."

"Don't laugh at me, Mom. You have tons of other books. You read all the time."

Setting the bun aside, Caroline twined their forearms and gave Jamie's hand a squeeze. Her palm was callused, another occupational hazard, and though hand lotion partnered with scented soap at every sink, it could only do so much. Not that Jamie minded. Her mother's skin was unique. Had it been smooth, it wouldn't have been Caroline's. Hell, viewers loved her toughness, too.

"Which is why," Caroline was saying, "I fell in love with this house. It came with shelves in most every nook and cranny, and what wasn't there, I built myself. I love the claw-foot tub in my bathroom and the antique fixtures in the hall, and the farmhouse sink in the kitchen is an original."

"It's porcelain."

"What's wrong with porcelain?"

"You need copper."

Caroline's silence said, quite eloquently, that she did not need copper.

Resigned, Jamie rested her head on her mother's shoulder. The ceiling beadboard was mint, a shade lighter than the outer shingles. Her gaze slid to the railing, which was the same pale blue as the rest of the trim, then the wood floor, which was a shade darker. The wicker swing was pure white only because its cushions were alive with florals that would mirror the riot of color in the flower beds at summer's height.

Jamie had to admit that the overall effect held appeal. Still, she would love to redo this place. "I want to design something special for you," she tried to explain. "Rehabbing old houses is what we do, but you've done nothing here."

"Not true. Look at my newel post and the crown molding in the bedroom and the detail work on the panels in the parlor. And my garage."

"That doesn't count."

Jamie realized her mistake even before an indignant "Excuse me?" came her way. Caroline adored her garage, which she had doubled in size and outfitted with new electrical and air systems even before she'd moved in. This was her prized workshop, where she made many of the more intricate pieces that other carpenters had neither the eye nor the hand to make. Oh yes, Caroline was a master carpenter with the years of experience to prove it.

Feeling like a traitor in light of what she knew that Caroline did not and how wrong the whole thing was, Jamie snuggled closer. She didn't care about sweaty skin. The heat couldn't compete with this deeper need. "The garage is for work. I meant living space."

"I painted," Caroline said in an indulgent way. "And installed new systems for heat, plumbing, and electricity. And added Wi-Fi. *And* got rid of the termites in the basement and removed the mold growing behind the bathroom wall, and what about the metal underlayment I added to my whole new roof?"

"I'm talking renovation, as in making it bigger."

"I don't need bigger. I live alone. Besides, this is my private space. I don't want a crew in here."

"You let Dean in."

"Dean's different. He's a friend."

"With whom you agree to disagree on a dozen little things."

"We have different tastes. That's all."

"Is he coming over later?" She tipped her head when her mother's phone chirped. "Speak of the devil. "

"No, baby. Dean's ring is a gray owl. That's a whippoorwill, which means Annie." Jamie was a chickadee and her grandfather a trumpeter swan. Her father, bless his misguided soul, was a duck with an annoying honk. Not that Roy called Caroline much, but even Jamie would recognize that sound.

Misguided soul. *No more so than now,* she thought, but, really, what else was new? Sensitivity had never been Roy's strong suit where Caroline was concerned. Phone calls to the house, gossip around town, photos with his arm around pretty young things—he wasn't fazed. And Caroline's lows when the divorce was finalized? He was oblivious. Not Jamie. She was twelve when he moved out, and in the subsequent months, she had been the one who followed nighttime footsteps to where Caroline stood in the dark kitchen staring out at an inky world. Jamie was the one who saw her ignoring the phone and avoiding people and moving more food around the plate than ever reached her mouth.

Eventually, she had found strength. Jamie never knew from where; she suspected it had been a combination of work, Jamie's increasingly complex tennis schedule, and a dawning realization that the judge-of-all-things was now gone from the house. The change didn't come overnight, but once the emergence began, it was steady. Anyone watching her now could see how comfortable she was with her life.

Indeed, her soft voice held confidence. "Hey, A. Yeah, I'm good. Jamie's here, can I call you back? Promise. Thirty max." She ended the call, put the phone in her lap, and picked up where she had left off. "Dean's bringing lunch."

Jamie had been counting on that. She didn't know if she could get back until late afternoon, and though Annie would be only one of a stream of other visitors, Dean knew his way around Caroline's house. And he was good company. They might argue about what she should do with the house, but Caroline did let him speak his mind. Maybe when he saw her laid up, he would talk her into making the place more liveable.

That said, the Victorian had its strengths. Taking a long breath, Jamie sank into the cushions as the swing gently rocked. She might fault Caroline's refusal to renovate, but she had to admit that the house was serene. Serene went beyond quiet. Her condo was quiet, but it didn't have the feel of home that this did.

The screen door gave a quick creak and slap. Seconds later, the swing jostled, and Master was settling his big body onto a sliver of cushion. He ended up half on Jamie's thigh, which should have been too much in the heat but was not.

"Oh, baby," Caroline warned, "he'll shed on your skirt."

"I don't care." She ran her fingers through the thick coat, from his wide collar to his bushy tail, then did it again. The resulting purr was hypnotic. "I'd get my own cat if I wasn't gone so much of the time." She sighed as she stroked Master. "Aren't I lucky you're willing to take the cats I fall for?" While Roy scoured the *Williston News* for useful buzz, Jamie beelined it to the weekly shelter column. Kittens went fast. Older cats? Harder to place, but they were the sweetest, most mellow creatures.

Master was one of three Jamie had given Caroline. The other two stayed inside, largely on the upper floors where the sun was strong and Master was scarce.

"I nearly got you a fourth for your birthday," she said now.

"Good thing you didn't. I told you, three's my limit."

"She was abandoned," Jamie went on. "By the time she was brought in, one of her eyes was so infected that they had to remove it. They're guessing she's eight or nine."

"Jamie . . ."

"Don't worry. She was adopted by the time I called."

Content with that, Jamie let the cat go. Just then, she was content with most everything. The air was hot and so much of her life murky, but as she sat here on the porch swing, with her fingers in the oddly cool hair of the cat and her mother's familiar scent spread by the ceiling fan, she was revived enough to pull out the thin package with its red ribbon. "I know you don't like me buying you gifts, Mom, but since you won't take another cat, this'll have to do. It's totally self-serving. Read the card."

Tucked under the ribbon, the card was handmade, as Jamie's to her mother always were. Caroline kept every one, occasionally pulling them out to show Jamie the progression. This year's was part computer-assisted, part cut-and-paste construction paper, all geometrically shaped navy and mint. And the note inside?

Caroline read it, set the card on her lap, and gave Jamie a chiding look. "A weekend with you at Canyon Ranch. I can't refuse that, which you knew." Slipping her good arm around Jamie's neck, she gave her a hug. "Thank you, honey. I will *love* it." Her eyes lit. "Let's go tomorrow."

Grasping the fingers at her shoulder, Jamie laughed. "We can't, because (A) your wrist has to heal, (B) I'm in Atlanta tomorrow, and (C) my calendar is crammed with meetings for the next ten days. The taping backed things up, speaking of which—" She hitched her chin toward the DVD case that lay on her mother's lap. Though its cover wasn't as handsome as what fans would eventually see, the red bow couldn't hide its identity.

"The uncut tape," Caroline said excitedly. "Perfect timing. I'll watch it later."

"No typing notes."

"I'll call Claire with a critique."

Oh no. Not good. "I'd hold on that, Mom. She wanted time off."

Without responding to that, Caroline angled herself and looked Jamie over. "I got used to seeing you in slacks while we taped. This is dress-up. Big meeting day?"

Grateful for the change of subject, Jamie gave her a rundown of appointments. She didn't mention having had breakfast with Roy and felt even more duplicitous for that. Wondering again whether Roy was behind the hosting change, she asked, "Is everything okay between you and Dad?"

"As okay as it ever is," Caroline mused lightly. "I rarely see him."

Jamie doubted her mother would have continued to work for MacAfee Homes if regular encounters with Roy were part of the job. They went their separate ways, his big-picture marketing to her detail carpentry. On the rare occasion that she went to the MacAfee Building, it was either to meet with the budget director or visit with Theo. She didn't seek out Roy.

"Which is good," Jamie said, considering.

"Which is good," Caroline confirmed.

"What'll you do when Theo retires and Dad takes the throne?"

"Work, same as always. Unless your father cuts my pay or tells me to use inferior material. I've been spoiled. Theo believes in top-notch everything, and he gives me free rein."

"He respects you." Jamie lifted her hair to cool her neck. "Besides, having a family business was always his dream. You may not be Dad's wife, but you're still my mom, which makes you family in Theo's eyes."

Truthfully, if Caroline had left the company after the divorce, Jamie might not have gone to MacAfee Homes straight from college. She and Caroline had always dreamed of working together, though, and her mother being on the family payroll was the clincher. The path to licensure was rigorous, and while Jamie's mentor at MacAfee had been patient and instructive, he was male. Her emotions weren't on his radar screen. But they were on her mother's. Caroline might glaze over when Jamie got going on a new piece of architectural software, but she was immediately, entirely present when Jamie needed encouragement.

And now this? Competitors for the same job? Jamie might have wanted that job in theory one day, but no way, *no way* could she take it today.

"You look troubled," Caroline said.

She gave a little headshake. "Sorry. I have a gazillion things on my mind and half of those on tap for today."

"But making wedding plans is not on the list. I thought that was Priority Number One once the taping was done."

"No," Jamie corrected, half-wondering if Brad had called Caroline to see how she was doing and mentioned his frustration, "wrist surgery was. You're key to my wedding plans. I can't go looking at venues with you laid up."

Caroline's phone cooed like the dove in the maple. "That's the hardware store. I gave them a tone because they call so much. They open early." She touched IGNORE.

"Maybe it's something important."

"Nothing's more important than this. Tell me what's going on with Brad."

three

Caroline liked Brad. He was a sweet guy who was a good lawyer and had a solid future with MacAfee Homes, which meant that Jamie would be taken care of whether she chose to work or not. And he loved Jamie. Caroline didn't doubt that. Other things, yes. But not that.

Unfortunately, she couldn't discuss those other doubts. For one thing, they were vague, more a niggling in the back of her mind than anything concrete. For another, expressing them might hurt her relationship with her daughter. Besides, Caroline didn't need to love Brad. Maybe all they needed was an easy rapport.

Jamie started the swing with her heel. "It started innocently enough. He said kind of what you just did about my needing to pick a date. When he kept pushing, I lost it a little. I feel like he's harping on it."

"Maybe he feels like you're avoiding it."

"That's what he said, and he started looking all wounded and dejected, which upsets me every time, because I know where it's coming from. He was a lonely little boy whose parents were always there but never *there.* He never felt loved." She watched a robin fly in and perch on the corner rail.

"She has a nest in the Andromeda," Caroline explained and, fully prepared to protect four helpless hatchlings, eyed Master. But the cat remained blissfully asleep under Jamie's touch. "Go on," she urged.

"He's such a nice person."

"So are you."

Jamie put her thumb to the underside of her ring. "I don't feel like it right now. I feel like a traitor." Her eyes shot to Caroline's.

Caroline wasn't about to judge her daughter. "Sweet people can approach things differently."

"Maybe." She focused on finger-combing Master's fur. "He says it's a matter of priorities and that if I love him, the wedding would be at the top of my list. But picking a venue isn't easy. Dad is adamant about it being a *big* wedding, which limits our options. I have to speak with people at each of the venues, but I just can't do it right now. That's driving Brad nuts."

"He's afraid you'll get away."

"I'm not *going* anywhere," she protested, still stroking the cat. "I keep telling him that. I text him all the time. I share my thoughts and show him my designs and ask his opinion, because I care what he thinks, and we talk about his work, too. I make his favorite dinner—well, pick it up at Whole Foods, but he's good with that." Her eyes rose. "Then he says, *You're too old to be afraid to commit.* Me, afraid to commit, like he has no idea where *I'm* coming from?"

Apparently not, Caroline mused. Jamie had learned commitment with a tennis racquet in her hand, playing at five, competing at eight. She had given her all to coaches, team sponsors, and opponents, and after discovering architecture in college had attacked that with the same fervor. Advanced courses, summer seminars, internships—she had front-loaded on all counts.

"Have I ever been afraid to commit, Mom?"

"No, baby."

"If I haven't had time to plan a wedding, it isn't because I'm afraid to commit but because I'm *busy,* and as for the too-old part, I'm only twenty-nine. I don't call that too old for much. How old is too old?"

Certainly not twenty-nine, Caroline knew. Women were getting married later and later, in part to establish careers, in part to be make sure they got the right guy. "Age isn't the issue," she replied, to which Jamie shot her a stricken look but said nothing. "You know commitment better than most." Her phone dinged. She glanced at the screen to read the text. "Taylor Huff . . . asking about my *wrist*?" She sliced Jamie a narrow look. "How did Taylor know about my wrist?"

"Uh, I may have let it slip. Inadvertently."

"Do I believe that last word?"

"People care, Mom. They *love* you."

Yes. Caroline knew that. And knew how lucky she was to be surrounded by people who cared. "Which brings us back to Brad," she said, returning the phone to her lap. "Your thumb keeps going to the backside of that ring, like you're either making sure it's there or it's irritating you. Are you worried Brad's right? Do you think there might be reasons why you haven't wanted to plan the wedding?"

"What, like subconscious ones?" Jamie separated her thumb from the ring. "Like what? Brad is perfect for me. He's smart. He works hard. He's our top lawyer at thirty-three, *thirty-three,* which means Theo has total faith in his talent. He's considerate and good-looking, and he adores me. Why wouldn't I be able to commit?"

"Maybe because your father and I committed and failed?"

The creak of the swing resumed at the bidding of Jamie's heel. "Your situation was different. You got married because (A) you were pregnant and (B) Granddad wouldn't hear of my being born out of wedlock. And you loved Dad back then."

It was a question without the question mark, but Caroline had known it would come. It always did. Her parents' relationship was Jamie's personal Achilles' heel.

"I loved him," Caroline assured her again.

"And you'd have loved him forever if he'd been a forever guy. *He* was the one who was antsy. But Brad isn't Dad."

"True."

Though Roy thought Brad hung the moon.

Which might be what bothered Caroline.

Which was certainly not a *rational* reason for Caroline's doubts.

Jamie pulled her cell from the waistband of her skirt. She flipped through messages, looking discouraged, then startled. She sat straighter, heels stopping the swing. "Oh, cripes, look at the time. I have to go. There's a problem that I have to work out before my eleven o'clock, and a couple of important phone calls."

"Think about it," Caroline said.

"About?"

"Commitment."

"Mom," Jamie said with audible frustration, "I do commitment better than anyone I know."

"Commitment to Brad," Caroline specified.

"I love Brad," Jamie vowed.

"Then there you go. That's it. You'll get through the rest." Caroline couldn't fight love.

But Jamie seemed upset at that, like she wanted more reassurance, like she wanted Caroline to tell her that Brad was the best thing to walk into her life. Lord knew, Roy said it enough. Well, Caroline couldn't gush over something she didn't feel. Besides, her focus was always on Jamie. If Jamie wanted to marry Brad, she was for it.

With a jingle of chains, Jamie shifted the cat so that she could shimmy herself out and push up from the swing. "Brad and I should elope."

"Your father would never forgive you."

"Would you?"

Caroline caught her hand and gave it a jiggle. "Absolutely, if it's what you want. I want you happy. Oh, baby," she said in alarm when Jamie teared up. "You'll get through this." She held out her arm and, when Jamie bent down, folded her in. "There's a reason why planning a wedding is so stressful. It separates the wheat from the chaff. Do you know how many couples don't make it?"

"No," Jamie whispered against her ear. "How many?"

"I have no clue, but there must be lots. It stands to reason, doesn't it?"

There was a soft snort. "You just made that up, then?"

"No. The Bible talks about separating the wheat from the chaff."

"I mean, the part about wedding stress."

"I'm sure I read it somewhere," Caroline said and gave Jamie a final hug before holding her at arm's length and thumbing away an unshed tear.

Jamie took a deep breath and smiled. "You're the best, Mom, know that?"

I'm only as good as you, Caroline thought. She hated that Jamie was upset, but loved that she was willing to share worries with her mother.

"It's weird seeing you doing nothing," Jamie remarked.

Caroline gave a facetious *ha.* "Enjoy it while it lasts. I'm not sure how much more idleness I can take. When I close my eyes, I'm in the garage working on that oak railing for the Millers' house."

"Don't even think it," her daughter warned and glanced at the books on the porch table. "You can read."

"Yes. I can read."

"Got something sexy and hot?" When Caroline shot her a look, she sang, "Your loss." But she was suddenly earnest. "Can I get you anything before I leave? Eggs? Cereal?"

"No thanks, baby. I'm good."

"Remember," she said as she edged toward the stairs, "I'm bringing dinner tonight. Lobster lazy-man style in honor of a one-handed birthday girl. Can I bring you more Tylenol?"

Caroline laughed. "It's only my wrist. I can walk." To prove the point, she stood and, taking Jamie's arm, escorted her down the steps, but they were barely at the bottom when they wobbled as a pair. "Maybe not."

"Oh please," Jamie muttered. "That's me." Reaching down, she freed her heel from the tiny crack between step and stone where it had caught, the front access being one more thing Jamie would have fixed had Caroline allowed it. "You're steady as a rock. Not that I wouldn't love to cancel everything else and stay here today."

"Don't you dare. You're behind already. Go. Really. I'm calling Annie back. She'll be here by ten. Then Theo's administrative assistant Allison's coming, then the LaValles, Rob and Diana, then Dean. I'm good."

Jamie started the car only when Caroline was back on the swing. Once on the street, she crawled forward to blow her mother a handful of kisses before giving the car gas. Seconds after the mint-on-teal Victorian was out of sight, though, she pulled over, picked up her phone, and tried Claire. When the call went to voice mail again, she tried Brian. Same thing.

This time, she redialed Claire and left a message. *Call when you can, and please, please, please, don't call Caroline yet. And don't mention the hosting issue to anyone else, please?*

Wondering how many other people already knew and, if the list went beyond three or four or five, whether it would be possible to put a lid on the secret at all, she headed for MacAfee Homes.

The MacAfee Building was several blocks from the center of town. A regal brick structure, it was designed to honor the Georgian Colonial style of the earliest homes built by the company. Its front door, which was oversized and paneled, had the requisite crown and columns, and its windows had multiple panes, but its six-story height had called for creativity. Though side gables and chimneys still rose at the top, its facade was a pastiche of those tall multipaned windows, with cornices, moldings, and pillared balconies strategically placed for visual appeal.

Jamie worked on the top floor, though not at the front of the building. That front, with its sunny southern exposure, housed executive offices that were spacious, one large desk per office and an assistant outside each door. At the other end, facing north, was the design team. Here, skylights allowed for available light, but none hit the computer screens so crucial to an architect's work. The floor space was open, broken by large L-shaped desks that were arranged in three-person pods to maximize the sharing of ideas and advice.

Jamie shared a pod with her about-to-retire mentor and an architect-intern. The latter was already at her desk, struggling with an egress issue as she moved tracing paper over one of Jamie's plans. Normally, Jamie would have leaned over her shoulder to see where she was headed and perhaps move the translucent paper around herself, but she didn't have time now for that. Waking up her computer, she checked for e-mail from Brian or Claire. Finding nothing, she set off to see Brad.

His office was on the floor below. The central area here held desks for a receptionist and secretaries, as well as comfortable chairs for guests. Glassed-in offices ran along either side, housing Brad, his paralegal, a one-person billing department, the MacAfee in-house real estate agent, and a resident computer nerd. Dean and two other general contractors, who were in the field more often than not but loyal enough to MacAfee Homes to merit dedicated desks, shared a large office at the end of the hall, as well as a conference room nearby for meetings with subcontractors, suppliers, and clients.

"Hey, Miranda," Jamie said, nearly beside the receptionist before the woman's eyes flew up.

Startled, she pushed the book she was reading out of sight. "Jamie," she said, blushing. "Hi. I didn't hear the elevator."

"I took the stairs," Jamie explained, but kept on walking to minimize the woman's embarrassment at having been caught reading on the job, much less reading a book with as recognizable a cover as that one. Miranda was as good a receptionist as MacAfee Homes had. She was attractive, personable, and efficient. She was also happily married and had three children in various stages of daycare and school.

Jamie might have wondered why she was reading erotica, if her mind hadn't been on Brad. She knew his schedule and had hoped to find him alone, but his clients had arrived early and were seated in leather club chairs while Brad reviewed their agreement with MacAfee Homes.

Her steps slowed. He was leaning against the front of his desk, his wire-rims on his nose, and he was a calming sight. Tall and rangy, he had short, side-parted brown hair. His blazer, slacks, and loafers were sedate and well tailored; they were nowhere near as expensive as Roy's clothes, but Brad wasn't about money or show. He was about competence. As he turned from one page to the next, he had his clients' undivided attention.

Then he spotted her, and she felt a moment's doubt. This wasn't the time to talk through the argument they'd had, certainly not to discuss Caroline. But his face lit with pleasure seconds before he waved her in. Yes, pleasure. Hard feelings from earlier? Gone, at least for now. She was barely through the door when he held out an arm, inviting her over in a gesture that might have been inappropriate in another place of business, but MacAfee Homes was about family. *Family Builds.* The words were on every piece of stationery, every contract, every bit of marketing the company used. It was hokey, perhaps, but Theo MacAfee couldn't say it enough.

Brad had become family. When he took her hand and drew her close, she felt safe. Not that clients intimidated her; she was with them all the time. Brad was particularly good with them, though. Content to socialize in ways she was not, he was the glove that fit her MacAfee life.

It had taken her a while to see that. He had already been with the company for several years when she joined it fresh from RISD—the Rhode Island School of Design—and there were no instant sparks. Jamie wasn't looking for a lover, much less a husband. She was focused on work. They became friends joking about everyone who *wanted* them to be more, only in time discovering that they shared other things as well. Once they started to date, sly smiles were rife, and when they became engaged, the celebration was office-wide.

The sense of safety was mutual. Jamie was Brad's security, too. She felt it in the way he held her to his side as he returned to his clients and said, "You remember my fiancée, Jamie MacAfee. Jamie, the Abbotts, David and John."

The two rose to shake her hand and were still on their feet when Brad said, "Would you excuse us for a minute?" and led her out of the office. In the hall, he whispered, "How did it go?"

Her meeting with Roy. "Awful," she whispered back. "They want me to take over as host of the show."

Behind his glasses, his eyes came alive. "He told you?"

"You *knew*?"

"I don't negotiate the contracts, since I'm not an entertainment lawyer, but Roy told me they wanted the change. This is so good, Jamie. You'll make an amazing host."

Jamie was startled because (A) he had known and hadn't told her and because (B) he thought it was a good idea. "I can't be the host. Not if it means kicking Mom out." Brad should have *known* that. He should have argued with Roy when the issue first came up. "Oh God. Dad asked you to side with him."

"He didn't have to. I think it's a good decision."

"You think Mom's not doing the best job?"

"She's done a great job, but so will you."

Jamie let out a discouraged breath. "I can't do it, Brad. This is my mother. And I have a *wedding* to plan." She squeezed his hand. "I'm sorry about this morning. My mind's been on too many other things."

He shrugged and, in the next breath, asked, "How's Caroline's wrist?"

"Better today."

"Did you wish her Happy Birthday for me?"

"I was barely able to wish her Happy Birthday from me. Thanks to Dad, we didn't have much time together. Can you and I talk later?" If Roy could enlist Brad to convince Jamie, Jamie could enlist Brad to unconvince Roy. Brad could also advise her on handling Brian and Claire. "What's your schedule?"

"Lighter than yours. You tell me. What time is good?"

She had clients coming at eleven for a second-round consult on the design of their home, a budget discussion over lunch concerning renovation of a public library, and, when that was done, an on-site check of the construction of one of her banks. Between it all, she had to review her Revit schematic and send it to the plotter so that she would have two full sets to take with her to Atlanta tomorrow.

"Three?" She had a short break then. "Out back, maybe?" There was a large patio behind the office, created to showcase MacAfee landscape designers. Client meetings were sometimes held there, though more often it was where employees went for coffee or lunch. It would be hot today, but there was shade. More important, there was privacy.

"Three, out back," he whispered. He kissed her lightly, raised a brow and grinned with a touch of mischief that said she was his, and returned to his office.

Jamie should have been reassured by his kiss, his grin, his conviction that she would make a great host. As she headed for the stairwell, though, she was uneasy. She wanted him to side with her from the get-go. He knew what her life was like, and he knew what she felt for her mother. He should have considered all that.

Shouldn't he have?

four

Caroline hadn't moved from the porch swing. Granted, it was her favorite spot, but she had never spent the whole morning here. She'd never spent the whole morning off her feet, period—or hadn't since she'd had the flu, what, four years ago? She was the healthiest person around, and she wasn't exactly sick now. Her wrist ached, but had it not been her right one, she would have been in the garage working. *Gut It!* might be done for the season, but other work went on. Most of it involved intricate carving, which was better done here. She had her best tools in the garage, plus ideal lighting and her own music. The guys she worked with liked hard rock. Her sound was more mellow.

Mellow was an apt description for what she felt now, she decided, eyes still closed through a stretch. She had fallen asleep sprawled on the swing after Annie had left, and though she felt sweaty, she didn't rush to sit up. The birds were quieter, either tired of socializing or silenced by the midday heat. Not so the MacAfee crew that was framing the new addition to a house two streets over. As muted as the hammering was, it was a tapping she knew well.

Then came a closer sound, a human one, and her eyes flew open.

Dean. He was leaning against the front rail, hands braced on either side, ankles crossed as long, bare legs settled in with a brush of hair on skin.

Eye candy, Jamie called him, no small compliment since he was close to Caroline's age, but her daughter was right. Everything about Dean worked: the dark hair that spiked over his forehead, the silver tips of his sideburns, the just-there scruff on his jaw, the muscled shoulders, the lean waist. Had he come from work, he'd have been wearing jeans and boots, but with the taping of *Gut It!* done, he was taking off for a week. He still wore black from the waist up, always black, but today in the form of a button-down rather than a T-shirt. His sleeves were rolled, his khaki shorts pressed, his eyes amused.

She tried to muster anger but was too logy. Besides, he was so much like a brother—why waste the energy? The best she could do was to chide, "That isn't very polite, Dean."

"What?" he asked innocently.

"Watching someone sleep without her knowing. How long have you been here?"

"Not long. How do you feel?"

"Great."

"Which is why you were sleeping just now."

"I was just sleeping off the last of the anesthesia. They called it a local block, but there was enough sedation in that IV to last a week." She eyed the mass of gauze and tape on her wrist, rolled it one way, then the other. It felt heavier in the rising heat. "This is just a gimmick to keep me from working. The incision is tiny." She eyed his knee. "Much neater than that." The scar there ran a jagged eight inches, the upshot of a hand saw misused by an apprentice carpenter several years before. It was usually hidden by jeans. "That still looks mean."

"It adds to my appeal, don't you think?"

"Absolutely," she mocked, though there was some truth to it. The scar fit the image of the rugged outdoorsman, and it wasn't alone. He had a white line over one eyebrow, a pinkie that didn't quite work, and numerous scars in other places habitually exposed to his work. Most people wouldn't notice; a man's skin wasn't smooth to begin with. But he and Caroline had a running competition. He showed her his; she showed him hers.

"I'm still ahead," he said.

"Only because you're reckless. I get credit for caution."

"Reckless has nothing to do with it. I learned the trade through trial and error. You learned it from a father who was not only a master at carpentry but totally protective of you."

She had been fortunate in that, and not only when it came to learning. Much as she loved both of her parents, she and her father had shared something special.

"Thinking of them?" Dean asked kindly.

Her parents, on her birthday? Of course. She had been a late-in-life child, "our little miracle," her mother always claimed. As though to prove themselves worthy of that, both had lived well into their eighties.

"They were proud of you. They loved watching the show."

"On some level," Caroline said with a sad smile, remembering the phone calls during the early *Gut It!* years. "Mom thought it was an ad, and Dad, well, Dad recognized me the first year or two, but after that he was too far gone. His mind just . . ." She flicked her hand toward nothingness and then, needing a regrounding, ran her eyes down Dean from head to foot. He was wearing flip-flops. Her eyes shot to the street. From where she lay, only the top of his truck rose over the porch rail. "No bike?" His passion was a Harley. He rarely skipped work without it.

"It's too hot."

Too hot. Definitely. Pushing up, she lowered her legs to the floor and stretched her back, then wiped sweat from her forehead with her good arm. She wasn't the only one sweating. Dean's tanned skin held a sheen. Naturally, it looked fine on him, which wasn't fair at all.

"I nearly brought you flowers. Good thing I didn't," he said with a glance at the porch table. "That is funereal."

Four arrangements had come, two from people who shouldn't have known about Caroline's hand. "My daughter has loose lips. But her intentions are good. Same with yours, though I told you not to cancel your trip." He was going fly-fishing in Montana, or so he claimed.

"I didn't cancel it. I just put it off a day."

"So who are you really going out there to see?" she teased as she always did, and as he always did, he smirked.

"No one you know."

"Meaning, a craggy old man who owns a fly-fishing business."

"Don't knock him. He's a find. He's fished the Big Hole River all his life and knows where the trout are best. He boats me in each morning and picks me up at the end of the day." His phone dinged. Taking it from his pocket, he studied the text. "Hick Weston underestimated the amount of piping he needs for the house on Smithfield. On. Its. Way," he said as he typed, then repocketed the phone. "Anyway, it's a solitary week."

Caroline actually believed him. He had been married for many of those Montana years and would never have cheated. In the three years since his divorce, those fishing trips had been pure escape from thinking about the woman who had rejected him, taken their then-eleven-year-old son back to her hometown, and reconnected a little too quickly with the childhood sweetheart to whom she was now married.

There had been anger, and when it came to his son, there was an ongoing sense of loss, though Caroline was one of the few to know about either. She might not be wild over things like his preference for dogs over cats and black over color, but Dean was a good man. If fly-fishing gave him a buzz, she was all for it.

Sitting forward, she pushed herself up. By the time she was standing, he had reached for her arm. "Where are you going?"

"The bathroom," she said drolly, "and no, I do not need help."

Hands up, he backed off. "Ooo-kay. How about I plate our lunch?"

Spotting the telltale bag on the floor by the door, Caroline's eyes lit. "Is it what I hope it is?" That would be a marinated chicken breast on focaccia, with Boursin, sliced tomato, and Bibb lettuce. It was Fiona's lunchtime specialty. Caroline could eat it every day, which Dean well knew, since they went there often enough. Not that he ate chicken breast with Boursin. His choice would be roast beef or ham topped with aged cheddar, hard and sharp.

Now he said, "Would I bring anything else on your birthday?" and shooed her off. When she came out of the bathroom, he was leaving the kitchen juggling plates, napkins, and drinks. His mouth was filled with something from the bakery stash Jamie had brought.

"Ah. You found the minis."

"Um-hmm." He finished off the mouthful. "I'd ask where you want to eat, except the front porch is the coolest place right now. You need AC, sweetheart."

Ignoring the remark, she took one of the bottled waters he carried and washed down a pair of Tylenol before following him out. After she'd set the water on the arm of the swing, she left-handedly peeled wisps of damp hair from her neck and pushed them into the knot above. Then she sank into the swing and took the plate he offered.

The side chair he pulled up was white wicker matching the swing, but large enough so that he didn't look silly in it. He had actually been with her when she bought both pieces, and had tried it on for size then. Now he sat back and sprawled his legs.

Content that he was content, Caroline closed her eyes as she took a bite of her sandwich. The first hit of flavor to her taste buds was always the best. "This is amazing. *Gracias, amigo.*"

"*De nada.*" He passed her a napkin. "So who else came by?"

"Allison. She brought roses from Theo. Then Rob and Diana." The LaValles, whose Cape *Gut It!* had just transformed. "Recognize the azaleas? They're from the shrubs Annie replanted. And Jamie was here."

"Are she and Brad getting away now that the taping's done?"

"I doubt it. She's backed up with work. Besides, she needs to plan the wedding."

In the silence that followed, Caroline felt a throb in her wrist. It was a quick jab, here and gone, but she feared it reflected a pang in her thoughts.

"How're you feelin' about that?" Dean asked quietly, surprisingly. Of all the things they shared, she had not told him her qualms.

She gave a little smile, a little shrug, a little look that said it wasn't her place to tell her grown daughter what to do. Again she wondered what her own problem was with Brad. Jamie certainly could have done a lot worse.

"Want me to get the Harley? It'd take your mind off things."

"Thank you, no." The Harley terrified her. "My mind is fine right where it is. Trust me, I am not obsessing about Jamie and Brad." She only thought about it when issues like wedding planning arose. The rest of the time she was fine.

Dean's phone dinged again. This time it was the foreman on one of his jobs calling about a problem with defective skylights, but it was nothing Dean hadn't dealt with before. His voice remained low, the phone was soon stowed, and stillness returned.

Then came the rumble of an approaching engine, and a van pulled up with another delivery. Caroline moaned. "Who all did she *tell*?" This arrangement was beautiful, though—white callas, blue delphinium, and the deepest of green herbs. She read the card. *"Heal well. You're still our carpenter."* She frowned at Dean. "Well, duh. That's weird. From our cameraman. See, this is why I didn't want anyone to know. Tell one person, and the whole world knows." He was suddenly looking a little too sheepish. "Oh, Dean, who did you tell?"

"Just Mike." Michael O'Shay was one of MacAfee's electrical contractors.

Her shoulders slumped.

"What's wrong with people knowing?" he asked.

"I don't know." She struggled for the right words. "It makes me seem weak. Worn."

"No way. It shows you're tough. You do jobs most men couldn't handle. That's a war wound, sweetheart."

"War wound," she echoed, doubtful.

He bit into his sandwich, chewed, swallowed. "You're just sensitive because it's your birthday."

"No, I'm not. I'm fine with my birthday. I like my life."

"Well, Mike's a good guy. I asked him to be on call for you while I'm gone, and since everyone knows how self-sufficient you are, I had to give him a reason."

"You couldn't lie?" she asked meekly.

He didn't respond. No, Dean couldn't lie. It was alternately his best and worst feature. Whether she liked it or not, she always knew where he stood.

One consistently good thing, though. He was comfortable with silence and didn't fill it when he had nothing to say, which she appreciated just then. She was feeling lethargic, no doubt a by-product of heat and surgery. Halfway through her sandwich, she couldn't take another bite.

After finishing his, he stood and pointed at the half she had left. "Can I wrap it?"

When she nodded, he stacked their plates and took them back to the kitchen. A short time later, he returned and handed her a mini scone. He was eating a second, with a third in his hand, when another van pulled up. Scratching the stubble on his jaw, Dean shot her an *uh-oh* look before trotting down the steps and meeting the deliveryman on the walk. The arrangement was huge. Back on the porch, he lowered it so that Caroline could remove the card. *"Happy Birthday,"* she read aloud. *"You're the best."* She smiled. "That's sweet. It's from Brian and Claire."

Brows raised in question, he hitched the vase toward the table.

"Living room," she suggested. The screen door slapped behind him. When she heard his flip-flops returning, she called, "Want to play Scrabble?"

"Nah." He came through the door. "You always beat me. And I have to leave." The door slapped shut.

She had another idea. "Jamie brought over the uncut tape. Want to watch?"

He shook his head to that, too. "I'm on vacation." His eyes grew shrewd. "Uh-uh, Caro. Don't work today. I know you love Facebook, but MacAfee has a paid staffer to monitor that. Marketing isn't your job."

"Right," she admitted. "It's Roy's."

"And doing it under his nose is part of the pleasure."

She had to laugh. "I like you, Dean. You get it." She was thinking what a good friend he was when she felt a sudden pang. "Oh boy. I'm so out of it. How did it go in Portland?"

He had been there yesterday. Given the demands of lead time in construction, planning for the spring *Gut It!* had to be under way even before the fall season taped. They had decided to renovate and enlarge a coastal cottage in Cape Elizabeth, and while Jamie only had partial designs done, Dean had enough to start interviewing local subs. "I was able to get a few leads, but it's hard to find women. We could bring up our own, but it's a trickle-down thing. Get someone local and they have local connections, which is a help when weather puts us behind schedule and we have to scramble. Besides, local people add flavor."

"Flavor" meant local accents, and Caroline had to agree. Most of the subs they used talked Boston, but Maine was unique. "It'll be a fun project," she said. "Very different from the one we're doing this fall." That one involved a small historical home that had been bought by empty nesters wanting to downsize. Jamie had no sooner finished a redesign of the house than two of the couple's sons decided to return home to live, so the gut-and-rebuild of a carriage house entered the mix. The last-minute change had caused mild panic, not to mention doubling Dean's work, but it made the project far more interesting.

Mildly disgruntled, Dean folded his arms. "I'm still not sure why the Millers want their kids in a separate house."

"You're confusing how much you wish you could be near Renny with the fact that most adult parents need a little space from their kids." Renny was fourteen and increasingly involved in a life far removed from Dean's. In Maryland for the last three years, the boy had embraced a new family, new friends, new school. Dean knew football; the boy was into lacrosse. Their Lego days together were gone. From what Dean could see, the boy's free-time pal was now his iPad.

Caroline felt his frustration, but she also understood this client. "The Millers are at a different place. And I hear what they're saying. I love Jamie, but I don't want her living with me, not after those last few years before she finally moved out. Her stuff was everywhere. Books, keys, hair ties, large purses, Sharpies, electronics, half-filled bottles of water—you name it, all in plain sight. Her bedroom was always neat, which is rare for a child, but common space in my house? Fair game. It was like she had to mark her territory each time she came home from school."

Dean's eyes remained dark. "Wouldn't it just have been easier for the Millers to buy a bigger house?"

"Then where would that leave us? I *like* this project." But she knew what he was thinking. "You wait. When Renny is older, he'll visit. You'll see."

"Not the same."

She understood that. Dean had clung to a bad marriage for the sake of his son. He went to Maryland often, but he was a spectator in his son's life. So no, it wasn't the same. And no amount of smooth talk from Caroline about things changing with time could help.

Again she pushed at the pieces of hair on her neck. They hadn't stayed put. Her left hand did a lousy job.

"I should brush your hair before I go," Dean muttered. "It's a rat's nest up there."

"Thanks a lot," she drawled.

"Hey. I'm just kidding. You look beautiful."

The compliment was unexpected. She wasn't sure she believed it, but along with surprise came an odd pleasure.

Seeming done with melancholy, Dean took a breath and pushed off from the rail. "Too bad you don't like fishing. You could come with me."

She was thinking that in another life she might when a bark came from the truck. She should have guessed Champ was in the cab from the way Dean had parked in the shade and lowered the windows. He knew not to bring the dog inside. A German shepherd, Champ had traumatized her cats enough times that they made themselves scarce at the first sniff of Dean. He did love that dog.

"Poor guy. Who's watching him while you're gone?"

"A neighbor. They have a shepherd, too. Champ'll be fine."

"Spoken wistfully."

"Well, he's my pal, like you." Leaning in, he put his soap-clean stubble to her cheek and his mouth to her ear. "There's a quart of yogurt in the freezer."

She drew in a fast breath. "Moose Tracks?"

"Um-hmm."

"My *favorite*."

She could feel his smile against her cheek. "I think I knew that." Straightening, he backed away and started down the steps. "Consider it a peace offering. I bought the country house."

Caroline was so taken off guard that she was a minute following. Then, "Oh no. No, no, no."

"Done," he said as his long legs ate up the walk.

She sat forward and called, "That place is in the middle of nowhere. It has water problems, zoning problems, *access* problems, *and*"—she raised her voice when he didn't stop—"it's so infested with carpenter ants that you'd be best burning the thing to the ground. You don't want that place, Dean! There's no way you can make it salable, and isn't that the *point*?"

But he was already in his truck, and once the engine turned over, her shouting was pointless. As he drove off, she grabbed her phone. It took her longer than usual to type, what with holding the phone steady against her bandaged right hand as she worked with her left. She had to delete numerous times until the letters made sense, and then it was simply *Big mistake.*

Thank you, Mom, he wrote back. *Be good while I'm gone.*

five

When noon came without word from Claire Howe, Jamie left a second message, as well as one for Brian Levitt. The fact that neither picked up or called back said they were avoiding her, which made her insane. Her fear was that the more time passed, the more word of the hosting switch would spread at the studio, and the more Caroline would be hurt when she learned it herself. At its extreme, Jamie's fear had someone at the station leaking word to a columnist at *The Boston Globe* and the whole world reading a blurb in tomorrow's paper.

She made it through her lunch meeting intact, though when she arrived at the site of the bank construction, she immediately knew something was wrong. What had looked fine on paper lacked the element of welcome that the bank wanted for its branch, which meant Jamie had to rework the plans. It was no big deal and could be easily fixed, but she hated getting things wrong.

She needed Brad, *definitely* needed Brad. By the time she crossed the back patio to the bench where he sat, she was feeling the heat. The air was thick, and she was desperate enough for support to set aside the issue of his knowing about the host change before she did. But when he opened with "Hey, TV star," she was not happy.

"Okay," she warned, "now's the time when I need you to say you're just kidding with that, because you know I don't want to do this yet, and you also know Caroline is still the best one for the job."

His gray eyes held steady behind his glasses, his voice quiet and smooth. "What I know is that you'll be a great host. The more I think about it, the more excited I get."

It went downhill from there. She rebutted his arguments; he counter-rebutted hers. And when she finally asked, "What about Mom?" he said, "She had her turn, now it's yours."

His confidence in her was as sweet as his loyalty. But there was a larger picture here, a more personal one, a picture of Caroline heartbroken at being ousted on account of age, by her daughter, no less, and he was so not understanding of that that she was beside herself.

He wouldn't help her with Roy, or he would have done it at the get-go.

And Roy had already made his feelings clear, which meant that they would only argue, which she did not, did not, did not want to do.

Her grandfather was her last best hope.

Theo MacAfee was eighty-two but as sharp mentally as a man half his age. The problem was his body. Bad knees, bad hips, bad back, bad cough. Fine to say he had brought the last on himself, but as he told Jamie whenever his cough alarmed her, "We were young and stupid. What did we know?" By some miracle of fate, whatever was there hadn't evolved into lung cancer, though there had been a melanoma scare a few years back—and it was fine to say he had invited that, too. But he first learned the trade by working construction himself, and how could he have possibly built a business in that field without spending time in the sun? Add foolhardiness to the mix, and he had been known until recently to climb a ladder in a snit and show a framer the *proper* way to mount plywood sheathing to the outside wall of a house.

He was a perfectionist, which was probably how Jamie came by the trait. He could be short-tempered when things weren't done right, and he could be painfully blunt. Beneath his impatience, though, was a kind heart. He treated his family well.

Jamie was counting on that now.

"Got a minute?" she asked, poking her head into his office and feeling a catch inside at the sight of him. When she was a child, she had always thought him tall and imposing. She had gained perspective on that as she had grown herself, but hunched over now, he seemed frail. He didn't smile when he saw her, but those blue eyes lit.

Theo was an older, more leathery version of Roy. He had a head of white hair that was only beginning to thin, and though his blue eyes were rheumy, they remained riveting. In his later years, finally accepting that he couldn't be harassing electricians at a job site, he had taken to wearing a jacket and tie, and his manners had grown courtly to match. He started to rise now. Slowly.

Hoping to spare his arthritic spine, Jamie scooted around his desk and eased him back down with her hug, then leaned against the mahogany not far from his trouser leg.

His eyes were keen, his voice gravelly. "I'd congratulate you, little girl, but you look like you lost your best friend."

"It might come to that," Jamie said with a little huff. "So you know about the *Gut It!* switch?"

"Your father told me. He said you were on board."

"That is not true."

"He said you asked for the change."

"To replace Mom? Why would I do that? Mom loves the job, and she's great at it. This isn't a good move, Granddad. You know it's not."

"No, I don't know it's not," he said as he calmly put his elbows on the arms of his chair and cupped his gnarled hands, one in the other. "It sounds logical. The producers want a younger face, and yours is a winner."

"What about age before beauty? Who always said that?"

"Your grandmother, rest her soul, but she didn't know the television business. Neither do I, which is why I defer to your father on this. Beauty before age seems to be the way of the world today."

Jamie was dismayed. "Is that why I'm working my tail off now, so that by the time I hit my stride, I can be laid off because I have wrinkles?" She searched her grandfather's face, finding wrinkles in abundance. "Is anyone saying *your* face is too old and asking you to step down?"

"No," he said with a dry quirk of his lips, "because I own the company, so I'm the one who decides, and I'm not ready to step down."

"What if Mom isn't either?"

"Has she said that?"

Jamie let out a frustrated breath. "No. She doesn't know about this yet. I'm hoping to get it changed before she has to. She'll be devastated. Think of what you'd feel if someone said you were too old to do what you do best."

"They'd probably be right."

"I'm serious, Granddad."

"So am I, but everything is relative. This is television, which apparently is a whole other ball game when it comes to age. Personally, I like seeing those little blondes reading the news in their cocktail dresses—not that I'd want your grandmother to know that," he said with a penitent heavenward glance. "But I do understand why the station wants you. Roy is proud."

"Roy is blind," Jamie countered, knowing that if she was out of line, Theo would blame it on her youth. And wasn't that an irony? "He isn't thinking about Caroline at all. But you love her. You always stand up for her."

"And I would now if I felt that show was her future. She's much more than a carpenter, and—no offense to you—she's much more than a host. I see her doing other things."

"On the show?"

"In this company."

"Like what?" Jamie asked, because, as gratifying as Theo's confidence in Caroline was, this was the first she'd heard of her mother doing other things within the business.

Theo only waved a knobby hand. "Not important right now."

"Okay. So right now, why not let her do what she loves? All it would take is a phone call."

"Oh-ho, no you don't," Theo scolded with a spasmodic shake of his head. "A phone call to any one of three people who have their minds made up? I've learned to pick my battles, little girl. This is one I'm not fighting."

"But *why*?" she asked, not understanding how after so many years of protecting Caroline, he could desert her now. "Mom's been loyal to you." She took his hands between hers. "Speak to Dad. Speak to Brian or Claire. Please? You can make them change their minds."

But Theo refused to commit, and she wasn't about to wheedle. *I've learned to pick my battles, little girl. This is one I'm not fighting.*

More and more, she felt like a lone warrior, but at least Caroline was still in the dark. When Jamie arrived at the Victorian to make dinner, her mother seemed as blissfully unaware of any problem as she had been that morning, so at least Roy was keeping his word on that.

With the heat so oppressive, Jamie had opted for lobster salad. No cooking was required, since she bought the lobster meat already boiled and out of the shell, and turning it into salad was so easy to do that she couldn't screw up. That was important, given how distracted she was. Theo was Theo; she could accept his position. But Brad? He was the one who gnawed at her as she cut the lobster into chunks. She didn't understand why he couldn't see her mother's side of things. Actually, she could. He wasn't close to his own parents. They lived in Minneapolis and didn't travel. Jamie had only met them once. They had been sweet enough to her in a polite, aren't-you-lovely way, but chatty they were not. Throughout Brad's upbringing, they had never shared thoughts, much less invited a discussion of problems. Caroline did both.

As Jamie took mayonnaise from the fridge and spooned it into a cup, she worried. Brad knew how important Caroline was to her, but hadn't made the connection that she should be important to him, too. He would in time. Only they didn't have time when it came to *Gut It!*

Cutting a lemon in half, she squeezed it over the mayo and stirred, then poured the mixture over the lobster chunks and folded it in. There was plenty for two, but not enough for three. She hadn't invited Brad.

From the start, she had envisioned Caroline's birthday dinner to be strictly mother and daughter, as it had been for so long. She wondered now whether excluding him was only perpetuating the distance between him and Caroline, causing jealousy, resentment, even dislike.

Knowing she was getting carried away, she reached for the tomato she had bought. It was huge and locally grown, which meant that it was likely a sin to discard the insides. "No problem," said a woman who stood beside her at the tomato bin. "Save the insides for salsa or, even better, for homemade Bolognese." Like she had the time to make either? Ignoring the guilt she felt, she sliced her tomato in half, scooped the innards down the drain, and piled in the salad. Once the stuffed tomato lay on a bed of Boston Bibb lettuce, with a mound of marinated mushrooms, a fresh baguette on the side, and a glass of wine nearby, the plate was gorgeous.

Where to eat? There was the Caroline-made dining table in the parlor, but that would mean seeing her own tension in her grandmother's Victorian lace, and the porch table was covered with flowers. So they ate on a quilt in the backyard, where the sun had fallen enough to allow for shade and a small breeze stirred the air.

Thinking that her mother was the only person on earth with whom she wanted to communicate just then, she turned off her phone.

The downside of that, of course, was turning it back on. Her home screen had barely appeared when the dinging began. She told herself not to look. Dinner had been great, an escape from all things unpleasant. But just cruising away from Caroline's with the streetlamps flashing sequentially in and out of her car, she felt her serenity begin to slip away.

The phone didn't help. It lay like a coiled snake on the seat beside her. She ignored it as she passed through the center of town and continued to ignore it as she approached newer homes. In contrast to Caroline's neighborhood, parts of which were settled in the early 1800s, this side of town had been farmland into the mid-1900s. Tract by tract, houses began to appear then, first a gaggle of ranch-style homes, then small regiments of Colonials, and then split levels that were a hybrid of the two.

Her condo complex was an eight-year-old MacAfee Homes development that captured the spirit of New England in shingled faces and gabled roofs. Each condo was two stories high, with its own walled patio and built-in garage.

Pulling into hers, Jamie turned off the engine and, resigned, picked up the phone. Why not? Every one of the day's worries was back anyway, from Roy's bombshell reveal early that morning to Brad's one-sided cheerleading to Theo's refusal to stop the change.

She studied the screen. There were several work-related messages. She skipped over them to the personal ones. *How'd it go?* Brad had texted an hour earlier. *Did she like the cupcakes?*

The cupcakes were birthday ones that she and Caroline had thoroughly enjoyed but that should not have been his first concern. She would have confronted him on it if he'd been staying with her that night. Just then, she was glad he wasn't.

Her thumbs typed *Yup,* then SEND.

His answer came in seconds. *No mishaps?*

Still not the right topic, but a wry one. He knew her well. *Nope.*

What time's your flight?

6:58.

Sure I can't drive you to the airport?

No need. Client pays for parking.

Okay. Have a safe flight.

It was an innocuous exchange that left her feeling empty as she sat in her garage. *And you, Brad?* came the snide little voice that was usually reserved for Roy. *Did that little back-and-forth do anything for you?*

She knew she was being unfair. A text was a text. Only he could have called once he knew she was in. Or asked her to call him. Or sent a longer e-mail. He might have even insisted on driving her to the airport so that they could talk, though attempting serious discussion at 5:15 A.M. was dangerous, as they had proven this morning with regard to choosing a wedding date.

Wedding date. *Gah.* Another problem to try to solve.

But first, Roy. He had texted her, too. More than once. She could guess why.

Grabbing her purse, briefcase, and the heels she'd kicked off to drive, she left the car and went inside, where she dropped her things on a glass table in the short hallway that connected the garage to the main living space. Right there, determined to face the devil before she stepped farther into her home, she pulled up Roy's texts.

Theo just called, he had written shortly after she arrived at Caroline's. *Why did you involve him?* Then, an hour later, *Have you told your mother yet?* And an hour after that, *Did you tell her?*

It was ten now. Like Brad, Roy slept with the phone by his bed, but Jamie couldn't bear to go into the *Gut It!* dilemma with him now. She was emotionally drained and physically tired, and she still had to run through a checklist for tomorrow. And, oh yeah, she had to be up at 4:30 A.M.

But she knew Roy. He would keep at it until she wrote back.

Quickly, she typed, *Just got this. Am leaving for Atlanta early tomorrow, back late. Talk Saturday.*

She hit SEND, connected the phone to the charger on the table, and walked away with only her briefcase and shoes.

Entering the body of the condo, she felt instant relief. The foyer was open to a small dining room, beyond which were an eat-in kitchen and a great room, all of it done in a soft white with accents in soothing shades of sand. Setting her briefcase on the island, she sank low in a leather sofa, put her feet on the limestone coffee table, and listened.

All was quiet. She appreciated that for all of two minutes, at which point she began hearing echoes of the day.

Needing to escape them, she was off the sofa in a flash and barefooting it up the stairs. There were two bedrooms here, one for sleep and one for work. Both were decorated in the same minimalist way, everything low and sleek, done in varying shades of white with sprinkles of sand—the bathroom marble, the bedroom dresser, the wall-to-wall on the office floor to soften the effect of the starker white desk and chair. Color came from art on the walls, though there wasn't much. What she had was large and contemporary, bringing in the neutrality of brown, khaki, and blue. She couldn't say what she loved about each, other than that it had spoken to her on a visceral level. Each was soothing and, regardless of hue, pristine.

She took slow, deep breaths as she undressed and pulled on a silky T-shirt and shorts, and she breathed her way into the bathroom to wash her face. When her freckles appeared, she eyed her mirrored self in despair. *She's had her turn,* Brad had said of Caroline; *She's fifty-six,* said Roy. *But me?* Jamie thought. Twenty-nine going on twelve, to judge from that freckled face.

Closing her eyes, she braced her hands on the marble countertop and continued to breathe, ignoring the voices as she focused on the movement of her diaphragm, belly, breasts, and hips. She really needed an hour with her yoga instructor. She used to do classes several times a week, but weekends seemed the only time for them now.

Saturday was the day after tomorrow. She could make it till then.

Clinging to that thought, she brushed her hair and piled it on the top of her head, then went back downstairs and opened her briefcase. Before leaving the office, she had packed it with every folder that she might have even a vague chance of wanting. Now, needing it as streamlined as her home, she sorted through. She did not need bubble diagrams, since she had two sets of formal plans ready to travel. Nor did she need printouts of every e-mail to and from the client. She did need her notes from multiple meetings with the client on his vision and the needs of his company. These she would reread during the two-and-a-half-hour flight, so that they would be fresh in her mind during her presentation.

She skimmed those notes now, along with the quote package Dean had prepared. The bottom line was more than the client wanted, which meant that there would be hard discussions. Best-case scenario, they could reach a comfortable compromise. Worst-case scenario, she would be paid for time spent and discharged. Hoping it didn't come to the latter, she repacked the briefcase. She had barely placed it by the garage door when she saw the message light on her phone.

That would be Roy.

Unable to deal, she headed upstairs to pick clothes. Her closet was built in behind a hinge-less white door and organized to the extreme, with full-length spaces for dresses and pants, half-length ones for skirts and blouses. There were a dozen drawers, as many open shelves, and more shoe cubbies than she could ever fill herself. Brad would help with that if he moved in. That said, he had a condo. She had a condo. Pooling resources, they could afford a house. They talked of this often—dreamed of it.

But she loved her place. It was the first one she'd ever owned.

For tomorrow, she picked a chocolate brown suit in a summer-weight merino that refused to wrinkle, and a pale silk tank. Once she had set her alarm for 4:30 and drawn off the fitted duvet cover, she climbed into bed with the remote. She didn't usually watch the news on television, preferring to read it online, where she could skim or not. The instant she tuned in now, though, she was riveted. *Personally, I like seeing those little blondes reading the news in their cocktail dresses,* Theo had said, and to her amazement, he was right. The co-anchors were female, with long blond hair and impeccable makeup. They couldn't have been any older than Jamie, and they looked disturbingly alike in a Barbie way. The main things setting them apart were their dresses. One was red, the other purple; one had cap sleeves, the other no sleeves; one had a plunging neckline, and the other was ruched to show just a hint of cleavage.

What had happened to chic business suits? Or to trying to win the respect given a man by dressing like one? Or, at the very least, to rejecting the stereotype of the sexy little woman?

Did Jamie hear the story being reported? No. She was too busy frowning at the cleavage on display and thinking how inappropriate it was to be dressed to the hilt to read the 11:00 P.M. news. She couldn't imagine either of these women actually going out into the field to gather information. Clearly, that wasn't their job. They were entertainers.

Did she feel confidence in someone her age who did this? No. They moved their hands, looked at the camera in a comfortable enough way, looked disappointed or downcast or jovial at just the right times. Did she trust that they had insight into world affairs? *No.*

Maybe brains didn't matter when there was someone else to write the words. In fact, the lead story, to which they returned repeatedly during the broadcast, was the weather. The heat and humidity would be around for another day at least, with no storms to bring relief until Saturday. Since Jamie was flying morning and evening tomorrow, this was good news.

Mesmerized in the way of morbid curiosity, she kept watching. *Beauty before age,* Theo had said, and that might work here, but not on *Gut It!*

Or did it? What if Brian and Claire wanted her to host solely because she was young and attractive? What if she were as noncredible, as *interchangeable,* as these women? If so, she hadn't accomplished anything in life, at least not where *Gut It!* was concerned. She was simply being rewarded for her age at the expense of her mother, who was being punished for hers.

It was all wrong. Caroline was a hands-on host who knew what she was talking about. Even when smiling, she had a gravitas that these two on the screen lacked.

The news ended, but Jamie was aggravated enough to be hearing voices again. Aware that she had to be up in five hours, she pulled up reruns of *American Idol* and let the music exhaust her.

Soon after dawn, she was on her way to the airport, and, yes, there were messages on her phone from Roy and Brad. Ignoring them, she read one from Caroline thanking her for the birthday celebration, and several from clients on project issues. Once she boarded the plane, though, she turned off her phone. Minutes later, the plane took off, and she was on her way to Atlanta, oblivious of the disaster about to unfold at home.

six

Caroline was sitting in the middle of her unmade bed, in a mess of fuchsia sheets and scattered sections of the newspaper, when she called the MacAfee shop Friday morning. Fresh from the bath, she had placed herself directly under the ceiling fan, so that it would cool her as it dried her skin.

At the other end of the line, she heard the high-pitched screech of a table saw, then the voice of the shop's manager. "McGinn here."

"Hey, Brady, it's Caroline. Just checking in. Have my dowels arrived?" The dowels in question were small pins that would anchor the top to the legs of a trestle table she was building from white oak. The pins were a hybrid of wood and steel that was new enough to the market to make them a special-order item.

"Hold on. I'll look."

He was gone for several minutes, during which time the upstairs cats joined her on the bed—Biscuit, the youngest, to bat at the newspaper, AnneMarie, the mama's girl, to stretch out along Caroline's thigh. Caroline was stroking her orange back when Brady returned.

"I don't see them. They should've been in by now. Want me to track 'em down?"

"That'd be great. Thanks, Brady. What's doing there?"

"Same old. Norris and Watts are working on prefabs for the Connolly house. Turino's cutting decking."

"Not on-site?"

"He says it's too hot. Me, I'd be out there anyhow. It's pretty hot in here, too."

Caroline didn't doubt it. Her house seemed to be absorbing more humidity with each passing hour, and though she had every ceiling fan running on high, they could only do so much when the moisture became entrenched. Lethargy was the order of the day, not that she was about to do anything strenuous, like take a wood chisel to teak. Her wrist was still achy.

Phone calls were fine, though. She made a few more before extracting herself from the cats, pulling on a white tank and denim shorts, and trotting barefoot down the stairs. The place smelled—cloyingly—of roses. She might have tossed them, had they not been from Theo.

She poured herself an iced tea, pulled a stool up to the kitchen counter, and opened her laptop. It was a minute before her e-mail began loading. One day offline, and an amazing amount piled up. MacAfee had a digital assistant whose job was to monitor *Gut It!* Facebook posts, forward notes to whoever of the cast could best answer them, and post their replies. As host, Caroline got the most mail. For that reason, and because she liked doing it, she wrote and posted replies herself.

Today, there were questions on refinishing butcher block, building bunk beds into a gabled alcove, and replacing an out-of-code banister, but she had barely skimmed the list when Master began weaving through her legs. She managed to haul him onto her lap—no small feat with only one arm and significant cat girth—but once there, he butted her chin with his furry gray head by way of thank you, turned a circle in search of just the right spot, and settled in.

How to restore salvaged barn board. She started with that. Her right thumb was a problem, since the bandage holding it in the proper position for her wrist kept hitting the space bar at the wrong time. Other than the occasional twinge, though, the typing caused no pain.

Caroline loved this part of her job. There were times when that still surprised her. Born and bred a carpenter, she had never dreamed of doing anything but working with tools. But now this—writing letters, giving advice, sharing her knowledge with people who turned around and put it to good use? Life was good.

The doorbell rang. Easing Master to the floor, she left the kitchen. And there, at the far end of the hall on the other side of the screen, was Claire Howe.

Caroline's first thought was that Claire would *not* like what she was wearing. She rarely did. Not that the woman was a sharp dresser herself. Tall and lean, she seemed oblivious to her sloppy appearance, as in ill-fitting skirts and half-tucked blouses. And sneakers? Even Caroline knew that flats or low heels were better with a skirt.

Not that Claire needed clothes to exert command. Her deep voice did that all on its own, and if not her voice, her eyes. They rarely blinked. The intimidation factor didn't bother Caroline, but she spent her share of time on the set soothing others who suffered a bruising Claire stare.

But they weren't on the set now. This was Caroline's turf.

"Claire. Hi." She smiled as she opened the screen. "This is a surprise—and before you say anything, I watched the tape. It's amazing. Our best season yet, don't you think?"

Claire didn't reply. She was eying the bandaged hand. "That looks serious."

Caroline turned the wrist back and forth. "Not to worry. This is by design. My doctor has a perverse sense of humor. And thank you for the birthday flowers." She glanced toward the living room, where the arrangement from Brian and Claire positively burst from its vase. "Come." She gestured. "You have to see these."

"I can certainly smell them," Claire remarked as she followed Caroline into the living room. She glanced at the flowers, said a dismissive "Pretty," and returned to Caroline with cautious eyes. "You look calm. Does that mean you're okay with everything?"

"With what?"

"The change."

"What change?" When Claire's eyes darkened in annoyance, Caroline tried to think of something she might have forgotten. The woman certainly wasn't talking about menopause; she never got personal. Caroline could only think of one possibility. "You mean the underwriting change?" A new sponsor would be on board for the fall. But Claire's frown said it wasn't that. Uneasy, she said, "Spill it, Claire. It's not like you to hesitate."

"It's not like Roy to lie," Claire shot back.

Ooooh. Caroline wasn't touching *that* one. "Please," she invited, "what *is* it?"

With a low chuff, Claire looked away, then almost angrily back. "We're changing hosts."

Pause. "Excuse me?"

"We're making a change in who will host the show." The words, enunciated in pairs, were barely out when she declared an irritated "I was not supposed to be the messenger here. We discussed this at length. Roy said Jamie already told you."

Caroline was doubly confused. "I was with Jamie yesterday. Twice. She didn't mention any change."

"Well, I don't know why not. She was the one who offered to tell you. This has been in the works for a while. We've been prepping her behind the scenes. She'll be taking over as host."

Caroline was floored. "Ex*cuse* me?"

"Jamie is the new host. We want a new face."

Caroline recoiled. "What's wrong with mine?"

"Nothing, Caroline," Claire said in a pedantic way, clearly still annoyed, "except you've been hosting for a while. It's time for something fresh."

Caroline had an awful feeling. "Define fresh."

"Young. Our backers feel strongly about this, and focus groups tell us that Jamie is the one they like best."

"At least they have good taste," Caroline managed to say. Jamie would make a great host, but that wasn't the issue. The word "young" was echoing, echoing, echoing. She felt blindsided, gutted just as she had been when Roy had told her she was no longer "young" enough to be his wife. "Oh boy," she muttered. "This is Roy's doing." It was the only thing that made sense. He loved everything about *Gut It!*'s success except her role in it.

Claire was strident. "Roy does not make the decisions here. He may know about marketing for your family business, but television is not his world. No, Roy didn't initiate this, but he's been on board from the start."

From the start? Like months and months? And Jamie knowing, too? That thought had her reeling.

"Jamie is good, Caroline. She won't let you down."

"Her ability isn't the issue."

"It was Jamie's idea to make a contest out of choosing the fall house."

"She's definitely savvy about marketing gimmicks, but how does that correlate to hosting *Gut It!*?"

"She's of the generation we want. It was her idea to bring Taylor Huff on as interior designer this spring. Taylor is thirty. Focus groups liked her, too."

"Who all were *in* these focus groups?" Caroline cried. "*College* kids?"

"Accept it, Caroline. It's a fact of life, and it isn't just television. Every entertainment platform puts a premium on youth."

"What about Oprah? She's not thirty. Neither is Katie Couric or Cokie Roberts or . . . or Diane Sawyer."

"You're no Diane Sawyer."

"And *Gut It!* is no *This Old House,*" Caroline shot back, because one put-down deserved another. But there was little satisfaction in it. Something inside her was withering. "I'm just gone from the show, then?"

"Oh no," Claire said quickly. "*Lord* no. We want you to stay on as master carpenter. You'll still anchor certain segments, especially if the wedding takes place during the taping, and Jamie and Brad are in Paris."

"Paris."

"Am I speaking out of turn? I thought they were honeymooning there."

The woman certainly knew how to stab and twist. Caroline felt the pain but refused to show it. "They haven't decided," she replied, though suddenly wasn't certain.

"Well, whatever. When it comes to *Gut It!* we want you to do everything that you've been doing."

"Like smoothing things over when you offend people on set?"

Claire stared. "Do you have a point with that?"

"Absolutely," Caroline said, perhaps brashly, but what did she have to lose? "I do a lot more on set than hosting, and it's because I am who I am at the *age* I am that I'm able to do it."

"And we appreciate your efforts. But the person facing the camera is going to be Jamie."

With that bluntness, Caroline was blindsided all over again. How to process this, when it didn't make sense? She and Jamie shared everything. Besides, hadn't Jamie just said she didn't have time to plan a wedding? Add hosting responsibilities to that—unless she was *already* factoring in hosting responsibilities?

"There'll be a learning curve," Claire went on. "She understands that. But you have to agree that this will lead to big things for her career. Her name will be front and center. She'll be a celebrity in architectural circles."

"I'm not arguing with any of that. But why *now*?" Jamie was twenty-nine. Caroline had been midforties when she took the helm.

"Because our new sponsor feels strongly about it. Jamie was instrumental in securing this sponsor, by the way. She was in on all the meetings last winter. It's about demographics. We want to aim for the twenty-five- to forty-year-olds."

"Well, that's very PC," Caroline said in a burst of pique, "but they're not the ones spending the money."

"Increasingly, they are. Advertisers know this."

"They should tell *that* to those twenty-five- to forty-year-olds, who either have low-paying jobs or—if they were lucky enough to go to college—huge debt to repay. In the ten years our show's been running, what was the youngest age of a homeowner?" In response to silence, she said, "Correct. Forty. Which is at the very top of that demographic. The average age of homeowners has been fifty. Our fall homeowners are nearing *sixty*. Do advertisers want that to change, too? Should *Gut It!* start focusing on redoing the one-bedroom condo that the average thirty-year-old might be able to afford?"

Needing fresh air, Caroline left the living room and went out the door to the porch. Oh yes, the heat was brutal, but that wasn't why she was sweating. Claire was poison. She wanted the woman out of her house. But even the porch was too close. She went halfway down the walk, where she put her hands on her hips and waited.

Behind her, the screen slapped. Hit by a new wave of bewilderment, she turned as Claire approached. "Was it something I did? Something I said? Something I *wore*?" Not that she was about to change her look. Viewers loved her color. She constantly got mail on that.

Claire said nothing.

"Just my age," Caroline concluded in defeat.

After another moment's silence, Claire waved away a fly. "So . . . are you okay with this now?"

They had come full circle, but Caroline was more confused than ever. "How could I be okay with it? I totally disagree with this decision."

"You don't want your daughter to move ahead?"

"Whoa," she cautioned with deadly calm, "I *always* want my daughter to move ahead. I've devoted my *life* to having my daughter move ahead. Do not *ever* think that I would do anything to hold my daughter back."

It was true. But Caroline knew that the issue here wasn't job advancement. It was caring. It was honesty, or the lack thereof, and the hurt it caused. It might even be betrayal, though she refused to go that far before she spoke with Jamie.

Claire was still backing her BMW out of the driveway when Caroline went inside and, heart pounding, tried Jamie's cell, but the call went straight to voice mail. Realizing that the plane might not have touched down in Atlanta, she waited another few minutes, then tried again. This time, after the beep, she said, "Call when you land," and clicked off.

Claire was gone.

Jamie was silent.

Caroline was too old.

Sinking down on the steps in the front hall, feeling deficient in ways she hadn't in years, she waited for Jamie to call back. Antsy, she wandered out to the front porch, frowning at nothing in particular until her eye fell on the flowers the *Gut It!* cameraman had sent. *Heal well,* his card read. *You're still our carpenter.* She had thought the wording strange at the time, but it took on new meaning now.

Who else knew? Claire and Brian, Roy and Jamie, the cameraman. Were e-mails making broader rounds even now? Was she the *last* to know? Had they purposely chosen to break the news when they knew she would be at home and out of commission?

Striding angrily down the steps and across the lawn, she paused at the junipers growing in the shade of a curbside oak. They needed pruning. But not now. Totally aside from the heat, her *wrist* wouldn't work.

Because she'd had to have surgery on it. Because she'd been using it for so long.

Discouraged, she went back to the steps, sat on the lowest one, and hugged her knees. A neighbor returning home slowed and waved. She waved back but was in no mood to talk. Instead, she went back inside and tried Jamie again, wondering if Jamie had forgotten to turn her phone on. She didn't usually. Whenever Caroline was with her, she turned on the phone the instant the wheels touched down. It was habit, even compulsion perhaps.

Unless she had deliberately not done it now because she didn't want to be reached. Unless she had actually, horrifyingly *planned* to be away so that Claire would have to break the news.

Trying not to panic, Caroline went through to the kitchen and out the back door. Even as she headed for the garage, though, her mind remained in the kitchen. Jamie wanted to renovate it. She had been increasingly insistent. Out of guilt? That would make sense if she had known about this for a while or, worse, had lobbied for it. Would she seriously have done that?

Roy sure as hell would. Caroline had no doubt about that, as she slipped into the garage. He might not have come up with the idea, but he was probably on the phone with Claire right now, grinning that cocky grin of his as he reveled in Caroline's demotion.

Inhaling the familiar scent of sawdust, she ousted Roy from her mind. She didn't want him here. This place was hers.

Up until five years before, she had lived in the house they shared while married, and though it was a dozen years before that when he moved out and signed over the deed, that house had never felt entirely hers. This one did—both the main Victorian and this garage, which had the same facade as the original carriage house but was a totally different beast inside. Oh yes, it had a small office in the second-floor loft, but more important to Caroline was the belly below.

The equivalent of a generous two-car garage, it was outfitted with superb lighting and the latest in ventilation systems to remove sawdust from the air. That said, there was just enough of it gathered at the feet of the worktables to bring her comfort. Add to its smell the fainter ones of glue, wood stain, even a lingering electrical smell from her new belt saw, and she was in her element. Her tools were on shelves and wall hooks, or mounted on tables, with goggles and gloves lying nearby. Mingling among them, though, and just as precious to her were the relics from her father's workshop. Most were small hand tools. Running her hand now over a palm sander that had been revolutionary in his day, she was taken back to her roots.

She was a carpenter. The scent of sawdust, like comfort food, was an anesthetic. She was okay, she told herself. She didn't need to host a TV show.

Momentarily soothed, she tried Jamie again, but when she hit voice mail, the soothing leeched away. Jamie knew. Jamie prepped. Jamie plotted.

But knowing Caroline would be hurt?

She thought about asking Roy and quickly vetoed the idea. All he would do was gloat.

Theo, on the other hand, was her champion. He might have insight into what was happening and why. But running to her ex-father-in-law at the first sign of trouble just wasn't her way.

Unable to work because of her hand and too unsettled to sit still, she left the garage and paced the yard as she waited for Jamie's call. But the cell in her hand remained silent, and the longer it did that, the more damning things seemed. Jamie was taking her sweet time returning her call, which was so not like Jamie that there had to be more going on.

Plane trouble? Back inside, she checked the airline's website. ARRIVED, it said.

She thought of calling Dean. But he was in the air somewhere in the middle of the country, and besides, his solution to life problems was either to ride on the Harley or to hunt.

Annie would be as angry as Dean. But she was doing a huge installation at a MacAfee project an hour away. And Caroline didn't want to involve anyone else until she talked with Jamie.

She wanted to convince herself that being upset was petty and that she'd be fine as long as she was still part of the show. She wanted to say she didn't care if Jamie hosted.

But the silence grew louder with each minute that passed, so that by the time Jamie finally called, Caroline was ready to believe the worst.

seven

Jamie's heart lurched when she heard Caroline's message. It was too short and too tense, not like her mother at all. And though Jamie was in a car with her client and needed to maintain a semblance of professionalism, there was no way she wasn't calling right back.

Picking up, Caroline said her name, just her name.

"What's wrong?" Jamie asked in the lowest of voices.

"Claire was here."

Jamie pressed her fingers to her forehead, as much to shield her voice from the driver as to keep herself calm. "She wasn't supposed to do that."

"How long have you known?"

"One day."

"That's not what she said. She said you've known for a while."

"Not true."

"She said they've been grooming you for this."

"I had no idea."

"She said you were all in favor of it."

"She lied."

"But you did know about it both times you were here yesterday."

"Yes. But the time wasn't right to discuss it." Nor was this, what with a client sitting three feet away. Voice even lower, she said, "I can't talk right now. Can I call later?"

She heard what sounded like a frustrated sound, then a click, and the line went dead.

Caroline's rational self understood why Jamie couldn't talk. The emotional one did not. Thinking that if Jamie was as innocent as she claimed, she would find a way to call back, she waited anxiously on the porch. She walked through the house. She spent time with the cats.

Again she considered calling Dean. He would get the aging part. Again she considered calling Annie. She would get the betrayal part.

I do not want this change, Jamie texted an hour later.

Caroline didn't reply. Texting was a cop-out.

But another came a short time later. *I did not ask for it. They just want it to look that way. I've been used.*

You're not the victim here, Caroline shot back. When she calmed a bit, she typed, *Who used you?*

Brian and Claire. Dad.

What did Roy do?

Supported the other two. He should have said NO.

Your father? Caroline wrote back with sarcasm aplenty.

Jamie didn't respond as they got into the lunch hour. Caroline's hopes rose when the phone rang, but it was Brad.

"Jamie is panicking," he said. "She's had two minutes in the ladies' room, no other time alone. She's worried about you. She's worried you're furious. How are you doing?"

"I've been better," Caroline said in what she thought was a commendably benign voice.

"She feels terrible about this."

"Which part—the switch or her role in it?" she asked and instantly regretted it. She didn't want to discuss this with Brad. Jamie should have called her during those two minutes in the ladies' room.

Apparently Brad didn't want to discuss it with her either. What he said was focused on the narrowest angle. "She doesn't want you angry at her. She's agonizing down there."

"Well, I'm agonizing up here, but that doesn't help either one of us, does it. Listen, I appreciate your calling, but Jamie and I really need to talk."

"Can I tell her you're okay?"

"No. That would be a lie. Hey, Brad, I have to run. Thanks for calling."

Stuck in a car with her client in thick traffic thanks to an accident, Jamie was late getting back to the airport, and then reached her departure gate only after a fiasco at security during which she spilled the contents of her bag. Frazzled and no small amount exhausted, she corralled runaway print tubes from under the conveyor belt while the security guards watched in amusement. Knowing the plane was boarding, she ran. It wasn't until her things were in the overhead bin—actually, in a bin farther back, since those over her own seat were full—and she had climbed awkwardly over the legs of a large man who chose not to stand, for some reason, that she was able to call Caroline. Her mother picked up right away, but Jamie spent so long trying to explain why she hadn't been able to call sooner that she sounded defensive even to herself.

"I'm landing at ten," she concluded as the flight attendant began the instructions for takeoff. "Can I drive right there?"

Caroline nixed that. When Jamie asked why, she said she needed time, and when Jamie insisted they had to talk, Caroline said, "Not tonight."

Jamie didn't mention Brad's call, though she knew he had made it. He had texted that it went just fine, but she didn't know what that meant, and she hadn't had time to call him to find out.

So she didn't stop at Caroline's on her way home from the airport. She did talk with Brad, but when she tried to pin him down about his conversation with Caroline, she didn't learn much. "She's feeling self-pity," he suggested.

"Seriously?" Jamie shot back, unimpressed with his analysis and thinking that her mother had a right to feel that and more. To his credit, Brad was contrite. He didn't offer to drive over to comfort her, though, and for a second night in a row, she was glad. He had meetings with clients Saturday morning, and she planned to sleep in.

In fact, she slept poorly and was glad for an excuse to stop trying as soon as daylight appeared. Though clouds covered the sky, she was able to drive to Caroline's with the top down, but took no pleasure from it this day. The stifling air reflected her mood, which undermined the comfort she normally felt approaching the Victorian. When she thought of her mother, she ached.

The truck was parked at the garage, but Caroline wasn't on the porch. When Jamie stuck her head in the front door and called, Master's meow was the only response. As she scrubbed the back of his neck, she heard a faint noise over his purring.

Ducking back out, she followed that noise to the garage. The shrill buzz of the table saw was as familiar to her as a lullaby. The sheer normalcy of it raised her hopes.

Caroline couldn't hear her over the noise of the saw. Nor would she catch movement, with her goggles distorting her peripheral vision. She wore a T-shirt so faded that it looked gray and very old, very worn jeans. With her hair in a high knot and protective gloves on her hands, she was carving a piece of wood at one of three worktables. If her wrist hurt, she was ignoring it. The intensity of her forward stance suggested full concentration.

Jamie was wondering how to get her attention without making her jump when it struck her that Caroline knew she was there. Her jaw had grown tighter. Likewise her forearm. And rather than surging and ebbing as she shaped the wood, the whir of the saw was steady, determined, angry.

Not good.

"Mom," she called, then did it again. Finally, with a sigh, Caroline silenced the saw and straightened. After raising the goggles, she removed her gloves—gingerly when it came to the right one. The bandage on her wrist was gone, replaced by a Velcro support.

"That's an improvement," Jamie said in a tentative voice. "Is it okay?"

Caroline brushed at the wood, smoothed it with her hand, and bent to eye it from a different angle. "It's fine."

But her mother was not. What little Jamie could see of her face looked pale. Her failure to look at Jamie spoke volumes. "You're angry at me."

"I'm angry at the world," Caroline declared in a resigned burst as she straightened to her full height. Jamie might have appreciated her honesty if those so-like-her-own eyes hadn't met hers then. They were guarded to the point of being foreign. "*Should* I be angry with you?"

"For not telling you myself? Yes," Jamie readily confessed. "For Claire's decision? No. I had no part in that, Mom. Didn't ask for it. Don't want it."

"Have you told that to Claire?"

"No. She won't return my calls."

"Did you tell Roy?"

"Yes. He said they'd just hire an outside host and that I'd be jeopardizing the show."

"He's right." She didn't blink. "It's our family that's associated with *Gut It!* One of us has to host it, and they don't want me to do it."

"But that's not *right*," Jamie cried. "They're discriminating against you because of your age. You have to fight."

"Oh, I plan to," Caroline informed her, "but will I win? Doubtful. Let's open our eyes here, Jamie. When I look at the rest of the entertainment field, this isn't unique."

"But you love your role on the show. You haven't been this happy since—"

"—the divorce." Caroline raised her chin and said, "So here's a question for you. I've gone out of my way all these years not to put you in the middle, but I need an honest answer. How hard is your father pushing for this?"

Jamie did feel sandwiched. She chose her words with care. "He says he wants it for me. He keeps telling me how good it would be for my career."

"Brad clearly agrees with your father. And they're right. This would be a great move for you. You'll make a fabulous host—and you're ready. It didn't occur to me, not once during the Longmeadow taping, but when I look back on it, you hosted more scenes than you ever have before."

"It didn't occur to me either, Mom," Jamie came back in a beseeching voice. "That's what I'm trying to say. It's only in hindsight that I can see what they were doing. I didn't plan it."

"Jamie!" Caroline shouted. "You were instrumental in choosing the next project and securing new sponsors. You brought in Taylor Huff, who is *your* contemporary. You even narrated segments on the hand-crafted built-ins that I made. How could you not see what was happening?"

"Did *you* see it?" Jamie asked. Her stomach was churning.

"No, because you're my daughter, so I wasn't threatened. Besides, I wasn't in on your meetings with Claire. But you did tell me you were meeting with her. As I recall, it was practically every Tuesday morning."

That was damning, Jamie realized. "Honestly? I just thought she wanted my perspective on things. I thought she was picking my brain."

"You also took her shopping."

"For shoes, because she has zero taste."

"You went to a concert with her."

"Because you hate Nine Inch Nails, and she got complimentary tickets."

"You told her you and Brad were honeymooning in Paris. You didn't even tell me that."

Jamie was livid. "*She* mentioned Paris. *She* said it would be a good place to honeymoon. I agreed with her because there was no point in arguing, but if I haven't picked a date for my wedding yet, how can I plan my honeymoon? Claire is a bitch, Mom. She's making trouble." She had a bizarre thought. "Are you *jealous*?"

"Of Claire Howe?"

"Of her thinking she's my friend. She isn't because (A) I have no time for friends and (B) you're the only friend I need."

"I'm not jealous. I'm just looking at the evidence and thinking that there's no way you could have spent that amount of time with her without knowing on some level what she was planning. You're too bright to have missed all the signs. You had to have known, even subconsciously, but you said nothing to me. This is my *life,* Jamie. Shouldn't I have been involved in the conversation?"

"*Yes,* but it wasn't my call, Mom. I guess I'm *not* so bright, but I did not know what they were doing until Thursday morning. I said I'd be the one to tell you, because Claire is abrasive and Dad is a bulldozer"—her voice rose—"but was I seriously supposed to tell you when you were recovering from surgery? And on your *birthday*? Was I supposed to tell you on your birthday that you were being replaced because of your age? Give me credit for sensitivity, at least."

"But you do want this job."

"Not at your expense. If it didn't mean replacing you, of *course* I'd want it. It's a dream opportunity. Who *wouldn't* want it?"

"There you go."

"That doesn't mean—"

"Call it subconscious, but you were lobbying for it."

"No, Mom. I've been doing what Claire wanted me to do. I'm the dunce here. I just went along."

Caroline stared at her before whipping the goggles off her head and tossing them on the table on her way to the door. "Poor Jamie. She didn't plan any of this. Well, poor Jamie is the one who stands to gain here." She stormed toward the house.

"You sound like Grandma."

Caroline whipped around. "Who was paranoid at the end because she suffered from *dementia*. Hah! The truth comes out—I am an old fool."

"Mom," Jamie moaned as Caroline whipped back and strode on, "I can't do this. I *hate* confrontation."

At the back steps, Caroline whirled around again. "Life lesson here. Confrontation is what happens when you are less than honest and you get caught."

Jamie was losing it. Her relationship with her mother was more important to her than anything else in the world. "Okay," she said, trying desperately to stay calm, "I'll do anything to make this right. I don't care about *Gut It!* Let it be canceled. Is that what you want?"

"Excuse me? Are you putting the burden of that on *me*?"

Jamie threw her hands in the air. "I can't win. What do you want me to say? Okay." She was beyond reason. "I wanted this. I planned it. Is that what you want me to say? It's not true, but do the words make you feel better?"

Caroline trotted up the back steps. At the door, she shot a look back, but her gaze was so forbidding that Jamie couldn't take another step. All she could do was to watch her go inside and close the door.

Driving back home, Jamie was beside herself. For the first time in her life, something stood between her and her mother. It wasn't a person or even a wall, but more like that screen door slapping hard in her face. She could still see her old mom—same wavy hair, same green eyes, same strong arms—but now on the far side that she couldn't reach. Anger was so not part of her mother's usual behavior that Jamie didn't know how to begin to handle it.

"How'd it go?" Brad asked, sounding concerned. He had been trying her, but it wasn't until she was inside her clean, neat, sleek white condo that she found the wherewithal to call back.

"She totally blames me."

"This is not your fault," he said innocently enough.

"No? I played into Claire's hands. I played into *Dad's* hands." She began wandering. "I should have seen it coming, but I didn't, and she's right, I'm the one who stands to gain from this. She used to trust me. Forget that now." Her feet stopped moving. "When you called her, Brad, what did you say?" Whatever it was hadn't helped, but she needed to know.

"I told her how worried you were."

"About her."

"Yes. That's what I got from you."

She felt a spike of frustration. She knew that Brad wasn't good with parents, but this was as much about his understanding Jamie as anything else. "Did you not tell her that I think this change is a mistake?"

"It isn't a mistake. It's a carefully crafted move to improve the show's ratings—"

"—which haven't declined. So it's a preemptive move."

"That's how successful ventures work. They have to stay one step ahead."

"This isn't a corporate venture. It's a family show. Does that not count for anything?"

"It's more than a family show." He barely paused. "By the way, did you hear the forecast? Bad storms are moving in."

Jamie couldn't have cared less about the weather. "*Gut It!* is about MacAfee Homes, and MacAfee Homes is about family. When it comes to the show, Caroline is the matriarch. She's the glue that holds it all together." With a quick breath, she begged, "I need you to hear me, Brad. I don't want this job. Maybe in the future, but not now. My mother earned it, she does it well, and viewers aren't complaining about the way she looks. If they're firing her because she's too old, that's grounds for a lawsuit." She paused, got no reply, finally asked, "Don't you think?"

"Actually, they're within their legal rights. Her contract runs from year to year. They're not kicking her off the show. They're just shifting the cast around. And I mentioned the weather because if we get torrential downpours, having dinner in Boston tonight may not be smart."

Their reservation was at a restaurant on the waterfront that had opened earlier that spring, but Jamie couldn't think about dinner just then. "Claire admitted it was about age."

"It might be, but this is entertainment. Actresses audition for roles all the time and fail to get them because they're too old. Do you see them suing? I looked into precedent, Jamie. Caroline can sue, but the case will be tossed out before it ever reaches a court, and she'll be out fifty grand for the attempt."

"MacAfee will cover it."

"We won't. I asked."

"Asked *who*?"

"Theo. Roy wanted to know. Neither one of them wants that kind of publicity. Listen, I know you're upset, but stand back for a minute. If she can't win this, wouldn't it be better to accept the inevitable?"

"You mean, go out with dignity?" Jamie mocked.

"Yes," he insisted with more enthusiasm in that single word than in any of the others preceding it, which annoyed her all the more.

"Okay, Brad. *You* stand back. Suppose I take this job. Suppose I hold it for a dozen years, and maybe the show has moved through a handful of mutations but is still going strong, and we're married with three kids—"

"Two kids."

"*Three* kids, and I'm over forty and maybe not so slim after the kids, and they decide they want someone twenty-five so they're easing me out, how would you feel then?" Silence. "How would you feel if they did that to *you*?"

"I'm in a different field."

Jamie simmered. "The correct answer would be 'I'm a man. That would never happen to me.' And you're right. But how unfair is that? Your dad is bald, so *you* could well be bald. Think MacAfee buyers will ask for a younger lawyer? No, they will not, because your age gives you authority. It suggests knowledge and experience. Well, the same is true of Caroline MacAfee."

"Jeez, Jamie," Brad burst out, sounding bewildered, "what do you want me to say?"

Jamie could think of a dozen things, but she refused to spoon-feed him. Either he felt the cause or he did not.

Right now, though, she wanted to get off the phone and go to yoga. There was a class at one, and after a disastrous time earlier with Caroline and now a disappointing discussion with Brad, she needed a break. Granted it was barely ten. One was a ways off, and the class wasn't far. But she had plenty to keep her busy, starting with the drawings for a residential project, for which she needed to visit a stoneworks company that MacAfee hadn't used before but that carried the fieldstone she desperately wanted to use on this house.

"Gotta go," she said.

"We have to keep talking. We don't agree yet."

"Brad, we're not going to agree on everything. I need to go to yoga."

"Watch the weather."

"Okay. I'll call you later."

Concentration was a problem. She couldn't sit still to work on the drawings, didn't see the fieldstone she wanted, and when she got to yoga, the instructor was so like Caroline in age and looks that Jamie had to keep her eyes shut. Without a visual example, she was distracted and kept reverting to shallow breathing.

Brad had been right about the weather. By the time her class was done, the morning's clouds had darkened to slate. Her mood was correspondingly grim. She needed Caroline.

As she drove home, she called. "Mom?" She paused. Nothing. "Are you okay?"

"I'm fine," Caroline said. She didn't sound it, but at least she had answered the phone.

"About this morning—"

"I don't want to talk about it, Jamie."

"We were both upset."

"Right, so I'm not going there. Let it rest."

"Nothing gets resolved if it rests." She realized she sounded like Brad.

There was a pause, then a quiet "When it's raw, it does, unless you want to do more damage?"

Invitation? Dare? Threat? Jamie felt like she might cry. "No," she conceded and swallowed, but an ominous lump remained in her throat. She had to clear it to ask, "What are you doing tonight?" It was a petty question, but it kept the connection going.

"Having dinner with Annie, Linda, and Dawn."

That was good. Jamie didn't want her alone. "Dawn?"

"From the nail shop. Like Linda. Their husbands are all going to Fenway."

"The game may be rained out." Jamie thought she heard distant thunder, until she saw a truck roll around the corner a block ahead. "Okay. Well, be careful."

"Yup." No *You be careful, too,* no *We'll work this out,* no *I love you, baby.* Just *Yup,* and the call ended.

eight

Jamie was bereft, which was why she caught a little breath of hope when she turned onto her street. Parked in front of her condo was Jess's silver SUV with its yellow TODDLER ON BOARD cling-on decal in the back window. Seeing Tad was the one thing sure to distract her.

When the SUV started to pull away, she honked and waved. *Wait! I'm home! Wait!* The SUV stopped. After pulling into the garage, Jamie ran back outside with her eyes on the backseat.

"Hey, Taddy!" she called, waving at the shadow that would be the boy, then at the real one when the window smoothly lowered. His milk-chocolate hair was a mop of soft curls that were longer than Roy wanted but shorter than Jessica did. His eyes were an even warmer brown, his little cheeks red as ever.

"Mamie, Mamie!" he shrieked.

She reached for the door just as it clicked to unlock, and shot a thank-you smile at Jess. Only Jess wasn't the one unfolding from the driver's seat.

Seeing Roy, Jamie felt a stab of dismay. He was the last person she needed right now. Granted, he wasn't looking as together as usual. He wore running shorts and a baggy tank, and his hair was messed. But his eyes were sharp, anger focused on her.

Stomach churning, she opened the door and released Tad's harness. "Hi, monkey," she said and scooped him up for a hug. His arms went around her neck, his legs around her waist. She closed her eyes, savoring. Tad always made her feel loved. Had from infancy.

Having rounded the front of the car, Roy kept the open door between them as he gripped its top. His voice was low to protect the boy, but nothing protected Jamie. The words came at her with a simmering ire.

"I can't tell you how disappointed I am. You promised you'd tell your mother, and you did not. You went behind my back with Theo and tried to do it with Claire. *She* had to tell Caroline herself, which made it harder for both of them, so if you were trying to protect your mother, you failed. I didn't ask you to tell Caroline, you offered, and I told Claire that you'd do it, so now I look like a fool and, by extension, so does MacAfee Homes." He threw up his hands. "What were you waiting for? Did you think I was kidding? That if you waited long enough, this would all just go away?"

Wearing Tad like a shield, Jamie kept her cheek tucked against his hair as she swayed from side to side. When the little boy sang her name, she drew back. His brown eyes held excitement. He babbled something.

"Say it again, monkey," she urged.

He pointed back. Fallen over on the car seat that it must have been sharing with him was a furry brown moose. "Oh my," she said in awe. "Is he new?" Indeed. The tag was still attached to its side. "What's his name?" She studied Tad's raised brows and caught in a breath. "Oh. No name yet. Should we call him Moose?"

Tad lit up. "My Moose."

"Absolutely, your Moose," Jamie said.

"Did you *hear* me, Jamie?" Roy asked, seething. "I'm not sure what your mother said, but Claire was pretty offended, so there's harm done on many fronts. Do you fully understand the stakes here? The station will go on with this show—don't ever doubt that—but if we can't come together and make it work, they'll remove the MacAfee Homes label from it."

Jamie burrowed the moose against Tad's neck. The child giggled and contorted.

"Maybe they should," she said softly and shot her father a look. His hands were on his hips, knuckles white, and his blue eyes sharp. He had clearly been stewing about this.

Tightly, he said, "I want you to call Claire and apologize. Explain why you didn't tell your mother on Thursday like you promised me you'd do, and tell her that you talked with your mother today and everything's settled. Tell her that your mother agrees with the reasoning behind the switch and is totally behind your moving up. Tell her you'll be *honored* to host the show from here on." Coming around the door, he reached for Tad. "Come on, boy. We have to go to the store for Mommy, and I want to do it before the rain comes."

With the child no longer in her arms, Jamie backed away from the car. "Wait," Roy ordered. After belting Tad in, he stalked her. "You want to feel loyalty to your mother, fine, but now is not the time. This is about loyalty to MacAfee Homes."

She didn't want to argue, but he was on a mission. When she stepped back, he followed.

"It's about business," he nearly shouted. "It's about MacAfee prominence. Did you not get it when I pointed out that Barth at Fiona's? Our competitors don't like what we have with *Gut It!* and would do most anything to have it fail. If it does, that hurts all of us." She took another step back, but he followed, hands on his hips now, upper body leaning in. "It's not just you, Jamie. You have a responsibility to the rest of the cast, too. Some have families to support, what about them? And what about your own future? Has it not occurred to you to get your foot in the door as host before you and Brad have kids? Once you've built a following, no one will blink if you're pregnant, and I'm talking about Brian and Claire, because they're the ones who count." He lowered his head so that their eyes were level. "Is anyone home? Can you speak?"

"You're crowding me," she murmured and took another step back. This time, when he followed, she held up a hand.

"I need you to speak now, Jamie. Tell me what I want to hear."

Her insides were knotted up. On a wisp of breath, she tried to be conciliatory with a mild "I think we're both upset." Caroline had said it earlier, so the statement couldn't be without merit.

Roy straightened, drawing up to his full height. "This is about your mother. That's your bottom line, isn't it."

It would be yours, too, if you had an ounce of compassion, shouted the voice in her head. The one that emerged from her mouth was less reckless. "Some things in life are just as important as MacAfee Homes."

"Like Caroline MacAfee—and hah, she wasn't so quick to give up my name, not when she was getting mileage from it. So what's the problem here? She's had her day in the sun. Now she needs to step aside and let someone younger host the show. Ah, but that's it, isn't it? You think for me it's all about age. You've always thought that. Well, let me tell you, it takes two to tango. Your mother was as much at fault for the failure of our marriage as I was. She knew I needed someone with pizzazz, but she refused to even try."

Jamie waved both hands spasmodically.

"Don't want to get into that?" Roy goaded. "Not your business? Well, you've made it your business with this . . . this show of misguided loyalty."

"Mom worked so hard to rebuild after the divorce."

"Ah, hell. She had lots of help. Theo worships her. But he's not stepping in on her behalf right now, is he? He knows when to let smarter people make the decisions. Your mother may be good at what she does"—he rolled his eyes—"but she's just a carpenter."

"If she's just a carpenter," shouted the angry voice in Jamie's head, "then you're just a salesman!" Only when his eyes widened did she realize she had actually spoken.

A sound came from the car. Tad.

Jamie was upset enough to ignore it. "I only say that because you did. If we're boiling it down to one word—"

"The difference being that your mother will always be just a carpenter, but I'm the next head of MacAfee Homes. Your calling me 'just a salesman' is not only insulting but ignorant."

Another sound came from the car.

Roy sent an aggrieved look there before it shot back to her. "Do you hear what I'm saying about all this? You won't listen to Brad, who is nearly as frustrated as I am, but I want you to listen to me. You're being selfish and shortsighted."

"You're being insensitive and cruel."

"Excuse me?"

She didn't apologize. He had insulted Caroline. He had insulted her. He had been pushing and pushing, spoiling for a fight. She was simply stating the truth.

Suddenly, he had a finger in her face. In a low, lethal voice, he said, "I named you my son's godmother because I thought you would be the most responsible person for the job. But if you can't behave like a grown-up—if you can't separate this fixation on your mother from what everyone else knows is for the best—I'll gladly change that."

"For what it's worth," Jamie burst back, hurt enough to be reckless, "as godmothers go, I'm a totally positive influence. I'll teach Tad sensitivity and compassion, which is more than you will."

"*Excuse* me?"

She stood her ground, staring at him in defiance. He seemed stunned, and understandably so. She could count on one hand the number of times she had stood up to him.

Tad began to cry full out. Swearing, Roy simmered for a last minute before he turned on his heel and strode off. Within seconds, the SUV peeled off from the curb, and Jamie began to shake.

She wasn't sorry, absolutely was not sorry. In a perfect world, she might have used a different tone, so that she sounded less bad-tempered and more adult. But this wasn't a perfect world, and she didn't regret the words themselves. They were the absolute, positive truth.

Still, she reran the argument constantly as she showered and dressed. She muttered some lines when her eye shadow was too dark, barked out others in the closet when a hanger wouldn't release the blouse she wanted. When Brad came to pick her up, though, she didn't mention Roy's visit.

She was having enough trouble processing it herself. Granted, Roy had goaded her. But now *both* of her parents were upset with her.

Then there was the line that stuck in her throat for a different reason. *You won't listen to Brad, who is nearly as frustrated as I am.* The implication was that Roy and Brad were talking and in total agreement about her stubbornness. She knew to beware. Roy was perfectly capable of twisting Brad's words, or worse, hearing in Brad's reply only what he wanted to hear. It was possible that Brad had in fact argued on her behalf.

But she doubted it.

Add to that the weather, and she felt totally off. The rain began even before Brad picked her up and continued through dinner without bringing a change in temperature, which meant that the very warm air was now also very wet. Her hair curled; her freckles bled through her makeup; her jeans stuck to her thighs despite all manner of shifting in her seat. Their dinner companions were Brad's law school friends, and she tried to be part of the conversation but didn't always succeed. Law talk wasn't exactly small talk, and it could be technical.

Returning from Boston, they drove through steady, heavy rain. By the time they got home, thunder had rolled in and was growing louder by the clap. When lightning joined it with a ferocity that confirmed Brad's prediction, it was reason enough to snuggle beside him on the sofa watching reruns of *Homeland*. They had to raise the volume. The rain that sheeted against the patio doors drowned out everything but what became near-continual thunder. Mix in a driving wind, with sudden, sharp gusts, and there were times when the condo shook.

Then came a deafening clap, a brilliant flash, and the power went out. Without lights or TV, they went to bed and made love. It seemed the only thing to do that didn't involve thinking too much.

Brad was happy. Feeling loved, he fell asleep soon after. Jamie wanted to follow, but her body wouldn't settle. She was on edge. Storm? Her parents? Sex?

She lay against him for a time, listening to the rain on the skylight as the flashes of light weakened and the thunder moved off. Eventually, she put on a robe and went downstairs, but bits of conversation followed—

her mother's distrust, her father's anger. Groping for a match, she lit the while pillar candle that sat in a clear glass lamp on the kitchen island. The candle flickered. Hoping to be lulled by the dance of the flame, she watched it, but long minutes after, she was as troubled as ever.

Wondering how far the power outage stretched, she opened her front door and leaned out. The rain had slowed to a drizzle, which fell off rooftops and trees to dapple an otherwise eerie silence. The surrounding houses were as dark as hers. She assumed that the problem had already been reported, and was wondering whether she should call herself simply to find out when the power would return, when a pair of headlights turned onto the street.

She didn't think a neighbor would be driving so late in such bad weather, and this vehicle being a car, rather than a truck, ruled out the power company. Startled, she watched the headlights pull up at her house.

Her first thought was that someone casing the area had seen her open door and that she needed to close it, wake Brad, and call the cops. Before she could, though, both car doors opened, casting enough light into the lingering drizzle to bounce back on itself.

It *was* the cops.

At her house.

At one in the morning.

The strangeness of it made her uneasy, no less as their flashlights made a path to her door. The men wore rain gear. When they were close enough, she recognized the younger as one of the officers who had been leaving Fiona's when she arrived there Thursday morning. The man in front of him, older, more portly, and plodding forward under the weight of the world, was the chief of police. Paul Logan was a local boy who had left town, learned the ropes of law enforcement elsewhere, and returned. He and Roy were high school buddies, close then and now.

"Paul?" she said uneasily.

He hitched his chin. His voice was rough. "Can we go inside?"

Heart pounding, she held the door open. "What's wrong?" A dozen thoughts went through her mind as she opened the door wider, but the scariest part was Paul. After he shook the rain off his cap, she got a good look at his eyes. They were filled with sorrow.

"There's been an accident."

She barely breathed. "Who?"

"Your father and his wife."

She was suspended in time. "Bad?"

He nodded, then looked past her as Brad approached, wearing jeans and an unbuttoned shirt. "What's up?" He was looking at Paul.

"Dad had an accident," Jamie whispered, terrified. "He and Jess." She forced her voice into sound. "*How* bad?" When Paul swallowed, she urged, "*Tell* me."

"Lightning hit a tree. It fell on their car." He paused briefly before saying, "Your father didn't make it. They're rushing Jess to the hospital, but it doesn't look good."

"Didn't make it," Jamie repeated, needing something more definitive.

"When?" Brad asked. "Where?"

"We're guessing it was when the last cell hit, but we won't be sure until forensics looks at the car. It was over on River Run."

Not heavily traveled, Jamie thought with rising panic. Dark as pitch unless the moon was full, which it wasn't even behind all those storm clouds.

"What do you mean, didn't make it?" she asked.

Paul's tired eyes said it all. "I'm sorry."

She might have swayed, but Brad was at her shoulder. *"Dead?"* she asked with barely a sound. It didn't make sense. There had to be a mistake.

But Paul was Roy's friend—*and* the police chief. Wouldn't Paul know? *Omigod omigod omigod.* She looked past him to the other officer, but his frightened expression said he hadn't had to make a visit like this before, which was telling.

Her eyes filled with tears. Unable to grasp *dead,* she focused on details. "A tree fell. Did it crush them, push them into another car, make them go off the road, maybe flip over? Part of River Run has a really steep drop-off."

Brad cupped her shoulder with a hand that said, *Not important now, Jamie,* but the police chief understood her. Gently, he said, "The car was on the road under a large tree. A forensic team from the state is on its way there now. We won't know whether the cause of death was blunt force trauma from the tree or from the sudden stop until an autopsy is done."

"Do you think it was instant?"

"For Roy, yes."

"Was Jess conscious?"

"No, but breathing. I don't know who of her family to call, and there's the matter of whoever's staying with Tad. Someone has to call Randi." Miranda MacAfee was Roy's only sibling. She lived in California, well removed from MacAfee Homes. "First, we have to tell Theo. Would you like me to do that?"

Feeling a soul-deep dread, Jamie looked up at Brad. His eyes were wide behind his glasses, but he did get this. "You should be with Tad," he said. "Should I go to Theo's?"

"No. Um, no. No." She cleared her throat. "Mom will. She'll know how to do it." Caroline was the *only* one who could tell Theo. Jamie had no doubt of that, but she was struggling with who else to call and what to say, trying to order her thoughts in a nightmare for which she was ill prepared. "Maybe you can go to the . . . scene."

Jamie didn't cry. There was too much to be done. After hurriedly throwing water on her face, she stuck her hair in a ponytail and pulled on jeans and a shirt. She grabbed for her phone with such a shaky hand that she nearly dropped it before getting a grip.

Brad had already put up the convertible top. He gave her a hug before she climbed in. "Are you sure I can't come with you?"

She nodded. "I'm okay."

As she headed out, though, she wondered. Jess might survive, but *dead* was final. Just as she hadn't been able to grasp her phone, she couldn't grasp that Roy was gone. Part of her wanted to go to the scene first. Until she saw her father's car, she wouldn't believe this was real. He drove a BMW. People didn't die in BMWs.

But Paul Logan had seen the car, and his pain was clear.

Hands tight on the wheel, Jamie drove over roads that were slick and littered with branches and leaves. At least the sporadic house light said there was power on Caroline's side of town.

Only as she turned onto her mother's street did she remember their rift. Rift or not, though, Caroline would be there for Theo. That was who she was.

The front walk was as littered as the street, the front steps soggy. Even the porch showed wear and tear from gusting winds. Ignoring the wrought-iron chair overturned near the table, Jamie reached for the doorbell and was about to press it, then pulled out her phone instead and dialed. Caroline slept with her phone on the nightstand—*in case you need me,* she always said.

I need you, Mom, she thought. *I need you now.*

She heard the phone ring inside once, twice, and pictured Caroline groping for it and squinting at the caller ID as it rang a third time. Just shy of voice mail, there was a groggy "Not now, Jamie. It can wait till morning."

"Dad's dead," Jamie said in a breathy rush. "I'm downstairs at your door. Someone has to tell Theo."

There was a long pause. Jamie was wondering whether she should ring the doorbell after all when she heard a hurried footfall descending inside.

The porch light came on and Caroline opened the door. *"What?"* she asked in quiet alarm as she pushed the screen open.

"Paul Logan just came to my house," Jamie said and rushed out the details she knew.

Her mother looked stunned. After a frozen moment, she gave a tiny headshake and wrapped her arms around Jamie. "I am so sorry," she whispered, "*so* sorry." Her hold was strong and precious. It wasn't long enough to stop the trembling deep inside, but Jamie was grateful nonetheless.

Too soon, Caroline drew back. Eyes clouded in disbelief, she asked questions, like where Roy and Jess had been and whether air bags had deployed, but they were filler, simply buying time for news that was unreal to sink in. Finally, plowing both hands—the right with its Velcro wrap—into her tousled hair, she held her elbows up and cupped her head. "Theo will be devastated. I'll go there."

"That would be huge," Jamie breathed. "Brad went to the scene. I have to call Jess's mother. She lives near Leominster and can be here in an hour, assuming she wants to come." Jess had no siblings, just a mother and stepfather with their own children, their own interests, their own lives. There were issues, Jamie knew, not the least being resentment of Roy and the easy life he offered Jess.

"Of course she'll come."

"They weren't on good terms." Nor were Jamie and Caroline, yet here they were. She raised tearful, fear-filled eyes. "What do I tell Tad's sitter? She's probably, like, fifteen. She'll freak out."

Seeming bewildered for a minute herself, Caroline finally inhaled. "Just say that Roy and Jess are detained—uh, that they're having car problems and that you're filling in."

"Dad usually drives her home."

"One of her parents will have to come. You should call them yourself."

Definitely. She could do that. Trust Caroline to know what to do. She was always level-headed. "Mom, about before—"

Gentle fingers touched her mouth. "Shhhh. We'll talk later. Right now, you need to deal with Tad."

"But how? What do I do? What do I say?"

"He'll be asleep a while longer, so you have time. If Jess wakes up, she can tell you what she wants you to say."

"What if she doesn't wake up?" Jamie asked. "What if she's in a coma for days . . . or . . . or in a permanent vegetative state?"

"Don't go there yet."

But how could Jamie not? *I named you my son's godmother.* They were the most innocent of the angry, vindictive words she and Roy had exchanged—their last words to each other on this earth—less than twelve hours before he died. Now they took on even deeper meaning. Two years ago, shortly after Tad's birth, Roy and Jess had asked, and Jamie had agreed, that she also be the boy's guardian should anything happen to them.

She hadn't thought twice about it. Nothing would happen to Roy and Jess.

Now something had.

Most people lost parents. It was the generational order of things. But so soon? So *suddenly*? She couldn't begin to grasp that Roy was gone. For Tad's sake alone, she could only pray Jess would survive.

nine

Theo MacAfee lived in a Tudor-style home at the east end of town. It had been one of the company's first showcase properties in Williston, and Theo's wife loved it too much to sell. Caroline had always thought it dark, though as she approached it this night, the darkness was internal. Roy was gone. Crushed. Silenced forever.

It was surreal. Oh, she knew he was human, knew it better than anyone, perhaps. But he had always been so cocksure of himself. Sudden death did not seem possible.

Other than a residual dripping from trees, the rain had stopped by the time she pulled under the portico and climbed up the broad stone steps. Her heart was heavy as she rang the bell. She waited, wishing she were anywhere else but knowing she had to be here. She was more vigilant when she pressed the button a second time, listening for the bell, hearing it, knowing it worked. *Patience, Caroline.* Theo had day help, but nights he was alone. He would be startled from sleep and slow to descend.

But descend he finally did, put on a light, and opened the door with a groggy caution. His eyes widened a fraction when he saw Caroline. Seeming to know that only something desperately wrong would bring her to his door in the middle of the night, he stood aside.

She slipped in, closed the door, spoke quickly and softly. For a split second, she saw panic in those blue eyes. He looked at the floor and swallowed once. Then, either because he was overwhelmed with too many emotions or simply unwilling to think, his face went blank. Caroline was midsentence, saying that Jamie was going to be with Tad, when he turned, went to the phone on the hall table, and punched in a number with a large-knuckled hand.

"MacAfee here," he barked. "Get me the chief." The police dispatcher must have been waiting for his call, because he was immediately patched through. Frozen in place with his shoulders bent, he said a gruff word here or there but mostly listened. The conversation was brief. When he hung up, he murmured, "Paul's coming." Holding up a shaky *stay* finger to Caroline, he went back upstairs to dress.

She would have waited even without the command. She couldn't leave him alone at a time like this. Sinking into a Louis XIV chair that was nestled into the newel curve, she looked around at old-world furnishings, original art, creative ceramics that Patricia MacAfee had collected. What she kept seeing, though, was the look on Theo's face in the instant she'd told him the news. Panic was one word for it, but it also held shreds of horror and loss. It was here and gone in a second, but she knew that look. Her father had worn a similar one at the beginning of the end—knowing what was happening, not knowing how to deal. The look was wrong in both men, the kind of expression that a person who had led a full and commanding life should never wear.

Feeling lost herself, Caroline thought about calling Dean. But without more information?

She shifted in the chair. With nothing to do but think, she had a growing sense of the enormity of what had occurred. Theo had lost his son, Jamie and Tad their father, Jess her husband. The town had lost a leader. MacAfee Homes had lost its heir.

At the sound of a motor, she jumped up. She reached the door just as a cruiser pulled in behind her truck. Paul approached wearing a devastated look.

"How's Jessica?" Caroline asked.

"On life support. They're not optimistic."

She pressed a hand to her mouth. Life support was more definitive than unconscious, not good at all. Jamie would need to know. Now that Paul was here, Caroline could drive to Roy's to help her there.

Just then, though, Theo came down the stairs. Seeming older and more frail, he was gripping the banister, taking one step at a time. He cleared his throat as he met Paul's eyes.

"I'll leave you," Caroline said gently, but the words were barely out when Theo grasped her arm.

"No." He shot her a look that reprised a world of fear, then said a lower "Stay. I'll ride with you."

Could she deny him? He had been her father-in-law once, and in the years since, he had been in her corner more times than she could count. He was such a solitary figure now—such a *tragic* figure—that, much as she wanted to be with Jamie, she couldn't leave Theo just yet.

Jamie had stopped trying to differentiate windshield spatter from tears. More than once, when she could barely see, she thought about pulling over. But she needed to be at Roy's. She had to let the babysitter leave and then call Jess's mother. She wasn't looking forward to that, but it was probably an easier task than the one Caroline faced.

Tougher, for Jamie, would be seeing Tad.

Her headlights cut a bleeding swath through wooded streets. As many times as she had visited here, she had never done it at this hour or with this burden. Her throat was an aching knot by the time she reached the house.

It was one of the newer French manor homes built by Roy on a triple-size lot. It was bigger than anything he and Jess would ever need, and far too pretentious for Jamie's liking. Separated from neighbors and surrounded by woods, its lights were a beacon in the dark.

As fate had it, the babysitter's mother was already there. Apparently, Jess had promised that they would be home by midnight, and when that had been missed by an hour with neither texts nor phone calls answered, the girl was worried enough to call home.

Holding it together by a thread, Jamie explained that there had been a problem and that she was filling in. It wasn't a lie. They would know the truth soon enough. Williston had a handful of citizens who monitored the police frequency for sport. For all she knew, word had already begun to spread.

Apologizing profusely, she overpaid the girl, saw them out, and headed for Tad's room. Despite the many times Roy had talked of buying a toddler bed, it hadn't appeared yet. Tad was in his crib, sound asleep on his side with an arm around his favorite stuffed dog, the new moose fallen over behind him, and a zoo of other animals scattered about. She barely breathed as she listened for his soft, steady sounds. The child was blissfully unaware of the unfolding tragedy.

Child? *Try "baby,"* Jamie thought. He was a *baby* who would now never know his father. How could that *be*?

Overwhelmed with anger and unable to help herself, she started to cry. She quickly left the room so that she wouldn't wake Tad, and ran down to the kitchen.

Struggling to stem her tears, just needing to get this done, she searched for Jess's mother's number. Naturally, it would be on Jess's iPhone, but that would be in the car, a brutal mental image there. Plan B had her opening Jess's laptop to pull up Contacts. But . . . password? Jamie had no idea. Plan C—and there it was, *Maureen Olson,* at the very bottom of the list of emergency numbers in the kitchen drawer. Jamie suspected it was wishful thinking on Jess's part that the woman would actually be there for her in a pinch.

Nonetheless, Jamie felt deep sympathy waking Maureen in the middle of the night with news like this. The woman was stunned. When she couldn't get a word out, her husband came on to ask specifics of the accident.

Jamie wished she knew more. She wished she didn't have to now call her aunt. She wished her father, whose last words to her—and hers to him—had been ones of anger, would drive up any minute and walk through the door. She wished her mother were here.

In lieu of that, she texted Brad. *Where are you?*

At the scene. You don't want to come.

Bad?

Yes. Happened earlier than we thought. Took a long time to find and extricate.

She pictured a large clawed machine being brought in to lift the tree that had fallen and remove the roof of the car. And the scene beneath?

Squeezing her eyes shut, she was trying to blot out the image when Brad texted again. *Your mother just got here with Theo.*

How is he?

Stoic. Did you call Jess's mother?

Yes. She's going to the hospital. Any news from there?

Life support.

Jamie let the phone fall to her side. Jess gone, too? No. No. If miracles happened, she could still wake up. But whole and functioning?

By the time dawn arrived, Jamie had wandered through the first floor of the house over and over again, library to living room to dining room to great room, hating the place more with each round. She felt like she was in a mausoleum. Aside from a small den filled with sturdy leather and toys, the decor was an ultratraditional mix of velvet and silk, with elaborate mahogany millwork and brocades of blue and gold. The walls were jam-packed with paintings, the tables with bowls, vases, and lamps. Had these things been family heirlooms, the effect might have been different, but the family heirlooms were at Theo's. Roy had simply bought what the designer advised, that designer being Roy's favorite, a longtime MacAfee employee whose style was too busy for Jamie's. She felt suffocated here; with so much stuff packed in, she couldn't breathe. And it wasn't just the current horror that made it so. She had never been able to handle staying here for more than a day or two; when she was watching Tad for longer, she brought him to her condo.

This house was a showpiece, no doubt about that, but the thought of raising a child here gave her the chills. Not that Tad had free run of the place. His things were consolidated in kitchen, bedroom, and den. He could also play in a finished basement, a paved driveway, and a huge backyard. He wasn't deprived by a long shot.

Not materially at least. But to lose parents who would be only the merest threads of memory? *Stuff* was worth squat compared to that.

The circles she walked didn't include the upstairs. She couldn't bear to see the room that Roy had shared with Jess. Rather, her base was the kitchen counter, where her cell phone lay beside the baby monitor, both of which lay beside the Keurig, which she had repeatedly used more for warmth than caffeine. She was chilled to the bone, perhaps because Roy kept the AC low, perhaps because she was in a state of shock. She hadn't slept, doubted she could have even if she tried. Her thoughts were a muddle of disbelief and fear, her mind a demon of gruesome images, and her insides wouldn't stop shaking.

Brad and Caroline were with Theo, and while she wished one or the other were with her, she understood Theo's need. She exchanged texts with them, but there was little of comfort to be had there. Nor did repeated calls to the hospital help. None offered good news.

When she heard Tad crying at six, she panicked. Praying he might fall back to sleep, she didn't move. Barely a minute passed before he called again, this time with more force. *"Mommmeee."*

Swallowing a cry of anguish, Jamie headed for the stairs. She knew the early morning drill—change diaper, warm sippy cup of milk, fix breakfast. She had stayed with Tad enough to know that when she opened his door he would be standing against the bars of his crib—and there he was. His milk-chocolate hair stuck up in random curls; his brown eyes were clear, his cheeks pink. His thumb was in his mouth but popped out when he saw her. In his innocence, he wasn't confused at all but cried her name in delight.

It was so sweet, so *sad,* that she thought she would die. He had no idea how his life had changed. It was all she could do not to bawl.

"Hi, monkey," she whispered so that he wouldn't hear the shake in her voice. He held out his arms as she neared the crib. Gathering him close, she left his arms around her neck while she unzipped his sleep sack. Then she scooped him into a tight hug, rocking him from side to side as she struggled not to cry.

Focus, Jamie. That's a big fat diaper against your arm.

Regaining a bit of control, she eased off the hug. "Did you have a good sleep?"

"I wan Moose," he said and reached back toward the crib. She put the pet in his arms and tried to lay him on the dressing table, but he squirmed until she set him on his feet on the floor. This was a change since she had stayed with him last. But okay. Doable.

That said, changing his diaper while he was standing up was a challenge. If he wasn't dancing off toward his Playskool garage, he was reaching for a dump truck or twisting to pick up the driver when it fell out of the cab. Thinking that he definitely needed to be potty trained—*would Jess be here to do it?*—Jamie struggled with the clean diaper. She had never been as adept at this as Jess, simply hadn't done it as much, and Tad wasn't helping her out. It took three tries before the tapes were tight enough, and then she pulled on a pair of jeans to hold the diaper in place.

Sitting on the floor, he played with the truck and a bulldozer, gathering other drivers, handing one to Jamie and telling her what to do. He was actually quite clear with his instructions. "Put man dere . . . No, dis one . . . Brrrrm, brrrrrrm . . . Dump, Mamie." Having her here was a game.

She was thinking how grateful she was that he didn't know better when without warning he ran out the door toward the stairs. Heart pounding, she caught him just as he might have tumbled, though once she was beside him, she saw that he was already holding the banister. He climbed down facing front, knew to take one step at a time and move his hands accordingly. Physical coordination had never been a problem for him.

Or for his dad, Jamie realized, *who would never see him ride a bike, serve a tennis ball, score a basket.*

Aching inside, she gave him his milk, which he drank as he wandered around the kitchen. Then she fixed him a bowl of cereal, put it on the island counter, and reached for him. He had long since rejected a high chair, but now refused even the booster seat. "Dis one, Mamie," he insisted, patting a stool, and when she set him there, he patted the stool beside it. "Mamie eat."

Jamie wasn't up for food, but after a few minutes, she went to the fridge for yogurt and fruit and, to encourage Tad, swallowed a few blueberries herself. When she put some in his cereal bowl, he howled in protest. *"No blues!"* She snatched them back out and crossed the kitchen to get another plate. By the time she returned, he had tipped the cereal bowl and was drawing pictures in the milk that pooled on the granite counter, and when she reached for a paper towel, half a dozen sheets left the roll.

She might have been upset if there hadn't been so much else on her mind—like what to do with Tad when breakfast was done. They could play inside, outside, or at one of the playgrounds in town. But how could she play? How could she smile and laugh and run with the sun rising on the saddest possible day?

Focus, she told herself again. But how to do that with God-only-knew-what-else going on? Tad was lucky. He was a child. He could be blissfully ignorant. Or not.

"Where Mommy?" Big brown eyes held hers.

Uh. Uh. Omigod. What to say?

"She had to go out" seemed the best stopgap, and yes, the child was blissfully ignorant of the absurdity of Jess going out at this hour. "You're stuck with Mamie today," she said and let him help mop up the milk. He had fun with that. She let him drag it out.

She barely made it to seven before texting her mother. It was a few minutes before an answer came, and the exchange that followed was choppy. Caroline was driving Theo home. There was no word on Jess. Funeral plans would wait until they knew more. Theo wanted her to start calling MacAfee people.

You can do this, Jamie, read her final text, and while Jamie needed more, she understood. It sounded like Caroline had her hands full with Theo, perhaps even more so than Jamie with Tad. Theo knew what was happening.

Brad's appearance at Roy's shortly thereafter was small comfort. His hair was mussed, his face pale, his eyes shadowed. When she asked for details of the accident, he just shook his head, then did it again when she asked how Jess was, and when she tried to verbalize what had been hovering in the back of her mind, haunting her, his bleak look cut her off before she said a word.

Had the remoteness of the scene affected the outcome? Would Roy be alive if help had arrived sooner? Would they ever know?

Thinking that the answer was no to all three, but that Brad was grappling with gruesome images and could probably use breakfast, she left him in the den to play with Tad, but within seconds of her leaving the room, the boy followed, and she didn't mind. His presence filled a void and kept her mind from dwelling on Roy. Brad might have been the one physically viewing the scene of the crash, but her imagination pinned her right there as well.

She returned to the den for pieces of the wooden train, then set it back up in the kitchen while Brad planted himself on a stool with his forearms on the granite and his eyes distant. When she rubbed his shoulder, he gave her a weak smile.

She could have used words of solace in return. But what did one say in a situation like this?

What one said, she discovered when, within the hour, the phone started to ring, was *Thank you, I appreciate your thoughts, Yes, we're shocked.* What one said, she realized when more calls came and the questions narrowed, was *I'm sorry, I don't know, Maybe, No plans yet.* And when the calls grew solicitous, she could only express gratitude. *I'll remember that, I haven't thought that far, Thank you for offering.*

The last had to do with watching Tad, even for the funeral, but she couldn't go there yet. She couldn't think beyond the next hour.

There was a certain cruelty to the sun shining after the havoc wreaked by the storm the night before, but Jamie needed to get out. Brad had barely eaten and remained in a visible pall. Was it easy for *her* to carry on? No, but someone had to do it for Tad. She told herself that the child was too young to grasp what had happened, but even apart from the occasional cry for his mother, if the way he was clinging to Jamie meant anything, he sensed something was up.

Before they could make it to the backyard, though, Maureen Olson arrived in a deluge of tears. Tests had shown an absence of activity in Jess's brain. The local team had even consulted with neurologists at two other hospitals, but "brain dead" stood. Machines were all that kept her alive.

Jamie was crushed. When her eyes filled with tears, it wasn't so much for Maureen as for Tad. He would never see his mother again. She would never be coming home. Jamie had always prayed that he wouldn't have to be a child of divorce, but this? Unimaginably worse.

Maureen spoke in a rush, explaining that she had begged the doctors to tell her there was even the smallest sign of life, had begged them to try something, *anything*, but they insisted that nothing would change what the tests showed . . . that she thought it better to let her daughter die with dignity . . . that she couldn't possibly take Tad back to Leominster with her, that her other children were grown, her husband couldn't take the noise, and she couldn't handle a toddler.

As if Jamie would have even considered letting him go?

Misinterpreting her horrified expression, Maureen blathered on about money, time, arthritis, even a planned cruise, until Jamie stopped it with a hand on her arm.

"Tad is mine," she said. Her heart beat wildly as the fact of that set in for the very first time. Needing an anchor, she looked back at Brad. "When he was first born, they named me his legal guardian, but I never,

ever thought . . ." With Brad looking as stunned as she felt, she faced Maureen again. "We'll bury Jess with Roy."

The woman simply nodded, gave Tad an awkward hug, and excused herself to return to the hospital.

Tad is mine Tad is mine Tad is mine. The words echoed along with the deeper meaning that they implied. With Brad remaining silent, Jamie shifted her frustration to Maureen, wondering how in the world the woman could so easily walk away from the only thing she had left of Jess.

Feeling rejected on Tad's behalf, she gathered him up and held his face to her shoulder. His warm little body settling into hers was an unexpected comfort. *He's all I have left of my father,* Jamie thought, but an even more terrifying thought came fast on that.

I'm all he has.

Without a word to Brad, she went out the back door.

ten

When Brad joined Jamie a short time later, Tad was gliding forward and back in his bucket swing. The movement was repetitive, predictable, mindless, all of which she needed. When the bucket came back at her, she gave it a push, then raised anguished eyes to Brad.

He looked drained. A living nightmare and zero sleep could do that to a person. But she was living the same nightmare, and she needed comfort. She needed reassurance that things would be okay, that they could handle this, that he would be a father to Tad.

Instead, he stood at her side without a word.

To get him talking, Jamie asked, "Will she have them turn off the machines?"

"I'd guess."

"I don't envy her that."

The swing returned. She sent it forward again. And again. And again. Brad remained silent.

Having been leaning over the front of the bucket, Tad straightened and looked back as the bucket approached her. *"Out, Mamie!"*

Catching the swing, she lowered it to a stop and lifted him, but the bucket twisted when his sneaker caught in the leg hole. "Brad . . ." She breathed a plea for help—he was standing right there—but by the time he figured out what to do, she had freed the sneaker herself.

The child took off for the sandbox, where he picked up a plastic rake and began combing the sand. Though Jamie's eyes were on him, her thoughts were on Jess. "I really liked Jess. She had a good heart."

"Not her mother."

"No. Jess became a third wheel the minute Maureen remarried. It got worse when the half sibs were born. I guess it's in character that she's washing her hands of Tad, but it still boggles my mind."

"She was being honest. She's not prepared to take in a child."

"Neither am I, but do I have a choice?"

Brad didn't reply.

"Neither do you," she said quietly. "This is my lot now."

"I didn't know you were his guardian."

"I never thought to tell you. I never thought it would happen."

"You're not set up for it."

"I can be."

"How will you work?"

"I haven't thought that far."

"You'll have to soon."

"Dad hasn't been dead a *day,*" she protested and might have said more if a sudden scream from Tad hadn't brought her head around. One look at him sprawled on his face, apparently having tripped climbing out of the sandbox, and she bolted forward in a fit of worry and guilt. Had she been standing right there, paying closer attention, she would have caught him before he fell.

By the time she reached him, he was on all fours and crying bitterly. Snatching him up, she saw dirt on his knees but no blood. Heart pounding, she clutched him to her. "It's okay, baby, shhhh, you're okay, I gotcha."

"I wan Mommy."

Jamie identified with that, oh boy, did she ever. There was something about letting it all go and sobbing for a mother to make everything better. She was bereft about Roy, distanced from Caroline, uneasy over

Brad, and Tad was crying his little heart out. She felt his pain, felt as lost and alone as he did.

Holding him back, she wiped big tears from his cheeks with her thumbs, kissed his forehead, and hugged him again. "You're such a good boy, Mamie's right here, I am not letting go."

And she didn't. Ignoring the phone, she held him while he ate a snack. When family friends arrived and began congregating in the kitchen and living room to murmur together in horror and shock, she escaped with Tad to the den, where she held him on her lap and read board book after board book. When he began to squirm, she took him outside again, this time to the toy-filled garage. The child wanted for nothing except a mother and father.

And how cruel is that? Jamie wondered in silent anguish.

Well-wishers joined them, speaking kind words that inevitably led to questions she couldn't answer. She did her best to be polite, but after a while, her mind clotted. Leaving them texting others in town, she pushed Tad down the sidewalk on his tricycle while he walked his feet along. She went farther than she should have and ended up walking back with him on her hip and the tricycle trailing off her hand. By the time she reached the house, Brad was gone, headed to Theo's to help make calls.

People left. More arrived. Some were personal friends of Roy and Jess, some friends of the business. They were devastated and didn't know how to help, but the best Jamie could do was promise to let them know when she figured it out herself.

By midday, the people who came carried food. Sandwiches and casseroles, cookies and cakes, a watermelon filled with cut fruit—all so generous, she knew. But the gift she appreciated most was the arrival of Desideria Carmel, who cleaned for Roy and Jess and was stricken. Desperate to help, she took over the kitchen.

When it came to helping with Tad, though, Jamie smiled a thanks-but-no-thanks. She needed to do this herself. Sifting through foil-covered dishes, she took bits of chicken and pasta and sat him on her lap. He didn't eat much. There were too many people around, too many voices droning on through the house. She had a little more luck with fruit, and total luck with a cookie, but even before the last of that was gone, he was rubbing his eyes with his fists.

He was exhausted. So was she. She carried him upstairs, changed him, and put him in his crib. He was asleep within minutes, and within minutes of that, slumped in a nearby rocker, so was she.

When the doorbell rang, she bolted awake. That brief sleep had been so deep that it was a minute before she got her bearings, at which point reality returned in a biting rush. Stomach knotting, she scrambled up to check Tad. Mercifully, he slept on. Likewise, mercifully, everything downstairs was under control. With more people than ever milling about, the dining room table was beautifully set and offered a spread of food and drinks. There were no paper goods here, but rather the fine china and crystal for which Jessica had registered before the wedding. The elegance of it all would have pleased Roy.

He would not have been pleased with Jamie's T-shirt and jeans—it seemed a lifetime ago that she had pulled them on—but there was nothing to be done. She refused to run home for nicer clothes lest Tad wake while she was gone, and a good decision that was. Nicer clothes wouldn't have worked. By the time he woke up, she had so OD'd on well-meaning friends that she knew if she didn't escape she would go mad.

The town playground was a five-minute drive from the house. Jamie had driven Jess's SUV often enough that the eeriness of doing it now wasn't so bad. But then, she had no alternative. Her convertible didn't have a backseat, and the playground was a must.

Always before, though, she had taken Tad here during the week. This being Sunday, the place was packed with families, so arriving alone with Tad was a stark reminder of their loss. She actually stood at the fence for a minute, wondering if she could bear it. If a break from people was what she needed, she could always drive around for an hour.

But Tad was standing between her legs, his little fingers clutching the links and impatiently rattling the gate. Telling herself that his needs came first, she lifted the latch. He ran off toward a broad climbing dome, and though she was quickly there, he knew this piece of equipment. Scrambling up, he sprawled from one foothold to another, reckless and unafraid.

Jamie was moving around the dome in anticipation of where he might fall off when she was spotted. Even wearing sunglasses, she was a familiar face, if not as a former classmate then as a MacAfee.

"Jamie! Oh my God! You poor thing," cried one parent. And another, "Jess was my playground buddy. We always sat here together." And a third, this a dad who sold flooring to MacAfee designers, "We heard the sirens, but had no idea it was Roy."

Nodding, Jamie continued to shadow Tad around the dome. When he slid off and raced to a nearby rope ladder, others migrated there as well. She kept her eye on Tad, saying only as much as was necessary to avoid rudeness, but all the while she was growing frantic, wondering how word had spread so fast and why these people couldn't see that she needed to pretend, for a few minutes at least, that this hadn't happened. She helped Tad climb to the top of the ladder, then lifted him off, knowing that he was going to have to learn how to climb down as well, but not today.

Today she needed a quiet corner. There was only one—the old sandbox, which was huge and contained many more pails and shovels than children. Only one little boy was there; she guessed him to be three or four. The man she assumed to be his father sat alone on a bench on the far side. He wore sunglasses and a ball cap and was reading a book.

Thinking that something about him was keeping the other parents away and that maybe, just maybe, the repellent would work for her, too, she sat down at the end of his bench. She had no idea if he saw her. He didn't say anything. Which was good.

Her eyes hung on Tad, who stood utterly still by the rim of the box as he watched the other child shovel sand into a pail, pack it down, and turn it over. The sand was damp; after last night's rain, it would be a while drying out. Climbing in, Tad went to within three feet of the child and continued to watch.

"Will you have custody of him?" came the low voice of a woman kneeling at Jamie's elbow.

Jamie hadn't seen her coming. She cleared her throat. "Uh, yes. I will."

A minute passed. Then the woman said, "Jessica adored Tad. She was good with other kids, too. She told me she wanted another one and that she was trying to get pregnant, but I guess it hadn't happened yet."

Jamie swallowed. She tried to let the words go over her head, but they only created another source of loss.

"If I can help, you know, maybe host a play date for Tad, will you let me know?" She rattled off her name; Jamie didn't catch it. She was thinking that she couldn't process play dates just yet when she saw Tad pick up a shovel and dig into the sand. Without a word to the woman, she left the bench and entered the sandbox. Pulling over a pail, she set to helping Tad fill it with sand. When it was full, she tipped it to make a mound beside the three that the other child now had. None was perfect. All were crumbling somewhere or other, but that didn't matter. Looking around, she spotted a plastic piece in a castle shape, but while the other child helped her fill it, Tad sat on his haunches and watched.

They worked in silence. Jamie thought about asking for the boy's name. Or his age. But doing something, anything, without having to think was a respite. So she let it go.

When she returned to the bench, the woman was gone. Jamie dug out her cell and called Caroline. She didn't care if her mother was busy. She needed to hear her voice.

"Mom," she breathed, bending over herself in dire relief. "Mom." Barely a sound.

"Oh, baby. You sound awful."

She took a steadying breath. "Is Jess gone?"

There was a pause, then a sad "Yes. Theo just got the call."

Jamie wrapped her free arm over her head. "Oh God," she whispered.

"I know," Caroline whispered. "The enormity . . ." Her voice trailed off, then, "I'm guessing the funeral will be Wednesday."

"Together?"

"Yes."

"How's Granddad?"

"Terrible. The house is swarming with people."

"Roy's, too. It's overwhelming."

"Here. Brad wants to talk."

"Wait—" Jamie wasn't ready to let her go, but Brad must have grabbed the phone.

"Hey."

"Hey."

"Can you meet us at the funeral home?"

"Right now? I, uh, no." She cleared her throat. "I'm with Tad." She peered around her arm. Tad was holding his own.

"Can't someone watch him? Someone at the house?"

"I can't leave him right now."

"What about the housekeeper?"

Yes, Desideria would watch Tad, but Jamie needed to be with him. "I'll have to let Mom and Theo handle it. Gotta run, Brad. Talk later."

Ending the call, she pocketed the phone and, hugging her stomach, huddled into herself. Tad continued to play, not so much with as alongside the other child. From time to time, he sat back on his heels, but even then, he wasn't looking for Jamie.

She half-wished he was. She half-wished she was so instrumental to his existence that he couldn't bear to have her out of his sight for more than a minute. That would justify her not going to the funeral home. But the truth? With Jess declared dead and Tad her own child forever more, she was having trouble breathing. Dealing with the reality of a funeral—burial clothes, hymns, obituaries—would have been way too much. She couldn't even think about picking out a dress to wear herself.

When her eyes filled with tears, she pressed a hand under her nose to squelch out-and-out crying.

"I'm sorry for your loss, Jamie," came a new female voice. "What a fluke accident. If only that tree had come down in the hurricane we had two years ago—" The voice suddenly stopped.

Startled by the abruptness, Jamie looked up, then followed the woman's gaze to the man at the other end of the bench. His hand was raised off his book just enough to say, *Enough. Leave her alone.*

Amazingly, the woman pressed her fingers to her mouth, nodded, and, seeming duly chastised, left.

The angst of the past few days notwithstanding, Caroline would have driven over to see Jamie if there hadn't been so much to do here. Each time she went looking for Theo to say she was leaving, the front door opened, and more people arrived. She knew them all, if not through work then through Williston, and if not through the town then through her marriage to Roy. With Theo looking as fragile as the antique French armchair on which he sat—"Patricia's favorite," he said each time she suggested he might be more comfortable elsewhere—she couldn't desert him. She guided friends his way. She reassured him that the picture of Roy in the newspaper obit would be a good one. At his urging, she dug through files in the library to read the write-up of Patricia's funeral and see which hymns were played.

She also brought him water and tried to get him to eat. "You need strength," she told him in a private moment, squatting beside his chair with her back to the room. "Roy would not want you to starve. Here's tuna salad. You like tuna." When he waved the plate away, she set it on the lamp table. "You're exhausted. Why not go up and rest for a few minutes? We'll all understand."

Seeming not to hear, he said in a rough murmur, "It wasn't supposed to happen this way. This wasn't in the plan. You think about the life you want, and you follow the rules and try to do the right things."

Caroline squeezed his hand. "You're a good person, Theo."

"And still he died." Sad eyes met hers. "Roy had his faults. But he was my son."

"He had many strengths. You raised a good man. He loved his family."

Indeed, she had never once doubted his love for Jamie. Wondering if Jamie knew that, she thought again about going to Roy's, but as she stood, Theo's eyes went to the door. "There's the president of the bank. Talk to him, Caroline. Answer his questions. I can't go through that again."

So Caroline talked with the president of the bank. When Brad showed up, she drew him in to take her place. This time, when she went to tell

Theo she was leaving, he came up with another person she needed to call, so she went into the library to use the phone.

While there, she left another message for Dean. It was the third one. He would want to know what had happened, and though she knew that cell reception was iffy on the river, she also knew that he would connect to a hot spot at least once a day for emergency's sake.

As the afternoon passed, exhaustion crept up, but her own strain was nothing compared to what she heard when Jamie finally called. Given that, she was annoyed when Brad suggested Jamie join them at the funeral home. She wasn't needed there. Nor was he, actually, and though he offered to drive, Theo insisted Caroline do it. He claimed she knew as much about Roy as anyone, and he was likely right. As distant as they had grown personally, she knew about the work that he did, could list projects that he had single-handedly made happen and charities that he championed.

Jessica was more of an enigma. Her mother had little to offer beyond basic biographical facts, given tearfully and tersely. Caroline texted Jamie a few questions, like whether Jessica was an avid athlete and what flowers she liked. The feminist part of Caroline regretted that Roy's life so overshadowed his wife's. But there was no help for it now.

As she talked about Roy at the funeral home, something else hit her. She had been so focused on everyone else's loss that she hadn't considered her own. Reminiscing with Theo and the funeral home director, she realized that a person who had been a part of her life for more than thirty years was suddenly gone. Love him or not, his death left a void.

She was feeling that emptiness when they returned to Theo's, which made Dean's call perfectly timed. They talked as she stood at the kitchen window, overlooking the lush beauty of Theo's backyard patio.

"Just like that, Dean. In a heartbeat, he's gone. I haven't loved him for years, but we shared a lot once. I've never lost a friend before. I've been lucky, I guess."

"You and me both," Dean remarked. He had asked question after question at the start of the call. Now he was subdued. "The guy was my age."

He fell silent. Still, Caroline took comfort from knowing that he was there. Finally, quietly, he said, "I'm just . . . stunned."

"Yeah." She sighed. "Me, too."

"How's Jamie?"

"Hanging on, I guess. She's young. She's busy. Theo's the shaky one. He has me driving him places. I'm not sure he'd get to where he's going alone."

"Is he confused?"

"Distracted."

"Well, you're doing a good thing, sweetheart. I'm coming back. I'll help."

"Oh no, Dean. Don't come back early. That's not why I called. I just felt you'd want to know." She had also needed to hear the voice of a friend.

"I should be there out of respect."

Well, there was that. But had Roy earned it? Dean didn't yet know about the *Gut It!* fiasco. When he learned about that, he would be livid.

So Caroline said, "There are too many people here already, Dean. Wait. Stay there. Stay fresh. That way you'll be even more of a help when you get back."

eleven

That night, once Brad had returned and she was sure Tad was asleep, Jamie clipped the baby monitor to Brad's belt and dashed back to her condo for toiletries and clothes. By the time she returned, guests were gone, food was stowed, and the monitor was on the kitchen counter.

Brad was slouched on a stool nearby. Wrapping her arms around his neck, she tried to focus on the familiarity of his warmth, but the old comfort wasn't there. Oh, the house was quiet and under control, but nothing else was. Not really. Death didn't stop at the end of the day; it was the one guest that refused to leave for the night.

Jamie's life had changed forever. She wasn't sure Brad was on board.

"Nightmare," she whispered and felt him nod against her cheek. "Want to stay?" Sex was the last thing she wanted, but maybe in bed she would feel his warmth? She kind of needed that. Yes, he was feeling the shock of sudden death and perhaps even instant parenthood, but it was *her* father who had died, *her* friend who had died, *her* half brother who was orphaned. Okay. Brad needed time to adjust. She didn't have that luxury, and if he didn't see that, if he couldn't rise to the occasion and be supportive, what hope did they have?

But he shook his head. "I need my own space for a few. I have to go the office early tomorrow, then to Theo's. Can you handle things here?"

Jamie thought she could. But Monday was a repeat of Sunday, the only difference being that she *started* it worn down by the house, the guests, the mood. When it became clear that even with the onset of the workweek, even with mourners at Theo's and at the funeral home, Roy's was still the go-to place, she knew she had to move. Tad was growing confused, his little brow increasingly furrowed, his baby voice crying for his mommy more often, his eyes filled with something just shy of fear. The constant flow of people in his home who weren't his parents had to be upsetting.

Or so Jamie guessed. She couldn't ask. How could a two-year-old understand the questions, much less articulate answers? She was on such shaky ground here. She needed a book on parenting. She needed *ten* books on parenting. Actually, she needed her mother, but Caroline was tethered to Theo.

The longer she stayed at Roy's, though, the more oppressive it grew. His assistant helped pick burial clothes and ran them to the funeral home, which was a huge help to Jamie but brought little lasting relief. As soon as the woman returned to help Desideria at the house, Jamie packed several duffels of clothing, baby supplies, and toys and took Tad to her place. Short-term, that was always a novelty for him, and at least it was quiet. They played on the patio, went to the market for milk, mac 'n' cheese, and mangos, and returned for lunch. This was familiar, she decided, thinking of other times she'd had him here, and refusing to think beyond.

Once he was down for a nap, though, she had no choice. She couldn't hide behind him forever. She was a MacAfee. Totally aside from the issue of responsibility, she wanted to see Theo, who was suffering. She also wanted to see Caroline, if only for a few minutes. They were at the funeral home, which was the last place she wanted to be. But Roy had attacked her during their last awful talk. *If you can't behave like a grown-up . . .*

She could. She *would*.

She had a sitter. The receptionist in her department, a longtime family loyalist, had a grandchild Tad's age and a sincere need to help Jamie. When she showed up at the condo with the makings for chocolate chip cookies, Jamie quickly showered, dressed, and left. She wished she had her convertible. It would have made her feel more herself. But how absurd a thought was that? Her convertible was at Roy's and not much good to her now, which raised a lifestyle issue she couldn't begin to deal with yet.

Heart heavy with dread, she approached the funeral home all too soon and parked the SUV beside Theo's Cadillac sedan. Once through the front door, she was surrounded by townsfolk, but her eye kept going to the pair of coffins at the end of the room. They were closed. The reason why was chilling. She went to the one with her father's picture on top, touched the polished wood with one hand and her mouth with the other, and began to cry.

Firm arms came around her shoulders, bringing a familiar scent that was so woodsy and light and perfectly Caroline that it brought more tears. Jamie had no idea how long she stood there sobbing quietly—two minutes, five, ten—only that there was nowhere else she could fall apart but in her mother's arms. When a tissue materialized, she pressed it to her nose, blotted her eyes, and released a shuddering sigh.

Turning Jamie's face up, Caroline kissed her forehead and gave her a sad smile. "Better?"

"Yes," Jamie whispered. "I'm not very good at this."

"Nor am I. Or Theo." Her gaze crossed the room and returned. "He's anxious to see you. Are you ready yet?"

Jamie took a breath and nodded, at which point Caroline guided her to her grandfather, who held out his arms. Jamie hugged him and clung. He was such a part of her heritage, and with an even bigger part of that now gone, she couldn't let go. His body wasn't as solid as Caroline's; she felt a tremor in the arms that held her. When she finally drew back and focused on his wrinkled face, those teary blue eyes were hollow, and Caroline was gone.

Though Jamie stayed for a time, Caroline always seemed to be engaged with others. *By choice?* Jamie wondered, and quickly dismissed that thought. Whatever problems they had with *Gut It!* paled in the face of untimely death. It was enough, Jamie told herself, that Caroline had held her for those few minutes. There was hope here, at least.

She returned to Roy's more for the sake of politeness than necessity. No one seemed to need her, and Brad was a far better host than she could be. He was content to stay until the last of the guests left Monday night, go home to his own apartment to sleep, and return Tuesday morning. Though appropriately subdued, he filled Roy's social shoes with ease.

Jamie was alternately pleased and annoyed. On one hand, in stepping up so comfortably, he made a statement about continuity at MacAfee Homes. On the other hand, his dismissal of Tad was increasingly disturbing. He didn't ask how the child was, didn't offer to help with him, didn't praise her, as so many others did when she said Tad was hers, other than to say that she had been wise to leave him at the condo before coming to the house.

The little voice in her head went to work.

Did he not understand that her father had specifically wanted her to raise the child in the event of something like this happening?

Did he not understand that there were priorities in life, and that, yes, she knew she would have to make changes?

Did he not understand that she *wanted* to do this?

No, no, and no—which meant, bottom line, a storm was brewing.

Tuesday morning found Caroline visiting a succession of major MacAfee construction sites. Given a choice, she'd have been in her own workshop. Her wrist was fine, with little more than a bandage covering the stitches, and she needed the therapy of drilling, shaping, and sanding, needed the smell of sawdust and her father's old tools. But having been with Theo every waking hour since Sunday morning, she welcomed a break—from Theo, from tragedy, from distress.

That said, when he asked her to site-hop, she couldn't say no. The gesture was a good one. Yes, every MacAfee higher-up had been personally called, and most had come to visit, but there were scores of hands-on workers who would be wondering what effect Roy's death would have on MacAfee Homes. Her personal appearance made a statement that the business would survive.

Unfortunately, delivering the message meant a juggling of sorrow and optimism on her part, and it was exhausting.

Emotionally drained, after talking with a group of carpenters who were doing finish work in an office, she walked out into the sun and saw a Harley parked by her truck.

Dean.

Her heart lifted.

She needed a friend, and Dean was that.

Smiling as much as several days of darkness allowed, she approached him and, shading her eyes with a hand, looked up. "I said you shouldn't come."

Sunglasses hid his eyes but not his smirk. "Since when do I listen to you?"

Never. But she was too pleased to see him to fight. Wearing a black shirt and midnight jeans, he was certainly dressed right. "Well, thank you for coming," she said, exhaling tension. "It's been wild here."

"Wild?"

"Tearful. Tragic. *Bleak*." And here was Dean, the antithesis of these things. His nose and cheeks were sunburned, which was saying something about skin that had started with a good base tan. "Looks like you did get some fishing in. I'm sorry it was only two days."

"Not your fault. You didn't make that tree fall on Roy's car."

"At least if I had, I could say that what I'm doing now is penance." That sounded bitchy, she realized, and explained, "Don't get me wrong. I choose to help Theo. He's like a father to me, and the poor guy is beside himself. No one ever thinks his child will go before he does. But it's awkward. Roy was my ex twice removed, and Jess was more Jamie's contemporary than mine."

"How's Jamie doing with all this?"

Caroline felt Jamie's agony acutely. "She's struggling. She has custody of Tad."

Dean gave a little start. "Seriously? Did she know she would beforehand?"

"Yes."

"Can she handle it?"

"She'll have to."

He considered that. "Talk about life turning on a dime."

"Mmm. Lots of complications hitting at once." Not the least being the *Gut It!* change, which would be an even greater challenge for Jamie if she was dealing with new motherhood at the same time. But of course, Dean didn't know about the show. She wasn't quite sure how to broach it.

"Keep frowning like that," he remarked, "and you'll need Botox."

She tried to think up a smart reply, only her mind went off in a different direction. Botox meant wrinkles, wrinkles meant old, old meant death, and death was as final as those closed coffins at the funeral home, an image that did nothing good for her frame of mind. She had been feeling shaky since Jamie had shown up at her door Sunday morning—had actually been feeling shaky since Claire had shown up Friday—and while's Dean's comment was just Dean being clever, something about his presence snapped whatever element had been holding her together. To her horror, her eyes filled with tears.

He jerked back. "What's this?"

It would have been so easy to swipe at her eyes with the heel of her hand and blame the past few days for emotions too close to the surface, but the words wouldn't come for that either.

"Hey," he said more gently, then, "I need lunch. Want some?"

She nodded.

"Follow me."

Fiona's was back in Williston, and Caroline wouldn't have wanted to go there anyway. Seeming to know that she needed anonymity even before she pushed huge sunglasses onto the bridge of her nose, Dean led her to a sandwich place not far from the site. He waited until they were seated, with the wood wings of the booth back shielding them from other diners. Then he waited again, until after they ordered, before he said, "I was kidding about the Botox."

"I know." They might bicker, but he wasn't malicious. "It just touched a raw nerve." Sitting back in the booth with her head against the wood, she considered his mottled green eyes, dark hair, and burnished skin. He was the image of honed energy and health. By comparison, she felt positively ancient. "It's like you've been gone a year."

Those eyes grew puzzled. "Why am I sensing something else going on?"

Perhaps because he knew her better than most and could read her too well, she realized, and gave a self-deprecating shrug. "It doesn't matter. It's silly to even be talking about in the same breath as two deaths."

"Spill it, Caro. Nothing you care about is silly to me."

"You're sweet."

"I'm serious."

Knowing that he was, she nearly teared up again. Before that could happen, she said, "As of fall, I'm out as the host of *Gut It!* Jamie's the new host." He flinched, but didn't speak. Clinging to the steadiness of his gaze, she told him about her meeting with Claire. She was still watching him closely when she finished. "You don't seem surprised."

"That they want younger?" A sound of disgust came from the back of his throat. "I read, I see, I hear. It's happening everywhere. I'm not happy that it happened here. To you." His eyes rose to the server who brought their sandwiches, roast beef for him, shrimp salad for her. Once they were alone again, he picked up half of his sandwich and considered it, then considered her in the same puzzled way. "Are you sure Jamie was involved in the decision?"

"No. All I know is that she knew before I did and had ample opportunity to tell me but did not, and that makes me uncomfortable."

"Uncomfortable?"

"Like she was hiding it because she agrees with the decision but knew that I would not." Having removed the bread from her sandwich, she waved a fork. "Roy's death has kind of taken over right now. Jamie's going through so much. I know she needs me, but at odd times, I feel a twisting inside." She mimed the motion with her fork.

"Anger?"

"Hurt."

"You need to talk with her." He opened the bag of chips on his plate and crunched one. When it was gone, he said, "You used to tell me to do that with my ex."

"And you used to say it wasn't easy." Caroline sighed. "You were right." She had always heard him out, then rebutted his arguments with a certain insistence. Now that the tables were turned, it struck her that she hadn't fully grasped the emotions involved. "I'm doing what I can to help her. My heart wants to do more, but my mind fights it."

"Your mind is going through a lot."

Where to begin on that? She felt betrayed, sad, and worried, and those emotions had to do solely with Jamie. Add the age issue, which had dredged up feelings she thought were long buried, and Roy's death and Theo's fragility, and she was hopelessly mired.

They ate in silence until Dean ran a napkin over his mouth. "Will she opt out of hosting the show because of Tad?"

"Maybe. I don't know. This is new ground for Jamie."

"What about Brad?"

"New ground for him, too. He wants her to do the show. She says she won't because of me, but if she says no and they threaten to cancel—"

"You could sue."

"How can I do that? It would only hurt Jamie." She set down her fork, studied her lunch and then Dean. "I love my job, but I love my daughter, too." Retrieving the fork, she ate another piece of shrimp.

"What's wrong with your bread?" he asked.

"Nothing. I just don't need two pieces."

"Since when?"

"Since I'm sitting around like a sack of potatoes that hasn't worked in almost a week."

"Like you're getting fat? You've lost weight, Caroline. How's the hand?"

Lost weight meant looking haggard, a dismaying thought there. "Fine," she snapped.

"Spare me the fight, and save it for Claire. You must be furious at her."

"Absolutely. And at Roy, like that'll get me far." She scooped a forkful of shrimp salad off the plate and in her mouth. Talking around the food, as if that would gentle the words, she said, "And then I come back to Jamie again. She may not have known what Claire was up to, but there's been a whole lot of girlfriend time between the two of them. Shouldn't she have seen where Claire was headed?"

"Not if she didn't want to see. Is the decision irrevocable? No changing their minds?"

"Claire said not, but that was before Roy died." She had probably said the words "Roy died" dozens of times in the last two days, and still they shocked her. It wasn't that she loved Roy. There were times she wondered if she ever had. But he was still the father of her daughter, and his death was out of the blue. It was going to take some getting used to. "The problem is that they need to know soon. We can put them off out of respect for Roy, but they won't wait forever."

Nor could Caroline. There was a slew of prep that she always did in the months leading up to taping, and promo for the station was the least of it. She had to get to know the homeowners, so that they were comfortable with each other. She had to get to know abutting neighbors, who would be physically close to the work. She had to get to know the town well enough to give viewers a feel for the location, and had to work through house plans with Dean and the other specialists.

If she wasn't hosting the show, these things wouldn't be her responsibility. They would be Jamie's. Like Jamie had time for all that?

"Aren't you eating those chips?" Dean asked, but when she pushed the bag across, he didn't rush to open it. "You like chips."

She shrugged. "I'm not real hungry."

"Well, *there's* a convenient excuse for every anorexic woman. Not real hungry."

"I have never been anorexic."

"Not yet, but I know what you're doing. Roy did a job on you about the age thing. So now Claire Howe is saying the TV show needs younger, and you're thinking you're too old, too wrinkled, too fat—"

"*Please,*" Caroline cut in, "this isn't the time."

He settled back and finished eating.

She might have done the same, if *too old, too wrinkled, too fat* hadn't continued to echo. "But I'm right to feel some of that," she insisted. "You can joke as much as you want, but I do have more wrinkles than I did ten years ago. I may not be heavier, but my shape has changed, and my voice isn't as rich. I know these things." Every woman of an age did. Changes like these came with menopause, which she had gone through several years before, though she wasn't saying that to Dean. In her few instances of big-time public sweat, she had been able to blame hot weather. Fortunately, her hot flashes had eased up. "But I didn't expect I'd be axed because of them. I thought it was my personality that viewers liked."

"They like all of it."

"Apparently not."

"Claire's full of shit."

"Maybe, but she and Brian get to decide, and their decision is to go with Jamie. So where does that leave me? I like hosting the show. I feel so . . ." She searched for the word. "So *whole* when I'm there." Once started, the thoughts spilled. "I didn't plan it, didn't even realize it was happening, but suddenly when someone tells me I'm off the job, I realize how much store I put in it. It's become my identity. If that's gone, where am I?" She closed her eyes and pressed her fingertips to the tight spot between them. "I'm sorry. I shouldn't be carrying on. Roy and Jessica are dead, which makes my problems petty, y'know?"

"Don't apologize," he grumbled. "What, are you supposed to be a robot and not feel things? You didn't ask for this." Grabbing the check, he dug his wallet from his jeans. "Let's get outta here."

Leaving him at the cash register, Caroline went outside. When he joined her, she said, "Don't be angry at me."

"I'm not. I'm angry at them." He put his hands on his hips and glared at the street. "This is a stupid decision. The only thing it has to do with is sex."

"What does sex have to do with the show?"

"Sex has to do with everything. It's right fucking there all the time."

Caroline was appalled. "Well, isn't *that* a macho remark. Women don't think that way." Shoving her sunglasses on, she set off past sidewalk tables that held the overflow of lunch.

"Not Claire?" Dean goaded, keeping pace.

"No. She just resents my place on the set. She hates it that the crew looks to me before they listen to her. If sex appeal is the bottom line here, it's coming either from advertisers or the media. They're the ones who stoke this." When they passed a table where a woman was reading, she muttered out of the corner of her mouth, "And there you go, a perfect example of the ultimate hype. Can you imagine picking up something with the title *Legs*? If I see one more person reading that book, I'll scream. Since when is eroticism considered literature?" she asked and answered, "Since the media latched on to those books. I mean, talk about a whole load of hot air." Tossing Dean a quelling look, she huffed, "Sex is *so* overrated."

He eyed her strangely. Then, turning on his heel, he headed back to the table where the woman was reading and ducked his head to see the cover of her book.

Caroline could not believe him. Mortified, she cut diagonally across the sidewalk to her truck and was grabbing the door handle when he joined her. She fully expected another macho remark. When it didn't come, she homed in on his face. He wasn't exactly amused, wasn't exactly startled, though there were elements of each. In the aftermath, his eyes held a dare.

"What?" she asked, impatient.

"I could prove you wrong. About sex."

She pulled the door open and drawled, "Sure you could."

"I could."

With a foot on the running board, she looked back. "How?" It wasn't a question so much as a drawled *yeah, right,* but he held her gaze and slowly lowered his eyes to her mouth.

Not what she'd expected.

Head jerking back in alarm, she pointed a finger at herself. He nodded.

"Oh no." She waved a hand and backed away. "No no no. I did not see that nod." Angry that he would think to raise something so wrong at such a wrong time, she climbed into the truck and tugged at the door.

He stood in the way. "You asked."

"Not. Appropriate. We're planning a funeral here, Dean."

"I'm not saying it has to be now. It's just part of the other discussion."

"How can you even *raise* it now?"

"Maybe because I'm a man. And because I'd rather think about life than death. And because I do think you're sexy."

"We work together. We're friends, not lovers." She tugged at the door. "Move, Dean." When he didn't budge, she gave him a testy look. "Don't you think that if there was an attraction between us we'd have felt it long ago?" Lord knew, they had spent enough time together, and not only for work. There had been hours at dinners, on front steps, or in pickups talking about Dean's failing marriage, his fear for his son, Caroline's concerns about Jamie, her frustration with Roy. Dean had walked her through her parents' death. But this?

He looked hurt. "You don't find me attractive?"

"You're *very* attractive, but that doesn't mean we should sleep together—and anyway, this is *so* not the time to talk about sex. Roy is dead, Jamie's distraught, and Theo's as needy as I've ever seen him, meaning I have one hour before I have to be back there, and since the funeral is tomorrow and I don't own anything black, I need to shop."

What Caroline bought that afternoon and wore to the funeral Wednesday was a black flared skirt and peplum jacket with an ivory tank. She couldn't recall the last time she had worn a skirt, and since this one barely hit her knees, she wore sheer black stockings with pumps. The heels weren't terribly high. Still, she thought the outfit was stylish and young, which hadn't been the point at all, but the alternatives? Matronly, every one.

"You look amazing," Dean whispered as soon as they were seated at the church. Theo, Jamie and Brad, and others of the immediate families were in front of them, and the pews behind were filling quickly.

Keeping her eyes on Jamie's tense shoulders, she whispered, "I suppose amazing is better than sexy."

"If I'd said that, what would you have done?"

"Moved to a different pew."

"Right." He waited a few seconds before murmuring under his breath. "Trust me, though. That outfit's a slam dunk. It's good for Brian and Claire to see."

Caroline felt a twinge of unease. "Are they both here?" She had figured Brian might be, since he was the one who had worked closely with Roy, but she wasn't in any frame of mind to see Claire.

Dean nodded.

She let out a long, low breath, but it barely reached her anxiety. Leaning forward, she gave Jamie's shoulder a soft little rub. Large eyes in an unnaturally pale face looked back, which only unsettled her more. "Are you okay?"

The girl shook her head, but the minister rose then, the crowd hushed, and Jamie faced forward before Caroline could say more. Not that there was much to say. Her heart ached for her daughter—and not just because Jamie had to deliver a eulogy or even because she had lost her father. Caroline knew what Jamie faced long-term perhaps more than Jamie did herself, and that knowledge tore at her.

Motherhood was a lifetime commitment. It didn't end with a church service or ease up after a month or a year. Tad might be with Jamie's receptionist again today, but the woman would be back at work tomorrow, along with so many others who had offered to help but would now be resuming their lives. Jamie would be on her own.

Then again, maybe not. Caroline was likely jaded on this score. Roy had been there for the good times, but show him a dirty diaper, a sneaker reeking of dog poop, or vomit, and he was gone. Jamie had Brad, who would hopefully be a more hands-on father. He was definitely kinder than Roy, more devoted to Jamie than Roy had ever been to Caroline, certainly less ego driven. But good with change? Unfortunately, change was the name of the game right now when it came to Jamie's life.

The funeral began. Hymns, readings, even the minister's words were as uplifting as they could be; still, the weight of tragedy was oppressive, all the more so when Jamie rose to speak. At no point did she blow Roy up into something he had not been, but there was good to be acknowledged—Caroline could admit that—and Jamie spoke from the heart. From time to time, her eyes touched Caroline's for reassurance, but the reassurance was as much Caroline's. Being Jamie's mainstay had been far more a part of her identity than hosting a TV show, which was precisely why she was so bothered by the rift between them.

She was losing Jamie—and not only to Brad, though his arm was the one that circled her when she returned to her seat, while Caroline's fingers remained locked in her lap.

A large hand suddenly covered them, gave a gentle squeeze, and was gone.

Caroline didn't react. To look at Dean would have been to give the gesture undue meaning. He had sensed her loss and was trying to help, as simple as that. And he did make her feel less alone. With the warmth of his touch fading, though, it struck her that she hadn't been actually physically held by a man in anything but a perfunctory way in a long, long time. She shared hugs and linked arms often with Jamie and female friends. But with men? No. With men it was all about being professional. For Caroline, who had to work with them daily, it was about being asexual.

She might have dwelt on the necessity of that if the church service hadn't drawn to a close and the trip to the cemetery begun. She drove alone and, dreading what was to come, climbed the knoll to the graveside. This was the part that always bothered her most, the finality of lowering a body into the ground and then leaving it to the cold and dark, and turning away. And what had the minister said, that the focus of death had to be on living? Caroline wasn't able to do that as she stood in the crowd with Annie Ahl and her husband. She didn't see Dean again until she started down the hill, at which point she was too disheartened to do more than glance his way. She had to do more, though, when she reached the road and Brian and Claire approached.

There were the obligatory cheek brushes and words of sympathy. Then Brian said, "Caroline, about what Claire told you . . ." He paused.

Not the best time to discuss this, Caroline wanted to say. But she needed to hear what he had to say. "Go on."

"I don't want hard feelings."

She considered that . . . considered everything she wanted to say in response . . . considered the time and place . . . and held her tongue.

Not so Dean. She hadn't seen him approach, but there he was, a solid presence by her shoulder. "You could rescind the change."

Brian spared him a glance. "It wasn't a random decision. The reasons behind it are very real. We've already started spreading the word."

"You could say you changed your mind. This is a dumb move, Brian. Caroline is the show."

"Are you saying Jamie can't do the job?" Claire asked, putting him on the spot with Caroline right there.

He smiled. "Nope. Not saying that at all. She can easily do the job. What I'm saying is that viewers will be expecting Caroline. When they don't get her, they may be upset."

"We'll ease Jamie in gradually. Caroline will still be there."

"What if I'm not?" Caroline asked. She hadn't planned to, but with Dean's warmth at her shoulder and his antagonism toward Claire on display, she felt bold.

"Are you saying that if you're not the host, you're gone?"

"I don't know."

"We could always cancel the show."

"Do that," Dean warned, "and we'll take it to another station. We're the show, Claire. The players are all MacAfee people. If we leave, they do."

"Well, aren't you full of yourself," she remarked.

Caroline was thinking that he had a right, that he looked authoritative as hell with his dark blazer and tie, shadowed jaw, and combed-back hair, when Brian said nervously, "This is not productive." He addressed

Caroline. "Feelings are raw right now. Once you get past Roy's death, we'll meet and hash this out. Agreed?"

"Absolutely," Caroline affirmed, but she wasn't thinking of any meeting when Dean walked her to her truck a short time later. She was thinking of Dean's hand at her back, guiding her with just the lightest touch. She was thinking that he hadn't ever done that before, that she should speed up her pace to shrug off his hand, that it didn't mean anything.

But it had been really nice to have him on her side against Brian and Claire.

Not that that meant anything either. These were extenuating circumstances.

Still. Given the hollowness she felt about so much of her life, a little protectiveness was nice.

twelve

The funeral should have been the end of it, but Jamie's phone didn't stop ringing with Willistonians wanting to remember Roy. She couldn't cut them off; she wanted to remember him, too. But between talking with them, keeping Tad clean, fed, and busy, and trying to squeeze in little bits of work, she was exhausted—which was likely why she didn't see the potential for trouble before it hit Friday morning. She was making breakfast at the kitchen island, alternately dicing pears, stirring oatmeal, and watching Tad play. He was on the floor with Legos, and while the blocks were large enough for him to be able to snap together, his great joy just then—hands clapping, squeals of "Look, Mamie, Taddy do it"—was loading them in a box and dumping them out, again and again. After a particularly enthusiastic dumping, several blocks tumbled behind the sofa. She saw him run there and felt a silent alarm even before her beautiful tulip floor lamp began to totter. Dropping the paring knife, she whipped around the island and lunged to catch it, but it crashed to the wood floor, missing the area rug that might have protected it and shattering all four glass shades.

Tad's eyes shot to hers. They were huge. She was feeling a stab of desperation thinking of her lamp, her home, her neat life that was wrecked, when the little boy's eyes filled with tears.

"Don't move," she warned him and, advancing only enough to grab him, stepped gingerly away from the shards. She didn't breathe until he was safely on a stool at the island, but his eyes remained large enough to destroy her. Roy would have yelled at him; he had certainly yelled enough at her when she'd been a child. Roy didn't like accidents.

How ironic was it that his life had ended in one?

But thanks to that Tad was hers now, and Roy had challenged her to be *the most responsible person* in his life. She had to deal.

Framing the child's warm little head with her hands, she lowered her face to his. "It's okay, monkey. It's only a thing." So Caroline had always said. She hugged him close, humming to Pandora's rendition of "Old MacDonald" streaming from her iPad.

"I want Mommy," he whimpered against her middle. He was saying it more and more, clearly not satisfied with the nonanswers she gave. She would have to offer more one day, but what to say?

She was spared it now when he asked for the moose. Retrieving it from the sofa, she included it in a group hug.

Most. Responsible. Person.

With a steadying breath, she ignored the fact that her pristine white condo was in shambles and said, "Accidents happen, Taddy. You didn't mean to do it. But those little pieces of glass need to be picked up or these bare little feet"—she squeezed one—"will be cut." She was looking around, wondering where to start, when Brad came in from the garage.

"Oh look, sweetie. Here's Brad," to whom she called, "Careful," though unnecessarily. The dismay on his face said he had seen the damage.

"You loved that lamp," he said.

She didn't need the reminder. The lamp sprouted from a wrought-iron base into four stems of different heights, each topped with a tulip-shaped globe. For all the small items she had put away in the name of childproofing, she hadn't thought to remove this—likely because, yes, she had loved it.

It's only a thing. Same with her favorite glass vase, broken yesterday.

It wasn't that Tad was destructive. He was two years old, active and curious, both good in the overall scheme—but that thought raised others. Was he developing normally? Was there a line between active and ADHD? Did he have learning disabilities or food allergies? How would he be socialized?

As an aunt, she hadn't had to worry about these things. As a parent, she did. Today was her sixth day in that role. Having no experience with other two-year-olds, she knew nothing. She had ordered a slew of books and had read site after site about what two-year-olds typically did, but no two articles were exactly the same, and none were as good as getting advice from her mother. But Caroline was busy with Theo and MacAfee Homes. And they hadn't resolved the host change, which hung like a sword over her head.

So she went with her new favorite mantra. "It can be replaced." Then, "Give me a hand here, Brad. Broom and dust pan first?" Holding Tad on her hip, she took the oatmeal off the stove and put the knife out of reach before setting him up at the lacquered dining table with a coloring book and crayons. His strokes were wild, and he held the crayon wrong, but she wasn't about to correct him. Instinct said that his self-esteem was more important than perfect form.

Or was this the kind of thing she had to correct before his muscles formed memory? She didn't know the answer to that either. Caroline would. She would ask.

Worried about when they would talk and whether, totally aside from their current rift, she could seriously ask Caroline's advice on caring for Roy MacAfee's child, she busied herself vacuuming while Brad swept. The exertion was good, though when she knelt to run her hand over the floor and peer at it from a different angle to make sure every last shard was gone, she found a tiny piece of that earlier vase. *Not* good. She was a novice at parenthood to begin with, and mistakes didn't make her more confident. Always before, when she set out to do something big, she had a game plan. She had lessons, courses, mentors, coaches, and practiced until she got it right. This, here, now, was walking a high wire without a net.

She *desperately* needed Caroline.

"You look frazzled," Brad said.

She closed her eyes and massaged tension from her forehead, but, hell, she *felt* frazzled. It didn't help that Brad was rested, freshly showered, and neatly dressed for work while she wore yesterday's tee and shorts, a slapdash ponytail, zero makeup, and an expression that had to be strained. Beside him, she must look like something the cat had dragged in.

"I'm not sleeping well," she told Brad, which, of course, he couldn't know, since he hadn't slept over since the accident.

"I thought Tad slept through the night."

"He does. The problem is me. I wake up stressing and can't fall back to sleep."

"Maybe you need to be at Roy's house."

The suggestion alone made her stomach clench. "What difference would that make?"

"There's more room. You could spread out."

Half a dozen family friends had said similar things at Roy's after the funeral. *This house is gorgeous . . . You're lucky to have it . . . Easy enough to sell the condo . . . The yard here is perfect for Tad.* But totally aside from her own distaste for Roy's, being there meant that Tad would be waiting for his parents to come home. He would be expecting things to return to normal, without understanding that normal had changed. Her gut told her he was better off at her condo for now, and as for the tightness of the layout here, she didn't want to be more than a single wall away from him at night.

She doubted Brad would understand. He was clearly disheartened as he looked beyond the broken lamp, and oh yes, she knew what he saw. All sense of urban chic was gone, replaced by scattered toys, one empty sippy cup, clean diapers and wipes, one *half-filled* sippy cup, a mound of clothes newly removed from the dryer, and, on the floor, the pajamas she had just taken off Tad—all now with Raffi singing "Baby Beluga" in the background.

Her sanctuary was decimated. There were times when she looked around and couldn't breathe, other times when she couldn't see through panicky tears. It wasn't like she didn't clean and neaten, but as soon as she did, there was another stained shirt, another dirty sippy cup, another disgusting diaper. And toys? She was *constantly* picking up toys. But here they were again, so why bother?

"Are you sure you want to do this?" Brad asked very, very quietly.

Her eyes flew to his. "What do you mean?" But she knew, oh yeah, she knew, and was shaking her head before he could utter the name *Maureen*. "No. Absolutely not."

"She's his grandmother," he said in the same low voice. "She's an experienced mother—"

"—whose kids are grown and whose husband doesn't want Tad and who didn't even have a good relationship with Jessica. She can't take him, Brad. I wouldn't let her. She doesn't love Tad like I do," Jamie whispered with force, horrified as much by Brad's insensitivity as by the idea of giving up her half brother.

But Brad wasn't done. He didn't raise his voice, never raised his voice. She almost wished he would, if only so that she could yell back. The need was building in her.

"You don't owe this to your father," he said.

"Excuse me? I absolutely do! I owe it to him, and to Tad, and to *me*. I *want* him, Brad." Staring at him in fury, she tugged the elastic off her hair and finger-combed the long strands into a fresh ponytail. "And anyway," she said, still glaring, "Desideria's coming Monday to clean."

Looking unsettled—she had never before spoken this harshly, but was tired of coddling him—he pushed up his glasses. "Okay." He was buying time. She could see him trying to think. And he had two choices, he realized. He could be positive, as in *We'll make this work. What do I need to do to help?* Or he could be negative.

Her heart fell with his opening *"but."*

"But it's only a stopgap, Jamie. You can't stay here long-run. It's way too small, and you can't do with only Desideria. You need a nanny. It helps that MacAfee is closed this week, so you haven't had to work—"

"Oh, I've worked," she cut in, annoyed that he would suggest she was slipping. "Our clients need jobs done. That's what I do when I wake up in the middle of the night."

"Where?" he asked—a valid question, since her office was now Tad's bedroom.

She eye-pointed to the table where Tad was happily coloring—and gasped. "Oh *no.*" She rushed over. "No, no, monkey, keep it on the paper." She showed him how, then scrubbed at one of several crayon marks that marred the white lacquer, but a bare fingertip wasn't much of an eraser. A cleaning spray would work—or hurt?

Taylor. Taylor had chosen the table. Taylor would know.

Brad stood nearby with his hands in his pockets, shoulders slumped. "You need a dedicated office, especially if you'll be working more at home. You can have that at Roy's."

"Not happening," Jamie insisted.

"Why not?"

"(A) That house is too big, (B) it gives me a headache, and (C) it's my father, not me."

"Redecorate, and make it you."

"Why spend the money? We're planning to build our own house anyway. I'll sell Roy's house, and we'll build something that's plenty big enough for us and kids." Not that she had drawn up any plans. She had kicked ideas around, both in her head and with Brad, but time hadn't allowed for more. And that was before Roy's death.

Brad looked troubled. He might want a house, but he didn't want Tad. He was so not ready for this. She was about to scream that he needed to be a *responsible person*, too, when the phone rang. She was upset enough to answer without checking the screen first.

"Jamie, it's Claire."

She grimaced. Claire had been calling daily, and though the messages she left never asked for callbacks, their regularity pointed to a motive beyond saying hello.

"Hey, Claire."

"How *are* you?"

Jamie looked around the wreck of her condo and said, "Hanging in there." She watched Brad lean over Tad and point at the lines of a clown's hat to show the child where to color. "Things are a little weird, if you know what I mean."

Fisting a green crayon, Tad scribbled over the clown's feet.

"I do. I wouldn't be bothering you if I wasn't getting pressure on my end. We need a final decision here. Publicity wants to put together preliminary pieces before the Fourth. Are you ready to commit?"

"Oh, wow. I'm sorry, Claire. I haven't been able to really think about it," which was a bald-faced lie. Jamie had thought about it for *hours*. She knew that if Claire could get a commitment from her, Caroline would back down—and Jamie's relationship with her mother would be permanently screwed.

Claire was using her again.

She might have said something to that effect if Brad hadn't been trying to reposition the crayon in Tad's hand. She was rounding the island when Claire said, "It's been a hard week for you. When you're ready to talk, will you give me a call?"

Jamie was about to remove Brad's arm when Brad did it himself in response to a cool stare from Tad. "Sure," she told Claire. "Thanks for understanding." She ended the call.

"I don't think he likes me," Brad murmured.

Well, duh, said the little voice in her head. *You don't like him. He feels that.*

With a defeated breath, she slipped an arm through his. "He doesn't know you. You have to play with him." Brightening on an idea, she said, "Stay home with us today, Brad? A few hours, and Tad will *love* you. You said it yourself. The office is officially closed."

His gray eyes ruled it out even before she finished. "There's still a skeleton crew, and a family member should be there. But I miss you. We haven't been alone together at all. How about dinner out tonight, just us two? Can you get a sitter?"

Trying to weigh his needs against Tad's, she said a sad "How can I? Right now, he needs me with him. It hasn't even been a week."

Sweet children's voices sang, *If you're happy and you know it wear a smile . . .*

She pegged a stare at the iPad. *Seriously?*

Brad shared her dismay, likely for a different reason. "What station is that?"

"Toddler Pandora."

. . . tee hee . . .

He wasn't amused. She saw disappointment, concern, maybe even annoyance—and she tried to understand. He didn't know where he stood now that she had Tad. He was feeling left out, feeling *unloved*. He needed reassurance.

But so do I!

Which basically put her between a rock and a hard place.

"Okay," she said as much to herself as to him, "maybe this weekend? If a sitter comes after he's asleep, he won't know I'm gone."

"What happens with work next week?" Brad asked.

She hadn't thought that far—actually, she had and had pushed the thought aside. That probably wasn't the smartest thing. Once the weekend was done, she would be down to the wire. "How do I find a nanny? How do I know who's good?"

Brad shot her a bewildered look. Then he glanced at his watch. "I have to run."

She might have begged him to stay if she felt it would help. But really? His being there was only one more messy thing.

"Say good-bye," she mouthed, hitching a glance toward Tad.

Brad ruffled the boy's hair. "Have a good day, sport."

Jamie walked him to the door, where he gave her a kiss that was sweet, gentle, and totally devoid of passion. For the first time, that bothered her—angered her, even. She needed something stronger, something that said he was on board with this change to her life, something with *promise*.

"About what you told Brian and Claire at the funeral," Caroline began, leaning forward to see past Champ, who rose from the backseat like a sentinel. They were in Dean's truck on the way to a new project for which he wanted her to build custom cabinetry. She had plenty of work of her own, but it was a small house—and the truth was, a new project was always a distraction, and she needed one of those. She ached when she thought of Jamie, ached when she thought of *Gut It!* She also ached when she thought of Theo, who seemed to be aging by the day, which she would do one day, too, and then what?

Dean seemed to know her frame of mind. Since the funeral, he had rarely let a few hours pass without checking on her. He hadn't said anything about sex. She wondered if he regretted mentioning it in the first place. That would probably be best, she told herself, though the part of her that was feeling old and unwanted was sorry. Whether she wanted sex or not, being pursued was a good thing.

"The possibility of taking *Gut It!* to another station?" she reminded him. "I've been thinking about it. It's not a bad idea."

"I've been thinking about it, too," he said in a voice that rumbled over a cracked road. Nudging Champ back, he shot her a look. "It sucks." No rumble there, just a deep voice disagreeing in a familiar way.

"Why?"

"Because the risk is too great. We're already with the strongest local station. No other one will do the show as well or be able to match the syndication schedule. Switching stations would have been easier if Roy was here to work a deal—"

"We don't need Roy."

"I can understand your being angry at Claire—"

"Anger doesn't begin to describe it, and I'm angry at Brian, too. It's fine to say Claire is into the power of it, but Brian is old enough to know better."

"He's listening to market research. He's answerable to moneymen up above."

"How can you defend him?" Caroline asked as he pulled up in front of a barely framed house.

After shoving the stick into park, he reached for her hand. It was a surprisingly gentle gesture, matched by his eyes and his tone. "I'm not defending him. I'm trying to understand. But there's another reason why we need to back off. If you start shopping around, Jamie will take it personally. You haven't talked with her about this. I keep telling you to."

"I can't."

"So you're suffering." He gave her hand a jiggle. "I'll bet she is, too. There are so many crossed signals here that every day makes it worse.

You need to talk with her, sweetheart. And you need to see the boy. They're a team now, those two."

Caroline wanted to argue. Only, he was right. Without Jamie, she was missing a limb. And his calling her sweetheart? He had done that in the past, but it sounded different to her now. Given the upheaval in her life, she needed the endearment, *and* the hand-holding. He seemed to know that, too. Even if he had changed his mind about the sex. Which was probably for the best, since they did have to work together. Which brought her back to *Gut It!*

"What if I talk with Jamie and she agrees?" Caroline suggested, mellow as she linked her fingers with his. "We need a bargaining chip. She knows how that works."

"Assuming she doesn't want to host."

It was a big assumption. Caroline wanted to believe Jamie, *desperately* wanted to believe her. Being the star of the show, though, was a huge lure, and Jamie had said that, yes, she wanted it, but only some day. So there was room for compromise here. Caroline could more easily accept a gradual transition than the abrupt change the station wanted. Every bit of common sense in her—every bit of maternal instinct—told her Jamie would agree.

Unless she didn't know Jamie at all. Which had occurred to her more than once lately.

Seeming to sense Caroline's fear in this, too, Dean said, "Tell you what. You talk with Jamie. If she's on board, I'll make some calls."

thirteen

The morning flew, as mornings always did when Jamie had nonstop meetings. She met with a checkout clerk at Whole Foods, one at the Container Store, and one at Toys "R" Us—the last, an emergency stop when Whole Foods didn't have the Huggies Tad wore.

Big mistake, that last stop. He threw a full-out tantrum when she tried to remove him from a Cozy Coupe that was definitely too big for her condo but ended up in the SUV nonetheless.

Next time, she would buy Huggies at CVS.

No. Next time, she would buy Huggies online.

Actually, next time she would get *lots* of things online. Taking Tad in and out of the car seat, walking him in and out of stores, and stopping to take things from his hands and replace them on shelves took twice as long as running errands alone.

Armed with a new respect for Jess and every other stay-at-home mom, she returned home to unload the car, switch towels from washer to dryer, and make lunch, all the while ignoring the marks the Cozy Coupe left on her polished hardwood floor as Tad propelled it round and round.

His nap brought a brief reprieve. She could have fallen asleep in a nanosecond herself, but time without Tad was too precious to waste. So she organized. By the time she was done, she had a bin for diapers, a bin for stuffed animals, a bin for Legos, and a bin for trains, which was all well and good until Tad woke up from a longer-than-usual nap cranky.

He didn't want his diaper changed, didn't want a snack, didn't want a story. He didn't want the Cozy Coupe or any of the toys now neatly housed in the den. He squirmed out of her arms when she tried to gather him in and lay back on the floor, crying for his mother.

The novelty of being with Jamie was clearly gone.

But what to say? Tad didn't know what death meant. Even if he were old enough to grasp the concept of finality, how could she tell him that he would never, ever see his parents again?

Frantic, she simply sat beside him with her stomach in knots and finger-combed his chocolate curls until he quieted and asked for milk, and all the while she felt like a fraud. She was an architect, not a mother. She was clueless when it came to baby moods, not sure at all whether she liked the pressure of being *the most responsible person* in her orphaned half-brother's life.

Needing a shoulder to cry on—and desperate enough to risk being rejected—she put Tad back in the car and this time headed for Caroline's. The mere act of driving the route held normalcy, and once she turned onto the tree-lined street, the familiarity was a balm.

Her eyes flew ahead in search of the dusty red truck, but the driveway was empty. Her heart fell. She needed to see her mother—physically *see* her—needed even just a hint of Caroline's lily-of-the-valley scent, whether they talked substantively or not. That scent, as light and delicate as the tiny white bells that appeared so briefly each spring, was ageless. Caroline's mother had worn it before Caroline, and though Jamie was always looking for something new to give her, it was never perfume. That fresh, subtle sweetness was resilient.

But it wasn't to be right now, and Roy had thrown down the gauntlet. *If you can't behave like a grown-up . . .*

Clearing the lump from her throat, she said with surprising enthusiasm, "See the trees, Taddy? They're called maple trees. They're very old. See how big they are?" He didn't answer, but the rearview mirror showed him looking out the window. "What color are they?"

"Blue."

"Blue . . . or . . . maybe green?"

"Gween!"

"Good boy! Annnnnd"—she turned into the driveway—"here we are at Mom's house."

She backed out and parked in front. Taking Tad from his seat, she carried him halfway up the walk before catching herself, setting him down, and taking his hand. She was holding him too much, wanting to shield him from loss, but the loss was a done deal, and he was starting to rebel. *No, no, Mamie, Taddy do it.* He wanted to move.

As soon as the screen door squeaked back and she opened the wood one, he ran inside. "Kitty, kitty, he-ah kitty." Amazing that he remembered, since she had only brought him here a time or two before. The two upstairs cats would be warned off by his high-pitched shout, but Master sensed a playmate and came close. While Tad crouched low, Jamie showed him how to stroke the cat from neck to tail, how to throw a scrunched-up paper ball for the cat to retrieve, how to drag a piece of string along the floor for Master to follow, and all the while Jamie struggled to capture the tiny wisps of woodsy scent her mother had left behind.

When the cat wandered off, Tad chased him. That was good for five minutes. Ten passed on the front porch with crackers and cheese, another five scrambling over the low arms of a copper beech in the backyard, and through it all, Jamie listened for Caroline's truck. Finally, she texted, *I'm at your place with Tad. Master was a hit. Where are you?*

Office, Caroline wrote back. *Theo is trying to decide who'll cover for Roy.*

It involved more than covering, Jamie realized with a stab of grief. Roy's death left a huge hole in the company. Brad wasn't a marketer. No one in the family was, which meant they would have to hire from the outside. Theo wouldn't be happy about that.

Not quite sure what Caroline's role with Theo was, she typed, *I need to see you. Want Tad to see you. He's my son now.*

The statement was blunt, provocative enough to warrant an instant reply. When none came, she felt starkly alone. Feeling suddenly unwelcome in Caroline's house, she bundled Tad back into the car. She was nearing the center of town when her phone finally vibrated. When she stopped at a light, she read, *I need to see you, too.*

Tucking hope into a snug corner of her mind, she headed for the playground to kill a few more minutes before having to think about another meal. This being a weekday, it was quieter than last time, with no big families and fewer cars parked by the gate. Two moms and what looked to be a nanny sat together watching little girls dressed in bright shorts, shirts, and bows. Well beyond them, off in a corner of the grassy playing field, was the dad she had seen last time. At least, she assumed he was the boy's dad. He wore the same sunglasses and similar nylon T-shirt and long shorts, but no hat today, and his hair and the child's were identically dark, straight, and neatly cut.

When Tad headed for them, Jamie followed. She stopped behind him at a baseline etched in the grass and watched the game on the diamond unfold. Standing at the ready ten feet or so from home plate, the dad rolled in a soccer-sized rubber ball. The boy's first kick grazed its top, sending it feebly to the side. Loping forward, the dad retrieved it, loped backward—a pretty cool move, Jamie thought—and rolled it in again. This time, the boy's kick was solid.

"Way to *go,* Buddy," the dad called and, shagging the ball, narrated, "He's rounding first." The dad trotted toward second base, made an exaggerated attempt to tag the child, and missed. "Bad move, *pitcher,*" he sang, "and the runner is heading for third . . ."

The boy wore a wide grin and, between mischievous glances at his dad, was running for all he was worth. Laughing, Jamie bent over Tad. "Are you watching, monkey?" she asked and drew him back a step.

The child barreled past, heading for home as his father made a show of trying to chase him down and coming up short. *"Score!"* the man shouted, arms raised. "That's six for the Bud-man, two for Dad." Snatching the boy up, he held him high and shouted, *"The winner!"* He slid him back to the ground and turned to Jamie and Tad. "He's getting too good for me." Tossing the ball behind him for his son to chase, he ambled over. He was loose-limbed and tall, well over six feet.

"How old is he?" Jamie asked as they stood side by side watching the boy.

"Three and change."

"I was guessing four. That tells you how bad I am at all this."

"Not bad," he said. "Just new."

So he did know who she was. She felt she should know him, too. There was a vague familiarity to him. "Thanks for helping me out last Saturday. With the moms."

"No sweat. They can be overbearing. I hide in a book whenever I can."

Tad had inched over the baseline and stopped. The other child was sitting on the ball, watching him approach.

Jamie leaned in from behind. "You can play, sweetie. Go on." She raised questioning brows to the dad, who nodded.

"Roll him the ball, Buddy," he called. The boy stood and gave it a try, but the infield grass quickly slowed it.

"Is Buddy his real name?"

"Nah. It's Baker, but no one calls him that."

"Is his mom around?"

"Nope." One word. No discussion.

The ball lay idle halfway between the boys. They continued to stare at each other.

"Show him how," the dad called to Buddy, who didn't budge.

"Tad's two," Jamie offered lest the dad think him older and wonder at his failure to engage. He was tall for his age. Roy had loved telling people that. "Twenty-eight months, actually."

"Does he understand what's happened?"

His parents' sudden death. "No. We're both in denial. I'm still pretending to be the aunt who's babysitting."

"That's as good a bridge as any to a brave new world."

She had to smile. The man did get it. "I'm Jamie, by the way."

"Charlie," he said and trotted out. "Okay, guys. We need an ice-breaker here." Squatting between the two, he pointed. "Buddy, Tad. Tad, Buddy."

The boys remained silent and staring.

"Super," said the dad—Charlie—as he snagged the ball with one large hand. He looked from face to face. "We're playing tag. You ever played, Tad? No? That's okay, there's always a first time." He rose, then folded at the waist, knees bent, elbows on his thighs, shifting slightly from hip to hip, the quarterback huddling with his squad. Jamie assumed he was explaining the rules, though his voice was too low for her to hear until he said, "Ready, set, *run*!"

She was thinking that Tad couldn't possibly know what to do—when he started running after Buddy. With Charlie chasing first one, then the other, there were high-pitched shrieks, lots of legs wheeling and bodies tumbling, and, bless him, though Charlie reached out numerous times with the ball in that one large hand, he just couldn't manage to tag one of the boys.

Finally, with loud panting sounds, he pulled up. "Time out. You guys are too good." Dropping the ball, he trotted over to stand beside Jamie again. Not in the least winded, he put his hands on his hips.

"You're good with kids," she said.

He shrugged and cupped his mouth. "Circle the bases, Buddy."

Jogging in an exaggerated way, Buddy headed for first, rounded it, made for second. Tad followed more slowly.

"Do you come here often?" Jamie asked.

"Couple of times a week. We have a yard, but this one's better for hell hour."

"Hell hour?"

"Five to six."

How could she not have guessed? She had resorted to Elmo videos the last day or two, although the playground was infinitely better. "Do you live here in town?"

Charlie nodded. "In my folks' house. I got it when they retired. They divide their time between Florida and Vermont."

Longtime Willistonians, then? She might have asked the name—might have recognized it—might have even gone to the same school as

Charlie at some point—if she hadn't been so needy for other info. "Are you a full-time dad?"

He snickered. "It sure as hell feels that way, but no, I have an outside job. Buddy's in daycare till four."

"Where?"

"First Unity." The church. "There are some other good ones, too." He watched the boys. Buddy had rounded third, lengthening the distance between him and Tad, but Tad didn't stop. "I'm sure you got a rundown from friends."

"I don't have friends," she stated. "Give me the rundown."

When he turned to face her, dark lenses didn't hide his skepticism. "How can a MacAfee not have friends?"

"I've always been too busy. What are my daycare options?"

Flipping his glasses to the top of his head, he rubbed the bridge of his nose and looked at her. "After First Unity, there's one at the Community Center. There's a pre-K at Underwood"—one of the elementary schools in town—"but he'd be too young for that." He saw her staring and replaced his glasses.

Too late. Jamie knew who he was now. Added to height and physical dexterity, those blue eyes gave him away. "Chip?" she asked in puzzled surprise.

"Charlie."

"Chip Kobik."

"Charlie," he corrected again. "Chip is long gone."

She might have asked more if, just then, the ball hadn't hit him square in the back.

"Whoaaaa," he drawled in a higher voice as he turned and, with slow challenge, said, "What. Was. *That.*"

His son apparently knew teasing when he heard it because, with a high giggle, he turned and raced off with his father in pursuit. The ball forgotten, they played tag using hands. The big guy quickly tagged his son, caught him up by the waist, and jogged over to deposit him beside Tad. When he said, *"Go,"* Buddy took off again. This time, Charlie scooped Tad up and raced off with him pinned to his hip.

Frightened, Jamie put a hand to her mouth—and not because Chip

Kobik was holding her child. Tad didn't know the game. He didn't know the *man.* And he was only *two.*

When Charlie turned, though, the child's face was filled with delight, and once Tad tagged Buddy, he squirmed to be put down. Both boys stood close in the huddle, with Charlie bent over between them. He was shifting his weight from hip to hip again—a cool move that was no mystery now. Chip Kobik, physically coordinated to the nth degree, had dropped out of college to play professional hockey. He had been incredibly talented.

Jamie didn't know what he said, but when he was done, he turned both boys in the direction of second base and sent them off.

Her throat tightened, eyes filled. Tad was joining right in, seeming older than twenty-eight months at that moment and content in a way he hadn't been since his parents died. His happiness was infectious. She basked in it, even for a short time.

Charlie returned to her side. He watched the boys go all the way to the outfield with Buddy leading, Taddy lagging but not stopping. "The point of this is to wear them out. Buddy'll be asleep by seven thirty." He shot her a look. "You okay?"

She was actually feeling emotional, but the practical distracted her. "Is seven thirty his bedtime?"

"Mostly, but I don't like to be rigid."

"He must be in a big-boy bed."

Acknowledgment came as a grunt. "Double-edged sword there."

"How?"

"His face in mine at six in the morning."

"How long? I mean, when did you switch him from a crib?"

"When he was two and a half."

"Is that the usual age?"

He stretched his neck, one side to the other. "Depends on when the child is ready." He cupped his mouth and yelled to the boys, who stood with their backs to the chain-link fence at the very end of the field, "Come on back!"

"How do I know if Tad's ready?" Jamie asked.

He cut her a half-smile. "Are you?"

"I have no idea, but I have to decide ASAP. The Pack 'n Play isn't big enough. Either I bring his crib over from the house, or I buy a bed."

"Buy a bed."

"With all the other changes in his life right now?"

"What's one more." No question. Because it made total sense. Like keeping Tad at her place to allow the past to fade and the future begin.

"What about potty training?"

"Use M&M's. Bribery works wonders."

"Should I be training him now?"

"Is he compulsively neat?"

"Omigod, no." She pictured her condo. "He could care less."

"Then wait a little. Buddy was slow. It's harder for boys anyway—y'know, two things to learn to do."

Jamie might have been embarrassed discussing male body function with Chip Kobic, except that she found herself breathing, truly breathing, *deeply* breathing for the first time in forever. She had gotten more solid information in the last fifteen minutes than in all of the last five days. Amazed, she looked up at him. "Who'da thought Checker Chip would have answers like this?"

"Who'da thought Just-So-Jamie would deign to ask?" he shot back.

Well, she deserved that. Chip Kobik had been two years ahead of her in school. They had never been friends, had never spoken to each other, but nicknames transcended social circles when it came to standouts. En route to the pros, Chip had played hockey on local and state squads and was widely considered an ace at checking, hence Checker Chip. King of the jock crowd, he had an ego to match. Jamie had no ego, at least not at school. Nor, actually, did she have a crowd. Just-So-Jamie, fastidious to a T, had been too focused on tennis to care.

Seeming to regret the sharpness, he said more gently, "It's Charlie. And I have a list of babysitters at home. What's your e-mail address?" Taking a phone from his pocket, he keyed it in. "They probably aren't a permanent solution, but they'll help for now."

"I'll take any help I can get." She was without pride. "I am up the proverbial creek without a you know what."

"Speaking of which," he called over his shoulder as he guided his son toward the gate, "there's Toddler Swim at the town pool Tuesdays and Thursdays. He'd probably like that. And story hour at the library. The days vary, but there are always other kids. It's good for socializing."

Checker Chip a parenting resource? Who *knew*. Jamie was amused enough, curious enough, *needy* enough for a frivolous break to explore the surprise. After putting cheese tortellini on for dinner, she settled Tad in the crook of her left elbow with her iPad streaming a Handy Manny video, opened her laptop on her right, and Googled Charlie Kobik.

He taught PE at Emory Elementary.

Not what she would have expected, though seeing him on the playground with the boys, it made sense. Still, it was a turnaround from the wild behavior reported in earlier articles. He had gone to Harvard to play hockey, then dropped out and signed with the Montreal Canadiens, the Buffalo Sabres, and the Pittsburgh Penguins in quick succession until his three-year contract expired and the NHL summarily let him go. After an undocumented period spent, she assumed, getting his act together, he had enrolled at UMass, earned a degree in education, and been appointed to the Williston School Department. Summers, he ran a hockey camp at an indoor ice rink. According to the *Williston News*, it was hugely successful.

There was nothing about a wife and son, but given how he sat by himself at the park hiding under shades and a hat, she figured he was making a statement. What he did on his own time was his own business.

And yet, there came his e-mail, as promised, containing the names of half a dozen babysitters. *You are a godsend*, she typed back. *Thank you SO much.*

With the phone at her ear while she drained the tortellini, she secured a babysitter for Saturday night, then called Brad in triumph.

"Great," he said but sounded tired.

"Will you stay over?"

"Of course."

"Want to come tonight?"

"Nah. I'll be here working a while."

"You could come later. Or how about tomorrow morning? I'm taking Tad bed shopping. Want to meet us at the store?"

"Isn't he too young for a bed?"

"Not according to the reading I've done." No point mentioning Chip. "We can get a bed that's low and has bars, and the floor is carpeted, so it's not like he would hurt himself if he fell out. Come with us, Brad? It'd be really neat if he associated you with his new big-boy bed."

But Brad had other plans. "I just got into a foursome." Golf. "I need the break. It's been a nightmare week."

Jamie stifled the miffed little voice in her head that wanted to point out that it had been a nightmare week for her, too, and that he was part of a family now. Only he wasn't part of the family that was her and Tad. He didn't seem to want to be.

They had to talk.

fourteen

When a sharp knock on the door woke Caroline from a deep sleep early Saturday, her first thought was Jamie. No surprise there. Thoughts of Jamie had kept her awake into the wee hours more times than she could count, and last night was bad.

But no. Not Jamie at the door now. Jamie wouldn't knock. She had a key.

Nor would Jamie drive over in Dean's truck, which was what Caroline saw when, bleary-eyed, she scrambled over cats to squint out at the street.

Dean, who had said *I could prove you wrong about sex,* whose hand on hers during the funeral had brought comfort, whose palm at her back following the confrontation with Claire suggested he was more than just a colleague, and whose sensitivity and gentleness yesterday in his truck brought tears to her eyes now—all of which was bizarre.

Unnerved, she climbed back into bed, but only until he knocked louder. Then, resentful of being woken after the night that had been, she threw back the sheet and trounced barefoot down the stairs. She was wearing an ancient MacAfee T-shirt, once red but now faded from a gazillion washes. It was big enough to cover her sleep shorts and any body parts that were also faded from a gazillion washes, and if that didn't turn him off more, the mess of her hair would.

Jaw tight, she pulled open the door.

His eyes widened. Recovering quickly, he grinned. "Hey, Sunshine."

"Sunshine?" She cleared her throat. "Not. Quite."

The amusement in his eyes didn't waver. "Got up on the wrong side, did we?"

"*We* didn't."

"Through no fault of mine," he said with such innocence that once upon a time she would have laughed.

Now, confused and feeling unfit to deal, she simply pleaded, "Why are you here so early? It's the weekend. You sleep late." She narrowed a glance back at the grandfather clock. "What time is it even?"

"Eight," he said, "and I brought breakfast makings." He pushed past her—close, tall body brushing, *deliberate,* and not entirely unpleasant—as he strode into the house and down the hall.

She considered making a statement by going back to bed. There were two reasons she didn't. First, she would never fall asleep with him in her kitchen, and second—*worse*—he might follow.

That said, she was not changing her clothes. She didn't care that he was newly showered, hair still damp, T-shirt and jeans fresh. This was her house, her Saturday morning, *her* routine. "And don't ask if I called Jamie," she shouted after him, "because since you last asked, nothing has changed." Padding down the hall, she found him unloading bags in her itty-bitty little space.

"Bacon, eggs, cheese," he listed. "And bread."

"I have all those things."

"Bacon? Really?"

"No. Not bacon. Bacon's bad for you."

"Not for me. And I doubt you have this bread, which is thick-sliced organic whole grain, fresh-baked this morning in town." He arched a questioning brow.

"No," she admitted. A quart of fresh-squeezed orange juice stood in a signature glass bottle from the same bakery. Taking out two glasses, she filled them. Dean was frowning at the lower cabinets by then, clearly not knowing what was where. She nudged him aside. "I'll cook."

"That wasn't my plan."

"Maybe not, but my kitchen is too small for both of us, and I know what's where. And if you're going to tell me it's too warm in here, you can go wait on the porch." She removed a skillet from a low cabinet, put it on the stove, and lit the gas. While it heated, she separated bacon slices and laid them in one by one. The sizzle accompanied the *whooshhh* of the Keurig.

"Want some?" he asked. The fridge opened; he added cream to his coffee.

"Tea, please. K-Cups are—"

"Got 'em." He removed one, studied the label, removed a second and did the same.

"Either is fine. Surprise me." While he brewed it, she cracked four eggs in a bowl, whipped them with a fork, flipped the bacon slices. Messy curls slid forward as she worked, blocking her vision so that she was startled to find him close when she turned to the fridge.

Whipping her hair out of the way, she stepped back and cleared her throat, but he didn't move. Instead, he set her tea down near the skillet and asked, "How's your hand?"

Thinking a diversion was good, she showed him her bright red scar. "The stitches came out yesterday. It's fine." Proving it, she used that hand to push him aside. "Please. Take the orange juice and these"—she plunked napkins and forks on the counter—"to the porch." After giving the skillet a shuffle, she stood waiting, watching as the bacon shriveled and curled.

She felt his warmth at her ear seconds before she heard, "Mmmm. There is nothing like that smell." Though he meant bacon, she was thinking coffee, which was on his breath as he nuzzled her hair. "And this. Is it shampoo or you?"

She swallowed. "Shampoo."

His voice moved off a bit. "It smells like you."

"Because I always use it." She had torn off a handful of paper towels and was in the process of forking up the bacon to drain when she felt a hand slide up her spine. Fork in hand, she whirled around. "What are you *doing*?"

He took a step back, actually seeming guilty. "Just wondering what's on under this."

She refused to look away. "Nothing, Dean. Nothing. I just woke up."

"You're gorgeous."

She wanted to yell, scream, kick him out. Only he seemed to mean it, and—*traitorous, vain self*—a little part of her ate up the words.

Embarrassed, wishing she had put on clothes or washed her face or at the very least used mouthwash, she turned back to the stove. After draining bacon grease from the skillet, she poured in the beaten eggs and shook on a layer of shredded cheddar.

"More," he urged from her temple.

She added more, and when his warmth stayed behind her in as clear a message as could be, she set down the bag of cheese and, sighing in resignation, sagged back against him for a single weary minute.

Actually, it wasn't a single minute. It was probably a quarter of that, and it wasn't weary so much as bewildered. There was warmth and strength here, and a commanding height. There was a sense of being enveloped that felt better than it should. There was familiarity, and trust, and something else that she hadn't felt in many long years. *Why now why now why now?*

Confused, she came forward, taking her own weight again. "Oh, Dean," she murmured, stirring the eggs as they cooked.

Not moving far, he turned to lean against the sink, where he could see her face. "What does that mean?"

"It means this is strange." She focused on the eggs. "I don't understand what you're doing or what I'm feeling. Why is this happening all of a sudden?"

His hazel eyes darkened. His voice was quiet. "There's nothing sudden about it on my end. I've always been attracted to you."

That startled her. "Even when you were married?"

He looked uncomfortable, finally shrugged. "I wouldn't have acted on it then. And after my divorce, our relationship was comfortable. I needed your friendship more than I needed sex."

She studied him, her fifty-six-year-old self wondering if he was reading *More.* But he was serious. "And what's changed?"

He considered, seeming puzzled, then just gave another shrug.

Caroline was just as puzzled. "I'm not soft or sexy or feminine."

"Is that what Roy said?"

"He didn't have to. I'm not blind. I look in the mirror every morning. I see myself through the eyes of dozens of men every week. Besides, I'm older than you."

"Which *is* what Roy said."

She scrubbed the air. "Forget Roy. Roy is dead."

Dean stood straight, eyes suddenly clear and intense. "That's it, Caro. Dead at fifty-two. And what is the lesson from that? I'm fifty-*three.* Will I be gone next year or the year after that? Maybe fall off a roof or crash the Harley? I don't know, I really don't, but suddenly I'm thinking of the things I'd regret in those last few minutes before death. You'd be one."

She didn't know whether to laugh or cry. "So I'm on your bucket list."

"Actually"—he didn't blink—"you *are* my bucket list."

Caroline swallowed, trying to digest *that.* "I'm a carpenter, Dean. I do man's work. I have calluses and scars. And I'll be *sixty* in four years."

"You're sexy."

"*Sixty* in four years."

"You're fixated on age because of Roy and Claire—"

"Just stating facts."

"Like they matter once you're past, what, forty? Come on, Caro. That's just dumb. I don't care how old you are. I think you're hot."

Hot. Well, there was a potent word.

Caroline searched his face. When she saw nothing but earnestness, she felt a tightness inside. Roy could sling the bull, sling it often and long. Not Dean. Dean was all down-to-earth, tell-it-like-it-is practicality. He wasn't driven by ego. His expression right now—*vulnerable*—attested to that, giving new meaning to *I could prove you wrong.*

What she had initially thought was pure swagger was not. This wasn't a dare. It wasn't a game for him. And *that* was the sweetest, most frightening realization of all.

"You look terrified," he said.

"I am. I don't know if I can do this. I don't know if I want to."

He shifted again, this time caging her with both elbows as he took the skillet from the stove. Then his hands closed on her forearms. Dark against her skin, his fingers were long and scarred, with a pinkie that didn't fully straighten but took nothing from the strength of the others. His voice was low and surprisingly intimate. "You think I'm not nervous? You think I don't worry I'm not good enough? You think I don't know the risk? Think again. But Roy was younger than me, and he died. That's a reality check. Put things off and they may never happen. Ever. At some point in life, you have to go for what you want."

"Fine for you to say," she mused. "Apparently, you knew you wanted this. I've been in the dark."

"You're not in the dark now. You either feel it or you don't."

"Those are words, Dean, just words. So is this a philosophical challenge?"

He paused. "Why do you ask that?"

"Because."

"Because why?"

"I can just tell."

"How?"

"Because," she blurted, "you're standing against me, and we're talking about it, and if it was really a *sexual* thing, I should feel, well, feel you, but I don't—" She stopped short when he brought his lower body against hers, proving her well and truly wrong.

Dean had barely headed off in his truck when Caroline speed-dialed Annie Ahl. "Where are you?"

"Sitting in weeds at the Blaine site." The home in question, a current MacAfee job, was more an external facelift than an internal redo, which meant that Annie, Jamie, and Dean were more familiar with it than Caroline was, but she certainly knew the address.

"I'll be there in ten minutes." She dressed in two, fed the cats in two, and drove in six, which was truly too fast, but there was an urgency here. Dean's erection had stolen her breath. She should have been angry or embarrassed, should have been *turned off,* for Pete's sake, not intrigued. That erection had been impressive. Add to it earnestness and vulnerability, both of which she had seen in Dean during their discussion, and she was about to OD on confusion.

Annie was her closest friend. Having met on a job fifteen years before, they had bonded over girl things, like mani-pedi afternoons, breast biopsies, brown spots, and menopause. Caroline hadn't told Annie about *Gut It!* yet. She hoped she wouldn't have to. Annie was even closer to sixty than she was; if the hosting switch held, she would fear for her own job.

Besides, *Gut It!* definitely took a backseat to an impressive erection.

Pulling up behind Annie's van, she spotted the silver-haired pixie in the garden, trotted over, and sat. "We need to talk."

"About what?"

"Sex."

"My favorite topic," Annie sang in her high voice as she pulled up a clump of weeds.

"Is it overrated?" Caroline asked. When Annie shot her a *where did this come from* frown, she said, "You've been married to Byron for thirty years. Your sons are in college, and you're not having more kids. Is sex still important?"

Annie was oddly wary. "Why do you ask?"

"Is it?"

"Yes."

"Do you think about it a lot?"

"Yes."

"As much as you used to?"

Annie started to blink and stopped, seeming not to breathe. "More."

That surprised Caroline. Puzzled, she asked, "Because of those books?" Annie made no bones about having read them multiple times.

"No." Annie tugged up another handful of weeds. "Because I'm not ready to have it end."

"Why not?"

"Because it's fun. It's exciting. It's a way to feel alive. And young. And *feminine.*"

Dean had certainly made Caroline feel feminine. He had also made her feel protected—a totally bizarre thought, since she could take care of herself.

Seeming halfway between cross and sad, Annie sat back on her heels. "I don't want to dry up. Use it or lose it."

"Then things are better with Byron?" Caroline asked. Annie had once confided that her husband was losing interest in sex. When it hadn't come up again, she had assumed an improvement. But her friend wasn't answering now. "Annie?" Silence. "Oh, whoa. What is going on?"

Barely above a whisper, Annie's words came in a rush. "Don't worry, it's not like that, I haven't done anything wrong. It's just, I *think* about it." She leaned closer. "There's this guy—"

Caroline cut her off. "Byron is wonderful!"

"Yes, he is, wonderfully the same, getting older and not caring, but I do. There's this guy—" She stopped abruptly. Eyes flying past Caroline, she broke into a smile. "Hey. Jordan. I thought you were paying bills while Mandy was at the hair shop."

"Your being out here is too tempting."

The man who had come from behind the house wasn't particularly tall, muscular, or young, wasn't notable in any way other than the intensity of his focus on Annie.

Taking a brief break, he extended Caroline a hand. "I recognize you from the show. Jordan Blaine, homeowner." They shook, but his hand was barely free when he walked on. Coming up behind Annie, he steepled his fingers on the top of her head and said to Caroline, "Is this woman amazing or what? On a Saturday, no less."

Annie tipped her head back to see him. "It makes sense to clean now, so that I'll know what to dig up next week before our crew starts tossing off old siding."

"I'm happy to dump all of these plants and start fresh. I told you that."

"But some of them are worth saving. If there's no place for them in front, there is in back."

He glanced at Caroline. "How rare is a landscaper who comes up with a high-end design and still wants to save me money?" His fingers slipped to Annie's shoulder. "I'll be inside. Ring the bell when you're done." With a little squeeze, he was gone.

Annie followed his departure before shifting wide eyes to Caroline. Wide, *expectant* eyes.

"Him?" Caroline whispered in surprise. She didn't find Jordan Blaine sexy in the least.

"He touches me, y'know? Byron doesn't do that anymore. I could be a piece of furniture that he happens to screw once a month," which was pretty much what Annie had told her before.

Caroline's heart sank. The touching she had just witnessed seemed more friendly than sexual, like Annie was building it into more, but even that was a shame. Byron was a gentle soul who was faithful and adoring. It didn't seem fair that he should be cheated on because of sex alone. "If it's still bad, you need to talk with him."

"I *did.*"

"Do it again. And again. You owe him that, Annie."

"I know," she wailed.

"Not to mention," Caroline remarked, "that there was a big fat wedding band on the hand that stroked your hair just now."

"I *know,* but, *God,* the attraction's strong. His eyes, his hands, his body—when we're alone, he's there."

Okay. Caroline's presence might have kept a lid on the fire.

"He doesn't even have to touch me and I feel alive," Annie went on achingly. Grabbing Caroline, she pulled her up and, linking their arms, put distance between themselves and the house. "Maybe all I need is the tease. There isn't any of that in my marriage. No tease, no mystery, no adventure, no spice. How can old marrieds not get bored?"

"You're asking the wrong person. My marriage never made it to the old-marrieds stage. We lasted twelve years. Roy was bored after one."

"Were you?"

"Not bored."

"Satisfied?"

Caroline looked at her fingernails. Given her line of work, she had no business painting them. Feet, yes, but hands? She had only done it because she had known the surgery would keep those hands idle. Now the orange polish was starting to chip. Roy had thought her hands masculine; hence the concept of hand care had taken root. Had years of moisturizing made a difference? Or sexy lingerie or designer perfume? Had sex with Roy been satisfying?

Tucking her hands in her armpits, she leaned against Annie's van. "Our sex was good the first few times. Then I got pregnant, and it went downhill. By the time Jamie was born, Roy had tuned out." She met her friend's gaze. "We still had sex, but he climaxed and was done. My pleasure wasn't part of the package."

Annie hung on her forearm. "I'm sorry. That makes my complaints seem petty."

"No complaints are petty. Everything is relative. You've had something with Byron that I never had with Roy. Yours may be on autopilot now, but Byron's still a good man."

"I know, I know, I know. But right there, that's the trouble. I *know* Byron inside and out. We're the same people, bringing the same cards to the table over and over again. I try to suggest new things to do, but he's no change agent. I tell him change is good and healthy and how we stay young." She wagged a finger between them. "How often do you and I change nail color?"

"Nail color." Caroline failed to make the connection.

"Okay. Bad example. Try hairstyle. I cut mine short, then let it grow long and cut it again. I drive Claire nuts, but I'm sorry, I like novelty when it comes to hair and nails and food. Shouldn't I like novelty in bed, too?"

Caroline thought of Dean. She didn't know how he made love, what positions he liked, whether he was silent or vocal. Anything he did with her would likely be a novelty after Roy, who had been a die-hard missionary guy and didn't welcome her input. For all she knew, Dean was the same. Worse, he could be addicted to another position that she liked even less.

"Variety is *good,*" Annie said into the silence, and Caroline couldn't argue with that.

"But we're older. Our bodies respond differently."

"Different doesn't mean worse."

"I hate my thighs. They're lumpy."

"Most people call that muscled, but there's a solution for that. It's called darkness."

But Caroline was thinking about things that lighting couldn't hide. With anyone else, she might have been more hesitant to be blunt, but Annie was Annie. "What about dryness?"

"CVS sells lubricants."

"Do you use them?"

"With Byron I do. I don't think it would be an issue . . ." Her eyes touched the house and returned.

"How do you know?"

Annie stared at her pointedly.

Ahhh. Wetness just thinking about it.

"I mean," the pixie burst out, "you and I are at an incredible stage in life when we don't have to worry about getting pregnant or even being discreet since we don't have kids around. Why can't sex just be pleasurable and fun, and if my husband doesn't want that, should I be punished? Why can't I once, just once before I go senile, have a hot, passionate, incredibly romantic love affair? I've been so good all my life." She paused. "So have you. I didn't know you when you first got divorced. Did you think about having affairs back then?"

"Yes. I tried with two different guys. It was disappointing with both."

"Was it more than one night with each?"

"Yes. I really did try." One was a client whose house they had finished, the other an independent furniture maker. She had chosen them carefully to avoid fallout at work. Dean, now, Dean was a whole other can of worms.

"You were on the rebound," Annie offered, bringing her back.

"No, the sex just wasn't great, and I've been okay with that," Caroline insisted. "I like my life. It's rewarding and full." Until now, if the *Gut It!* change held. Being on the show as the host emeritus would make her feel older than God. Not that having sex with Dean would change that.

"But I see guys watching you. Aren't you ever tempted?"

She thought about that—and about why she had been totally unprepared for Dean's move. "Sex just . . . hasn't been on my radar screen."

"You've repressed it."

She considered that and conceded, "Maybe."

"Because Roy sucked at it."

She smiled sadly. "Either Roy or me."

"Roy," Annie said. "Every woman *feels.* It just takes the right man to make things combust. So Roy wasn't right, and clearly neither of the other guys was. But aren't you curious?"

"Curious enough to risk awkwardness, embarrassment, and pain?" Which raised the issue of why she was even *beginning* to consider sleeping with Dean. She wondered if Roy's death was a wake-up call for her, too, a red alert that she had to go for what she wanted while she still could. Granted, she hadn't thought she wanted sex. But she was getting older. If her recent birthday hadn't told her that, being put out to pasture by *Gut It!* would have, which brought her back to the issue of sex for a woman her age.

You either feel it or you don't, Dean had said, and a week ago she would have denied feeling a thing. But she was here talking to her best friend because she had felt something. Dean's erection—God, it was weird thinking of him that way—his erection had made her buzz in a way that made his argument real. He had put his money where his mouth was, which raised an interesting thought. His mouth. They hadn't ever even kissed. It was all well and good to be eye candy, but if his kiss turned her off, they had a problem that no advice from Annie would solve.

Still, that erection had given her a quick blast of heat.

"How long has it been?" Annie asked.

Caroline had done the math more than once since Dean had changed their relationship with his challenge. "Seventeen years since the divorce, ten since I last had sex, or tried."

"I knew you ten years ago. You never told me—"

"Because we weren't that close then, and it was bad. Oh boy," she breathed. "I am *so* out of my league here."

Annie's sidelong stare lasted long enough to make her squirm before a breathlessly high voice said an amazed "You're considering it! That's why you wanted to talk. Oooh, this is good, Caro. Who *is* he?"

Caroline moved a hand *no*. She couldn't tell Annie. Annie knew Dean. It would be unfair to implicate him in something that might absolutely never come to pass.

Mercifully, her friend let the identity piece go and chided softly, "You're thinking of doing it, and you're scared. Do not be, Caro. If the guy is right, it'll work, and if he isn't, it's no loss." Caroline was thinking that it wasn't so simple, that a working relationship was at risk, not to mention a friendship, when Annie said, "I'd give my right arm to be as free as you are. Sex is an integral part of womanhood. When I think of never feeling that . . . that *rush* again, I feel incredibly sad. It would be a loss."

"Loss of?"

"Pleasure. Possibility. Power." Annie raised hope-filled eyes to hers. "That's what I get from those books that you refuse to read. It's like they remind me that my body is capable of doing more, like I have to let go of preconceptions, like I can open my mind to growth in this, too." Her voice fell to a whisper. "I have not done anything with Jordan, I swear I haven't, but when he touches my shoulder or my hand, I feel powerful, like I'm the one making it happen. Don't you want to feel that?"

Actually, no. Power wasn't part of Caroline's equation. Hers was less lofty. She knew what it was to feel passion for work and for her daughter, but stripped-naked, bare-ass passion with a man? Exposure to the extreme? Being *that* close with another person, that *trusting*? That might be something she did want to feel.

But with Dean? It could either be the best thing that ever happened or the worst.

fifteen

Dinner with Brad Saturday night was a disaster. Jamie had hoped that eighteen holes of golf would loosen him up, and that since the other three in the foursome had kids, he would warm to the idea of being a father himself. But beyond color on his cheeks, his features were their usual calm selves. She had always found that reassuring. Now it angered her. If ever they needed to actually share thoughts, this was the time, but he remained distant. He nodded when she told him about organizing the condo and did it again when she said she had possible nanny contacts. His eyes glazed over when she described her dilemma at the furniture store that morning, and when she asked his opinion, toddler bed versus twin bed, he held up his hands and said a gentle "You'd know better than me" with an infuriatingly sweet smile. By the time he had given versions of the same answer with regard to staying with Jessica's pediatrician, feeding Tad the sugary breakfast cereal he wanted, and, finally, formalizing his adoption in court, she'd had it.

"I'm not asking for a definitive answer, Brad, just an opinion. What do you *think*?" She had lost interest in both the steak on her plate and the garlic mashed potatoes topped with onion rings that she would have normally devoured. She was too filled with annoyance to eat.

"I don't know," he said helplessly. "I have no experience in this."

Sorry, bud, said her irate mind-voice, *helplessness does not work here.* "You *do.* You spent a law-school summer interning for a lawyer who specialized in child custody cases."

"That was after my first year, and I hated it so much that I did a one-eighty the next summer and never looked back. I'm a real estate lawyer, Jamie."

"But you know how this state works. I want to know whether I should ask Theo to pull strings and speed things up."

"Why do you need speed? It's not like there's anyone else who wants custody."

Jamie recoiled. "Like Tad's a booby prize?"

He gave a tiny frown and silently reached for his wine.

"You think he is," she charged. She kept her voice low; it wasn't in her to yell. She couldn't control the tiny tremor in it, though. Her heart was breaking. She shouldn't have to work so hard to remember why she loved Brad. But after spending the week tiptoeing around him, soothing his ego, and giving him time to adjust, this issue remained huge. "You and I swore we would talk things out, so let's talk. You don't want Tad."

Yes, I do, he would have insisted in an ideal world, because Tad was an adorable, smart, healthy little boy whose now-dead parents had named Jamie his legal guardian. Just as important, how could Brad not want what Jamie so badly did?

Instead, he was silent as he considered his answer. It was only after a pensive swallow of wine that he set down the glass and said, "It's not Tad. It's fatherhood. I was hoping we'd have time to ourselves before that."

"Well, so was I. Do you know how often I think about the fact that if my father had been on that road five seconds sooner or later he'd be alive now? No," she answered, still quiet despite the ache inside, "no, you don't know, because I'm afraid to tell you, because it's so obvious that everything about Tad annoys you."

"Not everything—"

"You hate his noise, his food, his music, his mess. You hate his existence in the condo, but on little more than a week's notice, I don't have a better option—and do *not* suggest Roy's house. You know my feeling on that. You also know that my mother and I are barely talking, and that she might have been a resource for me if it hadn't been for the *Gut It!* mess—and that's *another* thing you and I disagree on. This is not the time to make a host change, Brad. My mother is too good at it, and I suddenly have a whole other job."

"The show is important to MacAfee Homes."

"And MacAfee Homes has always been my first priority, but it isn't now. Tad is." She knew Brad well enough to recognize the flash of hurt in his eyes, and she nearly caved. He needed love. But so did she. And so did *Tad.* So she whispered, "Don't, Brad. Please don't. Selfishness doesn't work right now."

"Selfishness?" he asked, sounding offended, but at least that was something. "It's not selfishness. It's concern for *you.* You've worked your tail off building a career. To just throw it away—"

"There's nothing throwaway about what I'm doing."

"You're an architect."

"And I can't be a mother, too?"

"You can, but it means compromise. You've never been one to do that."

"Brad." Frustration beyond belief. "Things *change.* What would you have me do? Where would you have me put Tad?"

He didn't answer.

"Where?" she repeated, desperate for an answer. If she and Brad couldn't find a middle ground, there was no hope. "Remember I told you how my father came over just hours before he died? He accused me of being selfish and shortsighted, and he wasn't talking about this"—she wagged a finger between them—"clearly he couldn't have been, but his words haunt me. He told me to act like a grown-up." Her eyes filled with tears, not very grown up at all, but when it came to self-control, she was depleted. "I'm trying to do that, Brad. I'm looking at a situation that was not my doing, and I'm trying to figure it out. Buying a bed for Tad may seem like a stupid little thing to you, but if it's the very first major

purchase I make as a mother, it isn't stupid at all. This is my life, Brad. This is who I am from here out. You're either on board or you're not."

He didn't take a stand on that, and Jamie didn't push it. Clinging to a last lingering hope, she told herself that he needed time to consider what she'd said. But the rest of dinner was awkward, and, though he came home with her, she wasn't sure why. She half-wished they were fiery people who fought and made love, fought and made love. But sex didn't happen that night either. Not that she wanted it. Still, he might have tried, at least.

And then they were barely asleep when Tad woke up crying. Naturally, the monitor amplified his sobs, which brought a groan from Brad, who murmured a groggy "Shut that off," which, Jamie later realized, said it all. At the moment, though, she was simply worried about Tad.

Taking him from his crib, she bundled them both up on the living room sofa, where they slept until she heard Brad let himself out at dawn.

Much as her heart ached, she didn't get up. Tad hadn't woken, and she decided he needed the sleep more than she wanted to run after Brad. Every minute of peace and quiet with Tad was a treasure.

So she lay on the sofa with him, appreciating the whisper of the AC, the cycling of the fridge, and the gentle sough of baby breath, as she alternately studied his rosy-cheeked face, fingered the ring on her left hand, and wondered how she could simultaneously feel so in love and so hollow. It wasn't until Tad opened his eyes and snuggled closer that she realized the "in love" part had to do with the child.

What Jamie wanted to do that Sunday morning was to race to Caroline's. She didn't because, for starters, Caroline hadn't called, which meant she was still angry. Then there was the fact of Tad being Roy's son, and Roy had been awful to Caroline for years. Finally, though, Jamie had to behave like a grown-up, and a grown-up didn't run home at the first sign of trouble.

Besides, she was a mommy herself now, and if she planned to be an architect at the same time, she needed to work. Her MacAfee inbox was starting to clog, and it wasn't that her clients were insensitive. Inevitably, they expressed condolences. But they quickly got to the point, which was wanting to know whether she had made progress on their house, office, or bank.

In nearly every case, she had not.

So she spent much of Sunday morning meeting with sitters on Chip's list. All three were warm and affectionate with Tad, but only one was interested in a nanny slot.

One was all she needed. Jamie hired her.

Wanting to thank Chip, she picked up her phone and realized she didn't have his number. So she e-mailed. *Good news. June Flores will be here tomorrow at seven. She's lovely. I can't thank you enough.*

Feeling victorious and more hungry than she had in days, she took Tad for lunch at McDonald's, where she proceeded to eat every last crumb of a Quarter Pounder and fries, plus more than a few crumbs of the Happy Meal she had torn into small pieces for Tad. Then, feeling too stuffed, she drove by Roy's for the jogging stroller. She didn't go into the house, simply backed up to the garage and piled in the stroller and as many other outdoor toys as the back of the SUV would hold. She had a patio, she reasoned, and Brad was already disenchanted with baby gear, so would a little more hurt? *No.*

She wasn't quite as bold when it came to Tad, though. Praying that he wouldn't notice where they were, she left him in his car seat, playing with his Happy Meal bendy dog. She was barely back in the car when he asked for his mother.

Her insides twisted. Buckling her seat belt, she said an apologetic, "Oh, sweetie, Mommy's not here."

"Daddy?"

She put the car in gear. "He's not here either." Her voice was higher now, filled with tentativeness, because how did one discuss such a cruel truth with a child? She had wondered it before, but the question plagued her. Blogs offered a dozen different answers. Which to use? Caroline would know, but she was temporarily off-limits. Next best bet would be a pediatrician or even a grief therapist. Now that she had a nanny, she could consult one, but what was she supposed to tell Tad at this very moment?

"Woof?" came his little voice, sounding curious but not tragic, and she was saved.

"Woof? Oh my *goodness.*" She couched her relief in exaggerated excitement as she started down the road. "That little dog on the wall?" It was a painting in Tad's bedroom. He used to wave at it when he walked by, but it hadn't occurred to Jamie to take it along. "Good *thought,* Taddy. We'll have to get him another day, because right now we are going for a nice, healthy run and then," with drama, "to a *puppet show.*" The show was held every Sunday on a green several towns over. Jess had never taken him, which was partly the point. It would be a new memory with minimal connection to things Jamie couldn't discuss, like death.

I'm glad June signed on, Chip e-mailed that evening. *She's motherly and mobile. Give her a car seat and she'll take Tad to kids' programs in the area. Are you nervous about leaving him?*

Oh yeah, he did get it. *VERY,* she wrote back in caps. *It's easy to leave him with a sitter for a few hours when he's sleeping, but leaving him for the whole day, mostly awake, is something else. But I don't have a choice. I have to work. BTW, what pediatrician do you use?*

Jake Babineau. He's with Williston Medical Associates, in the center of town. He went into private practice after a stint at Children's, so his qualifications are good. I like his way with Buddy. And he's good with me, too. He's alarmist enough to take my alarms seriously, but not so alarmist that he makes me alarmed. Does that make sense?

Absolutely, she typed with a smile of relief. *And I appreciate the vote of confidence, since he's the one Jessica used. Tad saw him right after he turned two, so he's not due again for a while, but I need some advice. He's asking for his parents more, and I don't know what to say. Does Buddy ask for his mother?* Jamie still didn't know the details of that. Several of the local articles, like the one announcing Chip's teaching appointment, mentioned his son, but only in passing.

He didn't used to. When he was little he didn't know that having a single parent was any different from having two. He's started asking now because some of his daycare friends talk about their moms. I tell him his mom loved him but can't be here. He seems satisfied with that for now. Each time he asks, I get nervous and think this is it, I need a better answer, but his mind moves on to something else pretty quick. Babineau says when he's ready to handle more, he'll ask more. He tells me not to push the issue.

Hadn't Tad's mind moved on to something else back at the house? Normal, then. She felt less guilty for having happily evaded the truth.

Does Buddy ever see her? Jamie wrote.

They had been e-mailing back and forth so steadily that she guessed he had to be sitting with his laptop the way she was—okay, maybe not curled up in a corner of the sofa . . . maybe, actually, in bed wearing nothing. *That* was a frivolous thought. The relief at being able to talk so freely with him was making her giddy.

He was slower to reply this time. Fearing she had overstepped and thinking that she could not afford to alienate a friend who was an amazing resource, she was about to apologize when his answer arrived.

No. She basically gave birth and handed the baby to me. She didn't want any part of either one of us. It's pretty sad when you think of Buddy, but once I embraced (haha) the terror of being a father, I was fine with it. She and I were together one night. Neither of us wanted more. We came from different places and were heading different places. She told me she was protected, so I thought it was over and that I'd never see her again. Turns out she didn't believe in birth control any more than abortion.

Would you have wanted her to abort? Jamie wrote back and instantly wished she hadn't. She feared she had overstepped here, too.

But this was what friends did, wasn't it? Okay, she had no close girlfriends to judge by, and Chip was male, but did that matter? If he didn't like the question, he could just not answer.

He did, albeit taking a little longer again. *I want to say no. But at the time, I wasn't sure I could take care of myself, much less a child. I had just finished college—slightly late, but I finally did finish—and I didn't know if I'd be any good as a phys ed teacher. I had to do a practicum to get my degree, but the school arranged that. I didn't know if I'd get a job on my own. Some of my past was, well, out of control. I think the only reason Williston gave me a chance was because I grew up here.*

Jamie figured that might have been part of it, but his e-mails were intelligent, his manner at the playground smooth. He had been something of a local hero before losing focus in the pros. He had charisma; she felt it herself.

That said, he was clearly haunted by his past. *Do you worry she'll show up someday?*

If she does, I'll just have to deal. At some point, Buddy may want to know her, and I'll have to let him. You're lucky that way. You may have inherited Tad with no prep time, but at least he'll grow up with a mom and a dad. I hear your fiancé is a nice guy.

Without conscious thought, she let her fingers fly. *Poor guy is pretty upset with me right now. I haven't had time to plan the wedding or draw plans for a house for us, which is especially critical now that I have Tad, who has taken over my office, meaning that I have no place to work, which is* especially *crucial since I won't be able to work the kind of long hours at the office that I used to or even be able to travel—I've barely thought about that. Sorry. Just broke out in a cold sweat. Must be a panic attack.* She sent it off before she could think twice.

His reply came quickly. *Want to talk? What's your number?*

She sent it. Her phone rang seconds later. Caller ID didn't identify him, but the timing would have been too coincidental for it to be anyone else. So she picked right up and said an embarrassed "Hey. I'm sorry. I didn't mean to lose it like that."

His voice was kind. "Think I didn't lose it at the beginning? Think I still don't?"

"Yeah, I think that. You seem totally on top of things."

"At the playground, sure. Sports are what I do."

"Do you miss hockey?"

"I teach it summers."

"I mean playing professionally."

"No. That became lethal for me. Do you still play tennis?"

"I call my old pro once in a while, but then I get out on the court with him and it isn't fun like it was. I'm totally out of shape."

"I can't believe that."

"I'm so bad now there's no way I'd ever win a match."

"But you're not playing matches."

"Tell that to my competitive self. It thinks I need to win and gets really, really upset when I serve into the net or hit one out. 'Course, I won't have time to do even that now that I have Tad. Tell me the parental panic gets better."

"It gets better."

"Are you just saying that because it's what I want to hear?"

"No. It does get better."

"I hope so." She took a deep, steadying breath and glanced in surprise at the clock. They had been going back and forth for an hour, and though only the last had been voice to voice, it had calmed her. "I should let you go. But thank you. I'm totally grateful for June's name."

"Any other questions, just text."

She gave a self-deprecating laugh. "You may come to regret that."

"Only if you tell the other moms. I try to keep this number to myself."

It was a warning. She held up a hand he couldn't see. "It's safe with me. No friends here, remember? But actually I do have another question. Toddler bed or twin?"

"Twin. Tad's tall. He'll outgrow a toddler bed in a year, and then you're stuck buying another. I suppose you can afford that."

"Maybe in terms of money, but not time. Twin it is. Thanks, Chip."

"Charlie," he corrected.

"I really like Chip."

"I don't."

"Okay. Charlie." She had to give him this, since he'd given her so much. "Thank you. Have a good Monday."

As the new week approached, Caroline was frustrated on three counts.

The first involved Jamie, who hadn't returned with Tad. No, Caroline hadn't called to invite them, but, having agonized over pros and cons until she was a tangle of nerves, she believed that Jamie had to be the one to reach out. Since she was the one laying the groundwork for a core family of her own, she needed to show Caroline her place in it. The idea that showing involved not calling or coming over sent Caroline into a tailspin.

The second involved Theo, who called often enough that Caroline was becoming unsure of her role. He seemed to want her in on discussions that went well beyond holding his hand. He was asking her opinion, as if she were in management, and, bottom line there, she didn't know what she was doing.

The third involved Dean, *Gut It!,* and work that perhaps, just perhaps, she shouldn't be doing. Over the years, she had made a practice of spending time with the homeowners well in advance of a taping, her belief being that for an unscripted show to flow, the major players had to be fully comfortable with each other. She had set a date with the Millers weeks before and might have canceled if Dean hadn't offered to go with her. They agreed not to mention a host change. But if the change went forward and Caroline's on-screen time was reduced, Dean would be able to fill in. Well beyond that rationalization, though, his presence was a comfort. Seeming to understand that she was feeling fragile, he kept his hands to himself when they were with the Millers and limited himself to a brief touch now and again when they were not. For the Caroline who was starting to look at his hands as sensual tools, starting to realize that he smelled like a river banked with pines, starting to wonder, still and again, whether he had lost interest, and if not when he would make his move, it was frustrating as hell.

So by the time Monday morning arrived, she was looking forward to doing her own work in her own garage with her own tools.

But the day started badly. When she went to the MacAfee shop to pick up the dowels that had finally arrived, she found herself disconcertingly aware of the men. Five were there. She had worked with each at one time or another. They were physical guys in a physical trade, which meant that on a virility scale of one to ten, all were seven or above.

Irrelevant, she told herself, but that didn't stop her from noticing things she didn't usually notice, like shoulders and chests. She even darted covert glances at a fly or two while she reviewed a stack of invoices relating to her work.

It was unsettling. Maddening, actually. She wasn't about to jump any of them, but after spending a lifetime of blending in with the guys, what she saw now made her feel very different from them.

Angry that Dean had awakened her to this, she grabbed her dowels, strode back to the truck, and was heading home to the sanctity of her garage, where she could work with no one to ogle, when Theo called.

"Can you come to the office?" he asked. He didn't sound imperious—Roy's death had scraped away that rough outer layer—but he remained firm.

Caroline released a disappointed breath. "Now?"

"Please. We have a Barth problem."

Oh dear. "Another one?" The first was the all-too-visible Dutch Colonial on the corner of South Main and Grove.

"Actually, a second and third."

"Where?"

"One is a small frame near the town line. They can do what they want with that one, but the other is the Italianate in the center of town."

A large house with a belvedere tower and arched windows, the Italianate was in as prominent a spot as the Dutch Colonial. "The Ellwells' house? Why did we not know it was on the market?"

"That's what we have to discuss," came the rasping reply, and she agreed. Totally aside from whether she should be in on those discussions, her competitive edge went on alert.

Pulling into the first driveway she came to, she turned around and headed back into town. She arrived at Theo's office to find Brad and Dean already there. Dean shot her a quick look to say that he was as puzzled by his presence as she was.

"Where's Jamie?" Theo asked Brad.

"She's not in yet. She had a new nanny coming. I'm sure she wanted to get Tad settled before she left. Her assistant knows to send her up as soon as she arrives."

Theo grunted. He looked from face to face. "I don't know what happened. We should have known about those other two houses."

"Roy would have picked up on them," Caroline said gently. "That's why we need to hire someone to fill his spot."

"No. This goes beyond marketing. It's about being part of Williston." He glowered at Dean. "That's why you're here."

"I was wondering," Dean rolled it right back. "I'm not family."

"But you know Williston as well as anyone here," Theo argued gruffly. "Have you not heard the rumors about Barth projects—framers defecting, plasterers stolen?"

"From us? Nope. Our guys are loyal. I'd guess the Barths are smart enough to use their own people. They start poaching our guys and they'll be in trouble."

"You can make that happen?"

"Oh yeah. Anyone who defects can kiss good-bye any hope of ever working with us again. Besides, the lumberyard knows me. One word, and Barths'll find their stuff on backorder. I'm guessing they'll use their own resources there, too, but I can spread the word. Once our guys know to look, they'll report back anything fishy."

Theo grinned. "And that, my man, is why you're here. You're the central clearinghouse when it comes to local subs."

Caroline chuckled, thinking the term was apt.

Dean tossed a chin her way and asked Theo, "What's she?"

"She's family."

"So is Dana," Caroline said, referring to MacAfee's in-house Realtor, "but she isn't here."

"She doesn't deserve to be," Theo groused. "She does fine when clients come to us, but she knows nothing about reaching out, and she doesn't know Williston. She doesn't live here. She doesn't even *like* the town. Send her over to Fiona's to schmooze and she sits alone in a booth eying her salad like it's crawling with bugs. She does more harm than good."

Caroline might have disagreed out of family loyalty; Dana MacAfee Langham was the daughter of Theo's long-dead brother. But Theo was right. Dana was off-putting. "Have the Barths affiliated with a Realtor here?"

"Don't know."

"We'd better find out," Caroline reasoned. "It's all well and good for Dean to sabotage the Barths while they're trying to build, but it'd be better if they had nothing to build in the first place. There are a couple of terrific Realtors in town who have an ear to the ground."

"If that's so, why didn't we know about the Italianate?"

"Because those Realtors aren't beholden to us. One of the best is a friend of mine." From the nail shop, but Theo didn't need to know that. "Would you consider putting a nonfamily Realtor on the payroll?"

Before he could answer, Jamie rushed in. Closing the door behind her, she slipped into the only free seat. "Sorry," she told Theo. "I just got the message. What's up?"

Jamie tried to focus while Brad filled her in, and again when Theo argued the pros and cons of *Family Builds,* but her pulse was racing from the dash to work and refused to settle down. The morning had been a nightmare from the get-go. Tad threw a tantrum when she put him in his SpongeBob T-shirt instead of the Handy Manny one he had worn the day before. "Hannymanny want Hannymanny," he kept crying, but Handy Manny was in the hamper with chocolate pudding streaks on the front. She pulled off SpongeBob, pulled on Bob the Builder, pulled off Bob the Builder, pulled on Diego. "Not dis not dis," he yelled until he saw Jake and the Never Land Pirates, but then he wanted her to read him the board book while she was trying to shower and dress. "June will read any book you want," she promised him through the mirror as she tried to cover her freckles, a hopeless task what with sweat from nerves. Tad either picked up on her nerves or wanted his mommy and not a nanny, because he took one look at the woman who walked in the door and, in a burst of tears, clung fiercely to Jamie, which meant that when she finally pried him off, she had to change her skirt—because she had tripped carrying his cereal bowl to the sink and forgotten to clean up the puddle, which Tad must have played in while she showered.

He was still crying when she left. She felt like the meanest mother in the world.

And now this meeting. Again she told herself to focus, but her specialty was design, not management, and, being so far behind in her own work, she didn't know why she was there. Brad must have seen that she was upset, but he didn't so much as squeeze her hand.

Caroline saw. Caroline knew. Jamie sensed both, but she was still startled when Caroline suggested that they needed to hire not only an experienced marketer and a Williston-based Realtor but another architect.

"Why?" she asked, feeling a chill as she faced her mother across a terrifying chasm.

"Because one-third of your team is retiring, which means you'll be the senior architect in your pod, and you could use the help."

"I'm fine," Jamie insisted and told herself it was true. But by the time she finally got back to her desk, she was alone with a lineup of folders that had her approaching panic.

When a hand touched her shoulder, she jumped.

"Are you really fine?" Caroline asked quietly, hunkering down beside her chair to keep their conversation private. As empty as Jamie's pod was just then, the two other pods were filled.

"I will be once I get some work done. Believe it or not, Mom, my clients want me, not someone else."

"You were offended."

Jamie hadn't called it, but yes, she was offended. Trust Caroline to home in on that. She had always been attuned to Jamie's feelings. Add a negative overlay, though, and you had Caroline seeing a Jamie who couldn't do her design work, or plan a wedding, or be a good mother without losing it over a dirty T-shirt, and therefore couldn't *possibly* take over as the host of *Gut It!*

Feeling a wave of anger, she was trying to think how to respond without provoking an all-out confrontation when Caroline said, "You've been telling me for a while that once Malcolm retires, you'd need to hire someone else. Why not now?"

"Because Malcolm hasn't retired yet."

"He's not even working half time, and most of what he does do is from his retirement place in Vermont. He's rarely in the office. He'd probably be relieved to have an excuse to clean out his desk."

That desk was perfectly neat, proof that the man wasn't around. Jamie's intern's desk was messier, though the woman was currently at a site rechecking specs.

"Yes, I know your clients want you," Caroline said. "I don't blame them. But why can't you be the name designer and the brain power behind a project while a new hire does the follow-up work?"

"Because," Jamie said as she swiveled to face her mother, "that isn't how it works. A good architect won't want to play second fiddle to me. (A) she'll want to work with her own designs so that she can build her own name, (B) if she's fully licensed, she's probably older than me, and (C), given (A) and (B), if she isn't a MacAfee, she'll feel threatened."

Caroline made a dismissive sound and stood. "The family thing has to change. We need a real estate agent, we need a marketer, we may well need a CEO if something happens to Theo, so what's one more architect? Okay, if you don't want to bring in a new person, what about shifting work around? We have two other design teams already on staff. Let them help."

Jamie told herself that her mother cared. But if she did—if she had a *clue* what Jamie was facing with Brad, with Tad, with her own insecurities—she wouldn't be harping on this.

"You think I can't do my job," she said.

"Which job are you talking about?" Caroline asked. "Seems to me you're working three right now." Her eyes softened along with her voice. "You don't have to do this all on your own, Jamie. When you were a singles star, it was just you out there on the court facing an opponent, and it had to be that way. But this doesn't. No one expects you to do everything yourself. There is nothing wrong with delegating."

Jamie barely heard. She was stuck back on *three right now.* Those three jobs would be as an architect, a mother, and what else? A wife-to-be? Maybe. More likely, though, a player in *Gut It!* Caroline hadn't specifically mentioned the last, but it was right there, under the skin like a burr. The message for Jamie, of course, was that if she couldn't handle the other aspects of her life, she shouldn't take on the show.

"I've got it, Mom. I'm on it. Trust me."

When Caroline folded her arms, Jamie glanced at her desk. She could have sworn the pile of folders had swelled since last she looked. She badly needed to work, which meant her mother had to go. But a hint of lily-of-the-valley hung in the air. Jamie didn't want to find comfort in it, but did.

In the next instant, the comfort dissolved. "Has Claire called?" Caroline asked. Her tone was too neutral.

"Not today. I think she got the point."

"Which was?"

"That I want her to back off."

"She won't. You know that."

Choking up with so much else on her plate, Jamie whispered, "I can't talk about this."

Caroline eased back. "But you did get a nanny."

"Yes." A breath of relief for both June and the return to safer ground.

"Thank goodness."

"Do you like her?"

"She seems great."

"Does Tad like her?"

"He didn't this morning. He was screaming when I left, but he stopped. I checked while I was driving here. She was taking him to story hour at the library."

"That's nice," Caroline remarked, seeming sincere. "How's he doing otherwise?"

"Who knows? He can't verbalize much. He wakes up crying in the middle of the night, needing to be held. He misses his parents." Jamie glanced at a clock on the desk. "I keep wanting to call the nanny."

"She has your number, doesn't she?"

"God, yes. Cell number, office number." *Your* number, she might have added, because it was right there on the list.

"Then you're good."

"Good" lasted until Jamie got home from work and found June Flores in tears. Something was terribly wrong.

sixteen

"What *happened*?" Jamie asked. She was trying to imagine what it might be, but the only thing that registered was Tad crouched on the floor putting Little People on a yellow school bus. He was clean and content.

But June was already gathering her things together. Bad news had come from El Salvador, she explained in an accented voice that was broken by tears. Her mother had died. She had to go home.

Jamie sucked in a breath, feeling the shock of Roy's death again. "Sudden?" she asked.

It was. Barely seventy and in perfect health, the woman had suffered an aneurism and died instantly. "I'm so sorry," Jamie repeated with each new bit of information, but it wasn't until she asked when June expected to return that the extent of the situation hit. As fate had it, June's father was the one who was chronically in poor health. With her mother gone and two brothers living on the other side of the country, June would have to be his caretaker in San Salvador. Having raised her own children in the United States, she would return to visit but not to work.

Jamie understood. She wouldn't have expected any different from a kind and caring woman. Digging out money, she paid June for a single day and smiled when the woman told her how sweet Tad was. Within minutes, though, June was gone and panic set in.

What to do what to do what to do?

Stay calm, Jamie told herself, but she was back at square one, with no names on a nanny list and only slightly more than zip accomplished that day at work. Maybe her mother was right. Maybe she did need help.

Grabbing her phone, she called Chip. "It's Jamie," she said the instant he picked up, "and this is probably a terrible time. Are you at the playground?"

"We're on our way home. I can talk. You don't sound so good."

Hearing his voice made her feel better. With only a handful of words, he sounded like he cared, like he *wanted* to talk. It was invitation enough.

"June's mother died today, so she's moving back to El Salvador. She was terrific, Chip. I called a couple of times because Tad was sobbing this morning when I left, but she was totally on top of things. I know it was only one day, but she was a lifeline, and now she's gone, and none of the others want weekdays." She paused. "You still there?"

"Still here," he said. "Keep going."

She tried to rein in her voice. She was a grown-up. "This is so wrong of me. Her mother died. I should be more understanding than anyone. I do feel bad for her. I have no right to feel abandoned."

"You have every right. You need child care."

Soothed, she spoke more rationally. "My gut tells me I should stay home for a while to bond with Tad. I also need to look for a new place, because my condo is *so* not going to work long-run. Only I'm falling so far behind at work that it could start reflecting on the company"—not to mention proving to Caroline that she *couldn't* handle things—"so I need a sitter for tomorrow. But if that person won't nanny, I'll have to find someone else, and isn't it worse to be passing Tad around? I'm thinking daycare, but honestly I can't bear the thought of spending tomorrow scoping them out, and I don't even know what to look for. You like First Unity, right?"

"I do."

"Then I'll call First Unity, but is there an application process? How long before he can start, and is it a problem if he isn't toilet trained—no, of course not, if they take babies," she thought aloud, "but will they even have room for him?" Meekly she added, "What do I do?"

"What you do," he replied, "is meet me at First Unity in ten minutes. Know where it is?"

"Yes, but it's too late in the day, isn't it?"

"It's a daycare center. They're open till six. That gives us twenty minutes."

"But it's such a bad time for you."

"Did I say that?" No. He hadn't. "Are you game?"

"I'm game," Jamie said before he could change his mind. "Ten minutes. See you there." She hung up, grabbed Tad, and raced out to the car.

There were only four children left at the daycare center, so Jamie didn't see the place in full operational mode. But three of those children were cleaning up a finger-painting project under the guidance of one patient teacher, the other teacher was cuddling a one-year-old who looked tired, and Chip was amazing. He introduced Jamie as a friend, and though there would normally be an interview with the center's director before accepting a child, he made it happen without. Granted, he exaggerated the critical nature of Jamie's work, and when he insisted that Tad wouldn't be a problem, it was like he knew the boy really, really well, which he did not. He also made sure, albeit in a subtle way, that the women knew what a coup it would be to have a MacAfee child enrolled.

"That was easy," he told Jamie when they walked to the car shortly after six. His was a Honda Pilot, parked behind her SUV.

Looking up at him to respond, she felt a spasm of shyness. He was tall and broad-shouldered, his sunglasses hung on the neck of his shirt in a way that showed a sprinkle of dark hair, and those blue eyes held hers. They were powerful, direct, *interested*—which, of course, she was seeing because she needed to feel the connection, which was probably not appropriate, but what was a single minute of make-believe?

Gathering her composure, she smiled. "*So* easy. Thank you. You went above and beyond. I'm sorry you had to bring Buddy back here again after you'd already picked him up. Did he not mind?" That Buddy was with Tad in the play yard, rather than hanging on Chip, said something.

Chip's lips twitched. "Oh, he minded. He counts on having his nights with me. I told him that if he came without a fight, I'd take him to Town House of Pizza for dinner."

"That's bribery."

"It works every time." He cupped his mouth. "Buddy!" He waved him in. "Bring Tad."

Jamie watched as Buddy reached for Tad's hand. He seemed to be a totally obedient child, certainly not like the Tad she had seen that morning. "When you say he 'minded' coming back here, how did he let you know?"

"Verbally. And physically. He started kicking the seat in front of him, *bam-babam-babam-babam.*"

She might have laughed at the way he said it, nodding sharply with each *babam,* if she hadn't been heading somewhere with her question. "Is he often physical?"

"Oh yeah. I'd say it's a boy thing, but I've seen girls get pushy and shovey on the playground when they don't get their way. The thing is, girls have an option. They can mouth off. Boys don't have that gene, so they kick." He tipped his head, ducked it, and asked a cautious "What did he do?"

The way he guessed her point—the way he asked—was adorable. She really liked Chip. Not caring in that instant whether it was appropriate or not, she related the T-shirt drama. "I was rushing to get ready for work and praying that June would actually show up, so I'm sure he felt my nerves, but when he continued to scream, I just yanked off one T-shirt after another. I mean, there was no finesse. How do you *deal* in a situation like that?"

He had long since straightened, and while he should have been studying her as if she were a pathetic mommy wannabe, there was no censure. His eyes were warm. They were appreciative. He liked her, too—and that meant a lot to her. From the corner of her mind came a whispered *tsk tsk,* but she was needy enough to ignore it.

"Sometimes not very well," he replied.

"What do you mean?"

"I lose it, just pick him up and put him in his room."

"Time out."

"Not that it's a solution if you're on the clock and have to get to work. Then I go with the two-choice rule. Two shirts, which do you want. Two sneaks, which do you want."

"What do you do if he refuses the choices?"

"Use force. I just put one of the damn shirts on him, usually the one I know he likes least, which is the pissed side of me coming out." Self-conscious, he scratched the back of his head. "So I get my satisfaction, and he learns that a little choice is better than none." He dropped his hand. "Kids this age want control, but they don't know how to make decisions. I can't tell you how many parents I hear offering choices their kids can't possibly make."

"Like?"

With a quick little jerk of his eyes, he lowered his voice. "That mom picking up the little girl over there just asked a wide-open 'What do you want for dinner?' That kid is probably eighteen months old. How in the hell does she know the choices, much less know which one she wants? Two choices. That's more than enough. You have to teach them a little at a time."

Jamie was charmed. "Did you learn that in college?"

"I wish," he said with a self-conscious snort. "No, I learned it by making every mistake first. I'm good at making mistakes."

If it was a reference to an earlier life, she didn't think it fit. "You're very good at parenting."

"Brilliant in hindsight. I've already been through what you're going through now, so I've mastered that stage. Now I'm muddling through the next one. Parenting is a work in progress. It never ends." He smiled crookedly. "I think I did get that from one of my ed courses. It's more profound than I am." He put a hand on Buddy's head. "Ready for Town House?"

"Yeah," the boy said enthusiastically.

"Join us?" Chip asked Jamie, but in that instant, leaning down to lift Tad, she dropped the daycare papers. She might have blamed it on being flustered at the prospect of dinner with Checker Chip, if she hadn't had such a history of fumbles.

Embarrassed, she knelt to gather them up. Chip was right down there with her.

"Sorry," she muttered. "Multitasking is always a challenge. I'm not the most coordinated being."

"I find that hard to believe," he said and passed her the papers as they stood. "I watched a tape of your last big match on YouTube."

She was ridiculously pleased. "You did?" Chagrin followed. "I lost."

"Daddy." A whine.

"In a sec, Bud," he told his son, then said to her, "You're very pretty to watch."

She was beyond ridiculously pleased. The way he was looking at her made her breath hitch. She had to swallow before she could say, "Was. But thank you."

"Mamie," Tad piped up, echoing Buddy's whine.

She took his hand. "I was eighteen then and totally focused. Real life is not that way."

"No." He eyed her, questioning. "What do you say? Town House?"

She wanted to go, *really* wanted to go, which confused her. She liked Chip a lot. Did that mean he was a good friend, like a girlfriend, only male? She worked with men all the time and considered many of them friends. This was different. She found Chip exciting—yes, because he had answers, and because he understood what she was going through, and because having a friend was a novelty for her, but also because he had strong hands, broad shoulders, and hips that could move in a purely male way. When he looked at her with those riveting blues, like he was doing now, she felt something deep inside.

Okay. So it was just a pizza place. But if they were seen together, word would spread, and though groups of parents and kids ate there all the time without sexual overtones, she wasn't feeling totally innocent in that regard. And it wasn't just her. She might not be as experienced with men as Chip had to be with women, but she knew enough to know when a man was interested, and he was. She would have been shocked by that alone even aside from the fact that she was engaged to Brad.

"It's not a big thing," he finally said.

"It *is*," she insisted and let her eyes say more, "but I should probably go home." It was safer that way. She couldn't focus when she was with him, but she needed to think about being engaged to one man and attracted to another. "I can't thank you enough, Chip."

"Charlie."

She blinked, laughed. "Sorry. I have this fixation on Chip—oh God." She felt her cheeks heat. "That so did not come out right. Chip is habit, okay?"

"Change it," he said, but she caught the edge of a smile on his cheek as he strode off with his son.

Jamie's confidence lasted until Tad was in bed and she was in the kitchen filling out daycare papers, at which point she took an objective look at what she was doing. In the panic of June's leaving and the nonexistence of replacements, she had rushed to the daycare option. Now she wondered whether she had been rash, whether Tad would get the same kind of care outside the home, whether the social experience of daycare would compensate for the lack of one-on-one attention a nanny could give.

She might have called to ask Caroline's opinion. But Caroline thought she should hire another architect and step back from the everyday grind, and Jamie wasn't ready to do that. It would take her out of the competition.

She might have called to ask Brad's opinion. But he had made it clear that he wouldn't have one. Besides, she wanted to put some distance between them. When she focused on him, she was angry. Their relationship had gone off the rails, and if he didn't see that—if he didn't care enough to come to her to discuss it—if he couldn't finally step up—if he was so *spineless* that he couldn't act, they were done.

That left Chip. But there was no need to call. She knew where he stood on the daycare issue, and she trusted his judgment. He taught kids. He would know what was best. Besides, she couldn't keep running to him every time something went wrong. She had to behave like a grown-up.

Her resolve lasted into Tuesday, when she dropped Tad at the center. It remained when one of the teachers called to say that he had begun crying inconsolably when asked to nap without Moose, prompting a truncated client meeting so that she could run home, get the stuffed animal, and drop it off. When she picked him up at the end of the day and smelled a nasty diaper, she reasoned that he might have done it seconds before climbing into the car rather than hours before, and when, the next morning, he didn't want to leave the house, much less leave the car when they reached the center, she told herself it was the strangeness of it all.

When she went for pickup late that afternoon and read the note that accompanied him, though, she lost it.

Head lice.

Two days into daycare, and Tad had been exposed to *head lice.* All parents were being advised to take precautionary measures, and while the note outlined what those would be, Jamie was too horrified to take them in. Stomach churning, she picked up the phone and punched in a number she now knew by heart.

"Guess who," she said the instant she heard Chip's voice. "I swore I wasn't going to keep calling you, but the idea of lice is freaking me out." She heard crying in the background. "Are you treating Buddy?"

"Against his wishes." His voice angled away. "The sooner we do this, the sooner we go back out." He sounded frustrated. Perversely, that made her feel better. Returning to Jamie, he said, "This isn't the first time a note's come home, so I have shampoo enough for ten. I'm at 403 Beech. Feel free to come." As the crying grew, he angled away again.

"Hold still and it *won't* get in your eyes." Then he was back. "Gotta go." He clicked off.

Beech was a rangy street that wove through meadows on the west edge of town. There was none of the dense greenery of Caroline's neighborhood or the sleekness of Jamie's condo, just a modest mix of houses, the spread of a tall tree on each acre, and lots of grass. Other than an occasional truck, the driveways held family cars.

Chip's home was a bungalow in the Craftsman style, shingled in weathered gray with black trim. A single wide dormer broke through the front roof above a generous overhanging eave. Beneath it was a white-slatted front porch braced by columns anchored in stone. The windows were multipaned above, single-paned below. The front door was wood and wide open.

Carrying Tad for the sake of expediency, Jamie climbed the steps and rapped on the jamb. "Hello?" she called and, shading her eyes, peered through the screen.

Buddy came running, wearing only shorts and a headful of damp, spiky hair. When he struggled with the door handle, she helped him out, then had to smile.

"Hey, Buddy. Your hair looks fabulous." But he was already running in the direction from which he had come, clearly having been sent to do a particular job.

"Back here," Chip called from what turned out to be the kitchen. She heard the clang of pots and the slap of a cabinet door. When she rounded the corner, he was just straightening. A dish towel draped his shoulder; overly casual hands hooked his hips.

"Were you seriously cleaning up?" she teased.

With a self-deprecating snort, he lobbed the dish towel onto the counter. "The place can be a sty. I don't put anything away that I may use again within a week." He reached for Tad and told Jamie, "There are different kinds of shampoo. I find the wet stuff easier to use. You massage it into the scalp for three minutes and rinse it off. No hair wash for twenty-four hours after that. You good?"

"I'm good."

"Okay. Here goes Treatment Number Two." He had efficiently removed Tad's T-shirt and laid him on the counter with his head over the sink before the boy could complain.

Jamie held his ankle to let him know she was there. "I could have picked up the shampoo at CVS myself, but the offer of moral support was too good to pass up." Still, she felt guilty. "Can I do that washing?"

"Do you seriously want to?"

"Uh, no."

He laughed. "Relax, then. I'm good. Close the eyes, Taddy."

When Tad scrunched up his face, Jamie braced for a scream. But he was simply . . . closing his eyes. He didn't even start crying when Chip started to scrub, not that he cried when Jamie washed his hair, but this wasn't your normal rubber-ducky-in-the-bathtub scene. Granted, his little body was stiff, but he clearly recognized authority.

Show. Authority.

It was a lesson for Jamie, but for another time. For now, she was very happy to cede authority to Chip. "I couldn't get myself to check his scalp," she confessed, grossed out even now by the thought. "Did you find anything on Buddy?"

"No, but a little shampoo doesn't hurt." He was cradling Tad's head with one large hand while he scrubbed with the other. "Be grateful these guys have short hair. Long hair sucks."

"Long hair *sucks,*" came an echo from his other side.

Chip drew in an exaggerated breath. "I did not use that word the right way, Buddy. What do we suck?"

"A juice box."

"But what goes in the juice box?"

"A *straw.*"

"Correct. What else do we suck?" When no answer came, he gave a hint. "What does Nana bring?"

"Lollies."

"Bingo."

"Do you see your parents often?" Jamie asked as she watched him work. If he was at all freaked out at possibly touching nits, he didn't show it. His fingers moved with efficiency and grace.

"They have a place in Vermont for summers, so we're back and forth. Winters, Buddy and I fly south when we can."

Jamie thought of Caroline, who lived five minutes away, and suddenly it seemed ludicrous that they weren't seeing each other all the time, like at least every few days. Caroline would keep lollipops in the house for Tad. She would take him to the garage and help him make something from scraps of wood. She would be a good grandmother, once she accepted the role, *if* she accepted the role. She might have easily done it if a grandchild had come the normal way, but now, especially after the *Gut It!* fiasco?

Yes, now, Jamie thought with sudden anger. Brad wanted children to come at a more convenient time. *That is not how it works, Brad. Get with the program, for God's sake!*

"You there?" Chip asked quietly.

She blinked, smiled. "Sorry. I was just feeling a wave of envy." When he shot her a curious look, she explained, "For what you have with your parents." She wanted to tell him what was going on with Caroline, but he already knew that she was a basket case of a mother and didn't particularly want him to think she was also a dysfunctional daughter. So she asked, "What's it like traveling with a child?"

He studied her a minute longer, as if he knew she was holding back and wanted to know why. Then he simply shrugged. "Better now that I can slap on headphones and a video. When he was little, I used to chat it up with flight attendants—you know, single dad, not good at this, desperate for help, hint hint."

Jamie tried not to laugh. "Did it work?"

"Every time," he said. "When they had breaks, they'd walk him up and down the aisles. The ones my age thought it might translate into a relationship, and the moms and grandmoms just couldn't resist a cute child and a helpless dad."

A *gorgeous* dad, Jamie amended. Between that dark hair and shadowed jaw, and a T-shirt that stretched over an impressive back and pulled up enough to show just a sliver of bare skin when he reached for the sprayer, he was totally sexy.

"You're shameless," she decided.

"When necessary," he admitted. His eyes met hers in a way that gave her a jolt. She could keep telling herself that she was imagining things, that Checker Chip was way too cool to be interested in her, but she had felt it before, and the look in his eyes now revived it. For a minute she couldn't look away.

Finally, he hitched his chin toward a clean towel lying on the counter. Refocusing, she passed it over. "Are you also washing the bedding and stuff?" The instructions from the center were extensive, and as disgusting as the thought of lice remained, it was safer than dwelling on an attraction she didn't know how to handle.

"I probably should, but Buddy wasn't itching, so I'm not too worried." He sat Tad up and began drying his hair. "Almost done, bud," he said, then, in answer to Jamie, "I'll wash what he brings to the center and do pillowcases, but that's it. You can go nuts with some of this stuff. I have to obey certain rules at school, but here I follow only one."

"Which is?"

"Common sense. And moderation."

"That's two."

"They're actually the same. Think about it." He reached for a small metal tool and held it up, like evidence at a trial. "Lice comb. For removing nits that are stuck on the hair shaft. Their shafts look pretty clean—" He paused for a split second, smirked into a wry little headshake, and went on. "It's probably overkill with our guys, but since they both have short hair, it's easy enough to do." He arched her a questioning brow.

She waved a hand. "Do it. Please." But he was right about common sense and moderation. For a minute she was silent, watching him start with the comb at Tad's nape. The child's body seemed frozen, only his eyes moving sideways toward Buddy, who stood in the middle of the kitchen holding a very wrinkled booklet and looking at Jamie.

"Whatcha got?" she asked and, crouching down, took the booklet. It was worn but intact. She didn't have to look far to see that it held instructions. "Whoa. Do you have wood blocks? *Real* wood blocks? I mean, authentic, *old-fashioned* wood blocks?"

"They're my daddy's," Buddy confirmed. "He said you could make me a building."

"Buddy—" Chip scolded, but Jamie spoke over his protest.

"So cool! I would *love* to make you a building. I'm a good builder." She ignored a snicker from Chip, but couldn't quite ignore Tad whimpering her name. "I'm right here, sweetie."

"Why does he call you that?" Buddy asked.

"Mamie? Because it's close to Jamie, which is my name." She considered. "Halfway between Mommy and Jamie, maybe?" But the whimper was a warning. "Can we do blocks when your dad finishes Tad's hair?"

"How many minutes?" The boy held up three fingers. "This many?"

"That's a good guess. You know your time. Like your dad knows his rules."

"Speaking of which," Chip said when she returned to the sink, "I'll contradict myself. What is *not* common sense is that if your child gets lice it has nothing to do with hygiene. Lice prefer clean heads."

She chuffed. "Not reassuring, but good to know." Leaning back against the counter, she looked around. "I like your house."

He shot her a skeptical glance. "It isn't your usual style. I've seen the homes you build. This one's old."

"So's my mom's house, but I love going there." She actually missed it—tight spaces, vintage fixtures, and all. Her condo was starting to look different to her. Sleek and clean was just fine until you couldn't keep it sleek and clean, at which point it just didn't feel right. "When was this built?"

"Thirty-eight years ago. My parents built it when my oldest sister was born. It was a stretch. Dad didn't earn a hell of a lot—"

"Bad word!" shouted Buddy.

"You are right," Chip said quickly. "Daddy forgot. Thank you, Bud." Under his breath, he murmured, "My mouth is a problem."

Jamie didn't think it was. His lips were lean, strong, masculine.

"He managed the hardware store in town and went out on a limb for this, but it served us well. They raised three kids here. They'd have made a bundle on it if they'd sold it on the open market instead of giving it to me."

"But they must have done okay if they have two homes now." When he was quiet, looking oddly guilty, a light went off. "Ah. You bought them those."

"It was the least I could do. Rink time at six in the morning, then a full day of work? My mom was a nurse. She did the night shift three days a week so she could be home while Dad was at the store. They'd be juggling my practices while one was coming and the other going." He set down the comb. "Done." He put Tad on the floor. "Want to take Tad to the backyard, Buddy?"

"Mamie promised me blocks."

"She may not—"

"Absolutely," Jamie cut him off "Where's the best place?"

"Are you sure?"

She smiled. She was unable to think of anything she wanted more. She wasn't ready to return to the real world. "Where should we do it?"

"The blocks are in a rolling bin in the living room. You could go out to the front porch."

"Inside, Daddy."

"Okay. Dining room table. We'll eat here in the kitchen. Is chicken-broccoli-ziti okay for you?"

Jamie had Tad's hand and was reaching for Buddy's when she realized Chip was talking to her. "Oh Lord, you don't need—"

"I want. Will Tad eat that?"

She was about to protest. After everything else he had done for her, dinner went above and beyond. But here, in this escapist moment, dinner was something she wanted to do even more than build with ageless wood blocks. "He'll eat it. So will I. Thank you."

"This is great," Jamie said an hour later. Having left a facsimile of First Unity Church standing tall and proud on the dining room table, she was now sitting in the kitchen with Chip, two boys on their knees on chairs as they ate with a mix of fingers and forks, and a near-empty casserole dish. "It's the single feature I most love about Craftsman-style homes. A breakfast nook has to be the warmest family element ever."

"Unless said family is bickering, which my sisters and I often did. This nook is small."

"Cozy."

"Small. The whole kitchen is small."

She took measure of the room. "It doesn't feel that way, because the cabinetry is on the perimeter, and besides, architecture is about proportion. This kitchen is perfect for the house. I like your Shaker cabinets. And the dark floor. And these," she said, smiling as she touched Tad's milk glass. He had needed help, but the problem was only partly drinking from an open glass. The rest was his wanting, at the same time, to look at the Bugs Bunny etched on the front. Buddy had Donald Duck on his, but he had made Chip take ones with Tom, Jerry, and Tweety from the cabinet. Lining them up and comparing them had occupied the boys between bites.

"Welch's jelly jars are vintage," Jamie marveled. "Did you get these on eBay?"

"Nope. PB&Js were staples in our house."

"You mean your parents saved the jars all these years?"

"They did. I want to say it was pure sentimentalism, but they were practical people. These are the right size, and they're sturdy."

"Can I be done, Daddy?"

With a glance at the boy's mostly clean plate, Chip slid from the booth to let him out. "Good job with dinner, Bud."

Tad didn't ask, just squirmed against Jamie, clearly wanting to follow. Though she would have sat a while longer, she followed Chip's lead.

"Show Tad your room, Buddy. Go Ninja on the stairs."

"Ninja?" Jamie asked, about to follow the boys. Stairs made her nervous.

"Hands and knees. Show him how, Buddy."

When Jamie would have still gone to help, Chip caught her arm. He held up a finger and listened. There were thumps, then lighter thumps, then lighter thumps still, then ample running footsteps overhead to prove both children had made it safely.

Gratified, Jamie began gathering up dishes.

"Don't worry about those," Chip said.

She made a sputtering sound. "I'm feeling incompetent about too many things, but I can load a dishwasher." She went at it while he cleared the table. "This dishwasher looks brand-new."

"The old one died last month, but it was time." He piled glasses and utensils beside the sink. "The hot water tank is up next, and in another year, a new heating system. I want to green up the place. Appliances today are energy efficient."

After standing the last of the plates on the bottom rack, she pulled out the top. "But expensive."

"I have the money. I just have to decide whether to stay here or move."

The glasses were easily loaded. As she reached for the forks, Jamie-of-the-sleek-white-condo surprised herself by asking, "Why would you move?"

"I grew up in this house. I worry I'll grow old here. I moved back when Buddy was born, because Williston is a great place to raise kids, and my parents wanted to leave. My sisters were both living away, so the house was here. But change is good. I keep an eye on the local market. When I hear of a place up for sale, I look."

Jamie envied him this house. Even all these years later, she felt tension when she thought of her childhood home. Then, unbidden, came the image of her grandmother's Victorian lace. She had always felt connected to it, all the more so after Caroline sold the big house and settled into her own. That lace was a relic of Jamie's past. She wished she had more.

"You'd leave these memories?" she asked Chip now.

"To make room for new ones, yeah. To start fresh. There are times when I feel like I'm hiding."

"From?"

He frowned, seeming unsure for the first time. The eyes he raised held vulnerability. "Myself. My future. Taking a chance. Being able to handle a challenge without going off the deep end."

"You can handle it."

"You didn't know me before."

"I see you now." She also saw herself in that instant, felt priorities shifting. Forget being an architect. Forget starring in reality TV. "Raising a child alone has to be the greatest change in the world, and you haven't gone off the deep end. You can handle a new house."

His lips twitched. "Says the woman who could sell me one."

"Who could *design* you one."

"Well," he sighed, "it's still hypothetical. I haven't seen anything great yet. The good news is that I did well when I went pro, so when I do, I can act. My dad insisted I bank half of what I earned. The money's grown."

Squirting soap on a scrubber, Jamie worked on the casserole dish. "I could tell you about land that's just been snatched up by our competitors, but I do not want you dealing with the Barths. Whether you move to a new place or renovate this one, MacAfee Homes is a better choice."

"I take it the Barths are your rivals?"

"Lately, yes. It's a game to see which of us can sniff out houses first and preempt a sale."

"Who's winning?"

She stopped scrubbing to look up. He was leaning against the counter on the other side of the dishwasher, all dark hair, blue eyes, and amused mouth.

"It's not funny," she said. "They've scored lately. That's not good for us."

"You'll come back."

"I hope so. Williston is a transitional town. It has a huge inventory of old houses ripe for renovation or teardown. There are cycles. Every five years, a different neighborhood starts to change hands. Yours is probably on the cusp. If you wanted to stay," she coaxed as she rinsed the casserole dish, "I could draw you some nice plans."

His mouth quirked. "I'll bet you could."

"I'm good." She held out the dish.

He took it and began to dry. "I know you are."

"I'm serious."

"So am I."

"You're humoring me, Chip."

"It's Charlie. And I'm not." He paused. Looking away, he opened his mouth, flexed his jaw, closed his mouth. Then, setting down the dry dish, he looked at her again, and in that instant, with humor gone, everything changed. "I have a problem," he said in a low voice. Intense blue eyes held hers, slowly falling to her mouth, then her breasts, before rising again. Everywhere they touched, she felt singed.

She didn't move, *couldn't* move.

Catching her left hand, he fingered her engagement ring. "I don't date much, Jamie. I haven't wanted to since Buddy was born, but I'm thinking about you a lot. I need you to tell me to stop."

She couldn't speak. She could barely breathe, her hand burned so, and the burning inside was even worse.

"Tell me to stop, Jamie."

"I can't," she whispered, because she had never, ever felt what she did now, and she couldn't think with him near.

•

It wasn't until she was back in the car on the way home with Tad that she realized there wasn't much to think about. That was when terror set in.

seventeen

Six had come and gone when Caroline finally finished her meetings and went down the hall to see Dean. He sat with a mess of open folders at one of three desks in the general contractors' office. Wearing thin-framed glasses, he was poring over what she knew were either subcontractor bills or supply invoices. Using a pencil to keep track, he darted her a glance over the glasses, then returned and made several notes.

Caroline liked seeing him this way. It was a different side of him. Perversely, she liked the glasses. They made him look his age.

Sinking into one of two chairs facing the desk, she put her elbows on its arms and exhaled.

He tossed the glasses aside. "You look exhausted."

"I am. How can four hours in an office do what eight at a worksite cannot?"

"Was it tough with the Realtors?"

She shot him a dry look. "Is Dana ever any other way? She had a chip on her shoulder from the get-go because of the time. She didn't want to get stuck in rush hour traffic, even though she lives in Boston and does a reverse commute. We couldn't meet earlier, because Linda had a closing, but our only other option was waiting until next week, which I didn't want to do."

Linda Marshall, Caroline's friend from the nail shop, lived in Williston. With four children who were not only attending local schools but were involved in every sport, she was in a prime position to know what was happening in town before it happened, and she had agreed to work with MacAfee Homes in that regard. Caroline had sold Theo on the idea of hiring her, but with the stipulation that she sell the idea to Dana; hence today's meeting.

"Dana isn't happy," she told Dean now. "No matter how vehement Linda was about not wanting to touch the buyer side, Dana just didn't want to hear. She likes things the way they are and doesn't see any need for change."

"Did she come around?"

"Grudgingly. Not that I care if she up and leaves the company. My gut says Linda is worth it. She just gave me tips on two houses we may be able to buy." She slid a piece of paper his way. Coming forward, he put on his glasses to study it.

"Interesting," he said, then, "Good. I'll check them out in the morning."

Dean was vital to a preemptive buy. With a quick look, he could tell how much a property was worth and what MacAfee Homes would have to spend in order to turn it around and sell it for more. His instinct rarely disappointed—which was why Caroline refused to begin to discuss the country house he had bought. That one was doomed.

Removing the glasses, he sat back again.

"I *like* those specs," she taunted, knowing he hated them enough to wear them only when his eyes were tired, but she was tired, too, and the country house was a bad move.

"You would," he said, undaunted. "Has she picked up chatter on the Weymouth place?"

"Only vague speculation."

"That's the land we want."

"Oh yeah." Caroline closed her eyes. "I dream of developing it for

Gut It! We could have three seasons right there—a continuing saga. We've never done that. It'd be great from a marketing angle." Opening her eyes, she saw reality in Dean's sympathetic expression. "Not that I'll be around for that, and if I am, they shouldn't listen to me anyway. I'm no marketer, which is why my interviewing marketing candidates for Theo was pointless." Just prior to the Realtors' meeting, she had spent time with three potential replacements for Roy.

"Not pointless," Dean argued. "You have years of experience working with marketing."

"With Roy. By comparison, none of the people I met today felt right—and trust me, I wanted to think one of them, at least, would be better than him." Weary and confused, she sighed. "I'm no executive."

"Theo is grooming you to take over."

"You think?" She did, too. It only added to her stress. "I shouldn't be here, Dean. This isn't my job to do. Yes, I can do it. Yes, I can handle people. But I'm *so* much better with wood." Wood was easy to nail down, and being nailed down was what her life lacked right now. Without Jamie to love, *Gut It!* to anticipate, even Roy to resent, she was feeling adrift—all that even before factoring in what she was or was not with Dean. "Lately I've been a little of this and a little of that, but not a lot of any one thing. So who *am* I?"

At first, he said nothing. She knew he was thinking of Jamie—could see it in the planes of his face. To hear him tell it, all it would take was a phone call on one of their parts. But it wasn't that easy. She had said it a dozen times and wouldn't say it again.

Seeming to sense the extent of her frustration, he began pushing papers into folders and folders into a pile. "Go home, Caro," he said as he stood and scooped everything into the ratty canvas messenger bag he had been using for as long as she'd known him. "I'll pick you up there in an hour." He put the strap on his shoulder. "Wear jeans."

And oh, she knew what that meant. "No, thanks. I don't want to ride on the bike."

"Too old?" he taunted, standing right before her now.

She looked up. "Too smart."

"What if I promise to go slow?"

"On a big, burly new Harley?" She snorted her disbelief.

"What if I promise to grill us some fish?"

That stopped her. "What kind?"

"Whatever kind I can get at the market."

"I want trout," she said.

"Would that make things better?"

She was about to say that nothing would when he took her face with his free hand, lowered his head, and kissed her. She was so taken off guard that she couldn't push him away, and then so curious that she didn't want to. His mouth was firm but fluid, controlling the kiss—and then gone. He raised his head and, while intense eyes held hers, dropped his hand.

"How about that? Did it help or hurt?" he asked quietly.

"I don't know. It was too short."

A slow smile spread across his face. "Good to know." Throwing an arm over her shoulder, he walked her to the door.

Caroline showered, put on dark green jeans with a sleeveless blouse in a matching green and orange plaid, and took care to tack her hair up in a way that might survive a helmet, because she was sure that despite her objections Dean would be on the bike—and she wouldn't refuse it. She needed an escape, maybe even needed danger or risk. He must have known that, which possibly explained why he had kissed her at that moment, in that way. The kiss was actually better than expected, not because she didn't find Dean physically appealing, but because she had always found kisses either too tame, as in closed-mouth and dull, or a slobbering mess. Dean's kiss had fallen somewhere in the middle—aggressive enough without *invading*. She hadn't felt violated. And as for being too short, that was perhaps why it had been good—as in, quitting while he was ahead.

Now what? He had taken his time making his first move. She wondered if he had anything planned for tonight. She assumed he would be taking her back to his place, a doddering A-frame several towns over that he was rebuilding and would sell for a profit when it was done. In the meanwhile, he had a grill on the back lawn and plenty of grass.

Last time, he'd done a mixed grill, steak for him, chicken for her. She liked the idea of trout. But the physical stuff? Not so sure about that. She had shaved for the sake of a sleeveless blouse, not Dean, and if she slathered on more body cream than usual, it was to counter motorcycle wind. She had also worn a bra, which on a warm night she might have foregone, but the blouse definitely looked better with lift.

Waiting on the front steps, she was restless. Master soothed her by rubbing one ear and then the other back and forth against her leg. She loved this cat, loved *all* her cats. They didn't care if her breasts sagged, her neck wasn't smooth, or her hand had an age spot.

Master's purr grew louder.

No, not Master. Dean's Harley.

Lifting the cat, she put him in the house, checked to make sure her phone was in a pocket, and locked up. She was midway down the front walk when the big machine arrived with its helmeted driver on board. His jacket was black, his belt wide, his jeans faded, his boots old. He silenced the bike, kicked down the stand, and climbed off. Setting his helmet on the handlebar, he came at her with a spare one, along with a jacket from the saddlebag.

She felt an alarming excitement, so much so that she might have turned and run if he hadn't already reached her. "The jacket's lightweight," he said, "but you need leather on your arms." He rolled the helmet on her front to back, pulled the strap tight, and, with a large hand spread, jiggled it to make sure it was snug. With the face shield still raised, he brought his eyes level with hers. "You okay in there?"

She was terrified, and not of the bike, not even of how tough and male Dean looked with his dark hair mussed from the helmet and his hazel eyes direct. What terrified her was the buzz in her own body. Again she thought about turning and running, but it was really too late for that now.

"This smells new," she said of the helmet.

"It is. I got red to go with your hair." She might have said red could easily clash with auburn, if he hadn't already been holding the jacket open like a gentleman, then zipping it before she could do it herself. The jacket was snug, bringing his fingers straight up her torso, but they didn't stray, just did their job and left.

Taunting, yes—but sweet, too. He made her feel like he was taking care of her, and, given that the weight of the world was on her shoulders, being taken care of was nice. He lowered her face shield, then turned and, after putting on his own helmet, straddled the bike. When he extended a hand, she took it and swung her leg over the back.

Too old? She'd be *damned* if she was that. She knew the moves, knew to put her Chucks on the foot pegs and her hands on his hips, knew to lean into corners with him and use her thighs to hold her in place. True to his word, he didn't speed—at least not until they passed through the center of Williston and hit open road, and even then she wasn't bothered. His body protected her from the force of the wind, and the Harley was surprisingly smooth. Imagining that the weight on her shoulders was lighter for the sheer unreality of the moment, she let him do his thing—until she realized that they were headed in the wrong direction.

She tapped him on the shoulder. He slowed fractionally and tipped his head.

"Where are we going?" she yelled.

"My house," came the muffled reply, followed by a resurgence of speed, and all at once she knew *exactly* where they were going, because there was only one house that Dean owned in the boonies.

Sure enough, he turned off the main road onto a side road, then again onto a rutted drive, and here the Harley wasn't so smooth. By the time it stopped, he had gone up a steep incline, and she was holding the back of his belt for dear life.

Riding on a rush of adrenaline and relief, she climbed off and removed the helmet. Her hair spilled free, its band God knew where, but she was too gripped by the house to care. It had the bones of a Victorian, but where her own spoke of age and charm, this one reeked of the dead. She had thought it spooky when he had first brought her here, and nothing she saw now changed her mind. This late in the day, with the sun low in the west, the house was all shadowed angles and peeling paint.

Dean traded her helmet for a bottle of wine. Taking two grocery bags from the Harley's trunk, he showed her up the side steps. He had gutted the kitchen, which was some improvement from the graveyard of broken-down appliances that had taken up space here before. In their place against the wall was a cluster of tools. A large worktable sat in the middle of the room. He set the bottle and bags there, then clicked on a single bare blub.

Wondering how he was going to pull off grilled trout, she folded her arms. Yes, she felt smug, because the how of it was not her worry. She was a guest. Since she was against this purchase, nothing here was her fault. She had zero responsibility.

Seeming off-balanced by her docility, Dean said in a tentative voice, "The grill's outside. And a table and lanterns."

She nodded.

He added quickly, "Just so you know, I had a geologic analysis done to pinpoint where to dig the new well to avoid rust, and the zoning board is granting an exemption from conservation land use. Rollers are coming next week to level the road." He frowned, tapped his forehead.

"Carpenter ants," she cued.

He straightened a finger. "Right. There were two nests. We destroyed them and treated everything nearby. I've already replaced the infected wood."

"Well, then," she said lightly, "you're all set."

He remained visibly wary. "You're still mad I bought it."

She had to laugh. "I'm actually not." She had seen enough gutted kitchens to be able to picture this one rebuilt, though she wasn't telling him that. Nor was she telling him that he was adorable when he was nervous, or that she felt removed from the world here. "I'm just tired and hungry and wondering if you're seriously going to be able to produce an edible meal."

That quickly, he grinned. "Just watch."

He was true to his word here, too. While she alternately explored a lean-to that held firewood and old farm tools, wandered to the edge of the woods to listen to the *yiiiip-yip-yip* of a coyote, and returned to sit backward at the picnic table and watch Dean work, he decanted wine, made a salad, and warmed French bread on the upper shelf of a grill while the trout cooked below.

She offered to help, but he refused, even when it came to serving the food. And she was tired enough, greedy enough for care, caught up enough in a time and place that was far from reality, to let him do whatever his little heart desired.

That included cleaning up afterward, although, given the lack of a kitchen sink, the sum of the task was stuffing paper goods and plastic wineglasses in a trash bag. The air had cooled by then, and it was dark, the crescent moon a hazy smile that left the job of lighting to the lanterns' pale glow. When she heard the coyotes again, she limited her wandering to an outcropping of rocks that she had earlier skirted. Easily climbing them now, she sat facing the woods and listened. The coyotes called again, though from a distance. From an even greater distance came the drone of an airplane. Looking up, she spotted its lights against a wavering backdrop of stars. A rustle came from the woods and, farther off, the trickle of a brook that, if Dean's home inspector was correct, had overflowed its banks and flooded the house during more than one spring storm.

Thinking to shout a reminder to Dean that he would need a good drainage system *and* sump pumps, she turned to face the house. The lanterns softened its edges, but with a turret still higher than she was, it loomed dark against a darker sky. She chafed her arms, as much against the cooling air as the gloom. Spooky was putting it mildly, and that was before a large figure blotted out the lanterns and approached.

Climbing the rock, Dean settled behind her with his legs flanking hers and his hands on his thighs, arms brushing hers. She tried to transfer fear of ghosts to fear of a hungry male. But she couldn't fear Dean. Not with the way he was taking care of her, now shielding her from coyotes that were probably no threat, but who knew? Certainly not with the way he smelled of wood smoke or the warmth he brought. With so much of her life in flux, Dean was solid and physical and *there*. The real world was not.

"So, what do you think?" he asked quietly.

Like the moment, her reply was hushed. "Of the house? I think it's a big job, but it's yours, and if you want to do it, you should. I also think that what I think doesn't matter, since you've already committed to it. And," she added, layering her hands on his with a squeeze, then leaving them there because her fingers were cold and his were not, "I'm guessing you approached Jamie before you ever put money down."

He chuckled. "I did. She roughed out some sketches for me to work from." He turned his hands to surround hers. "Cold?"

"Good now. She didn't tell me."

"I told her not to. I didn't want you riled up. I figured I'd wait until I addressed some of your issues."

She angled sideways to look at him. "It shouldn't matter what I think."

He pushed her hair back with his chin. "It does."

"Why?"

"Because I trust your judgment."

"That's very sweet."

"It's very true."

His thumbs had been moving on her hands, sharing warmth as his eyes did now. Such a small movement, but oddly intimate, and Caroline didn't fight it. With the rest of her life treading water on the other side of town, she was here, with trout in her stomach, wine in her blood, and a growing curiosity.

She had barely faced forward when he circled her waist and pulled her close. Her breath caught.

"So?" he asked.

"So?" she managed. He was definitely aroused, and while the ramifications of that were clear, her curiosity kept growing.

"Do I have your approval?"

"For what?" She couldn't think straight. His forearms were inches—*inches*—from the underside of her breasts.

"Buying this place?"

"You have it," she whispered and forced herself to breathe into sound. "Grudgingly. I still wouldn't want to be alone here in the dark."

"No." He put his mouth to her ear. "I heard voices at three this morning."

She squeezed his thighs in punishment. "You're making that up."

"I am not."

"Why were you here at three in the morning?"

"I've been sleeping here."

Bracing her hands, she looked back in surprise. "On *what*?"

"A bed."

"*Where*?"

"Uh, the bedroom?" he suggested, amused.

She hadn't gone upstairs this day. Last time had been bad enough. Now, though, the idea of a bed in an otherworldly room lent itself to certain imagery.

He smiled. "Makes you think, doesn't it." Taking her head, he faced it forward and drew her back again. This time, his hands went to her shoulders, massaging in circles.

"What were the voices?" she asked, feeling those fingers dip under the edge of her blouse.

"I assume they were ghosts." With another round, then another, his fingers went deeper.

"And that doesn't make you nervous?"

His mouth touched her ear. "When was the last time you heard of a ghost doing anything violent?"

Caroline had no answer for that, and when his fingers grazed the top of her breasts and she arched to meet them, she had no answers at all—not for why this was happening now and with Dean, or for why her body craved things that two weeks ago she wouldn't have dreamed of, certainly not for who had just moaned like that.

Closing her eyes, she focused on sensation. A distant corner of her mind knew what he was doing. It was called foreplay, and it was exquisitely arousing. The anticipation of having Dean's hands—*Dean's* hands—on her breasts was stoking a startling heat.

"Tell me what you like," he said in a hoarse voice.

"I can't," she wailed with barely a breath.

"I want it to be right."

"What you're doing is right."

"What about this?" When he went all the way to her nipple, she cried out. He snatched his hand away. Laughing, she caught it and, feeling like a wild thing, pressed it to her while she scrambled not-so-gracefully around to straddle his lap.

"Now do it," she breathed against his mouth, and while she looped her arms around his neck, he explored her breasts, her belly, even the notch between her legs. And she touched him, *touched* that erection, which was all the more impressive in her hands. The fact that she wasn't embarrassed was as stunning as everything else. She didn't know this creature she had suddenly become, which was as liberating a fact as the distance from home, the wine, the dark, and Dean's obvious need.

But the creature was real. The fire inside her was real. No nineteen-year-old virgin, she knew exactly what she wanted, and with that realization, something snapped. Suddenly, she had no patience. She needed more, needed it all.

"I want you in a bed," Dean gasped and in seconds managed to get them down from the rock. Holding her fast to his side, he crossed the grass in rapid strides and half-ran into the house and up the stairs. Ghosts? Caroline couldn't *begin* to think of ghosts with the way he was touching her, removing clothes, laying her on the bed and following her down. He took care to make sure she was ready, but she didn't need his fingers there to tell her. She felt the wetness. And she wasn't embarrassed. This was what being a woman was about. Besides, she needed him too much to be embarrassed. The creature she was—the one *he* had created—was hungry for everything she had pretty much forgotten.

Later, she would remember, time and again, that single first moment when he was fully inside. For now, it was about climbing hotter and higher until he brought her to orgasm, then let himself follow.

For a time, there in the dark of a bedroom that she would later learn had rotted walls, moldy rafters, and no furniture other than a king mattress on its frame, the only sounds were of shortened breath and stunned laughs.

"Who knew?" Dean finally asked against her hair. His voice was hoarse. "A wild woman. Where's she been all this time?"

Burrowing close, an arm across his chest, Caroline smiled. "Minding her own business. Well, at least, some woman was. I have no idea where this one came from. Actually, I do. You taunted her into existence."

"Taunted?"

"A look here, a touch there. It took you long enough to get to the main event."

"And whose fault was that? You didn't say a freaking *word,*" he protested. "Did you invite me over and open the door wearing something skimpy and black? Did you promise not to sue for sexual harassment? Did you say you *wanted* this?"

"I said your kiss was too short."

"Yes. You did."

"Did you plan on this happening tonight?"

"No. I only wanted to get you away. You've been down."

"*Some* woman was down. This one's feeling pretty good."

"So," he asked cautiously, "what do you think?"

"About?"

He pinched her hip. "This. Do you still think sex is overrated?"

Tipping her head back, she met his gaze. "You're good. I have to say that."

"Good is not great."

"Tonight you were great."

"Well, *that's* a qualified endorsement."

"Once is once. Things are always great the first time."

"I'm up for a second."

"Now? You aren't." The wild woman slid a hand down his belly and, at the same time that she wondered how she could be touching *Dean* this way, discovered that he was. Up for a second. "Oh my."

"Is that a yes?"

"No. My thighs are screaming. I'd give anything for a bath."

"No bath here. No hot water here."

"I have both at my house. Take me home."

"Only if I can stay the night."

Caroline couldn't say no. By the time they were back in her Victorian, by the time he had showered and she had kicked him out of the bathroom so that she could soak alone, by the time lotion was soothing whisker burns on her breasts and the cats were ousted from the bed so that she could slip in with him—naked, because he was, and because it was still dark, and because a part of the wild woman had survived the return trip on the Harley and was still feeling bold—she wanted to sleep skin to skin. He was a quiet sleeper, breathing just shy of a snore, and he liked contact, maneuvering so that a part of him always touched her. Though she was used to sleeping alone and liked her space, much of which was now taken by his larger-than-hers body, the connection was novel enough to be pleasant.

With the summer solstice around the corner, though, dawn woke her early. She was instantly aware of Dean—could hear and smell him even before she opened her eyes—but was still startled to see his dark head on her pillow, his large body tangled in her fuchsia sheets. She might have lingered watching him, had she not needed a semblance of normalcy.

Ignoring the protest of hips, thighs, and private spots that had been stretched to the max, she slipped quietly from the sheets and wrapped herself in the towel she had dropped by the bed the night before. She tiptoed to the dresser for a tank top and shorts and, taking care to coddle a few notoriously creaky treads, went downstairs to dress. Once she had fed the cats, checked the *Gut It!* website, and taken a shawl from the kitchen hook, she carried her tea to the porch.

The air was cool, the sun bright, the tea fragrant. Sipping it slowly, she let memories of the night drift back. None were bad. Some startled her—namely, her own hunger and forwardness. But she didn't regret what she had done. Dean had satisfied her—actually, had done way more than that. She felt good. She felt feminine. Even despite that little bit of stiffness, she felt energized.

She thought about calling Annie. *So* much to tell.

But no. She wasn't ready to tell Annie what she had done, and as for what she felt, she was barely beginning to break it down. She had been someone else last night. Where that fit into the *Who Am I?* debate, she didn't know. And yet, in spite of that, in this early Thursday morning moment, she felt strong. She might have even felt *complete,* if things had been right between Jamie and her.

If she talked with anyone, it had to be Jamie.

Suddenly, doing just that seemed urgent.

eighteen

Jamie might have woken Thursday morning with her stomach in knots if she had actually slept, but what she had done the evening before wouldn't let her. After leaving Chip's, she had driven slowly home. Determined to contain the terror she felt by acting in a deliberate and responsible way, she took her time getting Tad ready for bed, methodically read and reread him his good-night story, stroked his hair until he was deeply asleep, and all the while, she took slow breaths aimed at calming her nerves.

Leaving his room, though, she felt no different from how she had felt leaving Chip's. A truth had emerged that couldn't be ignored. Nor would it wait.

In the kitchen, she picked up her phone and called Brad. "Can you come over?" she asked softly.

"Now? I'm still at the office. There's a ton more to do here."

Much as she respected the work Brad did, time was passing. Her conscience couldn't have him choosing the office when doing the right thing meant acting now. "This is important, Brad. I'd come to you if I had a sitter, but I don't."

Her words were blunt, her tone no-nonsense. After a moment's silence, he sighed. "I'll be there as soon as I can."

Forty-two minutes later, he pulled up at the condo. The time wasn't quite long enough to say he was making a statement, though it was plenty long enough for her to suffer. There were no second thoughts. She had to do this. But with each passing minute, her sense of dread rose. The last thing she had ever wanted was to hurt Brad. Now, she didn't see how she could avoid it.

In hindsight, she would think about the lack of a kiss when he arrived and wonder if he sensed what was coming. He wasn't angry to have been drawn from work so much as wary. He slipped his hands in his pockets, seeming determined to be cool.

She thought of gesturing him in, having him sit, maybe pouring him a glass of the Pinot he liked. But that seemed inappropriate. This wasn't a social visit. He seemed to sense that when she took up a position just inside the door. There was neither a glance beyond to see the state of her condo nor a glance toward the stairs to indicate an awareness of Tad. He stood with his glasses in place, his shirt collar open, and his eyes on her as he waited for her to speak.

For a final moment, she held her breath, knowing that once she did this, there was no going back. In that moment, she felt a last tug of conflicting emotions—loyalty and hurt, compassion and resentment, even love and dislike. Had he broken the tension with warmth of any kind, she might have reconsidered. But his aloofness validated her decision.

Carefully, she removed her diamond ring and held it out. "This isn't working. I think we both know that."

He stared at the ring, then at her face. His own was as composed as when he was with clients, but she had to believe he was feeling something inside.

"I do love you," she hurried on in an effort to soothe, "but we want different things now. You need a woman who wants those things, too."

He frowned, but remained silent, and right now that was fine. Jamie knew what to say. She had enumerated all the arguments in those forty-two minutes he had taken to arrive.

"I suppose it's good to find out before we're married," she said. "I mean, maybe there are other things we see differently, things we've just disregarded because in so many ways we're right for each other. But this is a big snag, Brad. I'd say it hit like lightning, except that would be crude, given how Dad and Jess died." She considered. "Only it did."

He didn't smile, didn't nod, didn't speak. So she said, "Remember the Logans? Theirs was one of the first jobs I did for MacAfee Homes. They spent a fortune on a teardown and wanted a rebuild that was as big as the footprint would allow. I had just given them completed designs when he had a heart attack, and suddenly they needed a lifestyle change and wanted something more modest. Those original plans weren't good anymore. They had to be totally redrawn. That's kind of how I feel about us. The situation has changed. I'm not the same person I was when we got engaged."

"I am," he said, as if the problem were all her fault.

"Yes." She would take the blame if it made him feel better. "You are. But you don't like the person I am now."

"I didn't say that, Jamie, but there's the issue of honesty." His gray eyes were cutting. "You could have told me you were Tad's guardian."

"When? Tell me. I mean, I didn't deliberately keep it from you. I honestly never thought to announce it, because I never *dreamed* anything would come of it. You and I were barely dating when Tad was born, so was I going to warn you before we got more involved, like it was a disease? When Dad and Jess asked me, I was honored. I figured I'd eventually have kids of my own, and what was one more. I assumed that any man I wanted to marry wouldn't have a problem with it. I just didn't think about it again."

"It's the timing."

"I had no control over that."

"You could have told me right after the accident," he charged.

"You mean, like when the police were here?"

"The first I learned of it was when you were telling Maureen."

"Should I have been thinking about it before that? Should I have assumed Dad and Jess were *both* dead?" In a frustrated breath, she said, "Good God, Brad. Even if I'd told you six months ago, would you seriously have rejected me as wife material, just like that? *Please.* You would have thought the chances of Tad coming to me were as remote as I did." Her voice rose on a wave of anger. "Tad is an amazing little boy who is smart and cute and friendly and warm. He would make an incredible big brother for our kids." Brad's stony look gave her pause. "Ahhh. But he isn't yours. Is that it? Well, what if I hadn't been able to conceive? What if I had some problem—what if *you* had some problem? Are you saying that we wouldn't adopt a child? That you would not take in a child needing a good home and love him like your own if he doesn't have your blood? You never told me that."

"You never asked."

"Like you never asked if I was Tad's guardian?" she goaded. Yes, she wanted a fight. She wanted *some* show of passion from Brad. Calm and soothing were just fine until life demanded more.

She didn't get more from him, though, not at first. It occurred to her that his passivity was a form of punishment. He certainly wasn't making things easier for her. And that infuriated her all the more.

"Say something, Brad."

"What do you want me to say?" he finally charged. "I'm human. All I wanted was to have a *little* control over my life."

Confused, she shook her head. "Control? Have you been forced into something at MacAfee Homes that you don't want? Has being engaged to the granddaughter of the president of the company deprived you of freedom? Is the idea of one day heading a company so bad that—" She cut herself off. "Gah. This is going nowhere. There's no point in fighting." She held out a rigid hand. "Take the ring, Brad. We aren't a good match."

That quickly it was done. He took the ring, closed his hand, and without another word walked out the door.

Angry at Brad, shocked at herself, sad and relieved and worried—she just stood there in the front hall for a time. Eventually, she went upstairs, but she spent the night alternately hot and cold in a tangle of sheets, her mind too agitated to rest. Oh, she had done the right thing. She knew that in her heart. But for the right reasons? The ones having to do with Tad certainly were. But those to do with Chip? The idea that, even only in part, she had broken up with one man to be with another was so uncharacteristic that she felt like a stranger to herself.

By the time the sun filtered through the shutters and Tad shouted for her, she was dressed and waiting. For a long moment, she simply held him, a silent little monkey with his arms and legs wrapped around her. He had done the same thing the last two mornings, as though he knew something primal had changed in his life, didn't understand what, but needed grounding from Jamie. Much as she loved that, she needed grounding, too.

Setting him down, she grabbed the phone to text Caroline. Before she could, Caroline texted her.

It's time we talk.

Yes. Now. Her thumbs shook as she typed. *Can we come over?*

Of course. I'll make pancakes. Does Tad need milk?

Just water. Give us half an hour. She felt such relief, she could fly there.

I'll be waiting.

Eminently satisfied, Caroline pocketed the phone and stayed on the porch a bit longer enjoying her tea. When she returned to the kitchen, she sifted through a small index box for the dog-eared card her mother had passed down from *her* mother, who had printed the family pancake recipe in ancient blue ink. The recipe wasn't unique. Caroline figured an online search would turn up dozens like it. But knowing that her grandmother had created this card, that her mother had used it when Caroline was young, that Caroline had used it when Jamie was young and would use it now for Jamie's child—*Jamie's child*—made it worth the sentimental moments she spent thumbing through other cards in the box.

It wasn't until she had mixing bowl, skillet, and eggs on the counter that she remembered Dean, which meant that she was either totally brazen, entirely comfortable with him, or in full denial.

She raced up the stairs. "Dean! *Dean*!" He was sprawled facedown on her bed, dead to the world. Knowing that he was naked under the sheet—knowing exactly what his nakedness felt like against her and struck by the newness of it—she felt warmth suffuse her body into a blush. She shook one bare shoulder. "You have to get up, Dean. Now, right now. Jamie's on her way." When he opened an eye, seeming confused, she leaned in and said, "You have to *leave*."

He finally focused and frowned. "Why?" His voice was morning rusty.

"She's coming for *breakfast*."

"Can't I come, too?"

"No, you cannot. She's bringing Tad. *Please*. She and I have enough to talk about without this." She tugged at his arm. "You have to go now. There's no *way* the Harley would be in my driveway so early if you hadn't spent the night."

"Sure there is," he said with a lazy stretch. "Work starts early. I coulda come over."

"If you were going to work, you'd have come in the truck."

"You and I know that. She doesn't."

"Please don't argue with me right now," Caroline pleaded. "I don't want her finding you here."

"Are you ashamed of me?"

She barked out a laugh. "*That's* a joke. I'd parade you around, if it wouldn't be like rubbing her nose in my fun when she's been going through such a tough time." When she started to rise, he caught her hand.

"You had fun?"

"You know I did," she chided and, tugging free, made for the door. "But I can't have you here right now, please trust me on this. Weren't you the one who wanted me to talk with Jamie?"

"What's for breakfast?"

"Nothing for you, pancakes for Tad and her. My pancakes are beyond belief. I'll give you a rain check if you leave now." She gestured emphatically. "Up. *Please*?"

Having run out of words, she hurried down the stairs. She heard the thud of bare feet overhead as she cracked eggs, heard the shower as she whisked in flour, baking power, sugar, and salt. She melted butter in the skillet and cooked a first batch, then cooked a second with one eye on the clock—five minutes, four minutes, three minutes until Jamie was due.

"Dean!" she yelled seconds before she heard his boots. At the foot of the stairs, she raised her mouth for the quick kiss he sought. How natural it seemed, but she didn't have time to dwell on that, either.

"You owe me," he grumbled.

"I know." She pushed him to the door. "Go." She would have squirreled him out the back if there had been any other escape route for the Harley but the street. Holding her breath while he helmeted up, climbed on, and backed out—cringing as the raucous sound pierced the still of the morning—she breathed again only when the bike turned the curve at the end of the street and was gone. With a little prayer that he wouldn't pass Jamie, she hurried back to the kitchen.

Jamie was preoccupied. Along with a muddle of questions, doubts, and fear came excitement. She loved that Caroline wanted her there enough to make Great-Granny's panacea pancakes, that she wanted Tad to have them, too, and that, on some starter level at least, she had forgiven Jamie.

Right there, she had three things to be grateful for. But what she was suddenly thinking about as she backed out of the garage was the shiny red convertible in the spare bay, disappearing inch by inch as the garage door lowered. She loved that car. She hadn't planned to buy it, had actually gone shopping for a sleek two-door sedan, but one look at the convertible and something had clicked. It was flashier than any car she had ever owned, not the safest vehicle but spirited. What did that say about her—that she had a hidden wild streak, a repressed need to break out, a craving for risk?

Did she seriously *know* this person?

Roy would not have. He would have *freaked* over what his daughter was doing—and the risk she was taking with *his son*? Selfish. Shortsighted. The words echoed from their very-last-ever-on-earth talk.

But she couldn't turn back. Could. Not. Which was why she was racing across town at six thirty in the morning, while the rest of Williston was waking slowly, sipping coffee, lingering in the shower. Other than work vehicles and a lone motorcycle, her SUV had the road to itself, which meant she would get there faster. Indeed, the familiarity of turning onto Caroline's street was a lifeline. Once she parked in front of the mint-over-teal Victorian, she put Tad on her hip and hurried up the walk. The squeak of the screen was actually reassuring. And the smell of time when she stepped inside? Heaven.

"Mom?"

Caroline ran barefoot from the kitchen, stopped short, and put a hand to her heart. "Mother and child," she breathed and slowly approached. Her hair was a wavy mess, and her face blushed in a way that made her look forty, but her eyes, moist now, held adoration. Wrapping a firm arm around Jamie, she said by her ear, "We will not mention the show. It has no place in this house with us right now, okay?"

Jamie hadn't even thought about the show, and certainly couldn't think of it with Caroline's soft, woodsy scent soothing her nerves and giving her strength. "Mom," she began, drawing back, but Caroline was studying Tad.

"Oh my. A real little boy. Hey," she said softly and touched his hair. Jamie felt the warmth of the touch, but Tad just stared without blinking. "I think I know you. Aren't you Theodore MacAfee the Second?"

Those very big eyes were somber as he shook his head.

"Who, then?"

"Taddy," came the baby voice.

"The Taddy who likes cats?" Caroline asked, to which he started looking around the floor, "or the Taddy who likes pancakes?"

"Pancakes, please," Jamie inserted. "I promised him we'd eat here. Mom—" She broke off when Master meowed. Setting Tad on the floor, she waited only until he had run after the cat before turning back to her mother and holding out her left hand.

Caroline frowned. "You're shaking." She had steadied the hand with her own before she finally focused on that bare ring finger. Wide eyes flew to Jamie's.

In that instant, with this first oh-so-important disclosure, it was real. Jamie could barely breathe. "I returned it. Brad and I split."

"What *happened*?" Caroline whispered, but quickly caught herself. Cupping Jamie's face, she said, "First things first. I don't have a booster seat for Tad."

"He'll kneel on a chair. He looks like Dad. Do you hate him for that?"

Tad was on his haunches on the other side of the room, waiting for Master to come out from under the spindle legs of a lamp stand.

"I should," Caroline confessed, "but how to hate a child? He may have Roy's coloring, but he'll take on your expressions, and soon enough he'll look like himself. Besides," she gave a gritty smirk, "it's not like your father gets the last laugh. If he thought I was a withered-up old hag—"

"He didn't."

"Yes, he did. Isn't that what booting me off *Gut It!* was about?"

"You said we weren't talking about that," Jamie begged, knowing that despite this nascent reconciliation, *Gut It!* remained a huge issue. Not talking about it wouldn't make it go away, but she didn't want the intrusion of it now.

Caroline seemed to agree. She spoke more calmly. "Your father's opinion of me went way back to our marriage, so this, today, here, now, is satisfying for me. How happy do you think he is looking down from heaven to see his son at my house, chasing my cat and about to eat *my* grandmother's pancakes, cooked by me in *my* kitchen and served on a table *I* made?"

The part of Jamie that resented Roy for what he had made Caroline suffer shared her mother's satisfaction. She might have said that, if Caroline hadn't gone from bold to unsure in a breath. "I'm not equipped yet, baby. Does Tad need a bottle for his water?"

"No. He's done with bottles. Just a little water in a cup will do, since I forgot the sippy." In her rush to get out of the house, she had also left Moose, which meant she would have to go back for him before dropping Tad off, which meant she would be late for her first appointment, which she couldn't reschedule because she had back-to-backs all day, which meant she would have to postpone to another day, which wasn't good.

But she didn't care. Just didn't care. Right now, this was where she needed to be.

Her mother looked amazing—colorful, energetic, somehow soft, even when she was fired up about Roy. Not that Jamie minded the last. The anti-Roy sentiment was an ally. He would *so* disapprove of what she was doing.

Caroline took her hand and touched her ring finger much as Chip had done. The effect was totally different but no less potent. "When?"

"Last night."

"Who initiated it?"

"Me," she said, and that easily, the story unfolded. "I asked him over. He started to say he was working, but I cut him off and told him he *had* to come. I've tried to be understanding, Mom. I knew he felt wounded and left out, but finally, *finally,* we had to talk."

"About Tad?" Caroline whispered.

Jamie kept her voice low so that the child wouldn't hear. "Well, he was the catalyst. Brad can't deal with a child—doesn't *want* to deal with a child—doesn't want to deal with someone *else's* child. But Tad's mine now. This is nonnegotiable." Thinking back to the scene last night in her front hall, she was angry all over again. "Brad wants a neat little life that goes according to plan. Well, so did *I,* only that's not what I got."

Caroline touched her cheek. "I'm sorry. I know you like plans."

"But there's more, more that I didn't tell Brad," Jamie said, thinking of Chip, only Tad had returned and was looking expectantly at Caroline.

"Pancakes?" she asked him with an inviting nod, then said to Jamie, "Hold that thought," and returned to the kitchen.

Scooping the child up, Jamie followed. Once there, she set him down and opened a low cabinet. She shifted pots around until she found the one she wanted, grabbed a wooded spoon from a clay jar that held similar ancients, and showed Tad the art of drumming. "Mamie loved doing this when she was your age. See these dents? I made those." She demonstrated, handed him the spoon, and straightened. His banging was effective cover for more serious talk. "Am I a selfish person, Mom?"

Caroline was rinsing strawberries and raspberries in a colander. "For what?"

"Dumping Brad. This is a critical time for the company. Think of the meetings we've had this week. The Barths are creeping in, and we're short-handed without Dad. Brad would have grown beyond legal and moved up in time, but if he and I aren't married, there's no way he'll be CEO. Theo wouldn't want nonfamily in that position."

"Theo may not have a choice. We're running low on MacAfees." Caroline turned off the faucet and shook the colander. "Will Brad stay on now? More important, do you want him to?"

Jamie didn't know how she felt. This was all raw, and then there was the issue of Chip and what would come of that, and if something did, how comfortable Brad would feel having to see it all the time, which came back to the MacAfee Homes dilemma and whether Jamie had acted without considering the larger picture. "Do you think Brad has what it takes to be CEO?"

Caroline tipped the fruit into a bowl. "I don't know. I haven't worked with him enough."

"Then as husband material—did you like him for me? And don't say that if I was happy, that was enough. I need your honest opinion. You liked it when I got engaged, but were you thrilled?" She shook her own head in reply. "Why not?"

Easing her aside, Caroline took a jug of maple syrup from the fridge. Then she sorted through K-Cups, picking a coffee for Jamie and a tea for herself. Placing a mug on the Keurig, she made the coffee.

"Mom?" Jamie prompted. The evasion should have been answer enough, but she needed the words.

Caroline shot her a guilty glance. "Theo and Roy wanted him for you. He was preapproved, so to speak. Bitchy of me to think this, I know, but there were times when I worried that was part of his appeal."

Jamie hadn't thought of that—at least, not consciously. Considering it now, she admitted, "It probably helped. But I also did like him myself."

"Love him?"

"Yes. Just not"—she paused, struggling for the right word—"not *wildly.*"

"He isn't dynamic or exciting or passionate," Caroline said in a burst, then gave a short laugh. "*That's* funny. I could never put my finger on it before. He's such a nice guy."

"But not dynamic or exciting or passionate." Chip was passionate. Jamie had seen heat in his eyes and heard need in his voice. "Am I those things, Mom? I mean, I broke my engagement at an unwise time, which is not the way I usually do things. Is what I did totally crazy?"

"Not if it's what you feel."

"You aren't shocked?"

Caroline gathered up food. "Honestly, I'm just so glad you're here that nothing much would shock me."

"What about sex?"

Her mother went still. "What about it?"

"How important is it in a relationship, really?"

Caroline blushed. "Uh, uh—hold *that* thought." Then she fled, which was the only word Jamie could use to describe the way she ducked into the parlor with breakfast. And the look of panic on her face? She had never been shy talking about sex with Jamie before.

Tad was still happily beating his pot—no attention deficit problem *there*—when Caroline returned for utensils and the fruit plates Jamie loved. Seeing the latter, Jamie teared up.

"Oh, baby."

"I'm okay. Just emotional."

"About Brad?"

"Actually," she realized and took a breath, "no. When it comes to him, I feel free. This"—she made a broad gesture to include kitchen, plates, her mother, and Tad—"this makes me emotional." Her voice broke. "It's a dream."

Caroline hugged her again, even tighter this time. Then, plying her with plates and utensils, she saw to Tad herself—kneeling beside him, talking softly, carrying him to the dining room and settling him on a chair. She put a pancake on his plate and cut it up. "Syrup?" she asked Jamie.

"Oh yeah. He loves sweets." She dribbled syrup on her own pancake, took a bite, and closed her eyes in pleasure. The issue of Chip, sex, and her future remained, but right now she was more aware of her past. Pancakes were her past. So were Caroline's fruit plates and the framed Victorian lace, which looked down at her now from the nearby wall as a patchwork of smiles. Swallowing a second bite, she set down her fork. "I am so not good without you, Mom. You have no idea. I've had decision after decision to make, and it's probably been good that I've had to rely on myself, but you have answers that might have saved me hours—*days*—of emotional trauma. Like daycare. Dad liked having Tad at home with Jess, but I can't be home, and the nanny I hired didn't work out, and now that he's in daycare, I like him there. It's totally different from what he had before, and he's with other children."

"Which is precisely why I put you in daycare way back," Caroline said. "You were an only child. You needed socialization."

"Did Dad like my being in daycare?"

"No. He didn't approve then and wouldn't now, but it's no longer his decision. I know that sounds harsh, baby, but it's true. Tad is yours. So are the decisions."

And the cleanup when things were a mess. "He's getting syrup on your table," she said as she started to rise. Caroline's hand stayed her.

"It'll wash off."

"My condo is a wreck."

"Your condo is a thing."

With a happy sigh and a grin, Jamie scrubbed her fingers through Tad's curls. "See, Taddy? Haven't I said *that* a gazillion times?" She sipped her coffee, thinking that half of those gazillion times had been aloud to Brad and had gone right over his head, but that was only one of many problems they'd had. "It was so weird."

"What was?"

"Last night. I'd been terrified of hurting Brad, but he was fine. Now I'm wondering whether I felt the pain and vulnerability more than he ever did. Did I imagine his sensitivity because I wanted him to be that kind of person?"

"Maybe. Maybe it was pride. Maybe he didn't want to show weakness, or, God forbid, beg for another chance."

Jamie had a different thought then and sucked in a breath. "Maybe he was relieved. Maybe he's drawn to someone else."

"Would that bother you?"

"Of course it would. We were engaged." In the next breath, she thought of Chip and was guilt-ridden. "Actually, it would make me feel better," she admitted. "I like to think our engagement wasn't working for him either. I know he's relieved about—" *Tad,* she finished with a glance. "Maybe he didn't want to be CEO either. Until the accident, that was hypothetical. Now it isn't. Maybe he's glad to be off the hook."

It was only speculation, though, and had little to do with who or what *she* was. Chip was never far from her mind. She didn't understand it. In high school, they had been at opposite ends of the social spectrum. He had a reputation for being fast. She was sure he'd slept around. Not her. But she couldn't think about much else now.

"So," she tried again, needing to get to it. "About sex."

Caroline set down the cup. "Sex? Hmm. Oh dear, let me get something for Tad's hands and face. He seems to be done." With a scrape of her chair, she rose and left the room.

Jamie leaned toward Tad. "Was that yummy?"

"Yummmmy."

"I loved pancakes when I was your age, and Nana Caro makes the best. *Mom?*" she called, so happy to be a daughter again.

"Yes?"

But Jamie suddenly spotted the fruit bowl. "Oh no," she said in mock horror, "we forgot raspberries." She spooned up a bunch. "Strawberries, too?"

"Noooo." He picked up a raspberry. There were six. Jamie was wondering how long he would take to eat them, and what else might hold his attention while she talked with her mother, when Caroline returned with a damp dishcloth, a pad of paper, and a pencil. The cloth cleaned up syrup; the paper and pencil bought time.

"I need crayons here," Caroline remarked. "Lead is lethal."

"It's okay. Pencils are made of graphite. But we're watching him. He won't put it in his mouth. What should he call you? I don't see you as a Grandma."

Caroline seemed startled. "Uh, no. Me, neither."

"Caro would be cute, only I want him to call you something no one else does. When I was talking with him a second ago, I said Nana Caro."

"Nana Caro. I like that. It feels . . . fresh."

Jamie sensed she had been about to say "young" but hadn't wanted to touch on age again, and Jamie was with her on that. *Gut It!* lay in wait, just beneath the surface but totally secondary to why she had come. "So, can we talk about sex?"

"Shhhh." Caroline hitched her chin toward the boy.

"Mom," Jamie begged, albeit in a hushed voice, "he doesn't know what sex is. I am not getting graphic, but I need to talk about this, and I have no one else."

"It could be," Caroline said, sounding baffled, "that I'm not the best one to ask."

Because she hadn't had sex in a while? But Jamie's questions were hypothetical. "What if I said it was boring with Brad? What if I said I didn't look at him and start to tremble?" Caroline's eyes went wide. "What?"

"Nothing." But she was blushing. "I'm good."

"Are you *embarrassed*?"

"No." She tipped up her chin. "I am not embarrassed. If Brad doesn't make you tremble, I'd say it's another piece to the puzzle of why you and Brad weren't good together."

"But how important a piece is it? A relationship can't exist on sex alone. Am I crazy to throw away a guy who may be good in every other way?"

"But he wasn't," Caroline pointed out with a nod at Tad.

"He might have eventually come around on that." Jamie grunted. "Or so I kept telling myself, stupid me. But I need to know about the other."

"Sex."

"Am I wrong to want more?"

Caroline considered. "No."

"How important is chemistry? Am I a sexual creature first? Second? Third? What proportion of a relationship should be dominated by sex?"

Her mother laughed. "Oh, baby. It isn't about proportions. Sex means more to some people than to others, and its importance in a relationship isn't static. It changes with life. And with time."

"I understand that, but shouldn't it at least start off pretty great? If it doesn't, what hope is there? I want it to be great, Mom. I want to look at a guy and melt."

Caroline was suddenly far away, dreamy almost, and, for the first time, Jamie realized she must have had lovers other than Roy. Her mother was sexy in an organic way, and her work constantly exposed her to men. As many times as she had sworn that she and Roy were in love when Jamie was conceived, Jamie doubted the sex had been great. Roy was too into Roy. History had borne that out.

Cautiously, Caroline asked, "Was it never that way with Brad?"

"I thought it would be, because he really is sweet, and he wanted to please me. But sex with him was typical of our relationship—sedate and comfortable and planned. Even when he came—" She winced and waved a hand. "Forget I said that." Instead, she tried to articulate what she had felt in those moments with Chip. "Maybe I don't want it to be intellectual. Maybe I want it to be impulsive and hot. What does that say about me?"

Caroline was slow to answer, then oddly puzzled. "It might say that you're reacting to your father's early death."

"I don't think it's that."

"Have you always wanted more than Brad offered?"

"I wasn't aware that there *was* more." Jamie hesitated. How much to say? It could all amount to nothing. Right now, though, it was vividly real, and, even aside from rebuilding trust, she wanted Caroline's approval. "I met someone."

"Someone?"

"Chip Kobik."

Caroline's face was blank at first. Then her brows rose in surprise. "The hockey player?"

"Not anymore. Well, he runs a summer hockey camp for kids, but mostly he teaches PE at Emory, and he's a single dad. We met on the playground last week."

"Last *week*."

"I know. It's wild." A normal person didn't meet someone one week and let it change her life the next. Unless she believed in love at first sight. Which was *really* pushing it. "I mean, he is so not my type—or he wasn't, but he's different now. He's alone and I'm alone—I mean, I really am, Mom, because I haven't had Brad and I haven't had you—and I don't mean that as criticism, because I understand why you think I had a hand in what Claire did, but with Dad gone, if I'm choosing between hosting the show and being a mom, there's no choice, and if Claire—"

Caroline's fingers covered her mouth; suggestive eyes went to Tad. He had stopped scribbling. Large brown eyes were staring at Jamie in mild alarm.

"Well," Jamie drawled for his sake when Caroline's hand fell away, "*that* was a trip. Mamie got totally off-subject. What are you drawing, monkey?" She left her seat to study a havoc of lines. "That's so pretty!"

"At least he holds the pencil right," Caroline said appreciatively. "You were slow when it came to fine motor skills."

"Which is why I took up tennis." She scanned the coffee tables. "Do you have any old magazines you don't mind losing?"

"Would a catalog work?"

"Perfect. He decimated my *Architectural Records*." Moments later, with Tad on the floor engrossed in a tool catalogue ("Wow, Taddy, I'll bet Handy Manny uses this!") and Jamie hip to hip with Caroline on the love seat, she was calmer. "What are we going to do about *Gut It!*?"

"The show's on hiatus."

"Claire will be after me to do advance work."

"I'm already on it, so it'll be done for you if you host."

"She won't give up. She'll play dirty."

"We'll play dirty back." Caroline linked their hands. "But we said we wouldn't talk about *Gut It!* Tell me more about Chip."

Jamie didn't need forcing. "He's been amazingly helpful, and I don't just mean giving me lists of resources. He actually, physically, went with me to the daycare center to get Tad enrolled. His son is a year older than Tad, and he's a great dad. He's fun to be with and easy to talk to, and when he looks at me"—she drew in a shuddering breath—"it's *there,* Mom, everything I never had with Brad."

"When all did this *happen*?"

"Yesterday, and I know what you're thinking," she added quickly, "and you're right. I barely know the guy. But it's electric."

"Does he feel it, too?"

Piercing blue eyes. A tight jaw. *Tell me to stop, Jamie.*

"Oh, yeah. So maybe I like him because he's good with Tad or because he has answers I need or because he's a bad boy, or was, which makes him a little dangerous, and I've never *remotely* done dangerous. But can you fake chemistry? Isn't it either there or not?"

Caroline was so long thinking about this that Jamie wondered again about other men in her mother's life. She was about to ask when a second hand closed around hers and squeezed. "No, you can't fake it. But it may be dormant, like there without your realizing. If you're focused on other things and aren't looking—"

"I *wasn't* looking. I swear, I wasn't. I've never seen myself as that kind of person."

"Me either."

"My life has radically changed in two weeks' time. I don't know who I am anymore. How do I define myself? What do I *do*?"

"I haven't a clue."

"You have to."

A gentle laugh. "Why is that?"

"Because I need advice."

Caroline's laughter was higher this time. "What if I said that the last two weeks have been cataclysmic for me, too, and that my self-image has been turned upside down, so I don't know who I am either?"

Even without direct accusation, Jamie knew she was responsible for much of her mother's angst. "I'm not hosting the show, Mom. That's my final answer. Maybe I would have wanted it once, but no more. It's too contentious. And I seriously, *seriously* do not have the time." That said, she checked the clock on her phone. "I have to go."

"Will you come again soon?"

"How about, oh, um, eight-point-five hours from now?" Jamie said with a snicker. In the next breath, she was self-conscious. "No. Maybe not."

"You want to see Chip."

"He calls himself Charlie. That's pretty much the only thing I have trouble with when it comes to him. And yes. I want to see him." Which was why she had so badly needed Caroline. "Am I awful for that?"

"If you're awful, I'm awful."

"Then you don't hate me for going from Brad to Chip so fast?"

"How can I judge you?"

"I need your *approval,* Mom."

"Well then, oooo-kay." She considered for another minute before taking a breath and letting loose an explosion of words. "Passion can take us by surprise, as in hitting suddenly, but maybe that isn't a bad thing. I'm thinking we can't overintellectualize life. Sex may be more important than some of us even *know,* because situations change, and life is a learning experience. Maybe your father's death is driving us, but if it's telling us that life is short, it's right. If we discover something better than we had, does it matter how we got there?"

"Is that an endorsement?"

"Um, yes, I guess it is. But be careful, baby," she added on a note of caution, "I don't want you hurt. And it isn't just you anymore. Now it's Tad, too."

nineteen

Brad must have asked the receptionist to buzz him the instant Jamie arrived, because he was at her desk minutes later, leaning over her to talk with the same outward calm he would have shown any other day at work. He looked tired, as if he had barely slept. Heart heavy, she waited for him to say that they were acting too quickly, that he didn't want to break up, that he couldn't envision a future without her in his life. In fact, his glasses were straight, his eyes their usual light gray, his voice low and close. But his words were something else.

"I've thought this through," he said, intimate and low. "I want to hold off on making a formal announcement. Have you told anyone?"

Not regret, then. Just stark, cold practicality.

It was for the best, Jamie knew. Still, she was stung by how wrong she had been about Brad. "Only my mother."

"I doubt she was upset. Did you tell Theo?"

"Not yet. What do you mean, 'I doubt she was upset'?"

"It doesn't matter. It's over. But please don't tell anyone else. There's no need yet."

Jamie certainly hadn't planned on sending an e-announcement. Still, when they had first become engaged, word had spread on its own. "I'm not wearing my ring," she murmured. "People will notice."

"You can say you forgot to put it on."

"What about tomorrow? Or next week?"

"By then, I'll know what I'm doing."

That gave her pause. "What do you mean?"

Behind his glasses, his eyes were unblinking. "I've always had offers from other companies."

She was startled, then annoyed. "You never told me," she had to say, because he had made such a big deal the night before about her not telling him about Tad.

"I didn't tell you," he said, "because they were irrelevant at the time, but they aren't anymore. One's with a firm in Minnesota. I like the partners."

"You were entertaining job offers from out of state?" She could understand that he would be recruited by local companies he met through MacAfee Homes, but something out of state would suggest he had been actively soliciting jobs.

He didn't deny it. "I've often thought I'd like to go home."

"You never told me that." She had broken up with Brad as soon as she recognized her feelings for Chip. To learn that he had been looking elsewhere while they were engaged, knowing she was tied to MacAfee Homes, knowing that her work, family, and hometown were here, knowing that Theo and Roy were counting on his taking over one day—she was *stunned*. "You said you didn't want to be in the same city as your parents. You said you didn't *like* Minneapolis."

"And I believed it, but when I thought about it last night, I realized I had to make myself dislike Minneapolis so I could like Boston. The truth is, I'm a midwesterner. Minneapolis looks pretty good to me right now."

He was wounded and lashing out. That was the only explanation Jamie could find. She had been engaged to marry the man. She had always thought him down to earth and totally transparent.

Only it sounded like he'd had this at the back of his mind for a while, like Plan B had been there all along on the chance that Plan A was nixed.

For a split second, she was hurt. In that second, she felt a whole new swell of anger, betrayal, dismay, not the least of it being how easily he had moved on.

But the second passed, and reality returned. She had moved on, too. Her heart wasn't here. And as she studied this detached Brad—she actually moved her desk chair farther from him—she felt better and better. She had believed him vulnerable for so long that the idea of his being strong and filled with purpose was a huge relief.

"Oh. Okay. I'm glad," she said and meant it. She had loved him, perhaps not the right way for marriage, but feelings didn't just vanish.

"So you won't tell anyone yet?"

There she balked. Feelings were one thing, principle something else. Brad might be moving on from MacAfee Homes, but she wasn't. She had her own credibility to protect. "I can't promise it. The best I can do, if someone asks, is to say we're on hold until things sort themselves out from Roy's death."

He studied her with what might have been pique before producing a sad smile. "You're tough."

"Apparently," she replied, sad as well, "so are you."

She should have known it, of course—should have known that there was a fine line between even-tempered and cool. What kind of man professed to want a family but couldn't open his heart to a two-year-old orphan who was his future wife's half brother and, PS, the son of a man who had given him so much and was now dead?

She should have known that a relationship so slow to develop might, in fact, be more convenient than heartfelt. And that two people coming from such different places might just be *too* different.

Whatever, he seemed so comfortable now with his independence that she stopped worrying about him, especially when greater worries came a short time later in a phone call from Claire. "Does the name Barth ring a bell? . . . What do you know about the company? . . . Do you personally know anyone there?" Apparently, one of the Barths had contacted her about doing a season of *Gut It!*

Jamie was horrified. "A *season*?"

"Not this fall or spring, but maybe in a year. I checked them out. They're well regarded."

"But *Gut It!* has always been a MacAfee show. Are you thinking of switching to an entirely new cast? Because of the *hosting* issue?" She found it unthinkable, both change and cause.

"No. This goes beyond that. Alternating crews may be another way of keeping things fresh. There would be continuity, since the Barths are in Williston, too."

"They're not here. Not like we are. Besides, part of the appeal of *Gut It!* is that we're women. They aren't."

"Well, that's a hook that could work to our benefit. It could be a competition between the sexes. Viewers could even vote on their favorite crews. What do you think?"

"I think it's *awful,*" Jamie cried, but Claire was unruffled.

"It's certainly something to consider if you don't want to host. Okay. I just wanted to mention it. Call me when you're up to it, so that we can lock things in."

Moments after ending the call, Jamie was on the phone with Caroline. "It's a threat, baby," she soothed, sounding sensible and calm. "She's trying to intimidate us."

"With Dad not two weeks dead?"

"Claire wants what she wants when she wants it. That's part of what makes her good on the set."

"Well, I'm not hosting. Period."

"You'd be a good host."

"Not now."

"What if the choice is between your hosting or our losing the show?"

"Hosting is *your* job."

"Yes," Caroline said firmly, "and I do not like someone saying I'm too old to do it. But we're not the bank, and if the bank is calling the shots, we may be stuck."

The bank? Jamie kept coming back to a single person. "It's about power for Claire."

"Maybe," Caroline agreed. "Maybe she's getting pressure from someone above. It could be political, like she botched some other project and fears for her job if she can't swing this change."

Jamie was amazed that her mother could be so casual, given how she had been screwed. "But aren't you *angry*?"

"Only when I let myself really think about why I'm losing something I love. I'm trying not to do that, Jamie. I'm trying to focus on other things I love, one of which is spending time with my daughter. And with her little boy. *And* in Toys "R" Us just now."

"You didn't."

"I did. Dean and I were doing research in Warrenville." That was the site of the fall show. "Claire would die if she knew, but whichever one of us hosts will need to know more about the town. Remember how tough it was the first few seasons when people had no clue what we were? Now they fall over themselves wanting to help, even with Dean looking slightly disreputable."

Hearing an odd fondness, Jamie said, "You used to hate that."

There was a pause, then an indulgent sigh. "So I did. But that look can be a turn-on. People who watch *Gut It!* know Dean and love him, but trust me, baby, they wouldn't open their hearts to any of the Barths that way. Claire's done us a favor by tipping us off about them. I'll let Linda know. She's connected. She'll do her best to shut them out." The more Jamie listened, the more she relaxed. "So, anyway, when we passed Toys "R" Us on the way home, I made Dean stop."

Jamie tried to picture it, but the truth was, she hadn't dreamed this far. Having Caroline buy toys for her child was as new a concept as Jamie's having a child at all. "Were you bad?"

"Awful. Dean was worse. I was picking up practical things, like sippy cups and toddler utensils and crayons and a plastic pool. He got toys. He said he knows little boys better than me. He's probably right." She paused. "Have you seen Brad?"

Warmed that Caroline was so accepting of Tad, Jamie was lighthearted. "Yes. No problem there. He's moved on."

"That easily?"

"I know. Seriously scary."

"Seriously upsetting."

"No. I'm relieved."

"Because of Chip?"

"Because the relationship was wrong. The scary part is my not seeing that. Brad doesn't want me telling anyone yet, not even Theo, but he'll be leaving the company. Will that be a problem?" Caroline did seem to be the one to ask, the one in the know, the one closest to Theo.

"*Definitely* leaving?"

"Oh yeah. Amazing, isn't it? He says he wants to go back to Minneapolis, which is the last thing I would've thought, which goes to show how much I did not know this guy. Theo won't be happy with me."

"I can handle Theo," Caroline assured her. "That's one advantage of being bumped up into the C-suite." She paused before asking in a gentler voice, "Does Chip know your engagement's off?"

"Not yet. He's at school till three."

"Jamie . . ." A warning.

"Caution. I know."

Caution haunted Jamie as the afternoon passed. Between meeting onsite with one homeowner and talking on the phone with two others, it occurred to her that she might have misread things and imagined something more than momentary lust on Chip's part. When that discouraged her, she pulled up her dream file, which contained whimsical plans for the Weymouth property. She added an arbor to the community amenities, had the computer insert wisteria, a few grapes, even a wedding reception. The last was telling. She hadn't been able to plan her own wedding. Caroline was right. Subconscious reasoning must have been at work.

And now? Caution meant leaving nothing to the subconscious, which meant understanding that Chip might have decided she wasn't his type at all, and that other than meeting at the playground, he didn't want to be involved with a single mom, which was likely the responsible thing, the *grown-up* thing.

Still, her excitement grew as the afternoon passed. It helped that Tad's day had been better—no crying jags and a nice long nap, his teacher reported. He had finger-painted Jamie a beautiful piece of art and chattered about it during the drive home. The chattering actually surprised her. Two days in daycare seemed to have jump-started his speech. Much of what he said was unintelligible, but his enthusiasm was catching. In that spirit, Jamie could always give an excited *Really?* or *That's so good, Taddy,* or *I love it!* And she chattered right back at him—she'd read a study during lunch about how toddlers benefited from hearing complete sentences with good grammar.

Of course, her own talking might have been from nerves.

Was from nerves.

Back at the condo, she changed from skirt, blouse, and heels to T-shirt, shorts and flip-flops. Once Tad had snacked and pooped, and the clock reached five, she packed him back in the car and drove to the playground.

They were there. At the swings, Chip pushing Buddy at the same time that he coached, "Pump! That's it, Bud, use the legs." Tad ran toward them as if he knew the drill, his head down, arms and legs going for speed. Jamie followed more sedately, reliving every fear that what she had assumed to be mutual was not.

One look at the vivid blue eyes that watched her approach, though, and she knew she hadn't been wrong. Suddenly shy, she simply smiled and said, "Hey."

"Hey," he said with an answering smile. He gave his son a push, then caught up Tad, lowered him into the bucket, and got him swinging. He easily handled both buckets, with his wide arm span. "I wasn't sure you'd come."

"It's hell hour." The term held new meaning now; the temptation to be with Chip was greater than ever. *Caution,* she reminded herself and swallowed. "How was your day?"

"Challenging." He gave another two pushes, darting looks at her between. "Less than a week until summer break, and the kids are ready. They were antsy as hell." He looked her over. "I wasn't much better than they were today. Kept thinking about you." His gaze stuck on her hand. "Where's your ring?"

No one at work had asked that. Not one single person. They simply assumed she was with Brad, ring or no.

"Gone." He looked at her quizzically. "I broke my engagement."

"For me?" he asked with endearing excitement.

"For me. He and I had other issues, but once I realized I was drawn to you, I couldn't let it go on."

He smirked. "'Drawn' to is putting it mildly. At least on my side." He kept double-handing the swings.

"Mine, too."

He shot her a wary look. "I may be a lousy bet."

"And I'm not? I haven't ever done anything remotely like this."

"You're a MacAfee, I'm a Kobik. You're Phi Beta Kappa, I'm a party animal—"

"Am?"

"Was, but still, you're a TV star, I'm a gym teacher. You can do better than me."

"How do *you* know?" she asked with enough indignation to shut him up.

She stood close beside him, acutely aware of his long body flexing and reflexing as he pushed, and for several minutes, there was only the *whoosh* of the swings, the laughter of two little girls playing princess on the adjacent jungle gym, and the occasional *"Higher!"* from Buddy. When the latter became demands for the sandbox, they made the switch.

Then they sat side by side on a nearby bench, leaning forward, each with elbows on knees and fingers laced. Their thighs—his muscled and hair-spattered, hers lean and clear—were inches apart, yet the heat was enough to make her tremble.

When he muttered, "I need to touch you," she went up in flames.

She couldn't find breath enough to speak, she was shaking so inside. The best she could do was to lean that little distance closer until skin met skin.

Moaning, he shot her a sizzling look, then hollered at the boys, "Anyone in that sandbox hungry?"

"Me!" shouted Buddy and scrambled out of the sand. Tad imitated both the shout and the scrambling exit.

"Is pizza pickup on the way home okay?" Chip asked Jamie.

"Perfect." Anything would be. She was so not thinking about food, but there were the boys to consider, and Chip was much better than she was that way.

She followed the Honda to the pizza shop, then to his house. Once inside, she helped set out plates, napkins, and glasses—tonight Fred and Barney for the boys, no choices there. Other than catching the pocket of her shorts on a drawer pull, which she couldn't have done a second time if she'd tried, she breezed around his kitchen. Working together, they quickly joined the boys in the breakfast nook.

Did Jamie know what she ate? No. Nor did she know what she said, though she kept up her part, dovetailing with Chip through a running conversation designed to include the boys. All the while, if she wasn't looking at Chip's hands, she was looking at his mouth, or his once-broken nose, or the shadow on his jaw. Everything about him was forcefully male, including, once dinner was done, the commanding voice that got the boys into the living room to watch Diego rescue dinosaurs.

"You guys stay here while Jamie and I clean up," he said with commendable nonchalance and, returning to the kitchen, promptly backed Jamie up to the sink. Framing her face with both hands, he tipped it up and held it steady, and a good thing that was. His kiss was hungry, slanting one way, then the other, using tongue, teeth, and lips in the undisciplined way of the starving—until Jamie was wild with need.

"Okay?" he whispered against her mouth. She had barely begun to nod when his hands were under her tee, and while he pushed up her bra and thumbed her nipples, he kissed her again. This time it was all tongue, provocative and deep.

Jamie had been fisting his shirt, then rubbing her palms over his chest, but she needed more. The thrust of his hips drove her. Frantic, she breached the waist of his sports shorts and found him with both hands. He was so magnificently erect that she gasped.

"Nnnnnn," he groaned into her mouth. Then he bodily lifted her, guiding her legs around his waist, so that he was right where she needed him to be, or almost. Having clothes in the way didn't work.

Breathing hard, he put his forehead to hers. "Buddy has a bunk bed. Can Tad sleep on the bottom?"

"He'll have to," Jamie said with a low laugh, because there was no way she was returning to her condo without having Chip inside her first, and there was no way that could happen until the boys were down for the night.

"Okay." He seemed in pain. "Okay." He sounded determined. "I'm a lousy dad for having pizza too often and for not knowing what in the hell we were saying to them at dinner and for sticking them in front of the TV while we do this, but right now I'm going to redeem myself by cleaning up here and then running their bath."

With measured movements, he set her on the counter. Determined to be similarly disciplined, she slid forward and promptly overshot the edge. She would have tumbled if he hadn't caught her, but he was kind enough not to say that. Without a word, he crushed the empty pizza box and put it aside, then began to load the dishwasher as she ferried things from table to sink.

"Do you think it's okay for Tad to be sleeping somewhere different again?" she whispered as they corralled the boys upstairs for a bath.

He began filling the tub. "I don't know, but I can't think of another option."

She couldn't either, and Lord knew she had tried to find one. She tried once more as she retrieved Moose and the diaper bag from downstairs, but she didn't have a sitter who would come instantly and stay late on a Thursday night, and she certainly couldn't ask Caroline. Caroline would talk about caution, but Jamie's body wouldn't listen.

"Let's see how he does," Chip said when she returned. "We'll only be two doors down."

Two doors down. In his bedroom. In his bed. Naked.

Hit with another flare of heat in her belly, she rocked lightly back and forth as she knelt by the tub, and though there was some foreplay—*way* wrong word—with a dozen rubber dinosaurs, they quickly got down to soaping the boys. She did Tad. Chip did Buddy. There was conversation in which Jamie did participate, though she didn't retain any more of what was said than Chip claimed to have taken in at supper. She did read the boys a story. It seemed only right to do that. She sat on the lower bunk with Tad tucked against her from the start, and though Buddy kept an initial distance, by the time Peter Pan backed Captain

Hook off the plank and into the water, where the tick-tocking croc awaited, he was sitting nearly as close as Tad.

Chip sat cross-legged on the floor, a distraction there. But he got to his feet—bare, lean, masculine feet—as soon as the story was done, nixed Buddy's request for a second, and hoisted him up over the safety rail and into the top bunk. There were kisses, instructions, promises, and good nights. Moments later, Jamie and Chip stood with their backs to the wall just outside the room.

Chip whispered, "He'll come down the ladder at least once for another animal." He took her hand. She could barely think over the thunder of her pulse and the pooling of heat in her body, certainly couldn't make out the low murmuring in the bedroom, but Chip did. "Giving Tad something," he whispered. "Likely a teddy."

Jamie wanted to say what a sweet child Buddy was, but Chip had swung around to press her into the wall and capture her mouth. Clearly still listening, he kissed her quietly, lips sliding along her neck and down to her chest. He paused when a sound came from the boys. Jamie felt his ragged breath and tried to tame the thud of her heart, but forget that. His mouth was warm on her skin and so close to her breasts that her insides sizzled.

She dragged him up by the hair. "I *need,*" she whispered in desperation, and still he waited another one, two, three minutes, rubbing against her in the most subtle undulation as those blue eyes seared hers. When no further sound came, he lifted her as he had done in the kitchen and carried her into his bedroom with her legs wrapped around his waist.

Freeing one hand to close the door, he lowered her to the bed and followed her down, and, that quickly, restraint vanished. His hands were everywhere, fighting with hers to remove clothes, touch what was bared, and see each part between kisses. It was frenzied, but not without care. As awed as she was by his size and by the rough texture of his skin, there was an answering wonder in his hands as they moved over her body.

His gentleness undid her. She was so ready for him that her body was weeping with need, but when he rose above her and thrust deep, she cried out. The fullness was beyond anything she had ever known, a sense of completion that brought even greater hunger. In a tangle of arms and legs, they rolled over, then over again, seeming to share the same need to feel more, deeper, *harder,* and when they came, it was in quick succession, overlapping, endless.

He landed on top, but when he made to roll off, she held him still. "Don't."

"I'm too heavy."

"You feel good." She loved his solidity, loved the musky scent of his skin and the way the late-day sun glanced off one broad shoulder. As her breathing leveled, though, a germ of responsibility returned and, conscience-stricken, she sought his eyes—blue eyes that looked down at her with satisfaction, admiration, and such incredible warmth that she forgot what she was going to say.

"Taddy," he prompted gently.

"He's not used to a bed," she said in a rush before she lost it again. They had padded the floor with cushions, but still he was used to having sides and would be afraid if he fell. "Will we hear if he cries?"

Holding her gaze, he stretched one long arm toward the nightstand. There was a click, then the whispery static of a monitor. When that long arm returned, it began to explore—and, oh, she'd been wrong about not wanting him to move. When he slid lower, his mouth did things to her she hadn't dreamed it could. And how his hands held her? And his words of arousal and praise? The pleasure was unfathomable. When she came, she sobbed with the intensity of it. She might have been embarrassed if his throaty cry hadn't quickly followed. He had waited for her, she realized. Both times, he had needed her to climax first.

It was a while before her body calmed, and even then, with his arms locking her to his side, she couldn't move far, not that she wanted to. There was too much to see. In the dying sun, he was positively golden—strong facial planes, wide shoulders tapering over a firm chest to a lean waist. He was athletic, but nowhere near as bulky as he must have been once. She trailed a hand through the whorls of dark hair that spread wide before arrowing down his torso to his groin.

He caught her hand and, carrying it to his mouth, opened her fingers and slowly kissed her palm. The gesture was unbelievably sweet, particularly when he flattened her hand over his heart and said in a voice that was husky and real, "You are my dream."

Her heart caught. "I'd say you're mine, too," she whispered, "only I didn't know I *could* dream this. It's crazy."

"Not crazy." The clarity of his eyes swore to it. "Just sudden. Let's get married."

She grinned. "Okay. When?"

"This weekend."

"Perfect," she said. "Makes total sense." It was way *way* crazy. "We've never been to a restaurant together, never celebrated a holiday together, never talked about what we want for our boys in two or five or eight years, never discussed work, like what we do in a day, never even met each other's families—"

He stopped her mouth with gentle-giant fingers. "Don't overintellectualize this, honey. Just feel."

Intellectualizing versus feeling. It was a potent choice for someone whose life had been dominated by deliberate thought—at least, before Chip. Since meeting him, it seemed, feeling had been major. Still, she heard her father's words and felt chastened.

"I'm trying to think like a grown-up."

"We are," he said in a measured voice. "But things happen—like death, like instant parenthood. I'm thirty-three. There are times when my knees don't work and my past makes me old, but I *see* better than I ever did, and I know what I want. Besides"—he gave a half-smile—"I did meet your father, more than once. He used to come up to me at Fiona's to talk sports. I'm sorry he's dead, Jamie."

"So am I." With each day that passed, she remembered more of the good and less of the bad. "There is an irony, you know." When he raised questioning brows, she said, "If it hadn't been for that car accident, we wouldn't be here now. If I hadn't inherited Tad, I wouldn't have been a basket case at the playground that day, you wouldn't have rescued me, we wouldn't have shared the parent thing and dealt with lice and had sex." She considered. "Dad would like you."

He made a dry sound. "You think? Talking sports with an ex-jock is one thing, letting one marry your daughter is something else."

She studied his face. "Are you serious about that?"

"Getting married? Completely."

"How can we? We just met."

"Only in the most narrow sense. Big picture, we've known each other for years. We're both Williston—grew up here, went to school here. We work here, shop in the same stores, know the same people."

Jamie was desperate enough to rationalize along with him. "Maybe we were totally aware of each other in high school and didn't know it. Maybe we were attracted back then. Maybe we were imaginary lovers. Did you dream about me back then?"

"I didn't dare. You were a MacAfee. Did you dream about me?"

"I didn't dare. You were too cool. I'm not sure I'd have known what to say to you if we'd ever come face-to-face. I don't even know what to call you now. I can't get used to Charlie."

His handsome mouth curved up. "Chip is fine."

Distracted, she touched a tiny white scar at the corner of his upper lip. "You don't have many of these. Aren't hockey players supposed to be missing teeth?"

He chuckled. "Face masks and mouth guards work when you use them. I got this baby playing street hockey when I was eight."

"Was it fun, playing street hockey?"

"Very. There was a whole group of us. I still see a lot of the guys."

"I'm envious. Tennis was solitary. But I can't call you Chip. You hate that name."

"It's different coming from you. Kind of unites past and present."

He was so easygoing, so sensible. She might have remarked on that if the monitor hadn't made a sudden noise. She froze, listening.

"It's Buddy," Chip murmured. "He's a noisy sleeper. Give him a minute."

That was exactly how long it took for silence to return, but for Jamie, the brush with reality lingered. "Being responsible for a child is huge. Whatever we do, it isn't just us." Caroline had said that, but Jamie felt it firsthand now. Marrying Chip on impulse was totally off the wall, even more frightening than stashing Tad in a strange bed so that she could have sex.

Have sex? Make love? If she was *feeling,* as Chip wanted, given the richness and depth of what they had just done, it was the latter. Still. "I've never been as impulsive as this."

"Me neither."

She felt a stab of self-doubt. "You've been with ten times as many women as I've ever had as friends."

"*Big* exaggeration."

"You know what I mean. Women chase professional athletes."

"They're called puck bunnies, and there weren't that many for me. For the record, I've never been with a woman like this."

"You mean totally crazy with two children down the hall?"

"I mean *meaningful*. I mean thinking about what I'm feeling and being humbled by it. Are you on birth control?"

"Yes, pills. 'Humbled' how?"

"Knowing you're a gift I may not deserve. I want more kids."

"So do I," she said with fervor. Brad had always limited it, another SLOW sign she should have seen. "I want *lots.*"

"See, there's another thing we share." And it was like he was in her mind. "What happened with your fiancé?"

She returned her cheek to his chest. "He only wanted two kids."

"Tell me about him."

"Not in this bed."

Gentle hands raised her head. His eyes were positively cerulean, earnest and clear. "I need to know, Jamie. My heart's at stake here. Are you and he really over, or are you just taking a break?"

She wanted to be offended. But how to be that in the echo of *my heart's at stake here*? Besides, he was only asking what any normal man would wonder. For all their talk about marriage and kids, they didn't know each other.

Wanting to change that, she sat up and wrapped a corner of the sheet over her breasts. "For the record, Checker Chip, I would never, *never* have been with you if Brad and I weren't completely done. It probably ended the day my father died, only I didn't see the writing on the wall until I wanted you so much. I'm actually amazed Brad and I lasted as long as we did. At the first sign of trouble . . ." Her fingers exploded into the air from a fist.

"Is it a problem that he's part of the business?"

"Only short-term. He's leaving. We'll hire another lawyer." She considered. "His being with the company may actually have been why we got engaged. I mean, he's a nice guy in every respect, but the office was watching. It became a game. Once we were dating, getting engaged was the next step." She reflected. "I couldn't get myself to plan a wedding. My mom thought I was afraid to commit because my parents' marriage failed, but I think it was because I must have known deep down he wasn't the one. We come from different places, Brad and I."

"Maybe you and me, too," Chip cautioned. "You're a MacAfee."

"Don't keep saying that."

"But it's true. You're out of my league."

As often as she had seen, or imagined seeing, vulnerability in Brad, what she saw on Chip's face rang true. There was nothing innocent and pure about Chip. She knew his past. But it didn't make a bit of difference.

No. That was wrong. His past gave him depth, which made him more attractive to her.

Rocking forward on her knees, she pressed a hand to his mouth and whispered, "We are *so* in the same league. I feel connected to you like I've never felt to anyone else." And completely comfortable, though he was sprawled naked on top of the sheets and she had her legs folded in a nonladylike way. When an inner stirring flared, she remembered the caution thing and sputtered a laugh.

"What?" he asked.

"All last night and today, I told myself to go slow. Like that was possible. What will Buddy say if he finds me here in the morning?"

"I don't know. It's never happened before. There's no way I would have had a woman in here with Buddy around."

Yet here Jamie was.

"Does that scare you?" he asked.

Scare. Funny. Had Chip Kobik looked at her back in high school, she'd have run in the other direction. *Anything* about him would have scared her, from his size to his looks to his radiating sexual appeal. Now? The grown-up Jamie had her own confidence. She could see substance, brains, a caring teacher, a loving father. The grown-up Jamie had more deep-down, visceral faith in him than in any other man she'd known. He had been tested and was a better person for it. The grown-up Jamie wanted to stake her future on him.

"Scare me? Are you kidding? It makes my heart sing."

He smiled and, reaching for her hand, wove his fingers through hers. "Heart sing, huh? I'm not telling the Bud-man that, but he'll have to get used to having you guys here." He was suddenly serious. "You okay with that?"

twenty

Caroline was in the garage shaping rosewood slats with a molder when Dean came from the house. She didn't see him enter, she was that focused on the wood. It was only when Champ, who had been sleeping against the cool wall, roused to greet his master that she silenced the molder and raised her goggles.

Thanks to the dog, she shouldn't have been startled to see Dean. But she was. Bare-chested, wearing jeans that were zipped but unsnapped, he looked like he had just rolled out of bed. Which he had. Which was still stunning to her.

"Will I ever get used to this?" she asked without asking.

He bent to rub Champ a greeting. Straightening, he approached her on bare feet, wrapped an arm around her chest, and gave her neck a smacking kiss.

She had to smile at the affection in the gesture. "Just wake up?"

"Pretty much." He nuzzled her hair for a lingering minute before releasing her and moving around the table to admire a dozen more slats. "You've been busy."

"Plantation shutters for multiple windows in six rooms makes for lots of work."

"Boring?"

"You know it is. I've long since finished the control rods and frames, but I've been putting these off." She ran her fingers over the newest slat. "Look at the veining here, Dean. The brown is so rich."

"It is. You've always liked rosewood," he remarked, then asked, "What time did you get up?"

"Five."

"If I were to guess from how focused you were just now, I'd say you're trying not to worry about Jamie. Ease up, sweetheart. It hasn't even been a whole day since you two talked."

"Well, I keep telling myself that," Caroline said, adding the new slat to the pile, "but right now, her life is—how to even describe it?"

"Busy is fine."

"Busy is inadequate," she countered and, checking to see that everything electrical was turned off, went out the door. "Try new. Or changing daily. Or *precarious*."

Closing the door, Dean fell into step beside her while Champ bounded ahead. "Why precarious?"

"Because she's stressed, and when people are stressed, they sometimes do things they come to regret."

"Precarious means dangerous, but you don't regret her breaking up with Brad, which means you're seeing danger in Kobik. He's a good guy, Caro. I asked around."

She stopped walking to looked up at him in horror. "You didn't. Oh, Dean. If Jamie thinks I'm snooping behind her back—"

"—you'd only be doing what any other mother would do. But this wasn't you, it was me, and I was subtle."

She sputtered a laugh. Dean Brannick was good at many things, but subtlety wasn't one.

"I *was*," he insisted and, taking her elbow, got her moving again. "Some of our guys' kids play hockey, and Kobik's camp is starting soon. They were talking about it, so I stuck in a few innocent questions. These guys think Chip Kobik is a god."

Of course they do, she mused as they reached the stairs. "Because he was a professional athlete."

"No. Because he's so good with their kids."

She considered that and sighed. "Given that Jamie has one now, that's a good thing, but still, he was a party boy for a while. I don't want her hurt."

"She's a big girl. And a sensible one. Besides, I don't see you rushing to tell her what *you've* been up to."

"I'm fifty-six. She's twenty-nine."

"Twenty-nine is adult."

"Fifty-six is more so."

"You're grasping, Caro." He opened the screen door. Champ scooted through. "Who was telling me that a mother raises her children to let them go?"

Caroline grunted as she went inside. She had told him that in a philosophical moment of self-restraint the night before.

"The same argument stands today, sweetheart. Don't call her."

"Fine for you to say. You aren't the one trying to repair a relationship. So I'm giving her space now, but I'm worried she'll think my not calling her is from lack of interest or, worse, anger, like I'm still blaming her for the *Gut It!* switch."

"Are you?"

"Only when I think about it." She opened a cabinet. "I've had other things on my mind."

"Me," he said sweetly, and her mood lightened, which was why she was pulling out pancake ingredients for a second day in a row. She had promised. And he had been very, very good.

"Are we arrogant?" she asked.

"Shouldn't we be? Last night was pretty damned amazing."

"Who *was* that in bed with you—"

"—she asks for the hundredth time." He opened the fridge.

"I'm sorry. The whole of me remains a puzzle." She was trying to settle on a self-image as safe as the one she had relied on for the past dozen years, but it seemed to change each day.

"Here's a clue. Who used her tongue last night—"

"Dean."

"Just asking." He had a block of cheddar cheese and a slicing knife. "For the record, sweetheart, the answer is one hot lady who should be eating crow by now."

"Gloating is not nice," she chided but without true bite. The sex kept getting better. She still wasn't ready for prime time, as in going naked in daylight or, more immediate to her needs, soaking her aching thighs in a hot bath while he looked on. But she was growing more confident. "Uh . . ."

He was feeding Champ her organic cheddar.

"He's hungry," Dean reasoned. "You can't begrudge him this after making him sleep in the garage."

"He upsets my cats."

"I upset your cats."

"Only Master. He has this alpha thing."

Snorting at that, Dean leaned down to scrub Champ's ears and told the dog, "Caro really does love you. She's just between a rock and a very hard cat." Leaving the dog, he came up behind Caroline as she put the skillet on the stove. Sliding his arms around her waist, he put his chin on the top of her head with a quiet intimacy that had her melting.

In a flashback moment, she remembered what Annie had said about being touched. She had been right. There was something about a man's hand moving over your skin that was special. Had she not missed this? Perhaps never had it with Roy, or simply been without for so long that it was new now? Or did age enhance the appreciation of little things, like a hand on an arm or fingers on a cheek?

Again she wondered how she could have been so close to Dean all these years and never wanted this. *Again* she wondered who she was.

A high bark came from the parlor, followed by a feline snarl.

"Champ!" Dean hollered. "Get back here!"

The dog came running. Freeing one arm, Dean pointed him to a spot by the door. With a shamefaced look, he slunk there and sat.

"At least he obeys," Caroline observed.

"More than Master ever will."

"Master is a cat." As far as she was concerned, that said it all. "Do you want pancakes?"

"Absolutely."

She could not cook with him plastered to her. There were some things that begged for space. "Then back off and let me cook."

He did. But his mind must have been hard at work the whole time she was making breakfast, because they were no sooner finished eating firsts under the watchful eye of her grandmother's smug-seeming lace than he said, "Marry me."

She nearly choked on her tea. Pressing her chest, she shot the lace a frown and caught her breath. "Where did *that* come from?"

"The heart."

Breath left her again. He couldn't have given a better answer. Still, *marriage*? "My *God*, Dean. How can you even *think* that word so soon?"

"Twelve years is too soon?"

"You know what I mean. Being friends is different from being lovers. That's a sea change."

"Not a sea change. An evolution. It's been brewing. Sex was the clincher. If we weren't compatible in bed, it wouldn't have been any good."

"Sex was a *test*?"

"Not for you," he said with a self-conscious look. "For me. I needed to know I could satisfy you in bed."

Put that way, as if the potential deficiency were in him and not her, she was more touched than she could say. Dean was taking responsibility for making her happy. Roy had *never* done that. "But why marriage?"

"Why not?"

"Uhhh, take the little thing about marriage being forever, with both of us having failed once, and what about love?"

"I've loved you forever. And you love me."

She might have argued that there was love and there was LOVE, though in truth, since they'd had sex, since he had been so caring of her in bed, since physical intimacy had deepened the emotional intimacy that had always hovered, the lines had blurred. "But why get married?"

"I want to know you're mine."

"I am yours."

"I want the *world* to know it." He scratched the back of his head, dropped his hand, and scowled. "Call me a throwback, even a Neanderthal, but it's how I am."

Caroline actually understood. She had grown up with a similar mindset, assuming that marriage was what women wanted in part to let the world know they were loved and taken care of.

But times had changed. Marriage didn't have to protect women. In this new world, Caroline could protect herself. She was single and proud.

At least, she had been proud until the hosting issue cropped up. She thought about the age issue through breakfast. Later, buttoning a blouse over her bra while Dean showered, she went into the bathroom and, speaking loudly enough to be heard over the water, tried to explain. "Here's where I'm hung up. We don't need marriage. We're not having kids, and we're both financially independent. We don't need a piece of paper tying us together. And a wedding—flowers and fanfare? I can't picture it."

When he turned off the shower and drew back the curtain, she passed a towel through the steam. The towel was pink, like her sheets, but it was plush.

He began drying himself. "It doesn't have to be fancy. We can go off, just the two of us, and get married at a little inn. Lots of them have elopement packages."

She drew back in alarm. "How do you know?"

"I looked."

She didn't want to hear more. The fact that he was bending and stretching to dry himself, casual with nudity in ways she was not, only added to her dismay. "There's something evasive about eloping. It's for people who either need speed or have secrets."

"You're afraid people will start counting months?"

"Cute. But what about Renny? If you want a closer relationship with him, how can you do something as momentous as get married and shut him out of the ceremony? Don't you think he'd be hurt? Jamie would be."

He wrapped the towel around his waist, his body all the more masculine against pink terrycloth. "So we'll invite them."

"But then it becomes something bigger, so what's the point? I don't want to elope. I don't want to get *married.*"

He was quiet as he went into the bedroom to take clean clothes from a gym bag. Then he turned. "Are you afraid to commit?"

Brad had accused Jamie of the same thing. Caroline wanted to think her daughter had sensed the relationship would sour before they made it to the altar. That wasn't the case with Dean and her. If Caroline was involved with anyone, Dean would be it.

But she was used to being on her own, cooking without a shadow against her back, coming and going as she pleased without reporting to anyone. *I'd give my right arm to be as free as you are,* Annie had said. Caroline liked that freedom.

She also liked knowing that no one could put her down for her age as Roy had done Fine, Dean said he didn't mind that she would be sixty well before he was—but once the novelty of their relationship wore off, would he feel the same? Roy had divorced her for being too old. Claire was firing her for being too old. She would be crushed if Dean changed his mind after a few years and was turned off by liver spots or varicose veins. At least if they weren't married the breakup wouldn't be quite so hard.

Here he was right now, though, waiting for her answer with his shorts in his hand, naked and exposed with his scars and his crooked finger and shots of gray through the hair on his chest, and well and heavily hung. Oh my. But she couldn't dwell on that, or even on her own fears, when his eyes held such vulnerability. That vulnerability touched her deeply. It made her want to protect *him,* which in turn made her realize just how much he did mean to her—and in ways that had less to do with sex than with the person. He might be a throwback, but he was honest and steady. He had been in her corner for years without wavering. She knew the truth about his marriage and divorce, knew how he agonized over his son. She didn't doubt that he loved her. And yes, she loved him.

"I'm not afraid to commit," she said. "I am totally committed to you."

"You are?"

"Would I have slept with you if I wasn't?" She tucked the tails of her shirt into her jeans. "And, for the record, sex is not overrated." She owed him that. "But at our age we don't need a piece of paper. No one will approve or disapprove if we sleep together."

"Not old-world Theo?"

"Theo doesn't matter. I'm a carpenter, and if my morals prevent him from naming me as his successor, I'm good with that."

"What about the show? Will Claire be happy if her host is sleeping with the GC?"

"I'm not her host, remember? She booted me out. So she may be jealous that an old lady like me can attract—"

"Old lady—"

"—a hunk like you, but the fact is, a romance on the set would *boost* ratings."

"*You* are no old lady. Would you wear my ring, at least?"

"A wedding ring without the wedding?"

"An engagement ring."

"To mark me yours."

With a growl of apparent frustration, he tugged on his shorts and jeans. By then, Caroline was feeling awful. Closing the distance between them, she ran an open hand down his chest. As gestures went, it spoke of intimacy in ways words could not. "It isn't you, Dean. I do love you. It's the institution I don't love."

"If I gave you a diamond, would you wear it?"

"Too *soon,*" she begged. "Can't we take it slowly?"

"Does that mean you won't rule it out?"

"Yes. It means I won't rule it out. Ask me again in ten years." When his eyes went wide, she pinched his middle. "Just kidding. Ten years is as ridiculous as two days. But haven't I been good about your country place?" She tried lightening things up. "I agreed to spend tomorrow helping you build a deck, though I still think that house is more trouble than it's worth."

His hazel eyes were chiding. "You agreed because you like the place. Admit it. It has sentimental value for you now."

She heard a distant ding. "Is that my phone?" As she headed for the stairs, she heard a soft "Coward" behind her, but she kept going, following the sound of the phone into the kitchen. She didn't want to miss the call if it was Jamie.

It wasn't. Nor did she recognize the number. Since her own was unlisted, though, it had to be someone with a personal connection. A new client, referred by a friend?

"Hello?"

"Caroline MacAfee, please."

"Speaking."

"This is Zoe Michaels, from the *Globe*." The words came in a rush. The woman sounded young and nervous. "Since *Gut It!* is homegrown, I'm doing a piece on Roy MacAfee's death and its impact on MacAfee Homes and the show. I was hoping we could talk."

Caroline had done many interviews. They didn't intimidate her, especially when the interviewer was as young as this one sounded. But the last thing she wanted was to talk about Roy. "I think you ought to call Theodore MacAfee. He's the head of the company." On one hand, she hated burdening Theo. Outweighing that, though, he could be a charmer when he wanted, and it would give him an outlet, even be a distraction. He was certainly an expert on Roy.

"He was the one who gave me your number," replied the reporter. "He said you were his spokesperson. My mother is a total fan of the show, so I know exactly who you are. You'll be perfect for me to talk with, seeing as you're the host."

Then word hadn't spread. That was something. It struck Caroline, though, that Jamie would be a better spokesperson. If she was taking over as host, she had to learn to handle the media, and as for handling Roy's death, as his daughter, she was in a better position to speak of it than his ex-wife.

Here was a perfect reason to call Jamie. But Caroline wasn't sharing her number with a reporter without checking first. "Can I call you back, Ms. Michaels?"

"I need to do this as soon as possible. My editor wants to run the story on Monday."

"Give me your number," Caroline said with authority, "and I'll get back to you." A minute later, she called Jamie, who picked up sounding breathless.

"Hey, Mom."

Breathless could mean busy or excited or just late. "Everything okay?"

"Everything's great. I'm just trying to get out of here."

Late, then. Perhaps the others, too, but if her tone said she didn't have time to talk now, Caroline couldn't very well ask. Quickly, she told Jamie about about Zoe Michaels. "You'd be perfect for this interview, Jamie. Should I give her your number?"

"God, no. Thanks, Mom, but you can do the interview."

"If you're the next host—"

"I'm not."

"Has Claire changed her mind?"

"I haven't talked with her. But there's no way I can take it on right now."

"Well, the reporter needs one of us ASAP. They're running the article on Monday. If I do the interview, Claire may be annoyed."

"*Good.* Do the interview, Mom, please?"

"Are you sure?"

"Absolutely. Thank you. You're the best. We'll talk another time, okay?"

Caroline knew when she was being rushed off the phone. Fearing Jamie might have even less time if she was with Chip and his son over the weekend, she asked a quick "Is Tad okay?"

"He's *great.*"

"Have you seen Chip?"

"He's great, too." The voice was higher and more breathy. "But I have to run, Mom. I'll give you a call, okay?"

Seconds later, Caroline held a silent phone, the sense that what she had heard was extreme excitement, and no clue whether to be pleased or worried.

twenty-one

Extreme excitement didn't quite cover it. Jamie was so totally in love—so *impossibly* in love—that she didn't dare tell Caroline lest her mother have her committed. What she was doing with Chip was crazy. *Crazy.* She kept coming back to that word.

But it didn't feel crazy when Tad began to cry at three in the morning and Chip bolted out of bed and carried him to her. Or when she woke up in the morning to hot coffee served in bed by a guy who already had the boys eating breakfast downstairs and was looking at her now as if she were priceless. Or when they met at First Unity later that afternoon and drove in a caravan to the pediatrician's office to discuss what Tad would be feeling about his parents' death and how best to ease both boys into a new relationship. Chip had arranged the meeting. He seemed determined to make their family work. She kept looking for signs of crazy in him but only saw commitment.

Stopping back at his house, they put Tad's seat in the Pilot and drove to Jamie's condo, and there, for the first time, a problem arose. As if Tad had actually heard their discussion with the doctor—which he could not have, since he and Buddy had been in the playroom down the hall—he was suddenly and fiercely possessive. Buddy picked up a toy; Tad grabbed it out of his hands. Buddy went for another toy; Tad started to cry.

"He's feeling loss without understanding it," the doctor had said. "He's at the age when sharing is difficult anyway. Let him cling to things that mean most to him—a stuffed animal or a blankie or a favorite toy—but teach him to share others. Be consistent. Be patient."

Wrapping her arms around him now, Jamie held him until he finished kicking and grew quiet, then softly explained that Buddy wasn't taking anything away, and he wasn't touching Moose. Didn't it feel *good* to share other toys, she asked, especially since Buddy would always give them back? "See, Taddy, he's already done with the farm."

Chip snickered from the sidelines. "Not a great attention span on my boy."

Jamie disagreed. "There's just a lot to see here. This is like a toy store to him, and he's been so good about sharing with Tad. Which of these should we take to your house?"

They picked a few. Chip played with the boys while she packed what she wanted for herself; then he joined her in the office to gather Tad's things. He ran a hand over her sleek white desk, admired her huge computer screen, studied drawings tacked to a corkboard, and flipped through design books—all the while asking questions about her work. He described the small office he had in a spare bedroom and vowed that any new house they built would have a large one, which got her thinking. She rather liked the connection he had with his childhood home and was inclined to stay there for now. Adapting it would be easy, starting with a simple addition. Her artist's eye saw modifications that would give the place a vintage-modern look inside and out.

Moreover, staying at Chip's would minimize change for the boys, and that was the responsible thing to do. His house wasn't pristine. But nor, any longer, was hers, and she was surviving just fine.

She was deciding that pristine had a sterile side when Tad wandered in, slid his little arms around her leg, and held tightly.

"Hi, monkey," she said. Kneeling, she cupped his face. "All done playing?"

He didn't answer, just looked up at her with such mournful eyes that she knew what he was thinking. They were the same eyes she saw when he woke at night needing to be held. He was a smart boy. Having gone through one life shift, he sensed another coming. One too many?

His lower lip trembled. "Where Mommy?"

Be honest, the pediatrician had said. "Mommy's in heaven."

"Wanna see her."

"I know, monkey, I know."

"Where my daddy?"

Jamie teared up. "He's in heaven, too."

"Taddy wanna go there."

"Someday."

"Now," he demanded, but he didn't resist when she hugged him close.

"I miss him, too," she whispered against his warm curls, rocking him as much for her own comfort as his. Despite their differences in those last days, Roy had been her father. So much had happened in the two weeks since his death, so much filling her mind, that she hadn't really had time to mourn, but right here, right now, emptiness hit her hard.

She might have wept if Chip hadn't suddenly hunkered down close, making her feel less alone. Cupping her head with one hand and Tad's with the other, he said in an exquisitely gentle voice, "Since we can't visit heaven right now, we ought to do something else. It's pretty warm outside. I have a sprinkler with Mickey Mouse on it. How about we play in the water before dinner?"

Jamie came forward just enough to press her face to his neck and breathe in his scent. That quickly bolstered, she faced Tad, who likely had no clue what a sprinkler was but would take his cue from her, and said an awe-filled "Mickey Mouse? Oh, Taddy, you *love* Mickey Mouse. Let's *do* it!"

Not only was the sprinkler a hit, but when Chip unscrewed the hose to spray the boys directly, he had them shrieking and running and tumbling over each other *and* over Jamie when she tripped, which she did repeatedly trying to escape the spray. Chip kept at it long after she laughingly retreated—kept the boys racing back and forth and around for such a long time that they could barely hold their heads up at dinner and were asleep soon after.

He checked on them while she showered. She checked on them while he dressed. When they were sure neither boy would wake, they headed out. Not only had Chip hired the trusted babysitter he used for school events, but he had made reservations at a restaurant on Beacon Hill, had brought along a bottle of champagne from his first pro signing, and seemed determined to learn every last thing about Jamie.

It started in the car—Jamie's convertible, so *cool* with Chip at the wheel—when the origin of the champagne got them talking about sports. What had Jamie felt when she won a tournament? When she lost? Where were her trophies, why were they packed away? Where were *his*? Had Chip regretted dropping out of college to go pro? Did he want Buddy playing hockey? Did she want Tad playing tennis? How to minimize the pressure of competitive sports? In what ways did sports ethics affect their current work?

Many answers were of the yes or no variety, because there were so many questions, *so* much to learn. By the time they pulled up at the restaurant, they were on to their jobs. What was Chip's favorite age group at school, favorite season, favorite sport? Were school parents a problem for him? How did Jamie choose between projects? Did she prefer commercial to residential? How did she keep up with the latest in technology?

Jamie learned that Chip blamed his early stardom for the arrogance that had led to women and booze, and that he dreamed of coaching hockey at the high school level to help ground budding stars. He talked about the growth of his summer camp, how it emphasized skills and teamwork over competition and partnered with a reading program at the local library. But he was as eager to know Jamie's dreams as share his own. So she talked of the drawings she had made for the Weymouth estate and her fear that the Barths would steal it away.

She had never been as thoroughly comfortable with anyone in her life. For all Chip's warnings about her being a MacAfee to his Kobik, the way he described his childhood made it sound identical to hers in terms of values. His family was firmly grounded—sisters functional professionals, one married, one not, parents still together after forty-some years. Could he be crazy, coming from that?

As they talked, they sipped champagne, split an appetizer salad, and munched on warm zucchini bread. Did Jamie see the restaurant's decor? Barely. She couldn't look at anything but Chip, which was why she was taken by surprise when a couple stopped at their table on their way to the door.

"We love your show," said the man, to which his wife added, "We watch it every week, even reruns now. Can't wait for the new season."

Much as Jamie resented the interruption, she couldn't alienate a viewer. Managing a polite smile, she said, "We just finished taping it. They're in the process of editing."

That led, when the couple moved on, to Chip wanting to know everything about *Gut It!* and Jamie telling him how the show had begun and what it meant to MacAfee Homes, but also about Claire's decree on switching hosts and Jamie's resulting rift with Caroline.

"Is hosting something you want?" Chip was careful to ask first.

"I thought it was. *Assumed* it was. But under these circumstances?" She shook her head. "Maybe someday, but not now. Especially not now," she added, reinforcing the *especially* with a meaningful look.

"I feel for your mom," he admitted. "Mine lost her job when the hospital where she worked was bought by a for-profit corporation. They said the cuts were part of the takeover, but it was mostly older women who were let go. Mom liked her job. Suddenly it was gone, and she was too old to find another."

"So she retired?"

"If you can call it that. She's a professional volunteer, her current passion being the library in the Vermont town where they summer. She's busier than ever."

They continued to talk over grilled snapper and rack of lamb, and when Chip ordered a side of sour-cream-and-chive fries, Jamie was in heaven. They lingered over cappuccino until thoughts of getting back for the sitter intruded, but they hadn't made it out the door when it was his turn to be stopped.

"Buffalo blew it when they sent you to Pittsburgh," said a man who was clearly a hockey fan. "You were the best right wing they had."

Less indulgent than Jamie, Chip thanked him, no conversation, and guided her to the car. "I always hate that," he muttered as soon as he slid behind the wheel.

"Why?"

"Buffalo traded me because I was a problem."

"You were a great player."

"Yeah, when I was on."

"You think of the bad behavior, Chip. People like him are thinking of the good stuff."

Taking a deep breath, he grabbed her hand and held it tightly as he drove off. "Keep reminding me, please?"

By mutual, unspoken consent, they avoided PDA at the restaurant. The fact that both of them were recognized validated that decision. The last thing either of them wanted was to find a cell phone shot posted somewhere online.

After the restraint, though, they touched constantly during the drive home. When Chip wasn't holding her hand, it was on the back of his neck or his thigh. He kissed her with promise when they pulled into his driveway, and made good on the promise after taking the babysitter home. She fell asleep in his arms, well and fully satisfied.

Jamie had trouble thinking about designing when she was with Chip, but she had fallen behind after Roy's death and was nowhere near catching up. She had always been focused on work, always. So it was near-compulsion that had the wheels in her mind spinning when she woke at five on Saturday morning. Naked beside him, she lay for a time just taking in the sounds and smells of the house. Her condo had few. Well built and new, it smelled nondescript, it didn't creak underfoot, and its systems were silent. This house was different. She smelled Chip, of course, all clean male, on her skin and his as he slept beside her. She also smelled wax on aged wood floors and heard the rattling of cool air through heating vents that had been adapted for AC only four years before.

Absurdly, she thought about flying. She was always more comfortable when the plane was hitting a steady stretch of gentle bumps. They gave her the illusion of being on the ground.

Likewise, the sounds in this house were grounding. Or maybe what gave the house roots were silent echoes from Chip's parents' time. They had raised a family here and had been happy. Jamie could *feel* that, as if the house had a character that lived beyond its inhabitants. It wasn't unlike Caroline's house in that sense. For the first time, she understood why her mother loved the Victorian so. Especially at a time when one's life was new, roots helped.

The AC cycled off, and Chip's rhythmic breathing was more noticeable. Turning her head on the pillow, she studied him—dark hair, shadowed jaw, broad shoulders, and good heart—and felt such a swell inside that she was beside herself. His body warmth was welcome in the air-conditioned chill he liked, but he wasn't physically holding her down. Rather, he had a hand tucked to her hip, as if the reassurance of her presence was all he needed.

But those wheels in her mind continued to whir, now joined by a little voice that cried, *Work!* That voice had been silent, not a peep since she had broken her engagement with Brad. And it wasn't snide now, just insistent.

With care, she gently slid away from Chip, but as soon as she sat up on the edge of the bed, he mumbled, "Where are you going?"

Miming writing, she whispered, "Work thoughts." She returned to kiss his cheek, then reached for a robe and crept down to the breakfast nook, where she sat with a paper and pencil making a list, by client, of work to be done. When the list grew daunting, she began shifting tasks to a second list, this for her assistant, and when that one grew daunting as well, she sat back.

Caroline was right. They needed to hire another architect. Jamie could still do everything herself, but did she want to? *No.* She loved designing homes, offices, and stores. But she had to learn to delegate, and some parts of her work couldn't be done by an intern. Oh yes, she might have trouble finding a licensed architect willing to take her runoff. Or not.

This would be a lifestyle change for Jamie. She had always been narrowly focused on one thing, first tennis, then architecture. She didn't go out with friends, didn't cook, and, other than yoga classes and the occasional tennis game with a local pro, didn't have any hobbies. But life wasn't all work. For the first time now, she wanted a mix.

Oh, and one more thing? She was absolutely, definitely, bottom-line not hosting *Gut It!* in the fall—didn't have the time, interest, or energy. She was thinking how best to break this to Claire and what the consequences might be when Chip slid into the booth snug beside her.

"The boys are up," came his deep, early morning voice. "I want a kiss before I go in there."

She kissed him—so natural, so sweet—then said, "I'll get them."

"No. You're working." He glanced at her lists. "Productively?"

She shrugged. "It helps when I organize things, but I need to hire another architect." Suddenly, though, she wasn't thinking about work. Laying her head on his shoulder with an ease that should have been years in the making, she said, "How can something so new feel so right? I keep waiting for a hitch."

"I like my house cool."

She smiled against his warm skin. "I noticed."

"And I leave the toilet seat up. Do you hate that?"

Still smiling, she raised her head to meet his gaze. "I might in the middle of the night, but hey, I like my bottles of hand soap, body lotion, and cologne lined up just so."

His blue eyes grew mischievous. "I noticed. I knocked them out of line last night when I was shaving, I think."

"It's probably good for me. I'm not exactly OCD, just organized. And clumsy? That's plain embarrassing."

"It's plain adorable. Like your freckles."

She spread a hand on her face. "I hate them."

He removed the hand, threading his fingers between hers, just as a call came from upstairs. "I need another kiss."

The second one was as sweet and satisfying as the first. It held comfort and ease and promise and love—yes, love. So bizarre, the speed of that.

"Can I make breakfast?" Jamie asked as he slid out of the booth.

He trailed his thumb along the line of her jaw. "I like cooking, you don't. I'll do breakfast, you do laundry."

Breakfast and laundry. They were mundane things to begin a day of mundane things that kept Jamie busy enough not to think once about work. When they hit the supermarket, she learned that Chip hated Brussels sprouts, liked his peanut butter chunky rather than smooth, and bought only organic milk. When they hit the drugstore for Buddy's allergy medicine, she learned that he refused to wear sunscreen himself but wanted 70 SPF on the boys. And when they hit the children's room at the library, she learned that he preferred nonfiction and read his books on an iPad.

Wherever they went, they were physically close. He seemed to need it as much as she did, which stunned her when she stopped to think. As touchy as she and Caroline were, she had never been this way with Brad. She hadn't thought it was in her nature to want to crawl all over a man.

That said, they were discreet. Seeing people they knew went with the territory in as small a town as Williston. Each time it happened, Jamie thought of Caroline. By rights, Caroline should be the first one to see her with Chip.

But how to see Caroline and not mention marriage? Because that was where they were heading. Once the boys were down for a nap, Jamie perched beside Chip on the arm of his living room chair. While one of his own arms steadied her, the other worked his laptop, which was open and searching. They found an inn in New Hampshire whose proprietor would issue a marriage license, officiate at a short ceremony, and provide music, flowers, and food for a wedding celebration, all on a Sunday.

"A gazebo," Jamie breathed in delight when the picture appeared on the screen. "I want it there."

"Then we're doing this?" Chip asked softly.

Sliding an arm around his neck, she searched his eyes. On level with hers, they held the same bits of terror, excitement, and determination that she felt. "I want to," she whispered. "I shouldn't. It's insane. But I want to. You?"

"More than anything. I love you."

She returned the words in a kiss, lingering with it until she couldn't any longer put off the only other major decision. "What do we do about our parents?"

Chip frowned, clearly struggling with that, too. "I'm not sure. They'll put a damper on this."

"The voice of reason," she remarked. By all standards, what they were planning was rash.

"They'll say we're rushing into this without thinking it through. They'll say it's infatuation, not love."

"They'll say I'm on the rebound from Brad."

"Or that I'm after your money," which he wasn't. He had shown her an investment statement in Friday's mail. He had way more money—and growing—in his name than she had in hers at the moment. That would clearly change once her inheritance came through, and Tad's inheritance would cover him for life.

"They'll worry that I'm desperate for a co-parent," she said.

"Or me a live-in maid."

"Or that I'm reacting to my dad's death and not thinking clearly. But I am. I feel like I'm thinking more clearly than I ever have, like I understand more what I want *because* of everything that's happened. We're not eighteen, Chip. We're fully grown, sensible, down-to-earth people."

He smiled. It was a sweet smile that matched the adoration in his eyes. "We are," he said, but his smile faded. "They'll still tell us to wait. They'll say we should take the time to plan a traditional wedding."

"Do you want a traditional wedding?" Jamie asked and caught the tiny shake of his head. "Me, neither."

"But if we elope, they'll be hurt."

She exhaled. "Yes." If there was any reason to wait, this was it. She had never met Chip's parents, but everything he said pointed to solid, loving people. He was as close to his family as Jamie was to Caroline, and then there was Theo. They would all be hurt.

Taking her hand, Chip pressed it to his mouth. His breath was warm against her skin, his eyes earnest. "All I know is that I've been happier in the last week, even when we were just talking on the phone, than I've been since I can remember. I love my son, but it isn't the same. I know what I want in a life partner, and it's you. We can rationalize this nine ways to Sunday, and it won't change how I feel." He kissed her knuckles, brushed them with his thumb. "We could wait."

"We could."

"We could get married in a month or two and have them there. It wouldn't be so awful."

"No," Jamie supposed, though everything in her objected to the idea. "On the afternoon he died, my father called me selfish and shortsighted. He may have been right about selfish, but our eloping wouldn't be shortsighted. It would give Tad a stable home with an amazing dad and brother, but even aside from that, this is *our life*. There would be something poetic about getting married so fast, given how we first got together. And the boys would be involved in the secret. They'll love knowing that."

"We're already living together," Chip added. "Done deal there. Do you have any doubts that we're meant for each other?"

Jamie did not. She had led a studied life, but not once in the shockingly brief time since she'd met Chip at the playground, not once since they'd become lovers, started living together, and talking marriage, had she had a second's doubt that he was her future. She had never been overly romantic, but if there was such a thing as a soul mate, Chip was hers.

Doubts, he had asked? "None," she replied and then, knowing that (A) she loved her mother and (B) she might be jeopardizing their already tenuous relationship but that (C) she was finally an adult and had to do her very own thing, on her own initiative, for the first time, she gave a definitive nod. "Let's book it."

Chip exhaled. "Consider it done," he said gallantly and clicked through for the phone number of the inn.

twenty-two

Caroline breezed through an hour with Zoe Michaels. She had done many other interviews, and while none of those media outlets had the prestige of the *Globe,* other reporters had been tougher. Perhaps the newness of Roy's death weighed on this reporter, or perhaps her age kept her intimidated. Perhaps Caroline was simply adept at answering questions she liked, sidestepping ones she did not, and religiously staying on message—message, in this case, being that while the MacAfee family deeply mourned Roy, he had set them up to succeed, which they would do. Though Caroline confirmed, when asked, that Roy had been one of the founding voices of *Gut It!,* she said that the show would continue on, starting with the fall season, in the manner viewers had come to love.

The interview was held in the courtyard behind the MacAfee Building, otherwise deserted early on a Saturday morning, and as soon as it was done, Caroline met Dean at his country place, where, in work clothes, goggles, and gloves, she sawed, hammered, and shaped wood for the bench that would curve in a corner of his fast-forming sundeck.

At least, she started out doing that, but there was something about

Dean in motion that caught her eye and stilled her hand. Too often of late, he managed schedules and crews rather than doing physical work. But he was a skilled builder, not to mention an impressive sight in the midday sun with his shirt off and his skin moist. As always during hands-on moments, he poured himself into the work. This was nothing new to her. His intensity attacking personal projects was what had initially invited her questions, which was how she had first learned of his struggling marriage. Later, in the darkest days of negotiating his divorce and dealing with his increasingly distanced son, he had been most able to articulate his feelings to her when he was pounding nails into wood.

There was something different about him today, though. She saw intensity without darkness, simply a man enjoying his work. Wanting to believe that their relationship was behind his lightened mood, she watched for a while.

He caught her at it, looking up absently, then doing a double take and sliding her a self-conscious smile. "Am I doing it right?"

"Absolutely," Caroline said and waved a hand. "Go back to it."

She did the same herself, but before long, she took another break. This one was for a cold drink, which she carried back outside in a single large travel mug. She had thought to bring lemonade but not insulated cups, and since she found only one of those in what could still barely be called a kitchen, they passed it back and forth.

They didn't have to talk. The companionship was just fine without sound—so fine, in fact, that when Dean returned to hammer and saw, Caroline grabbed her e-reader and sat on the grass nearby.

"Not a real book?" Dean called over at one point.

She held up the device. "A gift from Jamie last Christmas."

"Ahhh." His hammering resumed.

At some point it stopped again, which she realized only when his voice came from close by her ear. Hunkered down behind her, he read over her shoulder in a voice that was naughty and low.

" *'I am naked and hot, nearly orgasmic, and he hasn't even touched me yet.'* Jesus, Caro. What book is this?"

It was the same one the woman on the sidewalk had been reading that day after lunch. Caroline was embarrassed for all of five seconds before realizing how ridiculous that was. Recovering, she said, "If you're not wearing glasses, how can you see the words?"

"They're pretty big." His voice lowered, intimate and teasing. "I take it you don't want to miss a one?"

"I set the font bigger so that I could read in the sun."

"I'll bet."

"I did," she insisted, struggling not to smile.

It grew harder when his stubble brushed her cheek. "But you don't want anyone knowing what you're reading."

"Of course not. That would compromise you."

"Really."

"Really. I'm only reading this now to find out what the appeal is of these books."

"You didn't want to know before."

"No. I didn't." She hadn't quite analyzed the why of that, only knew that the woman she was back then hadn't been the least bit curious, while this one was.

He moved a bare shoulder against her back. "And?"

"And what?"

"Is the book as hot as we are?"

"Hotter," she said, unable to resist, and, laughing, caught the hand that slipped inside her shirt. "I'm just kidding, Dean. It's a pale imitation—*oh no,*" she cried when he flattened her to the ground and came over on top, "I am not doing this here, not in broad daylight where anyone can see, not with rocks digging into my back and that air compressor going on and off, and both of us sweaty as hell."

He slid his bottom half to the side but left his bare chest hovering. "Can we read the book together tonight?"

She made a show of considering before saying, "Only if we finish this deck first. Think we can?"

By way of answer, he quickly pushed himself up and went back to his tools. Joining him, she finished her part first and then lent a hand with his. As midday moved into afternoon, though, she wasn't thinking about sex with Dean. Increasingly, she felt a nagging unease. She hadn't talked with Jamie again, and yesterday's call had been too breathy.

No cause for concern, she told herself. *She's having fun. This is good.*

She kept thinking up reasons why the silence might not be good, though—notably, that Chip wasn't the great guy Jamie had thought but that she was too embarrassed to tell Caroline that, after the buildup she had given him. Caroline didn't want her daughter hurt. So she worried.

Dean wanted to cook out for dinner, but she wanted something more distracting, like milling crowds at a sidewalk café in Boston. They compromised on a suburban restaurant overlooking the Charles River that was popular enough to be packed without requiring a trek through city traffic. The last meant that Dean could take the Harley, which he claimed he badly needed, given the workweek that had been.

Caroline knew about that week. Cell constantly dinging, he had juggled crises ranging from the mundane to the not so, including a shipment of cracked marble, a surprise raccoon den with kits, and a framer suffering a major heart attack on-site. For Dean, working at the country place, where the sounds of their tools were solitary and he was in control, was therapeutic, too, but the Harley was his joy. She couldn't begrudge him this.

First, though, she was having a pedicure. The nail shop had started to empty when she arrived. Preferring it that way, she and Annie always took the last appointments of the day, customarily on Saturdays to enjoy their toes without work on Sunday. Linda Marshall often joined them, though there was no sign of her today.

For a time, they talked about nothing—a new varietal of peony, a summer salad at Fiona's—while they sat side by side in pedicure chairs, backs vibrating, feet soaking. Only when the whirlpools went off and their feet were taken over by practicians who spoke little English, ensuring privacy, did Caroline ask about Jordan.

Annie shrugged. "I finished the job Tuesday, so I haven't seen him much."

Her voice was predictably high, but something about the way she kept her eyes on her toes made Caroline ask, "You opted for prudence?"

A soft snort. "You could say that."

"Oh dear. What happened?"

Annie sank deeper in the chair, moving her silver hair against the headrest to stretch her neck. "I think my imagination got the best of me."

"How so?"

She shot Caroline a look of chagrin before refocusing on the pedicurist's work. "The last time I was there, I went inside to let him know I was leaving. A crew was installing draperies, so I knew he wasn't alone, but that made it safe to talk—you know, maybe arrange another time to see each other. I called his name and went looking, and there he was, testing the new Roman shade in the itty-bitty little first-floor powder room with the only female member of the crew. They weren't doing anything improper, and he wasn't embarrassed or awkward seeing me. He didn't take his hand off her arm, just gestured me in with his head. He touched my shoulder when he introduced me to her, and he touched her hair when he introduced her to me. He thumbed my chin when he talked about his shrubs and tapped her cheek when he praised her shade. Apparently, he's just a toucher."

"All touch, no action?"

Annie looked wounded. "It isn't funny, Caroline. I felt desired when he touched me, and I thought it meant something." She took a self-deprecating breath. "I thought it meant something—because I wanted it to, because I miss being touched."

Caroline twitched as the pedicurist hit a ticklish spot near the dry skin on her heels. She hadn't wanted Annie fooling around with Jordan in the first place, but her friend's disappointment was real.

"I'm sorry," she soothed.

"I told Byron."

"About *Jordan*?"

"Yes, because nothing happened, but it made me realize what I need and how badly I need it. If it isn't Jordan, it'll be someone else."

"You told him that?"

"I did," Annie said in a voice devoid of regret. "Byron needs to know I'm not just blowing off steam when I tell him I'm lonely."

Okay, Caroline realized. Annie wasn't giving up on her marriage yet. That was good. "Did he hear you?"

"He heard. Whether he can do anything about it is something else."

"I'm sure he can."

"I'm not, but we have to try. We're going on a 'date' this weekend. Overnight."

"Good move. I know a really romantic place if you want one." She snickered. "Dean's country house."

Annie eyed her curiously. "The house you say you hate but seem to be working on a lot?" She paused, frowned. "Romantic?"

"Well, aside from the ghosts, but if a man can't protect you from those, what good is he?"

"Romantic," Annie repeated, clearly suspicious now. "Am I missing something?"

Caroline wouldn't have chosen this particular time to tell Annie this particular bit of news, but something subconscious must have been at work, a tiny little imp of excitement craving expression. Denying it now would be lying.

Romantic? "Oh yeah."

"Dean?"

She nodded.

Seeming not in the least jealous or disturbed, Annie angled into the seat to face her more fully. "Oh. My. God. Tell me all."

"No one else knows."

"Or will." Annie's fingers locked her lips. "Tell me *all*."

Caroline wasn't about to do that. Much as she treasured the honesty between her and Annie, some details were too personal to be shared. What she had with Dean was special. She didn't want to dilute that. "One thing led to another," she said simply. "It's been nice."

"Nice," Annie echoed.

"Fun."

"*Fun*? I can't believe you are talking so calmly about being in bed with Dean Brannick."

Caroline shushed her with a glance toward the women who were now rubbing cream into their skin. For all she knew, despite assumptions to the contrary, they understood every last word. First names were one thing, but first and last could incriminate.

Annie's only concession was to lower her voice. "Do you know how many women daydream about that? How many see him on TV and take him to heart? How many women think of him while they're making love with someone else?"

"You don't know that," Caroline chided, though the possibility of it gave her a little thrill. Dean was hers. She still had doubts about her body, but it seemed to please him. He had said it enough—*touched* it enough—that she was starting to believe.

"Is he good?"

"Very good," Caroline said softly. He deserved that credit.

"And it worked? Everything you were worried wouldn't?"

Caroline blushed. She remembered their discussion—*so* hard to believe it had been only one week before, given all that had happened since. "He makes it work," she said now.

"Wow. Atta *girl*. Does Jamie know?"

"No, that's what I'm saying," Caroline replied with hushed urgency. "You're the only one. I don't know what Jamie'll say. She has so much else going on in her life right now, what with Tad and all." She couldn't mention Chip to Annie without mentioning Brad, and it wasn't her place to do that. No one at MacAfee Homes even knew the engagement was off. "I worry about her. I can't help it, Annie. I get nervous when I don't hear from her."

"When was the last time you talked?"

"Yesterday morning." At Annie's dry look, she added, "I know. Not so long ago, but we used to talk all the time." That was, of course, before the *Gut It!* crisis, but Annie didn't know about that either. "Most women have nine months to get ready for a baby, plus whatever time they spend thinking about getting pregnant. Even those who adopt think about it beforehand. Jamie had no warning. Overnight, she became a mother. She must have constant questions about dealing with Tad. I want her to call me with those."

"Her generation goes to the Web."

"I don't want Jamie doing that. I want her getting answers from someone who sees the world the way she does."

"Meaning you, but parenting has changed since we had kids. When my assistant talks about equipment or food or discipline, it's like another language to me. Jamie speaks that language. She needs current sources."

Caroline grunted. "That's what Dean says." Strong hands worked at the tension in her calves, her heels, her soles, her toes. "I'm trying to give her space, Annie, really I am, but it's hard. When she was playing tennis, I had to be involved, because Roy wasn't about to do the driving to practices and all. I was her on-call therapist when she was in college, and we see each other now at work and even more during *Gut It!* tapings. She's my daughter. I love her."

"This has nothing to do with love. She needs space to grow."

The sensible, down-to-earth, intuitive part of Caroline knew that was true. The part that worried continued to worry.

"Sometimes," Annie went on, "out of sight, out of mind is better."

"That's easy for you to say. You have sons. It's different with boys. Jamie isn't only my daughter, she's my friend. And right now, she's going through the biggest change of her life."

"If she needs you, she'll call. In the meantime, she may be wanting to do things her way."

Caroline thought about Jamie's broken engagement and now her infatuation with Chip, and sighed. "Dean says that, too. He reasons it all out, and then gets me doing something distracting."

There were more subtle things going on, too. Being with Dean made her feel good about herself. Not that she had been aware of feeling *bad*, though Claire had given her moments of late. But being with Dean, being sexual for the first time in years, was adding a *glow* to her life. Claire might have told her she was old, but what she did with Dean proved she wasn't dead yet. It said there was more to come.

Which didn't mean sex was the be-all and end-all of life.

It absolutely was not.

But it was nice.

"I'm glad you're with him," Annie said. "It means you're finally making a life for yourself beyond Jamie."

"What if she makes a mistake?" Caroline asked. This was her greatest fear. There were so many potential pitfalls in Jamie's current path.

"Then she makes a mistake. We all do."

"What if it's a big one?"

Gently, confidently, Annie said, "Then you'll be there to help her pick up the pieces. That's what mothers do."

"Dean said that, too. Did you talk with him?"

"I did not, but if he said it, he's both sexy *and* smart. Speaking of smart—" Her eyes went to the door just as Linda breezed in.

"Oh, good," the Realtor said with visible relief. "You're still here. I was hoping to catch you before you left."

Caroline surveyed the back of the shop. "I think Van is gone." Van was Linda's usual pedicurist.

"I'm not here for toes." Perching sideways on the next pedicure chair, she bent toward Caroline with her elbows on her knees. "This may be nothing, but I just overheard talk at Timmy's lacrosse game. Two guys were discussing the market, one telling the other that if he wanted a really good house he should wait until the Barths start building on Weymouth land. When I asked him about it, he said he had just met a local Barth and was talking with him. Their kids are playing summer soccer together. On my way here, I called friends from two different brokerages. They hadn't heard about any deal, but they've both been approached in the last week by the Barths asking about available property."

Caroline felt a twinge of anger. What else to think but that the Barths were taking advantage of Roy's death to move while the MacAfees were down? She had no trouble losing a few houses to them, but losing the Weymouth acreage was unacceptable. Even beyond what it would say about MacAfee Homes without Roy, it would be a blow to Theo, who had worked hard and long to own Williston and the surrounding MetroWest suburbs, and a blow to Jamie, who had already sketched out dream designs for that land. And *Gut It!*—hadn't Claire told Jamie she was considering a Barth season? The Barths buying the Weymouth property would ensure that.

Caroline had never been anywhere near as competitive as Roy and Jamie, but she felt a personal drive now.

"Well then," she told Linda with new determination, "we need to shop aggressively ourselves, and if that means playing dirty, so be it. We can start with the local connection. Weymouth roots run deep in Williston soil. So do MacAfee roots. Barth roots do not."

"My understanding is that only one of Mildred Weymouth's three sons is still in Massachusetts."

"John," Caroline confirmed, "in Boston. I never knew him personally." She turned. "Annie? You grew up with them, didn't you?"

"That was years ago, and we weren't exactly close."

"Why not?"

"I was beneath them," Annie said, and while another person would have heard upset in that high voice of hers, Caroline knew better. Annie was fiercely proud of her roots. "My dad cut grass for a living," she said with her chin up. "He didn't speak English well, just drove around town with a cigar in his mouth and a mower in the bed of his truck. Needless to say, he never cut Weymouth grass, though, in fairness, neither did any other locals. The Weymouths had a full-time gardener on staff. Clearly, those days are gone. From what I hear, most of the trust money has been spent, hence their need to sell the estate. That land is their only remaining asset."

"So they'll want top dollar," Linda warned, "which is why we can't risk driving the price even higher by getting into a bidding war with the Barths."

"What's their idea of top dollar?" Caroline asked.

The Realtor speculated. "Thirty acres of prime wooded land, with twenty-six of those acres able to support a new build to sell at a million, plus or minus? That's allowing two acres for a rec area and two for the manor house, which needs work but has good bones. The manor could be fixed up and sold as a single for two million, or broken into four condos selling for five hundred each. You do the math. The Weymouths will."

"And the Barths," Caroline murmured. "Bottom line for us to buy?"

"I'd guess a million for the house and three for the remaining land."

Four million to buy, with turnaround potential approaching twenty-eight million? Granted, building costs would be high on high-end houses, which these would be. Still, Caroline had lived long enough in the right circles to know a good profit margin when she heard it. She would have to talk with MacAfee Homes' banker and with Theo, of course, but, totally aside from the political advantage of developing the Weymouth property, she couldn't see them ignoring the money.

"That's assuming the Barths don't bid," Linda warned. "Right now, I don't see any other competition, but that could change once word gets out that the property is on the market. Inventory is low in all of MetroWest. Interested parties may appear out of the blue."

"Then we'll act quickly," Caroline vowed. "That means making the Weymouths an offer they can't refuse. How high do we have to go for that?"

"I'm not sure. Let me do a comp study. The key will be getting the brothers in a room with you and making a presentation. Do you have plans you can show them?"

Caroline thought of Jamie, who was off doing whatever she was doing with Chip Kobik and certainly not home designing for a project that had been hypothetical until now. What sketches she had were rough. That said, Caroline knew Jamie could embellish them. She would pull all-nighters if necessary. She wanted the project as much as Caroline did.

"We'll have plans," Caroline assured Linda and turned to Annie. "Do we assume we'll be dealing with John, since he's the one who's here?"

"I wouldn't. The three of them don't get along. One won't trust the other to make the final decision."

"Where are they now?"

"The oldest, Ralph, is a turnaround specialist in San Francisco. He buys companies, builds them, sells them. He keeps insisting that one of his companies will develop the land, though he's strictly West Coast and hasn't been able to get an operation going anywhere near here. The middle brother is Grant. He's an impoverished artist."

"Needs money."

"Big-time. And our local yokel, John, is a hotshot plastic surgeon."

Caroline knew that. His name consistently appeared on the Best of Boston lists, more often associated with Botox than with surgery.

"He rakes it in," Annie went on, "but spends it as soon as he makes it. He keeps telling the brothers that he wants the estate for himself. I heard something about his wanting to run a clinic out of the house, which the town would never zone for, but John hasn't given up on the idea.

My guess is that Herschel Oakes is key. He's the family lawyer, more likely the family referee. I'd start with him."

Caroline agreed, though reluctantly. She knew Herschel Oakes, had actually dated him once after her divorce. Once was enough. The man had been thoroughly self-absorbed. There was zero chemistry then and would be zero now, but if she could play on the local connection to make an inroad to that land, she would.

Time was, Theo would have done it, and after him Roy. Her own experience had taught her that a male might be more successful talking business with a male, but she didn't want to involve Brad.

Dean would help. But he wasn't a MacAfee.

Jamie could do it. But she was both female and young, two strikes against her, and she was a designer, not a salesperson. Not that Caroline was an expert in sales either, and she certainly didn't have management experience. But who else was there?

The buck stops here.

How often had she thought that when she was raising Jamie, and Roy dropped the ball on one parenting event or the other?

Time didn't change certain things. Or maybe it did. She was fifty-six. If she could corral the cachet that came with age—the brains, the poise, the guts—she might be able to play the MacAfee champion as she couldn't have done even ten years before.

She wanted the Weymouth project—wanted it for Jamie, for Theo, for MacAfee Homes. She wanted it for *Gut it!* And she wanted it for herself. The carpenter in her dreamed of creating some of the effects Jamie had put in her sketches. Add the challenge of winning at her age—of showing *all* of them what she could do?

In light of recent events, that was suddenly very important to her.

Caroline actually hesitated before calling Jamie. It was Saturday evening. If she didn't have plans with Chip and the boys, she would have called Caroline, wouldn't she have? And Annie's warning was fresh in her mind's ear. *She may be wanting to do things her way.*

But that was personal.

This was business.

Hesitation overridden, she thumbed in the call on her way home from the nail shop. When it went to voice mail, she said, "Hey, baby, sorry to bother you, but something's just come up. Linda Marshall has the distinct impression that the Barths are working behind the scenes to ink a deal on the Weymouth land before we even have a chance to bid. If we want to beat them to it, we have to act fast. I can coordinate everything except design plans. They're yours. Give me a call?"

Waiting for the callback, she held the phone palmed against the wheel during the drive home, and though that took barely five minutes, she was impatient. As soon as she pulled into the driveway, she sent a text.

Just left voice mail. Let me know you got it. Kinda urgent.

Fifteen minutes passed. Her phone was balanced on the rim of the sink as she stepped out of the shower when a reply finally came.

This is happening right now?

So Jamie wasn't pleased with the timing. Well, hell, neither was she. *We have to arrange a meeting with the Weymouths for early this week,* she typed back. *Where do your plans stand?*

Long minutes passed. Caroline had a helmet on her head and was about to climb on the Harley behind Dean when she felt a vibration against her thigh. Pulling out the phone, she read, *They're just sketches.*

How long before they can be more? she typed back. She didn't want to pressure Jamie, but she needed something of presentation quality.

The answer came more quickly this time, actually while they were on the road, and though Caroline was anxious to read it, she wasn't yet comfortable enough on the bike to take one of her arms from Dean's. The minute he parked at the restaurant, though, she accessed it.

Wednesday, maybe?

Any chance of Tuesday? The Barths are breathing down our necks.

I'll try.

twenty-three

Sunday dawned warm and heavily overcast, but not even the occasional drizzle could dampen Jamie's spirits. She refused to think of the promise she had made Caroline and the juggling she would have to do to be ready for a Tuesday presentation, *refused* to think about how much she wanted that project and feared losing it.

Today was her wedding day. Even the brief text exchange was foggy now, seeming to dissipate along with the mist. By the time they hit the New Hampshire line, the sky held patches of clear, and the sun was positively beaming on the small Colonial inn by the time they pulled up.

As omens went, it was a good one. Jamie vividly recalled the rain on the night her father had died, and suspected thunderstorms would shake her for the rest of her life. But sun, here, now? She chose to believe Roy was smiling, knowing with a heavenly wisdom that her marriage to Chip was right.

The innkeeper was waiting. True to his word, he had the appropriate papers ready to be signed, and within the hour, with Chip and the boys in pressed shirts, shorts, and sandals, and Jamie in a sundress, the ceremony began. The gazebo was woven through with wild roses that matched those in Jamie's bouquet, and while a violin-cello duo played softly, she and Chip exchanged the simplest, sweetest, most heartfelt of vows.

It barely took five minutes, which was a good thing, since the boys wanted no part of standing still when lush gardens beckoned, but those five minutes were still beautiful and extraordinarily emotional for Jamie. She didn't know whether it was all that had happened of late, or whether she would have cried at her wedding even if they had waited a year, but her throat was tight and her eyes moist as they held Chip's, and her heart was filled to overflowing the entire time.

There were pictures taken by Chip's camera—a sophisticated digital SLR that he proved expert both at using and at telling others how to use. There were toasts with champagne for adults and apple juice for kids, even a dance for the newlyweds. There was an elegant picnic by the brook, with the innkeeper's wife arranging plates on a fine linen cloth and serving a hearty peasant bread, sliced filet mignon, and an asparagus and endive salad to die for. When the boys balked at the meat, she produced peanut butter sandwiches from her cart. None of them had trouble devouring freshly frosted wedding cupcakes.

They spent the afternoon between the garden, the brook, and the hot tub, and when it was time to head home, there were sandwiches for the car.

Jamie couldn't imagine a more perfect day. She had roses to press, pictures to frame, and memories to last a lifetime. Most important, she had a husband she adored and who adored her. He was forever lifting her hand to his lips as he drove, forever glancing at her with the same stunned pleasure she felt, forever citing one part or another of their wedding day as being *the* most special.

The boys fell asleep in the car on the way home, which meant that they were up later than usual into the evening, but Jamie loved even that. And when the house was finally silent, she had Chip. They didn't have to speak, were of like mind in what they wanted. Their lovemaking was slow and sweet, deeper and more meaningful than ever before.

She fell asleep in his arms and woke up feeling blessed. Eyes wide, she lifted her hand and looked at the ring he had produced in the middle of the ceremony. It was a total surprise; they hadn't talked rings at all, neither of them needing the physical symbolism. But the emotional one? When Chip was in Boston buying shirts for himself and the boys, he had gone to the Cartier boutique—not that she needed that either, but he had.

Three entwined gold bands, white for friendship, yellow for fidelity, rose for love—he had explained this while slipping the ring on her finger. All three bands were encrusted with diamonds, and though he didn't say it aloud, she knew he wanted the diamonds he gave her to be totally different from any diamond she had worn before.

"Hey," he murmured, smiling sleepily when her eyes flew to his.

She smiled back. "Just admiring my ring." She cupped his jaw. The dark morning stubble made the ring look even more delicate.

"Did we actually do what this ring says we did?" he asked.

"We did. Are you having second thoughts?"

"Not me. You?"

"Nope."

Grinning, he scooped her close and was about to act on an impressive arousal when the boys trailed in, at which point it seemed more important to make them feel loved. And that was heavenly, too—her adored baby half brother, soon to be her son, tucked up against her with his thumb in his mouth and Moose in his arms, grinning around that thumb as he watched Chip tickle Buddy, who squirmed and contorted.

As an only child in a house that had grown even more quiet after her parents' divorce, she had always dreamed of having a large family. This, here, now, was what she wanted. She didn't fear that Chip would tire of her, that Buddy wouldn't accept her, or that the children she and Chip had in the future wouldn't be wonderful.

Her only fear was what Caroline was going to say when they showed up at her house that morning.

Caroline was on the front porch with Champ and her laptop, researching Herschel Oakes's recent activity, when a Honda SUV turned into her driveway and parked behind Dean's truck. It was a minute before she realized that it was Jamie with Chip and the boys. Excited, she glanced at her watch. Not yet seven thirty? The implication of that didn't sound like the caution she had urged for Jamie, but she was so hungry for contact that she was relieved nonetheless.

Closing the laptop, she returned Jamie's wave, motioned Champ to stay on the porch, and started down the walk. Her eager eyes were first and foremost on Jamie, who was dressed for work, summer chic in a skirt and silk tank, auburn hair daring to curl past her shoulders. She took Tad out of the backseat, shifting him to a hip as Chip and his son rounded the SUV. And how could Caroline not stare at the man? More casual than Jamie in sneakers and jeans, he was also taller and darker, but if looks were the basis of a relationship, her daughter couldn't have done better. They were a striking couple, a *modern* couple dressed for different jobs.

Taking his hand, Jamie drew him alongside her, and in that instant Caroline saw beyond a handsome pair to a tight foursome, the quintessential all-American family. Her gut said that there was commitment here, though whether it was infatuation or true feeling she didn't know. Her gut also said Jamie wasn't here to talk about the Weymouth land.

They seemed nervous. But so, in her own more mature and experienced way, was Caroline. Anything Jamie was committed to, whether brief or long-term, mattered to her.

Meeting them at the head of the walk, she smiled and extended a hand to Chip. "I'm Caroline. I'm sure our paths have crossed at some point."

His handshake was firm. "Charlie Kobik. I'm honored. You've raised an amazing daughter."

"I think so," Caroline said in faint warning that Jamie was hers, would always be hers, and that Charlie Kobik could go by whatever name he chose, but it wouldn't change Jamie's parentage.

Lowering Tad to the ground, Jamie said a breathless "Mom—"

She had never been breathless where Brad was concerned, yet here it was again. Unsure of the meaning of that, Caroline bought time by dropping to a knee. "Hey, Tad," she said and was pleased that the child didn't resist when she drew him close. She reached out to Buddy. "You must be this handsome man's son. I'm Caroline, Jamie's mom."

"Where da cat?" Tad asked.

"You have a cat?" Buddy asked.

"Three," Caroline admitted.

"Mom—"

Caroline rose with a hand on each boy's head and her eyes on Chip. "I'm not one for formality. Do you mind if I'm on a first-name basis with your son?"

"I'd like that."

"Mom," Jamie demanded with too much force to be further denied, and held out her left hand. The fact that it was shaking gave Caroline a feeling of déjà vu. Last time, the ring finger had been bare. This time it was not.

Meaning? Caroline wondered uneasily. Three days after breaking her engagement to one man, her heretofore prudent daughter was engaged to another?

"We got married," Jamie said, visibly holding her breath.

Caroline's eyes flew from the ring to Jamie and Chip. Neither was laughing, winking, or taking it back, and there was nothing remotely bogus about the diamonds in those three entwined rings. She didn't have to be a jewelry buff to recognize the design. It was stunning, high end, and authentic.

But *married*? After knowing each other, what, *half a day*? And . . . and without a word to her mother?

Jamie wouldn't do that. They were more than mother and daughter. They were best friends.

"Where da cat?" Tad repeated, standing inches in front of Caroline, looking up at her.

"Uh, oh, sweetie, he's inside. Upstairs, actually. I believe he's sleeping." She didn't know for sure. Having ceded the front porch to Champ, Master could easily be hiding in the parlor, waiting to attack when the dog invaded that space, too. Whatever, Caroline couldn't let anyone in the house, certainly not to the second floor.

"Is there a ball in the car?" Jamie softly asked Chip, who immediately loped off. Her eyes followed. Caroline couldn't miss the way they clung, seeming to take strength from just looking at him.

But still, marriage after knowing each other such a short time?

Chip returned with two kickballs, rolled them off across the grass, and leaned over the boys, who took off seconds later. As Jamie's vigilant eyes followed, Caroline struggled to find words, but she didn't know where to begin.

Helplessly, she listened as Jamie listed the arguments against what she and Chip had done, preempting Caroline's raising them, but insisting that their marriage was right, that they loved each other and the boys, and that, *believe it or not, Mom,* she knew Chip better in this short time than she had known Brad in four years.

Caroline could believe it. She had never been able to open to Brad, in part because he hadn't opened to her. Charlie Kobik looked like a different sort, stronger and more dynamic, but either of those traits could have a dark side.

She was thinking he might have somehow enthralled Jamie, forcing her to act in a way she would never have done on her own, when he said in too normal and sensible a voice, "For what it's worth, my parents will be as shocked as you are. They'll have heard of Jamie, but they'll be upset that they've never met her, and they'll be hurt not to have been included in the wedding. I apologize to you, and I'll apologize to them. I know this is sudden, but I know my own heart. I also know what I want in a family, because I grew up in a good one. Jamie's the first woman I've ever been with who wants the same thing. I love her, Caroline. She's it for me."

Caroline fought liking him, but the words resonated. His family had an outstanding reputation in Williston—which she knew how? Quickly she remembered. When Chip made a mess of his hockey career, the buzz around town had been what a shock it was, given his parents' goodness.

Did that make him the black sheep with emotional problems?

Champ had come off the porch, apparently as impervious to Caroline's authority as Jamie, and was eying the kickballs. Tad inched away. Buddy simply froze.

"He'll want to play," Caroline called gently. "Try rolling him the ball."

"Why is the dog here?" Jamie asked. "Why is *Dean* here so early? I thought he wasn't a morning person. Is he working in the garage?"

Caroline could not go into that. When Chip trotted toward the boys to show them how to befriend the dog, she turned to Jamie. "I'm just stunned, baby." Her voice was hushed. "I never expected you'd run off to get married. When did this *happen*?" There weren't many choices, but she needed to know.

"Yesterday, at an inn in New Hampshire."

More pain. "You knew you were doing this when we texted Saturday night?"

"We had just decided, like a few hours before. The innkeeper is a justice of the peace, and there was a beautiful gazebo covered with roses. His nieces played violin and cello, and his wife served a picnic lunch."

Something felt familiar to Caroline. She gasped. *Dean*. Hadn't he said they could avoid a wedding? That there were elopement packages? Had he put them up to this?

But no. That thought was nearly as preposterous as the one saying her daughter had just gotten married.

Needing a visual—something, *anything*, to make the unreal more real—she asked in an aching whisper, "What did you wear?"

"My pink sundress."

"From J. Crew?"

"It's my favorite."

Yes. Caroline knew that. The dress was adorable. "But we were going to shop for a gorgeous gown. You wanted a big white wedding."

"Not me, Mom. Brad, Dad, and Theo. Did *you* want that for me?"

"I only wanted what you wanted."

"Which is Chip," she pleaded softly. "I love him, Mom. He's everything I could have asked for."

Caroline told herself that Jamie was a good judge of people. But all she could think was that her only daughter was now legally tied to a man she had known for too short a time, that marriage was hard enough without this kind of rush, and that Roy would *die* if he knew.

Which was a ridiculous thought, of course.

Needing to blame him somehow still—Caroline had never set this kind of example for her daughter, had agonized for years before getting a divorce—she asked in the same hushed voice, "Does this have to do with your father's death?"

Jamie's voice was as hushed. "No. Chip and I discussed that, too. I'm telling you, we looked at every angle to find one that would tell us to wait. It wasn't Dad, per se. He and I were close, but he wasn't my best friend." *You were,* her eyes said, but the compliment stung.

"If I was the close one, how could you not tell me what you planned? How could you keep the most important thing in your life a secret? We talked Friday, and you said nothing. We talked Saturday night, and you said nothing. You could have come over any time in between, and you didn't. I could have kept a secret, Jamie."

"I know that, Mom, but I knew you'd tell me not to, and I didn't want anything spoiling my joy. I love Chip. I want to be with him."

"Couldn't you just live together to make sure it would work? Couples do that all the time."

"We could have," Jamie conceded. "But we know it will work. There's no question. Plus, we have kids. We didn't want anything tentative for them, and Tad, especially, has gone through so much. He needs permanency."

"Knowing someone for three days guarantees that?"

"I've known Chip more than three days," Jamie argued. "It feels like *forever,* like he's lived through the same things as me, like our lives ran parallel for years until last week, when they finally intersected and fused." She held out a hand to Chip as he returned, and when he wrapped an arm around her neck, she brought their linked fingers to her throat.

As lovely an image as her words produced, as sweetly as she was tucked into him, as truly connected as they seemed, Caroline ached inside. The rift Claire had caused over *Gut It!* had been bad. Jamie had sworn she was simply a pawn in that, but she had withheld information. This time, she was no pawn. This time, she had actively done something she had known would hurt.

Speechless, Caroline wrapped a hand around her own neck in an effort to get a grip.

"My son means the world to me," Chip told her—and though she wanted to shoo him away and say this was between her and Jamie, it wasn't. He was a key player. "I would do nothing, *nothing* to harm him. If I'd had any doubt that this marriage wasn't right, I'd have waited. And this isn't about my getting a live-in sitter. I love spending time with Buddy. It's what my dad always did with me and what I always dreamed of doing myself. I always knew I wanted a wife, but there was too much at stake for me to risk it all with the wrong woman. I never even brought a woman home before Jamie. I love that she has a career and that my work hours conform to the kids' schedule, so that I can be at home with our kids when she can't. I love that she considers Tad hers and that I have two kids now, and I want as many more as she does. Getting married may be sudden, but I knew from the first time we talked that she was the one. If we'd gotten together in high school, I might have saved myself a lot of grief."

"No," Jamie responded as if they were alone, "it wouldn't have worked back then. We weren't ready. We were both one-dimensional and self-focused."

"And you think marrying on a whim isn't self-focused?" Caroline asked, immediately regretting the words and their tone, but lacking control.

Jamie eyed her sadly. "(A) we didn't marry on a whim. Sudden doesn't necessarily mean on a whim. We considered it from every angle. And (B) I'm not afraid of marriage. You are, and I understand why. You're afraid of it not working. But Chip is not Dad."

Caroline gave a self-deprecating huff. "I didn't think Dad was Dad when I first married him either. That's my point. It's hard to know a person deep down in the best of circumstances." She didn't finish. Jamie was suddenly focused behind her.

Even before Caroline turned, she knew what she would see. There was Dean. Trotting down the steps. Striding down the walk. "Hey," he said to the gathering in general with a nonchalance totally at odds with the situation.

Jamie's startled eyes flew to hers.

Caroline might have denied it if he had been wearing a shirt and boots, but coming from the house rather than the garage, in jeans, a coffee mug, and little else, was incriminating. But—*whoa*—cause for shame, given what *Jamie* had just done? Absolutely not! "I'm fifty-six," she told her daughter, "and I'm *not* getting married."

"So she says," Dean injected as he shifted the mug to his left hand and offered his right to Chip. "Dean Brannick, and I sense something intense. What did I miss?"

"They got married," Caroline cried. "Eloped." She folded her arms, trying to cushion herself from the hurt.

Dean had the audacity to put a comforting hand on her back. She would have stepped away, if that hand hadn't made her feel less alone.

"You're *sleeping* with Dean?" Jamie asked. She looked surprised, but far from scandalized.

Caroline gave a dismissive wave. "It's very new."

"How new? Like, last night? Saturday night?"

"Honey," Chip cautioned, seeming to sense her point at the same instant Caroline did, but Jamie didn't listen, which probably was a strike against enthrallment.

"You didn't tell me, Mom. You could have, but you didn't." Her eyes went wide, dawning. "Last *Thursday*. I was driving here to tell you I'd broken my engagement, and it was early enough so that there weren't many cars on the road, only a few work trucks. And. A. Harley. He was heading out after spending the night, wasn't he?"

"It doesn't matter."

"It sure does," Dean argued. "Wednesday night was the beginning of the rest of my life."

"Dean," Caroline cried in exasperation.

"There you go, Mom," Jamie declared. "You've been sleeping with Dean longer than I have with Chip, and you didn't tell me."

" 'Sleeping with' is not the same as 'married to.' "

"If you and I are best friends, it is. But you said nothing. Omigod," she cried, clearly seeing even more, "we talked about sex. About whether it's important. You acted like you had no idea. You said you weren't the best one to ask, which was a total *crock*—"

"No, I *had* no idea—"

"It was the perfect opening, but you said nothing. Why is it okay for you to withhold vital information but not for me to do it?"

Caroline was upset enough to mimic her daughter. "(A) I'm your mother, and (B) I'm old enough not to have to report in."

"So am I," Jamie argued. "I'm older than you were when you married Dad. Did you ask your mother's permission before you accepted Dad's ring?"

"No—"

"And you were married within weeks."

"I was pregnant. You're not." She had a sudden, awful thought.

"No," Jamie confirmed, having one right answer, at least, "but Chip would have treated it like his if I was, which is only one of the reasons I love him. Look at his family. Look what he does for a living. He has the biggest heart in the world—but even if that weren't so, you need to respect my choice, because I'm an adult and now a parent and this is *my life*. Marrying Chip is probably the very first thing I've ever, *ever* done without consulting you, but he and I knew that what we had was real, and we wanted to act on it. Yes, it was fast, and people will talk, but we don't care." Her brow furrowed, eyes suddenly reflective. "So . . . so maybe Dad's death did have something to do with this. He died too early. Maybe the message is that if we put off the things we want, we may die before we get them."

"That's a recipe for disaster."

"My marriage is not a disaster."

You could always get it annulled, Caroline thought and might have said if not for Dean.

"Caroline," he warned, a single low word.

But Jamie seemed to have heard, too, because she was suddenly emotional. "Mom, *listen* to me. In other circumstances, we'd have wanted our families there. But this—here, right now," she wagged a finger between them, "is exactly why we didn't. Yesterday was beautiful. It was meaningful and intimate. Other than being with our families, I wouldn't have changed a thing." Her eyes grew moist. "Be happy for me, Mom."

Caroline had always wanted that, and she did hear shreds of common sense in the arguments, but it was overshadowed by a sense of loss.

"I wish I could be," she whispered. "This is just so not what I expected from you."

"Nor is this," Jamie said with a look at Dean, "but it's okay, Mom, because it's clearly what you want, which is the lesson you always taught me. You know, if we're talking about who's the most honest, you or me, it's kind of a draw."

Still Caroline fought. At some level, she knew she shouldn't, knew that she didn't fully understand her own reaction, but Jamie's actions hit at the heart and soul of the stability she had always tried to provide. "What about Brad? What about everyone at work? Marrying this fast after breaking up with him, you'll be called a cheater. Do you care?"

"Yes, I care. I've always cared about MacAfee Homes, but this is my life, and it's right, and they'll just have to accept that. If they want to think the worst, I can weather it, because I'll be with the man I love and our kids, and, by the way, that man will be covering for me at home while I work up designs for the Weymouth land, so you owe him for that, and as for Brad, he's outta here. He texted me last night—*after* I got married—to say he's accepting the position he wanted in Minneapolis. So who cheated? He was looking to change jobs and leave town while we were still engaged. I wasn't looking for anything, and broke my engagement the minute I realized I *wanted* to look. I'll talk with Brad this morning. But he's giving his notice today, so Theo has to be told."

Caroline held up both hands, palms out. "You're on your own there."

"I need to work on the plans."

"Sorry."

"You said you'd handle Theo."

"That was before this. I'm not *touching* this."

twenty-four

Normally, Caroline would cling to the sight of Jamie's car until it rounded the curve, but not today. For one thing, it wasn't Jamie's car, for another, she was furious with Dean, and for a third, her cell was ringing in the front hall. Entering the house, she snatched it up. She knew who was calling even before she glanced at the screen. She had seen the *Globe* piece herself first thing and had actually thought it quite good, but the *Gut It!* EP would not.

Phone in hand, she strode barefoot deep into the parlor and looked at her mother's Victorian lace as she clicked into the call. Even with the reassurance of the lace, she was feeling ornery enough to dispense with pleasantries. "Yes, Claire."

"What possessed you to do that interview?"

She imagined that the Victorian lace had just stiffened, like her spine. "I got a call from the reporter and thought the publicity would be good."

The screen door slapped a second time. Dean. Turning her back on him, she went deeper into the parlor until she came up against the hand-hewn walnut of the dining table.

"You couldn't have called me?" Claire asked.

"Why would I do that? The reporter wanted to talk about Roy's death and MacAfee Homes."

"And *Gut It!*"

"Oh, Claire. That wasn't the purpose of the interview."

"Of course, it was. *Gut It!* put MacAfee Homes on the map."

The show had certainly given the company good exposure, but a little perspective was in order. *Gut It!* wasn't the be-all and end-all of life. Hosting it had boosted Caroline's self-esteem, certainly in her post-Roy years. But she could live without it. She saw that now—actually *felt* it, perhaps for the first time since the threat of losing it had arisen. Moreover, MacAfee Homes had been in existence long before *Gut It!* and would definitely outlive it.

Feeling remarkably calm, Caroline said, "The *Globe* covers local businesses. That was the context of the interview. This was about business, not entertainment."

"Jamie should have done it."

"Actually, I called Jamie. I felt that since Roy was her father, she might want to comment on his death. She was busy"—and didn't *that* suddenly take on new meaning—"so she opted out, and since I'm more into MacAfee Homes management right now than she is"—which actually felt quite good to say—"it made sense for me to do it. The reporter was on a tight schedule."

" 'Tight schedule' " Claire scoffed, in rare form for so early in the day, "means either 'I screwed up and forgot about this assignment,' or 'I need to do this interview now to be free later for a more important one.' Reporters can be handled, Caroline. We have professionals who know how to do it, which is another reason why you should have called me. That interview was a golden opportunity, and now it's lost. A *Globe* piece would have been the perfect vehicle to start shifting the show's leadership—"

While she ranted on, Caroline held the phone away from her ear and stared at Dean, who, incredibly, was finishing getting dressed in the clothes he had deliberately chosen to leave on the newel post on his way down the stairs earlier.

"—and you didn't even mention Jamie's name," Claire concluded.

"Oh, I mentioned it. I mentioned it plenty. The reporter chose not to print it."

"You made it sound like *Gut It!* was all about you."

"No, Claire. I am simply the MacAfee Homes spokesperson, which is clearly what's pissing you off."

"You didn't *mention* the station, but the station is crucial here."

"Not for this interview," Caroline insisted with renewed defiance, "and, in fact, maybe not at all. If not your station, another station"—which Dean had suggested and subsequently vetoed, though his judgment was *lousy*—"but you know something, Claire? I have more important things to deal with right now. I'll have to talk with you another time." She pressed END, tossed the phone onto the table, and swung her irritation on Dean.

He was beaming at her. "Well, *that* was impressive," he crowed. "Good for you!"

"Flattery won't work," she declared, further annoyed by the tingle she felt seeing him there with his belt hanging loose. A week before, she would have been mortified if his jeans had been unsnapped, but she knew now what was under his clothes—or *someone* did, though she still wasn't sure who that woman was, especially when he irked *this* woman so. "And there you were, barely dressed, trotting down the front walk bold as brass. Why did you do that? It was *my* place to tell Jamie about us, at *my* time, in *my* way."

He tucked a black tee into his jeans. "Given how you were dragging your heels, I'd have been dead before you got to it." He zipped his fly.

"Dean. It's been *five days*."

He grinned, unrepentant as he sank down on the ottoman to put on his boots. "Counting, are you?"

"Did you have any inkling what Jamie was telling me?"

The grin faded. He paused and braced an elbow on his knee. "Actually, I did. Since you don't have AC, your windows were wide open. I heard what was happening and heard it heading nowhere good, so I figured it wouldn't hurt if I came down."

"Looking like you just rolled out of my bed."

"Which I had."

"Dean." She wanted to strangle him. "You changed the whole dynamic

of the discussion. I was making headway, and you gave her what she needed to turn my single best argument against me."

"The friendship one?" He went back to lacing his boots. "Oh, come on. It's not like she waited a year to tell you. They went off for the day yesterday, and she came here first thing today."

"She could have come over last night. She should have come yesterday morning, *before* she went off for the day."

"And given you a chance to say no?" He snorted. "She wouldn't have listened, Caro. All you'd have done would have been to rain on her parade, and please, *please*"—he speared her a quelling look as he reached for the second boot—"don't go on about her rushing into marriage. Yes, she rushed, but it wasn't just her, it was him, and it was their thinking about two little boys who they thought would be best off with two parents. They're adults, Caro. You might have acted differently had you been in her place, but this isn't your life, sweetheart, it's theirs. Besides, do you think time guarantees success? You took your time with Roy, Jamie took her time with Brad, I took my time with my ex, and God knows none of those relationships worked, so maybe time isn't the answer. Maybe it's about gut instinct and basic animal attraction."

Sex. "Why did I know it would come to that," Caroline muttered.

Both boots on, he stood, seeming too large and too right. "You didn't. You're just spoiling for a fight. You want to argue with Jamie, only she isn't here."

"Well, do you blame me for being upset?"

He held up a crooked-pinkie hand. "No, I do not. Being upset is normal. She's your daughter, you love her, and she did something that shocks you. But stop for a minute, Caro. Think about how she looked and how she acted."

"I don't know him."

"You don't have to. She does. And Williston does. He's a known entity here."

"Not all good."

"Pretty damn close, of late. So I repeat. Think about how she looked and acted just now. Think about the life she's making for herself. Is it all bad?"

He sounded so rational that Caroline couldn't ignore what he said. Jamie had an instant family—not just Tad now, but Chip and his son. Even without the Weymouth project, her life would be ten times busier. And richer? Maybe. She had always wanted a slew of kids, hadn't made any secret of that. If Chip's words were to be believed, he wanted the same and would carry his weight.

So, had she looked happy? Not when she faced Caroline. When she looked at Chip, though, or held Tad or said Buddy's name, she was happy. And she hadn't blown her hair stick straight, unintentional if she had run out of time. Or symbolic? It had looked prettier. Softer. Natural.

Dean's eyes were knowing. "Not bad at all," he confirmed, "but it is a life she's making for herself. If any one thing has you upset, it's that. She took her life in her own hands and acted without consulting you. So for you it's about control."

"It is not," Caroline argued. She *refused* to think she was a controlling person. "It's about closeness and trust. And—and *respect*. If she respected me, she would have told me what she was doing."

"It's about control," he insisted as he approached. "Why do you need it, Caro? You have your life, and she has hers. She's twenty-nine. Why can't you let go?"

Feeling personally attacked, not only by Dean but belatedly by Annie, who had said much the same thing Saturday at the nail shop, she raised her chin. "Maybe because I'm a difficult person who wants to rule people's lives. So now you see the real me. Now you can just"—she gestured toward the door—"just walk out of here and never look back and be all the better for it."

That quickly, he was inches away. "Oh-oh-oh no, you don't get rid of me that quick. I'm not leaving, Caro. You're making a mountain out of a molehill, but I'm not running away, because I am not the problem. So what if Jamie knows we're sleeping together? You've always wanted her happy. Don't you think she wants the same for you?"

Caroline opened her mouth to answer, but thought twice.

"Are you happy with me?" he asked, suddenly vulnerable.

She supposed.

"I'll take that as a yes," he decided, his hazel eyes warming in relief, voice dropping, "because I *do* like sleeping with you, and it isn't just basic animal attraction. I like touching you in the middle of the night—just touching—and if you didn't like it, you'd move away, but you don't. There are times when I'm awake watching you, and in your sleep you scootch closer, like you want to make sure I'm there. Know how that makes me feel? Like a million bucks! So I don't care if the world knows we're together, and that starts with your daughter. She's not going to think less of you for it, unless you're with me for some other reason that I can't figure out, when deep down inside you're really miserable."

"You know I'm not," Caroline grumbled.

He brushed her cheek with a gentle fist. "So what's really bothering you? It isn't just that Jamie got married without asking permission. You're not that small a person."

His gentleness did it, stripped away her fight. She was horrified when her eyes filled with tears, but she couldn't will them away. "I feel like I've lost her."

"Because of her tie to Chip or your behavior just now?"

Wrapping her arms around herself, she confessed a soft "Both. You said it. She made her own life. I'm not part of it."

"Of course you are."

"She doesn't need me. Certainly not like she used to. So where does that leave me? If I'm not a mother, who am I?" *Who am I?* How many times she had wondered that in the last few weeks. After years of stasis, so much had changed.

He grasped her elbows. "You're her mother, her friend, her confidante. You'll always be those things."

"Her confidante? Like she confided in me this weekend?"

"Oh, Caro," he breathed and, drawing her in, wrapped his arms around her, "you're confusing confidante with consultant. She didn't consult with you beforehand, but she confided in you as soon after as she could."

With his chin on the top of her head, her face fit his neck just under the stubble that was his salt-and-pepper not-quite-scruff, not-quite-beard. His skin was warm and his pulse strong, and though he didn't speak, she felt a dense emotional support. Having always been her own best backup, she had never leaned on anyone quite this way.

Daring to let down her guard, she said a self-conscious "So maybe it is about control. But it's hard, Dean, hard letting go."

"Is that why you won't wear my ring? Afraid of sharing something with someone? Of losing a little of that autonomy?"

She considered that, trying to figure out if it was true and, if so, where it came from. "I've just been the one in charge for so long. My parents were Poughkeepsie-centric, so I was on my own once I left, and Roy—well, Roy opted out soon after Jamie was born. When he was around, he ruled, but the rest of the time I was on my own. Jamie was mine. But I swear I didn't push her. The whole tennis thing came from her. I was just her manager."

"And cheerleader."

"Of course. What kind of mother would I be if I wasn't? But I tried to give her space, honestly I did, especially when she was at RISD, and still I was the one she came home to. So now she's going home to a *husband,* and the powers that be say I'm too old to host *Gut It!*"

"The powers that be don't know their ass from a hole in the ground," Dean said with such fervor that she had to believe it. "You're not too old. Jamie's too young to do what you do with the show, but she's better suited than we are to chase little kids around 24/7. Would you want to be in her shoes, starting out raising a family?"

Caroline thought about tired muscles and wrist tendonitis. She thought about quiet time with her computer each morning, minimal cleanup after breakfast, pedicures with Annie, and quality time with her cats. She thought about what she was doing this very instant, arms around Dean, deep breathing, quiet comfort, no interruptions.

Would she want to be starting out raising a family? "No *way.*"

He chuckled. "Me neither. I kind of like being near the top of the MacAfee Homes food chain. You're higher'n me, and you'll go even higher if Theo has his way."

"Oh, Dean, I'm not sure . . ."

"If you want to run the company? You keep saying that, but it isn't so much filling Roy's shoes as paving your own way. What you did with the *Globe* was great. Jamie couldn't have done that—no offense, sweetheart, but she doesn't have the experience or the gravitas. She will someday, but not yet. And what you're doing with the Weymouth acreage? Look how you've approached that."

"It's only one meeting." Later that morning with Herschel Oakes in his Boston office, and she was not looking forward to it. She was actually surprised he had agreed to meet—surprised he had even returned her call on a Sunday afternoon. If he thought she wanted to try them again as a couple, he had another think coming. She was perfectly happy where she was.

Dean's throat moved, sound vibrating past his Adam's apple. "I'm talking about the way you've taken the lead."

She sighed. "There's no one else to do it."

"I'm talking about you, Caro. You know what you're doing."

"I'm flying by the seat of my pants."

"You have good instincts. You make decisions. You act."

Letting the argument go, Caroline was quiet for a time, listening to the dove in the maple, to the patter of kitty paws overhead and Champ nosing at the front screen, wanting in. Superimposed on it was the steady beat of Dean Brannick's heart, not a bad moment at all, when removed from the rest of her life.

She tipped her head back so that she could see his eyes. "I made a mess of things with Jamie again, didn't I."

Wisely, he didn't respond.

"Only it's worse this time," she added, "because it isn't just Jamie, it's Charlie Kobik, who is now her husband, and the two little boys who will be calling her Mommy before long." She took a deep, resigned breath. "One bad thing about age? Hard to accept change."

"One good thing about age?" Dean, her hero, pointed out. "Realizing you need to do it."

"Well, *that* went well," Chip remarked.

"It was a *disaster,*" Jamie cried, only then shifting her eyes from the windshield and catching the grim look on his face. The fact that he agreed with her was small consolation for how upset she was.

"Consider it a dress rehearsal," he warned. Indeed, now that the hour was more reasonable, they were heading home to Skype with Donald and Helene Kobik before Chip dropped off the boys and headed for school. "My parents won't be much better, and there are two of them."

Chip's parents actually were better precisely because there were two of them. Don calmed Helene when she got caught up in many of the same arguments Caroline had. Jamie couldn't help but think, slightly hysterically, that the two moms would get along just fine if they could get past the suspicion that their son or daughter had been bewitched by the other's daughter or son.

Presenting a united front beside Chip during the video call, Jamie tried to look as unbewitching as possible. She tried to look as *together* as possible, when her insides were a tangle of nerves. She tried to reassure Helene as Chip had done with Caroline, and while there was no Dean to compound the argument, the call ended only marginally better.

"Should we have waited?" Jamie asked the instant the live feed ended.

Still bent over his laptop, Chip looked back at her. "Do you think so?"

"I asked you first."

He straightened. "My answer is no. What's yours?"

"No," she said, relieved that they agreed here, too, especially considering the big deal her mother had made over needing time to know a person. She hated that Caroline had planted even the tiniest seed of doubt. "I like your parents, Chip."

"You do not," he muttered and pushed a hand through his hair. "Hell, you'd think I was twelve."

"You're the baby of the family. Your parents worry."

"They had cause once," he said, seeming momentarily lost in that old regret. His eyes held sincerity when they focused on Jamie again. "They really are good people. They'll love you once they get to know you."

"So will my mom once she gets to know you, but I'm sorry about earlier, Chip. She came across as a bitch."

He arched a brow at her leg, to which Tad was clinging. Whispering,

"Ooops. Gotta work on that," she knelt to give her baby a hug. His warm little body was reassuring. Funny, given how recently he had become hers, but he was now a constant in her life. She was still trying to decipher his reactions and moods, but even his little tantrums were easier to deal with than, say, Caroline's right now.

Putting her chin on the top of Tad's head, she looked up at Chip. "She isn't usually so rigid. If she was talking about anyone else, she would have been more forgiving. I'm her daughter, so the rules are different. I get that. Still, given our ages, you'd think she'd be less uptight."

"Same with my mom. At what point do they ease up?" he asked rhetorically, then called into the other room, "Buddy, use the potty before we leave!" Back at Jamie, he said, "At least the men kept the moms sane."

Jamie frowned. "The men."

"My dad and Dean." He paused. "What?"

"(A) that remark borders on stereotypical, and (B) Dean didn't quite keep my mother sane." When Tad squirmed for freedom, she kissed his head and let him run off. More pensive, she said, "Dean and Mom—why didn't I see that coming?"

"Maybe because they've known each other so long. Do we like him?"

"Yes, we like him, but why in the world she needed to keep it a secret is anyone's guess." She considered, then added a meek "It is a little weird, though."

"Imagining your mother with Dean?"

She stood, sighed. "Imagining my mother with *anyone*."

Sputtering a laugh, he slid an arm around her waist. "I can't *begin* to go there with my folks. As far as I'm concerned, they've had sex three times. Period."

Thinking that he knew so well how to handle her, she locked her hands at the small of his back. "They have a right to do it."

He snickered. "You think?"

She did, which was why she wasn't truly upset thinking of her mother and Dean together. It actually made her feel better to know Caroline wasn't alone, since now she herself had Chip. She had never felt that way about Brad, probably because he had never fully occupied her the way Chip did. Even now, with so much urgency on her mind, he took her away, if for only a minute or two.

"Anything beats thinking about telling Theo, but I do need to do that, seeing as he's my first stop. Not that I have time for this right now." Chip had already offered to drop off the boys, so that she could see Theo and then go on to the office. Presentations were crucial. If she had a prayer of having something done by tomorrow, she needed every possible minute.

Chip drew her to him, his eyes the riveting blue that never failed to send a little thrill through her. "Are you sure I can't go with you?"

"I'm sure. Mom was right. I need to do this myself." The thought of it tied her in knots all over again. She would love to have her husband with her as backup. But her grandfather could be unfiltered when it came to pithy remarks. She didn't want Chip hearing that.

Knowing where Theo would be and that he would be softer there, she drove to his house. Though the Tudor structure was totally old-world, with its half-timbers and stucco over a fieldstone skirt, its second-floor gables, its grand portico and broad stone steps, the house had always called to Jamie. She had never once dreamed of redoing it, though many of her recent designs involved updates on the Tudor style. Theo's house was Theo's house.

More to the point, Theo's house was Jamie's grandmother's house. Though Patricia was long dead, her generous spirit lived in the antique furnishings and exquisite art she had personally bought. These things evoked her memory at every turn, but nowhere was that more true than on the back patio.

That was where Jamie headed. Circling around, she walked over well-mown grass, passing beds of heirloom flowers in staggered states of bloom, a stone chimney, and shrubs of varied greens. The patio was soapstone. Patricia had herself set the stones, which were a richly veined gray and held enough of a pattern to delineate three large vaguely circular shapes, one each for lounging, grilling, and eating.

Surrounded by an outer yard of ancient trees in full leaf, the patio itself was lush. Jamie vividly recalled Patricia on her hands and knees, weeding the gardens that bordered the stone. A subservient woman doing her husband's bidding? Only the ignorant would think that. Patricia was strong and quiet. She was also insistent when she believed in a cause, whether that cause was building a pergola, which was right now covered with lilacs, or raising money for the church. Though she had never been directly involved in the operation of MacAfee Homes, she took joy in the house her husband had built her. That joy shimmered over the gardens even now.

By contrast, Jamie's first glimpse of Theo so alone squeezed her heart. Wearing suit pants and a shirt, he would add a tie and jacket before heading to the office. For now, his neck was open, sleeves rolled to expose forearms whose skin was marbled and loose. A creature of habit, he was drinking orange juice, eating the last of the scrambled eggs and toast that his housekeeper had made, and reading the newspaper.

He didn't see her until she slipped into the chair closest to him, at which point he looked up with a start, then came alive. Gleeful, he slapped the paper.

"See this?"

Jamie had seen two things that morning. First, she had seen Chip, the boys, and the beautiful wedding ring that she kept looking at in amazement but that Theo hadn't noticed. The ring was stunning and held a world of meaning for her, but the subtlety of it would camouflage its meaning. Second and haunting now, she had seen Caroline's disappointment.

"What's there?" she asked.

"Your mother's interview. She did a damn good job, *damn* good job. She keeps saying no to it, but she's a fine spokeswoman for the company. You need to tell her that, too." He pushed the paper aside. "So, little girl, if you aren't here to talk about the *Globe* piece, why'd you come?"

Jamie tried to still her nerves. "I have news, Granddad," she said. Spotting the housekeeper approaching to offer food, she shook her head. The instant they were alone again, she faced Theo. She hated doing this to him when his spirits were high. She hadn't seen him animated since Roy's death. But her news wouldn't wait.

His creased face grew progressively drawn as she told him about her broken engagement, about Brad's plans to leave the company, and finally about Chip. By the time she finished, he was frowning, his blue eyes confused. Seeming older, he turned away for a moist cough, then shifted gingerly on the cushions of the iron chair to face her.

"Brad is leaving?"

"Yes. He misses his hometown."

"I thought Williston had become his hometown."

"Apparently not."

"What about loving you?"

"I'm afraid we were both wrong about that. I'm sorry, Granddad. I know the last thing you need right now is having to hire a new lawyer."

Theo's mouth was a pale line. "Bad timing, so soon after . . ." *Roy's death.*

"Yes," she said and waited. Brad had only been half of the news she had delivered. She had no clue what Theo was thinking about the other half. Giving him time to process it all, she remained quiet.

Finally, screwing up his face, he asked, "The washed-up hockey player?"

"But he's not washed up," she rushed out with a promising smile and sat straighter. Earlier, with Caroline, she had felt like the little girl Theo always called her. Now conviction gave her new force. "He teaches here in town and runs a successful hockey camp for kids each summer. He has a three-year-old son he's raising himself, lives in the house he grew up in—"

"Living back home?" Theo broke in. His implication was clear, made all the more so by the disdainful tone of his gravelly voice.

"Actually," she countered, "he bought his parents two homes to retire in. He has plenty of money."

Theo gave a guttural grunt. "He made a mess of his life."

"He knows that. Trust me, he does. He hit rock bottom but pulled himself up. He's gainfully employed, has a family behind him and a son needing him, and his instincts are good." She hurried on, unable to resist the argument. "We all liked Brad. But Brad didn't want a child, couldn't even open his heart to an orphaned one, who happened to be your namesake grandson. So we can intellectualize his merits all we want, Granddad, but on the things that matter most, he fails."

Theo continued to scowl. "You could've raised Tad yourself."

"I could have. And I would have. I had a good example of single parenthood in Mom." It was a slam against Roy, but it was the truth. Theo didn't deny it with so much as a raised brow. "Believe me, I was in no rush to get married, certainly not on the heels of breaking up with Brad. Tad is not the reason I married Chip."

From inside the house came a distant phone.

Theo seemed not to hear it. His eyes didn't waver. "What is?"

"I love him."

"That quick?"

"That quick," she replied, driven by determination, even a smidgeon of anger. If the ringing phone meant Caroline wanted to share her feelings about Jamie's marriage, grit was needed. "Call my behavior impulsive, Granddad. Lord knows, Mom did. But when it comes to Brad, at least, he was happy to let me go and take a job halfway across the country—a job, PS, that he'd apparently been considering for a while."

Guilt stopped her. She hadn't meant to sound resentful. "I'm sorry. That was unnecessary. Brad served MacAfee Homes well. But he has an assistant who can cover until we hire someone else, and in the long run, the company will be stronger for it. As for Chip, I've never been so sure of anything in my life. He and I think alike. We've both done the superstar thing and understand about passion and focus. Right now, his focus is on his son, and on me and Tad. That said, I understand your caution. I shouldn't have snapped at you. I'm sorry."

Theo surprised her with a sly grin as he sank back in the wrought-iron chair. "I always wondered if you had it in you."

"Had what in me?"

"Your father's spunk. It makes me feel like I haven't completely lost him." His gaze shifted as the housekeeper came toward him with the phone.

"Brian Leavitt," she murmured apologetically. "He said it was urgent."

Jamie was still trying to grasp what had to be a major compliment—at least, she thought it was—when the identity of the caller sank in. An urgent call from Brian could only mean that Claire was up in arms about the interview Caroline had given the *Globe,* and if Claire was upset about that, she would retaliate by upping her demands about *Gut It!*

Jamie took a deep breath to still her racing heart, but it made barely a dent.

"Yes," Theo barked into the phone. He listened, then said reasonably, "I thought it was a good piece," then, without remorse, "I'm sorry you feel that way," then, watery eyes meeting Jamie's, "A meeting is an excellent idea." She saw him sit straighter, as if his spine had had an infusion of steel. "No, tomorrow won't do, or Wednesday . . . Yes, Brian, I understand that time is of the essence, but I run a business . . . Thursday morning is fine." His eyes warmed. He was enjoying himself. "No, not at the station, at my office . . . Yes, that's all well and good, but I'm eighty-two, so you can just come to me." *Home field advantage,* he mouthed to Jamie and winked. "MacAfee Homes is my major concern. Yes, Brian. Yes. I know Claire is upset, you already said that. A word of advice? Have her tone down the rhetoric before she gets to my office. I don't do well with ultimatums." A final pause, then a nod. "Thank you."

Jamie didn't know whether to be excited or nervous. "A meeting with Brian and Claire?"

"And your mother and Dean and you."

For an instant, Jamie wondered if Theo knew that her mother and Dean were involved. Then she realized that (A) Theo would have probably assumed they had been involved long before this, and (B) Brian would have requested Dean be there, so what Theo thought was moot.

"What did he threaten?"

Leaning on the arm of his chair, Theo came closer. His eyes, remarkably clear, held both challenge and amusement. "He threatened to cancel *Gut It!* What he doesn't know is that I don't *care* if he cancels *Gut It!* It was my son's baby, not mine. And that's a message for you, too. If you and your mother want it, you'll have to fight for it." He sat straight again, watching her closely. "Married?"

"Married. I love him."

He was silent.

When she couldn't take the suspense any longer, she coaxed softly, "Say something, Granddad."

"Do I know his parents?"

"If you're asking whether they run in the same social circles we do, I'd say no, but they're well thought of in town."

"Tad is named after me. I don't want him called Kobik."

She felt a tiny breath escape. The beginning of acceptance? "He won't be. Chip and I talked about that. I'm keeping MacAfee, too."

Again he was quiet. Then, his voice more gentle than she'd ever heard it, he asked, "Is this what you want?"

Jamie's throat tightened. Given how brusque her grandfather typically was, she had driven here fully prepared for a dressing down peppered with lots of *little girl* this and *little girl* that. Now, though, he was different, perhaps mellowed by age or by the death of his son. She almost imagined he was standing in for Roy. That was enough to bring tears to her eyes—and if not that, then the fact that Caroline had always been the one who wanted for Jamie what she wanted for herself, but was closed off to it now. Theo's gentleness couldn't have come at a better time.

"What?" the man asked gruffly, clearly unsettled by the tears in her eyes.

"That's the nicest thing you could have said. Yes, it's what I want, and yes, it's going to make me happy, and yes, I've thought of every reason why someone who doesn't know the situation may call it crazy, but I love him, he adores Tad, he's a fabulous father, and he treats me like gold. Tad will always be my first priority. He has to be. But this will give him a stable home with a mother and father who want him." She paused and chanced a tentative "Mom is pretty upset—the speed of this and all."

Theo made a dismissive sound. "I proposed to my Patricia the day we met. We married a week later."

Jamie had known that but hadn't seen a correlation. "Times were different back then."

He did a thing with his white brows that said he didn't think that was important either. And since he didn't, she had a thought.

"Maybe you could remind Mom about you and Grandma? What with everything that's happened, she's probably forgotten. I would greatly appreciate your help with her."

"It doesn't come without strings."

"What strings?"

"Convince her to take my job when I retire."

Blindsided by how serious he was, Jamie was momentarily without words. There were so many reasons why she might not be Theo's best advocate, the most immediate being that Caroline would assume Jamie wanted her anywhere that would get her off the set of *Gut It!* so that Jamie could host.

"I've been testing her," Theo said with that same earnestness. "She's good at what I do."

"I'm not sure she agrees."

His smile was wily. "Then it's your job to convince her."

twenty-five

Caroline's outfit of choice for her meeting with Herschel Oakes would have been armor. He had never taken potshots at her directly, but she had seen him target others enough to know to beware. He wasn't a trial lawyer; his smooth zingers rarely reached a judge. They were aimed at everyday people, especially family members who were thinking of contesting a will for which he was the executor. Whether Mildred Weymouth had filed her estate plan with him to discourage one of her sons from doing that, or simply because Herschel had Williston roots, Caroline didn't know. All she knew was that he was a serious hurdle to cross in making a deal for that land.

Lacking chainmail, she went with the black flared skirt, peplum jacket, and ivory tank that she had bought for Roy's funeral. The outfit was as close as she owned to clothing that was both executive, as in I-am-MacAfee-Homes-take-me-seriously, and feminine. She did own slacks and blouses that she had recently worn to meetings calling for more than carpentry gear. But she thought the funeral outfit stylish and young, and

Dean thought it sexy—not that that counted for anything other than making her feel attractive.

Actually, it did count for something.

Actually, it counted for a lot. The more attractive she felt, the more confident she would be. There were moments—fleeting, here and gone, back in an hour or two—when she still wondered what in the devil she was doing with her life. She was a carpenter. Her specialty was working with wood. She was happiest under a veil of sawdust in the quiet of her garage, not negotiating Boston traffic in Theo's Caddy sedan, which he had insisted she drive. Yet here she was, dressed for business, following a GPS in a spanking clean and quite comfortable car, and it wasn't all bad. Interspersed with those moments of doubt were ones that said she was growing, trying new things, evolving. The terror she would have felt doing Theo's bidding even a month or two before was now mixed with anticipation.

She hadn't seen Herschel Oakes in more than a decade. After he had sold his Williston house and moved to Boston, there was no more running into him at Fiona's or the town dump, and while she had absolutely no personal interest in the man, she wanted him to think her a powerful woman. Powerful women who were also stylish, youthful, and sexy were impressive. If he was impressed, he might be inclined to help her.

Call her backward. Call her politically incorrect. Call her an embarrassment to every feminist in New England.

But she wanted the Weymouth land.

Herschel's firm occupied two floors of office space in the Financial District. The elevator that zipped her up had a brassy gleam, the twelfth-floor lobby was done up in a handsome navy lit by a wall of windows overlooking the city, and once her presence was intercommed through, the man who came out to greet her was as impeccably dressed as ever. His suit was Italian, making him look slimmer than she recalled, and his salt-and-pepper hair remained thick. But he looked much older. His skin didn't have the high color it used to, and his eyes, though still dark brown, were tired.

Older didn't disturb her, but something about him did.

After giving her a light hug, he guided her back to his office. A large mahogany desk dominated the space, but he passed up its high-backed chair—his throne, she thought dryly—and took the companion armchair to hers, where he folded one knee over the other and sat back. Surprisingly polite, he asked about Theo and Jamie, and congratulated her on her the success of *Gut It!* When he expressed condolences on Roy's death, adding as a caveat that he hadn't known Roy well and had never particularly trusted the man, she didn't reply. But when he told her how good she looked and tacked on "Roy's death must be agreeing with you," she couldn't be still.

She opened her mouth to protest.

He beat her to it. "I'm sorry." He actually looked sheepish. "That was mean-spirited. It's hard to change a lifetime of crass remarks. But I am trying."

"Why?" she asked, still startled.

He did a thing with his mouth that said it wasn't important and moved on. "So. You're interested in the Weymouth property."

Three times in the course of their one failed date he had complained about people wasting his time. She remembered it clearly, in part because he had been so focused on himself the rest of the evening that she had gone home convinced her own time had been wasted. So it didn't surprise her when he cut to the chase now. This was the man she remembered, and this was why she had come.

"MacAfee Homes would like to buy it."

"Before someone else does."

"If that's the case. We've been eying that land since Mildred died. We hoped we'd get a fair shot at it once the brothers decided what they want to do. Lately, the name Barth is cropping up a little too often. Is there a deal?"

"No."

"Would you tell me if there was?"

"Yes. I wouldn't share details, of course."

"Of course." More lightly, she added, "But can you tell me if anyone named Barth has sat in this chair in, say, the last six months?"

"They've tried. The Weymouth brothers aren't ready to act yet."

"Is it just a matter of waiting for the right offer?"

"I don't know," he surprised her by saying—surprised, because it seemed too honest an answer for the wily lawyer she remembered Hersch Oakes to be. That man would have hedged, simply to imply that the right offer would have to be high. If he were on top of his game, the man she had known would mention a recent golf outing with one of the Weymouths, to let her know how close they were.

If he were on top of his game, came an echo.

Her gut said he wasn't. Something about him was muted, as if he were a windup toy whose key needed turning. Perhaps he had just mellowed, but if so, it was unexpected.

"Are you okay?" she asked gently. "You seem—" She hesitated, not wanting to offend.

"Seem what?"

"Tame," she sang out, deliberately making it sound like a high compliment.

His brown eyes were steady. "Isn't that what life does as you age? You're aging. Aren't you more tame?"

She didn't have to weigh that for long. Strength, daring, passion—all had been front and center in her mind of late. "Actually, I think I'm bolder. But if I'd been as brash as you fifteen years ago, maybe I'd be tame by comparison now, too."

"Brash, huh?" His smile was wry. "I should have expected that from you. It was one of the reasons we were wrong for each other. You were totally honest and I was totally not. You saw right through me."

"Only partly this time. Something's different with you."

"And with you."

"If not now, when?" Caroline quipped in offhanded explanation, realizing only after she said them how true the words were. Wasn't she at an age where if she didn't try something, didn't do something new, didn't dare to push the envelope, she never would? Hosting *Gut It!* had been a challenge. She hadn't dreamed she could do it until she actually did it. Now that she faced losing it, she was discovering other things she could do, like pleasing Dean Brannick in bed. Like playing CEO. Even like arguing with Jamie.

Thinking of the last, she felt a painful curl near her heart. Needing to get back to the here and now, she eyed him and said, "Menopause. That's my excuse. What's yours?"

He huffed a soft chuckle at her response. When she didn't add anything, he said, "Ach," and waved his hand, though his wrist didn't leave the arm of the chair, "just tired."

"Just?"

"Cancer, actually." She gasped, but he went on. "I was diagnosed three years ago. The treatment was aggressive. Right now, I'm in remission. It will kill me eventually, assuming a client doesn't kill me first."

"I'm sorry," Caroline breathed. "I had no idea."

"No one did. That was the point. It was important to maintain the appearance of strength. Unfortunately, my energy level has never quite gotten back to where it was." He grimaced, bared his teeth, shook his head. "Now, there is another not quite honest remark. My conscience is what took the hit. When you face mortality, you start looking at your life, and when you overhear things like 'Couldn't happen to a nicer guy,' or 'I want his office the minute he checks out,' you start taking stock of where you've been."

Caroline didn't have to like the man to feel compassion. "People can be cold-hearted."

"If that's the example set for them by their mentors," he said with audible self-recrimination. "But the slowing down hasn't been a total waste. I've gotten to know my daughters. I have five grandchildren now."

"Five."

A smile softened his fatigue. "Two boys and three girls. They're pistols."

She eyed the photographs on the credenza. Most were of young children caught in spirited moments. "If they're pistols, they take after their grandfather," she remarked.

"Their grandfather made it work only to a point." He shot her an amused frown. "Why am I telling you this?"

"Maybe because we go back."

"It won't get you the Weymouth land," he warned smoothly. "I don't care how hard up MacAfee Homes is—"

"We're not hard up."

"Then why fight for that land?"

"Because it's a breathtaking parcel."

"It'll cost you a fortune."

"It'll make us a fortune."

"Well," he said and took a minute, seeming energized now as he regained command, "you may be barking up the wrong tree, because I'm not the one who owns the place. If I was, I'd have sold it months ago."

"It's that much of a drain on the trust fund?"

Lacing his fingers over his middle, he studied her with amusement. "I didn't say that. I said if I owned it, that's what I would do. I sold my place in Palm Beach—you knew I had one, didn't you? I held it longer than I should have. It was a greedy mother that cost a bloody fortune to keep looking good even when there was no one there, which was most of the time—but it had the right address and was just off the fifteenth hole. It was a great place to entertain. Evening guests, weekend guests, I'm telling you, you have no idea what you missed. I had a live-in cook who could prepare gourmet dinners for twenty, hell, sometimes thirty. When you offer guests a free meal that's better than the one they can get at the club—" He stopped, closed one eye, grunted. "There I go again."

Talking about himself. She smiled kindly, remembering that long-ago date.

He tipped his head. "If you owned the Weymouth estate, what would you do?"

Caroline didn't mistake his casual curiosity for anything other than what it was, namely an invitation for her to make her case for MacAfee Homes buying that land. So she began with the company's roots and ended with its love of Williston, and in between she spoke of Jamie's award-winning designs, other local projects they had done, the roster of local craftsmen they used, and the possibility of *Gut It!* involvement. "If the Weymouths choose MacAfee Homes," she concluded, after covering all of her major points, "they'll be guaranteed a quality product that will preserve the spirit of their childhood home."

"What spirit is that?"

"Elegance. Success. Beauty. Warmth."

"The Weymouths aren't any of those things."

She smiled. "But I bet they wish they were. Home development is about wishful thinking. It's about capturing a dream."

"That sounds very pretty."

Turning mockery to her advantage, she said, "It will be very pretty. We've done this before, Hersch. We know this land, we know this town, we know this business. We get things done, and we're willing to work with your clients to make them comfortable with everything we do. We'd like to meet with them. Can you arrange that?"

She imagined she saw a glimmer of admiration before he put on his game face again and clicked his tongue. "That may be tough. Like I said, they're not ready to act."

"That," she said, coming forward, "is because they haven't talked with us yet. You said it yourself. The trust fund is taking a hit."

"I didn't say that. You did."

"And you didn't deny it," she countered. Facing this man who, regardless of its cause, wasn't quite the demon she remembered him to be, she felt surprisingly strong. It struck her that she was almost enjoying herself. "You just told me about your place in West Palm. Given the weather up here, the Weymouth house has to cost far more than that one to heat. Throw in electricity, the cost of a live-in caretaker, the standard lawn cutting and snow plowing, homeowners insurance, alarm company fees, and property taxes—should I go on?—and it adds up."

He whistled softly. "You're good."

Studying him, she sat back. "*Are* you mocking me?"

"No," he said. "I'm thinking that I may have missed something in you."

It was high flattery, she supposed, though she couldn't return the compliment. Even mellowed, the man held less personal appeal for her now than he had then. Zero chemistry was an understatement, now that she knew what real chemistry was. Dean was such a total *man* compared to Herschel Oakes.

But that counted for nothing when it came to the land she wanted. Herschel was the man here, and she couldn't offend. Laughing softly, she raised a hand. "Oh, I am not touching that, but trust me, when it comes to the company that will do the best job in developing the Weymouth acreage, I'm right. The Barths don't have a feel for this land or this town, and as for your clients not being ready, Ralph hasn't gotten his act together enough to send a crew out to even look at the property in the year since his mother died, John may want the house for himself but will never be able to pay the trust as much as we can, and Grant is so desperate for money that he'll take *any* sale."

She wouldn't have dared be this blunt with a nonfriend, but her knowing all this told Herschel Oakes that she hadn't come on a whim.

"Here's the thing, though," she went on, striking while the iron was hot. "We want to act quickly. Arrange a meeting, and we'll talk money and designs and whether the brothers want the land featured on our show, but now's the time, Hersch."

"You want a preemptive deal."

She nodded. "We do."

"Why right now? Is this a play to show the world that the company can survive without Roy?"

"No. We know others are interested in it. We want that land before someone else gets it, because we know we're the best ones to develop it."

"Why are *you* here? Last I heard, you were a carpenter. Isn't that what you are on the show?"

Ignoring the put-down, she smiled. "Ever watch it?"

"Reality TV? I think not."

"You should watch ours. It's good."

"You didn't answer my question," Herschel countered smoothly. "Why you? Is it because we have a little, uh, itty-bitty little bit of history together, so Theo felt you could sway me for old times' sake?"

She actually laughed. "You and I both know that would never have worked, though I have to say I like the new you better than the old one, cancer and all."

"Cancer is no laughing matter."

Studying his earnestness, thinking about his reformed manner, and having the sudden thought that other things in his life might have changed as well, she glanced at one of the photos on the credenza. No family shot, this one showed a woman who was dark-haired, middle-aged, and seemingly down to earth. She wasn't his ex-wife or either of his daughters. Her face was kind.

Caroline hitched her chin toward the photo. "Is that someone special?"

"She's my therapist."

She might have laughed at the idea of one's therapist holding a prime spot among family photos, if he hadn't remained so serious. "Literally?"

"Yes. She helped me when I was first diagnosed. Not my usual type. She works."

"Works, present tense—as in continues to treat you?"

"Works as in goes to work every day. I always liked my women to be available. That was one of the problems I had with you. You kept me waiting an hour for our date while you finished a job."

Caroline smiled. "And here I thought you were going to say I had dirt under my nails."

"I could never see that," he mused with a glance at her hands. "You kept them polished, even back then."

"There's no dirt."

"And Alice isn't my therapist anymore, at least, not in any official capacity."

"Ahh." A romantic link, hence her presence on the credenza. "That's nice, Hersch. I'm glad for you." And she meant it.

"So, I ask again, why you?"

She could have said that Theo wasn't as mobile as he used to be, or that they hadn't yet picked a replacement for Roy. She could have even admitted that yes, it was because she and Hersch sort of had a past. The truth held bits of all these things. It held other things as well, like Theo wanting her in management and Dean wanting her in bed and the money behind *Gut It!* wanting her fifty-six-year-old face out of the limelight, meaning that she had something to prove by orchestrating this deal, but Herschel Oakes didn't need to know those things.

For now, she simply said, "Because I care about that land."

"If you care so much about a piece of land," Dean responded the instant Caroline finished her blow-by-blow over a late lunch at Fiona's, "then you need to care more about Jamie."

Startled, Caroline held her chicken-breast-on-focaccia midair. "Whoa. Where did that come from?" She had been feeling good. Suddenly, she wasn't. The little nagging that had been hovering just beyond the periphery of her consciousness sprang forward and squeezed her heart.

"Have you called her?"

Carefully, she replaced the sandwich in its wicker basket. She looked at her watch, then across the booth at Dean. She had been expecting praise for having held her own with the lawyer. Feeling defensive now, she said, "It's barely one o'clock. My morning was busy."

"You said you'd call her. Things weren't left well, and if you've taught me anything about handling my son, if you've learned anything since the last fight with Jamie, it's not to let moss grow on a festering stone."

A *festering* stone? "Did I ever use those words?"

"Fine. Not those, exactly," he conceded without backing down, "but you get my drift. You said you'd made a mess of things with Jamie. You said you were going to call her while you were driving to Boston."

Sitting back in the booth, she kept her eyes steady on his. "I thought I would, but then I wanted to stay focused on my meeting." She was challenging him straight on, having found that when she did, he was slower with barbed replies. She wanted him to think before he said more. Jamie was her point of greatest vulnerability.

Lifting the last of his ham-and-cheddar-on-focaccia, he studied it before dropping it again. Pushing the basket away, he wiped his mouth with a napkin, set it down, and met her gaze. "You could have called her on the way home. It's important, Caroline."

He wasn't letting it go. Frustrated, she shot back, "You think I don't know that?" Planting her elbows solidly on whatever newspaper article was under the glass that covered the table, she said, "Please don't lecture me, Dean." She lowered her voice. "Just because we're sleeping together doesn't give you the right to tell me what to do." She had been a free agent too long for that. "I'll call Jamie when I get my thoughts together enough to do it. Besides, she hasn't called me. And don't make a comparison between your son and Jamie. He's fourteen. She's twenty-nine. If she's old enough to decide to get married one day and do it the next, she's old enough to know that she hurt her mother and needs to make amends—*and* that she has no right to judge me for what *I* do in bed." She knew she was getting wound up, but couldn't stop. He had hit a nerve. "Did I cheat on her father? No. Did I have men in the house after my divorce? *No.* But all these years later, she wants me to stay chaste?"

His hazel eyes chided. "That's not what she meant, Caro. As I understand it, the argument was about your not telling her."

"I don't *need* to tell her."

"And she doesn't *need* to tell you. So you're even."

"Which is why she can call me," Caroline said, sitting back. "I have a lot on my plate right now."

"So does she," he said so reasonably that, perversely, she had to keep up the fight.

"Of her own choosing."

"Not all. You were the one who asked her to have preliminary Weymouth drawings done for tomorrow. And you're right, she's older than Renny, but you're older than she is."

"I'm older than you, too," Caroline said. Her anger was starting to fade—it had been stupid all along—leaving her embarrassed and, to cover that, hurt. "How about a little respect?"

He took a drink of his Coke and set the glass down, then, coming forward, put ropey forearms on the table. His brow was furrowed, his eyes puzzled. "You express your opinion of things that I do or don't do. Can't I do the same?"

"I don't attack you," she said quietly.

"I wasn't attacking."

"It felt that way."

"Then I used the wrong words or the wrong tone or the wrong look. And don't give me that bit about being older than me, because at our age months don't matter."

"It's years," she corrected sourly.

"It's twenty-nine *months,* and the only time I'm aware of that is when you remind me." He sighed and said in a conciliatory way, "All I wanted to do was remind you that Jamie is a priority. The longer you wait to call, the harder the call will be."

Caroline said nothing, simply listened to the surrounding blur of voices, the tick of utensils on china, the calls from the kitchen. A woman she knew approached and introduced a star-struck friend from out of town to her and Dean. Too soon they moved off, and the flash of pride she felt broke apart.

She looked at Dean. He was fingering the knife he hadn't used, turning it this way and that. Seeming to feel her gaze, he raised his eyes, showing her the vulnerability that never failed to touch her.

"I'm sorry," she said quietly. "I overreacted."

He reached for her hand. Usually they were careful, but now he wove his fingers through hers in plain sight on the table. "I don't want us fighting."

As uncaring as he was about who was watching—getting things right between them was suddenly more important—she squeezed his hand. "We've been fighting for years. It's who we are."

"Bickering is different from this." He seemed worried. "We were doing okay on the bigger things, weren't we?"

The bigger things. Like Champ. And the country house. And action movies that she couldn't stand and for which he now wore headphones when he watched in bed late at night. And even her baths, which she preferred to his showers, but for which she still liked privacy.

"Yes," she acknowledged. "And we are. We're doing good. It's just . . ." She tried to figure out what had set her off and explain it to him. "I was feeling triumphant."

"And I burst your bubble."

"I will call Jamie."

"I'll try not to attack."

"She really could call me, too, you know. She was pretty judgmental."

"You were judgmental on the bigger issue. Her husband is her life now. If you don't accept that, your relationship with her is screwed." He paused. "You're the adult."

"Seems to me you said she was one. She certainly said it."

"So who'll be more adult?" He stared at her and waited.

Caroline let out a breath. "We'll see."

"That's the best you can do?"

"Yes. This is still raw."

"Want to go back to your place for a little—"

She cut him off with a sharp stare.

"I can't help it," he said, eyes touching her torso. "You're wearing my favorite outfit."

"The one I buried my ex in?"

"Exactly."

"You're bad."

"But you love me anyway."

She sighed. "I do."

"Enough to marry me?"

"Please. That is one more thing I can't deal with right now. Theo's waiting. He wants to know about the meeting."

Relenting, Dean smiled. "You did good, sweetheart."

"Did I?" she asked. "For all my brilliant campaigning, Hersch wouldn't commit."

twenty-six

Encouraged by Theo's blessing, Jamie might have made progress with the Weymouth plans if she'd had nothing else to do at the office, but first there was Brad. Less than a week before, she had been wearing his ring. Her grandfather might not have noticed this new one, but someone else at the office was sure to. She owed it to Brad to tell him herself.

He was in his office when she arrived, and his anger when she told him about Chip shook her. She had hoped he would be as detached as when they last talked, but no such luck. Gray eyes cold, voice low in a way she had never heard it before, he accused her of cheating on him, didn't want to hear her denials, and went on about it way too long, so that she grew angry herself.

"You're a lawyer," she interrupted with enough force to make him listen. "There's all kinds of evidence in phone and text records to show that I didn't *know* Chip Kobik until he gave me advice on Tad, and there's an e-mail trail a mile wide proving that I was never alone with him until after you and I broke up. But if it makes you feel less guilty—"

"Guilty?" he cut in, pushing at his glasses with a slim finger. *"Me?"*

"For job-hunting months ago, for considering a huge move on the sly, for not being able to give of yourself to a *child,* Brad—that was the real eye-opener for me—then, fine. Believe what you will." Shaken as she was, she forced calm into her voice. MacAfee Homes needed Brad for one last task. "Theo knows you'll be leaving. All we ask is that you honor the two weeks' notice your contract allows. There may be action on the Weymouth property this week. It would be much easier if you were to handle it for us. If you ever had any feeling for me, I'd appreciate your help there, and if you can't do it for me, do it for Theo or for Roy. They treated you well."

To his credit, he remained silent. She wasn't sure if he would do what she asked, but she didn't have time to press him on it. Too much was weighing on her. Thinking about the work she had to do, she hurried upstairs to her office.

She might have made progress on the Weymouth plans then, if the phone hadn't started to ring. Each time it did, her pulse skittered on the hope that Caroline was calling. The morning's argument was like a paper cut with a constant little sting. If being a daughter was the only role she had to play, she might have been better able to deal, but being a wife, a mother, and an architect who was falling further behind each minute, she was raw. Caroline could make it better if she called.

But no. Not Caroline. Clients. They wanted progress reports, of course they did, and sending e-mail that Jamie might put off reading was too easy. How to tell them that their projects weren't her first priority just then? She did her best to reference details of each, pulling up the applicable screens on her computer, trying to make it sound like she was on top of things, when all the while she was thinking that she was losing precious time.

One call ended. She returned to the Weymouth project. Another call came in. Had Caroline been on the phone, Jamie would have happily talked, but designers and contractors, even a town official with setback concerns? Seeming of one mind, they had decided that she'd had enough time to mourn Roy and was now free to work.

They had *no clue.*

At the end of another nonproductive hour, she asked her assistant to hold her calls. That was when the woman noticed her ring. Jamie considered dodging the issue by saying it was her grandmother's ring or even her mother's, but a bigger part of her wanted the world to know about Chip. She was proud of him, *proud* that she had recognized how perfect he was for her and had acted on it. Just picturing him now brought a soothing wave into her turmoil.

But that was a lot of dirt for her assistant to handle, between a broken engagement and a wedding. The woman asked if she could tell people. Figuring that word had to get out sometime, Jamie didn't say no.

Big. Mistake. Her assistant told the receptionist—that was all, she swore afterward, but it was enough. Jamie was finally getting into the Weymouth plans when MacAfee people began texting her. Texts she could ignore; physical bodies, strolling into the design department and right up to her desk, wanting to see her ring? Most had no idea that she and Brad had even broken up.

"Nightmare," she told Chip when he called after his last morning class. "There are too many interruptions. I can't focus."

"Did you make any progress at all?"

"Not much," she said, trying to stay calm. She didn't want her new husband thinking she was prone to hysterics. And she wasn't. Not normally, at least. Of course, she didn't normally have as little time to prepare for something she wanted as much as she wanted the Weymouth job. "You saw my designs. They're dreams, that's all, dreams. My mother wants me to do something in two days that I would normally spend two weeks on, and it isn't all CAD work, it's imagination. You can't force that."

"Call her. Discuss it with her."

But Jamie knew how things worked. "There isn't much to discuss. We need the Weymouth project to undercut the Barths and be able to go into the *Gut It!* meeting Thursday from a position of strength. I just have to get going. Normally, I'd do a ton of site work beforehand, but it wasn't like I could hire a surveyor or walk the property taking pictures and measurements when the land isn't even formally for sale, and now, well, I just don't have time. The town assessor's office is faxing me a land plot, but it'll be primitive."

"How much detail do you need?"

He was right. She didn't need much. But detail wasn't the problem right now. "I need enough to convince them that we love the place and have a vision for it, and they'll want that vision to be beautiful and innovative and still preserve some kind of old-world feel—at least, I'm guessing that's what they want. I don't know them."

"I do."

Jamie caught her breath. "You do?"

"I played hockey at Harvard with Alex, son of Ralph. He was two years ahead of me, but the team was pretty tight. His dad used to fly in for games all the time. He was every coach's worst nightmare."

That didn't bode well for Jamie. "In what sense?"

"Egotistical. Larger than life—a big man with a big voice and big expectations. You won't need details with him. All he'll want to see is the big picture."

"Luxury?"

"I'd say so. As over-the-top as your dreams go."

"Ralph is one of three. Will the other brothers want that, too?"

"Not necessarily, but it'll stroke their egos to see something grand. I haven't seen Alex since I left Cambridge. I could call. If his dad thinks I'm a loser, the contact might backfire. Should I try anyway?"

"Not yet. And not because of that," she added quickly lest he worry. "You're no loser. You made the pros, Chip. That's phenomenal. It's just . . ." She tried to express it. "Old habits die hard, I guess. I really wanted to do this myself. The problem is that when I feel so scattered, I can't concentrate, and when I can't concentrate, self-doubt moves in. Maybe my vision isn't grand enough. Maybe they'll think I'm too young for the job."

"Age is just a number, honey. We've talked about that. Look at your portfolio. It's top-notch. Besides, if there's a meeting, Caroline will be there. And Theo and Dean. They'll add the element of age."

"But I'm the designer."

"With impressive designs."

She wanted to believe him, wanted it badly. "You think? I've only shown you dreams."

"Impressive dreams."

"You're biased."

"Absolutely," he said with a smile in his voice. "So here's an idea. Your condo is quiet. Could you work there?"

She could. The room where Tad had slept was a home office. When she thought of the place, though, she felt cold and alone.

Seeming attuned to her thoughts, Chip said, "How about I get someone to take lunch duty for me here. Meet me at the condo now, and we'll move your office to the house. My old bedroom already has a desk and Internet hookup."

"You need to work there. Student evaluations, all the paperwork for camp—"

"If I push my stuff to one end, there's still room for yours. We can pick up another table tomorrow at Home Depot and in the meanwhile put the printers on nightstands. The room'll be thrilled. It's getting bored with my work."

She laughed. "Like the room has a mind? You sound like my mother. Her house is always telling her not to renovate. She claims it wants its history intact."

"Wise woman," he said, but he didn't ask that she call Caroline again, for which she was grateful. More than any other distraction, her mother hovered in the periphery of her consciousness, a little ache that wasn't debilitating, just always there.

"I mean it," Chip insisted. "We talked about you working in that room until we could build on. It won't take us more than an hour to get the basics moved from your place and hooked up in mine if we do it together." He was a whiz at technology, from what she had seen of his Wi-Fi setup, which included not only Internet but music, television, and wireless heat control.

Feeling a glimmer of excitement that came as much from the idea of seeing him as from being able to work in a place that was emotionally warm, Jamie glanced at her watch and calculated the amount of time it would take her to collect what she needed and drive to the condo. "Ten minutes?"

She heard another smile. "Ten minutes."

Thirty minutes later, he said in a voice that rumbled, as intimate as nakedness, body heat barely cooled, and the mess of sheets on Jamie's bed, "We need to keep this place. It sure beats a motel for a tryst."

Jamie was logy in the wake of two mind-blowing orgasms, and if those hadn't done it, breathing him in would have. He had a unique scent, very male, now tinged with sex. "Tryst?" she managed to tease.

"That one word is the grand total of what I got from the literature course I took at Harvard during my abbreviated tenure there," he drawled in self-deprecation, but his eyes were on her mouth. Rolling on top again, he wound his fingers through hers, anchoring them on the pillow on either side of her head, and gave her a lingering kiss that ended with one to her freckles, which he claimed to love. "But you have to work."

Work? What was work? She hadn't been thinking sex when she drove over—well, maybe a kiss or two—but one look at Chip in gym shorts that hung from lean hips, with his dark hair spiked over his brow and his blue eyes hungry, and she was lost. Easy to subdue the attraction when they were preoccupied with getting the boys to dinner or bed or daycare, but the chemistry between them remained potent. Tryst? He might be onto something. *Thank you, Harvard.*

But yes, she had to work. The sudden twist in the pit of her stomach had nothing to do with arousal. Reluctant, she checked her watch. "So do you. Do we still have time to move the office? I should probably work here today."

"Are you okay with that?"

"No. But I'll suffer."

Grinning, he stretched over her again, moving a certain part of him against a certain part of her to remind her exactly *why* they hadn't had time to move her office. She arched up to catch his mouth a final time before giving in to that other shrieking need.

•

Several consecutive hours of quiet helped. Shifting between an old *Williston News* photo, Google Earth, and her memory, she made a computer rendering of the main house, which, in its heyday, had been a grand French country estate built of stucco and brick, with tall windows that rose from the second floor into the eaves, drawing attention to three high, steep hip roofs, each with a large chimney. Time had taken its toll on the real thing, but her drawings depicted a restored glory, which was how her mind's eye had always seen the place. Refining the image that had taken shape on her screen, she cleaned up the stucco and repointed the stone, pruned back ivy and overhanging trees, replaced rotted wood framing the windows, and added gables to lift the entire facade.

Lost in the work, she didn't notice the passage of time until she reached for her liter of Poland Spring and found it empty. Grasping the bottle, still in the kind of semitrance that came when she worked on something she loved, she stood back from her desk and studied the screen. She did adore this house. It had always seemed lonely to her, perhaps because for as long as she could remember Mildred Weymouth had lived by herself, perhaps because it had been so sadly neglected. Working on these designs reminded Jamie why she had dreamed for so long of this project and why she had to do it right.

When she went down to the kitchen for more water and glanced at her watch, though, she realized it was almost pickup time at First Unity. Chip would get the boys. But what would Tad be thinking when she didn't show? He knew Chip, but she was the one who had seen him in the hospital within minutes of his birth and been a fixture in his life since. If she wasn't at pickup, he might fear that she was gone, like his mommy and daddy. He seemed like such an easy kid, taking to Chip and to Buddy, adapting to two new homes in quick succession. She wasn't sure, though, if he was happy or simply on change overload—whether he was so lost without his parents that, other than the occasional crying jag, he just went along.

She needed him to see her. And she needed to see him. As priorities went, Tad came first.

That was why, when Chip pulled up in the silver Honda, wanting to see how she was doing before he went for the boys, she said, "I'm coming."

"You owe me for this," Herschel Oakes announced straight out when Caroline picked up her phone. "Wednesday at one. We'll videoconference from my office. John will be here in the flesh, Ralph and Grant on the screen."

Yessss. With the passing of the afternoon, she had grown doubtful. But he had come through! "Wednesday."

"At one," he repeated. "Will you be prepared? I'm going out on a limb here. I don't want to waste anyone's time."

Of course he didn't, but Caroline forgave him that. The timing was perfect, or as perfect as it could be given the meeting Thursday morning with Brian and Claire. If they had even a preliminary deal with the Weymouths before then, they would neutralize the Barths.

Tomorrow would be hectic. She wouldn't get much carpentry done, what with meeting with Theo and the MacAfee finance people. While Linda compiled a comp study, Caroline had to bring Dana Langham into the loop. She also had to talk with Brad, which might be fine, since he was likely as shocked by Jamie's marriage as Caroline was. Well, maybe. Actually, probably not quite. But Brad was still on payroll. Marketing presented a problem, since they hadn't hired a replacement for Roy. Well, between Theo, Dean, and her, they would come up with something. She would drive Theo into Boston herself.

"We'll be there," she promised. "And yes, I owe you. Anything, Hersch. This is a huge help to me. It's the act of a loyal friend. Thank you."

As soon as she ended the call, she texted Jamie.

Jamie might have ignored the phone if she hadn't suddenly realized it was still on vibrate, which was the only way she had been able to get any work done. When she saw Caroline's name, she sorted through a score of messages to this one.

Just got call. Meeting with Weymouths 1 PM Wednesday. Work for you?

No, it did not work for her. She needed twice as much time, *four* times as much time, to get the designs right. But if she wanted to show Caroline that she could do it all—marriage, motherhood, work—she would manage it somehow.

No problem, she texted back and broke out in a cold sweat.

"Everything okay?" Chip asked, darting her little looks as he pulled into the First Unity lot.

"Yup, yup, everything's fine," she said in a high voice and pushed it out of her mind. She was going to be with her boys. Her eye was already scanning the playground.

When Chip stayed behind to talk with one of the teachers, Buddy spotted her and came on the run. Bending over him, she slipped an arm around his shoulders. "How was your day?"

"Good." He pointed. "Taddy's there. He was crying during rest."

"Uh-oh."

"I think his stomach hurt him." He looked past her. "Where's Daddy?" When he spotted Chip, he broke free and ran.

Jamie turned her attention to Tad, who was standing off to the side, watching three kids on the seesaw. His aloneness broke her heart.

She was on her way to rescue him when she was waylaid by one of the teachers. "Don't let this fool you. It took him a while to settle down during quiet hour, but he's had a good day."

Watching him now, though, Jamie worried. "Is he afraid of the seesaw?"

"A little. He climbed on earlier and fell off. He didn't hurt anything but his pride. But this is how they learn. He'll get the knack."

He spotted Jamie then. Face lighting in recognition—breath-stopping, *that* was—he forgot the seesaw and ran to meet her, little legs churning so fast that he tripped, sprawled on his belly on the dirt, and began to cry, breaking her heart for a second time in as many minutes. Rushing to him, she scooped him up and buried his face in her neck, finally holding him back to wipe the streaks from his face. "Hey, monkey," she crooned, as she brushed at his clothes, "you run so well." It was true. He was fast like Roy, maybe prone to tripping like she was but the way he had lit up when he saw her made her day.

When he babbled something or other, the teacher interpreted. One of the children had a birthday, and the mother brought cupcakes.

"Rainbow sprinkles?" Jamie asked, brushing a crumb of one from the corner of his mouth.

"*Wainbow,*" he cried with a big smile, tears lingering on his lashes but forgotten. He was that easily distracted.

As was she, she realized. She loved being with these guys. Oh yes, work lurked in the background. When she let her mind go there even for a second, her stomach clenched. But she wanted to be here with Tad, needed to be here. Determinedly, she stashed that other part of her life in its own little box as they started back to her condo for her office equipment.

Two minutes into the drive, Tad fell asleep with his chin on his shoulder, his cheeks pink, chocolate curls sweaty. The heart-melting sight of him was further distraction, along with the finger painting Buddy pulled from his backpack. When they turned into her condo complex, whose entry bore a *Family Built by MacAfee Homes* sign in blatant reminder, she felt a twinge of guilt. In the next breath, she banished it. Relocating her office to help her work was a form of work, wasn't it? Soon enough, her office equipment was packed, half in her car, half in Chip's, and they were on the road again.

This time, passing a MacAfee truck brought back the guilt.

Again she pushed it away. But it made her think. Compartmentalization was apparently a learned art. Like a backhand slice on the tennis court, like Tad on the seesaw, it would take practice.

"Like deking," Chip added as they talked on the phone, car to car.

"What's deking?"

"Short for decoy. It's when a player handles the puck in a way that misleads his opponent—you know, feints left, moves right, that kind of thing. The opponent gets out of position. The player moves past."

"Clever. How long did it take you to learn?"

"Years." He turned the corner onto his street.

Putting her blinker on, she followed. "I don't have years. I've never had to wear so many different hats."

Chip didn't respond at first. Then came a low "Oh shit" and an aggrieved sigh. "Brace yourself. You're about to try on another."

twenty-seven

Jamie was about to ask what he meant when he pulled into his driveway beside a black BMW. A woman was leaning against it, hands flanking her hips, eagle eyes tracking the Honda. Jamie's first thought was that it was Buddy's mother. As she got closer, though, she realized the woman looked exactly like Chip.

Jamie barely breathed. "Which sister?"

"Samantha," he murmured and, ending the phone connection, called out his window, "Hey, Sam."

Samantha Kobik was the sister who lived in Manhattan. Black leggings covered slim legs, and though her tunic top was stylishly voluminous, her arms and face were lean. Her hair was long and caught in a high ponytail, but it was as dark and thick as Chip's, her eyes as blue, her jaw as square.

Jamie knew other things about her from stories Chip had told her, but could she remember them now? No! All she could think, with an edge of hysteria, was that she had promised Caroline a presentation on Wednesday—*No problem!*—and that being with Chip and the boys alone would eat up more time than she had. She couldn't be meeting a sister-in-law right now, much less a hostile one, to judge from the sharpness of those eyes.

But what choice did she have?

Parking behind him, she climbed out in time to hear Chip say a facetious "That was fast."

Samantha had straightened. "Look who's talking."

He kissed her cheek and gave her shoulder what Jamie thought to be a conciliatory squeeze. "If you're here to do Mom's bidding, save your breath."

"Do I ever do Mom's bidding?"

"Always."

"I do not. I do my own thing."

"Which is always on Mom's approved activities list," Chip said. "You're her first child. You don't break rules, and you strive to succeed. You're her dream child."

"Who isn't married."

"Who has two graduate degrees and a choice job, who travels all over and earns a ton of money."

"Who isn't married," Samantha repeated, only then shifting her gaze.

Opening an arm, Chip drew Jamie close. "Wife, meet sister Samantha. Sister, meet wife Jamie."

Samantha held out a hand—no hug offered, for which Jamie was grateful. "Sister-in-law" was a technical term. A hug would have suggested a relationship, which they didn't yet have. No, a handshake was fine, and Samantha's was firm. Jamie returned it in kind. If her father had taught her anything, it was that.

"I'd say I'm pleased to meet you," Samantha said, "but right now we're all stunned."

Jamie said the first thing that came to mind. "You should talk to my mom."

"She should talk to *my* mom, or maybe not. Mine was pretty steamed, and not only at Chip."

"If she's angry at Jamie," Chip said, "she's totally off base. Jamie's my other half."

"A little advance warning would have been nice."

"We didn't have advance warning."

"Exactly. *That* reassured her. Did you not upset her enough back when you were boozing it up?"

"Sam—"

"Or when you kicked them out of this house?"

"I did not kick them out."

"You said you could raise your child alone. You said you didn't need them."

To Jamie, Chip muttered a tight-jawed "That's not what I said. I'm getting the boys." He strode off.

Jamie wasn't sure she wanted to be left alone with Samantha. Little things were coming back, like the fact that this oldest sister was a perfectionist, which would be a disaster for Jamie, who wasn't sure she was doing *anything* right just then. But she couldn't move. Piercing blue eyes were pinning her in place.

"You're an architect."

With a serious deadline. "I am."

"Dressed like that?"

"I was working at my condo."

"No wonder. In a town like Williston, no good deed goes unnoticed."

Jamie laughed. She couldn't help herself. Broken engagement plus sudden wedding equals town gossip. The woman did know her Williston.

"I'm sorry about your father," Samantha said in a way that wasn't soft or sympathetic, just fact. "I read about it on the company website. MacAfee Homes was an institution when I was here. If half of what's on the website is true, it still is. I haven't watched your TV show. Is it any good?"

"I think it is," Jamie said. Just then Chip approached holding Tad, and she took him and made the introductions. Tad just stared at Samantha, clearly not knowing any more than Jamie did whether the woman was friend or foe.

Buddy, on the other hand, was no sooner released from the car than he made a beeline for his aunt. Stopping short inches away, he rocked back on his heels and grinned up.

Samantha gave him a thoroughly Chip grin, which made Jamie warm to her a little. "Hey, big guy," she said with genuine enthusiasm and bent for a hug. "I'd pick you up, but . . ."

"But what?" Chip said, approaching with Jamie's computer in his arms.

"He's too heavy."

"Then I won't give you this. If you want to make yourself useful, take the boys inside and make dinner. There's ground beef in the fridge." To Jamie, he said, "She likes to cook. Mom molded her."

"Taught her," Samantha corrected, "and it's a good thing someone learned something from her, because my brother sure didn't. Marriage is a major thing."

"Sam—" Chip began.

"You could've called me, y'know." She swallowed once, then again, and seemed to be taking a deep breath even as she asked, "Why did I have to hear this from Mom?"

"Because Jamie's mom wasn't happy, and our mom wasn't happy, and I didn't want more not-happy from you and my sisters, and Jamie and I had to get to work. She has a killer deadline on a major project, so I need to hook up these machines ASAP. Are you staying the night or driving right back?" As an aside to Jamie, he said, "She does that sometimes. Important people don't take time for family, which may be one of the reasons she isn't married."

"Chip," Jamie scolded softly. Marriage was a touchy subject for some unmarried women, and his sister seemed to have gone pale.

But she didn't back down. "Actually," she said, "the reason I'm not married is that I've never been able to find a guy who was anywhere near as solid as Dad. I've been looking. Trust me, I have. And yes, I'm staying the night." She swallowed again. "But I didn't bring my key, so if one of you could unlock the door, I could use a bathroom."

She was looking a little green. Jamie wondered if she was sick. Shifting Tad on her hip, she went to the side door, unlocked it, and stood back. Samantha had grown up in this house and knew her way around. She made a beeline for the closest bathroom.

When Tad squirmed, Jamie set him down near the fridge. Buddy was suddenly there. "Mamie, can I have apple juice?" he asked.

"That's just what I was coming to get," Jamie said with a smile.

Buddy was a sweet child, and even if that hadn't been so, the fact that he had accepted Tad so readily would have endeared him to her.

Removing two juice boxes, she tucked one under her arm while she fixed a straw first in Buddy's, then Tad's. She unwrapped granola bars and set the boys up near the toys in the living room. Retracing her steps, she heard the toilet flush as she passed the first-floor lav. Wanting to give Samantha as much privacy she could, she went straight on through the kitchen and out the door. She reached the car as Chip was gathering a second load.

He straightened, looking hassled. "I'm sorry. I figured I'd hear from her at some point, but I didn't think she'd leave New York so fast. You don't need this right now."

Thinking that she was so far behind in work that a little more wouldn't hurt, she tugged at his shirt to lighten his mood. "She doesn't seem so bad to me. Do you think she's okay?"

"Okay how?"

"She got really pale there."

He snorted. "Being brilliant can be draining."

"Be kind," Jamie chided. "She's your sister. She wants you happy."

"I'll be happy if she makes dinner," he said and, carefully extracting a machine from deep in the SUV, headed back to the house.

Jamie followed with a carton of typing paper, traceing paper, packs of Sharpies, pens and pencils, and correction fluid. When she saw the bathroom door still closed, she set the box on the kitchen table, went into the hall, and knocked softly.

"Samantha? Are you okay?"

There was total silence from inside. Then the handle turned and the door cracked open.

An invitation?

Thinking that she didn't have time to accept it but that this was Chip's sister and she couldn't turn away, she gently eased the door back. Samantha sat sideways on the closed toilet with her head bowed and a damp cloth pressed to the back of her neck.

Frightened, Jamie slipped inside and shut the door to keep the boys out. "What's wrong?"

"Morning sickness is only supposed to last three months. I'm going on six."

"Pregnant?"

Confirmation came with a snicker. "Not on the approved activities list when there's no husband."

"Who's the father?"

"Donor XR 21899."

Jamie gasped. "Not an accident, then."

"Oh no. I picked him carefully. He's six-three, comes from a large family, did a Peace Corps stint, and is currently a pediatric resident at a major hospital God knows where. I was lucky. I got pregnant on the first try."

Chip hadn't mentioned a pregnancy, which meant that either his parents had chosen not to tell him or . . . "Your parents don't know?"

"No." Samantha rocked gently. "I knew they'd be against it. They'd want the husband to come first. They'd tell me I'm not that old, and they're right, but I've always wanted kids, and my life is perfect in so many ways but empty in others, and I seriously do not like the guys I see out there. My folks say I need friends." She made a disparaging sound. "Like I have time to make friends?"

Boy, could Jamie identify with that. She didn't have time for friends *or* for a sister-in-law. Yet here she was, chatting it up in the bathroom with one. And mothering Tad? Granted, she'd have chosen any other way of getting him than having her father and Jessica die—but she loved her baby. Had it not been for him, she wouldn't be with Chip, with whom she was over-the-moon crazy in love. Nor would she be stressed to the max over time demands, or setting up an office in a house she would never have designed but in which she felt totally at home, or terrified about meeting in-laws. But she wasn't turning away from any of it.

Samantha set the cloth on the edge of the sink and raised nervous eyes to Jamie. "If I don't have time for friends, do I have time for a baby? I mean, what was I *thinking*? My lifestyle is crazy. I work long days, and I'm gone overnight all the time." Jamie remembered now; she did publicity for a restaurant group that had started in New York but was spreading steadily westward. "I can't do that with a baby. My boss may can me when I tell him I won't travel."

"He can't fire you because you're pregnant."

"No, but if I refuse to do the job he hired me for? Travel was always part of the package. I signed on to the deal. So I think about that, and I think about my teeny apartment, which is a walk-up, which I love for the exercise, but which may not be cool once I have a baby and a carriage and groceries, and the nausea's been so bad that I've used up my sick time, and this is all before childbirth, which terrifies me, and I haven't *begun* to consider child care."

"You're thinking too far ahead."

"But shouldn't I have done that before I got myself into this?"

"Would you do anything different if you could go back?"

"No. Mothering is the job I want." Closing her eyes, she put a hand on her stomach and drew in a slow breath through pursed lips. Exhaling the same way, she said, "Except when I feel sick." She breathed in again, out again. "Okay. I'm good." But she bent forward again.

Not knowing what else to do, Jamie freshened the cloth, refolded it, and returned it to her neck. "You don't look pregnant."

"A mixed bag, there," came the muffled voice. "I didn't tell my parents during the first trimester on the chance that the pregnancy wouldn't hold, and once I knew it would, I kept putting it off. I haven't seen them in a while. Besides, I've always worn leggings, and tunics are in style." Moving the cloth to her throat as she straightened, she smoothed the wide tunic so that her middle showed.

"Oh my," Jamie breathed. The baby bump was small, but definitely there. "Is it healthy?"

"She is."

"A girl!" A momentary excitement caught her up. "I want one of those next."

Samantha snorted. "Mom always said she loved that her first was a girl. Wonder what she'll say about her first girl now." She grew earnest, seeming to want Jamie to understand. "It's not like they won't want the baby. They just won't like how I got her. I was waiting to tell them until I felt better, so my third month became my fourth, and now that I'm well into my fifth, I tell myself that they'll just have to accept it the more of a done deal it is."

"Like Chip and me getting married," Jamie said.

Samantha was quiet. When she finally lifted her head, her eyes were defiant and ashamed at once. "Want to know my first thought when Mom called this morning with your news? Pure glee. I kept thinking, *My being single and pregnant will be small potatoes compared to Chip marrying one of his bimbos.*" Her defiance faded, leaving apology on its own. "Only you're not a bimbo, are you."

Jamie smiled. "No. But I'm horrid in the kitchen, and I'm in a state of panic about a deadline that my mother, who, by the way, isn't speaking to me right now, set for a project she wants done by Wednesday. So if I get you crackers, will you be able to make dinner while Chip and I set up my office?"

"I could do that," Samantha said but was suddenly cautious. "Which one of us tells him about the baby?"

Jamie didn't think it was her job to do that, but she heard a tiny thread of pleading in the question, and the part of her that had never had a sibling wanted to be involved with one now. She actually felt bad for Samantha. Jamie had had Chip with her when she broke the news of their marriage to her mother. Samantha was alone.

Leaving the cook munching Goldfish as she searched the cupboards, Jamie got another armload from the car. She carried it upstairs, where Chip was just finishing the computer hookup.

He took a step back. "Try it."

She tripped on the carpet as she crossed the room and would have fallen if he hadn't caught her. "Why do I *do* that?" she cried, glaring at the carpet as he took the box.

"To make the rest of us feel better, since you are otherwise perfect."

"Hah. I couldn't hook up these machines if my life depended on it."

"Do we know anything works? Try it."

Instead, she put her back to the computer and her palms on his chest. "I need to tell you something first. I don't want you to say anything until I'm done, and before you speak then, you need to know that I think it's good."

His eyes were large and scared. "Ah hell. You want out."

She nearly laughed. "Excuse me? *Never.* This is about your *sister.*" Quickly, she outlined the facts, watching his expression go from relief to surprise to disbelief.

"Pregnant? Miss High and—"

Jamie put a finger across his lips. "Let me finish."

He struggled with that. She could see him wanting to insert editorial comments when she described the sperm donor, and when she told him told him why Samantha hadn't told her parents, she could see he was dying to speak.

Finally, she said, "I like her, Chip. She's vulnerable—"

"*Samantha?*"

"Yes. She did something she wanted to do, just like we did, and not everyone will agree with her choice, but I want to. It's a baby, Chip, a little girl."

"If it was a boy," he said with a grunt, "it could play with ours."

"And a girl can't do that? Hello?"

"She was wrong, Jamie. When she said I kicked them out of this house?" Clearly this was bothering him. "Mom and Dad were looking to move, so I bought them two houses in exchange for this one, and I never said I didn't need them. I said that if they weren't there, I'd have to finally grow up."

"You have." Standing on tiptoe, Jamie kissed him.

By the time she lowered herself, his arm was around her waist and his grin was smug. "One thing's for sure. This'll give the folks something to think about besides us."

"Samantha is counting on our marriage helping her the same way. That's one of the reasons she got here so fast."

"Her timing couldn't be worse. You need to work."

"I will once the boys are asleep. So, do we support Samantha?"

Chip made a no-brainer face. "Of course, we support her. She's my sister."

He was right about Samantha being a good cook. In no time, she had whipped up their mother's chili recipe, baked cornbread, and made a salad. And Chip behaved well. Granted, Jamie was standing guard, but he didn't give his sister a hard time about the baby. He was actually reassuring about being a single parent, having just gone through three years of it himself, though he described the raw panic he had felt when he opened his front door to a woman he had never thought he'd see again but who was carrying a week-old infant she claimed was his son.

Yes, he said, mostly for Jamie's benefit, since she was hearing the details for the first time, he'd had a paternity test done, though the timing of the baby's birth, vis-à-vis its conception, made that a formality. For Samantha's sake, he listed some of his early mistakes taking care of Buddy. They were hilarious.

Of course, he had had his parents to help, even long distance. Samantha didn't have assurance of that yet.

Nor, right now, did Jamie. She kept thinking about that as she watched Chip and his sister, kept thinking about her father being dead and her mother being alive and the precious time they were wasting being angry at each other. Right now, she might have asked Caroline whether Tad's clinginess during dinner was a factor of yet another new person in his life or something else. He refused to sit in his own chair, whining for her lap, and while she loved the feel of his warm little body, she imagined it was too warm. He didn't eat much, just crumbs of cornbread and one or two tiny pieces of chili, and by the time Samantha pulled chocolate chip cookies from the oven, his little eyes were closing.

"I don't think he feels great," Jamie said, holding him tight as she stood. Her eyes were on Chip, who knew better than she what to do in this situation. "A quick bath and bed, maybe?"

He started to get up. "I'll do it. You have to work."

She pressed his shoulder down. "I'll work once he's asleep. Bath, Buddy?"

Buddy pouted. "I want another cookie."

"You go settle Tad," Chip told her, running a reassuring hand up her arm. "I'll bring him along in a few."

Tad took little settling. She stretched out beside him to read a story, but he was asleep before two pages were done. Worried, Jamie rolled to her side. She knew she should get up and work, but she couldn't just yet.

Breathing in baby-soap sweetness, she watched him for a while, listened to his breathing, monitored the rise and fall of his little chest. She knew he was bound to get sick at some point. No child made it to kindergarten untouched by other kids' germs, especially not a daycare child, but that wasn't reason to take him out, was it?

He still felt warm to her. But he slept through the sound of the bath being run and he didn't stir when, a short time later, Chip deposited Buddy on the top bunk.

"*Now* you work," he whispered as they crept from the room.

"What about your sister?"

"I'll handle her."

It took Jamie time to get organized—putting things where she could reach them, adjusting the height of her chair, connecting to the Web on one computer and the MacAfee network on another, hooking up the monitor to hear if Tad woke—and all the while, distracting tendrils of thought came and went. Some had Tad's name on them, some Samantha's. Thoughts of Chip soothed. Not so thoughts of Caroline. The ache remained, along with serious self-doubt, so when she was finally able to pull up her design of the main house, she was surprised to find that it was actually good. If her goal was to make the Weymouths proud of their family home, this was a solid first step.

That said, if the first glance at a presentation mattered, and the estate was to be truly inviting, the entry had to be more imposing than the narrow lane of cracked tar that it was. *Natural speed bumps,* she could hear the ghost of Mildred say, and while that might be true, there were more gracious ways to discourage speed. Widening the drive, she paved it with bricks made of recycled materials that gave it a slightly uneven, almost cobblestone feel. When it reached the house, she swung it into an elegant circle, with a trio of river birch in the middle and ample space for guest parking around the curves.

"How's it going?" Chip whispered from the door. An hour had passed.

She gave him a thumbs-up. Returning to her screen, though, she realized she couldn't show guest parking without addressing resident parking.

That could be in clones of the existing carriage house, which she would tear down.

No. Not carriage houses. She wanted attached garages.

But that meant a redesign of the back of the house, for which she needed a rear exterior view. Turning to the second computer, she searched earth-view sites in vain. The *Williston News* had photos from long-ago backyard parties, but they showed people with only slices of grass, lawn furniture, or trees. What memories Jamie had herself were too vague to use.

Imagine, she told herself. *Create.*

But another half hour had just passed with nothing to show.

Frantic to draw something—*anything*—she turned her back on the house and, on a fresh screen, re-created the woods. She set the outline of three carriage houses along its rim. No, freestanding carriage houses weren't her first choice, but they were charming, certainly practical with storage space above, and if they differed from one another, the visual interest of the presentation would be enhanced.

But three? Or four? With walkways connecting one to the other and the house? Would the Weymouths like seeing a circle out back with a courtyard in the middle?

Not if there was a circle out front.

A landscaped courtyard might work if it had grass, flowers, and benches.

Then came another thought. There had to be access to the pool and tennis court from the main house. But how close should they be? Too close and those owning the condos would hear noise. Too far and they'd need a frigging *golf* cart to get there.

She glanced at her watch. Another hour gone, with too many decisions, too little input, and little progress. She was starting to hyperventilate when Chip appeared.

"Ignore me," he whispered, pulling a chair up to his own computer. "I need printouts for tomorrow."

She gasped. "The field day." She had been so obsessed with her own work that she hadn't thought about his. "I'm so sorry, Chip. I forgot. And here I left you alone with your sister. Where is she?"

"Sleeping. It's after ten." He shushed her with a finger to his mouth and pointed at her screen. "Work."

She would never have been able to—would have sat watching him do his thing—if she hadn't been so aware of the time. After ten? The clock was ticking.

Postponing exteriors, Jamie turned her thoughts to the interior of the house. The Weymouths had memories of growing up there. She wanted to tap into memories, but intimate and close didn't work. She wanted the condos branching off from an impressive foyer that incorporated a grand staircase in the front hall. She had made sketches of this in her dreams.

But, again, how many condos? If four, each unit would be smaller and more reasonably priced. If three, the units could be larger, with luxury elements like his-and-her walk-in closets and a solarium. Which would the Weymouths prefer? Which would potential buyers prefer?

Roy had been the marketing genius. He would have known instinctively which route to take. In his absence, Caroline might have thoughts, since she was taking the lead in this project. But Caroline hadn't called, and design was Jamie's thing.

She went with luxury, partly because of what Chip had said about the Weymouths, but even more because three units would take less time to draw than four.

But wait. She had no existing floor plan, no starting point. She told herself that was fine, since the brothers wouldn't have a floor plan handy either, but she had never worked this way. It was disorganized. It was *messy.*

Thinking that she had *no choice,* she was about to start when she heard a gagging sound, then a shrill cry.

In a flash, she ran to the boys' room. Tad had thrown up and was sitting on his bed in a gross mess, crying pitifully. She snatched him up and cradled him, cooing softly, "It's okay, monkey, Mommie's here." But she wasn't a vomiter, had never seen Tad do it before, didn't know *where* to begin to clean up.

"The bathroom," Chip said with a calm hand at her back. "Put him in a tepid tub while I change the sheets."

She might have marveled at his composure if she hadn't been so concerned about Tad, but the bath seemed to work. The water soothed him. Once she had him soaped and rinsed, she refilled the tub so that he could soak in clean bubbles, and all the while, ignoring her fear-filled heart, she played with him as if it were just another night in the bath.

"What now?" she asked Chip when he appeared.

He touched Tad's forehead. "He's cooler. That's good."

"What *was* it?"

"Who knows. Maybe something he ate. Maybe something going around at school."

"Do I call the doctor?"

"Nah."

"Give him Motrin?"

He considered that. "Let's wait. If his temperature spikes—"

"I don't even know how to *take* his temperature."

Chip slid her a tired smile. "Not to worry, wife. I do."

Tad's temperature was only mildly elevated, no cause for alarm, Chip assured her. She gave the child water to sip, but he seemed happiest clinging to her, arms and legs. So she brought him back to the office and let him doze against her that way while she tried to work—"tried" being the operative word. She couldn't settle into it. She was a creature who worked with facts and figures. Without them, she was groping around in the dark.

Thinking she might do better if she set the manor aside and worked on the rest of the acreage, she pulled up her work e-mail and scrolled through a fearsome list until she found the plot map that the Williston town assessor had sent. Unfortunately, it was as crude as every other assessor's plot plan she had ever seen.

Disconcerted, she bowed her head against Tad's warm curls. If construction ever became a reality, MacAfee Homes would bring in engineers to determine the location of access roads and the positioning of each house. But she had no engineers now. She had no marketing advice, no Realtor advice. She had no Caroline. She had no Chip, who had finally gone to bed. She had Tad, who woke each time she tried to put him down, and she was exhausted. It was past midnight. Fear alone kept her at her computer. But fear wasn't conducive to design.

Thinking that an hour or two of sleep might help, she tucked Tad close and climbed in with Chip, who stirred. "I don't know if this is allowed," she whispered, "but he starts to cry when I take him to his own bed, and I don't want to wake Buddy, and I need to feel you here."

His answering whisper came against her hair as he drew her back into the curve of his body. "It's good. Sleep."

An hour was all she managed. This time it was Buddy who got sick, and they were up again, repeating the drill of bath and laundry. Though Jamie felt less guilty knowing it was *Chip's* son now and that she was doing her part, she was exhausted.

The good news was that both boys settled down in their own room.

The bad news was that it was three in the morning before that happened.

Determined to work, she made coffee and went to the office, but where to start? Forget the manor. Forget carriage houses and courtyards. Forget even the clubhouse by the pool, which would double as an event room and be constructed in the style of the main house . . . or in the style of the original carriage house . . . or maybe in the style of one of several different house plans she envisioned for the outlying acres. Forget the gazebo and the trellis and the huge fire pit. That was all detail.

She needed to think big picture, bird's-eye view. *That* would impress the Weymouths. But not only didn't she have an engineers' report, she had never walked through the wooded part of the land, didn't know which sections were wet and which were not, which were underscored with granite that would require blasting, which were embedded in stands of pine or birch or beech so dense and beautiful that removing even a single tree would be wrong.

Caroline would understand this. She had a keen perspective on these kinds of issues and might have pertinent thoughts. Jamie would have given anything to call her, if for no other reason than to share the responsibility. But this was her job to do.

Just do it, she ordered herself. *The Weymouths won't know where boulders or trees or low-lying wetlands are. Scatter homes over the land in a way that looks interesting. You've done this before. Just do it now.*

Desperate, she did. She spaced houses on the computer in a way that looked plausible. Pretty. Maybe even interesting. Same with siting the swimming pool, tennis court, and clubhouse, though she hated working this way. It reminded her of the year she had tried to bake gingerbread for Caroline's birthday and, not having molasses, used honey instead. Caroline had said it was perfect. But Caroline was her mother, what else would she say? Jamie tasted the gingerbread and knew it was flawed.

Flawed was how she felt about what she had done here.

She redid it once, then looked in on the boys. Back in the office, she saw more flaws, so she redid the design. She was in the kitchen filling her third cup of coffee when Chip hurried in looking as tired as she felt. It was seven. He had showered, and his messenger bag was stuffed, but he sidled up close to her as he reached for a travel mug.

"How's it going?"

She waggled a hand and opened the fridge. "At least the boys haven't thrown up again. Will they?"

"There's not much left in their stomachs," he said as he filled the mug with coffee. "They'll need liquid, but make it watery."

She topped off his coffee with cream. "What about milk?"

"Only if they ask. If they keep down lighter stuff, it's probably okay. If there was ever a day when I'd stay home and help . . ." He scowled. "Make Sam watch the boys."

"Is she staying?"

"Tell her if she doesn't, I'll call Mom and rat her out. And I'm serious." He screwed the top on the mug, looped an arm around her waist, and pulled her in. "Will you be okay?"

"I have to be."

"You can always call your mom."

She didn't answer, just mined his blue eyes for strength.

"I'll call in sick," he offered.

"You will not. It's the last day of school. You've been planning this field day for weeks. Go." She pulled away.

He leaned in for a kiss, started off, came back for a second, then left.

twenty-eight

Caroline was twisting to get a rear view of herself in the cheval mirror when she saw Dean staring at her from a corner of the glass. Much as she'd grown used to having him around, there were times when it was embarrassing. Blushing, she felt the need to explain. "My hips look big. Should I tuck in the shirt?"

The outfit was new—a slim white skirt that ended in a soft flare at the knee, a fitted brown silk shirt with clingy tails, and cork wedge sandals. Jamie would approve. But she hadn't bought these things for that reason alone. She had important meetings this week, and her funeral outfit had exhausted its stay. It was black. She didn't like black. Dean did, and a good thing *that* was, or he would clash with the floral wing chair in which he was now sitting to lace his boots. Today's black shirt, already tucked into belted jeans, had its sleeves rolled to the elbows and its neck open.

Holding her eyes in the mirror, he left the chair and came up behind her. "Your hips aren't big, and leave the tails out. You look very chic. Grown up but still you."

She gave him a puzzled smile. "Grown up?"

"Sophisticated."

"Am I not usually sophisticated?"

"Yes, but in a craftsman way. This is cosmopolitan." He paused, speculative, but not quite. "It could use something, though."

Frowning at her reflection, Caroline touched her watch, then the studs in her ears. She wore a hand-carved silver ring on the middle finger of her left hand. It was a gift from her parents, marking no special birthday, but its heft so fit who she was that it she wore it often. Her mother's own filigree bangle-and-cuff set was a delicate heirloom, and though Caroline treasured it, she would no more wear it than she would wear a wedding gown of Victorian lace.

Then again, who'd have thought she would willingly buy a white skirt and wedge sandals, much less feel good in them? But she had, and she did. Who'd have thought she would be power dressing—well, as much as her carpenter side would allow—and auditioning for a role that she didn't want? Or hadn't wanted. Only it wasn't so bad. She was actually good at it, mainly because it entailed dealing with people. That was what she loved about *Gut It!*—not the eye of the camera or the public recognition, but working with people to produce something that other people would enjoy.

The woman she saw in the glass was interesting. Oh, she looked her age. Neither her neck nor her hands were as smooth as the silk of her blouse, and her bare legs no longer tanned as evenly as Jamie's did. But there was something different about this woman. With Dean's nearness evoking the memory of sleeping with him last night, she might have said that the something different was confidence. She might have even added the word "complete" had it not been for Jamie. There was nothing complete right now in Caroline's role as a mother.

But that couldn't have been what Dean meant when he said her outfit needed something. He was a literal guy.

One hand left his pocket, then both touched her nape, and suddenly something was sliding down a platinum chain to nestle between her breasts. By the time her fingers were there, he had both hands on her shoulders and was looking at their reflection in the mirror, his ruddy skin less ruddy as he waited for her response.

"Dean," she warned softly. She knew just what it was, but that didn't prepare her for the real thing when she found the nerve to pull it out and look. He had chosen an emerald-cut diamond flanked by vertical baguettes—and her very first thought was how much more the straight stones fit her than the round stone she had once had. Set in platinum, the ring was simple but elegant, traditional but new, exquisite any way she put it.

His fingers found hers inside the shirt, work-roughened skin against the swell of her breasts. "Wear it for me?" he whispered. His hazel eyes, always magnetic, were suddenly a truer green, as if the brown had been overrun by a surge of life inside. Her heart positively ached.

"Oh, Dean."

"Don't you like it?"

"I *love* it," she said, closing the ring in her fist. "But I don't want marriage. I like what we have."

"So do I. That's why the chain. It's a long one. No one needs to see the ring."

"But you want people to know. You said that."

"I changed my mind. This isn't about other people. It's about us."

That was the moment she knew it would happen, the moment she knew they were both old enough to make it work. It was the moment when she realized that the important part of growing older was the growing part, and that resisting change meant forever standing still, which was a sad way to live.

It was also the moment when she saw that holding little grudges was as paralyzing as insisting on hosting *Gut It!* season after season.

Letting the ring settle between her breasts as it seemed made to do, she turned, looped one arm over his shoulder, and framed his whiskered cheek with the other. "Thank you."

"Is that a yes?" he asked with such boyish hope that her heart squeezed again.

Through a sudden sheen of tears, she smiled. "It is."

With Chip gone, Jamie set the monitor beside her computer. It gave her a full view of the bunk bed, and while she was desperate to creep in for a real look at Tad, she resisted the urge. One boy shifted, then the other; neither was sleeping soundly. But both were alive, and with no sign yet of Samantha, she grabbed at the chance to work.

Worried that her bird's-eye view was *BLAH* but not sure what it needed to make it *WOW,* she saved what she had, pulled up a new screen, and focused on individual houses. All she needed for tomorrow's meeting was a prototype or two to show what MacAfee Homes would build on Weymouth land.

She had dreamed of designing *six* different options for buyers, each derivative of the manor house but with its own unique personality. Among them would be an elegant miniature manor house done in brick, another done in stucco and stone, a lake cottage option, a farmhouse option—the presentation would be awesome. But which to draw first, whether to aim for luxury or charm, whether to aim for the Weymouths or the buyer, whether to site it flat or on a knoll—and how could she determine the last without detailed knowledge of the lay of the land?

Forget reality, she cried, losing patience with herself. *Reality doesn't matter. Just take an image from your head and draw it on the frigging screen.*

She was about to start when Samantha wandered in asking what the middle-of-the-night activity had been about. Hearing her voice, Buddy got up, and when Tad, still in bed, began a woeful "Mamie . . . Mamie," work was shot.

Daycare was out of the question. Both boys were still warm, unusually pale, and generally lethargic. If the constancy of the AC was any indication, it was hot outside, not that Jamie had been out to look. She could see patches of condensation on the windows where hot and humid air met cooler glass.

"What do we do?" Samantha asked. Despite her caution about lifting Buddy yesterday, she was holding him now.

Jamie had a quick vision of different-color construction paper cut in triangles, circles, and squares, with toothpicks and string, markers and glue, a perfect sick-day project for boys who didn't feel great. She had grown up on projects like this. Art was her thing. She would do this with them *in a minute* if she didn't have to work.

But she did. So in lieu of arts-and-crafts?

Pressing Tad's face to her throat, she said, "You're asking the wrong person. I've never done this before. They need to stay quiet, but we can't just hold them all morning. What do mothers do when their kids are sick?"

Samantha didn't answer. Nor did she think for long. She simply walked into the living room and turned on the TV.

Caroline's smile was gone, her eyes were dry, and while one hand touched the ring, her new talisman, the other held the wheel of the dusty MacAfee truck that should have detracted from her sophisticated look but felt right. The look was vintage modern, she decided—old car, new woman, traditional ring, new meaning. June magazines were filled with ring ads picturing two and three rows of tiny diamonds, sometimes in different colors, around a central stone, but that wasn't for her. She liked the timelessness of what Dean had picked.

Old, new. A person who blended the two was flexible enough to listen and hear and grow. She wanted to think she was that kind of person. She might have a shot at it, if she could fix what she'd botched with Jamie.

Time worked against her. Jamie had to be feeling pressure right now even apart from being a new mom and new wife, which Caroline was still struggling to digest, and her own morning was booked solid. Rather than texting, *Hey, when can we talk, ooops, no, not then,* or worse, having Jamie tell her not to come, she figured that she would just show up.

First, though, a breakfast meeting with the Realtor. Over boiled eggs at a blessedly air-conditioned Fiona's, Linda Marshall led her through a comparative market analysis that gave Caroline a grounding on the latest in recent sales of other MetroWest properties, broken down by the age of a house, its location, and its size. Linda didn't notice the necklace, but that didn't mean Caroline forgot it was there. Not for one minute. *It's about us,* Dean had said, and the words were never far from her mind. She pressed her fingers to the ring often, as if she were catching her breath or suffering heartburn. In a sense, she was. With each touch, it radiated warm little shocks of pleasure, pride, and comfort, and while a woman who was self-confident enough to dress chic and drive dusty shouldn't need comfort, she did.

Armed with Linda's report and a realistic grasp of the kind of homes they could build and sell, she sped to the MacAfee Building to see if Jamie was there.

As helpful as her sister-in-law was in keeping videos streaming and the boys hydrated, she couldn't help Jamie with work. And Jamie tried, really she did. Running downstairs and back up every few minutes to check on the boys, she managed to draw the beginnings of a house on one of the acre lots. Then, when her mind skipped around, she worked the upstairs of one of the condos into an odd part of the manor house roof. Desperate to jump-start her productivity, she turned away from the computer and made drawings by hand. That was how she often began a project. But even if caffeine hadn't been making her hands shake, she knew that sketches wouldn't impress the Weymouths.

She returned to the computer, but the harder she tried, the more frightened she grew. Mothers didn't stick their kids in front of the TV when they were sick. They sang to them, played with them, held them. So Jamie was as lousy a mother as she was an architect—with one big difference. Short-term, the boys would survive. This project would not. At tomorrow's meeting, there might be negotiation over money or timing or the wisdom of showcasing the project on *Gut It!* But if Jamie couldn't get her act together and make a stunning presentation, they could kiss the whole thing good-bye.

The weight was on her shoulders. Scores of jobs and priceless publicity were at stake, as well as enough money to keep MacAfee Homes afloat while the company recovered from Roy's death and Brad's departure. And Caroline? If she was truly taking over from Theo, and Jamie's incompetence spoiled this chance for her to shine, how awful would *that* be?

Once inside the MacAfee Building, Caroline went looking for Jamie. She wasn't there, but any number of other people were, all jumping at the opportunity to talk about Jamie's marriage. Extricating herself as quickly as possible—"Theo's waiting," she said more than once—she hurried on down the hall, fully understanding why Jamie hadn't come here. How to work in a bee's nest? The buzz would have made it impossible.

She shared Linda's report with Theo, who then added final instructions for her before she went to the bank. She might have saved time by simply phoning the banker. But Theo was insistent. "The bank is in the center of town, and Fred McDonough has been a solid adviser. He'll feel he's valued if you make time for a face-to-face meeting." The subtext, of course, was Theo wanting Caroline to begin the stroking of locals that he and then Roy had done. She would have had no problem with that if she hadn't been impatient to get to Jamie, but she figured that a few more minutes wouldn't hurt.

Besides, Fred McDonough was a convivial guy, who did seem impressed that she'd taken the time to come. He talked about Roy for a while, and asked in depth about Theo. He wanted to know when Jamie and Brad were getting married, and while Caroline was gratified to know that word hadn't spread so far so soon, what could she say? Much as she didn't want to spend time talking about this, she couldn't lie.

So she gave him the bare facts and smiled at his startled expression. "Sudden, huh? They just met. No shotgun wedding, just love at first sight."

Saying the words made them real. As she touched her own ring for the grounding it brought, she couldn't help but compare Jamie's handful of days to her own years and years. So different. Perhaps that was how it should be?

"It's been a rough month for her," Caroline said, "but she's really happy. I'm counting on you to assure people of that. Yes?"

"Yes, yes, of course, I've known that girl since she was born," Fred reminded her, "and, of course, the Kobiks have always been clients here." She waited for him to remark on Chip's past, but he did not. Rather, seeming all the more dedicated to MacAfee Homes, he gave her a vote of confidence on the Weymouth project and a promise to study the Realtor's comps alongside the MacAfee accounts, and let Caroline know by day's end how high they could bid.

Leaving the bank, Caroline drove to Jamie's condo, where there would be a fully equipped office and a guarantee of silence. But the place was deserted—no car in the drive, no gooseneck lamp in the office window.

Of course not, Caroline. She doesn't live here anymore.

Still, she unlocked the door and checked inside, only to be met by a telling heat.

She headed back to the office, needing to study Dean's cost estimates before he gave them to the banker. Then she drove to Emory Elementary. The street was lined with cars, and the playground was mobbed. Curious, she parked and approached the chain-link fence.

The entire school appeared to be there, with teachers milling around and groups of parents watching from the sidelines. The students were divided into teams. Orange shirts kicked soccer balls at a goal; blue shirts shot baskets. Greens dribbled a kickball around an obstacle course, while reds and whites competed at tetherball. The tallest adult on the field, Chip was with a large group of children who stood body to body holding the edges of a large round parachute. Purple was on the left half, yellow on the right half. Chip held a kickball ball over his head for a moment, pointing around with last-minute instructions before tossing the ball onto the chute and blowing his whistle. Instantly, the children began feverishly waving the parachute up and down in an attempt to get the ball into a hole on their side. Once it fell through, he called out the score, tapped a student to retrieve the ball, then began the game again.

She watched three cycles before he spotted her. He did a double take, eyes widening before he waved over another teacher and trotted to where she stood. His face was sweaty, but his look of fear was worse. "Is everything okay?"

"Yes. No. I need to apologize to you, but this is clearly not the time. More immediately, I need to see Jamie. The silence between us is deafening, but she isn't at the office."

"She's at my house, and she really needs you," he said, seeming suddenly very young and as frightened as he had been in command with his students seconds before. "The boys were throwing up all night, so Jamie couldn't sleep *or* work, and my sister showed up unannounced, which may be good or bad, I don't know." He swabbed his forehead with an arm that left his hair sticking up. "I need to be there with them, only this is the last day of school, and field day is my thing, it's becoming a tradition. I'm texting her, and she says everything's okay, only I know it isn't, and I can't leave here for a couple more hours. Not that there's a whole lot I could do to help her. I'm just a meathead, she's the brains. She knows what she wants to draw, but she's second-guessing it all and looking at the clock and panicking. This is the first time she's had to deal with illness, so she's worried about the boys. She may be furious I'm telling you all this—she's so damn independent when it comes to work, and the whole thing with you is eating at her. I'll be home by four, but if you could stop off before then, I'd be forever grateful. Do you know the address?"

Of course she did. She had looked it up in the town directory the first time Jamie mentioned Chip. Gently nudging him back to the field, she returned to her truck, called Dana MacAfee Langham to delay their midday meeting—*No, Dana, it can't be helped, I know you don't like rush hour traffic, but two isn't terribly late, yes, that's fine, if you can't make it I'll understand*—and headed for 403 Beech.

Jamie felt sick to her stomach. She did not have, could not have, *refused* to have what the boys had. There were plenty of other reasons why her insides were jangly, like lack of sleep, lack of food, lack of faith that she was heading anywhere good with the plans she had drawn. Just thinking of that made her sweat, so she lowered the thermostat again.

Tad was napping against her with his thumb in his mouth, his small legs straddling her hips, and Moose's head sticking up between his arm and his ear. She touched a tiny swell of baby fat that lingered at the crease of his elbow, then uncoiled a long curl from his forehead. He needed a haircut. She kept putting it off, letting the summer air simply tighten the curls. This was all hair that his parents had seen and touched and kissed. Cutting it off would be severing a part of that tie. She knew she would have to do it eventually, but not yet, not yet.

She kissed his forehead; he cuddled deeper. In that instant, she wished she could walk away from the computer and just be a mother for the rest of the day.

But her empty screen haunted, *taunted*. Desperate to fill it, she kept Tad framed by her arms while her hands worked between keyboard and mouse, constructing the house to which, in her dreams, she would take the boys for quiet soothing the next time they were sick. It would be in a secluded corner of the property, maybe a hilly spot surrounded by hemlock and pine, with thick grass for rolling here, boulders for climbing there. She gave the house vertical interest, with tall windows, gables, and a steep-pitched roof reminiscent of the manor, but then, tired enough to be foggy, she just let go and tossed in features that she loved.

She was horrified when Tad's stirring woke her from her own stupor and she saw what she had built. It was *all wrong*—looked more *Victorian* than French country, which was not at all a style that would work for the Weymouths. Realizing she had just wasted an hour of irretrievable time basically *playing* with design, she felt her heart begin to pound.

That was when the computer went dead. And the TV. And the AC. After only the briefest winding down of moving parts, the house was completely and utterly silent.

Panicked, she raced down the stairs with Tad in her arms and a hand on the rail. She could *not* afford to stumble on the stairs, not with Tad, not with a deadline.

The thermostat in the living room was blank.

Convinced that she had just pushed the AC unit too hard, she lowered Tad to the sofa beside Buddy and ran first to the kitchen, then the laundry room in search of a fuse box.

"Not a fuse," Samantha announced, dressed in a shirt and shorts as she rose from the basement. "It must be something bigger."

"Oh God," Jamie breathed, frantic. "I can't afford to lose power right now. My condo was always okay." Of course, it hadn't been on the night Roy and Jessica died, a thought that gave her a chill but did nothing to cool her body heat. "Do you lose it here often?" If so, the power company would immediately know what to do.

Samantha shrugged. "Beats me. I haven't lived here in almost twenty years. Back then, not as many houses had AC, so the grid wasn't strained."

"And Chip has no generator." If he had, it would have already gone on. A generator was a *must*. MacAfee Homes *never* designed a house now without one. She couldn't believe it. Could. Not. Believe. It.

"What happened to the TV, Mamie?" Buddy asked.

Fighting terror, Jamie pulled him close. "I'm going to try to find out," she said and, cell phone in hand, searched the kitchen board for the emergency number of the power company. "It's not even eleven," she murmured mostly to herself as she tapped in the numbers, "*not* the heaviest usage time." An automated voice. *"Gah."* A menu. As she worked her way through it, she muttered, "It has to be routine maintenance, though why they had to pick today . . ." She listened. Not routine maintenance; an outage in the area, a crew was on its way, that was it. *"When will the power be back?"* Jamie yelled into the phone, though, of course, the recording didn't hear.

"Mommy," Tad shrieked in a way that said he wanted his mother, his *real* one, not Jamie but Jessica.

Racing back to the living room, she found him on all fours facing the sofa back, clearly having dozed and woken with no idea where he was, but stuck, neither here nor there, not knowing which way to go or how to get a foothold and save himself, which was exactly how she felt. And suddenly, as she closed convulsive arms around him, the fact of no power, no computer, no work, no mother was too much.

That was when the doorbell rang.

twenty-nine

Jamie took one look at Caroline on the other side of the door from Samantha and burst into tears, just stood in the living room sobbing above Tad's head, unable to move or think or speak. There was little relief until she felt her mother's arms wrap her up in the scent of spring and the earth, and then the comfort was too visceral for words.

"Oh baby," Caroline murmured against her hair the way she had done since Jamie could remember, "it's okay now, everything's okay, you're going to be fine."

"I don't . . . know . . . *how*."

As broken as Jamie's voice was, so Caroline's was whole. "You do. You've always known. You were born with an instinct for knowing how things work and what to do when they break. Isn't that what you did for me when my marriage fell apart?"

"I didn't fix anything."

"You did, you fixed me. You gave me a reason to hold my head up. And now, here you are, with a wonderful husband and a beautiful son and *another* beautiful son who is now clinging to a person I'm guessing is his aunt because she looks like his dad, and he said she was here."

A faint chuckle came from the door.

"He called you?" Jamie asked, too tired to be angry if he had.

"No, but I think he would have if I hadn't shown up on my own. This has gone on too long, Jamie. We're not meant to be on opposite sides of anything, especially not now, when there are so many good things going on. I was wrong about the wedding, baby, not about keeping secrets or wanting a wonderful celebration for you, but about suggesting that your judgment wasn't good. Only a guy with a big heart can do what Chip is doing right now with a gazillion kids running around and him worried sick about you." She held Jamie back and grimaced. "Is it hot in here or is it me?"

"It's *hot,*" Jamie wailed, because though the temperature hadn't had a whole lot of time to rise, between Tad's heat, her own heat, anticipation of heat, and stagnant air, the place felt stifling. In a hysterical burst that included her abysmal designs, she led Caroline right up to the loss of power. "My computer's gone, the kids are sick, and I am so far behind—"

"*Shh.* Wait." She pointed her finger and voice in the direction of the now-closed front door. "I'm Caroline, Jamie's mom, and I don't know your name—"

"Samantha."

"Samantha, I need my phone. It's right there in my purse. Would you dig it out for me, please?"

When Samantha knelt to forage, the absurdity of the instant hit Jamie. "Purse? Why are you carrying a *purse,* Mom?"

"Because these CEO clothes have no pockets." She touched Tad's cheek and cooed a soft "Hi, baby boy" before taking the phone from Samantha. Several touches to the screen and she said, "Okay, gorgeous, we need you ASAP here at Jamie's, 403 Beech, and bring Tommy Mello." She smiled, laughed softly. "No, but I will . . . Yes, now." She ended the call.

Gorgeous? It wasn't so much the word as how Caroline said it. Jamie wasn't sure she had ever heard that tone from her mother. She sounded almost gleeful, intimate in a deeply affectionate way. "What was that about?"

Caroline continued to smile. "A portable generator and this." Reaching into the V of her very beautiful navy silk shirt, she pulled out a ring.

Jamie forgot exhaustion, throw up, and flawed designs. This was her mother. A few weeks of crossed signals couldn't compete against twenty-nine years of adoration. Caroline was also her best friend, and this was exciting! "Oh. My. God. *When?*"

"Maybe four hours ago. No one else knows but you, me, and Dean. And now Samantha and these boys, not that the boys know a real diamond from a ring in a Cracker Jack box, though they probably don't even know that, poor things."

"Can I tell Chip?" Jamie asked. It was the first thing that came to mind, the second being that she wanted him here now to see the cool person that her mother really was.

"Absolutely. But no one else."

"Engaged?" It was *very* exciting. Jamie trusted Dean. He had loved Caroline for a long time, which Jamie hadn't seen then, since there was love and there was LOVE, though looking back, LOVE was a *duh* thing. Caroline deserved this.

"Not engaged," her mother warned. "I'm not brave enough to say that word yet, which is why this came on a chain."

Tad reached for the ring. Jamie opened her mouth to caution him when Caroline stroked his curls and said, "It's okay, baby. It won't break."

Jamie wasn't sure whether the baby just then was Tad or her, but it didn't really matter. She was her mother's child, so *so* grateful to be back. And that sounded like a betrayal.

"I love Chip," she said quickly. "I adore Chip. He's competent, and he just fills me up with hope and happiness and love. But I'm glad you're here."

"Well, isn't *that* one of truths I've come to accept?" Caroline asked. "He and I aren't in competition. We fill totally different needs. Your family with Chip is your future, Jamie. I never want to stand in the way of that. But if I can't be here to help with a problem I caused by giving you a deadline that you might have trouble meeting because (A) you just got married and (B) you have two sick little boys and (C) no power, what good am I?"

Jamie was the enumerator in the family. "You're mocking me."

"No. It's about organizing my thoughts. I'm learning from you."

Jamie felt an oppressive fatigue edge back. "Maybe you shouldn't. I am so in trouble. Is there any way we can postpone the presentation?"

"We can. But do we have to?"

"I'll show you my stuff. It's awful."

"It isn't," Samantha put in, approaching them. "It's not bad."

"Not bad won't get us a deal."

"It's *impressive,*" Samantha told Caroline, who glanced at her watch. "We still have a full day before the meeting."

"I have no computer, two sick kids, and a mind of mush."

"We're here to help," Caroline said so gently that Jamie choked up again. "First, you need sleep." She smoothed a tendril of hair from Jamie's cheek, leaving her hand there. "Until gorgeous Dean gets us some power, you can do that."

"But Tad—"

"I'll take Tad." Caroline offered her arms.

Jamie was about to say that he was caught between Mamie and Mommy and probably wouldn't go to her when he held out his little arms and went. That easily, he settled in against Caroline, who patted Jamie's cheek and pointed upstairs.

Caroline should have been nervous. She wasn't used to deadlines. A carpenter didn't have rigid ones, or maybe her clients were forgiving, or she was simply always ahead. Same with *Gut It!* Not so business administration, with a progression of appointments that led from one into the other with a domino effect. Yet here she was, digging Popsicles from her son-in-law's freezer, and she wouldn't be anywhere else. If Tad's coming to her like that didn't melt her heart, nothing would. She didn't even care if Roy was cringing. It wasn't about revenge anymore. She felt good doing this.

She actually felt so good that nothing would slow her down. Seeking out Chip had been a win-win move. In helping Jamie, she was helping herself. She needed to be needed. She was needed here. He had said that, as had the look of relief on Jamie's sweet, tired face.

Caroline could do power loss. She could do sick kids. This was where experience paid off.

And Samantha? Well, Samantha was interesting. She wasn't meek or resentful about taking Caroline's help, actually welcomed it, which made Caroline wonder whether the small bulge at her middle was from an affinity for hot fudge sundaes with whipped cream, or something alive. Caroline wasn't about to ask—had made *that* awful mistake more than once in her life. And really, did it matter right here, right now whether Samantha was pregnant? No. She seemed as clueless as Jamie about what to feed a child who had been throwing up. At Caroline's direction, she searched the freezer until she found a second box of Popsicles and then fixed dry toast, and when Caroline asked if Chip had a little swimming pool, she rummaged around in the garage until she found one.

The pool was a godsend. Water from the outside tap was tepid in the heat, actually perfect for keeping little bodies just cool enough. Once in it, the boys perked up, and while Caroline stayed close, especially to Tad, who was the younger and the less experienced of the two, they were surprisingly adept in the water. Neither was old enough to play with the other for long. Rather, they splashed randomly, or filled and dumped the plastic containers Caroline had found in the kitchen. When she gave them straws, they blew bubbles for a time.

Samantha brought her a lawn chair. "You're dressed too nicely to be on your knees."

Caroline had to laugh. "I've been on my knees all my life."

"Not when you're on TV. I watched several episodes last night. You're good. Both of you."

It was a golden opportunity. Caroline couldn't resist. Deliberately speculative, she asked, "So, when you were watching, did it bother you that I'm old?"

"You're not old."

"Old enough to be your mother."

"My mother is old. You are not."

Caroline didn't know Samantha's mother, but the woman had to be close to her own age. "Why do I want to tell you to be kind?"

Samantha studied the boys for a minute before raising her eyes again. "Because you're right. I'm just . . . dealing with something." With a little breath, she left it. "I look at you on that show, and you're not old. You lead. I expect my leader to be older than I am."

The remark was validating. "Thank you. You put that well. I'm dealing with something right now, too." Taking Samantha's arm, she urged her into the chair. "Watch the boys for a couple of minutes while I make some calls? I need to delay a few meetings."

"You can go to your meetings. I'll help Jamie."

But it wasn't only Jamie. A month ago, Caroline had been a mother and friend. Now she was also a mother-in-law, grandmother, and significant other. The newness of it all had her feeling her way along, but she rather liked the purpose. "I want to be here, too. My meetings will hold a few hours."

She called Dean first, just to hear his voice. Buoyed by that and by the knowledge that he was on his way, she called Theo. He listened while she explained where she was, sympathetic only to a point before asking when she *would* be in. She called Fred, who said he would stay at the bank as late as she needed. She called Dana, who bowed out entirely, which was fine, since Caroline was only including her as a formality. Linda was Team Caro, and it was Linda she called next. Once she had a feel for the Realtor's schedule, she called Brad to reset a time for the three of them to meet.

Having temporarily ceded responsibility for her life to Caroline, Jamie fell into an immediate deep sleep. She was so far out of it that she had no idea what was on her cheek until she brushed it and found lips.

Chip.

She inhaled. Eyes still closed, she wound her arms around his neck and hummed her pleasure. In the next second, the heat registered and she remembered why she was in bed in broad daylight. Her eyes flew open. "Omigod." She listened. "Silence is not good."

Chip smiled. "We're minutes from cool."

"The power company came through?" she asked with cautious hope.

"Dean did. He's out back with two experts hooking up a generator."

Dean. Caroline. *Gorgeous* rushed back. "He gave Mom a ring, Chip. She swears they're not engaged, but I think it's the fifty-something version of that." His hair was sticking up, his skin tanned and moist, which reminded her where he was supposed to be. "Why are you here?"

"School ended at noon. The kids left, so I left."

"What about teachers' meetings this afternoon?"

"They'll live without me. I need to be here. Your mom can't stay all day. Her meetings are important."

Mention of those caused a tightening in her gut. "She and I have to talk. She needs to see what I've done before she goes ahead with all that." Jamie tried to get up, but his torso was angled over her in a way that prevented escape. "Chip," she protested, but he was studying her face, playing with wayward strands of hair.

"You are so pretty."

"I'm a *mess*." But even a little sleep had taken the edge off. Prolonging the escape just a bit longer, she touched his mouth. "How are the boys?"

"Better," he breathed against her fingers. "Your mom has them drinking warm Jell-O. They're asking for cookies."

"And Samantha?"

"Not asking for cookies, but asking the guys a gazillion questions about the generator. It's a whole-house one."

Her hand slid to his neck. "Oh no, Chip. I don't think so. Whole house ones have to be ordered."

"I thought that, too, but Dean insisted that MacAfee Homes installs enough of them in new construction to have special access."

"But whole-house generators take a full *day* to install."

Chip's blue eyes were smug. "Not when you have three guys who know what they're doing. Dean didn't see the point of wasting time on a Band-Aid when he could do the full fix."

"Are you okay with that?" He looked it, but they were treading in new territory.

"Why wouldn't I be?"

"This is your house. It should be your decision, not Dean's."

He laughed. "Your mom must have been thinking the same thing when she told me it was a wedding gift. Like I mind a generator? Besides, it's not my house, it's ours, and I trust your mom's people." On cue, a low hum spread through the house. His grin widened. "She's an amazing woman, Jamie. I like having her here, and it isn't about child care. It's about family. My sister may be bossy, but her heart's in the right place, and your mom is resourceful and calm. She's one together lady."

With that, for Jamie, reality returned. "She won't be once she sees what I haven't designed."

Caroline didn't know what to expect. She understood that her very professional daughter was shaken. But by the time Jamie had gone through her questions about the land, the marketing decisions she couldn't make, and the designs she would draw if she only had more time, Caroline was seriously worried.

Standing over Jamie's shoulder a short time later, she was silent, eyes on the screen as page after page of designs appeared.

When she had seen enough, she said a soft, "You little stinker."

Jamie raised stricken eyes. "That bad?"

Caroline shot her a punishing look before asking Samantha, who was at Jamie's other shoulder, "Are they bad?"

"They're incredible."

"Incredible," Caroline confirmed. "The details you added to the manor exterior are simple but have a profound effect. The foyer inside is just detailed enough to show how elegant the entries to the condos might be." She gestured for Jamie to go back one screen, then another. "What you've done with the front drive makes a statement, the carriage houses in back are charming, and this house . . ." She had to smile. The single new build Jamie had designed looked suspiciously like Dean's country house might look once the rehab was done. Caroline wouldn't quite admit the potential to Dean, but there it was. "This house is totally inviting."

"It has a younger feel than the manor," Samantha observed. "What demographic are you targeting?"

When Jamie looked to Caroline for the answer, Caroline opened her phone. Seconds later, she connected with Linda, and minutes after that, Linda was headed their way. While they waited, Caroline studied the designs again. Together the three of them had listed a dozen questions by the time the Realtor arrived.

Over the next hour, while Tad napped, Chip watched Buddy, and the house cooled, the four women skimmed over things that they would explore more if the project was theirs, focusing instead on demographics, cost issues, and buyer trends. Beyond that, it was about brainstorming what would work in winning over the Weymouths. By the time Linda left, Jamie knew what she needed to do for tomorrow, which had been Caroline's goal.

Leaving her to work, Caroline found herself talking with Samantha in the kitchen. "Would you buy a house here?"

"If I could afford it."

"Would it bother you if other buyers were empty nesters?"

"You mean older?" She popped a Goldfish in her mouth and offered the box to Caroline, who shook her head. "No. I love having older people around. They're family when family can't be there."

"What if they resent the presence of young children?"

"Are you worried the Weymouths will?"

"Maybe."

"Don't they have kids?"

"Grown ones." Even as she said the words, she had her phone out and was calling Herschel Oakes. Minutes later, she had a helpful piece of information. "Between the brothers? Seven grandchildren."

"Family builds," Samantha remarked. "That has to be the theme of the pitch."

Caroline smiled, bemused. "It does. Why didn't I think of it before?"

"You may be too close to the project, or just not a marketer. But you're talking a lot of homes here." She pushed in another Goldfish and talked as she chewed. "Williston was on the outer edge of commuter towns when I was growing up here, but that's probably changed. The home prices the Realtor mentioned aren't out of sight for Greater Boston suburbia. Quality-of-life issues here compensate for the commute. Yeah, I'd buy a home here in a minute." Her eyes stopped blinking as they held Caroline's. "I'm pregnant."

And no husband, said that look of defiance. She was daring Caroline to criticize her. Not that Caroline would. She liked Samantha. Her gut said that this was a strong woman who would come to be Jamie's good friend. Caroline wasn't about to jeopardize that.

"I was wondering," she mused.

Samantha touched the bump. "I'm eighteen weeks. My parents don't know."

Caroline had an instant reaction to that but bit her tongue. After a moment's thought, she came at it a different way. "Jamie and I have always been this close." She held up two fingers. "We hit bumps this month—"

"She said you weren't talking."

"We weren't. There was a lack of honesty—no, a lack of *forthrightness.* It was hurtful and stupid and counterproductive. The longer it lingered, the more it took on a life of its own. Don't make the same mistake we did, Samantha."

"I already have," she cried in a slightly hysterical way.

"Then correct it soon. This conversation we're having, you and me? You've mentioned family more than once. It's on your mind."

Munching on a handful of crackers this time, Samantha considered that. Finally, seeming regretful, she said, "My family was always close. I could really use the emotional support." She nodded. "Family builds. It's a good sales slogan. I say that as a slightly impoverished version of your quintessential first-time home buyer."

Caroline was thinking the girl was correct in that, too. She did represent the younger face of the market. If the slogan appealed to her, it would appeal to three brothers whose children had to be somewhere around Samantha's age. She was also thinking that someone who was articulate, direct, and had a certain marketing savvy might impress the

Weymouths. On impulse, she said, "I'd like you at that meeting. Can you come?"

If sheer numbers counted, the MacAfee side would have won hands down. Theo led the team, looking debonair in his old-world way. Caroline sat beside him, wearing another of her new outfits, while Dean flanked her, looking ruggedly Dean. Caroline was amazed at how stunningly Jamie presented herself, despite being thoroughly sleep-deprived. Samantha wore a slim-fitting white top over her narrow skirt, a very New York bump-flaunting look that was actually a clever marketing choice, Caroline thought, in that it portrayed MacAfee Homes as totally modern. Granted, Samantha didn't work for MacAfee Homes. Nor did Chip, who looked sporty and god-awful handsome as he sat in the background, ostensibly present for moral support. Annie Ahl was there. And Linda. And Brad, looking awkward as hell.

Conversely, the Weymouth presence was limited to Ralph videoconferencing from San Francisco, Grant on speakerphone from Santa Fe, and, in the flesh, John the hotshot plastic surgeon who'd had plenty of work done on himself, and Herschel-the-lawyer-with-ties-to-Caroline.

Unfortunately, since the Weymouth brothers owned the land, they held the cards. Seeming disgruntled from the get-go, they had pithy remarks about Jamie's designs, Linda's real estate savvy, Samantha's *Family Builds* image, and Caroline's offer. They questioned whether Dean's green installations were pure gimmick, and whether Annie's landscaping plans would preserve their mother's aging dogwoods. Ralph wanted to know why the Barths, who he claimed were about to affiliate with Sotheby's, wouldn't be a safer choice, and, by the way, if Theo was still the one in charge, why wasn't he talking, and what role would he play anyway? John declared that he didn't want Web marketing, which, he said, might create a conflict for someone Googling his name; Linda explained that any URL would simply include the address, and Samantha, having done her homework that morning, pointed out that nine in ten home buyers used the Web at some point, with 52 percent citing it as their first step.

When they seemed to run low on criticism, Ralph asked Chip why he was there. "If you think your friendship with my son will get you brownie points, think again. You let down your teammates at Harvard and made a mess of your life. I wouldn't want you involved."

Chip held up a respectful hand. "I'm just the chauffeur."

Jamie took exception to that. "He's my husband. He's here to support me."

As much to prevent Jamie from saying something that might anger Frank as to make a protest of her own, Caroline put in a quick "Chip doesn't work for MacAfee Homes, but if there was a position, I'd hire him in a heartbeat."

Dean added, "I second that. My subs rave about how he is with their kids."

"You're all biased," Ralph scoffed.

"Actually," John told his brother, "I just heard the same thing from one of my patients. His kids go to Emory Elementary."

That touched off a bout of arguments among the brothers, starting with the state of the local schools but quickly moving on to whether the prototype houses should resemble the manor, whether an imposing front drive was practical or pretentious, whether their father would roll over in his grave if tennis courts were built at the expense of a golf course.

Caroline was still smarting from Ralph's remarks about Chip. When the brothers began suggesting terms of a sale, like mandating that freestanding houses be built on two-acre lots and sell for no less than $1.5 million, she began to feel that these weren't people she wanted to deal with at all. That was when Brad passed her a note.

All posturing. They know they have to sell. Let them talk. Once they settle and agree to a sale, I negotiate with Oakes.

Caroline was grateful for his words. Actually, she was grateful that he had agreed to come at all. Yes, his job called for it, but he had one foot out the door and could have pleaded a dentist appointment or a migraine or whatever. For all his emotional shortcomings, it had to be hard for him sitting in clear view of his ex-fiancée and her new husband. Much as Caroline wouldn't want Jamie with him, she felt a brief fondness.

Then she heard Ralph Weymouth's strident voice. "Why twenty-four hours? Twenty-four hours is ridiculous. We can't consider competing offers in twenty-four hours. Twenty-four hours won't work."

Caroline knew what to say, but hesitated. Ralph was the toughest of the three. She had watched him during her presentation and could still hear him archly ask what role Theo would be playing. Here was a man's man. Age wasn't the problem; her being female was. She could fight that, push through, be strident right back at him. But she had dealt with enough men in her life to recognize counterproductive before it happened. Meeting with Hersch on Monday had succeeded because of their past. She had no past with Ralph. Her gut said that a reply to him was better coming from someone in pants.

Touching Brad's note, which had been tactically sound, she gestured for him to answer.

He didn't touch his glasses, didn't glance at the papers before him. His eyes remained locked with Ralph's on the video monitor while, with his trademark calm, he said, "This offer stands only that long. We're willing to pay a premium for a preemptive sale—"

"MacAfee Homes isn't the only game in town."

"No, but it's the best one for this job. We've made the arguments why. If you agree, then the decision isn't hard to make. Absent a preemptive sale, our offer changes."

He was calling Ralph's bluff. Caroline would have done the same, but with less chance of success. Even coming from a male, though, toughness could backfire. She wanted to look at Theo to see if he was uneasy, but knew he wouldn't show it even if he was. She wanted to lean into Dean, but vetoed that idea, too. For a split second, she thought about the simplicity of carpentry, where her greatest decision might be whether to use rosewood or oak. In that split second, she wanted only that.

Then she directed her mind's eye around the table, thinking that she cared about these people and that helping them create something bigger was a worthwhile challenge. Yes, there were risks of giving a twenty-four-hour window. But the risk of letting the fire cool and the competition into the game was greater.

Also, on a personal note, there was *Gut It!* The whole point of rushing to meet with the Weymouths was to have something secured before meeting with Brian and Claire. Before that meeting, though, Caroline and Jamie had to talk.

Chicken Fingers and Spring Rolls, Crispy Beef with Broccoli, Chicken with Pea Pods, Kung Pao Shrimp, white rice, brown rice, and fried rice—Caroline's dining table was covered with takeout containers by the time Jamie and Chip arrived with the boys. Samantha wasn't with them. They had barely left downtown Boston when she announced that she planned to pack and head north.

"When?" Jamie asked in alarm, seeing Samantha as part of the team and therefore deserving of a celebratory dinner. Not that celebrations were in order. Soon after Brad's ultimatum, Herschel Oakes, who had been quiet until then, finally spoke. "We have a lot to discuss," he told the brothers and, shifting his focus to Caroline, stood. "I think we have the information we need. Thank you for coming. If you'll excuse us now . . ."

It was a less than encouraging ending. Seeming to agree, Caroline leaned close in the elevator and said a quiet, "Hersch was being deliberately abrupt so that the brothers see him as in charge. We don't know what they're saying up there now."

No, they didn't. So that was disappointing. And now Samantha. Totally aside from her help at the meeting, Jamie liked having her with them. More important, she sensed that Chip did, too. Two days were not enough.

Samantha's explanation came from the backseat. "I need to get there before I lose my nerve. Or fall asleep." Her hand touched Jamie's shoulder. "You'll give the boys a hug for me? Tell them I'll see them soon?"

"Will you?" Chip asked more sharply than Jamie would have.

Apparently, Samantha agreed with her. "Don't be a prick."

"I'm not," he said, darting glances at her in the rearview. "I'm your brother, and I'm serious. I'd like to see more of you."

"*We* would," Jamie amended, twisting to look back. "There's always room, you know. It's your house."

Her mouth, so like Chip's, tipped into a crooked smile. "I think you just want me here when you meet the folks."

"That, too," Jamie said, only half kidding. She had an ally in Samantha and actually felt bad that they weren't driving north to support her now. Tomorrow's meeting made that impossible.

But life was too short to be distant from family, which was why, after they watched her drive off and then picked up the boys, they went straight to Caroline's—that, and the fact that Jamie was too tired to even think of dinner but was famished.

Tad did amazingly well. Ever prepared, Caroline had applesauce and bananas for anyone whose stomach might still be sensitive, but Tad insisted on sitting on Jamie's lap and finger-feeding himself bits of broccoli and rice. The last ended up less in his mouth and more on her lap and the floor. Champ's tongue swept the floor, and, having changed into shorts, Jamie didn't care about her lap.

Nor, actually, did she care about the fact that Herschel Oakes hadn't called yet. Given the brothers' negativity, she sensed they would wait until the last minute, even if they'd already made a decision, and while that annoyed her, she couldn't sustain anger. She wanted to blame her placidity on the Chardonnay Caroline had opened, but it had more to do with exhaustion from two nights of little sleep. And relief that the presentation was done. And a more immediate and unexpected pleasure.

Looking through the back screen as she carried dirty dishes to Caroline's sink, she thought about the teeny family she'd grown up in and her dreams of it being bigger. That dream was coming true—and on the heels of that realization came one that said the Weymouth project didn't matter all that much in the overall scheme. Effort mattered, and yes, she felt she had done the best she could in a limited time frame. Health mattered. The boys were fully recovered, both of them strong. *Love* mattered. Caroline had Dean, who was at this moment on his hands and knees in the backyard digging up something or other for the two little guys. And Chip, her Chip. He was out there, too, having a ball with the boys in the dirt but also giving Jamie a chance to have her mother alone. If she didn't already love him to bits, his sensitivity to that need would have pushed her there.

She watched Caroline slather on hand lotion before pulling on rubber gloves. With the scent of woods and spring rising from the gloves as they warmed under hot water, Jamie set down the dishes she held.

"About *Gut It!*—"

"About *Gut It!*—"

Jamie hurried to speak first. "I need you to believe me, this change was not my idea."

"I know, baby," Caroline said with a smile. She kept adding soaped dishes to the pile to be rinsed. "I probably knew it all along, but I was feeling vulnerable and I got defensive. Defensiveness is a cloud, sometimes so thick you can't see through it. It's gone now. I feel better about myself."

"Because of Dean?"

"Yes. And because of Theo."

Barely two days ago, Jamie had agreed to lobby on Theo's behalf to convince Caroline to succeed him. She hadn't done it—*such* a conflict of interest—and yet, here was her mother, looking the part, right down to a dusting of blush and mascara, and the neat twist of hair at the nape of her neck. Not even the neon green, soap-covered gloves that went to her elbows detracted from that. Jamie felt positively inelegant beside her.

Taking a dish towel, she began to dry what Caroline rinsed. "Will you take over for him?"

Caroline touched the back of one rubber glove to her chest. Jamie thought she was trying to still a racing heart. But no, she was feeling her ring. It clearly gave her something—*Dean* clearly gave her something. "I fear I may want to," she finally said. "If you think that doesn't terrify me, think again."

"You can do it." Jamie had no doubt whatsoever. From nowhere came memory of the harsh words she'd had for her father before he died. *She's just a carpenter,* he had said of Caroline, to which Jamie had replied, *If she's just a carpenter, then you're just a salesman.* They were both wrong. Seeing Caroline coordinate every detail of today's presentation, Jamie had a new respect for the job. "You've been doing it since Dad died. And now you come home to Dean."

"Actually, I come home to my garage before I'm much good to Dean. I'm a carpenter, baby. That's my first love. I need to make things. I'll always need that. It clears my mind. It *settles* me." She rinsed several more dishes before saying, "Your father died too young. When someone tells me I'm getting old, like Claire did—"

"She was wrong."

"Not entirely. "She rinsed another dish. "I don't believe I'm too old for *Gut It!,* but I am getting older. We all are. I look at what happened to Roy. There's a lesson in that." She handed over the dish, then braced the heels of her gloved hands on the edge of the sink and looked at Jamie. "I have things I want to do besides host. Like this." She hitched her chin at the counter filled with empty takeout containers. "Like working on Dean's house, spending time with your family, going to Canyon Ranch with you. And yes, I want to help Theo. The little I've done has been satisfying. I didn't expect that, but it is. I'd like to give heading MacAfee Homes a shot."

Here it was, Jamie's moment of truth. If Caroline didn't have time to host the show, they were in trouble. Jamie couldn't do it now. "Mom, I . . . I . . . I . . ."

"I know. Not the right time for you."

"But Claire needs to know now."

"Yes." Caroline studied her face. "Your own family has to come first. That's the way it should be. And it's one of the reasons why the changes in my life are good. They'll keep me busy. So. You're busy. I'm busy. Which of us is less busy right now?"

Jamie bit back the quick *You* that was on the tip of her tongue. Both of their lives had gone from simple to complex in the instant when a tree was hit by lightning and fell on a car. If she respected that Caroline was wearing new hats, too, she had to be truthful. "I don't know."

Caroline did. "Me, baby. I don't have kids. I don't have a whole new family to get to know. You'll sort it all out. Things will line up for you. Until then, I'll stay on as host and ease you in as soon as you're ready."

It sounded like a plan, with one possible glitch. "Will Claire agree to that?"

"If we get the Weymouth land, she will."

epilogue

The rain had let up several hours before, and though the late afternoon sun was more hesitant than Jamie might have liked, she couldn't be greedy. The western sky, framed by the new window in her new kitchen, showed resilient swathes of orange just over the trees, as a dry June breeze pushed gunmetal clouds east.

How to describe what she felt as she stood at her new counter, which was a sandy granite with very practical, kid-friendly veins of burgundy and gray? Grateful for the weather, yes. But now, still, nervous about the food.

This was their first time having everyone in their new home, which actually was the old country house that Caroline had not wanted Dean to buy but then had helped rebuild. By the time it was done, Dean had already purchased another house, this one right next door to Caroline's Victorian. With Caroline insisting that her cats shouldn't have to suffer his dog full-time—and that, BTW, adults needed their own space, too—it was the perfect solution.

It was also the perfect solution for Jamie and Chip. With the prospect of more children in the future and frequent visits from his parents, they needed rooms. The old country house had plenty. And hadn't Jamie drawn the plans that Dean followed in his gut-and-rebuild? Hadn't this exact home design, which so captured her dreams, helped win the Weymouth project?

So Jamie and Chip had bought the country place from Dean, giving his parents' place to Samantha, who was now outside with her eight-month-old daughter Maisie, Caroline and Dean, Chip's parents Donald and Helene, Theo, and the boys, while Jamie frantically whisked a third attempt at dressing.

When Chip appeared at her shoulder, she raised a spoon to his mouth. "Still too sweet?" She was making homemade cole slaw. Well, not entirely homemade. Just the dressing. The cabbage was out of a bag—*no one* seriously cared who cut the leaves—but she had wanted to make the dressing herself. Hamburgers and hot dogs took no brain power. Dressing for cole slaw did. She had a bottle of store-bought, just in case. But this had become her cause, and, with the smell of sizzling burgers drifting in, she was down to the wire.

He licked the spoon, licked his lips, and smiled in a way that would have distracted her if she weren't so focused on the task. "It's *good.*"

"I want it great."

"It is great."

"You're just saying that."

"No, it really is. Everything you make is great."

"Is that because I make so little that you're pleased when I make anything at all?"

He rolled his eyes, pulled her close, and kissed a freckle. "It's because even a year later I'm madly in love with you, and because you're a better cook than you give yourself credit for, and because this dressing really is good."

"Yeah?" she asked softly, losing that focus. Even a year later, she was madly in love with him, too.

"Yeah. Mix it in. But first . . ."

He gave her a full-on kiss. Even a year later, that was still special. Every. Time.

"Besides," he said against her lips, "no one eating with us today is as discriminating as you are."

Jamie drew back to disagree. "Your mom is. Look what she brought—three different dinners for the freezer, plus baked beans, pasta salad, and seven-layer bars for today, all homemade."

"She loves cooking. It's her hobby. And she has more time than you do."

"Mommy!" Tad cried, racing in, "Bud-man isn't sharing!"

Buddy was on his heels. "He took Maisie's toy, and he wouldn't give it to her."

"But I didn't have a turn playing!"

"Maisie *wanted* it!"

"Buddy—" Chip began. Jamie stopped him with a touch. Sibling rivalry was still new and not easy for either adult, and while she adored that Chip looked out for Tad, she couldn't let him blame Buddy just because he was older. Tad was three and had to learn to share. Besides, if it was Maisie's toy, Buddy was right.

Bending low, she put an arm around each boy and said as much—and didn't *that* say something? She was the ideological parent, Chip the blunt one. She was the rainy-day activity expert, he the one who taught them all to laugh when they fell. She was the one who still researched problems ad infinitum, while he solved them with a hug.

Tad pouted. "I didn't get *my* turn."

For a minute, Jamie couldn't speak. The child was so like his father in perseverance that she was alternately horrified and touched. She would tell him stories when he was old enough to ask. For now, she simply kept pictures of Jess and Roy on his dresser. He knew to call the faces Mommy and Daddy. But he seemed perfectly fine calling Jamie and Chip the same.

The reminder was apt. His turn? "With a yard full of other toys? Theodore MacAfee, you are far from deprived. There are a dozen trucks in the sandbox, a water table on the deck, a lawn mower on the grass, and Transformers that Poppy just brought. But what happened to the tee?" She looked questioningly at Buddy. "I thought you guys were batting off it."

"Poppy got tired of shagging the ball," Buddy said, and while Jamie was thinking, *Well, yeah, because the two of you hit more than you miss,* Chip was more blunt.

"And one of you two couldn't do it?"

Buddy looked up at him. "Fido peed on the deck."

"Oh *no,*" Jamie cried, thinking of the sweeping they had done just an hour before to rid her beautiful deck of rain debris.

Fido was the German shepherd pup that Dean had given them as a housewarming gift. Oh, he had checked with them first, causing one of the few arguments between them. Jamie wanted a pair of quiet, clean, self-sufficient cats. Chip argued that a cat wouldn't run with boys who clearly needed to run. When she argued that cat shelters were overflowing, he pointed out that the puppy Dean had chosen *was* born in a dog shelter. It was three against one. So Fido had arrived. They tried to rename him, alternately calling him Oliver, Chester, and Remington over the course of a week, before returning to Fido, which fit the dog, just as Dean had originally said. Now they just had to get him house-trained.

"Oh God, Chip. We're *eating* on that deck."

"Not to worry," Caroline said as she entered the kitchen. "Dean hosed it off." Her eyes were on the boys. "Is anyone here ready for a hot dog?"

"Me!"

"Me! Can I get mine first since I'm older?" Buddy asked.

"Baker." From Chip.

"I think," Caroline said, "that Dean will hand them out at exactly the same time." The two raced out. "Cole slaw done?" she asked Jamie, who shot Chip a *what-do-I-do* look.

He mimed mixing, which she quickly did and handed the bowl to Caroline. Just as quickly, Caroline passed it back to Chip with an affectionate grin.

"Would you take this to the table, like a good boy?"

Chip winked at Jamie in a way that said he got a kick out of her mother, which meant the world to her. Then he, too, was gone, leaving her with Caroline, who had the same huge heart as always, but today a different facade. For one thing, her nails, fingers and toes, were neon blue. For another, her shorts and blouse were white. The irony, of course, was that Jamie, who had lived in a pristine white world before becoming a mom, didn't dare wear it now. But Caroline wore it well. Between those blue nails, her auburn hair, and her green eyes, she was as colorful as ever.

So color wasn't what made her look different.

It wasn't even the diamond ring that hadn't once left her neck.

No. There was a richness to her now, an inner beauty, as though she'd come into her own long after she thought she already had.

That said, she smelled the same. Lily of the valley. Or was Jamie smelling the scent as it rose from the edge of the woods, where yards and yards of the real stuff carpeted the ground, green except for those tiny spikes of little white bells? The smell was ageless. It fit her mother perfectly.

"Are you nervous?" Caroline asked softly.

"With Chip's parents here and Theo—" Distracted, she broke off. "He looks good, Mom. How did his tests go?" Theo had had a minor stroke the winter before, hastening Caroline's ascension. Though he remained president of the company, he had named her CEO from his hospital bed. In the six months since, she had hired good people to help, including a CFO, a new legal head, and Samantha.

"He's fine," Caroline assured her. "Cagey as ever. There are times when I wonder whether he didn't stage that little TIA just to get me on board."

"But you and CEO are a fit. Better than me and kitchen. Yes, I'm nervous." She indicated a Post-it on the wall by the fridge. "I have lists of what all to remember to put out—ketchup, mustard, pickles, olives, and—"

Caroline stoppered Jamie's mouth. "Everything out there is terrific. The table is *full*."

Jamie had a sudden thought. "Lemonade." She started for the fridge, but Caroline caught her arm.

"It's on the table, and if you'd forgotten, someone would have asked, you'd have come back in for it, and all would have been well. You don't have to be perfect, baby. We've talked about that."

"I know."

"But that wasn't what I meant," Caroline said. "Are you *nervous*?"

Jamie didn't follow, until her mother's conspiratorial tone registered. Then her eyes lit. "You mean about watching the tape?" That was the second purpose for the party today. How could she have forgotten? Hel-lo. She'd had a few other things on her mind, like new sneakers for the boys, finishing touches in the guest room for Helene and Donald, and cole slaw dressing.

"It's your debut," Caroline said.

The hosting switch was complete, in part because Theo needed Caroline in the office, and in part because Jamie had taken to it so well. Caroline had hosted the fall project, to which Brian consented once he had a promise of the transition. They had just finished taping the spring project in Maine, with Jamie hosting from start to finish.

"It's also Gina Anderson's directorial debut," Jamie pointed out, pinching back a smile. "Do we miss Claire?" The question was rhetorical. Her absence made things immeasurably more relaxed. And no, the Weymouth property wasn't on the show. It never would be. The brothers were firm about that, and Jamie and Caroline had come to agree. They didn't need *Gut It!* publicity to help sell the development; within months of inking the deal, MacAfee Homes had preliminary contracts on nearly every lot. Without the Weymouth property, the Barths hadn't held much of a lure for Claire Howe, who decided that *Gut It!* didn't hold much of a lure for her anyway, what with Brian intent on keeping the MacAfees and the MacAfees standing as one on who should host. An interim EP had directed the fall project, allowing Jamie and Gina to start fresh in the spring.

"If you're nervous," Caroline said now, "there's no need. Your own personality emerged, and it worked, so if you're worried about what the raw cut will show"—she tipped her head toward the great room, where a huge flat-screen awaited the postcookout showing—"do not be."

'I'm not," Jamie said and realized that she meant it. "I'm really not. Not that *Gut It!* doesn't matter. I mean, I love that we're still doing the show, and the new coffee table book is going to be amazing. But it isn't the only thing in my life."

"That's an understatement," her mother drawled and asked, "I take it you're happy with the latest new architect?" Jamie had actually been through two before finding a woman who could execute a similar architectural vision. Moreover, she had kids of her own, which meant that she was comfortable, in essence, job sharing with Jamie.

"Like her a lot," Jamie declared, more concerned about dinner on the deck. Wanting to make sure everything was where it should be, she linked her arm through Caroline's. They had no sooner left the kitchen, though, when her attention caught on her grandmother's Victorian lace, which now hung on her own dining room wall.

"I feel guilty having this here, Mom."

"Oh, no no no. Do not. This is where it's supposed to be, one generation to the next." They stood together before it. "What do you see?"

"Maybe it's laughing at me and my cole slaw, because I see a bunch of big wide grins."

"Those are happy grins. Satisfied grins. *Fulfilled* grins. I see them, too. What do you think that means?"

Jamie didn't answer. Her throat was suddenly tight. She had her mother back with an even greater appreciation of their relationship, but that was just the beginning. Looking past the dining room, through the great room and out the French doors to a colorfully food-filled deck, where her husband was standing with Caroline's would-be husband, flipping burgers on a huge gas grill, while the boys wandered from adult to adult eating hot dogs and chips, she was overwhelmed.

Then Theo looked their way. His wrinkled face broke into a grin, seconds before an arthritic hand gestured them out.

Neither was about to refuse.

acknowledgments

Do I seriously have to write about things I don't know? How easy it would be to stick with the tried and true! Unfortunately, it would also be boring. I've always prided myself on making every one of my books different, so I naturally gravitate to the new. Or maybe I simply like new things, and if I do, I feel my readers will, too. Writing about new things is slightly scary at times. Trust me, there was plenty of insomnia where *Blueprints* was concerned.

My medicine for that? Good people, willing to share their expertise with me. I start by thanking Susan Wornick, television personality extraordinaire, who gave me enough information on how the real thing works to make *Gut It!* credible. I also knew nothing about architecture until Jenne Whitelaw and Peter Darlow filled me in enough so that I could picture a real architect's life. My thanks to them. In the field of construction, huge thanks to Bob Gavill and to Ed Foran, for answering my questions. And Ed's crew, which unwittingly made my book real. They were here in my house doing renovation work while I watched and asked questions. And they thought my curiosity was idle. Hah! My apologies for any deception, along with admiration and thanks.

Writing about these fields, I've taken liberties in the name of fiction. All mistakes are mine and mine alone.

My thanks, as always, to my agent, Amy Berkower, and to my editor, Hilary Rubin Teeman, and her talented and dedicated team at St. Martin's Press. Thanks to my assistant, Lucy Davis, whose work exceeds assisting, to Linda Kay, for references and a ready ear, and to Eric MacLeish, for sharing child custody info in answer to every last question I posed. And to my family, truly the footprint on which my own personal blueprints are drawn. Much thanks and love forever.

Finally, my readers continue to be my greatest professional pleasure. With the landscape of the book world constantly changing, they continue to read my books. I never forget that.

Kerry Brett

Barbara Delinsky is the author of more than twenty *New York Times* bestselling books. She has been published in twenty-eight languages worldwide. A lifelong New Englander, Delinsky earned a BA in psychology at Tufts University and an MA in sociology at Boston College. She lives in Massachusetts with her husband, more books than she'll ever be able to read, two tennis racquets, and enough electronic devices to keep in close touch with her children and their families. You can find her online at www.barbaradelinsky.com and on Facebook (@bdelinsky), Twitter (@BarbaraDelinsky), and Instagram (@BarbaraDelinsky).